CARPATHIAN

CARPATHIAN

An Event Group Thriller

DAVID L. GOLEMON

THOMAS DUNNE BOOKS

ST. MARTIN'S PRESS ✷ NEW YORK

THOMAS DUNNE BOOKS.
An imprint of St. Martin's Press.

CARPATHIAN. Copyright © 2013 by David L. Golemon. All rights reserved. Printed in the United States of America. For information, address St. Martin's Press, 175 Fifth Avenue, New York, N.Y. 10010.

www.thomasdunnebooks.com
www.stmartins.com

Library of Congress Cataloging-in-Publication Data

Golemon, David Lynn.
  Carpathian : an Event Group Thriller / David L. Golemon. — First Edition.
      pages cm
  Includes bibliographical references and index.
  ISBN 978-1-250-01300-2 (hardcover)
  ISBN 978-1-250-01301-9 (e-book)
  1. Event Group (Imaginary organization)—Fiction.   2. Quests (Expeditions)—
Fiction.   I. Title.
  PS3607.O4555C37 2013
  813'.6—dc23

                                                            2013009117

St. Martin's Press books may be purchased for educational, business, or promotional use. For information on bulk purchases, please contact Macmillan Corporate and Premium Sales Department at 1-800-221-7945 extension 5442 or write specialmarkets@macmillan.com.

First Edition: July 2013

10 9 8 7 6 5 4 3 2 1

For my band of Gypsy wanderers—
The road will someday lead us back home . . .

ACKNOWLEDGMENTS

For Pete Wolverton and Thomas Dunne for their hard work and dedication—we grow ever closer to the tale's conclusion!

PROLOGUE

And they burned the city with fire, and all that was in it. Only the silver and gold and articles of bronze and iron, they put into the treasury of the house of the Lord. . . .

Cursed before the Lord is the man who rises up and builds this city Jericho; with the loss of his first-born he shall lay its foundation, and with the loss of his youngest son he shall set up its gates.

Joshua 6:24–26

THE FLOODPLAIN OF YAM SUPH
(THE SEA OF REEDS), 1556 BCE

The great multitude of humanity stretched out as far as the eye could see. The eight-hour trek had been filled with hardship and death for the Hebrew tribes as they continued to slog across the floodplain of the Sea of Reeds. The lost nation from the land of Goshen had made the passing of the large body of shallow water before the tide set upon them.

As the many tribes neared the end of the desperate gamble made by an even more desperate general, the rearguard element of Israelite soldiers came under grievous attack by the lead scouts and charioteers of Libyan axmen. The axmen were the forward vanguard of Crown Prince Amun-her-khepeshef's grand army of one thousand chariots. Amun-her-khepeshef was the firstborn son of Pharaoh Ramesses II and was chosen specially for his historically ruthless treatment of all enemies of Egypt, and would lead the army of Ramesses to avenge the loss of so many during the plagues cast down upon the Egyptian people by the Hebrew leader—Moses the Deliverer, the onetime great-uncle to the crown prince himself and one of the greatest generals in all of Egyptian military history.

The rear guard of Hebrew forces was fashioned from elements of the twenty-two tribes of Israelite pilgrims. The shabbily clad soldiers held their ground for as long as they could against the fierce axmen of the Libyan deserts. The rear guard was meant to hold off the lead infantry soldiers of the army of Pharaoh until the signal was given to break off the defense of the floodplain. This would be done just before the larger lines of charioteers entered the trap set by the prophet. The sun was just starting to reach the fourth hour past midday. The Hebrew retreat had not rested for more than four days since the flight from Pharaoh and his two lands of Upper and Lower Egypt.

The main cohort of the Egyptian army hesitated at the edge of the muddy seabed. The battle-hardened soldiers watched as the last of the Hebrew rear guard, after brutally attacking their lead elements, fled back into the mire and stinging nettles of the Sea of Reeds.

The path of the 128,000 men, women, and children, along with their vanguard of many beasts of burden, was made clearly visible in the mud and the beaten path made by this great multitude of humanity. The trail was more than a mile wide and snaked across the muddy plain until the trampled earth disappeared into the late afternoon sun. The lead chariot stopped and watched as the last of the Hebrew soldiers vanished into the tall reeds that lined the retreat of the Exodus from the land of Pharaoh.

"Great one, we should await the coming of the morrow sun to continue the pursuit," said Amun-her-khepeshef's commander of the Egyptian host as he stood beside the crown prince just as the perfectly matched set of black horses pulling his chariot pawed at the ground nervously. The wind had started to pick up and the smell that struck the Egyptian's nostrils was that of the returning sea. "The tide comes in and we have little time to cross the sea as it rises. We must wait lest our main strength and advantage of chariot and speed of horse will be lost in the mud and rising tide."

"This ends today. The pursuit has carried on far too long. I have a thousand chariots filled with weary soldiers who tire of the chase. My father wishes this put to an end and until I have the head of Moses on the tip of my spear we will continue. Look at the retreat of the Hebrew army and people. Their God is as bad a general as Moses is a prophet. Spy to the east, Commander," he said pointing. "The sea is now at his back and this shallow pond is no obstacle at all to the Egyptian host."

Crown Prince Amun-her-khepeshef raised his right hand with his spear pointed to the long trail of retreat and thrust the bronz-tipped weapon forward. The action brought the thunderous roar of two thousand horses to action as the first of the charioteers rode into the low floodplains of the Sea of Reeds. For almost an hour and a half the grand army of Ramesses II chased the remains of the fleeing Hebrew nation into history and legend.

The charioteers rumbled through the quickly drying mud and sand. The wind was now nearing gale force and the many soldiers of Ramesses II knew the day had turned to an evil portent of things yet to come. Prince Amun-her-khepeshef's chariot was in the middle of the fast moving units as they pursued the rear elements of the Israelites.

The horses were tiring as they fought for footing in the drying seabed. Mud covered most of the soldiers' bodies and equipment of war, and the well-trained army was now growing as weary as their animals as they became weighted down by the sticky, thickening mud.

Without warning the lead chariots started slowing, and as Crown Prince Amun-her-khepeshef's chariot followed suit he saw the reason for the abrupt halt. The first light waves of the returning sea splashed among the horses' hooves and the wheels of the chariots. A nervous flutter flitted through the four thousand soldiers of the Egyptian host. The rumors of the strange abilities of the Hebrew prophet had slithered down to every man, woman, and child of Upper and Lower Egypt. Most of the soldiers had the deep-seated conviction that they would never see the Nile River after this day.

"The tide is coming in, Great One, we must turn and await a better time to cross," said his general of the host as the horses started to rear up against the fast rising sea.

"I can see the trailing elements of the traitors' animal herd. We are close to finishing this bloody errand—it ends here—it ends today," Amun-her-khepeshef said again as his brown eyes flashed in the dying light of day. "These ungrateful people will pay for the lives lost and the traitorous way in which they have treated my father and the land that sustained them for centuries."

As he spoke the wind died as quickly as it had sprung up and then they heard the rush of water as it covered the lower half of the chariot's wheels. The force of the returning sea frightened the battle-hardened soldiers of Pharaoh's army until they were told that the saltwater would rise slowly for the next three hours and never achieve the depth they need fear. The crown prince knew then that they would have the time needed to do their butchery before the sun had set that day.

The prince ordered the pursuit to continue as the sun became hidden behind the black and ominously roiling clouds that now covered the sky from east to west and north to south. The pitch-black heavens in the late afternoon were something the men of Pharaoh's army had never seen before the coming of this day. The clouds seemed to be spinning in a terrifying rush to close off the heavens from the sight of men. As the prince looked around him he saw the thousands of horses of the army start to stomp at the water and shy away from the approaching tide of the returning sea.

"Great One, there to the east, look!" his general called out as he tried to pierce the sudden darkness of the false night as he fought the reins to control the matched black horses.

Off to the east on a small rise of land that was an island when the tide was in stood a figure flanked by two other men. The tallest of the three stepped forward and even though the men were more than half a mile away, the crown prince knew exactly whom he was spying.

"The Great Deliverer awaits the host of Pharaoh's army," the crown prince said as he once more raised his spear to the sky. "He is not the weak man I had taken him for. So be it, onetime uncle, today you meet your one true God!"

"Some say he is the greatest general of the two kingdoms and is led by a singular God," the general said as he watched the man close to a mile away raise both arms and spread them wide and then suddenly lower both and tap the ground beneath his feet three times with his long, crooked staff.

"This is quite enough. Bring me the head of the false Egyptian!" the crown prince shouted as he ordered the host forward into the deepening Sea of Reeds.

The thousand chariots started forward slowly as their wheels began to get mired in the mud, swirling sand, and rising waters. As they started to get bogged down in their haste to reach the Hebrew army they saw the man on the slowly shrinking island raise both arms once more to the blackened sky.

The attack signal had been given.

Before the men of the Egyptian host knew what was happening they were assaulted from all sides. The black shapes sprang from the water. They struck from behind large stands of reeds and from the mud. The crown prince heard the shouts and the screams of men as they were taken from their chariots by unseen forces that had sprung seemingly from the bowels of the underworld. He watched as a black, mud-covered shape shot up, shedding water, black mud, and sea grass and took the general that had been standing next to him but a moment before and all that was left was one of the man's sandals.

Screams of men and horses pierced the false night around him. Arrows were loosed in a frenzy to get away from the unknown and deadly attackers. Un-aimed arrows flew around the prince like angry hornets as men fought for their lives. More shouts of frightened soldiers sounded when the large, black-fur-covered animals vanished after mauling a quarter of his chariot force. The Libyan axmen taking up the middle of the Egyptian formation had been decimated by the ambush. As soon as the last of the beasts had disappeared back into the mud and water, the archers of the Hebrew forces started loosing arrows by the thousands into the dark sky.

Amun-her-khepeshef took the reins of the shaking and rearing chariot and snapped the leather straps to get his twin black Arabian horses back to the attack. Before the horses could take purchase in the mud and water something rose from the sea and made the horses rear up to protect themselves. The beast was enormous. It tossed one horse to the side and that harsh action forced the other large Arabian to follow suit. The momentum of both horses going down twisted the chariot until it became airborne, throwing the crown prince into the rising foulness that was the Sea of Reeds.

Amun-her-khepeshef came up spitting vile saltwater from his mouth and dripping from his nose. Before he could catch his breath amidst the screams of torment of his many thousands of men, he was taken by the throat and lifted from the stinking mire. The long fingers of the animal were something the crown prince could not believe he was seeing. As his eyes widened at the sight of the humanlike digits he tried to move his head to see the beast that was going to kill him. As his eyes rose they came face-to-face with an animal he had always heard tales of from his Hebrew servants. They had been mere stories to scare all Egyptian children about a mighty beast that guarded the eastern gates of the empire. The Golia were mythical animals sent by the god of the Egyptian underworld for the defense of the two lands. Now the prince saw that the subject of those tales that had been meant to frighten him as a boy was now staring right at him. The beast's yellow eyes glowed brightly as its huge muzzle opened wide to allow the prince to see the sharp teeth and the saliva dripping from them. The mud covering the animal was crusted and smelled of dead things and that was when the prince, the firstborn son of Ramesses II, knew these animals had buried themselves in the mud of the plain after the tide had left and waited until the sea had returned to spring their trap.

The onetime children's tale raised its muzzle to the sky and the howl of triumph filled the blackened sky as the crown prince of Egypt was slowly torn limb from limb.

A half a mile away the old and weary man was assisted down from the island and eased into a small ark. His gray hair and beard were covered by thick robes as he bent his head in utter weariness.

"Is it over?" one of the Hebrew soldiers asked as the two men pushed the small dugout toward the eastern shore of the Sea of Reeds.

"This day the Lord has sent us the true deliverers of the people to do battle for us, and after this night you will see the armies of Pharaoh never more."

The men saw the old man lower his head and cover his face with the fold of his robe. The killing was far from over and their flight just beginning and the awful truth of their situation was sitting before them weeping and forever crazed by events never meant for a human to experience. The old man rested for the years of fleeing ahead of them.

The men around him knew Moses the Deliverer was dying.

THE PLAIN OF MOAB, ISRAELITE ENCAMPMENT AT ABBEL-SHITTIM, 1520 BCE—THIRTY-SIX YEARS LATER

In the fading light of the setting sun the elder stood upon the rise and looked to the west as a freshening breeze brought the smell of desert water to his nostrils. He slowly reached up and pulled the shroud from his head—the hair was once brown with strength but now it was colored gray with age and to the elder that translated to the color of guilt. If the tribal elder strained his aging eyes into the setting sun he could almost see the shimmer of the River Jordan many miles distant. He knew this to be wishful thinking on his behalf, as the river ran deep, cutting itself into the small valley beyond the hills and plain of Moab—thus impossible to see from this great distance. As he watched the sun finally set beyond the great sea to the west he saw the oil lamps of the city start to illuminate the desert surrounding the last obstacle standing in the way of a promised homeland for his people.

"The city seems to come to life after the setting of the sun. But the real truth be it never sleeps. The city is a live, breathing animal—an animal that stands between your people and their new home."

Joshua didn't turn at the sound of the deep voice behind him, instead he once more placed the shroud upon his head.

"The task before us is great," Joshua said, "even more so than our flight from Pharaoh. The walls of Jericho are too thick, too high, and there are too many Canaanites defending them. I fear they outnumber the forces of our Lord five to one."

"There will be no trick of light or mysterious plague that delivers the city of Jericho unto you. The walls must fall and it will take an effort unlike any that has come before, Joshua, son of Nun. As before, brother, you stand against the impossible."

The smaller man finally turned and faced his visitor. The five-man bodyguard, men who were now Joshua's constant companions, watched the much larger elder of the tribe of Jeddah. Joshua, the leader of the Israelites, tried to see the eyes under the many folds of the hooded robe, but the darkness there was as complete as the night sky.

"They have caught every man and woman I have sent into the city to gather the information I need. My forward elements tell me their heads are even now spiked to the front gates of that cursed city."

The visitor to the encampment stood silent knowing Joshua had not finished what he had to say. Even after three years of separation the visitor knew Joshua better than all but one man.

Joshua ben Nun of the tribe of Ephraim placed a hand on the shoulder of his guest as he gestured with his other toward the open tent and the welcoming smell of cooking meat.

"Come, friend Kale, we will break bread and share the meat offered by our new homeland. It has been three very long years since we spoke, my friend. The tribes of man have missed your tribe and its brotherhood. Your rearguard action against our many enemies has brought us through the harshest of lands to this, the home Moses has led us unto."

The large man hesitated as he saw the women of Joshua inside preparing the evening meal. He stopped short of the tent's opening and refused entrance into the house of the man who had replaced Moses the Deliverer. The new leader of the chosen saw the fear in the women's faces as they finally spied just who their guest was. When their eyes saw the robed figure next to their husband and father, they scurried from the tent, not waiting long enough to serve the master of the house. The women, with eyes lowered, were all careful to skirt past Joshua with heads bowed, but even more so in deference to the hooded figure next to him.

"Forgive them, old friend. Old fears never leave us, they just settle in like mud between your toes and harden like the hearts of men. And even if you remove that mud the stain of filth is still there."

"The fears of women and children do not concern me, brother Joshua. You and the Deliverer before you have perpetrated the falsity of my tribe to the others, thus necessitating their fears. We are nothing but butchers and witches— nothing more than a tribe of magicians and tricksters to them. And it has been three years, two months, and eighteen days since the Jeddah have joined with other men of Israel."

Joshua gestured for his guest to sit. Kale refused. When offered bread, another refusal.

"I will break bread with my people tonight," Kale said. "The Jeddah have been on the march since the turning of the season. The treasure wagons are still months behind."

Joshua finally removed his shroud and then shook his head.

"I am the most tired man on God's great earth, brother Kale. We heard of your battle against the Canaanite charioteers near the plain of Deeab." Joshua noticed the lowered head of his oldest friend and the greatest warrior he had ever seen in action for the Egyptians, or against them. "Did you lose many warriors of the tribe of Jeddah?"

"All told since the Great Exodus, the Jeddah have been sacrificed to the count of one thousand soldiers."

The tent was silent as Joshua bowed his head in a silent prayer. He slowly raised his face to the highest part of his tent as if he were seeking wisdom from the highest of sources. Joshua took a deep breath.

"A heavy toll, brother, but a necessary one I fear, just as the task ahead will also take a heavy toll on the chosen," he hesitated momentarily, "and of the Golia. Thirty-six years of wandering, Kale. Of never finding the home promised by our Lord. We need your soldiers and your animals this one last time."

"We have lost all but twelve of the Golia. And there are only two females left to continue the breed. The remainder cannot be risked." Kale softened his voice when he saw that Joshua was actually pained by not only the loss of the soldiers of the Jeddah tribe, but also because of the battle deaths of the magnificent animals that made their Exodus from the land of Pharaoh possible. The special breed of beast were slowly being killed off nearly to extinction for the benefit of the other tribes. "The Golia alone broke the son of Ramesses at the Sea of Reeds while the Hebrew army escaped and crossed the wetlands. An escape made possible by the loss of twenty of the most prized male Golia. And then last month on the plain of Deeab, eight more males and three of the remaining females were lost when they attacked the enemy of Israel as they lay in ambush of the relief army you sent searching for us—or more to the point, the people's spoils from the conquests of Egypt and Canaan."

"Old friend, we owe the Lord's greatest creation our very existence. Without the Golia, we never would have escaped the two lands—"

"As Moses promised me many years ago and you agreed, Joshua, I am taking the Golia and the tribe of Jeddah out of this land God has given unto the people. I am taking them to the far-off lands of the north where the Golia and the tribe of Jeddah can once again grow strong." Kale looked his old friend in the eyes. "We have done the bidding of the Deliverer, and that of our Lord God. We have done what was said could not be done. We have died for the people of Israel and we have been their host of war. It is time to allow the Golia to live free once more."

Joshua touched the shoulder of the much larger man. "You have taken the Jeddah and camped far from the other tribes this night. I had prayed that you would be among the children of Israel after your long journey into the land of Canaan. You have not broken bread with the other tribes since the Exodus from the land of Pharaoh."

"You and the prophet before you know the many reasons why the Jeddah cannot live among the people. It has been this way since the days of Joseph, and before that, Abraham. They too found it a matter of convenience to hide us and the animals away until needed."

"Your people, your tribe—are they not part of the chosen? Are they not a part of the plan of Moses, and therefore of God? In essence the Jeddah are God's people . . . therefore, *my people!*"

"Do not overstep your bounds, Joshua. Moses found himself punished and banned from this land for far less arrogance. The Lord God of Hosts did not mean for us to kill off his greatest creation outside of man, the Golia."

"Enough, Kale, I am not Moses! I do not have the gift of divine intervention. I am but a man—a very tired and worn man at that. No prophet." He lowered his eyes, unable to meet those of Kale. "Some would even say no war general," Joshua finished ashamedly as he finally looked up into the face of his greatest soldier. "We . . . no, I have need for the Jeddah and your—your very special kinship with the Golia one last time."

"No!" Kale said loudly as he took a step back. "We have fought for the people since we fled Egypt. Now there are but two hundred men, women, and children left in the tribe of Jeddah, and half of those will not make it to see another summer."

"It is your animals that are needed. The walls of Jericho must fall tonight."

"The Golia are dying, dying for the tribes of Israel. They are dying, being killed off by the enemies of the chosen people. And what is the reward we offer them for their service to God and all of Israel? You offer the one thing the animals have come to hate, Joshua. They hate death. They hate their dishonor. They are sickened by what they have been asked to do against our brother man. You offer yet more carnage and then and only then can the Golia's days of peace commence for an animal we turned warlike in nature. Only there will not be one animal left to cherish that peace, and their caretakers, my Jeddah, will not be far behind them in death."

Joshua's anger was legendary, but Kale did not flinch as the new leader of the Hebrews bound to his feet. The only movement Kale made was to lightly touch the bronze sword just under the folds of his large robe.

"Jericho must fall . . . it must fall tonight!"

"Then you had better marshal all your soldiers, old friend, because you take the city without the Jeddah and absent the Golia. I will not risk one more man of my tribe and not one more of the remaining animals will ever do murder for the people again."

"Is it murder to kill for the sake of seeking a home for all of the children of Israel?"

"Find a home, but live among the people of this new land. Soldiers of the enemy may need to die, but not their women and children—a murderous task you have become rather adept at, Joshua."

"Kale, after this night you and the Jeddah are free. The Golia will make the sojourn to the north with you. Take them and go as brothers."

Kale stopped at the tent's entrance but dared not ask the price of this surrender by Joshua.

"If you allow the Golia to accede to my battle plan, this city will fall tonight. After the walls of Jericho fall and the city burns you will be tasked with an even greater mission for the people of Israel."

Kale allowed his shoulders to slump as he was now informed of Joshua's true intent. The leader of the Jeddah knew Joshua as the most knowledgeable of men. Far more clever than even the prophet Moses when it came to the long-term plans of the children of Israel. Kale waited for the truth of his visit.

"After the fighting has finished in this land awash with water, tree, and fruit," Joshua explained, "I fear the people will never have true peace even then. I fear it was not meant to be so." Joshua went to Kale and touched the large man's shoulder and the Jeddah leader turned to face his old friend. "The people's treachery against God at Sinai has angered the Lord of Hosts and his punishment against his people for arrogance will be centuries of battle against the people and tribes of Canaan." Joshua looked at Kale with pleading eyes. "Only two of the Golia will be risked for the chance at not only life for God's beasts, but life for the Jeddah and a lasting chance for the people to have their heritage saved for them. In future battles we could lose our greatest treasures to the peoples of this land. After the fall of the city you will take that heritage with you and you will allow no man of any land and also no man of the chosen to ever know where our heritage lies hidden. That is your task. Leave us for your great stone mountains and I swear no man shall follow the Golia and the Jeddah. Two Golia and the casting of the spell—that is what I ask of the great Kale."

"You swear on the stone tablets that you and the chosen will not follow my people and the Golia to the north?"

"After this night the Jeddah are free to take the Golia and Pharaoh's artisans and engineers to erect the greatest temple in all of creation for the heritage of the people. Hide it well and you will never come to harm from the people of Israel."

"What are you doing, brother? You are giving away king's ransoms and our greatest gifts from God for what? So they will not be taken from the people when other greater armies come for you in the land of Canaan?" Kale stepped up to his old friend. "You lie to me, brother, why?"

Joshua turned away from Kale and removed his sword and then looked at it in the weak light cast from the oil lamps. "Because if we don't hide away forever that which has been taken as spoils in battle and the gifts from God himself, the people will never become one with the land and we will be fighting the Canaanites for a thousand years to keep this land. As long as the riches of Egypt and the gifts from

God remain with the people we will forever be fighting to protect that which is not important for life."

"You may not speak with God, but you truly speak for the people of God. If they discover you have given away the greatest gifts God has bestowed upon the people, they will curse your name, brother. You give the Golia and the Jeddah the gifts from God to hide among the rocks and ice of the north and you will be cursed."

Joshua laughed for the first time in what seemed like years.

"What could be worse than the gift of leadership that was bestowed upon me by Moses? No, my friend, I will not be killing my people off to protect treasure and heritage when it could all just vanish with you and yours into the night. The people fear the Golia, they will not follow. Build me my temple in the great stone mountains in the land of snow and frost and bury the treasure forever."

"I will instruct the Golia. I will inform you of the plan of attack. After this night Jericho will fall, Brother Joshua. Then I will take my people and the Golia and leave this place of death forever."

Joshua nodded. The deal had been struck and the Jeddah would do God's bidding one last time. He gestured for Kale to look upon the map of the great city and he pointed out his plan for the final battle of the Golia for God's chosen people.

In less than an hour Kale had summoned his two finest warriors for the casting of the spell and the link with the Golia.

The two guards in the south tower watched as the Hebrew army marched and demonstrated outside the city walls, their many thousand torches blazing a path of its march around their walls. The trumpets had started at sundown as they had every night since the four-month siege had started. One guard turned away and lifted a cloth from a bowl. He reached down and took a large chunk of stale bread, tore it in two, and tossed the smaller half to his companion. "Music makes me want food and drink." He shook his head at the moldy bread in his hand. "But I guess rock-hard bread will have to do."

The second tower guard accepted the bread and then turned to watch the drummers and the trumpeters, followed by sixty spear- and shield-wielding Hebrew soldiers continuing their march around the city walls.

"Those trumpets are maddening. They even invade my sleep." The guard looked at the bread in his hand and then tossed it over the side. "They even steal the taste right from your mouth," he said as he watched the bread sail over the edge of the tower and into the darkness below. "When will they attack?"

Chewing the bread with a look of disgust, the first guard paced the few feet to his companion and then tossed his own bread over the wall.

"They haven't enough soldiers to do anything but lay siege. They will move on when they see that the walls of Jericho cannot be breached."

The second chunk of five-day-old bread hit the rocks at the base of the six-foot-thick wall and rolled to the base of a small pomegranate tree. It was ignored by the large snout of the beast as its nostrils sought out other smells beyond that of the rotten food. As the bread came to rest only inches from the nose of the beast, the yellow eyes opened wider and the long muzzle of the wolf rose into the air and sniffed. The male could smell two men of Canaan. They were a hundred feet above the hidden male as it waited for the trumpets and drums to pass. In the darkness of the night the male slowly came to all fours directly under the guard tower. It sat and waited, smelled, making sure there were only the two men at this post. The beast sniffed the air once more and then turned its massive head to stare out at the small hills surrounding Jericho. At that moment two more of the Golia males slipped from hiding and with two great strides made it to the base of the wall.

Kale watched from a hidden location a mile away from the south wall. He saw the first animal as it watched its two male companions run past. Then the first beast raised his right paw upward and examined its padded foot. Slowly, methodically the Golia saw the clawed appendages coming from the knuckle just above the running pad, then the long fingers of the beast, which had been curled into a fist when not in use, extended until the long, slim, but powerful digits extended. The eight-inch black and purple claws were shining brightly in the moonlight on this, the last night in the history of the city of Jericho.

Kale looked back at the small fire and the two female attendants who watched over the two male warriors of the Jeddah as they sat silently and with eyes closed around the small fire. The women wiped sweat from their brows and dampened their mouths with water-soaked swatches. Both men of the Jeddah lay in a trance delivered from the spell and didn't move except for the rising and falling of their chests as they breathed. The Golia were in control of the two men and would not relinquish that hold until their mission had been completed. Kale concentrated on the third animal at the base of the wall—the alpha male of the pack.

The giant beast felt Kale's presence in its large brain. The leader of the tribe of Jeddah was reaching out to it. The beast shook its massive head, slinging the long, upright ears to the left and to the right. Saliva flew from its open muzzle as Kale came unbidden to its mind.

One of the attending women used a small cloth and dabbed at the spittle that flew from the Jeddah soldier closest to the fire.

The beast at the base of the wall stopped and listened, tilting its head first right and then left as Kale's words struck its mind in picture form. The animal used the raised right hand to push itself up higher until it was balanced on its two hind legs. Again the toes of the beast uncurled—it would not need the running pads on its feet for what needed doing this night of nights. The foot looked far more human than it had a moment before. The giant beast tested its footing on the loose shale beneath the wall. The eyes narrowed and the orders it had been given came clear to its thoughts. The animal, which now stood as tall as two men upon one another, raised its long powerful muzzle to the night sky, and then just before it shattered the night with the howl it wanted to loose upon the sky, it was bidden to hide once more from the man thoughts in its mind. There would be no howling, no fight before the walls were taken. Instead it lowered its head and then fell to all fours once more.

The two animals to the left and right of the alpha male sat at the base of the wall and both Golia knew what had to be done from the link with the two soldiers sitting a mile away from the walls of Jericho. The first wolf sank its claws into the clay and stone wall. Then it raised its powerful hand once more and sank the second set of claws deep into the wall. Then it started to climb, quickly followed by the second Golia. The same was happening on the other darkened walls of Jericho. The black-on-black movement of the beasts was undetectable on the moonless night. Joshua had only requested two Golia for the attack, but Kale had used five. This would end tonight.

The drums and trumpets became even louder as the Golia struck the guard towers with a fierceness the men of Canaan were not capable of withstanding. The attack on Jericho had started and now there was no stopping the Golia from opening the rear gates of the city of Jericho. The magic was happening again, just as it had on a thousand different nights when the Golia fought for their brothers.

Joshua stood upon the rise three miles from the burning city. As the screams and sounds of fighting came to his ears he collapsed to his knees. The leader of the people pulled the shroud of his robe over his head and prayed forgiveness for the carnage he had set loose in the city of Jericho. The screams of the women and children and the shouts of his own soldiers could clearly be heard across the River Jordan.

"Lord God, forgive my weak use of your words. The needs of the people have driven my mind to madness. I need guidance to—"

"He is not listening to you this night of nights, Joshua."

His prayer interrupted, Joshua froze as he recognized the voice. It was Kale.

"I cannot stop the screaming in my head."

"The voices of the children of Jericho will forever haunt your mind. That is your price, Joshua," Kale said and then added, "as it is my own."

"Our losses?" Joshua asked as he pulled the shroud from his head.

Kale looked up and across the River Jordan. The flames were now a thousand feet high in the center of the large city. As he watched, a great watchtower along the southern wall collapsed into the streets below, sending a fresh wave of screaming and shouting into the night sky.

"The tribes have lost no more than three hundred in the attack. The Jeddah have lost eight soldiers, and we have . . ." His voice trailed off to nothing as his eyes saw another section of the great northern wall fall and even more of the Hebrew army charge over the smoking ruin of rubble.

"You have lost Golia?"

Kale was silent as Joshua rose to his feet.

"Two males were near the southern wall when it collapsed. After they silenced the guards in the tower, it was they who opened the smaller southern gate for your soldiers. They were near there when the wall fell, crushing the life from their bodies." Kale gestured behind him and Joshua turned to see two men being carried by other Jeddah soldiers and the two attending women, who cried into their veils as they left Joshua's encampment. They had died, just slumped over and fell dead the moment the lives of the two Golia were crushed from the falling stone of the walls. Their faces and bodies were covered but Joshua could see an arm, mangled and broken, as it fell from the side of the dead soldier.

"Old friend, the task has been done. Take the treasures and spoils of the chosen and go—"

"We have already taken that which was offered by the people." Kale leaned close to Joshua so he could see the elder's eyes. "Only we have taken one more item that was not offered. One that will ensure you never come north to find my tribe or the Golia. We will destroy the very heritage of the people if any attempt is made. Your charade against Israel after the death of Moses will destroy the people if known. Come for us and we will give you a war the likes of which you have only seen in minority. Come for us and the Jeddah will release the Golia among the chosen." Kale turned and started walking away. "Leave us be, Joshua, and send no soldiers to find us. This land of milk and honey has been closely won with the blood of the Golia . . . and your own people."

"What have you taken?" Joshua shouted. "Kale!" He gestured his five-man guard to stop the much larger Kale from walking away.

Kale smiled as he continued to walk. The sun had just started to rise above the far eastern mountains when the guard came within a spear tip of reaching Kale. Suddenly the five men in braided leather and rope armor saw the three animals sitting on the top of the small ridge. They had risen out of the ground fog that had slowly moved in from the Jordan. The black animal in the middle slowly rose to all fours, and then to Joshua's and the five-man guard's amazement the beast actually stood on its hind feet. The long and powerful arms were stretched out along its side and the clawed fingers opened and closed. In the early morning light they could see the blood-soaked muzzle of the animal after its night's work inside the fallen walls of Jericho. The beast was the alpha male that had linked with Kale outside the walls of the city. The other two beasts stayed on all fours and remained unmoving, but their menacing glare never wavered from Joshua and his guard. Kale finally stopped and turned.

"Use us no more, Joshua. We are free of Pharaoh. We are free of the chosen people. Come for us and I will send what remains of the Golia south once more."

Joshua watched as Kale vanished over the small rise followed by the two beasts on all fours while the third remained. The yellow, glowing eyes moved from the armed men to settle on Joshua.

Joshua swallowed back the rising bile in his throat, as this was the first time he had seen one of the male Golia up close. His wife, Lilith, took hold of his arm as she too saw the wolf for the first time. As the great beast stared at him, Joshua saw the lip curl up over eight-inch-long canines as a low growl issued from its throat.

It suddenly went to all fours and in one great leap jumped over the rise and vanished. The warning had been delivered.

Joshua was ill. He had never felt the fear he had when the animal looked upon him. He then remembered the words of Kale and then angrily tore free of his wife and ran for the largest of the tents a hundred yards away. As the city of Jericho burned below on the other side of the River Jordan, Joshua, leader of the chosen people, ran past the twenty-man guard and into the tent. His eyes went to the center and his heart fell. It was gone. The one item he could never lose had now been taken. His eyes roamed to the far side of the tent and that was when he saw the massive tear in the rough-hewn fabric. He then spied the massive claw prints in the sand. The Golia had gotten in past the twenty-man guard and stolen the one object that could bring down the trust of the chosen people and the love they had of him as a successor to the Deliverer.

"Joshua, what is it?" Lilith, wife of fifty-two years, asked as he collapsed to the sand. Then her eyes widened when she realized what was missing from the tent that held the Hebrews' greatest religious objects. "What do we tell the people?" Lilith asked as she turned away from the empty space where the gilded box had lain. "The covenant is still here. Why, my husband, would the Jeddah take not the Ark of the Covenant, but take the—"

"The people must never know what was taken. Never."

"What will you do, my husband?"

In the distance the sound came. It was loud enough that it filled the early morning sky and even drowned out the sound of butchery across the river in Jericho. The sound echoed off distant hills and was not absorbed by the fog as sounds often are. The roar of the beast was a challenge to the world—the Golia were now free and they would never follow the death words of men again.

"I pray that Kale builds my temple and lays to rest for all time the heritage of the people; to be locked away behind stone and earth. If he does this he will never have fear from me or mine. Let him travel to the stone mountains, let Kale and the Jeddah be. Let the Golia be."

The roar of the giant wolf was followed by the sound of howling that coursed through the valley of Moab as every remaining animal left of the family of Golia mourned the loss of the two irreplaceable males.

The Jeddah, along with God's last magic found on earth—the Golia—moved into the distant, barren, and foreboding lands far to the north.

The Lost Tribe of Jeddah would forever dwell in the land of darkness beyond the lands of the Hittites—in the lost world of the stone mountains of the great north.

HONG KONG HARBOR,
APRIL 1, 1949

The gleaming white yacht sat anchored in the bay of Hong Kong glistening in the illumination cast from a full moon and the festive multicolored lights that had been strung from bow to stern. The largest yacht inside the harbor was hard to miss as it sat motionless at a minimum of two miles from any fishing or harbor patrol boat, creating an island unto itself in the great expanse of the harbor. The only vessels allowed near the gleaming white hull of the *Golden Child* were the rented whaleboats that had been cleaned and lined with satin pillows for the invited guests as they traversed the busy waterway on their way to the largest auction of Palestinian and ancient Canaanite antiquities the world had ever seen.

Golden Child was owned by a man known as Charles Sentinel, a Canadian commodities broker of some ill repute. It boasted accommodation for forty overnight guests and had an interior salon that measured 182 feet in length and could handle a party of hundreds. Tonight however, the salon would only accommodate thirty. The remaining space would be taken up by the items everyone on the *Golden Child* had come to see. The evening belonged to Lord Hartford Harrington, who had agreed to the astronomical lease price for the ship of $2 million for the weekend. There could be no other more secure location for the greatest antiquities sell-off in a hundred years.

As the third to the last whaleboat wound its way around the tied-up water taxis made famous in Hong Kong, the woman saw the *Golden Child* in the distance for the first time. As her green eyes roamed over the shape and silhouette of the ship her mind raced. This was the first time she had assigned herself a field operation, and also the first time she had disobeyed an order from the director. If he knew she was four thousand miles from home with no field security team in place she may as well find somewhere to live inside China because she could never go home again. *"Garrison would kill me,"* she mumbled to herself as the whaleboat slowly made its way to the large staircaselike gangway that had been set up on the starboard side of the three-hundred-foot-long *Golden Child*.

Twenty-one-year-old Alice Hamilton was outfitted in the finest dress her limited bank account could cover. She had to borrow the wide-brimmed white hat that matched the dress. The gown itself was a satin turquoise one-strap item that made her feel a tad uncomfortable. It was almost embarrassing that her field equipment was listed as one party dress and one borrowed hat while the other field units in her department had to settle for desert camping gear and weapons hidden among their picks and shovels. If she were lucky, Alice thought, she might be able to come up with a fingernail file for protection. She wondered once more for the hundredth time if she knew what she was doing.

Alice tried to hide the large intake of breath as a line was tossed to one of the deckhands waiting on the bottom platform of the yacht's gangway. Here she was getting ready to step into the den of some of the most ruthless dealers in ancient art and antiquities ever assembled and she was going in with possibly a nail file and a knockout dress. But Alice knew she had to chance it once word had reached her desk at the Event Group that something unusual in the antiquities world was about to take place. Alice had used every contact, informant, and had even called in favors owed to her by the FBI and the new CIA to get the location of the auction.

This was her baby and not even General Garrison Lee could bully her into not taking this chance to stop some of the theft of the ancient world.

Alice Hamilton was the widowed wife of one of Garrison Lee's men from his old Office of Strategic Services days during the war. After the surrender of Japan the young widow had gone to work for the new director of Department 5656 in September of 1946. The man named Garrison Lee was a beast and by far the hardest man in the world to work for. The former senator from Maine was a thinker who covered every aspect of field operations, and one of his staunchest rules was that no office, lab, or academic personnel could go on field missions without a covert military police escort. She smiled at the standing order. Alice knew she was none of those. She was the personal assistant to one of the most ingenious men she had ever known. And now she wished he were with her.

As she was assisted to her feet by the white-coated helmsman of the whaleboat, she thought about Lee and what his reaction would be when he found out her little vacation to visit her mother back home in Virginia had turned into a weeklong trip to the South China Sea in search of stolen artifacts. She had fought for the assignment but Garrison Lee had said no—that it was not part of the Event Group charter to retrieve stolen antiquities. She knew this to be the largest lie that Lee had ever told her. He took chances time and time again to recover items from not only the past of the United States, but that of the world.

Department 5656 of the National Archives, or better known to its scientists, archaeologists, teachers, professors, and military personnel as the Event Group, was a creation of President Abraham Lincoln in 1863. It became a chartered section of the National Archives in 1916 and signed into American law (albeit secretly) in that same year. Its mission was to discover the true history of the world's past. The Group's job was to ensure that the United States avoided the pitfalls stumbled into by mankind throughout history by learning the truth about how we got to where we are, and to learn where the world was going. The Event Group protected the United States from committing the same sins as our forefathers and their ancient European or Asian ancestors.

Alice loved the concept but had found the actual work chosen for her by her boss, Garrison Lee, mundane and boring, more that of an academic investigator than team leader, and that was not Alice and Lee knew that. The general could not keep her caged up as he had the past four years: he was overprotective of her and that infuriated the twenty-one-year-old widow no end. Thus this one chance to prove she could be a field operative and handle the very worst of people.

Alice adjusted the stole around her shoulders and the fishnet, large-brimmed white hat that half covered her beautiful eyes. As she made her way up the gangway she experienced her first hint of nervousness as she spied the two men at the top of the gangway who were watching her move slowly up the steps. Their eyes saw the shapely body beneath the expensive dress and the subtle movement of her breasts that were hidden very badly in the French-designed fashion. Alice felt so humiliated knowing the dress was not anything like her. She was far more comfortable in men's pants and shorts and far happier with a shovel and pickax.

As she reached the top of the steps she saw that the two men were armed with weapons poorly hidden in their waistbands. She knew the men *wanted* her to see that they were armed.

The first man half bowed and held out his hand. Alice swallowed and then pulled the invitation from her handbag. The gilded, gold-embossed invitations were numbered and a security code printed on the front ensured that no one uninvited would be allowed to board this ship. Again Alice swallowed hard but managed a smile as she handed the forged invitation to the large guard. The security man looked it over and without hesitation handed the invitation back to the young American.

"Welcome to the *Golden Child*, Mrs. Hamilton, your host eagerly awaits your opinion on his collection. Please, follow Mr. Chow into the salon."

Alice was about to speak but her words caught in her throat as she realized that she was far more frightened about what she was doing than she thought she would have been. Instead she nodded her head and followed the largest Chinese man she had ever seen onto the boat deck. As she did she heard the engines of the *Golden Child* start and then the sound of the anchor being raised and felt the rattling of the teak deck. She stopped momentarily as the great yacht surged forward in the calm bay of Hong Kong.

"Don't worry, ma'am, the *Golden Child* will anchor ten miles out to sea for . . ." The Chinese brute smiled down at Alice. "Security reasons."

Alice knew then that if she needed help of any kind it wasn't going to be found beyond the territorial limits of Hong Kong. That meant if for any reason her true intent was discovered she would find it hard swimming the ten miles back into the bay, especially with a few bullets in her back and sharks stalking her. She knew then that she may have made the biggest mistake of her young life.

The *Golden Child* put to sea.

Alice Hamilton, a girl of twenty-one from the town of Manassas, Virginia, who until this year had never been farther from home than Nevada, found herself being escorted to the fantail of the magnificent yacht. As she rounded the corner she took a deep breath and told herself to relax. As she told herself this she felt the slow movement of the *Golden Child* heading for the open sea. The departure wasn't noticed by the many men and women on the fantail standing and sipping drinks as waiters and other servants wound their way through the expensively dressed guests.

Alice momentarily froze as she stood looking at the white dinner jackets and budget-breaking gowns. As they stood with martinis and other drinks in their manicured fingers, she realized that as soon as she opened her mouth to any one of these people they would know immediately that she didn't belong. They would eventually see right through the forged invitation that had been prepared for her by the intelligence element inside Department 5656, another little item Garrison would be furious about. She swallowed, wanting to jump off the fantail before the ship was too far out to sea.

"The water is extremely cold and you would more than likely get run over by a water taxi—that is if the sharks don't get to you first."

Alice felt her heart catch at the sound of the thick and even voice behind her. Masked beneath the dark veil of her hat, her eyes closed as she tried to gather her courage. She opened her eyes and turned.

"And I hope that dress didn't come out of the petty cash drawer in your desk."

Alice looked up and into the face of Garrison Lee. He was dressed in a white dinner jacket, bow tie, and of all things horrid in the world, a bright red cummerbund. His eye patch was over his right eye but that didn't stop Alice from seeing that the scarred brow itself was arched in that way Lee had of intimidating those who worked for him. The brown hair was perfectly combed and the small touch of gray at his temples made him look far more menacing than she had remembered.

"We don't have a petty cash box, and if we did I would have told you to use it to buy another tuxedo—or at least a cummerbund that doesn't look like you're wearing a stop sign," she said with as much indignation as she could muster, trying to get the upper hand for the battle she knew was coming.

His brow furrowed even more as he self-consciously looked down at his waist as Alice walked past him and toward the group of high-stakes antiquities players. She deftly reached out and took a glass of champagne from a passing waiter without missing a step.

The six-foot-five-inch Garrison Lee watched her leave and then looked down at the bright red cummerbund once more. He was now actually confused as to how Alice had turned the tables on him before he could get her into a corner about vanishing like she had from her desk at the Event Group complex. He grimaced and then followed her into the milling crowd.

"Well, we're here so I suspect you have a plan?" Lee asked the retreating form of Alice. "Most field agents have a plan before going in. Or at the very minimum ask their director to assist in formulating that plan."

"Champagne?" She suddenly turned and thrust a glass into Lee's hand. As he reached for it she suddenly pulled it away. "Oh I forgot you're a bourbon man," Alice said as she turned for the bar near the far stern railing.

Lee smiled and nodded at those few guests that had heard the brief exchange. He nodded and embarrassingly made his way toward Alice, who had her back to him while standing at the ornate bar. He stepped to her left and leaned against the bar, letting his cane dangle uselessly at his side, his anger spent for the moment. A few of the high-priced guests near the couple looked up and saw the scarred, very large man leaning next to them and then they smiled uncomfortably when they noticed Lee's facial scars and ducked away.

"You know, Hamilton," Lee said as his eyes followed the three guests as they exited the bar area of the fantail, "I counted no fewer than four suspected murderers, two known antiquities thieves, and a well-known and respected British lord who purportedly was raiding dig sites throughout the Middle East during the British occupation. And I noticed all of this in just the past few seconds walking over here. You, Mrs. Hamilton, are out of your element. And that will get people killed." Lee didn't turn to face her; he just reached out and took the proffered drink from the bartender.

"How am I supposed to learn anything stuck in that underground hell you call a complex?" she hissed as she smiled at the bartender as he passed her another glass of champagne.

"Listen, I—"

"Ladies and gentlemen, welcome aboard the *Golden Child*. I believe we have a very special evening in store for your pleasure."

Lee and Alice turned at the announcement. The man was impeccably dressed in a white tuxedo with a black cummerbund.

"I told you, red cummerbunds are so tacky," Alice said softly through the side of her mouth.

"I apologize for not having the same taste as our host, Lord Hartford Benetton Harrington, the seventeenth Lord of Southington."

"Sounds made-up," Alice said as she looked the stately host over from head to toe.

Lee glanced over quickly as he took in Alice for the first time without his anger blinding his one good eye. He saw her eyes beneath the black veil watching their host make his greeting. The perfect jawline coupled with her slightly turned-up nose usually calmed Lee down like no sight in the world—but this night was different. Her looks now had the opposite effect on him as he realized what a dangerous situation the girl had placed herself in.

"Tonight you will be witness to one of the truly great collections in the world. We will present to you, ladies and gentlemen, many items of history and from the dawn of man and his understanding of not just himself, but that of his God, or gods." Many of the guests nodded appreciatively. Lee just watched on with distaste. "These are not just mere antiquities that will thrill and enthrall you at each viewing, ladies and gentlemen, they will mesmerize you—and of course checks will be acceptable."

The gathered guests chuckled at the humor displayed by the Englishman, who smiled and nodded at the men and women as they passed him heading for the salon belowdecks. The man had the appearance of a smiling shark as his prey swam around him.

"Since we're here, do you think you could put my perceived shortcomings on the knowledge of field operations aside long enough to allow us to do our job?" Alice said as she pulled the stole around her shoulders and made ready to follow the others. She half turned and her green eyes settled on Lee's blue one.

"I had already come to that conclusion and told you so before you stormed off half-cocked." He looked at her with intense gaze. "Don't think this is over, Hamilton."

"Believe me, I know it's not over," she said as she extended her left arm. "Now, shall we see what all of the fuss is about, General?"

Lee smiled enough that his teeth blazed, as it was hard enough to do without breaking off his teeth in his anger. "By all means, Mrs. Hamilton."

As they fell in line with the crowd walking through the gilded glass doors of the salon, Lee felt many eyes on them. Thus far he had counted at least seven armed guests. At least five heavily armed guards, and of course that wasn't counting the crew. He now felt he and Alice were walking into the bowels of a pirate ship and he also knew they were making this up on the fly. He leaned in close to Alice when he knew no one was in hearing distance.

"We observe and we make mental notes of what we see being auctioned. Then we report everything to the Hong Kong police. If we're real lucky we can get the information on what's here and where in the hell it came from. All our department is interested in is the history of the pieces involved, not their value, but their provenance. Our job is not recovery. Our job is to document the history of the pieces and discover if we have a historical precedent to alter the perceived historical reference to those items or the location in which they were discovered. Agreed?"

"I never intended anything different," was her curt reply.

As the guests walked down a wide carpeted stairway, Alice was the first to see the black satin-covered objects set up in the massive salon of the *Golden Child*. Spotlights had been arranged for maximum effect once the black dustcovers were removed. To Garrison Lee it was nothing more than antiquity thieves making thievery as legitimate-looking as possible.

Some of the objects were massive, while others were small. Alice quickly counted eighty-seven objects. As the guests were again offered drinks and champagne, the satin covers were slowly pulled away from the items to be sold.

"Ladies and gentlemen, the items on sale here tonight have all been authenticated and a provenance has been established for the . . ." the British lord smiled almost embarrassingly, ". . . the more controversial pieces." The seventeenth Lord of Southington raised a flute of champagne. "Please, peruse the collection and enjoy, the sale will commence as soon as everyone has viewed the items."

Lee turned slowly, taking in the faces of the buyers. Alice momentarily watched Garrison. She knew his mind was one of those rare things in the world that make one afraid to know someone too closely. As the former OSS man looked at the faces around them as the guests moved toward the illuminated objects, she knew he was mentally taking a picture of every face he saw. He had a photographic memory and never once forgot a name he had been given or the face that was attached to that name. The senator had made Alice extremely uncomfortable before she got to know him in the years since they met at Walter Reed Army Hospital in 1945 where he was recovering from the devastating wounds received at the end of the war.

"Well, are they all arch-criminals?" she asked as Lee accepted another drink from a waiter.

"While not arch-criminals, nonetheless, there are some very seedy characters here," he said as he pretended to sip at his drink. "And a few others that don't belong here at all." His eyes wandered over to a man who stood in the far corner with a small plate in his hand. The man was slowly eating caviar on toast points and Lee saw that the man wasn't that good on his surveillance techniques. "Like this gentleman in the far corner, he seems quite interested in you far more than the antiquities at auction. I suspect the revealing dress is more fascinating to him than any old broken pottery. "

"Is there anyone else that doesn't belong in this den of thieves, General?"

"A few," he answered and then turned away. "I think we better split up, we seem to have attracted the attention of our host."

Alice smiled and then slowly turned and saw Lord Harrington conferring with a uniformed crewman and two of the plainclothes security men and they were looking right at her. Alice moved into the milling guests as they started to examine the artifacts.

Lee moved off to the far end of the lined exhibit, stopping in front of two urns that had been braced upon the tops of columned pedestals. The director of Department 5656 was just starting to look away when he decided that he needed a closer look at the two urns. His interest was piqued. The urns were faded and both had several large cracks coursing through their surfaces where the artisans had taken painstaking time in their reconstruction. Lee saw designs and artwork he wasn't familiar with. He could see they were possibly of Canaanite provenance in construct but the images were unlike any he had ever seen before. The former OSS general leaned closer and read the placard attached to the pedestal:

THE BROTHER AND SISTER URNS
UNEARTHED AT TELL ES-SULTAN—THE ANCIENT CITY OF JERICHO
12/8/1943

"Son of a bitch," Lee hissed beneath his breath. The exclamation was loud enough that a French woman next to Lee gave him a distasteful look and moved away to the next exhibit.

"Those were almost my exact words when these two exceptional beauties were unearthed."

Lee closed his one good eye and then gathered himself as he straightened after reading the placard. He smiled and nodded at the smaller man standing next to him. He had a pencil-thin mustache and his cheeks were reddened to the point Lee suspected the man to be wearing rouge.

"You must be Lord Harrington?" Garrison asked, placing his hands with his cane behind his back instead of offering his host his hand in greeting.

"The very same, uh, Mr. . . . ?"

"Kilroy, Addison Kilroy," Lee said as he held the man's eyes with his own. Neither man blinked at Lee's use of the infamous cartoon graffito of a million American servicemen during World War II—the famous *Kilroy Was Here*.

"Ah, I see. Many apologies, Mr. Kilroy, so many invitations were sent out I failed to recall sending yours."

Lee reached into his dinner jacket and produced the wax-sealed invitation forged by the same agent at the complex that created the fake documents for Alice.

"Sir, I have no need to see your invitation. I just wanted to greet my guests and offer any explanation of the items that I may."

"Well," Garrison said as he replaced the forged invite into his jacket, "I must say these are two very important pieces—if they're real, of course. I mean, the ruins at Tell es-Sultan are closed to archaeological study, ordered by your government in the forties and the no-dig policy has been carried over by the new state of Israel."

Lord Harrington smiled and nodded his head. "Yes, the ruins at Tell es-Sultan have been closed, as you can see for very good reason. There are some unscrupulous people in the world today that would take advantage of such marvelous finds, Mr. Kilroy."

Lee nodded his head and smiled crookedly. "There are indeed, sir, very unscrupulous people. I mean, the mystical city of Jericho? A lot of people would call that blasphemous to dig there." Lee leaned in close to Lord Harrington, who stood his ground not too comfortably against the scarred and very much larger Garrison Lee. "I mean, the city was supposedly destroyed on the orders of God himself. Frightening stuff," Lee said with his brow arched high above his eye patch, waiting for a reaction from his host.

"Fairy tales to scare the unenlightened, Mr. Kilroy."

Lee smiled, broadly this time. "I've learned that fairy tales, when ignored as such, tend to be more truthful in the end than first thought and that they also usually come back and bite you right in your hindquarters when taken too lightly, Lord Harrington."

The smile from the American was unsettling to the Englishman, enough so that he half bowed and slowly backed away, nodding toward his security people that this man was to be watched. Lee lost his smile as he turned back to the stolen urns.

Alice nervously looked over her shoulder and saw that Lee was holding his own with their host. She closed her eyes and nearly walked into a woman standing in her path.

"Oh, excuse me," Alice said as she placed her empty champagne glass on the tray of a passing waiter. Then her eyes locked on the young girl she had nearly collided with. They were approximately the same age. As Alice looked closer at the raven-haired woman she could see that the dark beauty had one brown eye and one green eye. She was a beautiful girl. Then Alice saw that she was also being examined, *or more to the point*, she thought, she was being sized up by the girl like she was a possible adversary.

"American?" the girl asked as her eyes roamed over the dress Alice was wearing. The strange young woman wore a plain black satin dress that was as gorgeous as Alice's expensive gown. Her equally black and shiny hair was straight and shiny and she wore large but not ostentatious gold hoop earrings.

"Yes, I'm American," Alice answered as she watched the young girl with the strange European accent and multicolored eyes look over every inch of her.

"Yes, I can actually smell the difference," the girl said as she finally stopped examining Alice and then looked into her eyes under the veil.

"Excuse me?" Alice said with that tinge of anger that exposed itself at most times unbidden—Garrison was rubbing off on her to her horror as she felt her defensive hackles rise.

"Well fed—Americans smell well fed," the gorgeous young woman answered as she turned to look at a large stone block. She crossed her arms and looked at the ancient section of wall that once stood at Tell es-Sultan—the ruins of the city of Jericho. "Interesting piece, don't you think . . . Miss . . . ?"

"Hamilton, and it's Mrs.," Alice said, looking from the girl to the giant block that appeared as if it taxed the carpeted salon deck with its massive weight. Suddenly Alice's eyes widened when she realized what it was she had been directed to look at. She didn't see the girl beside her smile as Alice leaned closer to look at the strange object embedded in the stone.

The granite block was eight feet high and as many feet thick. It had been rough-hewed and quarried thousands of years before. The tool marks were still clearly visible on the block's leading edges, a surefire way of determining the provenance of the piece, as the tools themselves were linked to a specific region of the Middle East.

However, it was the relief carving in the dead center of the stone that froze the heart of the American girl from the farmlands of Virginia. The raised outline of the animal was clearly visible. The stone block looked as if the relief was carved around the depiction of something out of a nightmare. The muzzle of the beast could clearly be seen and even the claws of its hands were in stark contrast to the surrounding stone.

Alice suddenly realized she wasn't looking at a carving of a deity of some kind from long-ago Jericho, she was looking at an animal that had been crushed between two massive stones. She could even see scorch marks from a long-ago fire. Her eyes went to the sand-colored and now petrified beast. The animal was massive and as Alice examined the piece others were drawn to the stone block. Many were crying hoax and some were angry at an obvious attempt at humor by their host, Lord Harrington.

The young European girl smiled and then without another word and with her eyes on the man that Hamilton had been speaking with a moment ago, the strange and exotic woman left the gathering crowd of skeptical bidders.

Alice never noticed that the woman had left her side, as she couldn't take her eyes from the block and the animal mysteriously encased there. Recognition sprang immediately to her memory.

"Vault 22871," she whispered to herself. Most of the gathered guests had already voiced their opinion on the stone block and its obvious defacement, or outright attempt at a hoax, and then moved on, leaving a stunned and shocked Alice, who knew she had to bring Garrison over to the stone block. The assistant to the director of Department 5656 knew she had stumbled onto something that even

the great General Lee could not ignore. As she turned, Alice came face-to-face with
a small and ancient-looking woman.

"You will have to excuse my granddaughter, things related to our distant past
do not impress her the way that they should."

Alice heard what the old woman was saying but nothing was registering in her
head. A well-dressed and appointed lady in a light but elegant white gown with pink
highlights. Alice placed her age at somewhere in the eighties. Her cane looked like
an old twisted wooden walking stick complete with what on closer inspection
looked like the Egyptian Eye of Ra embossed in gold on the handle. Not an ordinary walking stick. Her clothes were beautiful. The dress satiny and fine and her
gold jewelry sparkled in the salon spotlights. Alice looked closer and saw a tattoo
that began at the woman's neck and disappeared into her dress. The top of the
tattoo was that of a pentagram, the five-pointed star, but Alice couldn't see what
the rest of the tattoo held below the neckline.

"I am Madam Korvesky." She turned to look at the stone block and the animal
that had been crushed to death by it more than three thousand years before. "We
have come a great distance to denounce this . . . this abomination." The old woman
smiled and then looked at Alice with her aged eyes. "But I can tell that you have
seen this sort of trickery before my dear, am I correct?" The old woman stepped
closer to the young American. "Yes, I see the recognition in your eyes, young
one."

Alice didn't say anything at first; she just raised her white-gloved hand and
slowly reached out and touched the petrified image of the beast.

"Don't do that." The old woman reached out and lightly took Alice's hand and
pulled it away, giving her another grandmotherly smile. "Bad things can come of
it," she continued, but her next action betrayed her warning as a lie as she herself
reached out and lightly ran her old and weathered hand over the stone-hardened
fur and teeth of the beast. Then the old woman's spell seemed to break and she
smiled and looked at Alice. "You seem not to belong amongst these people." She
looked around with distaste etched on her wrinkled features. She tapped her
cane on the carpeted deck once, and then a second time. The old woman became
serious and fixed Alice with a gaze that froze her blood.

"You don't seem to belong either," Alice finally managed to say.

"I belong nowhere, my lovely girl. We belong nowhere." She leaned close to
the American woman and whispered in a voice steeped in an East European accent, "You seem kind, not like these . . ." she gestured around her at the men and
women eating, laughing, and preparing to buy the stolen items taken from an illegal archaeological dig at Tell es-Sultan, ". . . people, these scavengers of our
shared history." The old woman bowed her head and then looked up minus her
warm smile. "Forget what you saw here tonight, and if I am correct and you have
seen something like this before, tell no one and keep your secret buried . . ." She
hesitated only a moment as she looked deeply into the eyes of Alice Hamilton.
"Wherever that may be." Her European accent vanished and her next words were
spoken in unaccented English and were far deeper in bass than her voice had been

a brief second before. "You have just twenty minutes to remove yourself and your one-eyed handsome escort from this ship, my dear. All of this," she gestured with her wooden cane, even going so far as to accidentally poke another American woman on her rather ample derriere, which elicited a shocked yelp and angry look, "Because all of this is going to be at the bottom of the South China Sea momentarily."

"What?" Alice asked, shocked at the slowness of her reaction.

The old woman had gone. She melted into the milling buyers as if she had never been there at all.

Lee was getting close to the explosion factor that made his early years in the Senate a legend, and one of the reasons it was suggested to him by his own party that he was maybe just a little too high-strung for politics. The general always found his temper hard to control when sheer audacity of privilege and corrupt people at every walk of life threatened his keen sense of justice.

As his good eye counted the varying degrees of thievery, his limited vision fell on two small items on display that made his stomach roll. Lord Harrington had actually uncovered human remains at Tell es-Sultan. A cursed thing to do at any archaeological find was to openly display remains that have not been studied and guaranteed to be something from antiquity. It was also something that any well-bred museum curator would find hard pressed to put in any exhibit. He saw a few of the English-bred buyers grimace in distaste at the open display of remains. Lee shook his head and decided at that moment this secret auction would remain so forever. These items would not find their way to the private sector because he would destroy it all first if that need arose.

"I see anger in that one, beautiful eye."

Garrison looked down to see the young woman who had been talking with Alice a moment before. Lee had seen her spying him from across the salon and was uncomfortable with the looks she was shooting his way.

"Then you should look closer, young lady, because what I see is sadness that this is happening. And if you're here to place your money on any of these artifacts, I would save it; I predict it's going to be a bad investment."

"I was just speaking with your most beautiful companion. I see in her eyes that she adores you."

Garrison looked closer at the raven-haired beauty. Her gaze seemed to go right through him. "Again, you better go take a better look, and study my companion a little closer. Soon enough she will reveal her cloven hooves, horns, and vipercated tail."

The young girl looked confused for the briefest of moments and then smiled and laughed—a disarming and innocent sound that made Lee look twice at the woman standing in front of him with her arms crossed over her breasts. Her one brown and one green eye took Garrison in from head to toe. The eyes lingered momentarily on the bright red cummerbund.

"Ah, I see how the game is played with you Americans. Even though you are emphatically in love with someone, you deny it and show nothing but contempt at the mere suggestion of it, even in the face of something so obvious."

Garrison Lee was stunned for a moment. He wasn't used to bandying words with someone so young, but this girl had a way of getting into his thoughts that was just a little unnerving.

"If I may be so bold, you were a soldier, am I correct?" she asked as she watched Lee's lone eye for a lie.

"I and many others."

"Not many aboard this pirate ship I think. If the rest of England knew about this very unscrupulous man they would hang him in Trafalgar Square," she said as her eyes left Lee for the briefest of moments to study some of the human waste that were the bidders of the world's past. Her double-colored eyes turned back to the general and this time she examined him as if she were looking for a disease. She tilted her head and Lee saw the beginning of a tattoo at the base of her neck that wound its way down into the black dress. "You are a keeper of secrets."

"Excuse me?" Garrison said as his smile tried to cover up his consternation at the girl's prognosticative prowess. "I think your crystal ball may be a little cracked, my dear."

The woman placed her small hand on Lee's lapel. "Leave this ship—immediately, Keeper of Secrets," she said as her smile was replaced with a seriousness that Lee found disturbing. He slowly pulled the girl's hand free of his jacket. Her smile slowly returned as Alice joined them, her eyes on the girl.

"I see, you espouse cryptic things to complete strangers like me and then you go off and flirt with a man that is old enough to be your father." Alice looked from the girl and then back to Lee. "Or your grandfather."

Lee's brow furrowed once again, only this time without much enthusiasm or threat behind it.

The young girl who reminded Lee of the Gypsies he met while on assignment during the war smiled even wider as she turned to look directly at him.

"My crystal ball isn't as cracked as you would like to believe." She bowed toward Alice and then to Lee. "Mrs. Hamilton, Senator Lee." The young woman turned and left without another glance.

Lee and Alice watched the young girl take her grandmother's arm and with one last smile at the both of them, the two strange guests of Lord Harrington left the salon.

"Strange, I don't think I—"

"Told her you were a former senator," Alice finished for Lee.

"And I don't fancy being lectured to by a twenty-year-old girl on the politics of world history." Lee looked down at Alice. "Or anything else for that matter."

Alice patted Lee's thick arm. "Calm down or your good eye will pop out of your head." Alice smiled at some guests standing near them when she leaned into Lee. "I got a tip that we should leave this ship posthaste unless we want to see this boat turn into a submarine." Alice looked right at Lee. "And for some reason I believe my source."

"I saw you looking at the block of stone." He turned and faced his assistant. "Get it out of your head. There is no relationship to Vault 22871." He held up his hand, his cane dangling as he stopped Alice from speaking. "Are you surprised I noticed? Who in the hell could miss that? That block of stone is a hoax—a forgery. I heard some genius in the peanut gallery say it was Anubis, the jackal-headed god that held sway over the dead, until old Anubis was ousted by Osiris, at least according to the Egyptian priests at the time. I don't think the god Anubis got slammed between two rocks during the actual historic siege of Jericho. This petrified monstrosity is as fake as that thing the Group has in Vault 22871."

"That is your opinion; everyone else thinks the animal remains in 22871 are viable. Our best people say there have been no postmortem alterations to the bones—the same alterations that would have had to have occurred to this animal right here. The articulated hips can clearly be seen under the petrified fur. The fingers and claws, Garrison, look at the fingers and claws for God's sake; they are exactly the same as the remains the U.S. Army recovered in France after World War I!"

Lee looked around as other guests started to pay them unwanted attention.

"Calm yourself, Hamilton, I believe *you* believe it. But this is ridiculous, Anubis, for crying out loud?" Lee wanted to walk Alice to the ancient stone block and take a hammer and chisel to it and prove that this display was nothing more than a curiosity that no one should take seriously. "There is one thing that really tears at my ass when it comes to our own science departments, and that's the fact that there has never been one of these animals ever found in the fossil record the world over."

"After inventorying every item we have in the Event Group vaults you have the guts to say that to me? No fossil record? Just when does that prove the non-existence of an animal? You of all people should know there are things out there we know nothing of, even the great General Garrison Lee is capable of being wrong once in a few hundred damn years."

Lee saw the anger in Alice's eyes and her words were scathing, almost the same exact speech he had given, no, shouted at his people at the Group since he took directorship of Department 5656.

Garrison looked around and nodded as people were passing by with their secret bidding envelopes and giving them looks that were making the American feel extremely uncomfortable.

"Okay, I'll give you that one, Hamilton, but—"

"Good evening, I couldn't help but overhear your conversation, as well as that of many other men and women here."

Lee and Alice looked over at a small man wearing the traditional headdress of the Palestinian people of the Gaza Strip—the kuffiyeh, the checkered head scarf seen on every male of the region. That was where the similarities fell off sharply, however. The tuxedo the small man wore was cut perfectly and fit the bearded man to a T.

"Mr. Kilroy," he said and then smiled as he turned to appraise Alice. "I don't think I have had the honor."

"Alice, this is Mr. Hakim Salaams Saldine, our resident Palestinian authority on ancient Jericho—Saldine, Mrs. Alice Hamilton, also an authority it seems on ancient Jericho and the animal life contained behind its ancient walls."

Alice ignored the small insult and held her gloved hand out as the man kissed it, making sure not to touch the hand itself.

"So, you are an authority on Jericho. What is your opinion on the talk of the auction?" she asked.

The man looked confused at first and then smiled. "I do not offer my opinion on things that are irrelevant, and believe me, my young friend, that is the most irrelevant piece I have ever examined—it is a hoax."

"You have been to Tell es-Sultan?" Alice asked as she looked deeply into the newcomer's reaction.

"Yes, many times have I ventured to Yeriḥo, I mean Jericho, I'm afraid it has never held that much value to us as a people. It was after all, a place of defeat for us."

Alice smiled and nodded at the man, and then she looked at Lee and the smile vanished. The man continued to insult her intelligence and she was getting seriously sick of it. It was time to put General Garrison Lee in his place.

"You do know where you made your mistake don't you, Mr. Saldine, if that is your name?"

"Excuse me?" the man said, trying to keep his features neutral.

"The ancient word Jericho is thought to derive from the Canaanite word Reaḥ, which you obviously should know already. I mean, since you are an authority and all and obviously a Palestinian." Alice smiled again. "This little Virginia farm girl learned at an early age in Bible school taught by her uncle, that Reaḥ in Arabic, or Jericho if you will, is pronounced totally different. It's spelled with a Y, not a J, which was clearly enunciated when you said the word very crisply." Alice smiled as she made a show of looking around the room. The man shifted from one foot to the other. Lee rolled his good eye, knowing Alice was hanging them both out to dry.

"What is your point, madam?" the man with the headdress asked, looking over at Lee, who just grimaced, waiting for the other shoe to fall.

"Mr. Saldine, you are no more Palestinian than Garrison Lee here. You are Israeli intelligence, maybe just a policeman, but definitely no Palestinian. When you pose as another nationality, at least make sure you stick with their language, not your own." Alice dipped her head and moved away.

"Who in the bloody hell is that?" the man caught in the lie asked.

"She's a royal," Lee said as he started to go after Alice.

"A royal?" the Israeli asked.

"A royal pain in my ass—Hamilton, wait a minute."

Alice stopped on her way to the salon staircase. She turned to face her employer.

"When are you going to stop this unrelenting testing of my knowledge? It took me all of a minute to figure out who your buddy was. Trust, Garrison, that's what's missing in your soul, trust." She started to turn away but Lee grabbed her arm.

"Look, his name is Ally Ben-Nevin. He just took over the Gaza region for state security. He's here to keep the Palestinian people and his own from having their shared history vanish into rich American, European, and Chinese mansions."

"And you're telling me he knows who you are?" she asked, skeptical at the very least.

"Of course not, President Truman would have me hung from the Washington Monument if that little secret got out. No, Hamilton, he thinks we work for the State Department."

"I'm shocked that you're competent enough to pull that little deception off without getting caught."

"Okay, that's about enough of—"

The tremendous explosion rocked the *Golden Child* from bow to stern.

Alice was thrown forward and Lee wasn't far behind. As the ship listed sharply to the starboard side, Garrison pulled Alice aside as the giant block from Jericho tilted crazily on its steel pedestal. Alice was able to get her legs free at the last second as Garrison pulled on her for all he was worth. The stone block hit the carpeted deck and then after a moment's hesitation the massive weight of the block smashed through the teak wood and then crashed into the bowels of the ship. Lee was stunned as a giant geyser of water shot through the opening and slammed into the ornate chandelier. Water and glass cascaded onto the men and women trying to pick themselves up off the deck.

"I believe our host may have angered someone. I do think this bloody ship is sinking," Ben-Nevin said as he helped both Lee and Alice to their feet.

With water already lapping at Lee's ankles he reached into his jacket and pulled an old Colt .45 automatic from his hidden place beneath his bright red cummerbund. He turned and looked at Alice and just winked with his good eye.

"Now you know why the giant red cummerbund, Hamilton." Lee nodded his head at Israeli intelligence agent Ben-Nevin and then gestured toward the large staircase where people were making their way out of the salon. "May I suggest we see if there's another mode of transportation back to Hong Kong?"

Around them horns and sirens were blaring and men and women were screaming. Lee just started pushing women and men toward the stairs. Alice turned and the last thing she saw of Lee was him disappearing into the panicked crowd of secret bidders. The lights flickered and then went out to the accompaniment of more screams and shouts. Somewhere in the darkness a gunshot sounded. Then that was followed by another. Garrison found a woman on the flooded floor and assisted her to her feet. It was the haughty French woman who had given Lee a most distasteful look earlier in the evening.

"This is unacceptable, unacceptable!" the woman screamed as she tried to push Lee's hands from her.

"Well, you're going to find out there's a hell of a lot more that's unacceptable in a minute if you don't get your fat ass up those stairs." He slapped her hard on her behind, sending the shocked socialite through the water. As Lee watched her leave he saw a small black-painted wooden statue float by in the churning water. His eyes widened when he saw the wolf's head and the articulated hands depicted on the carved wood. Lee reached out and grabbed one of the surviving auction pieces and then shoved it into Ben-Nevin's jacket pocket. "Get this to your people and tell them they're hemorrhaging antiquities and the bloodsuckers are getting rich. Now go!" Lee pushed Ben-Nevin away even as his eyes didn't understand.

As the eighty-plus guests and crew fought their way through the jumble of broken artifacts and buffet items, Lee saw that the water was rising far faster than the men and women were moving. The ship must have taken a shape charge directly to her waterline and possibly one to her keel. A very professional job if he were correct.

The last twenty men and women were close to the top of the stairs when something blew. It knocked several people back and over the top of the darkened stairs. Lee saw agent Ben-Nevin hurled into the far wall where he hit and slid into the water and then slowly regained his feet. Garrison pulled the intelligence agent to his feet and pushed him toward the now bent and burning stairs.

The fire was now spreading across the ceiling of the salon. Lee's escape was blocked both at the main salon entrance and the exit leading to the galley.

"Oh, this is good," he said as he shoved the Colt back into his pants and then scanned the interior of the darkened and fire-lit salon for Alice, but she was nowhere to be seen. For the first time in many years, Garrison Lee was frightened. Frightened that he had lost someone he really cared about. He shook his head as the flames and the water were coming close to meeting in the middle, one from above, the other from below.

As he fought his way back into the center of the salon, he knew then that he loved Alice, had from the very first moment he had laid his one good eye upon her in the hospital in Washington, D.C., in 1945 when she had come to inquire about the husband she had lost in South America during the war. Why he thought the most beautiful woman in the world would, or even could, love a man as scarred as physically and emotionally as Lee, he could never figure out. But Lee knew he had to try. As flames reached from above and water from below Garrison Lee made a quick decision and then dove headfirst into the gaping hole where the stone block and its strange animal had vanished when it crashed through the deck to the spaces below.

"You!" The shout came from behind Lee just as he surfaced into chaos on the third deck. As he turned he saw their host, Lord Harrington, standing between two of his guards. They had guns pointed his way. The Englishman was soaked and his hairpiece looked as if it had hit an iceberg. "I don't know who you are, but you did this!"

Lee was beginning to wonder if his real identity and intentions had been stenciled on him. First the girl and now this antiquities thief seemed to be excellent guessers at his true vocation. Garrison felt the weight of the old Colt .45 in his cummerbund but knew he would never reach it.

"Who sent you?" the Englishman shouted as another, even larger geyser of seawater shot through the massive hole in the deck. Garrison saw his opportunity as he was obscured at the last second by the eruption. He pulled the gun, ripping away the hated cummerbund, and dove for the water. Lee surfaced and with the biggest guess of his life took a chance and started shooting as soon as he surfaced. The first two .45 caliber rounds missed. The third struck one of the armed men and sent him backward into the roiling water. The Englishman's eyes widened as Lee took quick aim at the second man and fired. The bullet caught the man dead center of the forehead. He slowly eased himself back down into the water, not feeling anything in his now dead brain. Garrison moved the barrel toward Lord Harrington.

"No, no," he shouted, raising his arms.

Normally Garrison would have had no compunction in shooting the thief, but he also realized that it wasn't his job. He lowered the .45 automatic. The look on Harrington's face was decidedly relieved. That was short-lived however when as Lee looked on in stunned silence a three-foot-long aluminum shaft slammed into Harrington. The small spear protruded from his chest as he stared down at the instrument that had killed him. He slowly looked up at Lee, who grimaced as he realized the man had been murdered right in front of him and amid the chaos of the sinking *Golden Child*. As he watched Harrington also slid beneath the water. Garrison looked around, aiming the gun in the darkness and the flickering electrical shorts, and saw what he was searching for. The girl smiled, lowered her diving mask, and then tossed the spear gun toward Lee. The young woman with the strange eyes waved at Lee and then vanished into the rolling water. Garrison saw one of her fins swipe at the air as she kicked away beneath the shattered deck.

Lee decided that the girl was showing him a way out. He dove after her, praying that Alice had made it to the main deck and over the side.

Alice Hamilton watched as the panic-driven guests fought their way to the main deck. She angrily removed the fur stole and her white gloves as she reached down to assist an elderly man to his feet and then unceremoniously push him over the railing of the heavily listing *Golden Child*.

"Damn it, Garrison, where in the hell are you?" she shouted at the many frightened faces jumping over the side of the ship. She kicked off her high heels and furiously started back toward the salon opening.

Lee held his breath as he felt the shudder come from beneath the *Golden Child*. Another scuttling charge went off, sending a pressure wave through his eardrums that came near to stunning him. The blast was obviously meant to send the $6 million yacht to the bottom of the South China Sea. The murder of the antiquities thieves and bidders had been meticulously planned out. The first charge was meant to send the guests scurrying off the ship. The second was meant to break the back of the *Golden Child* and send her to the bottom. A tactic Lee had used himself on numerous occasions during the war, both in Europe and South America.

As he swam though the darkness a fresh rush of seawater struck him from beneath. The powerful explosion placed along the keel of the ship sent a torrent of heated water upward, where it slammed Lee into the very block Alice had been mesmerized with not fifteen minutes earlier and that now sat at the lowest portion of the decking near the engine spaces.

Garrison was starting to lose faith that he had enough air left in his lungs to escape through the bottom of the *Golden Child*. As his hands fought for purchase against the rush of incoming sea, his fingers tore lose a large section of the stone block from Jericho. He held on to the small piece of stone as his vision started to tunnel and his lungs were close to exploding.

He knew he would never see Alice again. And he found that was the only regret he had. Alice.

Suddenly his leg was tugged on and he felt himself being pulled further down into the water. Whoever had his leg was not too gently pulling him to the bottom of the engine spaces where all hell was breaking loose. As Garrison fought to keep consciousness he saw the floating bodies of many of the *Golden Child*'s crewmen. Most were burned and some had parts of their bodies missing from the two powerful explosions. He was pulled even further along the hull. Then suddenly Lee and his savior were free of the *Golden Child*. The water was much cooler as he felt himself rising from the depths. When he broke the surface of the choppy sea he didn't think he had enough strength to take a deep breath, then just before he did he felt his face being slapped hard.

"Don't you know when you abandon ship you head to the deck, not the engine room?" the voice said as a life preserver was thrust into his hands.

Lee tried to catch his breath as he saw who his rescuer had been—the young Gypsy girl from the salon. She was treading water not inches from Lee's face. Her smile caught the senator off guard.

"Don't think us cruel," she said as her swim fins kept her easily above the choppy water. "I set the first charge to scare the guests, the second to sink the ship, but I'm afraid it went off too early. I'm really not that good with explosives."

"Who are you and who made you judge, jury, and executioner?" Lee said, spitting saltwater from his mouth.

"I am no one, Mr. Lee, but the woman who gave the execution order is that pig Harrington's judge, jury, and executioner, and also my queen." The girl smiled and lowered her dive mask. "Your woman is your equal American, but don't allow her to follow us. It will only bring her grief. If we ever meet again, Keeper of Secrets, it will not go so well for you."

Lee started to say something but the girl turned away. Lee watched her swim away as sirens and patrol boats from the distant harbor were starting to get closer to the scene of the tragedy at sea. Lee looked for the girl but she was nowhere to be found.

"Thank God!"

Lee quickly turned around.

"Hamilton!" he said as he reached for her.

Alice placed her arms around Lee and then they both just remained that way as the seas lifted them and then lowered their floating bodies back down. As Lee held her he noticed that they were being carried away from the survivors and the arriving rescuers.

"We better start swimming or it may be a while before I can apologize for being such an ass."

Suddenly and before Alice could speak a splash sounded next to them. As Lee looked up he saw that an inflatable raft had been tossed into the sea.

"As I said, my crystal ball may be cracked, but it still shows a pretty clear picture of future events. Mrs. Hamilton, Mr. Lee, good luck, and swim that way."

Lee and Alice looked up onto an ancient-looking Chinese junk. Standing at the railing was the young raven-haired girl. She was wrapped in a blanket. Standing next to her and leaning on the old wooden railing, the girl's grandmother stood with her arm through that of the girl for support. The junk was slowly pulling out of the debris field left by the sinking *Golden Child*.

"Remember, Mrs. Hamilton, what you have seen here tonight cannot be." She slowly waved her small hand, as did her grandmother. "God doesn't have that kind of sense of humor. After all, animals like that cannot, should not exist. God wouldn't have it," the girl shouted. The junk slowly vanished into a fog bank and was gone.

"That has got to be the strangest girl I have ever met."

Lee didn't answer Alice, he just yanked the ripcord on the CO_2 cylinder and the raft immediately inflated. He pulled himself in and then Alice after him. As the sirens and the screams slowly started to fade because of distance, Lee looked into the fog after the fleeing ghostly image of the Chinese junk.

"What are you thinking?" Alice asked as she slowly pulled the expensive gown over her head and then tossed it into the boat. Her slip was soaked through and Lee could see that Alice was in no mood to care who could see her body underneath the thin material—especially Garrison Lee.

As the small boat bobbed in the water and searchlights started to poke through the mist, Lee reached into his jacket pocket and pulled out the piece of stone he had torn from the block after it had fallen through the deck. He looked it over and then pressed the large piece into his palm and closed his fingers around it.

"I'm thinking we had better take a closer look at what we have in Vault 22871 when we get back to the complex."

Alice tilted her head as she also tossed the wide-brimmed hat into the sea. She shook out her long brunette hair and then caught the item Lee tossed to her.

"Because I have never seen anyone go that far to create a hoax."

As Alice brought the chunk of block closer to her salt-encrusted vision, her heart froze. "Yes, I think we may have something a little more to investigate at Jericho than just the ancient ruins of the city, because something else was happening a few thousand years ago that isn't recorded in the Bible."

As the small piece was rolled in Alice's hand the bone was clearly seen underneath the petrified fur of that long dead animal. What antiquities forger would think to do that, place bone under the petrified skin of a hoax?

Alice Hamilton and Garrison Lee of the Event Group had learned that night for the first time that things do go bump in the night and there is always the beast under the bed and in the closet. *So yes, Mrs. Hamilton,* Lee thought, *there really may be monsters in the world.*

PART ONE
OLD SCORES

We cry "Our Father!" we that yearn
Upward to some divine embrace,
And dimly through the mist, discern
At times a lovely awesome Face,
Whose darkened likeness haunts our race.

—Caroline Spencer,
"On the Dark Mountains"

1

As she reached for the small piece of broken block her hand lightly rubbed against the stronger hands of a man she hadn't felt the touch of in nearly a year. All thought of that long-ago Hong Kong night vanished during the daylight hours only to reappear when sleep claimed the eighty-four-year-old woman. As the small rubber boat bobbed up and down in the cold waters outside Hong Kong harbor she remembered the feel of the piece of stone block and the touch of Garrison Lee's fingers as the dream continued. In her sleep the woman wanted to cry out that she didn't want the relic, she wanted him. As always in her dream all Lee would do is smile and wink that irritating wink he always did to make her think everything was all right—she knew it wasn't. This was the same dream Alice had been having for the past six days and it always ended the same way—with the feeling of massive loss and the sharp pain of her heart breaking every time she saw Garrison in the dream.

"Hamilton, you're obviously dreaming this for a reason—*now wake up!*"

The voice of a man gone for a full year woke her as she lay at her small desk in her bedroom. She had fallen asleep again at her computer terminal and as she looked at the screen she saw the jumbled words in one long and continuous sentence, the result of her head lying on the keyboard.

Alice Hamilton reached out and angrily punched at the keyboard and cleared the screen of all the nonsensical words. As she yawned she looked at the clock on the wall. It was four-thirty in the morning and for the fifth straight night she had fallen asleep while in the midst of her research, and that in turn brought on the dreams of Garrison Lee and the time they spent together in China in the forties.

Alice straightened in her chair, finally remembering what had prompted this dream in particular. She frantically searched the scattered papers on her usually neat desk.

"Where is it, where is it!" she asked herself, almost fearing the letter itself was part of her sleeping remembrances.

"*Calm down and think*," came his voice. This was a tool she used many times. Garrison always told her think and then act.

Alice stopped her searching and then squeezed her eyes closed and thought. She opened them suddenly and reached for her robe's front pocket. She took a deep breath as her fingers touched the two-page letter that had been overnighted from Rome.

"Thank you," she said as she pulled the letter from her pocket and opened it, sitting back in her chair as she did. Alice again closed her eyes realizing that she just thanked a man gone from her for what seemed an eternity. She swallowed and then caught herself and mentally shook the tears from her eyes before they fully developed and then opened the letter. She read it once more for the umpteenth time in the twenty-four hours since receiving it.

"Europa, am I still signed in?" she said aloud as she folded the letter but this time held it tightly in her hand as she forced herself to relax. Alice was finally feeling her age after many years of keeping up with the best of them.

"Yes, Mrs. Hamilton, User 0012 is still logged on," came the sexy Marilyn Monroe–voiced Cray supercomputer located at the secure center inside the Event Group complex underneath Nellis Air Force Base ten miles from her house.

"My apologies for being rude and dozing off on you," Alice said as she pulled her robe tighter around her.

"Computer center activity is light, access should be uninterrupted until 0600."

"Well, thank you anyway, Europa. Now, can you . . ." Alice stopped briefly to stifle a yawn, making herself realize she was getting far too old for these all-night research digs. "Excuse me, can you give me the status of security element Goliath please?"

"Security element Goliath has not reported in as of this time."

"Europa, I am expecting a package through the complex communications system and I want that e-mail package to come straight to me and is not, I repeat, is not to be entered into the incoming communications log. Is that clear?"

For the first time in many years Europa didn't answer right away. Alice thought maybe her systems were still being disrupted from the troubles a few months earlier when her mainframe was attacked from an outside source.

"Mrs. Hamilton, your request cannot be granted due to security regulations."

Alice closed her eyes knowing that she could seal the incoming e-mail off from everyone—except one man, and that was the head of Event Group security and the smartest man outside of Garrison Lee and Director Niles Compton that she had ever known—Colonel Jack Collins. As far as she could see there was no way around Jack not seeing the e-mail, especially from a source as important to Department 5656 as anyone could ever remember—Goliath, a code name for one of the security departments and Director Compton's most guarded deep opera-tives. The information this agent gives the Group is as important as any historical intelligence they had ever received from any one source. Goliath was deep—the deepest any security element had ever been before, and only Jack, Niles, deputy director Virginia Pollock, Captain Carl Everett, and Alice knew who it was and where he, or she, was buried.

"I understand, Europa, but no one else gets copied on the package. I hope I can handle Colonel Collins on this one security oversight."

"Incoming packet has arrived, Mrs. Hamilton."

Alice was stunned at how fast her requested data from their deep operative came as a follow-up to the first communication, which had set Alice on a course of action she had wanted to take since 1951.

"Put it through, please," she said.

The coded pictures sent by Goliath slowly started coming up on her monitor as fast as Europa could decipher them. As she scanned the screen trying to figure out what the coded pixels were starting to form, her eyes started to widen and then recognition struck and with her usual self-control lost for the moment, Alice clapped her hands together and let out a yelp. She stood and hopped once as she picked up a picture of Garrison Lee that sat upon her desk. She kissed it, knowing in real life that gesture would have caused an immediate rebuke if it had not been done in private. She looked at the pictures once more as Europa broke them down into a four-square shot and they all clearly showed the item she had for so long searched.

"You were right, damn you, you were right! This would have been something that had to have been covered up. And it was your idea to get someone inside—oh, not for this, you old goat, but I figured our agent was in place anyway so why not have him do a little private searching for me?" She kissed the picture again. "Now I've got to kiss Jack and Niles for getting our agent placed!" Alice stopped danc-ing and then looked at the picture of the one-eyed love of her life. "Jack and Niles are going to hang me out to dry for this one," she said sadly, and then she sud-denly smiled. "But what the hell, Europa, I'm fully vested so they can't take my retirement away." This time it was Alice who winked at Lee as he grimaced back from his eight-by-ten glossy.

"Mrs. Hamilton, should I code-name and secure the file in your private pro-gram?"

"Yes, Europa, I also want you to place all files developed on the contents of Vault 22871 with this new file and secure it."

"Yes, Mrs. Hamilton. Do you wish a code name for the new combined file?" Europa asked in her sexy voice that Alice never quite noticed any longer.

"Yes, code it—Grimm."

VATICAN CITY,
ROME, ITALY

The young Vatican counsel held the door open for a young woman. He nodded as she went past. Once outside he placed the black hat on his head and looked around the building. The cybercafe wasn't as crowded as it would be when the students hit just before classes started in less than an hour.

As he turned toward Vatican City a mile distant he felt the eyes on him just as he had the day before and then again this morning—both times coming to and from his office and then from his office to the cybercafe. Now he was feeling it again. His training was either kicking in or he was starting to lose it. He dipped his head as he passed another young lady on the street. As he did he used the opportunity to glance in the storefront window to his right. Beyond his own reflection of black robe and collar he saw a lone woman about fifty feet behind him. Her gaze seemed just a little too intent on him. He quickened his pace.

Crossing St. Peter's Square he felt more secure as the crowds grew thick with tourists and others seeking the comfort of the city. He no longer felt the eyes upon him as he had. As he made his way back to his office inside the Vatican archival building he stopped and leaned down to tie a shoe that needed no tying. He again looked around and his heart froze. Not twenty feet away from where he had stopped that same young woman he had seen on the street was staring right at him. He was tempted to turn and walk toward the girl just to see what reaction he would get, but his training told him to cut and run and then report, let others far above his pay grade make the decisions. He did however reach his cell phone and then he brazenly straightened and started taking pictures like he was a normal tourist. He framed the young woman in his fourth shot of the milling crowd. For good measure he took another just as her face went stern and she turned away. The young Vatican archivist smiled and turned away himself.

The man deep undercover at the Vatican, United States Army Second Lieutenant Leonard DeSilva, knew he would have to report to Colonel Collins in Nevada, because if his cover inside the Vatican was blown there was going to be hell to pay.

The young priest, who had spent the past year and a half after graduating from Notre Dame fighting for his assignment at the Vatican, knew he would have to call home for instructions—and that entailed a call to Department 5656—the Event Group.

TEL AVIV,
ISRAEL

Lieutenant General Addis Shamni slowly laid down the report from his agent at the Vatican and then slammed his hand down upon it. He raised that same hand to his forehead and then cursed his bad luck.

"With everything going on in the world I have to deal with this!" he said aloud as his hand left his furrowed brow and slammed into the report once more. "How in the hell did someone get a man inside the archives when the Mossad couldn't get into the damn lobby just for a research paper!"

Lieutenant Colonel Avis Ben-Nevin sat silently in his chair as he listened to the general angrily curse the file in front of him. The colonel with his meticulously trimmed pencil-thin mustache saw the fear in a man's eyes that up until now had never known the feeling. He knew this involved the Vatican, an area the lieutenant colonel had a special and vested interest in. Ben-Nevin was known as the religious factor inside the Mossad. Anything and everything that had to do with religion inside the state of Israel, Ben-Nevin had a firm grasp of it and the event happening at this moment in Italy had a firm hold on the colonel's imagination.

"Colonel, you may have to get on a plane to Rome and find out exactly what is going on here. I need someone on station that knows just what in the hell they're doing. Young Sorotzkin is one of the best but she may be out of her element where Ramesses is concerned."

"Perhaps if I could be briefed on Project Ramesses I could—"

The general looked up with an arched graying eyebrow.

"You could what, read something that could possibly get you killed by someone higher in rank than myself? Colonel, outside of this office that code name is never to be mentioned. Your father knew of it and took it to his grave." The eyes of the general bore into the younger Mossad officer. "You are to evaluate the situation with Major Sorotzkin, then report back to me. Nothing is to be done with this American spy. This may be our chance to get into the archives and find out exactly what the Holy Roman Church knows about our history."

Ben-Nevin knew he was on the trail that his father had discovered four decades earlier in Hong Kong and the trail just got a little warmer.

"You are not to bring your normal religious zeal into this mission. Get to Rome, evaluate, and report back."

"General, I know I am considered the religious laughingstock around here, but anyone who believes that our religion has nothing to do with how we are viewed, or even perceived in our world, especially our near world, well, that's a bit naive on your part. Our heritage is what makes us strong and any evidence of that heritage we can uncover will go a long way to proving we should reign in this part of the world."

General Shamni slowly stood and placed his thick arms on his desk and then leaned forward. "Reign, Colonel Ben-Nevin? We are just trying to survive here. If we can be friends with our neighbors through cooperation and mutual respect then that is our goal. Not to point to them and say, 'See, we were right and you were wrong and God is on our side.'" This time the general smiled but the gesture was not meant to be sincere in the least. The general hated Ben-Nevin and the colonel knew it. "If there's one thing our young state has learned, Colonel, is the very real fact that God has never been on anyone's side. As a matter of fact I have come to the conclusion that if he ever was, he's cut the apron strings on us—as the Americans like to say. We are too far along to be killing people over these ancient tales."

This time Ben-Nevin smiled. "This stuff is the manna of our history, proof that we were meant to be here. If Operation Ramesses could prove the world wrong in that regard, why we could—"

"Enough!" This time the hand came down and its impact shook the desk lamp. "Colonel, you have pushed and pushed on this very closed loop matter far too long, and the funny thing is I couldn't give you the details of Ramesses even if I knew them. Our policy on the operation has been in place since the time of David Ben-Gurion. And your assertion that Ramesses can save the situation in the Middle East is highly dubious at best, especially since you know nothing of its details. From what I understand Ramesses would do, at least according to our experts, is ignite a wave of religious fundamentalism the likes of which the world has never seen. That cannot happen and will not happen as long as this administration is in place—and every administration of whatever political stripe after. Now get to Rome."

Ben-Nevin gave the general a halfhearted salute and then turned on his heel. The general didn't see the small smile lift his thin mustache.

"Sergeant Rosen!"

"Sir?"

The general looked up as his assistant popped her head inside the door.

"Get me the prime minister," was all he said as he inadvertently picked up the field report again and cursed his eyes for reading the words. He didn't acknowledge his assistant as she ducked out of the office.

"The prime minister is on line one, General."

With a minimum of motion the general snatched up the phone and hit the flashing button.

"Mr. Prime Minister, a trail to our heritage may have been discovered by unknown sources." The general paused to rub the throbbing that had just started coursing through his temples. "Sir, we have a problem—a three-thousand-year-old nightmare from the past kind of problem."

After the general's conversation with the prime minister's office was completed, exactly thirty-two minutes later the elite commando arm of the Israeli Defense Forces; the Sayeret—one of the best trained killing forces in the world—went on full combat alert.

As the colonel stepped from the general's office he looked around the deserted hallway and then stepped to the nearest door where he took out his private cell phone and punched in a preprogrammed number.

"There has been movement on Project Ramesses. I'm not sure, but the report was generated by General Shamni's wunderkind inside Vatican City." The colonel nodded at a young man as he quickly slipped by Ben-Nevin with a file report. He waited as the man disappeared. "Look, if I do this my career in Mossad is over. If I get caught that will be the least of my problems. My father had his life ended when he discovered the old antiquities in China and reported them to his superiors. I will not make the same mistake. You have your religious principles and I have mine, and my principles include enough wealth to retire somewhere that the general, the prime minister, and any other left-wing government official cannot track me down and hang me for this small betrayal. I'll get the location of Ramesses, but then I'm on my own. You can take your holy relics and I'll take what's important to me. Then we're finished . . . I will no longer be a citizen of this country and that is where you and your Knesset friends come in. You make sure that after I kill the Gypsy major, that Mossad soon forgets the name Ben-Nevin."

The small smile slowly made its reappearance and then Ben-Nevin closed the cell phone. The mystery his father uncovered that night long ago in Hong Kong had finally come home to roost and Colonel Avis Ben-Nevin was finally going to collect payment for lies and cover-ups by the Israeli government as far back as three thousand years. As he started to walk away to pack his bags for the last time as an Israeli agent, the colonel heard the yelling coming from the general's office.

GOLD CITY PAWN SHOP, LAS VEGAS, NEVADA

The 2005 Jeep Cherokee bounced into the parking lot beside the Gold City Pawn Shop. Luckily the parking spaces for the business were near empty due to the earliness of the hour—even in Vegas people slowed down pawning their lives away at six A.M.

Alice Hamilton took a deep breath before opening her door. She looked at the package of research material piled on the passenger seat next to her: the culmination of sixty-three years' worth of research and another lifetime of bitter disagreement with men Alice Hamilton respected more than any two men in the world—Niles Compton and Garrison Lee. They both had always failed to see the direct connection she proposed between the magnificent animals she proclaimed had once lived amongst man and the changing theory of how exactly a few of the more celebrated and ancient biblical battles were really won. Her theory she knew always lacked the necessary proof so an Event mission had never been called. There just wasn't enough evidence, both Compton and the late Senator Lee had told her. Oh, she knew both Niles and Garrison wanted to believe in the animals, and she thought they did. As a matter of fact she was positive Garrison believed it as he saw the relic himself, but being the bureaucrats they were they were handcuffed about calling an Event with such a small sampling of evidence. Alice had sworn to Garrison Lee that she would continue to search for that proof and let Niles decide if it was enough.

Alice set her lips and then reached for the nine-inch-thick folder, and unlike the other red-bordered top secret folders used at the group, this folder was a standard size manila type—nothing special, and surely nothing secret—until this morning that is.

She stepped from the Cherokee and made her way to the glass-encased front door of the Gold City Pawn Shop. Before grasping the old-fashioned thumb depression plate she looked closely at it. As soon as she took hold of the handle and her right thumb went down upon the thumb plate, Europa, the Cray Corporation supercomputer, would read the minute valleys and swirls of her thumbprint. That image would be studied by no fewer than five security men inside the building at all times. Five was the minimum number of U.S. Marines, Army, Air Force, and naval security personnel needed to secure and guard Gate 2 of the most protected federal reservation in the United States—the Event Group complex, the home to Department 5656.

Alice took hold of the handle, knowing that Europa would send an automatic report to the Security Department notifying them that she was at Gate 2 and would soon be passed on to the complex itself. Alice only hoped that at six A.M. Jack Collins and Carl Everett, the two men in charge of that department, were out running or eating breakfast. She opened the door and stepped into the pawn shop.

Captain Carl Everett had showered, shaved, and dressed after his four-thirty A.M. run around the indoor track facilities on Level 18. On most mornings the captain was joined by the director of Department 5656 security, Colonel Jack Collins, but today, as well as for the past several weeks, the colonel had been missing from their morning runs. As a matter of fact, Everett had noticed that Jack Collins was MIA at most anything not directly related to his military duties at the Group, and Everett knew the reasons behind it.

The captain now stood at the door to the main security office on Level 8. He took a deep breath in anticipation of a conversation that was weeks in coming. He went in.

The staff duty officer this morning was Sergeant Gabriel Sanchez, an Air Force enlisted man now in his second year of duty at Group. He looked up from his shift paperwork just as Everett stepped inside the still quiet office.

"Tell me he's still in bed and hasn't reported yet," Everett said as he noticed the closed door to the colonel's office.

Sanchez slowly shook his head in the negative. He used his ballpoint pen to point at Jack's door.

"Never left. He's been in his office all night and Europa says he's been logged on his terminal since 2250 hours last night."

A grim and determined line formed at Everett's mouth as he moved past the several rows of desks yet to be filled by the day shift of the Security Department in less than an hour. He figured now would be the best time to confront an old friend about a serious problem, and that problem was Jack Collins himself.

"Sergeant, take ten and get some joe down in the cafeteria," Everett said as he paused at Jack's closed door.

"I don't drink coffee, Captain, I—"

The words fell short as the sergeant saw the stern look on the captain's face.

"But a donut would be nice," Sanchez finished as he stood and left the office.

Everett without hesitation knocked twice quickly and then went through the door.

"Good morning, Jack, restful night?" Carl said as he perched himself on the front edge of the colonel's desk.

Jack was studying a printout from Europa and still hadn't looked up at the U.S. Navy SEAL and a man that had, over the many years, became the colonel's closest friend.

The colonel, without looking up from his printout, replied, "Restful enough, Carl." Collins finally looked up as if he had been waiting for this conversation as much as the captain had. Jack laid a yellow highlighter next to the printout and then waited for Everett's size thirteen shoe to fall.

"Anything?"

Jack held Everett's gaze, his face neutral, and the captain couldn't read what was behind the mask. He was relieved when Collins visibly relaxed.

"No." Jack lowered his head and folded the printout and placed it in his desk drawer and then looked at his watch.

"Jack, let me in, will you, you can't do this on your own."

"The murder of my sister by someone in government service is what I consider a personal matter, Carl. As much as I appreciate the offer, this is something that I have to do on my own. Can you understand that?" Jack's blue eyes bore in on Everett's and didn't waver.

"No, Jack, I can't. I can't justify you doing this alone. We all knew and liked Lynn. I think Sarah McIntire, Will Mendenhall, and Jason Ryan, and even this dumb swabby captain need to be a part of tracking down whoever did this to your sister. It's not just you, Jack."

Collins once more with flair looked at his watch and then back at Everett. "I appreciate the offer, but no. I have to do this and will not risk one more individual of this organization to track her killer down. Stay out of it." Once more the watch was glanced at. "We have a departmental meeting in an hour. I have work in another department so I'll need you to cover that staff meeting."

Everett watched as Collins stood, placed a hand on Everett's shoulder.

"The lives of you, Sarah, Will, or even Ryan will not be put at risk." He looked directly into Carl's eyes. "I appreciate your offer, but this has to be done without you."

Everett watched Jack leave the office without another word. As he stood from the top of Jack's desk he noticed that the colonel hadn't logged off from Europa. With little shame and far less hesitation Carl leaned over and looked at the computer monitor. As Everett saw the picture on the screen his heart leaped in his chest. Colonel Henri Farbeaux was the face staring back at him. The Event Group's most feared enemy and the world's greatest antiquities thief had been in custody as early as the month before right here at the Event Group facility. Circumstances however soon dictated that Farbeaux be set free due to personal reasons between

Jack and Sarah. The entire incident was kept quiet out of respect for the couple's privacy. He saw the flashing message just under the picture of the arch-criminal. *"Message received from Avignon, France, at 0235 hours this date, Farbeaux, Henri R."*

Everett reached out and tapped the power button for the computer's monitor and then slowly stood and rubbed a hand over his chin. To have an open communication with a man the FBI considered the second most dangerous man in the world and speaking with him was a treasonable offense. Everett knew Farbeaux had been blamed for many despicable things in the past in his work to gather the world's greatest antiquities, but thus far he and Colonel Collins could come up with no concrete evidence that he had ever done an American citizen harm. He realized that Henri could be, and on occasion was, a cold-blooded killer, but only when the need arose and only if his life depended upon his aggressive actions. For Henri Farbeaux killing was just too expensive a commodity for his line of work. As he turned for the door Everett became more afraid than ever for Collins.

"What are you and old Henri up to, Jack?"

Alice stood at the security arch leading to the vaults on Level 63. The entire level was dedicated to artifacts that were deemed interesting on an individual basis, but they were also items that held little value to the security of the United States as a whole. This level of vaults was the junk closet of the Event Group.

"Ma'am, are you feeling all right?" asked Marine Lance Corporal Freddy Allen.

Alice stood before the security arch, holding the thick file clutched close to her breast as if it were in danger of jumping free. The lance corporal looked into the tired face of a woman that held sway over Department 5656 as a living legend, right up there with Lincoln, Wilson, FDR, Ike, and Garrison Lee.

Alice didn't answer the security man's question. Instead she slowly leaned over the duty desk and placed her right hand on a glass pad. The scanner glowed green, flashed red and then green again; the color remained steady.

"Finger, palm, and pad print confirmed. Now if you'll please step to the security arch and place your left eye to the scanner." Alice did as requested.

Suddenly the archway illuminated with a soft blue light; this indicated the laser and gas security systems had been "safed" for Alice's entry into the vault level after the device correctly read her scanned and stored retinal data on file with Europa.

"Thank you," was all she said to the blue-clad Marine as she moved into the vault level.

"You're welcome, ma'am," the corporal said as she disappeared beyond the security arch. With his eyes on the slow-moving figure of Alice the security man reached for the phone. "Captain, this is Lance Corporal Allen on Level 63. I think you need to come down here. Mrs. Hamilton just checked through security and she looks . . . well, sir, she looks exhausted."

Second Lieutenant Sarah McIntire was just leaving the large and very well appointed mess hall, or as the civilians at group called it, the cafeteria, when she saw Jack speaking in hushed tones with the director of Department 5656, Dr. Niles Compton. She saw the stern look on the director's face and she also noticed that Jack was doing all the talking. The director shook his head from time to time and then the conversation was over. Collins briefly looked up and noticed Sarah just outside the glassed double doors of the cafeteria. He nodded his head once and then turned to leave the now crowded hallway. Sarah decided that the silent treatment from the man she loved was getting to be too much for her. With everything that had happened to the Group in the past two years she was tired of being the last to know everything, especially from a man who used to be able to tell her anything of a personal nature.

"Colonel, do you have a moment?" she asked when she caught him at the elevator tube.

"Lieutenant?" Jack said without turning to face her.

"You didn't come to see me last night at the Ark. You stood me up, Colonel Collins—again."

Jack finally turned to face Sarah. He forced a smile and knew it had been a miserable attempt.

"Short stuff, I was just swamped last night," he said, the lie easily flowing from his lips, something he had never developed a talent for over the years, even for security-oriented situations, much less those on a more personal level. "That's not true," he corrected his lie quickly. "We'll talk later, okay?" With that he attempted to smile and again failed.

The elevator hissed to a stop and the doors opened. Collins stepped back to allow the passengers off and then quickly stepped in and then the door closed on Sarah.

Sarah McIntire slowly lowered her head as others in the hallway passed by on their way to breakfast. After a moment she turned away from the closed doors of the elevator.

"McIntire!" came the call from down the curving corridor.

Sarah turned toward the voice and saw Captain Everett and the deputy director of the Event Group, Professor Virginia Pollock. The tall but beautiful assistant director looked worried as she and Carl approached. It was strange seeing Virginia out of a lab coat while on duty.

"Come with us, Lieutenant." Virginia didn't wait for Sarah as she stepped quickly into the next empty elevator. The trip to the vault area was silent as they rode the air-cushioned elevator to Level 63.

"We're losing Jack," Sarah said as she leaned her head against the polished aluminum of the elevator doors.

"I know," Carl answered as he pulled McIntire back from the doors. "He won't let any of us inside."

"His sister's murder has reacquainted Jack with his recent combat past and no one is going to stop him from finding out who the traitor was at either the CIA or FBI," Virginia Pollock said as she looked at Sarah, and then tried to give her a reassuring smile, but like Jack a few moments before it failed. The doors slid open to Level 63.

The sister of Colonel Jack Collins, Lynn Simpson, was murdered three weeks before and the only clue left behind was a memo generated from either a computer desk at Langley and the CIA, or D.C. from the J. Edgar Hoover Building and the FBI. Someone in one of those two dark agencies had lured Jack's sister to her death because she may have uncovered something at one, or even both departments, and Jack was determined to track down the killer and administer his brand of justice to the scum that ambushed his sister in Georgetown.

"We have to let him play this out for now and then we'll see if he comes back to us," Everett said and looked down at Sarah and knew that was a point she didn't really care to hear about. Carl reached out and squeezed her small shoulder. "And he will come back. Besides, I think there may be more to his shutting me out than either you, Mendenhall, or Ryan. I can't place it but he's pushing me away from him even harder than he is you or the others."

Sarah nodded. She had noticed the distant way Jack treated Carl since his sister's murder. As the three reached Vault 22871, indicated by the illuminated light blue numbers to the left of the vault, it stood open, and they entered to see Alice Hamilton on her hands and knees retrieving papers that had spilled to the tile floor. Lance Corporal Allen was assisting her.

"What's up?" Everett asked as Virginia and Sarah entered one of the smaller vaults on this level.

"I'm afraid I startled Mrs. Hamilton when I came inside the vault. She was engrossed in looking at the specimen and I must have caught her off guard."

Everett leaned over and gently helped Alice to her feet. "Come on now, the lance corporal can get those. What are you doing here this early, Alice?" Carl asked as he looked her over. The captain shot a quick look at Sarah and Virginia and then gestured by a dip of his head that he needed their help with her.

"Oh, I'm all right, just startled me is all. I wasn't expecting someone to come up behind me when I'm looking at that," she said with a nod of her head toward the specimen inside the glass enclosure.

As Everett released Alice into the more familiar arms of Alice's closest friends at the complex, he glanced at the contents of a vault he had never been in before. He saw what looked like a display of bones laid out inside a hermetically sealed Plexiglas enclosure. His eyes went from the bones to the lance corporal as he handed the captain the large file.

"She was carrying this file like she had nuclear launch codes stashed in here," the Marine said quietly.

"Thank you, Corporal, you can return to your duties."

"Aye, aye, sir."

Everett looked over at Alice, who was being helped into one of the many seats lining the interior of the vault. She was shaking and insisting to her two friends that she was fine, repeating that she had just been startled by the sudden appearance of the corporal. Carl then glanced at the file he held in his hands. He opened it, not really wanting to see anything of a private nature but he considered Alice the mother he had never had and his worry drove propriety out of his thoughts. His brow furrowed when he saw the first few pages. After reading it he shot Alice another look. Everett shook his head and then walked over to where Alice was sitting and knelt down in front of her.

"How are you doing?" Carl asked, slapping her knee lightly with the thick file.

Alice started to answer and then saw the file in Carl's hand. She reached out but Everett simply moved the file a few inches away.

"Alice, I need to know what you're doing here," he said pointedly with a glance toward the open vault door—it was empty.

"I . . . I need to make a presentation to Niles and the other department heads . . . I . . ." Alice's words trailed off and she looked confused and then just as quickly snapped out of it. "This is important," she finished, looking first into Carl's eyes and then Sarah's and Virginia's in turn. The sadness and determination were set deep in Alice Hamilton's face. "Can I talk to Niles?"

"Well, of course you can, why in the hell would you think he wouldn't see you?" Virginia asked, angry at the thought that Niles Compton's oldest friend in Alice would ever think that.

"Of course she can see me anytime she likes."

Everett squeezed his eyes closed. Even though it was on his orders that Niles be notified about Alice's presence in the vault area when she wasn't scheduled to come in at all for the next three weeks, he realized now it had been a huge mistake. Now there would be no way to keep the contents, or at least the pages he quickly scanned over, out of the chain of command. Niles Compton stood in the doorway. His white shirt and black tie were freshly cleaned and pressed and everyone could see that he was getting ready for the start of the day at the Event Group complex. Beneath his glasses all could see that his eyes were focused on Alice. As they looked up, Jack Collins stepped into the vault right behind Niles. He looked at Alice, Carl, Virginia, and then Sarah in that order. She could see his jaw muscles clenching and she knew something wasn't right.

Everett stood and faced Collins. He held up the file and everyone saw Alice flinch and almost start to reach for it once more.

"Colonel, I think you need to see what's—"

"Carl, we'll be placing Alice into protective custody. For the time being she will be restricted to the complex. Her house will be secured by our personnel."

"What?" Everett asked, incredulous at what he had just heard. Carl was so highly trained it was a shock for everyone watching how fast his reaction to Jack's order was. Never had he questioned a command from Collins in front of anyone.

"This is a joke, right?" Sarah asked as she stood to face Jack.

"No, Lieutenant, it's no joke. The action is on my orders." Niles Compton walked into the vault and most noticed him give the specimen enclosure a look;

then his eyes moved quickly away and he walked over to Alice. He smiled down at one of his closest friends and the woman who had trained him in the art of running a federal facility unlike any in the world. Niles held out his hand and Alice nodded as if in resignation, and then allowed Niles to help her slowly to her feet. He placed an arm around her and turned her away from the other shocked occupants of the small vault.

"You're angry, Niles," Alice said. "You and Garrison have that same *I'll disarm them with kindness* approach."

Niles squeezed her closer to him as they walked to the vault door. "Angry? Not at all, and I know better than anyone here that I would never try to psych you into submission. Hell, Garrison knew that also." He glanced up at Jack as they slowly walked by him. Collins's look softened and at the same moment he reached out and also squeezed Alice's shoulder as they passed by.

"Jack's pretty hot too, I can tell," Alice said quietly as she stepped over the threshold of the vault and into the curving corridor.

"Not mad, Alice. He's just concerned with certain activities you've been up to lately."

As the soothing voice of Niles Compton slowly faded away in the hallway outside, Collins turned to Everett.

"Carl, get that file up to the conference room. Also get three security men dispatched to Alice's house. I want her Europa link to the complex severed. Her off-base security clearance is hereby suspended until further notice."

"What in the hell is—"

Jack held up his hand while not looking at Sarah as he cut her off. "Look, Alice and a few others may have compromised security. They also may have placed an agent in jeopardy. This is just temporary until we find out what she's up to."

The look on Sarah's face and also that of Virginia made Jack cringe.

"Short stuff, she's not under arrest, she's in protective custody."

"Yeah, a nice euphemism, Jack . . . I fail to see the difference."

"Damn it, Lieutenant, Alice just may have compromised the most important deep cover agent the Group has ever placed, and to tell you the truth that operative is in a rather unforgiving place to be caught and accused of being a spy."

"Jack, it's Alice Hamilton for crying out loud."

Collins lowered his head and didn't wait for Sarah to catch up as he headed for the vault door.

2

The medieval castle was nearing completion. The magnificent one-half-scale stone structure was built right into the solid but craggy face of the mountain. The stone had been aged by the artisans at a cement and stone plant in Bucharest, making the facing look as if the ancient defenders of Walachia would rise to the parapets to do the bidding of their prince, Vlad Dracul, or as he was known to history: *The Impaler.* One of the many items that immediately smashed the illusion was the eight cable car lines running from giant tower to giant tower as it snaked its way a mere three miles to the art deco nightclub and restaurant that would entertain guests the year-round, snow or sunshine. The new cable car system was one of the more expensive developments of the massive main project far below in the small valley—The Edge of the World Hotel Resort and Casino.

The castle-nightclub was the only element of the project that was behind schedule. With the opening a mere three weeks away electricians were still fighting to get the power on and stable. Running the thick electrical lines up the side of the mountain had cost money and, much more importantly, time. With the lines placed dangerously close to the cable cars the safety factor had been ignored due to those very same time pressures. Presently there were sixty-two workers housed directly inside the castle to save the time of moving them about at the end of every work shift by cable car. The makeshift plan for the electricians had worked and it looked as if Dracula's Castle would be online and on time.

As over fifty of the workers slept on cots inside the massive nightclub, several of the men were still completing some last-minute work on the outside floodlights that would highlight the scarred cliff face the castle was pressed into. Two of these men walked silently to the patio stairs and hopped over the old-fashioned wooden railing that was actually tube steel and made their way out of the glare of the floodlights. One of the men pulled out a small bottle.

"Here, this ought to help you sleep tonight."

The second man accepted the bottle and, tilting his hat back on his head, turned up the container of fiery liquid. The Romanian equivalent of American moonshine called Ţuică burned its way down the small man's throat. He held the bottle up until the second, much heavier man pulled it away.

"I said help you sleep not put you in a coma," his friend hissed as he wiped his dirty sleeve over the mouth of the bottle and then capped it. He looked around at the ancient rock face. "This wouldn't be the place to be if half that mountain decided to come down on top of this damned monstrosity."

"Landslides and avalanches in the winter aren't the real danger here and you know that. As beautiful as this place is, the valley below, the pass above, even the villages scattered throughout both mountain and valley can't hide the fact that something is wrong here."

"Ah, it's just rumors and old wives' tales the old-timers inside told you about that's got you going. Stop staying up late listening to those old beards and you'll find sleeping may come a little easier. Now," the man burped and then slapped the smaller man on the back, "we better get back up there before they cut the power to the lights."

The two electricians looked at the deep shadows cast by the lighting hitting the crags and deep scars in the face of the small mountain, and at that moment you could understand the tension the workers at the makeshift construction site felt when the old stories were repeated. Even the old Hollywood films from Universal Studios were brought up and why those old films had always turned their nation's legends into running jokes. The old-timers said the entire world had always underestimated the tales coming out of Romania and that the world most definitely had it wrong about this area of the Carpathians.

As they started to make their way up the small incline of loose rock to the railing above to pull themselves back onto the outdoor patio they both heard the sound of falling rubble from above them in the darkness of the mountain. It wasn't a large slide, but enough that it echoed in the crags and minute valleys of stone above their heads.

"Maybe it's a few more of the men leaving in the middle of the night—it's always on this shift that they quit and make their way down to civilization."

The younger man was clearly frightened and just hoped that was the case. His friend knew just like everyone else that indeed several of the night shift work detail had quit and moved on, with several leaving their small bags, backpacks, and a suitcase or two—one even left some very expensive tools behind in his haste to leave the mountain and the hard conditions working inside the castle.

As the large electrician reached the rail a few feet above his head, the floodlights illuminating the mountainside went completely out.

"Damn it!" hissed the man as his hand missed the rail on his first attempt. "We'll be lucky if we don't break our necks out here."

"Hurry up, it's not that dark, I can see your hand, it's only—"

Suddenly a shape that was just a blacker spot on the black night shot out from the patio deck and grasped the large man by the wrist, snapping it in five places. Then to the horror of the second electrician the man was pulled straight up and over the railing of the darkened patio. The action only took three seconds and not a sound was made outside of the snapping of bone and the sharp intake of breath from the man that was now gone.

The smaller man's eyes were wide and he felt the shivers start as he neared a state of shock brought on by the suddenness of the assault on his friend. The young Romanian swallowed and then slowly started shaking as he reached up and removed his hat just to keep his hands busy.

As he placed one foot in front of the other he allowed the hat he held in his left hand to fall to the loose shale at his feet. He held tightly to the stone facing of the fake blocks making up the castle walls as he slid first one, and then the other foot along. His left hand rubbed the wall as the night seemed to get even darker than it had been before. His hand touched something that wasn't the fake veneer of the stone blocks. Whatever it was it moved and that was when the floodlights above flickered and then came back on. The man closed his eyes, refusing to see the thing that he knew was blocking his path to the front of the castle. He heard some soft clicking noises that moved to his front and then disappeared above him. The man opened his eyes to nothing ahead of him except for the shadows cast by the bright light from above.

"God," the man whispered in his native Romanian. And that was all he could say in his relief at being alone. He turned his head back toward the patio to make sure there was nothing there staring back at him.

The small electrician took a deep breath when he saw that the night was perfectly normal behind him at the rear of the castle. As he turned his head to start forward again he felt the wetness as it struck his hatless head. He reached up and felt his hair and pulled it away. A clear substance was running off his shaking fingers as he looked up to see what exactly had drooled on him. His eyes again widened as he came face-to-face with his own personal nightmare. The beast was actually hanging upside down, its claws dug so deeply into the stone veneer that it held itself perfectly straight above the frightened man.

"Oh," was all that was uttered in shock before the claws and teeth went to work.

Another two workers were unaccounted for at breakfast the next morning. It was assumed that they had quit after their shift and like the others had made their way back down the mountain to save them the embarrassment of admitting that the dark, foreboding countryside frightened them.

The newly built nightclub that would service the brighter gem of the project below in the valley had claimed a new chapter in the sordid history of the Carpathians.

As in the time of Prince Vlad Tepes, the new Castle Dracula had been christened by blood.

Janos Vajic stood on the blade of a Japanese-made bulldozer and surveyed the hotel, casino, and hot springs garden dome that covered the nearly forty-square-mile resort and was satisfied that the $2.7 billion project was nearing completion and he would be open on time and under the budget forced upon him by his partners—partners with a history of being unforgiving toward failures where their investments were concerned.

Vajic watched on satisfyingly as the last bit of Italian marble was placed around the 72,000-square-foot hot springs bath, gardens, and the magnificent tropical

Environ Dome that would bring many thousands of visitors to see the most exclusive plant life in the entire world located in one place. The dome was his personal architectural wonder and actually disguised the control housing for the massive cable car system that ran up the mountainside well enough you couldn't even tell there was a system. Tourists would board the cable car one hundred feet in the air at the top of the magnificent glass dome.

As he watched the final phase of construction nearing completion he spied the black Mercedes as it approached along the new highway built by the Romanian government so the public could get to the remote location at the southern tip of the Carpathian mountain range. He shook his head as he deftly jumped from the blade of the bulldozer. He was immediately approached by his assistant, Gina Louvinski, a Russian-born, Cambridge-educated general manager who spied the cursed vehicle at the same moment as Vajic.

"Well, this is it," Gina said as she approached her boss and friend with her clipboard held firmly, ready for any and all questions as far as budgetary matters were concerned. "Shall we meet inside the hotel? I'm sure we can find a quiet ballroom somewhere where there aren't a thousand workers still lingering."

"No, the reason this magnificent hotel was built here was because of the beauty of the mountains. I will let the Carpathians do the intimidating," Janos said as he made sure his coat jacket was buttoned. He looked at the clearing sky knowing that he would indeed be open before the fine summer weather started in this, the part of Romania that used to be known as Transylvania.

The two watched the Mercedes as it approached slowly, obviously so his main investor could see the progress that had been made since his last visit in January. As he watched the progress of the Mercedes, Janos looked over at Gina. She was dressed as a woman, not a woman trying to fight for legitimacy from a male-dominated Eastern society. Her business skirt was just above her knees and her white blouse was no-nonsense. Her gray jacket was devoid of any design save for the small pendant she wore on her lapel. The pendant was designed after the hotel's main attraction, after the gaming aspect of the property of course: three mountains with the largest in the center lined with small golden flowers—this was the symbol for the multibillion-dollar hotel and casino project known by the name The Edge of the World Hotel and Resort Casino.

The Mercedes pulled to a stop and two men stepped from the front seat. One, from the passenger side, placed a hand inside his coat pocket and scanned the area around the car. The large man's eyes settled on Janos and Gina and then moved on. He soon nodded to the second man, who then reached over and opened the rear passenger door of the black luxury car. A medium-sized man with a black-on-gray Armani suit complete with turtleneck stepped from the car and smiled widely as he scanned the area. He placed a large pair of expensive sunglasses on and then looked over at Janos and Gina. He raised a hand in greeting and then slowly approached, followed closely by the big man, whose hand was never far from his inside coat pocket.

Russian-born Dmitri Zallas was head of the investment group that supplied the funds and the bribes needed to complete the most luxurious hotel and casino this side of Monte Carlo, and one with a much better view. Zallas had come to Romania during the height of the rule of Ceausescu and never left, having stolen his spoils from the enslaved population during the reign of communism.

"My brother Janos, I see we are well on our way," he said while ignoring the extended hand of the 35 percent owner of the Carpathian resort. Vajic lowered his hand, embarrassed that Gina had witnessed the disrespect the Russian had toward anyone he considered weak—which was everyone who wasn't Russian.

"Yes, we will make the grand opening in three weeks on time and on schedule."

"Magnificent," Zallas said as he removed his sunglasses. He looked over at his limited partner. "By the way, friend Janos, we will be having a special gala affair the weekend prior. For three days we will host the most influential people in all of Europe."

"The week prior, we won't be ready!" Vajic quickly stated, which elicited a withering glare from Zallas.

"Oh, I think you will be."

"Who are these people and how many are we to accommodate?"

"They are very special guests that look forward to a long weekend without worry or interference from the government." Zallas cleared his throat. "Any government."

"Russian and Romanian gangsters are what you mean," Gina put in.

Zallas shot Gina the same look he had with Janos a second earlier, only this time the look remained.

"Ms. Louvinski, for a Russian-born patriot I am surprised you would think that." The smile came on but the brightness of that gleaming gesture never reached his dark eyes. His teeth were actually showing underneath the well-trimmed beard. "After all, there is no such thing as a Russian mob, and most assuredly not Romanian." He chuckled. "I don't believe they are capable of organizing anything, much less crime. No, Ms. Louvinski, they are just tourists looking for a relaxing stay before the official grand opening."

"Dmitri," Gina objected, "the cell phone towers will not be up that weekend, the German contractors cannot adjust their schedule. There will be no phones with the exception of the landline and you know the phone service inside Romania is spotty at the best of times."

"Oh, the guests will be warned to leave their business behind and just enjoy the resort."

"But—"

The look from Zallas stopped the hotel's general manager cold from persisting with her questions to Zallas and his suspect weekend guests.

"There will also be several friends of the Edge of the World Reclamation consortium from the Interior Ministry of your country, men that made this land grant possible. Men we have invested inordinate amounts of cash to."

"The men who took land protected since the time of the Boyars and Vlad the Impaler and turned it over to a foreign national, men who—"

"You bore me, madam, to no end, and I don't like to be bored in the slightest. Leave me and my friend to speak in private, please." The "please" was purely a habit on the part of the most ruthless drug kingpin and organized crime leader in the history of the Russian people.

Gina turned on her heels and left the two men, all the while Zallas's bodyguard kept a close eye on her shapely figure.

"I want no more distractions. The work is to be completed and the hotel in full operating mode. The casino will remain open and at our guests' disposal twenty-four hours a day for the entire weekend. Full staff, I don't care about the budgetary concerns you may have. The hotel will be reimbursed many times over by the favors that will be granted to us in our endeavors here in the Carpathians." Zallas looked around him and took a deep breath as his eyes took in his pride and joy embedded in the side of the mountain, the reimagined Castle Dracula, the jewel in this Carpathian crown. "This is truly a magnificent location and I must say that is a fantastic site, my friend."

Janos's eyes followed Zallas's as he scanned the rocky mountain range above them and the meadows of flowers leading up.

"What of the troubles you have been having at the castle?" Zallas asked while replacing his sunglasses.

"Every time we send men into the mountains to survey the terrain to ensure there will be no rock slides or avalanches during the snow season, they either come back with tales of terror or of being stalked and watched. Just last night we had two night shift electricians who didn't come back at all and the rest of the crews are starting to make noise about it."

"Give the missing men, or surviving families, a complete compensation package, or kill the damn families, I really do not care, Janos."

The stunned look on Vajic's face elicited a much larger smile from the Russian. "Surely you're joking?"

The smile remained. "Surely."

"My point of all of this is that the castle will remain behind schedule if we do not get the main cable cars operating. We need them not only for the last of the kitchen equipment delivery, but also food and beverage. These items cannot be manhandled up the mountain or travel by the small cable car; we need the four resort cars for transport. The men are frightened out of their minds by old wives' tales and the isolation of working seven days is driving these workers mad. That is the reason they vanish in the middle of the damn night. It has to be the local villagers and those damn Gypsies that roam through this area constantly. And to tell you the truth we don't need that sort of realism for the castle. I mean Gypsies, real Gypsies. I thought they were extinct in these parts." He looked self-consciously at a man with little sympathy for frightened workers, or junior partners for that matter. "We need security posted at the castle with my workers for the remaining days we have left to complete the project."

"Oh very well, I have a few men that have experience at this sort of activity.

I believe all you're dealing with here are a few peasants and transients, maybe even student protesters mad at us for using once protected lands. Kids, or Gypsies, or mama and papa villagers that are angry their mountain range and precious sheep meadows are no longer a sanctuary for backward people made possible by two thousand years of inept and clueless government."

"What of them?" Janos asked as his head dipped toward the mountain.

"Who?" Zallas asked as if he was annoyed.

"The Gypsies in the villages up there."

"Gypsies? Please, Janos, Gypsies? They dress differently than the other mountain people for sure, but to call them Gypsies? That's a little much." He smiled. "I think you've been listening to some of those tales these peasants tell around here." He smiled. "Gypsies—that's funny, friend Janos, perhaps one too many American and British Dracula motion pictures, you think?"

At the insult to his intelligence and his country, Janos closed his eyes momentarily. When he opened them again Zallas was stepping into his Mercedes.

"A man will contact you immediately about your mountain peasant problems." The door was pushed closed without another word.

Once inside the Mercedes, Zallas stared up the mountain in the direction of the unfinished castle. Then his eyes moved upward from there to the Patinas Pass covered in clouds. As he watched he knew the cursed Gypsy was also up there watching him. He knew what the attacks at the castle were about and he would have to put a stop to it. He removed his satellite phone and made a call. As he looked at the phone in his hands he decided to bring in his own communications equipment for the opening weekend, that would cure the problem with no cell phone towers.

"Yes, I need you here by tomorrow and bring some men with you. No, not a hunt but you will want to be protected while you're in the mountains. No, just a payment delivery." Zallas placed the satellite phone back in its cradle as he watched the mountain above him as the car drove away. "Yes, I received your message loud and clear," he said as he spied the clouds above the pass where he knew the Gypsy was watching. He looked away from the window. "In a few days you will receive my message, my backward Gypsy inbred."

One mile up into the low foothills, eyes watched the progress of the hotel and the land surrounding it. Then the bright yellow eyes dimmed as they moved to the castle above. From the shadows of the thin line of trees a low growl was heard. The eyes then settled on a lone figure that was clearly seen in a grayish haze caused by the daylight hours. The object of the growl was looking back at the mountains. This time a much louder growl rumbled and shook the loose earth around the stand of trees—then the tree line became silent once more as shadow melted back into stone.

For the first time in their long and ancient history, the inhabitants of the region—sheep men, dairymen, and huntsmen of the Carpathian highlands—were afraid, and when they became afraid bad things would start to happen in the world of men.

EVENT GROUP COMPLEX,
NELLIS AIR FORCE BASE, NEVADA

Alice sat in the office she had spent her entire adult life working in and at the moment felt as uncomfortable as if she were in a hospital waiting room. As Niles went about canceling the morning's departmental meeting and field assignment assessment teams in lieu of the recent security developments—Alice herself—she looked about the office once occupied by the man she had loved since the end of World War II—Senator Garrison Lee, whose new portrait hung on the wall in a place of honor next to the oil painting of Abraham Lincoln, the creator of Department 5656. The painting of Lee was a portrait she had never seen before and one obviously made without her knowledge. She found she couldn't look at the man she faced every day of her life for the past sixty-five years until his death in South America the previous summer.

Known as the strongest personality in government service, Alice Hamilton had intimidated presidents from every decade of her service. Now she was basically under house arrest and was also sitting in her friend's office like a student caught cutting class—*Well, maybe a little more serious than that*, she thought to herself. Alice knew this was going to be the end result of her using the asset Jack and Niles had placed so carefully inside the Vatican but she knew she had to take the chance and ask the agent known as Goliath to search for the items she so desperately needed for her Event package.

Alice looked up as the double doors opened and Niles Compton, Jack Collins, and then finally deputy director of Department 5656 Virginia Pollock all came in and then sat around the smaller of the two conference tables in the large office of Director Niles Compton. The exception was Collins, who knelt beside Alice.

Alice confidently looked up and into Jack's blue eyes. He placed a kind hand on her knee and looked into her eyes.

"Been busy?" the colonel asked.

"Jack, I'm fine. I know I went against protocol but I have good reasons for doing so."

Jack nodded and then straightened. He glanced at Niles, who hit the intercom switch to his outer office.

"Please tell the security element of Lieutenant Commander Ryan to go ahead and remove the Europa link from Ms. Hamilton's house and then secure the location for hardware removal. Tell Ryan that Pete Golding will be assisting." Niles turned the intercom off and then took a deep breath.

Alice would not blink nor would she shy away from Niles's saddened features.

She knew everyone in the room was thinking the same thing—that she had gone over into Alzheimer's land never to return.

"In 1947 you and Director Lee forged the rules of secrecy here at Department 5656. In the ninety-five-year history of the Event Group there has never been a prosecution for treason or dereliction of duty." Alice hung her head but when she looked back the old fire was back in her eyes. "Usually these things are dealt with in-house and never make it to the courts as you all well know."

"This is Alice Hamilton we're talking about," Virginia interrupted, "and in case you hadn't noticed, Niles, she's right here in this room."

"If I may finish, Virginia?" Niles said as he forced his anger down once again, mad as hell that no one but he and Jack was seeing that an absolute and serious security breach had occurred. He quickly walked over to his desk and replaced his glasses.

"Apologies," Virginia said and then looked over at Alice, who was taking this thing far better than herself.

"Alice, you know as well as anyone in the world what could have happened if the Europa system had been compromised by using her capabilities outside of the complex. I gave permission for your home link to Europa be made available to you in your retirement, but since you are who you are, a legend here at Group, Dr. Pete Golding didn't place any constraints on your activities at home as far as the use of Europa was concerned. He gave you full access to the Cray system. Dr. Golding and I will discuss this after we are through here. Colonel Collins, your department will prepare an incident report and list Dr. Golding as responsible for the massive security failure. He is hereby suspended from active duty until I figure a way to hang him without actually killing him."

Jaws dropped around the table, with again the exception being Jack Collins.

"Europa, are you online?" Niles asked, looking at the large eighty-five-inch monitor in the center of the conference room.

"Yes, Dr. Compton."

"List the names of departmental personnel who have signed onto the home terminal of Alice Hamilton, please."

"Date of user login 12/3/2013 1350 hours—Hamilton, Alice, Jean—Executive Director, Department 5656. User login 12/3/2013 1415 hours—Ellenshaw, Charles, Hindershot III—department head—Cryptozoology. User login 12/3/2013 1510 hours—Golding, Peter, Maxwell—Director, Computer Sciences Division, Department 5656."

"Thank you, Europa. Were there any more names listed as active on the home system of Mrs. Hamilton?"

"No, Dr. Compton, the only other user login was made 6/23/2012, Lee, Garrison, Donner, former director, Department 5656—deceased."

With the name mentioned Alice perked her head up and then looked over at the portrait of Lee, which was staring back at her with that "*I told you so*" look that always infuriated her. The others felt horrible that the name was mentioned by

Europa. They all looked at Alice, who had a change come over her as she straightened in her chair and then actually slid it up and placed her hands on the tabletop and folded them. She looked up at Niles and the fire in her eyes was palpable—this was the face they all knew from Alice Hamilton.

Niles placed his hand on the thick file and then sat down next to Alice. He shook his head and took a deep breath.

"Do you see what your persistence in this quest has done? I'm leaving it up to Jack on what to do with Charlie Ellenshaw, but I believe a year's suspension is in order—the same for Pete Golding. Of all the personnel who know the importance of keeping Europa secure it is Dr. Golding. If the president had a mere suggestion of what happened here we would all be looking for work, if he lets us off that easy. This is a major crime. You just didn't break a rule; you may have compromised an agent of this department. A man it has taken Jack, Senator Lee, and me six years to get into place."

"I know how long it has taken; it was I who suggested the young man in the first place."

"Alice, we have a man inside the Vatican archives who may have to cut and run, and that action by a member of the Vatican staff would surely leave the Swiss Guard and even the Italian Carabinieri to conclude that he was an agent. And if they ever found out it was not only an American agent, but a second lieutenant in the United States Army, well, I don't know how the president of the United States could ever explain that one to the Catholic faith. And with the recent religious developments in the world this country does not need to antagonize another religion. They already think the president is against all religion, which he is most definitely not."

This time Alice did hang her head.

"The only people who knew about our man in the Vatican archives were Niles, Virginia, me, and you," Jack said.

"All for a possible Event that we have not been able to prove since all of us have been here," Niles said as he opened the folder. "The only consensus on that animal in that vault since the day it was found buried in France in 1918 is that it cannot be real. Our own people believe it was a hoax perpetrated on the people of Bordeaux in 1187. That is the science here, Alice. Even your co-conspirator, Charlie Ellenshaw, doesn't believe an animal like that ever existed."

"Damn it, Niles, do not dare to sit there and quote me the fossil record data. Was what we found in South America listed in the fossil record? No. Were the animals of the Stikine River in Canada listed in the fossil record? No. And were the symbiants' life-forms we found deep in the Marianas Trench and the Gulf of Mexico in any fossil record? No. Of anyone in this room I have earned the right to believe in the impossible after working in this basement menagerie for over sixty years."

The room became silent as the tension hung in the air between Alice and Niles Compton. It seemed that Alice, who suddenly had come to life and back to the strong woman who used to run the Event Group like she was Genghis Khan, had been reborn in just the few seconds it took to get riled up after her project was basically called a fairy tale.

"I think we need to know what Alice here is subscribing to, Dr. Compton," Jack said as his curiosity came to full boil when he saw how adamant Alice was. For the first time in many weeks he was not thinking about the murder of his sister. The colonel was now fearful that he was losing a great friend, and he wanted to give Alice every break possible and allow her to explain why she would risk so much.

"Alice, in her compromising of our man at the Vatican, thought she hit the jackpot with what our agent found buried in the archives." Niles chose a picture out of the file and then slid it toward Collins, who picked it up and looked it over.

"A dog's skull?" he asked.

Alice reached out and removed the photo from Jack's fingers. "No, not a dog, but an exact duplicate of the specimen we have preserved in Vault 22871. Niles, I had convinced both you and Garrison, and now I have the proof, and what's more, I think we may have a real problem with ancient artifacts that have been showing up on the black market." Alice looked at one of her oldest friends. "Niles, you believed in this once also."

"Believing is one thing, Alice, but you know we move and act on proof. Alice, I do believe you. I know the things we've seen here defy description. But I cannot justify an Event call based on an animal carcass. I need proof. For right now the issue is closed—there is not going to be an Event declaration on this."

Niles saw Alice set her mouth in that straight line that always announced she was about to dig in her heels and not budge while he was pushing. Niles closed the file and then slid the folder down toward where Jack was sitting.

"But I will have Jack take a look at your new evidence." Niles nodded toward the colonel. "He's unbiased and will give you a fair shake. I have to step back from this call."

"I do apologize for jeopardizing our agent. But when you see all that has changed in the past few days you will know why this has to be evaluated immediately."

Niles nodded and then smiled.

"Your apology still won't save your partners in crime."

"Niles, leave Pete and Charlie alone, you know how scared they get when someone threatens them, and I did mention a little something about killing them if they didn't help me."

Most in the room smiled as Alice finally lightened a little. Even Niles smiled and then nodded.

"I'll leave that up to the colonel also. But I think a little more fright need be placed on those two. Don't you think, Colonel?"

Jack raised his brow. "You bet."

Alice silently nodded and then with a last look at the file in Jack's hands left the conference room.

"So you have believed Alice and her tale of strange animals all along?" Virginia asked Niles.

Compton laughed. "After Alice reminded us of what we have run across on our missions? Yes, I have always believed. When someone like Alice Hamilton says something is out there, you damn well better believe there is something out there." Niles looked at Jack and then smiled wider. "Besides, she needs to sweat a little for placing our Vatican man in danger."

"And that's not why we are angry, Virginia," Jack said as he hefted the thick file and stood. "It's that she didn't come to us and tell us she was doing it. Our man is buried at the Vatican archives for a reason, and Alice using him is what we have him there for. She just has to inform us so our young lieutenant can take the appropriate precautions."

Both men could see that Virginia, after shaking her head at the two men, was also embarrassed as she left the conference room.

As the doors closed behind the nuclear sciences director, Niles looked at Jack with a far more serious face.

"Colonel, I'm afraid I have to ask you to postpone your trip to Washington to meet with your contact there about your sister. This," he pointed at the thick folder, "has to take priority, because if Alice thinks it's important enough to break security protocol over then we better check it out. And frankly, Jack, I need you here." Niles stood and reached out and hit the intercom for Europa. "The pictures that our man at the Vatican took of his tail in Rome, well, Europa got a hit on her identity, and our problem, Colonel, just went into the red. Europa, place the information you received via secure link from Goliath please."

Jack knew his agent at the Vatican, Lieutenant DeSilva, was code-named Goliath.

On the large monitor a picture of a young girl came up. She was beautiful, more of a student look about her than anything.

"Europa, have you identified the subject centered on the screen?" Niles asked.

"Affirmative, Dr. Compton. She has been identified through facial analysis derived from photos and cross-referenced with the CIA Ice Blue program at Langley. The subject's name is Mica Sorotzkin, a Russian-born female of Jewish heritage now living in Israel. Employment verification through the offices of the National Security Agency listed as intelligence gathering—Mossad."

"Well, that just about does that—damn it!" Collins said as he realized they had just lost their cover inside the Vatican archives. "Mossad." Jack knew the Israeli intelligence arm was one of the best in the world. "How in the hell did they tag him?"

"We need to get Everett to Rome and prepare to bring our operative out of the Vatican. While Carl is in Italy," Niles tapped the file folder with Alice's evidence, "I need you to look through this with a fine-tooth comb and see if there's anything else that has been compromised over this. And also check Alice's evidence and see if there's anything there we can move on."

Jack knew the request by Niles placed his personal investigation into the murder of his sister on hold. He looked at the file in his hands.

"Why is she so obsessed with that damn vault? If Sarah hadn't told me about the thing inside it I would never have known it was even there."

"Jack, she didn't believe it either for the first few years she worked here. But she slowly became obsessed with the cryptozoology issues as far as animals' walking upright were concerned."

"Walking upright?" Jack pulled the picture of the skull received from the Vatican archives and looked it over. "She believes this thing walked upright?"

"That's not only her belief, but, damn," Niles started but looked embarrassed, "I believe it too. But I'm a little more practical. Show me the proof and then I can act."

Collins placed the photo back into the file. "I'll look it over," he said as he stood and left the conference room. As he did Niles slammed the intercom button down once again.

"Get me Professor Hindershot Ellenshaw III out of his dungeon on Level 82 and get him up here, and while you're at it bring his accomplice, Dr. Peter Golding when he returns from Mrs. Hamilton's house."

It was time to put the fear of God into both of the wacked-out geniuses.

Carl Everett was in the process of inventorying the components removed from Alice's home computer system. The link had been destroyed and all relevant hard drives removed. Several hundred files, most of them unclassified departmental investigations, had been recovered. Everett slammed one of these files onto the table, making both Will Mendenhall and Jason Ryan stop what they were doing and stare at the captain.

"If Alice believes this, why in the hell can't the director? I mean if she believes, that settles it for me."

Both Mendenhall and Ryan were silent as they let Everett get it off his chest. They knew it wasn't just the situation with Alice. It was more Jack cutting everyone out of the loop as far as finding his sister's killer was concerned. Will looked at Jason wanting to know if they should comment. Ryan, the one usually to shoot his mouth off, just shook his head for Will to leave the matter alone and then went back to cataloguing files.

The door opened to the Security Department and Collins walked in. He looked at the mess on the large table as everything Event Group related had been removed from the house on Flamingo Road. Jack reached out and slowly picked up an eight-by-ten photo of Garrison Lee and Alice at a small birthday party. Alice had her arm around Garrison and was kissing his cheek. The eye patch was askew and his face held a picture of pure annoyance as he was smooched by his longtime love. Collins swallowed and then placed the picture and frame back down. He tucked the thick file folder that once belonged to Alice Hamilton under his arm as he faced Everett.

"Mr. Everett, get to your quarters and pack. Europa will have State Department identification waiting for you. Get to Nellis. Ryan, you will fly the captain to Rome."

Everett looked at Jack and knew what was wrong.

"So the rumor is true, Goliath has been compromised, it's a fact?" Carl asked.

"Get there and get him out. No computer communication or cell phone. Make contact and get him to the plane. Access the situation, but more than likely you'll have to pull him out."

Jason looked at Everett first and then nodded his head. "Yes, sir."

"This is a priority. In the meantime I've been ordered to go through this file and see if Alice dug up anything that can be used to back her theory—whatever that is."

Everett nodded as Collins turned for his office door and then entered without another word to his best friends in the world.

"There he goes again. Now he'll be on the phone and communicating with Europa until tomorrow sometime." Will Mendenhall placed a folder on the table and looked at Everett and Ryan. "I'm telling you he's talking to the Frenchman. I saw his face when he talks for hours with the man. He's planning something regarding the death of his sister and Farbeaux is in on it."

"In lieu of us, are you kidding? He hates that man," Ryan said.

"The colonel respects Farbeaux and you know it. He believes just like all of us that the Frenchman has been blamed for a lot around here that he didn't actually do. Jack is willing to bet his reputation that old Henri isn't as bad a man as he likes to make out sometimes."

Everett looked at Ryan. His theory about Henri Farbeaux was nearly correct. But there were one or two things that Ryan and Mendenhall didn't know that he himself did—Henri might be respected by Jack Collins but to use the word friendly in conjunction with Farbeaux was another issue altogether. That and the fact that the French antiquities thief was in love with Sarah McIntire placed the whole situation into the realm of the surreal.

Everett suddenly placed his hand to his temple and closed his eyes in thought. "Mr. Ryan, I see a Learjet 60-220 Executive Air in your near future."

Ryan nodded and smiled at the way Carl had closed the conversation about Jack. "Shall we go to Rome, Captain, and leave this peasant Mendenhall to cover us while we vacation?"

Everett smiled for the first time in hours. "Yes, let's do leave the Army peasant to do the easy work while we toil away in Rome."

"You guys can kiss my—"

"At ease, Lieutenant, and get to counting," Ryan joked as he cut off Mendenhall's curse. Both he and Everett left the security office as Mendenhall tossed a pencil at Ryan.

ROME, ITALY

Mossad Major Mica Sorotzkin had retraced the American priest's steps back to the cybercafe he had used on no fewer than three different occasions. She had first used one, and then two, and then finally the third computer she had noted the young priest had used during his visits. In just minutes and without any of the five people currently in the small café, Mica had successfully removed all three of the hard drives from the PCs without being noticed by anyone but the counter clerk, who just admired the beautiful woman with the carefree ponytail as she sauntered past with over a thousand dollars' worth of his equipment. Mica Sorotzkin batted her two differently colored eyes and smiled as she nonchalantly left the building.

Three hours later the hard drives were being forensically studied by no fewer than six Israeli computer technicians at a Mossad safe house two miles from Vatican City. As she waited for further orders, Mica studied the file on the man the Israeli intelligence arm suspected had infiltrated the hardest area of Vatican City to get into—the archival department. It was so vast and so closed to the outside world that most authors of fiction get the description of its depths and contents totally off the mark. Mossad had been trying to get an agent placed for the past fifty years with no success. Now they suspected the American CIA had penetrated the most guarded religious archives in the world—*Yes*, she thought—either the CIA or another arm of the American government.

"Major, the general is on the secure line, it sounds urgent," said one of the safe house security men.

"When isn't it urgent with General Shamni? I swear the man sees Palestinians coming out of his oatmeal in the mornings." She picked up the phone at her desk. "Major Sorotzkin."

"Your priorities in Rome have changed, Major. Your concentration is to be focused on whom the young priest works for and to whom he is secretly sending information regarding Project Ramesses. Your mission to possibly turn this young man and make him work for us is off for the moment."

"Sir, I don't have any intelligence on that particular project, what is it?"

"Listen, Major, your computer forensics team believe they will have the hard drives broken down in a few hours, they will give you the information this covert priest is sending out. We want that information and if it leads to certain . . . sensitive projects we will have to act and act strongly in defense of Israel, is that clear?"

"No, General, not at all."

"Major Sorotzkin, I am ordering you to pack your bags. You are hereby on alert for assignment change if and when we find out if Project Ramesses is compromised. I am sending Lieutenant Colonel Ally Ben-Nevin to debrief you and to evaluate the importance of this young American. He will take command of the station when he arrives."

"General, that religious zealot can only mess this up, I want him—" Mica leaned forward with a slap onto the file compiled on her American priest. "General, I have been working this man for the past year and I'll be damned—"

The silence on the other end of the phone told the Mossad intelligence major she was talking to no one. The general had given his orders and had nothing else to say or hear, it was just that simple. Mica hung up the phone as gently as she could to control her need to throw the instrument through the window.

"Damn it!" she said with her one green and one brown eye, and then not being able to contain her anger at the obvious misstep by her superiors any longer, the major slapped the desk and then angrily slid the file she had put together piece by painstaking piece on the actions of the archival priest off her desk and onto the floor.

"Are you all right, Major Sorotzkin?" one of the technicians asked, looking around nervously at the scattered file.

"I hate this damn job sometimes."

DACIAN HOT SPRINGS, ROMANIA, EDGE OF THE WORLD HOTEL AND RESORT CASINO

Janos Vajic and Gina Louvinski sat at one of the two thousand tables inside the massive restaurant named Vlad's. It was a name that Vajic absolutely hated but had no choice in using. He didn't consider it very good advertising for one on the world's foremost kitchens to be named after Vlad the Impaler. They were going over the recent wine, liquor, and food delivery. The food and beverage manager had just taken away a large folder of added expenses for the long weekend planned before the private grand opening.

"Mr. Vajic, you have a visitor here to see you, sir."

The Romanian-born Janos looked up from his work and he and Gina both saw the worried look on the trainee manager's face as he stood before them wringing his hands.

"Well, bring them in," Vajic said in annoyance.

The man looked back through the large plate glass window that separated the giant restaurant from the large bar.

"What in the hell is the matter with you?" Gina asked when the manager trainee didn't speak. "Show whoever the hell it is in."

"The gentleman is in the bar with some rather unscrupulous-looking men. I . . . I didn't think you would want their kind in the restaurant."

"Oh, for Christ sake," Janos said as he tossed his pen down and stood and started to follow the man. "You would think you had Frankenstein's monster in the barroom."

Janos froze at the large sliding glass door that connected the restaurant with the barroom. The five men were standing at the bar dressed in black pants, black leather jackets of varying styles and lengths, and they all wore sunglasses. Vajic saw four men standing separate from the fifth, who leaned against the bar drinking from a glass slowly and deliberately while his companions were loud and boisterous.

As Gina slid in beside him and started to move forward trying to buffer her boss from these rather dubious-looking locals, Janos took her arm and stilled her. He nodded to the items leaning against the bar railing. Several large cases held what must have been very powerful weapons. There were more than fifteen different cases.

"I believe Mr. Zallas's solution to our problems in the mountains has arrived," he whispered.

Gina froze as she realized she was looking at men who were sent here by the Russian mob.

Janos took a deep breath and approached the five men. As he did, the solitary drinker looked up and into the gilded mirror behind the bar. He raised the large glass of water and drank. To Vajic's surprise the ruffians were all drinking water. He had thought the men were tossing down vodka at an incredible rate. The man standing by himself straightened and turned to face his approaching host and hostess. His eyes lingered only a moment longer on Gina than on Janos.

"You are Janos Vajic?" the man asked, his face hidden behind a thick beard and mustache. The eyes were nowhere to be found hidden underneath the thick-lensed sunglasses. Vajic wondered how the man could see at all.

"I am he. And you are obviously Russian," Janos said, not holding out his hand for the official introductions. "This is Ms. Louvinski, my general manager. We have many—"

"The general manager," the man asked in passable Romanian. "So you are the person I am to see when this problem in your high country is solved?"

Gina looked from the small man with the beard to Vajic, who nodded his head that she should answer.

"Yes, whatever that problem is of course."

"I suspect the men are frightened of the mountain dark. It is a dark that never ends."

Gina looked at Vajic once more and rolled her eyes and stepped back.

"As I said, you are Russian," Vajic repeated. "What makes you think you know this area well enough that you can solve something we don't even know needs solving? This could be just a case of men working away from home and becoming homesick, it happens all the time."

The man reached over and retrieved his black fur hat and then placed it on his head.

"As you said, I am indeed Russian, but my companions here are not. They are Romanian like yourself and Ms. Louvinski here. They are all former Departamentul Securității Statului, the now defunct department of state security. All of these men used to work directly for President Nicolae Ceaușescu. I admit that they failed to protect him in the end, but then again it wasn't really their job. What they do is special. These men, like me, hunt for a living. I admit that we usually hunt men," here the small brute smiled for the first time, "but we can be persuaded to hunt myths and legends . . . or just see if every Romanian worker is scared of the darkness."

"I take it you will start your search in the high country above Dracula's Castle?"

The men all smirked at the name of the project they were sent here to protect.

"That is our concern, not yours," the large Russian said as he reached over and gathered four of the gun cases and slung them over his shoulder.

"Well then, 1 guess we'll leave it to you to do whatever it is you do," Janos said as he half turned and then stopped. "By the way, my friend, I wouldn't advertise the fact that these idiots used to work for one of the largest mass murderers in Romanian history if I were you, or there may be five more men missing in the high country. Nicolae Ceauşescu wasn't too popular, even in an inaccessible place like this. A lot of people are still angry at the deaths he caused just to remain in power—like another country I could mention." Janos Vajic couldn't help it. Romanian citizens just weren't that fond of their former partners in communism and he had to get in a dig at the small man for his country's transgressions against his nation.

The man just smiled and then moved toward the door.

"The main cable cars are now functional and moving up the mountain so that will save you time in your climb to the castle."

At first both Janos and Gina thought the man was going to leave without comment to Gina's information, then the man stopped amid his companions and they all looked back at Janos and Gina.

"No cable cars and no hot meals at the castle. We will walk, study, and learn more in our travel up the mountain than you have ever known about this region in your years of building here. No, we walk."

As the men filed out of the bar Gina shook her head.

"I hate those goddamn secret police bastards."

"Cheer up, maybe they'll find what it is they seek."

The Russian and his men were going to a region of Romania once known to the world at the time of the dark ages as the Transylvanian Ridge, a little known name for the most inaccessible area that hosts the bleakest, darkest mountains in the entire world—a place where men have always feared to tread. This was the ancient mountain that guarded the southern approach to Romania from the Danube River. In the Old World tongue of ancient Wallachia, the language of the Boyars and Vlad himself, it was also known as the Land of the Blood Moon.

3

Niles Compton watched as Professors Pete Golding and Charles Hindershot Ellenshaw III slowly walked out of his expansive office as if they had just witnessed their puppy being put to sleep. Niles had read them the riot act, but despite his earlier promise to crucify them both for assisting Alice with her Vatican break-in, he let them off with a written warning and a write-up in their 201 file. The one thing Niles realized about both brilliant men, neither one refused to say that they would not help Alice in the future, nor would they refuse anyone in their small group of managers. To Compton that was good enough. He allowed them to leave with the warning to stay clear of Colonel Collins for a while, and it was that alone that hurt their feelings more than anything.

After his punishment had been meted out, Niles turned and went back to his desk to finish his paperwork. He looked down at the forms on his otherwise clean desk and then he threw off his glasses once more and placed his hands so they covered his face as he realized how badly he had hurt Alice by his refusal to move on her Event. He just hoped Collins could find something in her files to help him help her.

Niles needed Jack Collins to help him find the provenance to move on this possible Event; if not he would seriously have to consider retiring Alice Hamilton. And that would eventually lead to Niles Compton resigning from the Group.

Jack Collins looked up from his chair at a small table inside the Group's single place to relax and have a drink after their working hours: the Ark, named after Department 5656's most prized and the very first artifact ever collected by the Event Group in 1864.

Jack reached for the cup of coffee he had allowed to go cold in front of him. He closed his eyes and then pushed the cold coffee away. He reached out and opened the thick folder and what Alice thought was evidence of either a lost or extinct animal or proof of a massive hoax perpetrated by a long-ago prankster. The first picture he saw was the photo that had been forwarded through their man, Second Lieutenant DeSilva, inside the Vatican archives. He examined the skull and read the exhibit note under the skull.

SPECIMEN EXCAVATED IN 1567 NEAR VENICE, ITALY.
SKULL RECOVERED FROM RUINS OF ESTATE OWNED BY
ROMAN SENATOR MARCUS PALETERNUS TAPIO.

Collins then picked up Alice's notes on the Italian find. He noted that the report had been written in 1966.

After exhaustive on-site research and unauthorized archaeological digging, it is concluded at this time that Roman senator Marcus Paleternus Tapio was indeed a Roman senator from year AD 19 to 27. Further research has shown that Senator Tapio was also a military leader who achieved the rank of centurion before family wealth pushed him into the Senate and the life of politics. Further notes as more information becomes available as to Marcus Paleternus Tapio's military campaign assignments: it must be noted that the animal skull, which I believe to be a species of large timber wolf, may have been a gift to Tapio when he was a senator. However, it is my theory that Centurion Tapio, not Senator Tapio, recovered the skull on one of his many military excursions for Emperor Augustus Caesar.

Collins shook his head after reading Alice's beautiful handwriting. He once more looked at the picture of the wolf skull that for some reason the Vatican archives, or maybe even the pope himself, had sealed away and buried among whatever else they had hidden from the rest of the world.

Jack was ready to close the folder and head for the Europa clean room to better understand what it was he was supposed to be reading, when a small padded plastic box fell out of the thick file. Collins picked it up and examined it. The case contained a small chunk of stone. It was only seven inches square and looked as if it were a carving of some kind. Jack read the words on the tag that had been attached to the plastic box since 1949.

Recovered by Senator Garrison Lee the night of April 1, 1949, aboard the vessel *Golden Child* inside Hong Kong harbor. Special note to self—the bone inside the relief has been proven to contain residue of bone marrow. Must have further analysis done to determine gene structure when and if possible.

Jack examined the piece of stone. He turned it over in his hand and then once more. The piece looked as if it had been broken from something far larger, and what was the most amazing thing about this small stone was the fact that where the break in the stone had been severed from its parent stone to his astonishment there looked to be a bone underneath the broken area of petrified skin and hair.

"What the—"

"Can I join you?"

Collins had been so intent on studying the small piece of stone that he failed to see Sarah McIntire walk up to his table. He smiled at her and then self-consciously slid the small stone back into the file folder. He looked Sarah over. She was wearing her blue military jumpsuit.

Jack held Sarah's eyes for the longest time. He knew the confrontation was upon him over the nonuse of Event Group personnel in the search for his sister, Lynn's, murderer. The real conversation with Sarah would not be just the exclusion of his friends in his personal search for killers, with Sarah it was her relationship with one Henri Farbeaux. The man had been a pain in the side of every Event Group security director since 1992. Garrison Lee announced before his death that the Frenchman was a direct threat to the security of the United States due to his proclivity of stealing the world's heritage. The problem with Sarah was that she had become attached to Farbeaux in a special way. Without moving, Jack lightly kicked out the chair opposite him with his shoe. The invitation to sit was offered.

Sarah kept her eyes on the man she had fallen in love with the first time she had seen his gruff exterior. The small scars etched on Jack's face like a road map declared to anyone who met him that yes, indeed, Colonel Jack Collins had done his thing for king and country. She slowly slid into the chair.

Jack watched Sarah as he moved Alice's thick file aside.

"I thought you were teaching a class at five this afternoon?" Collins asked.

"I had my assistant take it for me. We need to talk about Henri."

"I don't think I want to discuss the Frenchman at the moment, short stuff. Whatever the reasons you may have for wanting to help him is your discussion."

"Because the man went to Mexico and saved my life, and I ask you for a favor that shouldn't have been asked and you allowed Henri to escape—for me. I appreciated it, but all you had to say was no. And now I suspect . . ." She stopped and rubbed a small hand over her face and then slowly looked into Jack's blue eyes. "You didn't even do it for me, you did it because you need him. You didn't let him go because he saved my life, Jack, you let him go because you need him more than you need us to find Lynn's killer. How's that for a forensic analysis?"

Collins didn't respond. He reached out and took the thick file folder from the tabletop while pushing his chair back.

"We just want to help, and I deserve to be let in."

"I think we need to be somewhere we can discuss this in private."

With that Jack took Sarah by the arm and instead of going out the front door Collins escaped with his charge through the back.

Seven hours later Jack awoke. Sarah was lying next to him and he couldn't help staring at her sleeping form. Collins had just broken a cardinal rule of the Group and especially the military—no private liaisons will be tolerated at the complex, and surely not with a junior officer, as Sarah was. As he looked at Sarah he knew there were no rules when it came to the small geologist. He knew he had been far too hard on her and he also knew there was no way around it—he loved the woman sleeping in his bed more than anything in the world and he didn't know how to handle it. He studied her breathing and smiled when she snored a second, rubbed her nose, and drifted back off.

Jack had relented as far as Sarah was concerned, but he wouldn't give an inch

as to allowing the men and women of this Group to become entangled with what
he knew he had to do in regard to his sister's mysterious killing. He wouldn't involve them in murder, and that's what Collins knew it would come down to. People
who murdered CIA personnel rarely if ever made it to trial. This was Jack's plan
and the reason he was using the talents of Henri Farbeaux to gain access to the
seedy world of double agents—if anyone knew how to catch a rat in the cupboard
it was another rat who wanted the cupboard all to himself, and that was the
Frenchman, Colonel Henri Farbeaux.

Collins leaned over and kissed Sarah on the forehead. He saw her hiccup and
then cry for a minute and then fall back into her dreamworld. Jack knew he had
almost pushed away the only woman he had ever loved. He shook his head and then
slowly removed himself from the bed, trying not to awaken Sarah. He threw on a
pair of white boxer shorts and then walked over to the desk. He reached down and
snapped on his desk lamp and rubbed his eyes. When he opened them they fell on
the file Alice had so meticulously cared for over the years. He shook his head and
sat down at the desk and opened the history once more. He removed the photos
stolen from the Vatican and then came to a rather lengthy report Alice had typed
out on an old-fashioned typewriter. His eyes scanned the pages and then he realized he was looking at Alice's follow-up report on the centurion who once upon a
time became a Roman senator. Jack yawned and then looked the story over. As he
read he became just a little more awake the further he read. After he was done he
went deeper into the file. He soon came across two pieces of rotted cloth encased
in plastic shielding. He picked them up and examined them. One small piece of
cloth was trimmed with what used to be fringe. Jack read the small tag Alice had
attached many years before.

Sample sent to me 2/6/1955—Levite cloth. Four vertical stripes on
pomegranate-dyed wool, analysis indicates Middle Eastern design.

Collins retrieved the second section of cloth and brought his desk lamp down
and looked the material over more closely. The designs were the same—four vertical stripes that were once red in color. The weave looked the same and the age
close also. He read the tag.

Sample recovered 12/25/1967—Levite cloth. Four vertical stripes on
pomegranate-dyed wool—analysis confirms Middle Eastern design style—
sample recovered south of the Danube River, Romania.

Jack, instead of figuring out what it was Alice had put together, the more he
read and saw, the more confused he became. What in the hell kind of trail was
Alice on? Was this ancient fashion she was interested in or was it an animal that
absolutely no one scientist at the Group believed in but Alice?

Collins replaced the sealed and protected cloth and then brought out something that made him lean closer to see. The photos were of two women. One was

young and raven-haired, the other older—far older. The only thing written on the small tag Alice had written was a name and that wasn't much at all. On the photo of the older woman, Jack placed her age anywhere from eighty to a hundred, was the small description:

Madam Ladveena Korvesky—Gypsy Queen—aprox. age 110 years old. Granddaughter is Leah Korvesky—heir to the Eastern European Gypsy hierarchy.

"What in the hell is this?" Jack mumbled to himself, "Gypsy Queen? What are you getting at, Alice?" Jack placed the photos back in the file and then picked up the next typewritten notes.

Sample 131-c recovered from privately owned vessel, *Golden Child*—Hong Kong–flagged yacht. Item recovered from vessel after said vessel was destroyed by sabotage the night of April 1, 1949, by Garrison Lee, General United States Army (ret).

Jack had a quick flash of memory as he rummaged through the file until he found the piece he was looking for—none other than the small chunk of rock he had examined before at the Ark—the small block of hewed stone with the petrified specimen inside. The tag read: 131-c. Collins played the stone in his hands as he thought about what was in the file—a file that made no sense as to the direction Alice Hamilton was taking with her investigation.

Collins made a decision and reached over for his phone. "Europa, Colonel Collins 5785 clearance—give me the locations on Professor Ellenshaw, Dr. Golding, and Alice Hamilton, please."

"Professor Ellenshaw is currently in Laboratory 1344 on Level 81, Dr. Golding is currently in the Ark, and Alice Hamilton is in her personal quarters."

"Thank you." Jack hung up and pushed another button. "Will, gather up Alice from her quarters and Doc Ellenshaw in his lab and get them to Level 63," he said quickly and then hung up.

He closed the file and that was when he noticed the code numbers and name Alice and Europa had given the file. It was strange he hadn't noticed it before, which proved he was thinking of his sister's murder too much for his duties at the Group. The code was File 890987—code name—Grimm.

"So, you're helping Alice figure out her little problem?"

Jack felt the small arms encircle his neck and he relaxed as Sarah kissed his cheek.

"Get dressed, short stuff, and go to the Ark and drag Pete Golding out of there and get him down to Vault 22871."

"Ordering your woman from your room at this early hour can force me to stop handing out the kind of loving you received last night for a very long time."

Jack smiled for the first time in what seemed like months as he turned and kissed Sarah and then slapped her on her rear end. "Now get some clothes on and get Doc Golding."

Sarah straightened and went for her jumpsuit, which was crumpled on the floor by Jack's bed.

"What has you so worked up after the workout I gave you—I must not be that good if you have this much energy."

"Baby, you're that good, I would promote you to major if I could, but for right now let's go help out a friend who everyone thinks has gone off the deep end about her wolves."

"You believe her about her animals?" Sarah asked as she zipped up.

"Not just yet, but I think I may have found someone who changed his mind somewhere along the line that adds far more weight to her argument—someone with the credentials that not even Niles could argue with."

"Who is that?" Sarah asked as she ran her fingers through her hair in lieu of a comb.

"Senator Garrison Lee."

ROME, ITALY

Everett reached over and hit Ryan on the shoulder as the taxicab came to a stop just outside St. Peter's Basilica. Ryan jumped at the sudden stop and the impact of Everett's muscled hand. Almost two hours of postflight, refueling and then getting a private hangar at Leonardo da Vinci International, one of the world's busiest airports, and then getting through customs, had placed an even harder burden on the naval aviator than just jet lag could produce. With Everett acting as his copilot on the nineteen-hour flight his sleep was off and on as Everett had to be checked on during his turn at the controls, even though most of the flight over the Atlantic had been flown by autopilot.

"Are we there already?" Ryan asked as he yawned and looked out the cab's filthy window.

Everett paid the driver and then looked at Jason. "Yeah, it only took us an hour and a half through Rome's midday traffic." He sat back in his seat as he opened the door. "If we have trouble we may have to find a different route back to da Vinci."

As Ryan looked at the crowds meandering through the wide walkways leading to the large square he shook his head.

"Our best bet on that occasion would be to walk out of here."

Everett nodded that he thought Jason was right. "Well, maybe we're just being paranoid about life in general lately. Let's go get our boy."

The two U.S. Navy men stepped into the thickening mass of humanity on their way to find their Goliath.

Mica Sorotzkin watched as the young American priest sat on the steps in front of the Basilica. His long black robe was easily played out at his sides as he opened his brown paper lunch sack. Major Sorotzkin had picked the priest up that morning as she spied him leaving his apartment on the east side of the massive property that was its own city inside of Rome—the Vatican housing area. She had been ordered to pick him up there and then again after he left work or at any time he was not in his highly classified office at the archives building.

As the major watched the young priest remove his sunglasses and wipe them on a tissue, she saw that he was actually far younger than he looked at the cyber-cafe the several times she had followed him there. She sat three rows of steps back from the American. She used a large carry-all and pulled out a small thermos and poured herself a cup of tea.

Mica had received a very urgent call from the general and that call now made her wonder why General Shamni had suddenly ordered constant surveillance on the priest after the hard drives taken from the cybercafe computers had been ana-lyzed and the results sent straight to Tel Aviv. It had been at three that morning that Shamni had called personally and ordered the "eyes on" until further notice—instructions would follow.

Mica didn't like the connotation of that last message. As she watched the young American she became worried that the general would order something other than an attempt to turn him into a working associate of Mossad.

The young American cleric known to his superiors at the Event Group as Goliath bit into his cheese sandwich as he watched the thousand milling tourists in the square and thought about how the day had changed not long after he had awoken.

That very morning he had received a coded message from Director Compton himself that came through his secure phone link bounced off several NSA com-munication satellites. He was going to be contacted at one this afternoon Rome time. He was to meet his contact at the steps of the Basilica and it would be Cap-tain Everett himself coming in for the field evaluation. Everett had assisted in his covert training and DeSilva knew the captain well enough to know that some-thing big was happening if they sent him all this way. He chewed on his sandwich. Behind his dark sunglasses the University of Notre Dame grad and U.S. Army second lieutenant scanned the crowd for the impressive form of the Navy SEAL, Carl Everett.

Major Sorotzkin flinched when her cell phone vibrated in her breast pocket. She reached into her lightweight blazer, past the Israeli-made, polymer-framed BUL Cherokee nine-millimeter in its nylon holster and retrieved the vibrating cell phone. She angrily hit the receive button.

"Yes?" she said easily into the phone as she took a sip of her lukewarm tea. She grimaced and was tempted to pour the tea onto the stone steps but held off as two highly visible Corpo della Gendarmeria walked past. The Corps of Gendarmerie of Vatican City State were highly trained at spotting trouble in crowded situations. She averted her sunglasses-covered eyes as the two uniformed guards walked past with just an appreciative look at the beautiful woman taking her lunch on the steps of the Basilica.

"Major," said the familiar voice of General Shamni, "are you in visual contact with the American agent?"

"He's about ten meters in front of me eating his lunch in the square, as he does every day the sun shines."

"We were unsuccessful in tracking the location of his contact. We suspect it's the American CIA or National Security Agency, or maybe even their FBI, but that has all become a moot point. The photographic material removed from the Vatican archives directly affects the security of Israel. Am I clear on this point?"

"Again, you're not clear at all, General. I need to know certain things if I am to perform my mission correctly. How is this man a threat and what about the written report filed with the photos to this American's contact?"

"Major, you are treading on harsh ground—ground that could collapse under you at any time if you step wrong. We suspect that his filing to his superiors can be found at Langley, Virginia, and that's something that will have to be dealt with at another time, for now the American priest is to be brought into the Rome safe house as soon as you can safely commit to the act, and once there you and the American can be debriefed by Colonel Ben-Nevin. He will burn all evidence of this priest's activities and that report filed with the photographs is to be burned. Are you the only person at the safe house to have read that particular report?"

"How can a report filed by a Roman officer be of any consequence to our security?" Mica knew the answer involved Operation Ramesses and she also suspected that the general knew she knew.

"Ben-Nevin will burn the documents and close the safe house down, and then your mission in Rome will be complete. If need be the American will be brought in for more detailed questioning."

Sorotzkin could not believe what she had just heard. "Brought in?" she asked on the secure cell link through an Israeli satellite. "I have a chance to turn this man, that's what I do. Counterintelligence, not snatching an unofficial allied agent off the street inside a friendly nation."

"Major, that harsh ground I mentioned to you earlier is starting to cave in as you speak. The American has learned of a key piece of Project Ramesses and cannot be allowed to connect that piece with any other that may have surfaced. And we must know what else he has uncovered. And don't even ask about the project, it's a thousand miles above your and also my pay grade. Clear?"

Silence from Major Sorotzkin's end.

"Colonel Ben-Nevin has been on-site for an hour and our American spy is being tracked as we speak. You will call from the safe house and let me know when Ben-Nevin starts his debrief of the American. Nothing is to happen to this boy; right now he is valuable for what he *may know*. And more to the point, Sorotzkin, there may be elements inside our own government—far more hard-line elements I may add—that want what the Ramesses project represents brought home. Get him to the safe house and the prime minister has guaranteed his safety."

"General, I have your word no harm will come to this American operative?"

"Major, the naïveté of that question is why I think your future is destined to be outside Mossad. Maybe I was wrong for handpicking you and that a transfer back to Army Intelligence would be best for your career; they are a little more suited in playing fair with the other kids on the block. We are not. But we do not kill Americans when it is avoidable, and this is one circumstance where it is still avoidable with your cooperation."

The phone went dead. Sorotzkin looked at her cell and then angrily closed it as she glanced up and saw the priest placing the remains of his lunch into his brown bag. Her differently colored eyes quickly scanned the area closest to the American but could see no familiar faces—and the pinched face of Ben-Nevin was easily seen and remembered.

Mica, like most field agents, absolutely hated men like the colonel due to the fact that they are blinded by the religion they profess to believe in. Men like him have slowly been weeded out of Mossad and mostly from political office thanks to the young people's trend toward voting for national security over religious heritage.

The black-robed archivist got to his feet and fastidiously brushed at the dust on his behind. Mica saw the two men too late. One bent to a knee and tied a shoe that needed no tying and as she watched a second, smaller, dark-haired man in a polo shirt held up a map and asked the priest a question. Sorotzkin saw the American point to the streets to the south and then the man with the map pointed in the same direction. She saw them laugh together and then the priest looked as if he had made a decision. The two men with the taller one taking up the rear started to leave the square.

Mica was thinking that Ben-Nevin's Mossad agents had arrived and there was little she could do to stop the abduction of the young American.

Major Mica Sorotzkin followed what she believed were the Mossad agents and the archival priest out of the square and into the darkest of hours that would conclude somewhere in the mountains of Eastern Europe.

Carl Everett kept pace ten feet behind Jason Ryan and United States Army Second Lieutenant Leonard DeSilva. Carl had been impressed on how easily the soldier playing a priest had taken his recall order, it was if the kid had been sensing he had been made before Everett informed him of the fact. When he felt he was being followed the day before he had acted quickly and got the evidence. The Mossad agent had been pinpointed from those grainy pictures taken from DeSilva's cell phone camera. Underneath the desert sands of Nellis Air Force Base it had taken Europa all of ten minutes to nail her real identity as an agent for the state of Israel.

As the three wound their way through the midday crowds around St. Peter's it was Everett who was the first to feel the prickling at the back of his neck. As he scanned the area through dark sunglasses he saw first Ryan, and then DeSilva become aware of the same feeling. They were being followed. Everett's SEAL training always paid dividends when it came to combat nerves, and with Ryan and DeSilva it was the same from the intense training they received at the hands of Colonel Collins.

Ryan, understanding the procedure, quickly left the priest's side and crossed the street where he vanished into the crowd of tourists and locals. He ducked low and then fought his way upstream to get behind Everett and the American contact. Ryan absentmindedly reached for his nine-millimeter Smith & Wesson but remembered this was supposed to be an extraction and not a gun battle. Everett had decided it had been too risky to try to get their personal weapons through customs. He grimaced and continued to try and come up behind the captain and their charge.

Everett was also mentally kicking himself in the ass for not going to the American embassy and meeting the Event Group contact there and getting some protection but had thought that would be unnecessary due to the fact that the extraction would take place in downtown Rome and close to Vatican City, so what could go wrong with getting the kid to da Vinci Airport? Maybe Jack was right, maybe he, Ryan, and Mendenhall weren't good enough to help the colonel track his sister's killer if he was going to make simple mistakes like underestimating a situation. He started walking faster. Just as he was about to approach from the back a child stepped up to Everett and held out a bag of oranges he was selling. Carl tried to sidestep the child but the boy stepped in front of Everett and then held out the plastic bag holding six oranges.

"Comprare le arance, la mia giornata è molto calda?" the boy said smiling up at the very large American.

Carl had been asked to buy the boy's oranges on this very hot day. Everett reached into his pocket and pulled out a twenty-dollar bill and gave it to the boy, who stopped and stared at the strange money he had been given. Everett didn't wait, he now stepped quickly to catch up with DeSilva even as the boy stood there with his small bag of oranges and the twenty-dollar bill.

Everett closed the gap between himself and DeSilva as the boy followed him with his eyes still looking at the unfamiliar money. Carl came up beside DeSilva and lowered his head as he slowly took a step past him as they neared a street vendor selling Vatican City T-shirts.

"We've been made, Lieutenant, it's time to—"

"Hello, gentlemen, can I interest you in a T-shirt depicting the Basilica at its finest?"

Everett looked up at the smiling man and realized he had spoken English. But by the time he realized it another man had come up behind DeSilva and quickly maneuvered him into a small antique shop that the vendor fronted.

At that moment Ryan appeared out of nowhere and tried to take DeSilva by the arm before the second man could get him into the antique shop.

"That is not wise, young man. You and your friends have been covered by no fewer than two weapons at all times since you left the square. If you don't want to see many innocent people hurt I suggest you step inside our small but trendy shop."

Ryan became defiant at the same moment that DeSilva decided he would not be led into a darkened store. Everett saw what was going to happen and stepped between the vendor and his two men.

"That is wise. I am not familiar with these men but I do know the people they work for. I promise you no harm if you just step into the shop."

Everett, Ryan, and DeSilva turned and saw the black-haired woman as she stepped up to the confrontational scene. It was the Mossad agent pegged by DeSilva and Europa—Major Mica Sorotzkin. Everett recognized her even with the over-sized sunglasses on her face.

Carl had no choice. With a wary look to Ryan and DeSilva, he nodded that they should do as ordered. They were led into the store followed by the major and five men who had approached unobserved.

The small Italian boy of twelve years of age looked from the closing door to the paper money in his hand, and then at the bag of oranges the tourist forgot to take. The boy was lost as to his next course of action.

The safe house was strangely quiet as Sorotzkin entered, followed by the eight men. Carl was pushed to the far wall of the small antique shop as the last man through the door closed it and then pulled down the dark shade on its roller.

Major Sorotzkin made her way to the back of the shop and looked through the security curtain. Her computer technicians were not there. Everything looked normal with the one black fact that the safe house was never to be abandoned for any reason outside of a break-and-run order, which could only come from Tel Aviv. As they had with Everett and Ryan a moment before, the major's hackles started to rise. As she turned and made her way back into the shop she heard a commotion.

"What are you doing?" she asked as she saw that the large blond American had been hit hard in the head and was just now trying to pick himself off the carpeted floor. Ryan was assisting Carl, but DeSilva had been placed on his knees with a Glock nine-millimeter pinned to the back of his head. With her fears confirmed, Major Sorotzkin slowly reached for her blazer and the BUL Cherokee semiautomatic. As she moved toward her weapon a hand coming from behind moved far faster and removed the gun. As the man to her rear pulled the weapon he intentionally allowed his hand to slowly press and glide over her left breast. She heard the sharp intake of breath from the man as he removed his hand and then stepped in front of her. Her eyes widened when she saw that it was General Shamni's special projects assistant.

"Lieutenant Colonel Ben-Nevin," she said as she gave the man a filthy and distasteful look. The pencil-thin mustache had a small line of gleaming sweat just above and below that made the major cringe. "The general will not like it if these men are mistreated," she said as Ben-Nevin tossed one of his men Sorotzkin's weapon and then turned and grabbed the major by the shoulders and brutally pulled the blazer from her body. He then turned her and slowly and perversely frisked her for other hidden weapons. Finally he stopped and ripped her sunglasses away. He smiled when he saw the two differing eye colors. He had always heard about the major's strange eyes but never saw them before today.

"Ah, the general, the prime minister, the people of Israel, they don't know what they like or dislike. It's whatever wind blows that particular day from the direction of Washington that sways them. Threats of sanctions over the West Bank make them think. The prospect of defense cuts from America gets them thinking even more. But saving the heritage of the people, nah, can't be bothered with that, no, no, no," he said as his hands made their way to the front of her pants and then deftly slid inside making the major jump and scowl at his treatment of an agent from his office. She realized something was very wrong at the safe house. The colonel roughly probed the inside of the major's pants and when he was satisfied that she carried no throw-away weapon he smiled and kept running his hand along her waistline.

Everett watched as he was helped to his feet. The blood that coursed down the left side of his head slowly made its way to his jawline. He shrugged off Ryan's helping hands as he watched the strange confrontation in front of him—a conversation that wasn't going this raven-haired woman's way at all.

"Where is my safe house team?" she asked as she squeezed her eyes shut as the colonel completed his frisking of her. He removed his hand and then winked at the major.

"I'm afraid they have retired while still on active duty, along with the agents that General Shamni had sent in to debrief this American spy. We'll be doing that," he said as his smirk brightened at the prospect. "My specially chosen men are good at recovering data from the human element."

"This is treason, Colonel. General Shamni will come after you like no agent in Mossad history. I had five brilliant technicians here, now what did you do with my people?" Her last few words came out far louder than she had intended. "Do you not think that the general has suspected someone in his office for quite some time was getting information to the extremist elements outside the Knesset?"

The major's eyes went from the injured American to the young priest and then at the smaller man, who had his hands in the air but looked as if he were just playing the game—a game Mica knew these two Americans had played before. The young priest may be new to this backdoor game of thrones, but not the blond American and his smaller friend—they have been here before and danger didn't really frighten them, and as she could see by the small dark-haired American it was a game they loved to play.

"After we find what we came for the general will have no choice but to become a part of what is happening. I daresay the people of our besieged nation will demand that the current left-wing regime take part in what we are going to do."

"Everyone in the service knows your appointment was a political move by the prime minister to satisfy the religious hard-liners in his own cabinet and those even harder men inside the Knesset. As soon as this traitorous act has been exposed you will hang in public." She looked around desperate for a way out of the situation she never saw coming. She needed time. "And what of these Americans, do you plan on killing agents of an ally state?"

The thin colonel looked over at Everett, Ryan, and DeSilva.

"Life is hard, Major, harder for some than others. But then again, we as a people know this, do we not? Now," the colonel said as he walked over to where one of his men had DeSilva kneeling with a gun to the back of his head. "I need to know where the written report was sent on the animal skull you took such fine pictures of at the Vatican archives." The colonel leaned over and patted the young priest on the back. "I think you know the one of which I speak. You sent it via computer to a secure source. Journal pages recovered from a villa in Greece describing a certain campaign of a Roman centurion later turned very important senator. Now, son, what was the name of that Roman soldier and senator, or better yet where was the campaign he was sent upon two thousand years ago? What country did he describe in his journal?"

"What?" the major asked loudly as another restraining hand held her in check. Her eyes took a quick glance at the taller American, who kept his eyes solely on her own.

"Look, I didn't read the filing," DeSilva said. "I don't know what in the hell you're talking about. I filed the report with the pages attached but I didn't read it."

Again there was a pat on the back from Colonel Ben-Nevin. "But I do not believe you, my young American friend. But we will get the truth out," Ben-Nevin said as the weapon was pushed harder into the American's skull.

Major Sorotzkin took a quick look at the front door and Ben-Nevin saw the movement.

"Major, there will be no daring last-minute rescue by the forces of good. I have arranged for an uninterrupted afternoon of thrilling historical discussion."

At that exact moment the bell above the door tinkled and the door opened sending sharp shards of afternoon light into the small antique shop. Everett's eyes widened and at the same moment one of Ben-Nevin's three men pointed his weapon in his direction as the boy stepped over the threshold of the door with his bag of oranges clutched in front of him.

"*Mister hai dimenticato la tua arance,*" the boy said with his big brown eyes flitting from the much taller American naval captain and then over to Mica, who was still being held in place by the disgusting hand of the colonel. The child held up the plastic bag of oranges. The colonel released Mica and then the weapon was slowly aimed at the boy. Sorotzkin reacted.

"He only wants this man to take the oranges he paid for. He's just a vendor. He's harmless, Colonel."

The boy didn't flinch as he took a cautious step toward Mica, which elicited a threatening point of the colonel's weapon at the twelve-year-old. Major Sorotzkin shook her head at the boy.

"*No, no, le arance per la American man.*" Mica explained that the oranges should go to the American who bought them.

The boy held eye contact with the major for a split second longer than was necessary. The boy then turned toward Everett. His eyes saw the blood on the man's face and where it had dribbled down into the collar of his blue shirt where it stained a dark maroon in color. It didn't seem to faze the boy as he took two steps toward the man. Everett felt the gun leave his back and knew his guard was going to shoot the boy.

"Hey, hey, my oranges, I thought you ripped this poor tourist off, kid," Carl said, hoping to defuse the situation, at least where the kid's safety was concerned. He felt the gun lower somewhat as Everett reached for the small bag of oranges. As he reached he saw the sparkle in the twelve-year-old's eyes and then the small smile that only the captain saw.

As soon as Everett's large hand closed on the plastic bag he felt the cold steel of something the child was hiding behind that bag. This was no ordinary child vendor. His eyes momentarily flitted over to Mica and he knew that the weapon had been purposely introduced into the store by the boy for express use by Mica. The street hawker was a plant, guard, and lookout, whatever the euphemism was these days for kids used by spies in their operations. As he saw the colonel and Mica looking at him he realized that the Mossad major had a look in her eyes that could only be related to excitement. He saw her slowly lick her red lips: this woman was watching and waiting for something that she was used to—extreme violence.

Colonel Ben-Nevin saw what had happened too late to react. The large American took the bag of oranges and the small pistol concealed behind the bulging bag and then swung the bag as hard as he could at the man to his rear catching him squarely in the face. Then without aiming Carl fired at the man holding Ryan at bay. The bullet struck the man in the side of the head and Ryan had his fallen weapon before his captor knew he was dead.

Mica realized that the American saved his friend first and that was about to cost him. As Ben-Nevin reacted slowly she brought her left wrist up and out catching the weapon just as it discharged, sending the bullet into the ceiling. The colonel swung back and caught Mica in the face as the third man in the small shop met his end when he tried to gain his feet from the staggering blow that had been delivered by the now broken plastic bag of oranges. Everett saw Ben-Nevin turn and break for the back of the store beyond the curtain. At that moment sirens started sounding as the loud reports of the guns had shattered the late afternoon solace of the tourists. Everett started forward after helping the small boy to his feet.

"Thanks, kid, now run like hell away from here," he said as he started after Ben-Nevin. "Let's go, Ryan."

Mica tried her best to stop the big man from going after the colonel. She turned and followed the two Americans through the curtain. As she went past the scattered desks she saw what had become of her technicians. They were all piled in a lump of humanity in the far corner of the communications center. With a shake of her head she finally reached Everett just as he pulled the back door open.

"No!" the major shouted just as five bullets struck the old wooden door sending splinters in every direction. Carl went to his back side, knocking Ryan down, and then reached up with his leg just as two more rounds struck the framing of the door. He kicked out, slamming the door closed, and then rolled free of harm's way.

"That bastard always has a plan," she cursed as she reached up and pulled the boy to her, who was watching from the curtain. She kissed him on the forehead and then held him at arm's length.

"Treceți, stiti ce aveti de facut," she said and then kissed the boy again on the forehead. The dark-haired child looked hesitant at first and then with a last look at the two Americans he ran for the front door and was gone. The sirens were getting closer.

"I was always terrible at languages, but one thing I do know for sure," Everett said as he pulled the clip from the small .32 caliber weapon. "That wasn't Italian you just spoke to the boy." Everett reinserted the clip and just before Mica reached for a fallen weapon from one of her deceased technicians, Carl reached over and placed the barrel of the gun gently against the dark-haired woman's temple. "Now I know *not* speaking Italian to an Italian kid isn't a capital offense, but I'm willing to make an exception for you, gorgeous. Until I figure out just what language you and the boy were using I suggest you produce no more surprises for the rest of the afternoon."

As Everett slowly allowed the major to rise from the floor, DeSilva stepped into the back room. He stood looking from Everett to the woman. Finally his eyes settled on Ryan, who saw a youthful look of arrogance come over the kid's face.

"Captain, I think our young friend here has something to say," Ryan said from the front of the store where he turned to look out the window by pulling out on the shade.

DeSilva stepped meekly into the back room with his head held firm.

"I want to go back," was all he said as he took in the bloodied Captain Everett.

"No, your cover is blown and one foreign agency knows of your existence. We can't take a chance that the Swiss Guard doesn't know either."

"Captain, I'll take that chance. It's worth the risk and you know it. I have to keep my job in the archives. If you could only see what I've seen inside, you wouldn't believe it."

Everett looked from DeSilva to Ryan, who turned away from the window with a large smile on his face at the kid's naïveté. The young agent thus far had not been given the tour of the vault levels at the Event Group complex.

"I'm sure they have great stuff stashed in there, Lieutenant, but you need to come home now. It's over."

"With all due respect, Captain, I think it's my call. My ass is on the line and I think the risk to that ass is acceptable."

Everett used a handkerchief to wipe some of the blood away from his scalp. He looked over at Ryan, who nodded his head in agreement with the young Vatican spy. Carl then shot the Israeli Mossad agent a look. She just raised that left eyebrow of hers and stared at Everett. He stared at the two differing colors of her eyes and then nodded his head as he turned away.

"Okay, kid," he said as he pocketed the bloody handkerchief. "The colonel and director will more than likely fry my ass for this." He shook his head. "But you're right, it took too long to get one of our people in there."

"Who in the hell do you men work for?" Mica asked as she slowly eyed her possibilities of escape. She was starting to piece together the idea that these men may not have the same restraints that officers of the CIA or FBI would have—she was thinking these Americans were totally capable of killing her and dumping her body in front of Mossad headquarters in Tel Aviv. Yes, she thought, these men worked for someone other than an intelligence agency.

"We happen to work for people that don't like ambushes, Ms. Sorotzkin," Everett said as he reached out and removed the Glock nine-millimeter that DeSilva was holding.

"And how do you know my name? My own people don't know me for the most part."

"We have files on many bad guys that are really pretty impressive. As I see it you don't rate up there with the bad people we do business with on occasion, you're a little different, Major." Everett gave her a dirty look. "You work for a supposed friend, and when you showed your true colors along with your Colonel Ben-Nevin, you made our decision making really very easy." Carl made sure a round was chambered in the Glock.

Mica saw the handgun lower for a split second as Carl started to raise the weapon and that was the only window of opportunity the young Mossad agent could see for getting the hell out of her situation. Mica's hand soon found an old-fashioned glass paperweight that lay on one of her technician's desks. She didn't hesitate as she grabbed it and threw the heavy silver inlaid paperweight, hitting Everett in the chest, making him automatically recoil and fire blindly at the blur of speed that had become the dark-haired woman.

Before Ryan could move past DeSilva, Major Sorotzkin had moved far too quickly and was through the curtain before Everett could react. He intentionally shot wide of his mark as he never wanted to kill the young woman. The round went through the flapping material of the curtain. The three men all heard the bell above the door jingle and then there was silence. The sirens drew closer to the small antique store.

"Damn, I lost two hostile agents in one day and now can't prove anything," Everett said as he looked over at DeSilva. "And now I'm going against orders and sending a kid back to face one of the harshest security teams in the world at the Vatican." Carl slammed the slide home on the reloaded Glock. "Yeah, this is a red banner day for the Navy, Mr. Ryan. I'm beginning to think Jack's been right all along," he said as he pushed DeSilva toward the back door.

"About what?" Ryan asked as he placed his head out the door and looked to make sure the crazy Mossad colonel wasn't lying in wait for the three men.

"That he would be better off hunting his sister's killer without us being in his way."

"Bullshit, he needs us," Ryan said, looking back momentarily to make sure the captain heard what he had to say. "Now, I suggest we get this young man back to school at the archives and we get the hell out of here to try and explain how an ally state tried to kill us all."

Everett nodded his head and then thrust his right hand out for DeSilva.

"Lieutenant, it will be noted for the record you refused to leave the post you were assigned."

"Thank you, Captain."

"Good luck, Lieutenant," Everett said, as he released his hand. Then he watched Ryan do the same.

"Good luck, Army," the naval aviator said, shaking DeSilva's hand.

"Thank you, sir."

Both Jason and Carl watched the boy leave through the back door after checking right and then left, and then one last look back at his two superior officers with a smile.

"The colonel does know how to recruit, doesn't he?"

Everett ignored the statement, not wanting to admit that Collins could do anything right, at least for the moment. "Let's get the hell out of here."

Carl looked through the curtain toward the front door. He saw the milling crowd to gathering outside.

"What are we going to do about the woman and that crazier than a shithouse rat Mossad colonel?" Ryan asked as he held the back door open for Everett.

Carl stopped in the doorway looking straight ahead. The Navy SEAL captain moved his head ever so slightly toward the interior of the safe house.

"That colonel needs a little bit of killing done to certain areas of his body, but the girl, I don't know, there's something not right there."

Ryan saw Carl smirk for the briefest of moments as if he knew an inside joke he didn't. He heard Everett's explanation as he started to run slowly down the alley.

"Her, I just want to talk to."

4

SOUTHEAST ROMANIA, DACIAN HOT SPRINGS QUADRANGLE

The British-made Land Rover moved slowly up the winding road that twisted in and out of sunshine to darkness two miles above the newly built attraction below— Dracula's Castle. The two teams of armed men wound their way through the second small village and the lead vehicle pulled to a stop. The leader of the motley group of huntsmen stepped from the vehicles and stretched as he took in the craggy rocks that lined the drive for the next mile up the side of the mountain to a spot that was rumored to be home to one of the hardiest groups of shepherds in all Romania. The Patinas Pass was a rugged but beautiful area that is usually not traveled by anyone outside of the tight-knit peoples of the high country. The tales of the Carpathian Mountains always fall far short in the description of the area. One of the more beautiful and scenic ranges in Eastern Europe, the Carpathians have been sorely and falsely depicted in literature and film. Instead of the brooding, sharp, and darkened sides of mountains that could hide anything of mythic proportions you had small valleys nestled into the sides of the mountains the further up you travel where people live a slow but comfortable life tending their large herds of milk cows, sheep, and goats and it was this life that the rest of the world didn't realize was part of the mystical mountain range.

The man who had spoken briefly with Janos Vajic inside the resort knew his job was simple; wait until nightfall and he would be met and then he could deliver the message from Dmitri Zallas. The men he traveled with were just window dressing for the peasants that work at the castle and those below. As long as they thought the Russian was looking out for them while they were tasked with building the monstrosity below was all Zallas was concerned with. Their safety was not a priority but their work schedule was. The men thought they were to be hunting wolves even though the Russian knew there were none in this region of Romania. Zallas didn't care about the animal life, he just needed his message delivered to the man responsible for the disappearances and that in and of itself would stop the killing around the castle—not hunting down something that couldn't possibly be in the region—wolves indeed.

The Russian mercenary looked at an area of Romania that had been protected by governments both elected and those where the rule of one man was absolute. He looked into the village and the growing number of citizens watching from the cracked and worn cobblestone-lined street through the small enclave. The Russian sniffed through his bushy mustache as he saw at least two of the villagers had the old-fashioned shepherd's staffs that looked as if they had jumped from a book of fairy tales.

The driver of the first Land Rover stuck a camouflaged arm out of his window and tapped the car door three times in rapid succession to get their employer's attention. He indicated with a dip of his head that they were being approached from the small causeway over the fast running river that led into the village. The leader of the two cars and six men saw the villager with the white beard and brightly stitched vest slowly step over the small bridge. The mercenary squinted his eyes as he looked at the bright sun as it neared the western edge of the mountains. He was losing daylight and wanted to get closer to the pass where he would meet Zallas's most silent of partners so he could deliver the envelope. He looked at the old man with the long white hair and equally long beard. The man from the small village held up his hand.

"Are you gentlemen lost? This is the village of Tyrell," the old man asked in his native Romanian. The question was delivered with what seemed genuine concern in expression and voice that these burly, ill-dressed men in their new vehicles were actually lost.

The Russian took a moment to translate his limited Romanian in his head. He scowled when he failed to understand it clearly enough to answer the old man. He felt a moment of relief when his Romanian driver joined the two men. The old man crossed his arms over his chest and waited patiently.

"Tell this old fool that we have come to see and possibly hunt in the pass above. That we have been asked to do this by very powerful men from far below."

At first the Romanian hunter looked uncomfortable as he thought about how to tell the old man what was said and not insult him with the "old fool" part. He said the words in Romanian slowly to the village elder. The interpreter saw the large cross around the man's neck. The wind blew his white hair as he came to a rigid stance, lowering his arms to his side as the statement, once translated, made the small valley suddenly grow cold as a cloud passed over the setting sun. The interpreter looked uncomfortable, as he didn't particularly care for the timing of the wind and temperature change.

"You cannot hunt the pass. Patinas Pass is not a place for that kind of foolishness. The only animals you will find there are sheep and goats and maybe some milk cows." The old man looked from the two men in front of him to the two Land Rovers. "Nothing more threatening for men such as yourselves."

"Wolves, old man, wolves."

The villager needed no interpretation of the word wolf. He laughed and as he did turned and looked back over the small causeway at the men and women gathered in their small square watching the exchange. The old man shouted "Lup!" as loud as he could, enough to make the Romanian hunter jump.

The villagers, about twenty-five in all, started laughing. Some of the women raised their aprons and waved them as if the statement about hunting wolves was the funniest thing they had ever heard.

The Russian never wavered as he watched the demonstration by the men and women of the high country; he just turned his head and looked toward the pass only another mile and a half up into the clouds.

"There are no wolves in the high passes. They have been gone for a hundred years. They were hunted by our ancestors to protect what little we have here. We have always been left alone and they—" The old man nodded toward the high mountain and the Patinas Pass that looked down upon them. "Have always been left alone by us."

"Tell the old man that we have no intention of speaking to more Romanians in the pass. We have come for the Lup, the wolf of the high country."

The old man laughed once again at the mention of the wolves. He shook his head and was about to wave the men away from his village when some rattling sounded from around the bend in the road leading to the village from below. As they watched, five vehicles of several different makes and models slowly wound their way up the mountain. The lead vehicle was an old and battered Toyota Land Cruiser that had seen far better days. That was followed by four more all-terrain four-wheel-drives, all in battered and rickety condition. The lead vehicle slowed as it approached the small meeting by the causeway. As the three men saw the occupants there was a moment of clear recognition to all. The passenger had his arm crooked in his open window and his dark eyes were perched under a bright red kerchief, a much smaller version of the female head scarf, that was tied off in the back and held a long, black ponytail in place. The music poured from the open window and the Russian realized it was an American song from the sixties fouling the air of the mountains. As the man with the black eyes watched the meeting on the side of the road the old Jimi Hendrix cover version of the Bob Dylan song "All Along the Watchtower" blared and echoed throughout the small valley.

The old villager raised a hand nervously in greeting as the Land Cruiser moved slowly past the hunters and the last small village before the pass above.

The man in the passenger seat moved his black eyes only but made no movement to return the greeting. With his well-trimmed beard and mustache and clean-shaven cheeks and jaw, the man looked as if he were one of Satan's henchmen. The Gypsy's arm and bloused sleeve of purple material screaming out in an outrage to fashion simply looked away from the hunters with what amounted to dismissal as the five cars moved off.

"Gypsies," the Russian said in English. He turned to the Romanian hunter. "Ask him how many Gypsies live in the pass."

The old man again seemed not to need the interpreter as he turned and raised his hand as he walked away toward the small bridge and his village beyond.

"Why do you care how many there are, you're here to hunt the great Lup, not hunt Gypsies. I wish you luck, gentlemen, with whatever is hunted."

The interpreter said the exact words of the old man to his Russian boss and then lowered his head.

"Gypsies and backward Romanian peasants, the best of everything. Come," he said as he retreated to his Land Rover. "Let us find the man we have come to see."

The sun had set an hour before and the two vehicles still had not gained the pass. The Russian directed his driver to pull off to the side. As the man behind the wheel looked to his right he saw nothing but open space and the same to his left. The road had sheer cliffs on both sides. Now everyone in the hunting party was thinking the same thing—suddenly the Carpathians looked as menacing as the old tales said they were. It did not take much to become believers in the children's nursery rhymes of their shared past.

The Russian pulled out his cased American-made .30-06 Springfield nightvision-equipped rifle. He unzipped the case and then waited until his men had gathered. The six looked at the barren terrain around them, which had changed in the very short distance between the small village below and where they now stood. The Russian switched on his scope as he raised the rifle to his eyes and scanned the area. The hue was green and captured the dark in a relief of grays and greens.

"We walk from here to the pass. We will not go into Patinas, there is no need.

We will avoid the sheep men and Gypsies and then find the man I was sent here to see."

"We are here to hunt, are we not?" asked one of the more experienced Romanian hunter-trackers.

"The only thing you will be hunting is the man I seek. You are here to guarantee my safety, nothing more. Now let us finish this business so I can enjoy my long weekend."

Some of the Romanian hunters looked around nervously. The wind had freshened and it brought the smell of old wood to their nostrils. In the air was also the smell of wood smoke from the few ancient villages dotting the mountainside leading to the resort. The lights of the castle could still be seen below and they could even make out workers as they applied the finishing touches to the attraction. The men each uncased their rifles and then made ready to move up into the Patinas Pass. The Russian saw that the men were not concerned in the least that they had been lied to about the hunt; they looked far more concerned that the sun had just disappeared behind the western mountains.

The dark eyes watched the six men from high above. The man with the red kerchief and dark features saw the intruders and their weapons that had been parked at the village below and sniffed through his nostrils. He shook his head as he watched from behind a large, crookedly broken, and very dead tree.

"They will not be harmed."

The man turned at the sound of the soft voice in the darkness.

"Grandmamma, what are you doing, do you wish to break your neck in the dark?" the man said as he saw the frail shape of the old woman as she leaned heavily against her old wooden cane. The man could see the thinly held together woolen wrap that covered her spindly shoulders. Her golden earrings gleamed in the light of the rising moon.

"I have been up and down these mountains for over eighty years; I think I can walk in the night without breaking my neck." The old woman took a step toward the man, who nodded his head and then turned back to face the men who had intruded from the abomination far below. "The past two nights you were not at your home. Where were you, child?"

The man slowly turned and the moonlight caught his eyes and to the old woman they shone brightly, catching the light that is hidden in the dark, as had his father and his father before that.

"I have not been a child for some time now, you know that." He watched the men far below as they started up the road in near darkness.

"Ah, yes, the child who will be king." She laughed as she slowly sat upon the broken and crooked tree. She took a deep breath and then moved a strand of gray hair that had fallen free of her head scarf. "Patience, man-child, your queen is still among the living."

The man finally turned and then went to the old woman and kneeled in front of her.

"And you will be among the living for many years to come. I am a patient man."

The old woman placed her right hand on the man's clean-shaven cheek. Her thumb lightly ran along his strict jawline. "Two lies in one breath taken." She smiled at him. "A man truly destined to lead the people."

The man of twenty-seven looked confused as he always did when his grandmother spoke in the old ways. He could never follow her train of thought as his younger sister was able to. The man knew he was the lesser of the two children, lagging behind his sister in intelligence and the desire to not be who they were meant to be.

"As I said, these, these hunters, they will go home without trouble from you, Marko, am I understood?" She patted the man's knee but he stood so suddenly that it fell on empty space.

"They have come to the pass to see me, Grandmamma."

"Or do they come to seek the beast that has murdered their own far below?" The old woman stood so suddenly that the man took an involuntary step back. She pointed her cane with the golden symbol on its handle into the man's chest. "I know it was you and Stanus, he's always been hard to control, much like my grandson. You have left our territory and have gone where the Golia is forbidden to go. If the rest of our people find that you have flouted the ancient laws I would have a hard time controlling their anger."

"The ancient laws were made to blind the truly faithful and give those others, those sheep you call our people, an easy way out. We have been lied to. Our lands, our mountains have been invaded." The man gestured wildly about him but his voice remained even as he spoke directly to his grandmother for the first time about his desires for the people. "I have taken an opportunity to secure our future. To make sure our lands stay ours—"

"We need no flatlanders to give us what has been ours. You need not make deals while I am still your queen." She reached out after cutting off his words and gently laid a hand on his arm. "Child, we have but to await the return of sister, then we will start changing the old ways to new ones, we will—"

The man continued as if the old queen had never spoken.

"—this land that has been deeded ours since the time of the Impaler, these very mountains that our ancestors settled when the Hittites were still crawling out of the rocks. Invaded by them," he nodded at the group of men, "and not defend ourselves? Perhaps the queen is too afraid of the men who come." He looked down at her as she lowered her head. "You sit and wait for sister to give you advice. I need not await something that will never come. She is not coming back—ever! So I have taken it upon myself to make sure our people are left alone."

The old woman leaned once more against the strength of the old wooden cane.

"We have been counseled," she spoke, "that the men below are on ground that may be untenable on a legal basis. We may have a chance to see the intruders leave the mountains without exposing the Golia. If that fails, we will move the Golia and the people to a place deeper into the pass. I agree with my grandson that times dictate our changing. Now listen to me, man-child, your sister is soon finished with her long task and she will be coming home. I am making the arrangements now and an old friend is sending her back to us."

"Grandmother, we play a fool's waiting game. The more men that come the more chance there is of everything being exposed. I will not allow that. If the deal I made for the protection of the people fails, then I will accept your way of things. This is the way it must be and the Golia will side with me on this." He half smiled. "I'm not sure you could convince Stanus to move his family anywhere—this is their home and they may fight with or without us."

"And you know this as fact, my grandson?" she asked as she took a step toward him. "You have been with Stanus the past two nights, haven't you? You and Stanus are the prey the men hunt. Tell me, does Stanus know you are speaking to men of the flatlands?"

"Yes, I and Stanus are the prey of those filthy flatlanders. Stanus is aware of what is happening and how it all could come to an end after three thousand years of hiding. Yes, Queen Mother, Stanus and the Golia are on the move to the lower climes. They sense the war that is coming to the pass and they are preparing. If the arrangement I made fails, the Golia will be uncontrollable." The man leaned over so his grandmother could see his face clearly in the moonlight. "And if you would become one with the Golia as you have many times in your younger years you would have known that the beasts are frightened of the things happening. I am the calming factor here. Without me controlling the alpha male, Stanus would not wait, the Golia would kill every man, woman, and child near that resort. My way is the only way to keep us and the Golia safe. We need allies, Grandmamma. And those men represent the man we need to secure our home and future. The days of herding sheep and milking cows and our people wandering the earth with no home are over. After we make our deal with these men we will finally have a deeded document to show the world that these mountains are ours."

"As long as I am queen the Golia will remain in and above the pass at all times. The sister, child, will have answers. When sister arrives she will find my answers. The gifts you are bestowing among the people, where do these expensive trinkets come from, Marko? How can a poor people such as us lavish such gifts as music players, violins, new clothing for the children of the pass and the villages below? Who supplies you with these gifts, or is bribes a better description? No, we will wait for sister before we move to stop this."

"Sister is as big a fool as our queen," the man said as he turned and left the old woman leaning meekly upon her cane.

The Gypsy queen watched her grandson move off into the rocks and the crevices, undoubtedly seeking Stanus. Little could she know that her grandson shed a tear as he walked away from the only woman besides his sister in his life. She did not know that the boy loved her and his sister but would not remain blinded by the old ways.

Somewhere high in the Patinas Pass the first howl of the night was heard. It echoed through the pass and down the mountain making the night animals scurry for the cover of burrow or nest.

The five men stopped and listened.

"Don't tell me that was a dog, damn it, I know a wolf when I hear one," one of the men hissed from his position across the hard-packed road.

"Silence!" the Russian hissed as he scanned the area ahead with his night-vision scope mounted on the Springfield. He could see nothing but swaying bushes caused by the wind. It was virtually impossible to see actual movement around them.

The men continued moving slowly up both sides of the road. Every six feet the Russian would hold the scope to his right eye and scan ahead. As he did, movement in the small batch of trees ahead caught his attention. He saw a flash of black on black as something he could not clearly see shot up a large tree and then vanished as if it had never been there. The man's experience in hunting dangerous prey made his hackles rise as he sensed the danger. As he lowered the rifle and scope he saw that the Romanians were starting to bunch together. He had seen this before not only hunting but also when he was serving in the Soviet army in Afghanistan in the eighties: men tended to bunch together like frightened cattle.

"Two of you into the woods on your side, go on, get over there, and you take this side and you and I will take the middle of the road and cover both sides with the scope." The man who had been doing the interpreting nodded his head, as he was relieved to be near the man with the night-vision capability.

The men stood their ground only for a moment and then decided it was probably safer to face a maddened sheep dog than the Russian. They did as ordered, only at their own slow speed.

The Russian paused as the men broke into their teams. Finally he raised the rifle and scope to cover the sheer walls of rock rising on both sides of the road. The man he was supposed to meet should have been here. His instructions had been clear—stop and wait before he arrived too close to the highest point—the pass itself. Zallas had warned him that if he went further it was on his own head.

"What is that?" the Romanian asked in a hushed tone.

"Music. Yes, it must be music from above us in the pass. Listen. I even hear a violin, bells, no a tambourine, guitars and . . . now it's gone."

"Are they having a village party up there? How can we hear the approach of anyone with that kind of noise—?"

The Russian felt the hot wetness strike the side of his face and the blast of air as something broke from the tree line and struck. He was knocked off his feet as he tried in vain to bring the muzzle of the Springfield to bear. The Romanian hunter was gone. One of his loosely tied boots was still in the roadway as the Russian fought to regain his feet. He swiped at the wetness that covered the whole of his right side. The blood smelled coppery, enough so that the large man slammed his hand into his pants to swipe the sticky liquid from his skin. He tried to raise the rifle but a loud thump from his left made him turn.

"Oomph," was the only sound made as a man vanished upside down up a large, thick pine.

The frightened hunter next to him stumbled backward as he aimed quickly and fired his old rifle up the tree. The report was loud in the darkness but not so loud as you could hear the man taken scream in pain as the bullet struck him somewhere in the bowels of the giant tree. Still lying on his back, the hunter fired again into the tree. As he took aim for a third shot a loud thump was heard and he felt the ground move as his companion's lifeless, headless body slammed the hard-packed ground. As the hunter opened his mouth in a soundless scream he heard the trees around them and the cliffs above them come to life with movement. Dark shapes darted in and out of the rocks and trees. Some of the shadows were the size of a normal man, while the others were far blacker shapes and were even larger.

The two men covering the right side of the road were frozen just a few feet off the hardpan track. Try as they might their eyes could not penetrate the thick woods and rocks. The moon was starting to play tricks on their minds and vision as it started to mix with the trees and the mist that was starting to settle onto the ground from the mountain above them. It was as if God had sent a cloud down to cover the hunters like a death shroud.

"The tales about these mountains are true, I knew it," one of the men said as he aimed into the night.

"Wait until you see something, you idiot," the large Russian said as he man-handled the man from the left into the group of two. "And make sure you shoot at an animal and not the man I have come here to see."

"We are two men down here, I think shooting into the trees right now and run-ning may be the best recourse available to us. Of course we don't have your experi-ence," one of the more brave hunters said as his eyes went left, right, and then left again.

"Calm down!" the Russian almost screamed as he himself was losing his con-fidence about delivering the message in his breast pocket to the man who controls the pass. "We will head back to the vehicles. Zallas can deliver his own messages."

The other three men didn't need persuading; they turned as one and started back down the road.

Before ten steps were taken the Golia were seen for the first time. They came from cracks in the stone wall to the right and left of the frightened hunters. They jumped from a hundred feet high in the air from the treetops, bounding from tree to tree only to hit the ground hard and then scramble to their feet. As the Russian raised his rifle to shoot, the animals all vanished. The leader of the remaining men lowered the scoped weapon to get a broader view of the road and the ground mist as it started to cover everything.

"Oh my God," said one of the men in Romanian.

All four turned and saw the shape rise from the rolling mountain mist. The beast rose until it seemed it was looking down upon them like some vengeful god making ready to vent its wrath. The darkened shape was completely upright and its arms were held at its massively muscled sides. The animal breathed in and out deeply, creating a hollow, boiler sound that made the men's hearts freeze. Its yellow, inner-glowing eyes found each man in turn. As the muzzle opened and its teeth were bared the men could see steam roll from the open orifice. The beast laid its long ears back and the black shape dipped its knees and then let loose a howl that shook the earth and awakened men five miles away who were asleep soundly in beds.

As the men closed their eyes against the onslaught of noise it ceased as quickly as it had started. The men looked around and saw that the giant of an animal was gone just as if it had never been there. The night around them had become as quiet as any of the men had ever experienced.

The Russian swallowed and then looked down at his American-made rifle and decided that he wasn't armed very well for this sort of action. As he lowered the powerful weapon he heard the deep voice from the woods and the rocks and it froze his blood. The Romanians heard their language being spoken and the Russian his native tongue. If any of them had figured out that they were each hearing differing languages they would never have stopped believing in the magic that was the Carpathians.

The Russian hastily reached into his fur coat and brought out the item he was given by Zallas. He held it in the air and then tossed it into the middle of the hardpan road.

"I have brought what you requested. It is signed by Mr. Zallas himself. You made your point and he now wants these attacks to stop. The papers for the ownership of these mountains will arrive in the next two days from the capital."

"Tell the Russian he has been warned one last time. The transaction has to be complete before certain of my family members arrive back into the pass. If not, our deal is off and we will retake what has been given to us by God. Do you understand my words, Slav?"

"Yes . . . yes . . . we will give him your message."

"Not we, Slav, the Walachians will remain here with me. They have crossed into territory forbidden to them and they will not live to tell the tale. Now leave, Slav, deliver unto Pharaoh that warning."

Without hesitation and very confused over the reference to ancient Egypt, the Russian turned and started running blindly down the mountain. The Romanians saw this and froze as the night around them became a liquid sea of black shapes as they made their way down the craggy sides of the mountain. The hunters turned and started running after their employer.

The night once more turned silent and, far off in the distance, traveling the length of the mountain and filtering through the trees from the Patinas Pass high above, they all heard the sound of violins, tambourines, and guitars. Lost in the mix of sounds old, new, and very ancient, the men that had accompanied the message to the pass began to scream. The Golia did what they have always done—secure the safety of the people and themselves.

The Carpathian Mountains had truly awakened for the first time since ancient Rome ruled the known world.

Miles down the mountain, past the workers installing the last of the supplies for the new Dracula's Castle, and even further down the mountainside to the resort—the Edge of the World—men and women turned to each other and for no other reason than an ingrained memory caught and expanded in their brains, they knew that something was out in the woods and mountains—things that men were not meant to see and the ancient memory of a time when man was not atop the food chain, things that once ruled the mountains were now loosed upon them once again.

Dmitri Zallas was being shown the interior of the casino and the plush accommodations of the hotel above. All the masonry was done in gothic-style prefabricated stone building materials that made the entire facility look as if it could have stepped from a novel of the dark ages. As Zallas was led on the tour by his junior partner, Janos Vajic, and his operations manager, Gina Louvinski, he was pleased with the staff training classes that were currently under way in the four-star restaurant and the inside the casino. The entire hotel staff was being flown in from Prague where Janos Vajic owned another property. Needless to say staffing a private party for twenty-two hundred guests was costing the partnership close to $18 million just for staff, food, and beverage, and that's not counting the money the resort would lose in room revenue.

As the trio stopped just short of the waterfall that led into the giant dome and the world's most expensive garden atrium, Zallas looked around at the private army of botanists and gardeners as they were also into their final preparations for the party two days hence.

"Now, how are we progressing on my pride and joy?" Zallas held up his hand when Vajic started to speak. "The short version, please, my friend."

"The castle is complete. The food and beverage department delivered the last of their supplies this morning by cable car, whose operation made the final push to completion possible. We were wearing resort vehicles out running up and down that mountain."

"Good, good. Now, may I see this marvelous cable car system that's the engineering envy of every designer in the world?"

"Yes, this way to the elevator."

As Zallas made his way past palms and many more plants that had no right to be in the desolate Carpathian Mountains, he saw the most expensive escalator system ever devised. It was wide at the base and narrow as it climbed the six stories to the top of the dome where the hotel's guests could see the broad expanse of the atrium and the casino beyond through the eighty-five-foot-high glass partition. As they rode the glass elevator to the top Vajic and Gina could see that they had impressed their Russian gangster. The elevator opened and the trio stepped out onto a broad expanse that resembled something like a subway platform only far more extensively appointed.

"My goodness, brother Vajic, this is impressive."

Zallas saw the richly decorated forty-five-foot-long car. Everything mechanical on the cable system was hidden with what looked like something out of an Indiana Jones movie. The sheer rock covering the opening to the four cable cars themselves looked as if it were a giant cave opening. Two long, rich mahogany-paneled cars were placed on the downhill side and two more on the opposite uphill side, which could not be seen from where they stood. The cars sat in what looked like one of the naturally formed cave systems the Carpathians are famous for. The caves were engineered to house the cars and give the hotel guests a small taste of Disneyland as they boarded the cars for the three-mile climb to the nightclub.

"You and your lovely assistant have done a splendid job, brother Vajic. I anticipate no problems this weekend; you have set my mind at ease."

Vajic looked from his partner to Gina and then grimaced as he knew the subject had to be broached before the inspection of the property was complete. As Vajic pointed out the massively thick cable lines that were needed to support such heavy and richly appointed cars, he dared bring up the touchy aspect of opening in two days.

"Dmitri, I hesitate to ask but what of the attacks above the castle?"

"The supposed attacks you mean?" Zallas shot back as he stepped into the nearest cable car and walked over to the bar tucked in the corner and rummaged around and then found what he was looking for. He poured a drink of expensive vodka and then fixed the resort owner with a stare that had frightened many men from St. Petersburg to Chechnya.

"These men you have sent up the mountain, will they solve this problem or are we going to have to bring in added security for the one night the castle is open for your guests?"

Zallas downed the vodka and then poured another. He stepped from behind the bar and paced to one of the large windows at the end of the car. He slid the window open and took in a deep breath of the air that filtered in from the outside. If he leaned over just enough he could see through the rear of the cave's opening and barely see Castle Dracula sitting three miles up the mountain. The lights were blazing and the night was still.

"I will have all of the extra security you will need. My guests . . ." Zallas hesitated and then smiled before downing his second large vodka. "My guests are the type of gentlemen," he bowed toward Gina, "and ladies, that feel more comfortable away from authority but well protected in their pursuit of enjoyment. They will have their own security, but we will be covering their security with our security."

"The attacks?" Vajic persisted, not showing how the information that every man and woman would be armed to the teeth inside his hotel scared him more than any children's stories.

"Stop worrying about fairy tales, Vajic. I have made several inquiries, even before I sent the hunters up the mountain. There have not been any wolf sightings in these mountains for two hundred years. It seems the locals wiped them out because they favor sheep over monsters."

"Then why did you send the hunters up there to hunt animals that don't live in the mountains any longer?"

Zallas turned from the open window and took in both his partner and the general manager. The Russian gangster waved a hand in front of his face as if he were a magician.

"Ooh, the true mastery is one of illusion, my brother. Make people believe they are safe and it usually turns out they are. Give them confidence that they will be taken care of."

"They don't intend to hunt?" Vajic asked, looking from the ruffian Russian to Gina, who couldn't believe what she was hearing.

"Hunt what, Janos? A sheep dog that's mad at the world? A maniac that's been driven mad by tending sheep for fifty years that lives in one of those remote villages up there? No, my man will deliver what was needed to another *mere* man up in the pass and there you have it, problem solved."

"Dmitri, what we have here is a real problem with the staff: they hear the rumors and the people in this area tend to believe the old tales of the southern Carpathians."

"Enough!" Zallas said as he tossed Gina his empty glass. "There is nothing mysterious up in those mountains. All you have is the superstition of a backward people that never knew the last century just ended. Vajic, there is nothing up there but men and women with the same weaknesses as everyone else in the world!"

As they stood by the open window of the cable car they all heard it.

Vajic looked out the window but the view from the small opening was limited. He could see the base of the castle but that was all. The tremendous howl of an animal that no longer existed in the deep mountains seemed to come from further up, closer to the Patinas Pass. Vajic straightened and then looked at his partner.

"That thing that can't possibly exist just answered the question for us."

"Can you feel it?" Gina asked as she stepped toward the open window.

"Feel what?" Zallas asked.

"Something has changed here. It's like the mountains have come alive after many years of hibernation."

"Oh, for the love of Stalin, am I going to have to get replacements up here for everyone who believes this crap?" an angry Zallas said as he turned and stormed out of the cable car. That left Vajic looking at Gina and they both knew that this was going to be a very stress-filled weekend ahead of them. The two followed the Russian. "Listen, the people we purchased these agreements from live up there. I am the only man here to handle them. I need certain information against these people and then we can move to secure the rest of the land."

"The rest of the land?" Vajic asked as he tried to keep up with Zallas.

"Do you think we stop at the castle, my friend? No, no. I have visions of an all-encompassing resort with the finest ski runs in all of Europe."

"The Patinas Pass?" Gina asked as she lowered her ever-present clipboard from her ample chest, sending the eyes of the Russian mobster down to her blouse. "It is my understanding that those villagers up there have no intention of selling or granting access to that area."

"That is my worry, not yours. After this weekend I suspect that many attitudes in and out of the mountains will be changing for the better."

Gina looked at Vajic and they both now realized that Zallas had plans they had never been aware of. To expand the resort into the pass not only would cause trouble with the locals, but also the government.

"Uh, Dmitri, the Romanian government has just signed the North Atlantic Treaty Organization charter. We are now a part of NATO, and they have designs on that pass for emergencies. They will have agreements in place with the locals of the pass that will secure their lands forever. As a matter of fact there will be NATO members in the mountains this weekend."

"Then we will have to invite some of them to the grand opening of Edge of the World." Zallas smiled and when he saw his small joke didn't play well he lost that smile just as fast. "Politics are my problem, Janos. The securing of the land is also my problem, and everything is lining up perfectly. We should have not only a fine opening for many influential men and women, but also a very good time."

Zallas walked away and the two Romanians once again exchanged worried looks as they both turned and looked out of the expansive dome toward the mountain above them.

Several loud reports were heard in the valleys of the mountain that night of mist and darkness. The gunshots faded to nothing after twenty minutes but the howling continued on throughout the night.

The Golia were on the move from the high peaks of the Carpathians.

EVENT GROUP COMPLEX,
NELLIS AIR FORCE BASE, NEVADA

The two desperadoes of the Event Group that night had broken regulations again. Charles Hindershot Ellenshaw III and Pete Golding had used illegal means to bypass security and broken into the Ark. The darkened drinking establishment was empty of all personnel at four-thirty A.M. and they had the run of the place. The rebuke they had received for assisting Alice had both scientists feeling hurt and bewildered.

Both men had tall glasses of something Ellenshaw mixed up that he claimed took the life of Jim Morrison back in 1971. After swallowing the multicolored drink Pete grimaced and forced his stomach to stay where it was designed to be anchored—in his body.

"God, that was awful," Pete cried.

Ellenshaw looked nonplussed. He took another pull from his glass, then quickly set it down on the bar and started frantically searching for his glasses in his wrinkled lab coat.

A pair of hands magically appeared and then reached over Ellenshaw's shoulder and pulled the scientist's glasses down from where they had been perched on his head. The wire-rimmed spectacles were placed on his nose and that was when the clear vision of Will Mendenhall appeared to Charlie Ellenshaw. Both he and Pete had their eyes widen until the lieutenant thought they would pop from their heads. Standing next to him was a zoologist from the San Diego Zoo neither Pete nor Charlie could recall meeting personally but knew by reputation and from their copies of the academic roster.

"Doc, why didn't you and Dr. Frankenstein come to Ryan or me with this Alice investigation? If you had you wouldn't be in Director Compton's doghouse right now."

The computer genius looked almost as wounded as he did inebriated. "We . . . we thought . . . you and Ryan would tell on us," Pete Golding mumbled as he tried to no avail to focus on Will's face.

"Then you really don't know me and Ryan all that well, do you," Mendenhall said while staring at both men. "The difference is, boys, Ryan and I would never have been caught. You two were. Now get up and come with me, you have a meeting to attend."

Ellenshaw's head shot up from the bar. "It's . . ." He looked at his wristwatch but couldn't focus on it at all. "It's . . . it's . . . boy it's early."

"Come on, the colonel's waiting for you."

Both scientists exchanged worried looks as they resigned themselves to further humiliation at the hands of the man they respected—and feared—most in the world: Jack Collins.

"Come on, it will only hurt for a split second and then your minds will go blank, almost like they are right now," Mendenhall said as he tried to hide his smile.

"Oh, God," Pete and Charlie said simultaneously.

Jack was the first one to arrive at the vault. On his way down he relieved the security man at the arch and sent him away to other duties on the vault levels. This would be a private gathering of the Event Group's best, or as Collins himself thought, the people most expected to go outside the lines of Group regulations. As Jack stepped over the steel threshold of the vault he looked to the center of the room and saw the glass enclosure that held one of the strangest specimens of animal life the Group had ever come across and the subject of the meeting.

He looked past the specimen and up into the darkness of the viewing gallery high above the floor of the vault. The area had seating for students numbering a hundred as did most of the vaults at the complex. Jack's eyes lingered on the darkness there for a moment and then his attention was taken away by three people moving into the vault.

Alice Hamilton walked through the stainless steel opening and into the small enclosure. She was flanked by her closest friends, Virginia Pollock and Sarah Mc-Intire. Jack nodded a greeting and then directed them to a table that had been set up on his orders. Collins smiled at Alice and then pulled out a chair for her. Alice returned his smile but the colonel could tell she was apprehensive. He was sure she expected to be set up by him and possibly Niles to convince her and the others that her proof of an animal that has existed alongside mankind for thousands of years just wasn't enough for an Event to be called.

Jack looked up and saw a shaky Charlie Ellenshaw preceded by Pete Golding step into the vault. They both stood in the doorway with their eyes not focusing on any one thing inside the hermetically controlled environment. Collins shook his head.

"Lieutenant, escort Baby Face Nelson and Mr. Dillinger to their seats, please."

Mendenhall smiled as did Virginia Pollock as Ellenshaw and Golding were led to two seats in the middle of the table as if to their own private inquisition.

Jack paced to the head of the table and retrieved Alice's thick file. He walked to the enclosure that held the specimen recovered from Bordeaux, France, just after World War I. He opened the folder, took a deep breath, and then looked up at Alice, who held Jack's gaze without shame and without flinching.

"Europa, Vault 22871—describe the history of its contents, please."

"Specimen stored inside Vault 22871 was discovered in Bordeaux, France, on December 11, 1918, by American Expeditionary Forces after the close of World War I. Specimen is believed to be part wolf but verification has not been confirmed by Department 5656 staff. The object was recovered during excavations by American forces and returned to the United States for analysis. The specimen has been declared a hoax perpetrated on the villagers of that region three hundred years before. Said specimen is scheduled for decommission and storage at the Virginia depository for Department 5656."

"Professor Ellenshaw," Jack said in a voice somewhat louder than normal startling Charlie until everyone present thought he had a stroke. "Please step up to the enclosure and describe what you know about the subject matter inside."

Charlie had seen this vault and examined the wolf no fewer than fifty times. The object always held a special place in the hearts of anyone who examined it. He also knew that the specimen had been ridiculed by every lettered academic in the Group and even some out of it to the point that he always voiced no opinion on it until Alice came to him and asked for his help. He himself was always afraid of even more ridicule toward his rather unorthodox department of Cryptozoology.

The remains of the animal were deposited on a white satin cloth inside the glass chamber. The beast was curled in a fetal position. There was very little of the deep black fur that once covered the animal. The skull, with the animal's nose tucked under the front paws, made the skeletal remains look as if it had just curled up and died. What was amazing about the exhibit was that the wolf had to have been eight hundred pounds when alive. Although shrunken with age and diminished by decomposition, the animal would have clearly stood well over six and a half feet long, or as in this case, almost seven feet in height.

"What we have inside the specimen case is what is typically known as *Canis lupus*, a relative of the jackal, coyote, and even the domesticated dog. This particular specimen has been tested out no fewer than five hundred times and has been tagged with and most closely resembles the North American timber wolf. However, fossil analysis cannot pinpoint the exact species of wolf." Charlie tried but could not stop the series of hiccups that erupted unbidden to his description.

"Europa, Slide 7879098, please," Jack said as he shot a quick glance into the student seating above them in the darkened gallery and then looked away.

"Yes, Colonel Collins."

Before Jack could thank Europa the entire wall illuminated with slides of X-rays and CAT scans that had been done on the animal for the past one hundred years. The slides were placed on a continuous circle of high-definition monitors. As the slides came up the lights dimmed and that afforded Collins a quick look at Alice, who sat stoically between Sarah and Virginia. She had the look of a woman sitting at a defense table and that made Jack nervous—that perhaps the old woman had given up and that didn't suit Collins at all.

"Professor Ellenshaw, what is the most obvious anomaly on this particular specimen?"

Charlie held a hand to his mouth as he tried to control his hiccups.

"Well, to anyone who has ever studied how the wolf works, plays, and eats, they can easily see that this particular specimen was born with two pelvic bones and two differing hip bones. Both made to easily slide one bone from the hip socket to easily slide into another. In other words we have two very distinct hip and pelvic bones. These bones are supposed to act like a snake's jaw, unhinging itself so it can consume prey larger than its mouth. Well, these particular hip and pelvic bones act in the same way. You see the socket that is empty on this X ray just forward of the rear socket. Well, this leg bone is supposed to remain intact at all times because the wolf is a quadruped. It is designed to run on all fours. Now this animal," he switched positions and pointed to a clear X-ray of the beast, "if we are to believe what we see has the capability to dislocate its upper thigh bone from its socket and then slide that thigh bone into the secondary socket forward of the original. As a model you can actually see the grooves that have been made by the constant movement of leg and hip bones into varying sockets."

"Bringing the leg into proper alignment with its body, making the beast capable of walking and running upright," Alice said with a defiant look in her eyes that Jack was pleased to see.

Charlie nodded toward Alice. "Yes, ma'am, that would be the result."

"But you disagree?" Collins asked, knowing that Charlie's blind faith in Alice would not stop him from voicing what he really thought of the animal and its validity.

"I . . . I . . . yes, I disagree. This is not a species of animal that ever walked the earth. There is nothing in the fossil record that shows any animal in history with this capability. The closest resemblance is with the bear, which is capable of walking upright at times of defense, but the animal of course cannot maintain that posture for an extended time."

"Because it wasn't designed to," Alice put in. "This animal obviously was. Through many millions of years they have adapted to use this magnificent ability to survive in harsh conditions and terrain."

All turned toward Alice as the light of the slides reflected off her eyes.

"I am quoting your own notes, Alice, and you have listed a professor of zoology from the University of Toronto. *'No animal was ever designed to do what this beast would have been capable of doing. If it did what we would be looking at is what our legends described as a werewolf,'*" Jack said and then turned his attention back to Ellenshaw. "What other anomaly stands out to you, Professor?"

"Well, this particular scan of the animal's paws, or in this case camouflaged paws. As you see this is also a very big impossibility as there has never been any animal outside of science fiction that has an articulated digit system. The very same system we humans and primates have. Only this is perfect. You see in this X-ray how the bones curl inward until it forms a paw shape. On the outside of the fingers when they are curled in for running, we assume anyway, are what we describe as pads, just like the toes of your dog, thick pads for protection against the rough terrain in which an animal like this would run. When the wolf would supposedly walk upright these particular paw pads are not needed, so the beast had the capability of extending actual and very articulated fingers."

Collins stopped in front of Alice and then nodded his head.

"Okay, Alice, this is your chance. Convince me."

Charlie and Pete exchanged glances but Alice looked at Jack with defiance in her eyes and then she smiled her old smile. It was like she was going into teaching mode, a job she handled often in her years at the Group. She stood and relieved Jack of her file. She opened it and then placed it on the glass top of the enclosure.

"I never thought about this vault twice, even when I first saw it in 1946. It didn't hold any interest for me. Then everything changed one night in Hong Kong. Garrison and I were . . ."

Collins listened to Alice tell her tale of the yacht *Golden Child*, and how the disaster came about that long-ago night in the cold waters of the Pacific. She ended her talk by showing around the small chip of block with the animal bone inside the petrified specimen.

"And it was that night which sparked your interest in this supposed hoax?" Collins asked.

"Yes."

"Doctors Ellenshaw and Golding, as men of science I know you both are not believers in this animal. But I see doubt in your reactions . . . why?"

Pete and Charlie exchanged a look and then Pete turned and spoke. "Because Alice believes it." He looked at her again and nodded. "And because I believe she is the most intelligent woman I have ever met. That's why we are now doubting the fossil record. We may not fully believe in the animal, but we do this lady."

Jack turned to Ellenshaw again. "Professor, you believe in some wild things. You have even gone as far as proving the existence of some these animals we discovered on varying missions around the world. Charlie, I will ask you point-blank if you believe in werewolves?"

The question took everyone in the vault off guard. Sarah for her part looked furious that Jack could be so cavalier about the subject that he had turned this into a joke just to show how foolish Alice has been. Virginia Pollock went so far as to stand up in protest, but Alice laughed and then waved Virginia back into her seat.

"No. I believe in many things," Ellenshaw answered, "but an animal that has the ability to change appearance into something it is not, not just in camouflage or the changing of skin colors, it is impossible."

"And yet because it is Mrs. Hamilton you believe?"

"Yes, as Pete said, I believe in her."

"Thank you, Charlie." Jack looked at Alice and pointed to the file. "Alice, what you did when you placed our agent in jeopardy is open a closet that should have remained closed. To take a chance on exposing our man at the Vatican over something that is not a national security issue for which reason we, including yourself, placed him at the Vatican in the first place, is an act that could end this department for now and all time. The president would shut us down in a moment if he knew we may have sacrificed an agent in the field for what, werewolves?"

With a glance at Sarah he could see that she and everyone else was growing a little furious at the attack on Alice. He continued.

"But then again it's not just werewolves you're after here, is it?" He moved to his left and looked up at the darkened gallery above, and then at Alice. "There is something pushing you, Mrs. Hamilton, something you're covering up by this wolf aspect. There's more to this fairy tale, am I correct? There *is* a legitimate reason that would send this immediately into an Event declaration, but because you have even less evidence of this particular aspect of your case you chose to go the animal route to that declaration. But now you see that's not enough." He looked at the older woman and locked his eyes with her own.

Alice finally realized what it was the colonel was attempting. She smiled so only Jack could see and he returned the gesture with a wink. Alice momentarily glanced into the darkness of the upper gallery. She raised her left eyebrow and shook her head, and then nodded at Jack.

"Yes, much more to the fairy tale."

"Let's start in the middle of this thing. What is in that report filed by agent Goliath at the Vatican?" Jack asked as he reached into his pocket for the message sent by Captain Everett less than an hour before this meeting started.

Alice opened her extensive file and then pulled out a three-page report.

"This was found in Greece. It is an account by a Roman soldier who later became a powerful senator. This account gives credence to the beast that lies under this glass. Europa will read the account as listed by this soldier. You will have to suspend your belief while you piece this together in your minds. This account was uncovered in the ruins of the senator's house in Macedonia sealed in jars and stored as if the senator wanted the tale told, but was ashamed to have it publicly recorded in his lifetime. The original report was later criticized by the Papal See and the Holy Roman Empire and done away with, until our agent found it among the list of items we wanted searched for. This keyword 'wolf' was inserted by me. Goliath searched and found this from the eyewitness account of Centurion Marcus Paleternus Tapio, future senator of Rome."

Jack leaned against the wall and watched as the report came up on the circular monitors that ringed the vault along with a Renaissance rendering of the famous Senator Tapio.

"This is factual history, as Roman officers never fudged a report of resistance anywhere in the empire. So what you read is an account of that night. It started in some of the worst weather seen in that region in a hundred years and . . ."

THE DACIAN KINGDOM
YEAR AD 12

. . . The rain was unrelenting. The water refused to soak into the hard scrub of the mountains and the result was that small lakes developed from the massive runoff and all stood in the path of the eighty-eight men of what was left of the expeditionary force of the V Roman Legion. They had been ordered detached from the whole of the legion and sent north from the Danube River thirty-five days hence.

The men of the Fifth were in ill temper as the deadly attacks had continued against their ranks after moon-fall the past three nights. They would await the coming of the sun, if it chose to show itself at all to the Romans, and then they would tally the dead from the previous night's horrors. During the darkest hours of the previous night there had been sixteen men butchered and left hanging on the scrubby small trees of the region, a reminder that the Romans, or anyone else for that matter, were trespassing on land that would be defended to the full capability of the local inhabitants of this bleak mountain range.

Centurion Marcus Paleternus Tapio was the commander of the expedition sent to the unmapped wilds of Dacia to punish the people of that region for their support of co-counsel Pompey Magnus against his onetime friend and brother Gaius Julius Caesar during the four-year civil war that ravaged Rome and its legions. Thus far in two months of campaign they had yet to come across a village or even one single man that had ever heard of Gaius Julius Caesar, or even of the Roman Empire that had invaded their country. The centurion's conclusion was that the people of the Carpathian region had not been involved in their homeland's ill-advised alliance with Pompey Magnus. The punishment campaign had been ordered by the legal heir to Caesar's fortune and power, Octavian, or as he was now known, Augustus Caesar, emperor of the Roman Empire and thus the most powerful man in the world.

Thus far they had burned over fifty small villages on their trek northward from the Danube. It had been that way until six nights before when they entered the mountainous region known to the locals as the Patinas Pass. The area was situated high in the Carpathian Mountains and was once thought to be controlled by the traitorous Dacian king, Burebista, but they had discovered that the Patinas region in the Carpathians belonged to no one man. The peasants here paid tribute to nothing but the land, the sky, and the animal life that existed in the rough mountainous range. It was in this place that they started to hear the screams of Roman sentries being murdered in the night. No matter the size of the stockade, moat, tangle foot, or sharpened barbs of spear or arrow erected for the night's camp security, none could keep at bay whatever nightmare was attacking and tearing his men apart.

Centurion Tapio looked at the list of men he had lost. The expedition was now down from eighty-eight to forty-nine men of the Fifth. The experienced Roman commander knew when it was time to cut and run from the region.

The centurion looked up at first spear of the cohort and his second in command, Julius Antipas Cricio. The man was well scarred from his many campaigns in support of first, Julius Caesar, and now he murdered in the name of Augustus. The large soldier stood at attention barely Bible in the shadow-inducing tallow-fueled lamp as it spit out its weak light.

"This campaign ends tomorrow. We burn the stockade at dawn. I want the fires hot enough that every man, woman, and child in the region knows that we are leaving this place of evil. They can have it and take it to hell with them."

The first spear centurion looked at his commander. Instead of sending for at least another cohort of legionaries or cavalry detachment, this element of the Fifth would tuck its tail between its legs and run back to the south, defeated, embarrassed, and disgraced among their peers of the Fifth Legion.

"There are but three or four men in the attacking party. If we are patient we can ambush them as they come in for their nightly attacks. We need not retreat in the face of this thing. We dishonor the eagle standard of the Fifth Legion," Cricio countered, hoping the thought of the golden eagle's shame would change his commander's mind.

"Then place a wheat sack over the damn eagle as we retreat, First Spear Centurion. I do not care about the honor of the eagle. I want what's left of my men out of these mountains. There is no honor to be found here."

"We run from peasants? The Roman Empire will be chased away by mere men that have a tendency for the dramatic in their way of killing. We can never live this down, Centurion, and I wish my protests to be placed in your report that I do not agree with your decision to retreat. We must stay and fulfill our orders from the Senate, the people of Rome, and Caesar Augustus."

"I will not do that, old friend, but I will allow you to take the rearguard action as we leave this pass. With these duties you can try and thwart this evil that has enveloped us since entering these mountains."

"I will heed your orders, and if I do manage to thwart these attacks in the night, may I expect a change of those orders?"

The centurion smiled for the first time in days. "You kill the evil that has befallen us and you will be in command of the expedition, not I. You will have proven your worth to Emperor Augustus."

The first spear returned the smile. "How many men am I to have in the rear guard?"

"Take with you the four Berserkers. We'll see if the natives of this backward land are as frightened of their legends as we. The Danube Berserkers may be better suited to fight whatever dwells in the night in this devil's region."

"The Berserkers it is." Antipas Cricio replaced his red cloak against the chill of the damp evening and then before leaving he faced his old friend. "That's all it is, you know, an old legend that only a fool would believe in. Animals that walk upright?" He laughed against the bitter feeling he was having against his own words of strength. "I think we'll find five or six old soldiers out there that have learned what it is that frightens the mighty Roman Empire—the unknown. I will be back by dawn. Don't move the remnants of the cohort too far down the mountainside, as I will bring you our silent enemies' heads."

The centurion only nodded as he turned away from the falling rain with a last look.

"I will wait until dawn and then I move out with what's left of my men." Again he looked his old friend in the eyes. "Bear witness to the night, First Spear Antipas Cricio, for there is something out there that is a silent and swift killer of men. Now leave me to worry this list of my dead soldiers."

As Tapio watched his old campaign warrior leave he knew he would never see him again. With a deep breath he called his aide.

"Sir," the aide said as he slammed his right fist to his chest.

"I want the camp broken in less than an hour. We move before the rise of the moon, full equipment, no tents or cooking material."

"Sir!" the aide said and then hurriedly left.

Centurion Tapio watched as the rain began to fall in earnest. Just as he reached for the tent's flap he heard one of the many wolves that roamed the region loose a howl that sent chills into Tapio's fragile system.

"Beware the beast in the night and be afraid for he knows what frightens you." Tapio shook his head in memory of a local saying that had been passed on to him before he was sent north from the Danube as he pulled the tent flap firmly closed against the chill of the evening. As he thought about the saying another deep-throated howl rent the night sky.

This time the cacophony was coming from the mountain high above them. The darkest of nights grew closer to the Romans.

———

The horns and drums had started an hour after he and the four Berserkers had taken up their ambush points. Cricio tried to peer into the blackness of the night to spy the locations of the men from the Danube River region of Dacia. They were known for their fierce bearing and unforgiving way of battle. One man would stake himself in front of an enemy and just wait for them to attack. While that was happening the other three Berserkers would strike from their concealed locations. As he watched he could discern no movement. As he looked on he saw that the rain was finally relinquishing its hold on the southern region.

The horns were blasting the night air somewhere miles up the winding pass of the mountains. As the first spear listened he was reminded of the battle horns used in Syria and Thrace. They were meant to frighten and confuse an enemy, and that meant, at least to his military thinking, that this was not some super-natural or magical event taking place against their men. It was nothing more than an experienced commander that knew how to fight a guerrilla war. He smiled at the thought. If they knew how to fight in that manner, they were mere men and not the devils every legionary had nightmares about. In the end Cricio knew they could be killed.

Suddenly the rain had ceased and to Cricio's consternation the moon broke free of the black clouds swirling around the mountains. He had just lost 50 per-cent of the advantage he had just a moment before. The horns suddenly stopped after a final flurry of drums and cymbals. The night became still.

Cricio slowly withdrew the gladius at his side. The coldness of the leather-covered hilt felt good in his hand. As the first glint of moonbeam caught the sharp-ened edge of the sword, Cricio heard sounds that were not natural to the forest. A low growl that seemed to weave its way in and out of the thick woods around them. Suddenly he saw a flash of movement in that same moonlight. One of the Berserkers charged from his hiding place with battleaxe high, breaking the point of being what he was, a Berserker who would wait until the exposed man was mo-lested. Evidently Cricio thought the Berserker must have seen a clear advantage in his attacking posture. The Berserker's sudden move was swift and silent. There was no scream from the small bundle of muscle and sinew. Cricio heard the loud grunt as the man from the Danube struck out at something Cricio himself could not see in the darkness. There was an animalistic scream and then he heard the man yell something in his native language he didn't understand.

As he started to move forward, Cricio saw another of the Berserkers charge through the growing ground fog to strike at the same target. The four Dacian Berserkers were not following their own rules of attack. They were not allowing the ambush to unfold—they were striking fast and hard. Even as these thoughts struck, a third Berserker joined the fray. Cricio charged forward at the sound of heavy battle.

First Spear Cricio held up by the trunk of a thick tree and listened to the night. The three Berserkers were battling something in the dark that spit and snarled, yelped and growled. Then a sound came that froze his blood. A howl rent the night sky and reverberated through the pass until it dwindled away high in the craggy peaks above them. Then the howl was repeated at least thirty more times in thirty different directions. Cricio lowered his sword as the howls faded into the night. As he entered a small clearing that had been soaked through with the relentless rain, Cricio saw the three Berserkers. One was lying on his back; the other two basically ignored their comrade and were knelt by a dark form. As Cricio approached he saw the injured Berserker as he held his insides in place with both his hands. Blood and gore oozed out with every beat of the crazy man's heartbeat. His head was shaking wildly and Cricio knew that the man was soon dead and suspected the Berserker knew at least that much himself.

Cricio kicked away the dying man's hand grabbing at his boot. As he approached the two Danube men he saw one of the battleaxes embedded deeply into the back of an animal. As Cricio knelt down to examine their, until now, unseen enemy, he was amazed to see one of the enormous paws of the beast. At first the human fist-sized paw looked normal, then when the moon broke free of the encircling clouds Cricio saw that the paw itself was malformed.

"This is no wolf," he said as he reached out and lightly touched the massive paw of the dead animal. He looked up as another burst of light from the now exposed moon illuminated the area. He used the tip of a small knife and slid the blade into the folds of the beast's fingers. As he pried at the malformed shape, his stomach turned over. He lifted, first one clawed finger, and then another. He saw that these were not the normal paw pads of an animal. As he continued to pull at the claw a long and elegant finger uncurled. The top of the clawed finger had a pad, like that of a dog, so when the animal ran the fingers would curl under.

He heard the sudden jabbering of the Berserkers as they saw the same thing as he.

"Quiet!" he hissed through clenched jaw. He slowly started to rise from the eight-hundred-pound animal at his feet. He looked around him and saw the Berserkers come rigid. Cricio used his booted foot to turn the animal's muzzle up until he could see the features. The mouth was open and he could clearly see the animal's weapons of choice. The teeth were long and curled and the muzzle itself looked as if it could easily slice through the steel of his sword. The ears were long and came to cruel points until they nearly resembled horns. The eyes were half closed and he could see the lifelessness there. As his eyes looked down upon the enemy the claws were clearly seen; eight inches long and as thick as a man's thumb. He estimated that this particular animal would have stood close to seven feet in height if it didn't run on all fours.

"Golia . . . Estaisasurfas . . . Golia," the smaller of the two Berserkers said while looking around the dark forest with wild eyes.

He had more ancient tales of terror to frighten children? "I think it is just a wolf," Cricio responded, "a strange wolf to be sure, but just a wolf." He again withdrew the gladius. "And a wolf that can be killed, so allow us to . . ."

The head of the fourth Berserker, whose absence had gone unnoticed until then, flew into the midst of the three men and bounded off the body of the dead animal. The head had been ripped, not sliced, but torn from the Berserker's body.

Before anyone could react the beasts were upon them. Cricio ducked just as a clawed hand swiped through the growing fog and ripped free his dark red cloak. He swung blindly. The blade struck something that was rock hard and just as unyielding. He heard a sharp intake of breath, then a short animal grunt of pain and then he found himself airborne. He hit the ground next to the first body of the Berserker who had slid into the afterlife some moments before. As Cricio tried in vain to catch his breath he saw the animal leap from a cluster of trees. As the screams and yells of the Berserkers sounded around him, Cricio knew the beast was going to crush him to death with its weight, and then use claws and teeth.

Cricio was frozen with fear and just before the massive animal reached him and just as he threw his arms up to protect his face, an arrow thumped into the side of the giant wolf. It yelped and then turned toward its new threat. Suddenly the area was alight with torches and yelling men. Cricio was pulled to his feet as the sound of battle flowed around him.

"Form circle! Form circle!" came the shouted order of Centurion Tapio as he held his second in command by the arm while waving his sword with the other. The gold helmet and red brush made Cricio realize that his commander had indeed come back for him. As the men of the Fifth surrounded the shaken Cricio and their commander, the forest became alight with heat and flame. "More pitch, more pitch!" Tapio shouted. "Burn it all!"

Cricio shook off Tapio's grasp when he suddenly realized what had happened.

"You used me as bait?"

In the flames Tapio looked at Cricio and then gestured to the rear. "As you said, old friend, we must not tarnish the gold of the eagle standard of the Fifth. And now I do believe it's time to make a hasty retreat from this god-awful region." Tapio suddenly let the stunned Cricio go and he knelt down beside the animal. With a grimace of disgust the centurion studied the features of the beast. Then he removed his sword and started hacking at the thick neck of the wolf. It took six hard blows to sever the head. Tapio removed his red cloak and wrapped the head inside. "No one can fault this cohort of the Fifth for cowardice in the face of this." He held the dripping cloak up for his men to see.

The forty-eight men of the Fifth Legion cheered and then went quickly back to work as even more howls started filtering down from the mountains.

"We'll need a lot more than just fire to escape this evil place," Cricio said, still angered at being used as bait by his old general.

"I am prepared to burn this whole country if it means a chance of escape. Archers!"

Ten men stepped forward and ignited their ten arrows. As the howling through the pass became more insistent, the flaming arrows were loosed into the trees beyond their position. They struck the pitch-soaked trees and a burst of flame ignited the woods around them. The howls became more insistent as the flames started running the lengths of the imposing trees that surrounded the legionaries.

"Form! Form!" Tapio called out loudly.

Men fell into order and started moving south, down and away from an advancing enemy that in their minds and memories of the real world could not possibly exist.

The remaining men from the detached element of the Fifth Legion escaped that night of nights and made a fighting retreat to the Danube where the tales of the battle for Patinas Pass would fade from memory just as would the wild tales of animals that stalk their prey upright would fade from Roman history.

Everyone around the table was silent as each conjured their own picture of the event two thousand years ago in a place called the Dacian Kingdom. The actual field report given to the emperor was a document three wide pages long—a meticulous account of the action involving the detached element of the V Legion. They each had their own thoughts after filling in the gaps to the report of Centurion Marcus Paleternus Tapio, future senator of Rome.

At the specimen case Alice pulled out the eight-by-ten glossy sent from the Vatican. As she did this, Europa placed the same picture on the circular screen. The image of the skull recovered from the Vatican archives was the exact duplicate of the one they were all looking at inside the specimen case. The only difference being in this photo you could see just how lethal this animal would have been if it did truly exist. The teeth were long and sharp. The canines were at minimum six inches long. There was even a chip in one of the larger front teeth. The skull itself as measured by the ruler in the picture was a broad seventeen inches wide.

"This was the proof I needed," Alice said as she stepped away from the case and watched differing views of the skull come and go on the large screens.

"But our proof . . ." Sarah said, and everyone noticed that she had said "our proof," automatically aligning herself with Alice. ". . . is right here in the case."

"And to risk a young man's covert cover, and possibly his life, for evidence we already had minus the field report of a long dead Roman officer," Jack said to Alice's back, "is pretty weak stuff."

"The proof I speak of isn't the skull, although the report helped confirm my own research, it was the link I needed—the trail of provenance that's required to declare an Event." Alice turned back to the case. "Europa, bring the lighting up 80 percent please and place Items 4564 and 4565 from the file coded Grimm."

"Yes, Mrs. Hamilton," replied the Cray supercomputer and before she was finished with her response the ring of monitors came alive once again with alternating pictures of two items, both looking as if they were some sort of cloth.

Jack nodded his head only slightly as he knew exactly where Alice was headed with her proof because he had studied the same pictures and read the same Roman report as she, and that was exactly why this particular meeting was taking place.

"The two items you see are what is known as homespun. The weave itself is common enough throughout the known world for the time and place these two pieces of material were in actual use. These items were recovered from a sepulcher of ancient Egypt—northern Egypt to be precise. The dig was sponsored by the American University in Cairo five years ago. The material was commonly used by a shepherd or herdsman. The two swatches of cloth were recovered from the ancient site known to the modern world as the land of Goshen, the Hebrew city located northwest of the Nile."

"A sepulcher? So you're saying that these items came from a Hebrew crypt that was located in Goshen?" Virginia Pollock asked as she stood to get a closer look at the weave and the design of the pattern.

"That's exactly what I'm saying. Now if you will notice as Virginia already has, the distinct pattern woven into the swatch. Red, although faded, and a darker red, also in the same condition. This pattern was worn by the tribe of Levi, who served the other tribes of Israel and did particular religious duties for the entire nation. This particular pattern, designated by the second stripe here," Alice pointed to the second of the three red-dyed stripes, "was worn by the men who were the suppliers of meat, milk, and grain for that particular tribe."

"So you have made a connection between the petrified animal specimen you saw in Hong Kong to this?" Virginia asked. "I don't see it. Where was this petrified animal bone recovered? You didn't answer that."

Alice smiled and looked at everyone around the table and ended with Jack.

"The ancient city where this specimen, the small piece of hewn stone encasing the flesh and bone of the animal, was recovered and then stolen from was the city of Jericho. A more exact location was the diggings at Tell es-Sultan in Palestinian-controlled territory."

"Jericho, the city supposedly destroyed by the archangel Gabriel with his horn?" Jack asked.

"The same, but I suspect that there may have been a little more to the story."

"Meaning what?" the colonel persisted.

"That maybe the attacking army laying siege to Jericho had a little more help in their assault than just Gabriel and his horn."

Virginia looked at Jack and shook her head just enough so that he saw the disbelief in her eyes, and if he and Alice lost the deputy director that meant that Niles Compton would never accept Alice's theory.

"That petrified bone was from a complete animal that Garrison Lee and I both saw on board the *Golden Child*. The damage to the remains had been great because it had been crushed between the two massive blocks that were widely known to have made the city impenetrable. The blocks had scorch marks dating back thousands of years."

"Alice, I believe you saw what you saw," Virginia said, "but actually saying this is a connection, well, that's pretty slim."

Jack had to agree with Virginia even though he knew different—was already convinced, whereas Virginia was not.

"Yes, slim until you put two and two together with the design of that material on the screen. That is a Levite section of cloth, there is no doubt of that. The city of Jericho was conquered by the Israelite army, which is a historical fact. An animal that is the exact match for the beast inside this case was found among the ruins of that city, entrapped at approximately the same moment as the city's downfall. This second pattern on the screen—not the cloth depicting the hierarchy of the Levite tribe—but the second tier tribe that served the Levite known as the Jeddah."

"I've never heard of them before," Sarah said, looking at the difference between the two swatches of woven homespun.

"There's good reason for that, Lieutenant. The Jeddah are one of the Ten Lost Tribes of Israel, only the Jeddah tribe became lost long before the other nine." She paused for effect. "At the same time as the fall of Jericho."

There was silence around the room. Jack glanced at Ellenshaw and Golding, who were following the same trail as he had earlier when scanning the file. Now he could see how Alice convinced the two scientists to help her.

Alice could see she was losing Virginia and possibly even Sarah. She acted quickly.

"The proof of that particular timeline is confirmed by none other than Joshua himself as he listed the Jeddah as destroyed many years after the battle of Jericho in one of the first citizen censuses of the new Hebrew nation."

Alice walked toward the specimen case once again. "Europa, replace the exhibits on the screen with Artifact 5657—Grimm, please."

Again, Europa complied. On the screen was what looked like the exact same picture as before. The weave in this material was exactly the same as the one previous. This was the exact same pattern as the sub-tribe known as the Jeddah.

"The same cloth design and the exact same weave, so I assume this is the Jeddah?" Virginia asked.

"Yes," answered Alice as she waited for Virginia's next obvious question.

"Where was this material recovered and when?"

"The material is the exact same weave, color, and design as the Jeddah tribe with the one exception; this vertical stripe right here. This is a warrior's mark. So we have another sub-tribe of the Levites. Still Jeddah, but this tribe was known as warriors that once guarded the northern gates of the Lower Kingdom of Egypt. They battled Libyans on a constant basis and are well documented through Egyptian accounts. This symbol and this design disappeared over three thousand years ago. This material in this photograph was recovered three weeks ago through a close contact Senator Lee and I have in Eastern Europe."

Everyone inside the vault, including Jack, heard Alice use Senator Lee's name in the present tense.

"This material is only one year old and is still in use in the high Carpathian Mountains of Romania, by villagers in the remote mountain passes of that country."

"And it is connected by . . ." Jack prompted.

"By this," Alice said, holding up a facsimile of the Roman action report filed by Centurion Marcus Paleternus Tapio. "It says the battle took place in a pass known then as Lup Pass, or in English, Wolf Pass, today known by the name Patinas. It was once protected land handed down since the time of Vlad Tepes, or as many of you know him, the Impaler, who sanctioned the area and kept hands off by every ruler on down the line as a reward by Vlad for aid rendered by that region's inhabitants during the invasion of the Ottoman Empire in 1456 through 1462. What that aid was to Prince Vlad is unknown, but well documented by none other than the Holy Roman Church, another small connection, or coincidence."

"The Patinas Pass is in—" Virginia started to ask.

"The Carpathian Mountains, located in a region once known as ancient Walachia, or otherwise known as Vlad Tepes Dracul's Transylvania. The land of vampires and werewolves," Alice said in a mysteriously mocking tone as she glanced at Charles Hindershot Ellenshaw III, who nodded his head in appreciation of her inflection.

"Perhaps you can explain why you think this region is noteworthy for the existence of your wolves," Jack urged as he looked closely at the cloth depicted on the many screens inside the vault.

"Because of this." Alice smiled at Jack, silently thanking him because now she realized what his game was. "Europa, display Exhibit 6758—Grimm on the screen please."

On the monitors around the vault appeared a hundred pictures of an old woman. They were differing views in a number of locations.

"She looks like an old-time Gypsy in some of the pictures, and in others she looks quite regal, not Gypsy-like at all."

Alice smiled at Virginia, who never missed anything. "Correct, she is a Gypsy, and she is regal indeed. Her name is, or was, Madam Ladveena Korvesky. In 1946 she was known as the queen of Gypsies. She was hunted by soldiers of Germany during the war and protected by soldiers of communist puppet Ceaușescu during the Cold War. She is an enigma. She had strange enemies and even stranger allies."

"What have you learned of her?" Virginia asked.

"What I've learned is what prompted me to involve our friends here, Professor Ellenshaw and Dr. Golding. We managed to track her movements by Europa's prowess at breaking and entering into other systems." Pete Golding beamed but stopped when he saw the scowl on the colonel's face. He just looked down after that. "The census for the last communist count inside Romania listed her in the region known as the Patinas Pass."

"Coincidence?" the assistant director asked.

"Not hardly. This woman here is the key. We know absolutely nothing about Gypsies unlike what we do of the other peoples of Europe and America, but we do know this woman is respected by every band of Gypsies around the world. The reason for this is unknown."

"Also because Gypsies have been long rumored to be one of the Lost Tribes of Israel," Charlie Ellenshaw interjected.

"Yes, along with the American Indian and also the Ethiopians, all ridiculous hypotheses," Virginia countered.

"Yes, on the surface, but couple everything with the fact that this woman and her granddaughter went on board the *Golden Child* for the specific reason of destroying that stone block with the remains inside of it, and to me there's too much coincidence here."

"And this is the granddaughter?" Virginia asked as she looked closely at the dark-haired woman.

"Yes, she actually admitted to the sabotage of the *Golden Child* as she mocked us afterward."

Jack looked closely at the picture of the young granddaughter that Alice had uncovered in her research. That was the face that had awakened him in his quarters after he saw those same facial features in another photo he had been sent. He listened as Alice continued.

"Look, the evidence is here, there are no coincidences. There are two mysteries here on why I believe an Event designation should be declared. Declared because I think history is changing right before our eyes. The answer to the riddle of the animals is tied to their role in helping and then hiding something that has been an actual legend for three thousand years—the location and circumstance of one of the Lost Tribes of Israel—and that, ladies and gentlemen, is why a history-altering Event needs to be declared."

This time the room fell silent. Even Charlie Ellenshaw and Pete Golding looked up with pounding headaches and saw that Alice had actually requested an Event. All eyes went to Jack, who stood looking at Alice.

"And what do you propose, Mrs. Hamilton?" he asked.

Alice looked from face to face and then glanced into the darkness of the viewing gallery above. She smiled and looked at Collins.

"This old lady thinks we should get to the Carpathians and see what sort of animal and Gypsy-style life may be hiding up there." She kept her smile in place as she looked again to the darkened gallery above them. "And maybe discover one of the hiding places of a tribe of Israelites that supposedly vanished sometime after Moses led his nation out of Egypt. That's all."

The stunned silence overwhelmed the small vault. No one could really talk, as proof as thin as this had never been accepted for an Event. Charlie was the first to lower his head.

Jack met the eyes of Sarah and slowly shook his head.

"Europa, monitors off, please."

The dim lighting held the vault in shadows as the monitors with the pictures of the two Gypsies from Alice's tale vanished. The room was silent as Collins looked at Alice and then turned toward the darkness of the student seating gallery.

"What do you think, Mr. Director? Does Mrs. Hamilton have enough proof to call an Event?"

"No, Mrs. Hamilton does not."

All eyes turned and looked up.

"Europa, lighting up one hundred percent please."

As the gallery lights came on to full power everyone in the vault saw Director Niles Compton as he sat stoically with one leg crossed over the other and his fingers steepled under his chin. Niles slowly stood from his seat and walked to the railing and looked down into the vault. His white shirt had its sleeves rolled to his elbows in his usual mode of dress, as was the tie halfway unknotted as he placed both hands on the railing in front of him.

"You know how long I have wanted to believe in this theory? Hell, I believe everything Alice has said. But everyone here knows what kind of pressure it takes to declare an Event. There's just not enough here."

"Niles, I—" Alice started to say but Niles held up his hand. Even Jack was now feeling uncomfortable, thinking this may have been a bad plan.

"Please, Alice, allow me some time here."

Alice lowered her eyes and nodded.

"Thank you. I have hated that thing, that pile of bones and fur, since I first laid eyes on it. It went against everything my education told me was possible. Even after all we have discovered in just my time here. It's unbelievable I could have had such a closed mind when it came to . . . well, what amounted to a werewolf. Even Charlie here thought the possibility was ridiculous many years ago." Ellenshaw again nodded his head. "But Alice, you got to the professor and eventually convinced him, and then Pete, and now Colonel Collins."

Jack looked at Niles and wondered where the director was going with this.

Compton removed his hands from the rail and put them in his pants pockets and started pacing along the railing over their heads.

"I can't fight everyone. It's an intriguing story, I will grant you that. I am also impressed with your research, Alice, but why should that surprise me? But until I get something that ties all of this together other than a few pieces of old cloth and a rock that has a petrified bone in it and a story about how a bunch of Gypsies have a connection to an ancient tribe of Israel, I have to say no. This is not an Event, and thus far there is no indication that history took a turn at that point . . . sorry, just not at this time."

The vault fell silent on the last word on Alice's Event.

"Colonel," the director said, "this situation may change if we come across more on this Mossad quest to find out information on Alice's wolves."

"I would like to present one more piece of evidence if I could that is related to that very subject," Alice interjected.

Niles pursed his lips and then nodded his head.

"Europa, bring up secure File 22167—Goliath, please."

On the screen the picture of the exact same young woman came up, only this one was in color and looked far newer. Alice turned to Jack and her face was a mask etched with questions.

"This can't be! How old is this picture?" Alice finally asked. "It's the same girl from the *Golden Child*, the granddaughter!"

"Well, if you're correct, Alice, the young woman you're looking at in this picture, the same woman you met in 1949 and caught in a picture that was taken just yesterday afternoon, is quite spunky for her age."

"How old is she, Colonel?" Sarah asked.

"The young lady would have to be well over eighty-seven years old."

5

BEIT AGHION, JERUSALEM, OFFICIAL RESIDENCE OF ISRAELI PRIME MINISTER

Mossad Lieutenant General Addis Shamni sat patiently in an overstuffed chair outside the prime minister's study. He felt uncomfortable having been led through the back reaches of the residence in order to avoid the constant throng of press and protesters that occupied most of the front area of the residence at the corner of Balfour and Smolenskin streets. Shamni adjusted his uncomfortable behind in a chair that seemed to swallow him whole.

"General, the prime minister will see you now," the stern-looking assistant said as she stepped from the study and held the sliding doors open for the general.

Shamni adjusted the civilian sport coat and plain blue shirt he wore in place of his usual army uniform and stepped through the threshold and into the chamber of the most powerful man in the Middle East. The general saw the prime minister as he sat at his desk with his head down and was writing furiously, with his nose only inches from the paper. Shamni stood at attention through force of habit.

"Relax, General, I know how you hate being drawn out of your lair in Tel Aviv, but no one's going to shoot you here for not acting like a soldier," the bespectacled man of sixty-eight said and finally stopped writing long enough to look at a man he had known for over thirty years. They had served in the same company during the war of '73 and had remained close ever since. "Besides, being a soldier here doesn't matter much because any infiltrator to the residence would go after me first and that would give you time to get out."

The general finally saw the smile he had known since the seventies and he did relax.

"So our problems in Rome seem to have gotten away from us, yes?" the prime minister asked as he returned to his writing after asking the direct question.

"I have to say I never expected that old lady to get one over on us like that."

"Not on *us*, General," the prime minister said as he looked up. He wasn't smiling this time. "But the Mossad. *Your* Mossad. The agency I placed into your most capable hands just for situations such as this. We were handed this shit plate bequeathed to us generation after generation and it has fallen on us to keep the lid on this thing." He tossed the pen he had been using onto the blotter of his desk. "How were they able to infiltrate the Mossad, Addie?"

"It's not like we were well briefed on this mess from the previous administration. We didn't know how brilliant that old witch truly was."

"Well, I guess you were well schooled this afternoon weren't you, General?"

"How she penetrated our screens and heritage checks is beyond me."

"This Major Mica Sorotzkin, do you think she's in on the selling of the people's heritage?"

"All we know is we started making the push on the Vatican archives because we had artifacts turning up that could not have come from anyplace else on earth other than where we know they are. It just so happens that Major Sorotzkin was the best expert we had on the ancient artifacts we knew existed at that time. It was just a stroke of luck that she came across the American agent and what he discovered, and that truly was just a coincidence."

"So, we may have been undone by a coincidence? If the press gets ahold of this and the religious right finally discovers where the temple is located we may have to go the extreme route. Agreed?"

"I have been begging for that since I learned of this Project Ramesses. If this is exposed we won't have peace in this country for a thousand years. It's now a matter of national security. Let's put this mess to bed for all time. The protected lands are no more. Someone is selling off artifacts that probably financed this conglomeration being built beneath the lands in question. I say we send in the Sayeret immediately and without a moment's hesitation and bring the temple down into the earth."

The prime minister slowly pushed back his large chair and then turned and faced the dead fireplace. He took a deep breath and placed his hands into his pants pockets.

"That wouldn't look too good on the evening news for our people to learn that we have invaded a sovereign nation because their government is selling off its own protected lands. No, General Shamni, let's see if we can find out if that old Gypsy is playing cards we didn't know were in the deck in the first place. If they have decided to sell off the treasure to finally get their just rewards, then we act. In the meantime we need to know what's happening and I fear that this Colonel Ben-Nevin of yours has really put a crimp in things." The prime minister turned and looked at the general. "If he finds out what land this Major Sorotzkin is really from the whole thing will be exposed. He's a rogue and he needs to be attended to. That man and the maniacs he works for in the Knesset will bring this nation down faster than any Palestinian insurgence. Am I clear on that, General?"

"Yes, sir, I believe if we wait he will come to us. In the meantime I have a plane to catch. We need to find out firsthand who's in charge in those mountains and if they have decided to get rich."

"I will order the Sayeret into the country. They will be at your disposal if needed."

"Thank you, Mr. Prime Minister."

"Old friend?"

"Sir?"

"Have you ever thought about us? I mean you and I being responsible for destroying everything that is dear to our people? To destroy the greatest objects in the Hebrew world has to be the gravest of sins."

The general felt for his friend and answered the only way an old soldier could.

"If it means saving thousands of lives from a fundamentalist push from our own people, I say bring the entire Carpathian mountain range down around their ears. I love my people and my country and will not see the progress we've made these past few years undone by ancient history that will never have a bearing on our position in the world."

"Then see to it, old friend. Find out if the old Gypsy has turned on the people. If she has, destroy everything." The prime minister held his gaze on the general. "Everything, General, and if resistance is met from the Jeddah—"

"Don't say it, Moshe, don't ever say it aloud. I know what I will have to do."

EVENT GROUP COMPLEX,
NELLIS AIR FORCE BASE, NEVADA

The vault was silent as all eyes were still intently looking at the woman Jack claimed would have to be well over eighty since it was obviously the same woman Alice had met in 1946 in Hong Kong.

"If that's the same woman, I'm firing my Avon representative," Alice said as she slowly took a seat and Sarah placed a hand on hers and smiled.

"Well, the problem as I see it, Colonel, is that you can't prove it and the president will say this is too flimsy," Niles said as he looked at the dejected form of Alice in her chair. "So, that's where you come in, Pete. I want you and Charlie to do some work and I need it done now." Niles looked Alice's way once more. "*We* need it done now," he corrected himself and he saw that his words helped as Alice slowly nodded her head.

Both Ellenshaw and Golding looked up with renewed enthusiasm. It seemed they may not be in the basement of that doghouse they now found themselves in.

"I need every single scrap of information you can dig up on that entire region. Myths, legends, fact, rumor. I want to know about the people of the Patinas Pass. Charlie, you take the zoology aspect of the research. I want to know if there is any way this animal could exist and why in the hell it is so equipped through evolutionary means to be the way it is. If this beast evolved like that I want the reasons why. Pete, the land, the history, who owns it."

Both men nodded as they took their notes. Niles looked down at Collins and they had a moment between them that said enough was enough. Niles wanted to help but he needed their help in order for him to meet them halfway.

"Colonel, get a team together and get me everything you can on why the damn Mossad is so interested in the activities of our agent, and why in the hell they would attempt to kill him over that information. Is it the animals, the region, is it anything that Alice has connected to. I also want this Lieutenant Colonel Ben-Nevin tracked down and handed off to the FBI and Interpol. We don't need this traitorous bastard anywhere near where we may have to go."

Everyone in the vault took a sigh of relief when they heard the words *"we may have to go."*

"Okay, Mrs. Hamilton, you have your wish. This is your call and for right now we are a go."

"That means you're declaring—" Alice started as she stood from her chair while looking up at the director.

"An Event—you have met the minimum criteria in my opinion and I will get the president to see it our way. It shouldn't be too hard when I inform him about the Israeli government's interest in Romania and what lives there."

"Okay, we move as soon as Charlie and Pete come up with the information we need. Now get to it. Virginia, Colonel Collins, and Alice, please meet me in my office—we have been handed something that may be a connection here."

Jack, Virginia Pollock, and Alice Hamilton were sitting in three chairs facing the director. Niles looked at each in turn and shook his head.

"I was just handed this report five minutes before the colonel called me to the vault level." Niles handed the paper to Jack from across his desk. "This may be one of the reasons everyone is so concerned about Mossad agents and their defectors and moles."

"What is it?" Jack asked as he handed the picture to Alice, whose eyes took in the object in the photograph.

"This is Midianite pottery," Alice said, "and not just shards, but the whole vessel. Never has a complete relic been found intact."

"What is a Midianite?" Virginia asked.

"Alice?" Niles asked, wanting her to quickly explain why this was so significant.

Alice smiled at the color photo of the pottery and its straight laced striped design. "Biblical scholars believe Midian was located on the Arabian Peninsula, or possibly modern-day Sudan. Midian was where Moses spent the forty years in voluntary exile after murdering the Egyptian. He married the daughter of a local tribal elder. Then he supposedly returned to Egypt and you know the rest of the story."

"And this is significant because?" Virginia asked, her scientific mind never relaxing when there were questions to be answered.

"Because of these," Niles said as he slid photos of more pottery and small golden objects of Egyptian design. Golden scarabs, small idols of gods, and even several Bronze Age weapons glimmered under a photographer's light.

"Where did all of these come from?" Alice asked. "There have never been items like this unearthed and in such pristine condition. These have to be copies."

"They were sold at auction five years ago. There are many more items that were contracted for the bidding process through a company called Perry Deiterman and

Associates Limited, out of Cologne, Germany. Thus far close to two hundred pounds of gold and artifacts like these have been selling quite nicely to the seamier side of Eastern Europe. These six items alone brought in close to $78 million."

The office went silent.

"That is why I accepted Jack's offer to join you in the vault. The border patrol in the Czech Republic recovered these from a Russian national. They even found a bill of sale when they found these items hidden in the trunk of a car. The rather seedy character was questioned and it was discovered that he was the highest bidder on a prayer tablet, one that was carbon-dated to 1557 BCE. Ladies and gentleman, nothing this fragile has ever been recovered intact. We have nothing remotely like it in our vaults. The only reason Europa filed the report with me is because Alice had placed her keyword search into the system twenty years ago. And now we have this stuff turning up in the oddest places." Niles waved his hand over the photographs. "Did someone suddenly decide to sell off their world's foremost collection of Egyptian artifacts? Or are we looking at items that have long been lost to the world and are just now miraculously showing up to the highest bidder?"

"I see your point," Virginia said.

Niles shook his head. "Not yet you don't. Look at this one." Niles handed Virginia a larger photograph. It was a complete robe and the design integrated into the weave was the exact match for the weave and design of the swatches Alice had uncovered in the Carpathians.

"Looks like an oversized foul weather poncho," Jack said as he looked at the photo.

"Carbon-dated to 1521 give or take ten years and authenticated by the University of Cairo. It went at auction for $125 million. This, ladies and gentlemen, is something the entire world would never have recognized—the design is from that Lost Tribe of Israel everyone around here is so hot on—this is a Jeddah tribal robe."

"Possibly—the design is off somewhat," Alice said as she raised the photo and looked at it more closely. "What is that smaller design inside the red-dyed stripe?" she asked.

Niles smiled and then handed Alice a magnifying glass. He could have used Europa for the demonstration but Niles still liked the old-fashioned hands-on approach, especially when it came to Alice Hamilton.

As everyone watched they saw Alice freeze and then look off into the corner of Niles's office. The photo slipped from her hand. Jack picked it up and then pried the magnifying glass out of Alice's tight grip. He raised the glass and looked closely at the picture but could see nothing. Then his trained eye saw what was indeed shocking to Alice. Embedded in the stripe was a weave that looked as if it didn't belong. It looked like a dog's head.

"The Egyptian god Anubis?" Jack asked while lowering his glass and handing it to Virginia.

"No, that is not Anubis," Alice said, looking at Compton, who still stood behind his desk. "Another coincidence, Niles? The Jeddah, a tribe no one in history outside of the ancient Hebrews knew about? Now the robe coupled with the animal head weaved into the design of a robe? That is a wolf, Jack—one of my wolves. This is far more significant than just an artifact from one of the Lost Tribes; this is something that could alter the history of not only the Exodus, but of the entire world."

Niles sat hard into his chair. He looked at Alice and then at Jack.

"As a close advisor to the president I am allowed access to the National Security Council and the minutes of their meetings with the president. I found this by accident. It seems we have had a small movement of troops from the Middle East heading north. Specialized commandos you may know something about, Colonel. It seems Tel Aviv is a little concerned about something in the region and the NSA picked up an alert and movement order. Recognize that unit, Jack?" Niles asked.

"The Sayeret," Collins said and took a deep breath. "If these fellas are on the move somewhere, whoever is at that somewhere is in for a world of hurt. These men are killers. That's what they do."

"Can you explain, Jack?" Alice asked.

"No. Our intelligence on the Sayeret is highly classified. They are the Israeli army's best, I mean the very best of their crop of young men. They go, do, and kill whoever is placed in front of them. If they're moving there's a reason for it."

"Well, the president has been brought up to speed on Alice's hunch. That coupled with our trouble in Rome involving the Mossad, and now with this movement of a unit that never moves unless the enemies of Israel need some ass kicking in a covert manner, and now we have word from our State Department in a memo that was read by practically no one that the Egyptian minister of antiquities and their Foreign Office have filed a complaint against Romania for the theft of Egyptian artifacts. The sale of these artifacts was traced to a broker who was listed somewhere in the fine print of the sales contract, a Russian national who just happens to be opening one of the most luxurious hotel-casinos in Eastern Europe. Worth in the neighborhood of two and half billion dollars, it is a surprising amount from a man the former KGB said never amounted to much in the world of Russian organized crime."

"That alone should—"

Niles held up his hand to stay Alice's complaint.

"To make a long story short, the president has given me the leeway needed to start operations. The Event has already been declared—target is the southern Carpathians—the area known as the Patinas Pass."

Alice lowered her head and then suddenly looked up at Niles.

"Yes, Alice, you're in the lead. It's your last Event, so make it count or the senator will never let you live it down when he sees you again. And you know he's watching."

Everyone looked at the spot in the office Niles was looking at. It was the new oil painting of former director Garrison Lee scowling at them from the gilded frame that sat next to Abraham Lincoln's picture.

They all stood to start the massive process of moving Department 5656 into Event mode, which would bring every departmental element inside the complex under the desert into the initial phases of getting a plan together. All personnel were now on full alert for a possible history-altering change in the human timeline—exactly what Department 5656 was created for—recognizing that change in history and sorting it out.

Alice lagged behind with Niles as she looked upon the portrait she absolutely hated. Not because of the scowl that everyone agreed was Garrison Lee in a nutshell, but because she knew Lee hated anything having to do with memorializing him or his life's work at the Group.

"I believe this is yours." Niles held the thick file Alice had worked on for almost half a century.

"Thank you, Niles." She placed a hand on Compton's chest and patted it twice as she headed for the double doors.

Compton placed his hands in his pockets and walked over to the large oil painting. He looked at his old friend and mentor and shook his head.

"The times they are-a-changin', my old friend."

PART TWO
REBIRTH

For the strength of the Pack is the Wolf, and the strength of the Wolf is the Pack.

—Rudyard Kipling

6

The two richly appointed cable cars were running normally up and down the massive eight-cable system. There had not been one flaw in the computer programming that ran the operation. With the cars operational and the final preparations for the extensive private weekend nearing completion, Janos Vajic was starting to get that horrible feeling in the pit of his stomach as they neared the beginning of what could possibly be the end of his dream.

Janos watched as several workers arriving from the castle exited the cable car. The men seemed to be in a far better mood since the actions of the night before in the mountains high above the castle. As Janos turned away he saw Gina step onto the cable car platform high above the atrium. She held out a flimsy sheet of paper.

"This was just faxed over from Bucharest."

Vajic took the paper and scanned it very quickly.

"What in the hell is Zallas trying to do to us? He has every known black marketer, gangster, and white-collar criminal in the world on this list. If the press were to sneak in here during the weekend we would never open, and I don't care if Zallas has the interior minister in his pocket or not. They will shut us down through international pressure alone!" He crumpled up the guest list and threw it over the edge of the cable car platform where it landed in a geranium bush.

"I figure all we can do is keep the security as tight as—"

"We will not be handling the security. The resort security staff is to step aside."

"What? This is a casino, Janos; we have to have armed security at all—"

"Zallas is handling the security for this weekend. His own people will be here and he says it's double our normal staff. He said the press will not get to within a hundred miles of Edge of the World."

Janos could see his general manager deflate. He put an arm around her.

"I have regretted my decision on partnering with this man from the first day. It's like he never had money before and now he's crazed about how to spend it. It's like the trouble with the villagers up in the pass: he sends a backward Russian up there in a pretend hunt, and only he comes back down, but the attacks have ceased. I just don't understand it."

"Where is that Neanderthal anyway?" Gina asked as she was led to the cable car that had just arrived.

"Look here," Vajic said as he gestured out of the large plate glass window in the rear of the car. He was pointing far below to the swimming pool, which stretched five hundred feet in the back of the resort. Sitting by the pool was the Russian. He sat in a chaise longue and didn't move.

"What's he doing?" Gina asked.

"He's been sitting there since the maintenance people showed up at four this morning. He hasn't moved. He refuses food and water. He just sits and stares waiting for Zallas to arrive."

"What's wrong with him, and where are the Romanian hunters that accompanied him?"

"They're missing. Or at least we haven't seen a trace of them since they left here last night. He just mumbles about the pass," he said as he glanced upward along the cables and the mountain beyond. "That's it. He won't move until he reports directly to Zallas."

Gina watched the still and silent man far below. Then she turned to Janos.

"I have the most horrible feeling that we are in the middle of something here that we have no control over."

Janos Vajic stepped to the front of the cable car and saw the black Mercedes approach from the south. He took a deep breath and then faced his general manager.

"Well, the man who is in control has just arrived."

As Gina followed Vajic's gaze she saw over fifty vehicles as they wound their way toward the richest resort in the Eastern world.

The criminal invasion of the Carpathians had begun.

EVENT GROUP COMPLEX,
NELLIS AIR FORCE BASE, NEVADA

Jack heard the knock on the door and Carl Everett, looking haggard and half asleep, stuck his head inside.

"I've noticed that the red Event lights are lit up like the Fourth of July around here. Fill me in on what we've missed?"

"You bet. Have a seat, Carl. We need to talk."

Everett opened the office door and stepped in. He rubbed his eyes and took a seat in front of the desk.

"I thought I lost you for a minute over there. Is Ryan all right?"

"He slammed into his bunk doing mach one. He'll not be with us for a while, double jet lag and all."

"What about you?"

Everett didn't answer for a moment as he took in the colonel.

"I'm pissed at a woman and a double-dealing little Mossad colonel who tried to kill us. But that's not what's on my mind at the moment. Can we go off subject for a second, Colonel?"

Jack leaned back in his chair and waited for the shoe to fall. He had noticed Carl had addressed him by his Army rank behind closed doors, something the Navy SEAL ordinarily never did. Collins nodded his head that he should continue.

"I think it only proper that I inform my commanding officer that I have applied for transfer to the new naval surface warfare center being set up at Cape Canaveral."

Jack's brows arched as he listened to his second in command, a man he had known in some tough times and a true friend. He knew why this was happening.

"The new euphemism for space warfare center? The surface part of the name has little to do with it. You're not a shipboard officer, Carl. You're something far more special than that."

"Some would say, Colonel. But then again you cut me out of the loop in the search for your sister's killer. That's personal to me because I knew and liked Lynn. I think it best that I get on with this new program and see if I can help out some."

"I wasn't worried about you and Ryan while you were in Rome. Even when I knew your lives were in jeopardy. I can live with that. I can allow you to go into harm's way as long as it's in the line of duty and under the auspices of this department, the one in which you are assigned." Jack stood from his chair and paced to the door and locked it and then turned and walked to his desk and sat. "I will not lose friends on a personal quest of vengeance when they find enough death around them every damn day right here in this madhouse of history. But that is to be expected and accepted. You dying performing a criminal act on my behalf is not, nor will it ever be, acceptable, Carl."

Everett didn't look away from Jack's glaring eyes.

"That's your mistake, Jack. If you can't see the basic problem here you are far blinder than you realize. You are making mistakes not only in judgment on how to best go about finding your sister's murderer, you're cutting off the sounding boards and genius that make things work here at the Event Group, and that's the people who believe they are more than just a goddamn team to you."

Collins was trying to get everything settled in his mind from Everett's verbal assault. For the first time in his adult life he didn't know how to proceed.

"This communication you have going with the Frenchman has to stop, Jack." Everett stood and faced his friend. "Farbeaux may be assisting you because you think he is better equipped to do what you plan on doing, finding the scumbag and killing him. But don't you see that Henri Farbeaux doesn't do anything without it benefiting Henri Farbeaux. He will kill you if he gets the chance—make no mistake about that."

"There is a method to my madness, Carl. He may do what you say he will—maybe just to get Sarah, who knows, but there is *one* element in this equation you're missing—that son of a bitch is expendable, you and my friends are not. No more people are being lost on my account. In the line of duty is one thing, dying for something personal is another."

Everett set his jaw muscles and for the first time that Navy SEAL stare was directed at Jack.

"Transfer request stands. I'm needed elsewhere with everything coming down all over the world."

Jack Collins took a deep breath and then sat into his chair. He looked at Everett and then down at his desk blotter. He nodded his head in agreement.

Carl Everett came to attention and saluted. Jack looked up and frowned.

"The Navy doesn't salute indoors, Captain—dismissed."

Everett allowed his gesture of respect to slip by the wayside. He turned abruptly and then unlocked the door and stepped out of the office.

As Europa sounded a tone over the speaker system embedded in the walls, Jack was staring at nothing. All thought of the past day's events had slipped into a neutral position. He had just lost one of the best friends he had in the world because of the stubborn streak Sarah had warned him about a million and one times.

"Attention all personnel, as of 1245 hours this date an operational order has been issued by the director of Department 5656 declaring an Event in the Carpathian region of Romania. All departmental supervisors are to report to the main conference room immediately. All personnel are restricted to base and Gates 1 and 2 are now closed. Alert 2 status has been upgraded—full security measures are hereby in effect."

Jack didn't hear a word of the supercomputer as she gave the Event alert. His mind was on his friends—the ones he was losing because of his fears and the fear of others above him in rank.

Outside the office the Event teams were forming. The assault on the Carpathians was now an official case file.

The Event Group was now in its element.

PATINAS PASS, CARPATHIAN MOUNTAINS, ROMANIA

The moon was bright and the villagers of Patinas were out in the cool of the evening. The village itself would be considered large for most in the region. The census taken in 1980 by the former communist government listed the occupants of that particular protected area as 752. The center square of the village of stone and wood houses was alight with the fire that was built every evening for the families of man to congregate and share stories on the events of their day. It had been a tradition for over two thousand years. The families gathered and laughed and sang and played their string instruments to the delight of the children. Most of the musical instruments were new and shiny and the electric lighting now coursing through the small village even newer than the instruments that began showing up the past two years as gifts from the man who would soon be their king.

As the Romanian Catholic church bell rang just once announcing the hour of nine, all those around the fire and sitting on the grass listening to the music started to say their good nights and good-byes to family and friends. As they all laughed their way to their houses or out of town for their farms and flocks, there was only one who remained behind. The old woman sat in her customary chair after waving off several of her nephews and nieces as they tried to persuade her not to sit out in the damp night.

When the villagers had all left the old Gypsy looked around her at what they had built over the years. She slowly stood and leaned on the wooden cane with the Eye of Ra inlaid in the handle. She slowly turned and looked at the mountain behind her that encircled the beautiful but small valley and pass that was Patinas. Her two different colored eyes fell upon the temple that only she could see. She shook her head. The steam escaping from several open vents along the mountain road leading to the pass high above was a constant reminder that somewhere far beneath the surface of the earth mother nature was cooking up quite a cauldron of fury that someday would be released into the valleys far below—a wrath of prehistoric power that could eventually level the 250-million-year-old mountain range. The hot water vapor from the hot springs that coursed through this particular mountain actually produced enough heat to change the weather conditions during the winter months as the vapors brought a false warmth to the village and the pass above them.

"We should have brought the entire mountain down upon you before it was ever completed." She jabbed her cane at the darkness above and the mountain it hid in the night. "You are a curse that we should never have dared to lay claim to." Suddenly her strength was gone and she turned and sat back into her chair.

"It would take more than that rickety old cane to bring down the temple, Grandmamma."

The old woman closed her eyes and placed her forehead on the cane.

"There was death last night on the road to the pass. You disobeyed me, manchild."

"No, one still lives. The message I wanted to deliver was delivered and the men that were with the filthy Slav paid the postage on that message. There will be no man allowed above that ridiculous castle. Never again will men come this way without invitation."

The old Gypsy raised the cane an inch off the ground and then brought it down again as she turned to look at her grandson. The man was dressed in a bright red shirt with his ever-present head scarf, this one royal blue in color. His black beard and leather pants gleamed in the light of the rising moon. As he watched, the old woman forcibly calmed herself.

"You have been missed at the fire lately. You seem unaware that your family misses you. And for one who has delivered such magnificent gifts to the people it would seem you would be more interested in the activities here than down there," she said as she jabbed her cane down the mountainside.

The young man snorted and then shook his head. "To sit around and sing old Gypsy songs that are just as much a lie as the ones we tell of the ancient times? No, I have no more interest in lies. It's far past the time to be mere caretakers to riches and the knowledge of the old ones. It's time we take what we have earned. And giving out a few small gifts as you call them is what a future king of the Gypsies does for his people."

The old woman couldn't argue the point.

"How many of our young men have you taken from the villages below?" she asked, fearing the answer.

"Enough to protect what is ours."

"You have been in the temple recently."

The man laughed. His grandmother always knew his fascination for the temple and what that place of magic held for him. Even as a small child he would wander into the mountain and sit for hours, sometimes days, just to speak with the guardians of the temple, his friends, the Golia, and marvel at the temple and plaza that surrounded it. She knew his love of the massive building blocks the ancient artisans built for a people that would never see it. He always thought about the sacrifice of his people for the good of men and women that had shunned the Jeddah since a time before the Exodus.

"Do not bother to hide your activities with another lie. Sister arrives on the morrow and she will discover what it is you've been up to, Marko."

The man turned and the smile was gone.

"Yes, for the first time in many years we will see the sister, child, and the truth will be found out. I do not know what deal with what devil you may have made but sister will know what to do. I pray to God you have not been lying to me, Marko—or the Golia." She smiled as she took in her grandson. "They are not quite as forgiving as this old woman."

"You send her away for years to learn the ways of the Jewish state and to keep an ear to the ground about the temple and what's hidden there. But I am left here to never see the real world. Never will I venture into the cities and live the real life that my sister was chosen for."

"Marko, she was better equipped, more even-tempered to do the duties I have laid out for her. It's not that I do not—"

Marko held up a hand, stopping his grandmother's lie from continuing. He did manage to force a smile.

"It will be good to see sister again." He turned and started walking away while looking up at the camouflaged temple. "It has been a very long time and I have indeed missed her."

As she watched Marko walk away with his fists clenched into tight balls of anger, a small lamb that had come into the village from the flock outside the main gates bleated as he approached. Her grandchild kicked the small animal and it squealed and fell to the ground.

The old woman slowly got to her feet and went to the lamb and placed her aged hand upon it and stopped its hurtful bleating. The old woman stopped petting the frightened animal when the lamb's eyes grew wide and the lamb regained its feet and bounced away toward the open gate. The old woman knew the beast was poised right behind her. She slowly and carefully turned.

The black-furred Golia was sitting on its hind haunches and was looking straight at her with its long ears up in a nonaggressive stance. As she examined the giant wolf she saw the yellow eyes take her in also with just as much curiosity.

"You have grown so, Stanus." She slowly took a step forward and raised her hand to the animal's jawline and used her short, broken fingernails to scratch the new leader of the Golia.

Stanus tilted its huge head to the left as the old woman scratched lightly. The eyes never left her age-lined face. As she scratched the alpha male as she had done on a million other occasions her hand slowly started to rise toward the left side of the animal's face just below the ear. Stanus saw the movement and lightly growled and then raised its right paw to its face. She watched as the fingers slowly curled open and extended outward and was so large that the slim fingers and razor-sharp claws wrapped completely around her small wrist and hand. As the beast lowered the offending hand from its muzzle it came up on all fours and backed away a step and then sat once more on its haunches. The yellow, intense eyes never left the old woman's face.

"Your trust is as empty as your den in the pass. Do you even know what Marko is up to, or are you just going along because you finally get to vent that stored rage you have deep inside—not unlike my grandson?"

The wolf tilted its large head to the right this time as it listened to the woman speak. She could see that the respect the animal had toward her was still present. She suspected that Stanus was conflicted. She was even receiving small bursts of knowledge streaming from the new leader of the Golia but she couldn't understand the animal's consternation. She smiled at Stanus as she looked up into those yellow eyes that stood a whole head higher than her entire height.

"How are the babies?"

The wolf whined deep in its chest.

"You haven't been to the pass, have you? You've been with Marko."

The low growl sounded once more.

"Whatever he is doing is against the will of his queen, and also against the family of Golia. I need you, Stanus, in the days ahead. We have to—"

The Golia suddenly jumped from its place. The giant leapt over the old woman and then jumped again and cleared the stone wall that lined the small village and vanished silently into the night.

The Gypsy queen turned and listened as the mountain came alive with the sound of many Golia who were not inside their dens or in the temple. There were more and more howls coming from the dark in recent months as more and more Golia defected to Stanus and Marko. It was not the fact that Marko wanted better for his people—as she was responsible for her grandson's rebelliousness because truth be told she herself had been fighting with tradition and ancient superstition for most of her years to allow the people to be free of the curse placed upon them three and a half thousand years before. She and Marko just clashed as to the best way to free their people.

The ground shook and the night became a silent and bleak artwork of desolate landscape that screamed against the sign of the times. The howling awoke the night world of the Carpathians and brought every villager for miles around to their windows to close the shutters of their humble homes and farms.

PALILULA, SERBIA.
THE DANUBE RIVER CROSSING

The woman known to Israeli intelligence and the Event Group as Major Mica Sorotzkin was sitting and watching her reflection in the train's filthy window. She saw the bloodshot eyes accompanied by the dark circles underneath and then she closed them against the worn and tired reflection. The raven-haired woman turned away from the nighttime countryside of Palilula, Serbia, as the train passed over an ancient trestle across the Danube. She closed her eyes and felt much safer as she entered Romania for the first time in nine years.

The car in which she rode remained virtually empty even though at the last stop before the Danube the train had made an unscheduled stop as over a hundred soldiers were escorted onto a few of the forward passenger cars. They were Romanian and they carried full field gear and packs and looked as if they were going on manuevers. The soldiers settled into their seats three cars forward and the weary woman thought nothing of them again.

Behind her closed eyelids she tried to bring to mind the memory of her last day in Patinas. How she had cried with a broken heart when her grandmother sent her away. First she had missed four years sacrificing her childhood for schooling in Prague under an assumed name. When that was complete her grandmother awarded her with another painful banishment—under her new name she would enter the military academy and finish her last two years of higher education. The academy just so happened to be in Israel. She was accepted with her new identity into the top secret military program called Talpiot. The academy is Israel's most selective institution and accepts only fifty students a year. The school trains its students in physics and other sciences that most military-funded academies skim over. Its mission is to produce future leaders of the Israel Defense

Forces who are not only capable of changing the "act first" attitude of a hard-line military, but to finally transform their armed forces into a model of efficiency.

She had performed so well in her two years at the Talpiot Academy that she drew the attention of the Mossad. The chance meeting was in the plan the whole time with the guidance of her grandmother, who seemed to be wiser than her years and always claiming that she was sending her to do the work of the people and it was something that her grandmother had had to do when her age so many years before, the only difference being that the queen had studied at Oxford and Cairo. They both had left home to learn the ways of the modern world to help protect the people.

She opened her eyes and looked out the window once more toward the distant mountain range hidden in the darkness beyond the clean and cold waters of the Danube. As her eyes scanned the darkness the dimly illuminated farmhouses along the train tracks slowly started coming to life for the hardworking folk of the soil-rich Danube valleys.

Mica half smiled as she realized that she was nearing her home and felt happy for the first time in years. She didn't turn away from the smile that was returned in her reflection but did notice that the face had changed over the nine years she had been gone. Not that it had aged badly, but because her face was now showing the worries for her people far more than when she had been a child. Now she was slowly learning that the mountains could no longer be protected. She would have to break this news to her grandmother.

The worry over the fate of the temple and the men and beasts who protected it faded as she thought about setting foot in the pass once more. It was a place where she used to run and play with animals that lived in myth and legend. The Golia awaited her return and she anticipated rekindling the friendship that was lost when she was sent away.

Lost in thought, she was taken aback when she felt someone slide into the seat next to her.

"The general never realized just how good you were. But I knew as soon as I transferred you to Rome and put you on the trail of the lost legends you would dig up something to assist the righteous and bring what is ours back home."

Mica turned away from the outside world and looked right into the face of Lieutenant Colonel Ben-Nevin. The pistol he held was low and aimed upward; its barrel, as well as his crooked smile, never wavered.

"Colonel, you and the people you follow have been listening to fairy tales that never had a basis in fact. Your kind has left Israel backward and alone in the world, and if it weren't for the power of a few carefully chosen friends Israel would be nothing but a barren dustbowl today."

"And this is coming from a tried-and-true patriot? I think not, Major." The gun came up a little further. The woman slowly moved her eyes to better assess her situation, which was not a good one. The train's car was nearly empty with the exception of a young boy and of all things he was accompanied by a goat. Welcome home, Anya, she thought to herself as she looked at the small boy at the front of the car and immediately regretted leaving her small cousin back in Rome, but she had thought it safer for the seller of oranges to stay safe for the time being.

The colonel watched her as she studied her situation and he smiled wider than before.

"Do not attempt it. I have over fifty men awaiting our arrival. You will lead us to the treasures of the Exodus so the true patriots of Israel can take back the people's heritage."

Anya Korvesky didn't bother to look at the weapon because she knew how ruthlessly men of the colonel's religious bent acted toward women. They were backward and only thought about their precious religious tilt. Most Israelis were now content to live in harmony with those around them, but others were far more resistant to making peace with people who didn't care for the heavy-handedness of Jewish rule in the occupied territories. The colonel was part of an organization called Masada's Patriots, named after the small mountain once laid siege to by the Roman army to settle a small revolt two thousand years before. She wondered if the colonel realized that every one of those long-ago patriots had committed suicide to escape Roman justice. Perhaps it was time to refresh Ben-Nevin's memory on that point.

"You know there is no place you can ever run to and hide. General Shamni will burn any asset, kill any informer, he will take your group hostage in order to track you down and the law be damned."

"And you, a favorite of his? Your betrayal will not sit well with the general just as mine will not. I'm afraid we are both in the same boat." The look on his face was that of a cat staring at a caged canary. "Only, I have many friends and very powerful allies."

Anya chanced a look around but still the only occupant of the car was the little boy and his goat far to the front. At four-thirty in the morning there just wasn't any help to be had.

"This can all be so easy. We would be hailed as the man and woman who recovered the history and treasure of the chosen people, to prove to the world that, yes, God was once on our side and here is the proof," Ben-Nevin said as his eyes widened and his breathing got heavier.

"It's nothing but old wives' tales to keep the people believing in their past when we should be looking toward the future. There is no gold and other treasure. There are no artifacts to prove God was once in our corner. There may be those who have scratched the truth but it will do them no good." She looked the colonel straight in his eyes and didn't flinch when he raised the pistol a little higher. "The Ark of the Covenant has been lost since the dawning of the Hebrew homeland—gone, Colonel. The treasure of the Exodus never existed. You have placed a warrant of death on you and your followers' heads and every Israeli asset the world over will be out to track you down and kill you."

"You can fool the general, Major, but I and my people are not as naive as many others. We know the truth. We know what Joshua did and we are destined to bring the truth back home to Israel despite what the general's and prime minister's traitorous moves are."

"The general is a good man and so is the prime minister. They will never allow you to continue."

"Good men always get better people killed. He and his kind will do anything to stop us from gaining the right to live—live and expand the borders of Israel."

"And you think the recovery of some trinkets will allow the Jewish people to rise up and take control of everything? The people are not what you think they are, Colonel. They have evolved from the days where a few fundamentalists can whip them into patriotic frenzy. That policy had its place and its time. Everyone pulled together, and now you wish to take them apart, split the nation." Anya leaned in toward Ben-Nevin, actually stunning him enough that he raised the gun fully into her face. "I'll tell you, Colonel, since I have been with the Israeli people I have learned one inescapable fact—they like living, they also like to see their sons and daughters come home without having a bomb go off on their bus. Mothers, fathers, and grandparents like peace and are willing to break with tradition to have it. They actually like living . . . stupid bastards."

"Some of us aren't as dedicated to righteousness as others in our group. Some of us still like the finer things in life."

"I know your kind, Colonel," she looked away for the briefest of moments, "because I have a brother not unlike you. He would also bring the world crashing down because of something he believed in above all else. But even I don't believe he would be capable of selling out his own people as you are doing."

"I don't seek the treasure," he lied with an expert's persuasiveness and Anya saw it in his eyes. "Israel needs living space and the way to achieve it is to make other lesser people realize that God has always been on our side."

She smiled, knowing the colonel trapped himself.

"Adolf Hitler, 1928. Your grasp of history is admirable, Colonel Ben-Nevin. I wonder if your efforts to create Lebensraum, or living space for the people, will find as much enthusiasm as Hitler's did in the thirties and forties. I seem to remember him butchering millions of our people to achieve that living space. He even attempted to track my people down thinking we knew such a great and devastating secret involving our shared ancestry."

"Hitler was a maniac. And by your people I am assuming you mean the Gypsies?"

Anya smiled and arched her eyebrows.

"That's just about as much of a history lesson I can take for one night, so why don't we—"

The colonel realized they were no longer alone. The small boy with the goat was now standing in the aisle and staring at Ben-Nevin.

"Go away, child. Take your goat and sit down."

The boy was about eleven or twelve and was looking from the man to the woman, who just now realized who the child really was. She hadn't recognized him at first, and to carry a goat along? Things had remained as crazy in her small village as they always had been and she knew the boy's arrival had been her grandmother's doing.

"Excuse me," the boy said in halting English. "Aunt Anya?"

Anya smiled back and then relaxed as she knew who the boy was now. She felt the tears well up in her eyes and tried not to show her weakness, but she knew she was nothing but a real woman and not the trained Mossad agent she thought she was. Anya now realized how much she had missed her home. As she studied the boy she nodded her head and the child's smile widened.

"Hello, Georgi, do you know you look just like Kinta, your cousin who lived with me in Rome?" Anya said, smiling even wider as the boy of twelve did also. "He's there right now but will be home by next week I hope."

"Ah, the boy who rescued the Americans—the child selling the oranges!" Ben-Nevin said, unable to hide his surprise. "You never cease to amaze me, Major. To have a child from your home on duty in Rome and you managed to keep it from the Mossad; you are far more resilient than even I thought."

Anya turned to face the colonel. "I am human. To have someone from my village kept me sane and on track to what I needed to do." She lowered her eyes for a moment. "And I have made my mistakes but having my nephew's help makes me realize what's important, just like this child right here." She smiled and looked up at the boy again, ignoring the colonel. "Yes, I am your great-aunt. Did Grandmamma send you here?"

"That's enough," Ben-Nevin said as he reached out and grabbed the boy by the arm. "Save family reunion time for later. He will come with us when I meet my people in Bucharest."

The boy just looked at the hand holding his arm. At the same time the colonel saw his eyes raise and then the goat bleated and tried to step backward in the aisle. Its eyes widened and then it fell to the floor of the car and tried to get beneath the seat it was near. The colonel saw the smile on the boy's lips widen even further and his eyes moved from the hand on his arm to an area behind Ben-Nevin's shoulder. A loud, low-throated growl sounded from behind him. The colonel actually felt the moist, warm breath on his neck.

Anya didn't know how it had happened, but somehow her young great-nephew had gotten one of the Golia on board the deserted train. She slowly turned her head and saw the animal sitting in the train's aisle. The yellow eyes were firmly placed on the back of the colonel's head. For his part, Ben-Nevin only swallowed and then slowly turned his head to see the giant black and gray furred animal sitting menacingly behind him.

"My God," he whispered as his gun slowly started to come around.

"That," Anya said with authority, "is not a good idea, Colonel. The beast would have your severed hand in its mouth before you could pull the trigger." Anya sat further up in her seat and then looked more closely at the Golia. Her eyes widened when she saw the notch missing from the right ear. She remembered as a little girl how the animal became scarred in a fight with its older and far more aggressive brother, Stanus.

"Georgi, is that Mikla?"

The twelve-year-old boy nodded as the wolf whined and then flicked its ears in recognition of its name, but the yellow glowing eyes never left those of the colonel.

Anya smiled as she turned back to face a Golia pup that was born just two days after herself. They were so close in age that her grandmother always included the black wolf with the gray-tipped ears and tail to her yearly celebrations. She loved the memory of the small wolf at her side with his ridiculous head scarf–birthday hat on. The giant wolf paid her no mind, as it was the vibes coming from Ben-Nevin that held its attention.

"This is impossible, what is this creature?"

Anya slowly reached over and relieved the colonel of his weapon and then pointed it at him.

"An old and dear friend that I have missed." She smiled and then saw that Mikla had turned his head and was now watching something far beyond her nephew's head and shoulders. She heard the low growl start deep within Mikla's throat. His ears slowly lay down and Anya knew that someone was coming and the giant Golia sensed it. Anya chanced a quick look up and her heart froze.

"It seems we are about to have company, Major—whatever your real name is," Ben-Nevin said as he also looked up and saw the soldiers coming down the aisle of the car in front of them. They were laughing and joking and one of the Romanian troopers had a large bottle of vodka and the three soldiers kept looking behind them as if they were sneaking away for a nice nip of the strong alcohol.

This time there was no mistaking the menace in Mikla's growl. The colonel cringed as he sensed the wolf change positions behind him. He closed his eyes as the growl became far deeper and far more menacing than moments before. The soldiers had reached the door of the car and were about to enter the connection to their own. Mikla took one leap and was in the center of the aisle ten feet in front of Anya and the boy as she kept the colonel covered with the gun.

"No, Mikla!" Anya shouted as the soldiers opened the door to their own car just as the giant beast took four more large strides toward the connecting door. Anya saw that the Golia was not going to obey, he sensed danger from the soldiers and was ready to defend her and the boy and there was nothing she could do or say that would dissuade the massive beast. Anya stood from her seat. "No, Mikla, no harm!" she shouted in the silent car.

Instead of obeying Anya, the wolf hopped onto its hind legs and the three people in the car heard the cracking and the popping of the bones as the hip and pelvis started to make the shift that gave the Golia its heaven-sent ability to climb straight up any wall, mountain, or building. First one hip popped and shifted, sending the beast to the right as its articulated fingers took hold of the two seats closest to the aisle. It used the seat backs as a stabilizing factor as the thigh bones fell into place in the secondary socket; this straightened the animal's spine and aligned itself for the change enabling it to walk upright. The legs became stronger, longer and that brought the wolf into proper proportions to stand as a man.

Ben-Nevin could not believe what he was witnessing. His eyes widened as he saw the beast could not even stand to its full height because of its size. The ears were laid back against the wood paneling of the car's ceiling and the growling intensified to the point that the Golia vibrated the windows around them.

The soldiers were in the space that separated the cars and were swilling the vodka and laughing. The Golia let loose another growl that froze the colonel's blood in his veins.

"Mikla, leave them be! Come—"

Ben-Nevin reached out and took hold of the weapon he had been relieved of moments before. He turned it on Anya and pushed her back and was about to turn the weapon on the Golia when he felt the pistol ripped from his hand, taking three fingers along with it. The colonel looked up in shock as the animal had moved so fast that he never realized he was being assaulted. The wolf stood over the smaller man with the gun clenched inside the massive hand of the animal. The beast sniffed at the weapon in its left hand and then the yellow eyes slowly rose to meet the frightened and shocked eyes of Ben-Nevin.

Anya saw what was going to happen and jumped over the seats and scrambled between the Golia and the man it was about to shred to pieces. Before she could do anything to save the man she despised, the door at the front of the car slowly opened and they all heard the laughter of the Romanian soldiers as they started to enter the killing field.

"Mikla, home, now!" she shouted as loud as she could as the door remained halfway open as the three soldiers hesitated momentarily to swig some more vodka.

The beast turned its large head to the right and saw the soldiers. Anya could tell the Golia was confused as to which threat to take first. The massive head swung back to the Israeli Mossad colonel, who fell to the floor of the car and threw his arm up over his face splattering his suit with blood from his damaged hand. The animal raised the pistol it held by the barrel and closed its hand around it and then threw it to the back of the train car. Mikla leaned in close to Ben-Nevin and began opening its jaws wide. The teeth were straight and clean and they were the largest the colonel had ever seen. Then as suddenly as the action had started it stopped as the beast straightened and turned and looked at the soldiers as they finished their drink. The beast growled heavily and then started to turn toward the oncoming threat to the woman and the boy.

"Mikla, home!"

The Golia turned back and faced Anya and then reached down in a flash of movement and snatched up the boy and his goat in one muscled arm. Mikla then easily tossed the boy and dangling goat onto its back and then looked at Anya and growled, angry it had been called off from killing the soldiers. Its ears came back up and the creature with its massive strength reached out and took Anya by the arm and tucked her under its shoulder and then took one large step toward the wall of the car, kicking out with clawed feet the three seats between it and freedom. Mikla brought its muscled right leg up and kicked out once, twice, and then a third time into the glass and wood lining the window. The entire section of aluminum and wood framing separated from the train leaving a gash eight feet in diameter. The beast leaned out of the car as the wind caught its fur. Anya's, the boy's, and the goat's eyes widened as the Golia leaned out into empty space as the train sped along. Mikla howled and then pushed off from the car, and the Golia and its frightened cargo fell free into the early morning darkness.

The Golia hit the ground at fifty-six miles an hour but the great beast never lost its footing as it caught the hardpan of the feeder road next to the tracks. The giant beast yelped in pain and then vanished into the breaking dawn.

The soldiers came through the open door and felt the wind before seeing the frightened and bloody man lying in the aisle. Their eyes went to the eight-foot hole in the side of the train car and the vodka bottle slipped out of the grasp of the man standing in front of the other two.

The next thing they knew their platoon sergeant was standing next to them. He looked at each man in turn and then bent over and picked up the half-finished vodka bottle. His eyebrows rose in a silent condemnation. The Romanian army sergeant just pointed back the way they had come.

"I think that just about covers drinking on duty—let's go."

PATINAS PASS, CARPATHIAN MOUNTAINS

The old woman held on to the side of the temple entrance where man-made materials met the natural stone of the mountain. She held fast as the air of the dawn cooled her face after the heat inside the massive structure. Madame Korvesky knew eyes were on her from just off the trail leading down into the mountain. The Golia were there and were watching her; some with only mild curiosity, and then there were the others with malice-laced thoughts. She knew these were the younger Golia—the males and few females that seemed to set out away from the rest. One of these was Stanus, who she knew was on his high ledge above the temple where he lay alone and watched everything occurring around the giant temple structure and the camouflaged opening that led deep into the mountain.

The heat inside had become unbearable for the old Gypsy to take at her age and now she was paying the price for staying so long inside. She managed a deep breath and felt the pain in both her legs from the ten thousand steps it takes coming and going from the depths of the great temple. She would have to make it home and drink as much bitterroot tea as she could stomach in order to ease the pain that would nearly cripple her when she awakened later. The tea alone she knew would probably kill her or constipate her so bad she would wish she *were* dead. She took another breath and then raised the flowered print dress to a spot just above her right ankle. It was purple and black and she knew that if it wasn't broken it was a close imitation of a break. She could barely place any pressure on the ankle and foot without streaking jolts of pain shooting up her leg.

As she placed her cane carefully and took her first tentative steps down the small dirt trail that led into her village she heard the laughter of men somewhere ahead. It was only a few steps later that her grandson appeared on the trail with four of the men that had been his constant companions the past six years. Three were from their village but the fourth was from a farm more than fifteen miles away. She trusted none of them. Her grandson stopped and the talk between the Gypsy men ceased as they all took in her ragged and unhealthy condition. Marko looked shocked and then moved to her side as the other four men half bowed to the Gypsy queen and then faded off the trail and into the trees that lined it.

"What are you doing up here, Grandmamma?" Marko took her by the arm and held her as the talk of his men faded from ear.

He waited to speak again until the men had vanished. "You were in the temple?" His tone was still one of concern but now it was also laced with suspicion.

"I believe I am still allowed the freedom to come and go from my own temple, am I not?" She looked up at him and even managed a smile but she soon lost the will and the strength to produce either the smile or to keep her head held high.

"I must get you home and into your bed, you old foolish hen," he said as he placed his arm around her and started her back down the trail. He grew silent as he walked. The sun was broaching the eastern edge of the mountains before he spoke again. "Stanus is quite agitated tonight. I think you could tell that from the fire pit this evening. I think one of his young ones is missing."

The old woman didn't respond. She just kept her walk slow and easy while using her cane as much as possible to lessen the pain in her right ankle.

"Of course it's the male pup, Mikla. He always was surly and the only brother Stanus has a hard time controlling."

The old woman walked in silence.

"Are you going to tell me what you were doing in the temple so late and without escort?"

"I could not sleep. And yes the encounter with Stanus tonight was the reason. I had to pray on it some. The alpha is conflicted about something." She slowed and then looked upward into the dark features of her grandson. "You wouldn't know anything about that, would you, man-child?" She knew she had caught him off guard and turned the tables on him because Marko stopped and then stepped away from her so he could see her fully in the false light of dawn.

"With all of the changes in the valley below and even upon our own mountain, do you expect Stanus not to be confused? He will settle down, you will see. Now, do you know Mikla's whereabouts?"

"Yes," she said, suddenly refusing to play this game with her own flesh and blood. "I do know where Mikla is."

Her right leg gave out completely and she collapsed almost to the ground before Marko's strength stayed her fall. He lifted her up and carried her to a small outcropping of stone that lined the trail. He removed her sandal and saw that her ankle was swollen at least five times its normal size.

"What have you done? Did you fall on the great steps?"

"Oh, it's only twisted; I do worse sometimes tripping over my own feet."

He looked at her and then removed his blue head scarf and started wrapping the horribly swollen ankle.

"Twisted? If it's not broken I would be surprised, Grandmamma." He finished tying off the wrapping and then placed his elbows on his bended knees and then looked at the Gypsy queen. "Where is Mikla and what did you do to him to make your ankle swell like that? Is the Golia all right? Do I need to send Stanus to retrieve him?"

"That would not be a good task, as Stanus is not at all popular with Mikla and a few of the other pups. And Mikla needs no help getting home; he's with two very reliable people."

"What have you done?"

"Protected the future of our people the best way I knew how. Now help me get home so *you* can make me some bitterroot tea because I just cannot stomach the smell," she said as she used his strong shoulder to pull herself off the rock.

Marko said nothing in response. He knew it wouldn't do any good, as the old woman had the longest stubborn streak in her since Moses himself. He took a deep breath and knew he had to slow down her suspicions until he was ready for what needed to be done. He remained silent all the way home.

One hundred and eighty miles to the west three forms lay in a drainage ditch beside a deserted feeder road. The boy was sleeping soundly after their crazed exit from the train and Anya hoped he wasn't in some form of mild shock. Her two young nephews, thanks to her grandmother, had saved her life twice in the past twenty-four hours.

It was Mikla she was most worried about. The Golia lay on its side and was licking the right rear paw and ankle. The beast had landed awkwardly when he jumped from the side of the car. The speed of the train was something the Golia was not familiar with and it had caught the great animal by surprise when they had landed hard. Mikla barely managed to keep his footing but soon had to stop to go on all fours until he had to rest his leg.

"Poor Mikla, it's my fault for making you run when all you wanted was to hold your ground and protect us." She reached out and ran her hand along his side. The giant wolf looked up and then whined and licked her hand. The young Golia held Anya's eyes for the longest time and then with the articulated fingers of its right hand extended and the claws gleaming in the sunshine, Mikla reached up and took Anya's hand and held it tight. The prehistoric wolf suddenly winced and closed its softly glowing yellow eyes and released Anya's hand as it lay its head down into the grass.

"We'll rest the best we can today and start out again tonight after it gets dark."

She rubbed his thick fur once again. "Maybe we can get you another train ride, maybe on top this time, huh?" she said with a smile and a hard rub of the black wolf's fur. The ears popped up with their gray tips and she knew the thought of riding on a train, while his first trip didn't end that well, still excited Mikla enough that he wanted to do it again. She knew his thoughts at extreme moments like this and his being excited and happy was easy to pick upon. But she wasn't sure if Mikla was excited about the train or more to the point that he was nearing home.

The giant Golia laid its head against Anya and was content to close its glowing yellow eyes that were now fading to green as the sun started to rise higher.

Mikla had done the task he was sent out to accomplish and for the day at least the beast was content as he lay with those he was sent to protect.

7

DACIAN HOT SPRINGS, CARPATHIAN MOUNTAINS, ROMANIA

Dmitri Zallas was most impressed as he toured the Roman mud baths and hot mineral springs adjacent to the Enviro Dome. Accommodations for a thousand or more guests who would undoubtedly enjoy the spa when it was fully operational were now finished. The steam from the natural hot springs and the mud that boiled through to the surface after being cooked for a million years far beneath the Carpathians made the gardens as lush as any tropical rain forest.

"I take it your man was successful with his foray into the Patinas Pass? Were you pleased?"

Zallas lost his smile as he turned to face his limited partner. "It was worth it, but very expensive. You shall have no more trouble in the mountains above the castle."

Janos Vajic pursed his lips and then wrestled with the question in his mind for the briefest of moments before blurting it out.

"The man is a mess," Janos said as he stepped to the geodesic dome. They were on the eighth floor nearest the cable car entrance. He pointed down toward the maintenance area a thousand yards away from the massive pool and spa. The man was sitting on the ground with his fur coat still on in the heat of the day with his knees pulled up to his chest as workers and maintenance personnel were forced to walk around him. He pointed his man out to Zallas, whose eyes narrowed to slits when he saw the hunter. "He's been like that ever since he returned without his hunting companions—who are still among the missing by the way."

"They are not missing, Janos; they just went home after failing this man. He did what I paid him to do." He turned and looked at Vajic. "I will have him removed."

"May I broach another subject with you?"

"Does it have anything to do with my guest list?" Zallas asked as he turned away and started for the escalator to head down to the casino.

"Well, although I have major concerns about several of the more . . . colorful names on that list, there is but one that makes me nervous. But I have to start with my first concern, which is obvious to any fool who steps on this property: the amount of private security you have brought in. You have over a hundred well-armed men; this will not look good, not only to the guests, but to the media."

"Get to the point, Janos, for crying out loud." Zallas stopped at the guardrail for the giant escalator and turned on his partner.

"There are certain members of the media who have started asking questions about how the land was transferred from the state to a private concern after so many years of protection. Dmitri, they are starting to ask questions. And look at this." He held out the large guest list with close to two thousand names on it. "Stephan Antonescu, the interior minister, is on the list. We cannot have him on the property—at least not now."

"The sale of the land cannot be traced to us through his office. Remember it was over the very loud and media-covered protests of our good interior minister that the land grant was enacted. He maneuvered the right element into the equation, one that no one in all of Romania could argue with. As a matter of fact the people believe this to be to their benefit—I mean what more powerful ally could we have than the most formidable military organization the world had ever known backing us through sheer necessity?" Zallas smiled as he took in the shocked features of his partner. "I mean with the security of a new nation at stake, what's a little resort when the government finally has control over the one pass in the Carpathians that not even the mighty German army could capture."

Janos Vajic heard noise coming through the glass panes of the dome and stepped over to the front of the great construction to look out toward the south where the new highway had been built to accommodate the resort. Lined against the afternoon sun was a long column of vehicles. Janos leaned closer to the glass as the long procession of trucks drove past the entrance to the resort and then continued west where they disappeared around a bend in the highway. He tried to see the vehicles in more detail but they were just too far away. Zallas saw Vajic as he struggled with the distance and he smiled and reached into his suit jacket pocket and brought out a small set of binoculars; gold-plated of course.

"Here, use these and allow the sight to ease your concerns. Look first to the lead vehicle's markings, and then to the rear, view the military designations on those vehicles and then I will accept your apology for your baseless concern about land rights."

Janos accepted the glasses and held the dark eyes of Zallas before putting the glasses to his own eyes. As he focused on the lead vehicle, an older military version of the venerable American jeep but built in the old Soviet Union, was leading forty two-ton trucks. He focused on the markings along the side of the hood next to the stenciled black and gray eagle: Brigada 2 Vânători de Munte "Sarmizegetusa"— 2nd Mountain Troops Brigade. He turned and looked at Zallas.

"The new Romanian mountain division?"

"Yes. Now look who's bringing up the rear, Janos, why, it's our saviors," he said with a smile, "and the people ultimately responsible, although they didn't know it at the time, for getting our land grant for us and almost forcing the new Romanian government to open up land that has not seen the outside world for nearly three thousand years."

The smile made Vajic far more nervous than the anger Zallas could show from time to time. He turned the small gold-inlaid binoculars toward the end of the long column and placed the glasses on the strange-looking vehicles bringing up the rear of the military column.

"Oh my God," he said as the lettering on the front of the vehicle's bumper became legible: 223-SFOD-D82nd USA.

"If you are having trouble with understanding what you are seeing I am not surprised. After all you're Romanian so there is no reason you should. I received the information last week about our guests down there. They are the 223rd Special Forces Operational Detachment—Delta Company—the famous All American Division. Those are American airborne troops down there, Janos, and what we are looking at is the one factor that gave us all of this," he said as he gestured around the giant glass dome. "I give you NATO. The North Atlantic Treaty Organization, the most powerful military force the world has ever seen."

"What are they doing here?" Vajic asked as he lowered the glasses.

"The reason this area is so important to them is the fact that the Patinas Pass is a vital passage leading to the north of the nation. It is what's known in military parlance as a choke point—one that was pointed out to our friends at the Ministry of Defense. Thus, our new NATO partnership has paid the full dividend. The pass is about to become militarized and the Americans are here to show them how to defend it against invasion from the south." He smiled as he slapped Vajic on the back. "They will stay in the lowlands today and tonight and then head to the pass tomorrow to evaluate the defensive planning for an invasion that will never come." He laughed. "It is so very easy to frighten a people that have lived under the yoke of totalitarianism for so long that they never recognize the real threat."

Dmitri Zallas may have been comfortable, but Vajic wondered what other deals were made that wouldn't be so beneficial to their resort.

"After the pass has been mapped and war plans made, the entire area will be up for leasing and improvement. That is my plan. The whole of the mountain will soon be ours and we will expand the property to the pass itself."

As Janos allowed the plan of Zallas to set in, a loud whining rumble came to their ears.

Shockingly to everyone at the resort three American-made Black Hawk helicopters swooped low over the resort and then banked hard right to follow the disappearing trail of NATO vehicles.

"You see, Janos, who needs friends when you have the biggest bully on the block leading the way for you?"

"I have another issue, Dmitri. We have a hard weather front coming up from the Danube. This could play havoc with the opening night of the castle."

"A storm?" Zallas asked with more enthusiasm than could ever have been warranted with such bad news for his opening night of Dracula's Castle. "Excellent! What better ambience than to have a storm that night of nights." He slapped Janos on the back.

Vajic watched Zallas turn on his heel and leave and he realized for the first time how deeply insane the Russian gangster really was. He wadded up the note and tossed it in a trash receptacle.

"Will this nightmare ever end?"

Four miles up the mountain and one mile above the new and improved Dracula's Castle, the dark eyes watched the activity below. The eyes turned angry as the helicopters arrived and started making sweeps around the resort and the foothills to his mountain.

Marko Korvesky turned away from the scene below and then placed a hand onto the nearest tree and leaned heavily against it. His eyes went to the castle just below and then to the resort at the bottom of the mountain.

"What are you up to, Zallas?" he said as he watched the men finishing up their work far below. The sight of the soldiers was one Marko had never expected. As thoughts of possible betrayal entered his mind for the first time, he froze as he felt the presence behind him. He slowly turned and tried not to react to what he saw.

"You should always let your presence be known, Stanus."

The giant Golia watched Marko for the longest time as it sat on a large boulder above the trail leading to the pass. The black fur was gleaming in the sun as its yellow eyes, now dulled by the daylight hours, moved from Marko to the valley far below. The man was getting mixed vibrations from the Golia as it sat silently and watched.

"That means nothing to us; the soldiers are nothing but more guardians for the people and the Golia."

Marko only hoped that the half lie was good enough to satisfy Stanus and prayed the great wolf could not smell the sudden fear that the man had falsely represented the risk to the mountain, the temple, the people, and the one-of-a-kind species known as the Golia.

When Marko turned around Stanus was gone.

EVENT GROUP COMPLEX, NELLIS AIR FORCE BASE, NEVADA

The proverbial last piece of the puzzle fell into place for the Event Group early that morning thanks to Pete Golding, who after being read the riot act by Niles earlier had gone straight to work with Europa, and the Cray system came through as always. She had successfully broken into the man Alice pegged as the leading authority on not only the ancient Jeddah, but also the wolves that accompany the legend. Pete had the floor inside the main conference room and he was out to impress. The circular monitors came alive with a picture of a bearded man with thick horned-rimmed glasses.

"Ladies and Gentlemen this is Professor Avi Feuerstein, former chair of medieval studies at UCLA."

All eyes studied the grumpy-looking man in the tweed jacket.

"The good professor here produced a series of papers and letters saying that the settlement of the Hebrew homeland in Canaan was not God-inspired but one of a pure military nature against the citizens of the region right around the time of the Exodus. The man refuses to discuss the subject with anyone because of the ridicule he received for his outlandish theories. The man is virtually destitute and living in a hovel where he does nothing but his research projects he finances with his meager savings and by tutoring children in ancient Hebrew history." Pete paused and nodded toward Alice, who was seated in her usual place beside the director.

"In all of his papers written on the subject of the Lost Tribe of the Jeddah he had never once mentioned anything about what he suspected of the Golia, who were the onetime protectors of not only the Jeddah but of all of the tribes of Israel and the northern and western borders of Egypt during the time of the pharaohs."

Niles Compton cleared his throat, impatient for Alice to get to her point. "Does this man have the evidence you were looking for about the Jeddah and your theory on how they assisted in the mass Exodus out of Egypt?" He looked from Alice to Pete.

"Some of the information recovered by Europa doesn't stem from Professor Feuerstein's information about Egypt, nor does it spring from Hebrew tribal lore. It seems the man discovered a partial section of wall in a private collection that had been unearthed in Asia Minor. This wall was covered in Hieroglyphic Hittite—a long-dead language of a vanished culture and a historical enemy of the Jeddah tribe. It tells of Hittites battling forces from the great deserts of the south and against a people not known to them and with many standards and flags."

On the many screens arrayed around the room depictions of paintings and artwork of the ancient Hittite culture shone brightly across the interested faces of the group.

"This was an army that was described in varying texts of the time as magical. They conquered all before it and no matter the tactic of the Hittite tribes they could not wrest their lands from these invaders. Soon the strange people and their even stranger god moved on to the great mountains of the north never to be heard from again." Pete paused for the moment to make sure they were all watching as the picture changed to that of the ancient Egyptian god Anubis in an a military type stance with a large spear. It was beautifully done in black lacquer. "The Hittites spoke of the magical animals that did battle for these strange people. Beasts described as black devils of the night—gods capable of walking as men."

"Where is this historically valuable wall the professor found?" Niles Compton asked.

"The section of wall was destroyed in a museum fire while in storage in Prague in 1974 according to Feuerstein's notes. The fire was investigated and arson was proven."

"Pete, I have about $20 million in support equipment and fuel waiting up at Nellis and they are awaiting our Group, can you get to the point," Niles said.

"Right, sorry. Europa ran into a firewall where the professor had his proof hidden." The lights changed as the pictures on the screen did. "Item number one," Pete said as a freestanding statuette was shown on a soft bed of red satin. The way the piece was displayed reminded Alice Hamilton of the way the artifacts on the *Golden Child* those many years ago had been set up inside their displays.

"Ramesses II, am I correct?" asked Charlie Ellenshaw.

"Correct. This item was recovered while at auction in Paris in 1999 according to his notebook. But not before the unseen bidder placed a $500 million placement on the seven-inch statue."

"It's the pristine condition of the artifact," Alice said as she studied the statue. "Not one item from that dynasty has ever turned up looking as if it had been carved and painted the day before. Whoever had this took extremely good care of it."

"The possibility of a fake?" asked Niles Compton, who was looking at the statue closely.

"Zero," Pete said as he pointed to the screen nearest him. "If you could lift the statue you would see the drill holes in the bottom of the carved pedestal. This was caused when the item was authenticated in 1977 by carbon 14 testing. The statue you're looking at has been verified as 3,600 years old plus or minus five hundred years, which places this item squarely in the hands of Ramesses himself, or someone he knew anyway."

That caused the group to nod their heads in unison as they realized Pete and Europa had done the impossible once again.

"Item number two." On the screen a photo of a large stone block appeared and then the next view showed the giant stone in two separate halves. Alice Hamilton smiled for the first time in what seemed years to her. She was seeing an old lost friend. "Here is the picture found in his secured file."

"Alice's werewolf of Jericho," Charlie Ellenshaw said aloud.

"Found inside the ruins at Tell es-Sultan, or, what's left of the biblical city of Jericho, just as Alice said."

"What is the professor's take on its disappearance?" Niles asked, awaiting the confirmation Alice was seeking above all else.

"Feuerstein said it disappeared sometime after the war."

Looks were exchanged around the table as Alice's tale of what was seen aboard the *Golden Child* was now confirmed.

"While I am a firm believer of the romantic story of the Exodus as told in the

Bible," Alice said, "and while it may have been God who sent the plagues to curse Pharaoh, we can now start to see that it was the Israelite army and the Golia who secured the freedom of the Hebrew nation from what they thought of at that time was bondage, or at the very least undervalued servitude."

"I believe you have one last item in your report, Pete?" Compton asked as he glanced at his wristwatch.

One more time the monitors changed and this series of pictures caught everyone's attention. It was a view of another statue, of the impressively muscled Golia sitting upon a throne wearing the double crown of Upper and Lower Egypt.

"I believe this is why Ramesses II allowed his indentured servants and northern army to leave Egypt. I believe the tribe of warriors known as the Jeddah, who served the house of Levite, were getting ready to overthrow the two kingdoms. This is not the only artifact depicting the animals on the throne of Egypt. There are many more, all collected over the years and hidden away. It's as if someone were cleaning up after the fact."

"What is the provenance of this piece?" Virginia Pollock asked as she studied the Golia rendered in heavily lacquered carved wood.

"This artifact was sold at auction seven months ago in Ukraine in a secret bidding. The statue is in superb condition, pristine craftsmanship, and undeniable scientific proof of its age."

"Who bought it?" Jack asked, already guessing the answer.

A photo of a bearded man with dark eyes came on the screen. "This is the recipient of the $34 million sale."

"Dmitri Zallas," said Collins aloud.

"Jack?" Alice asked, not knowing the name. As she looked at Niles she could see that he also knew the man whose face stared at them from the many different screens.

"Former Russian Ten Most Wanted. He left Belarus ten years ago for more sunny and profitable climes. Current residence is unknown but he is a killer anywhere he goes. His hands are in any double dealing of antiquities the world over. He is more in the market for selling than buying. Europa, get me everything you have on Zallas and his whereabouts."

"Yes, Colonel," Europa answered.

"Can I make a point that Charlie and myself have been raking around for a while?"

Niles nodded his head.

"History is where our answers lie, just as it always is. The real key here is the Levite material Alice uncovered that says we have a starting point in Romania. For instance we now know the Roman Empire was terrified of that region. The Turks once chased Prince Vlad Tepes into the interior of his own nation and forced him to hide among the Carpathians to escape their wrath. Then suddenly and for no apparent reason the Turks began losing every battle against Vlad the Impaler now documented to have happened. He turned the tide of war after he found allies among his own people he never even knew existed, and ones that were brutishly ruthless—thus the horrific tales and vampiritic nature of Vlad Dracul's reputation. A reputation I might add that may have been earned and based solely on the teeth, claws, and weaponry of not only the Golia, but one of the Lost Tribes of Israel—the Jeddah."

Niles nodded that he agreed with Pete's conclusions much to Jack's and Alice's relief.

"Lieutenant McIntire, have you filed your geological report with Alice's team on the makeup of the Patinas Pass range in Romania?"

"The outstanding feature is the thermal makeup of the pass. The plates under the Carpathians are quite active in European terms as far as tectonic activity is concerned. The waters are boiled many miles below the mountain range and breach the surface in several areas creating natural hot springs in several small valleys below the mountain. The hot springs are actual weather variants that can change the temperature and makeup of their winters; the only section of the Carpathians that can lay that claim." She smiled. "It may be one of the reasons that region is so full of old legends; fog appears from nowhere, sudden rain falls out of a clear night sky. The old tales of vampires and werewolves sprang from this very area."

Sarah completed her report and then sat just as a Navy signalman walked in and handed Colonel Collins a message. Jack scanned it and then passed it over to Niles Compton. After reading the communiqué he cleared his throat. He looked down at Alice as she spoke in low tones with Virginia.

"Ladies and gentlemen, the situation is changing rather rapidly as unforeseen influences in Romania are starting to make this look far more serious than just a few stolen artifacts. This may involve Romanian government corruption at a high level, thus it is now a major concern for our nation's military—Colonel Collins, would you please explain what I mean?" Niles asked and then went to his desk and picked up his phone.

"The person going about selling artifacts from the Exodus is known as Dmitri Zallas as we learned earlier. But one thing that just came to light is what he was investing in. Europa, NATO satellite image 1245 central Romania, please."

On the monitors an image from space.

"Enhance grid coordinates 3489 and 3412. This is a high-altitude shot from one of our military Blackbird satellites taken five years and two months ago. As you see it's just a beautiful mountain and valleys—nothing there but several small villages. Okay, Europa, yesterday's satellite pass-by of the same coordinates."

On the screen a massive resort complex came into view and Jack read from the report hastily compiled by Europa. "I give you the Edge of the World Hotel Resort and Casino, owned by none other than Dmitri Zallas. It sits four miles from Patinas Pass high above it—a pass that our new NATO ally Romania is now in the process of evaluating for possible invasion scenarios coming from the south. It's a routine examination that all NATO selectees go through—the evaluation of their country's defensive positions for possible future use."

"What does this have to do with Alice's investigation?" Virginia asked.

"Europa, enhance grid 29-b."

On the numerous monitors, including the seventy-eight-inch screen in the center of the conference room, appeared an aerial shot of the Patinas Pass.

"Thus far we have counted no fewer than thirteen small villages near the pass, with the largest being this village dead center of Patinas." Jack used a laser pointer and hit the exact location on the gridded photo. "This is the village of Patinas. We can't get an exact census report until Europa gets it for us." Jack looked at Pete Golding, who only nodded his head that he understood the unspoken directive.

At his desk Niles was speaking quickly and deliberately into his phone.

"This is a point of concern here. With the NATO question at hand the CIA did some digging for the U.S. Army that Europa kidnapped before the report went to the Pentagon and stored until it was collated with the name Zallas by my information request. The land that surrounded the Patinas Pass south of the mountains and north of the same range was all protected land. This we know, but what we didn't know was the little known fact that the land is now owned by our friend Dmitri Zallas—the very same gentleman who seems to have struck it rich in the antiquities market. His resort opens for a private party day after tomorrow. That is one of the ways into the valley we can use. The other is NATO. We can get more people in theater by also using them as a front. Dr. Compton has already cleared it with the president, so half of our team will enter the valley with invitations to the private party and the other will travel to the Patinas Pass with the NATO element of the 82nd Airborne and Romanian army engineers. Captain Everett and Lieutenants Ryan and Mendenhall will accompany Alice to the pass."

The hands of Pete Golding and Professor Charles Hindershot Ellenshaw III shot into the air as both were about to protest their absence on the list of field representatives.

"Lower your hands, this isn't third grade," Niles said angrily, knowing that Jack had already requested the two professors be on the team because of Charlie's knowledge of ancient legends and Pete's computer genius—Collins figured they would need them both. "You'll both be on Colonel Collins's team. And you *will* follow orders."

Both men smiled and nodded that they understood.

Collins sat down knowing Sarah's eyes were on him. He kept his own eyes on the director as he continued.

"This Event was called because the mounting evidence Alice has presented was compelling. However, that is not the full measure of what's happening here. We now have one-of-a-kind antiquities being sold off to private, unscrupulous characters. We're going to find out where these artifacts are coming from. Number two, we have now confirmation from a State Department memo that the land granted to this Russian criminal was possibly attained through bribery and corruption, which could affect NATO's ability to include Romania in the alliance. Most importantly this is an Event that has gone viral quickly. We have a chance to rewrite several very confusing pages regarding the history of the Exodus—pages that have vast implications as to the history and heritage of most everyone in the Palestine region. In other words, this is a very sensitive issue that needs to be handled by us, and us alone." Niles looked at the clock on the wall. "Jack, how are you coming with the invitations to this gangster's shindig he's throwing with Jeddah money?"

"I have a fax coming through in a few minutes that will enable Europa to make exact copies of the invitation and to give her the opportunity to backdoor the computer system of the resort management company to enter the names we choose as invitees."

"With permission." Carl Everett spoke up for the first time during the meeting. "May I inquire as to the source of this invitation that is being provided to you?"

"The source is secure at this time."

Carl looked away and over at Sarah McIntire, who knew exactly what it was Carl was thinking. There was only one man dark enough to have received a legitimate invitation from a man of such dubious distinction as Zallas and his international antiquities ring—Colonel Henri Farbeaux. Both Everett and McIntire knew this for a fact as soon as Jack couldn't meet their eyes that his miscreant contact was indeed the Frenchman.

"The equipment to be used has already been loaded onto our 747-C at Nellis. From there we will fly to Bucharest. Once we land we will break into the first group consisting of our discovery team. They will penetrate the social function to ascertain the connection that exists between the resort ownership and the artifacts that have magically appeared over the last eight years. Lieutenant McIntire, Lieutenant Commander Ryan, and you, Pete, will accompany Colonel Collins and his team to the resort. Pete, you will need a secure cell link with Europa as you may need her if something turns up. I want one for my team also. The aerial photographs show the cell towers being erected but thus far are nonfunctional. We may have communication problems with the outside world, so see what can be done."

"My duties?" Sarah inquired.

"You and the colonel will assess the situation and report back to me at NATO command at the base of the mountain. Lieutenant, you will evaluate the strata surrounding the resort for anomalies that may explain why the developer," he made a face at the euphemism for the Russian gangster, "was so intent on building there. It may just be the hot springs, but look into it."

Sarah wrote down her notes, deciding to hit the computer center before they left for Nellis so she could study the geological makeup of the Carpathians one more time.

"My base element will be going in as a civilian survey team there to get a good look at the pass. That means we will be going up with members of the 82nd Airborne to the villages below, and then the main village higher into the pass. This small village of Patinas seems to be the hub of all social activity in the area."

"Why is that, Niles?" asked Pete Golding.

"The hot springs flow from the mountain near Patinas and the springs feed the entire valley system below. Besides, the larger cattle and sheep herds are near the village."

"What personnel will be making up your team?" asked Alice as she slowly looked up from her notes and fixed Compton with her determined eyes.

"My team will be consisting of Captain Everett, Lieutenant Mendenhall, and Professor Ellenshaw, who will be using the link with Europa in the field if we can get communications up and running. So get with Pete on its operation, Charlie, in case we can figure out the COM problems. Also, Dr. Gilliam will act as both teams' only physician. You will notice I am cutting the security element and the support teams from the list. The rest of the departments will stand down. This man may be far too dangerous to have a large Event team in the field, since we may have to get the hell out of there in a hurry. Virginia, you will see to it that all departments stick to their class schedules and their historical research." Niles waited for Virginia to let it soak in that she wasn't going into the field. She accepted the decision and then nodded her head.

Alice waited in silence and then looked up at Niles.

"Alice, you will accompany my team to the Patinas Pass."

She breathed a sigh of relief at her being added to the Event. She thanked Niles with a slight nod of her head.

Charlie Ellenshaw got up from the table with a curious look on his face. He walked up to the monitor, which still held the aerial view of Patinas Pass. He looked hard into the image and then turned to face Niles.

"Niles, do you have any information on what this out-of-place structure is?" he said tapping the big screen monitor. Compton picked up the report Europa received after backdooring the real estate managing firm operating the resort.

Niles read the name and smiled.

"Well, since we're going to the country whose name used to be Transylvania, I think it apropos that we also visit the nightclub known as Dracula's Castle."

Ellenshaw looked up and over at the others while muttering to himself.

"Oh, this is getting better and better."

8

DRACULA'S CASTLE,
PATINAS PASS, ROMANIA

The view was spectacular in the late afternoon light. As Dmitri Zallas watched the preparations far below at the resort, workers behind him were putting the final touches on Dracula's Castle, the nightclub to top all nightclubs. Zallas turned from the false parapet that was actually a ten-foot-by-eight-foot plate glass window and saw the stand-up cardboard cutout of the famous American crooner and onetime child recording star Drake Andrews, fresh from a ten-year run at the Las Vegas Hilton. He would be the first star to open at the resort and was booked for the next fourteen months. Zallas smiled at the lobby cutout of the famous star and lightly tapped the lifelike appearance.

"You have as much soul as that piece of cardboard, Zallas."

The Russian looked up and his smile vanished as if it had never been there. He released his hold on the smiling Drake Andrews and looked around quickly to make sure his bodyguards were paying attention—they were. There were four large men in black jackets that stood at various locations throughout the interior of the falsified medieval castle. He also had over a hundred workers blowing fake cobwebs and setting up the last of the mood lighting that would illuminate the outside of the castle. The crazy Gypsy wouldn't dare start trouble here.

Marko Korvesky stood defiant in the middle of the dance floor, forcing the workers to walk around him. The head scarf he wore was satin black and matched the all-black-leather clothes he wore with the exception of the bright purple shirt under his vest.

"You should not be here," Zallas said as he stepped up to the edge of the dance floor waiting for the Gypsy to come to him. He didn't.

"This mockery of our heritage should not be here, Slav."

"I told you not to call me that," Zallas hissed and then stepped onto the broad wooden dance floor in one wide and menacing step.

Marko smiled as he saw Zallas stop a few feet from him, well out of reach. "You're not a Slav?"

"I don't like the word, that's all I have to say on the subject."

"I understand. Let us try another." Marko placed his hands on his hips. "How about this for a name, Russian, just pick one—liar, cheat, gangster? I can go on."

This time Zallas looked at his men and they stepped forward in a grouped warning toward the Gypsy.

"I had to build this. Just look at it, this is a moneymaker." He gestured around him at the manufactured blocks of stone and plastic and Fiberglas that made up the castle. "It's just one little change to our agreement." He became serious as he looked back at the Gypsy and his enthusiasm was instantly absent from his features and voice. "A change that did not dictate your murdering my workers over."

This time it was Marko who smiled. "Certain factions around these mountains didn't take your intrusion above the castle all that well. It took some convincing to make them see things differently, which will cost you far more than you realize at the moment." He paused while his eyes moved toward his bodyguards and then back at the Russian. "Now we hear and see soldiers in our valley. We hear the sounds of helicopters as they fly low over the pass. We see more soldiers coming from south of the Danube and beyond. Yes, Zallas, there will be more owed to us than our original agreement called for. The initial investment money we gave you with our artifacts has a very steep percentage rate. You see I am more of a businessman than you thought," his smile returned, "or hoped for."

"You're worth millions upon millions right now, what more do you want?"

"Nothing. The money I received will ensure that my people are not without as they have been for so many years. No more sheep, no more cows and chickens. We deserve better and now we are going to live the way we were always meant to live." Marko took a menacing step toward the Russian mobster, making the bodyguards move toward him. But a hand held high by Zallas stopped them. "If you go north of this toy castle I will not be able to control . . . control some of my friends."

Dmitri Zallas saw Marko turn and start to walk away and then stop and face the Russian once more.

"You also need to have these fools of yours," he gestured to the armed men in black coats, "looking for a woman with black hair in the company of a small boy. She will be coming your way on her trek to the pass. It would be to your benefit to have this woman held and then brought to me. She is not to be harmed in any way."

"Ahhhh, now I see, the little sister returns to the fold. I can see why you're so hard to deal with lately, my friend. Not to worry, she cannot get through my men. They are the best there is. The resort is the most guarded property this side of the Kremlin, I assure you."

Marko laughed and then turned away but the laughter remained.

Zallas watched the Gypsy leave and then he snorted and pulled up his pants. He looked at his guards until they all turned away. He walked back to the window looking down upon the cable car lines and the resort far below. He swallowed and then closed his eyes blocking out the visage of Marko Korvesky, the bearded man who was the only person in the world that frightened Dmitri Zallas.

He soon gestured toward the larger of the bodyguards. The man was a Spetsnaz commando from the former Soviet Union and was linked to Zallas by pure meanness.

"Yes, Mr. Zallas?"

"Are we ready for Saturday night?"

"That Gypsy will lead us to it and there will not be anything this side of hell that can stop us from getting the information you seek from him."

Zallas nodded just once as he turned to the opposite window and watched Marko walking the trail that led to the mountain above. He was there with his ever-present guard of four of the burliest-looking Gypsies Zallas had ever seen. They walked slowly and then disappeared into the trees. He turned and faced his man once more.

"If what I think is true, our limited partner has a secret that may make this resort's worth pale in comparison. Yes, our Gypsy friend will let us in on that secret very soon and then I suspect we will discover where all of this ancient finery is coming from." He smiled. "Have your former friends from your formative days been alerted that we move on Patinas on Saturday night at the latest?"

"They have arrived on the property and are awaiting your orders."

"And they will have no problem doing the tasks I have set for them?"

"They will wipe out every man, woman, and child in that village if the need arises."

Zallas turned away and watched the spot where the Gypsy had vanished into the tree line.

"For what he has hidden up there, believe me, the need will more than likely arise."

As he watched the tree line he saw the shadows of the afternoon play against the gentle sway of the thin pines that made up the woods in the area. He could swear the shadows shifted shape against the force of the wind. He shook his head and sent the thought of things that go bump in the night out of his head.

As Zallas turned away from the window he failed to see the giant wolf as it slowly slid onto the crag on the side of the mountain beside the castle only ten feet away from the window where he had just been standing.

It was three hours later that Marko saw Stanus sitting beneath his grandmother's window. The beast did not see the man's approach, which was strange as nothing escaped the notice of the alpha.

Marko stopped twenty feet from the small cottage and the spot where the giant Golia lay on its stomach with its muzzle pointing up near the open window of his grandmother's bedroom. He looked around and saw that most of the men of the village had not yet returned from the high pastures of the pass and the womenfolk were busy with chores and preparations for the evening meal.

Marko watched Stanus as the muzzle lifted once more and the Golia sniffed the air. Then the head of the alpha turned to the human. Stanus stood up so fast that Marko flinched, which was never a good idea when startling a Golia. The beast growled. It was not loud and not even menacing. It was the alpha letting Marko be aware of the power that stood not twenty feet from him.

"Is Mikla home?" Marko asked. The dimmed yellow eyes took in Marko and that, in and of itself, was unsettling. "Stanus, is Mikla back home at the temple?"

The Golia stared at Marko and then its ears lay back and the giant beast yawned. Stanus shook its head as if it was just waking up from a long sleep, and then without another gesture of any kind the Golia stood on its hind legs. Marko heard the distinctive resetting of the hip and pelvic bones as they slid into their secondary sockets and joints. Marko was like anyone who ever witnessed the change. He never ceased to wonder over the Golia's ability to physically alter its shape. He watched in amazement as the right paw lifted and the fingers came free of the folded fistlike appendage. The clawed digits and thumb grasped the windowsill of his grandmother's room and then using the sill as leverage pushed itself up and over the back wall and then disappeared into the rocks lining the village.

Marko was confused as to the way Stanus was acting ever since Mikla vanished. Then Stanus went out of control with the workers at the castle and killed three of them because of what the Golia perceived as an invasion of their land. It had taken Marko over fifteen hours of hard mental contact to get the great wolf to understand that the change was necessary and that killing these men could only bring more men to the pass.

Marko walked to the front of the small cottage and then stopped at the wooden front door. He reached out after taking a deep breath and lifted the iron latch and stepped into a darkened house.

"Grandmamma?" he called out as he looked at the cold stove. Not even her ever-present teapot was warm. He quickly went to the only other room in the cottage, her bedroom. He saw her lying on her small bed. She was holding the blankets up close to her chin and she was shaking. "Grandmamma, what have you done now?" he asked as he rushed to her side.

He saw her ankle placed on the bed outside the blanket. His eyes widened when he saw the purple and black swelling. The ankle was cocked off to one side and she moaned with pain in her sleep.

Marko shook his head. He knew she had somehow broken the ankle and now she might get gangrene from the injury if not set by one of the women in the village very soon. As he started to sit on the bed to rewrap her ankle he heard his grandmother call out in her sleep.

"Mikla, hold still, you must hold still!"

Marko's eyes widened and he stood from the bed, stirring the old Gypsy queen to wakefulness. She looked around, wincing at the pain in her leg. Her eyes settled on Marko.

"Talking in my sleep was I?" the Gypsy queen asked as she lay her head back on the thin pillow that was made up of old clothes and a flour sack.

"You really did it, didn't you?" he asked. "Where is Mikla? Is he with my sister?"

"You leave them be, Marko."

"You cannot do this. You are too old to be making the spell. Look at what it has cost you, old woman. We will have to take that leg off if you do not get better. Sever your link with Mikla now because you will not survive the amputation of your leg with only half your brain working to fight the infection. Let Mikla go so you can heal."

"Would that not be a benefit for the man-child? Would not my death bring you the power you seek among the people, maybe even the Golia?"

"You talk with a feverish mind," Marko said as he calmed and then sat on the edge of the bed once again, lifting her swollen leg to his lap. "You know that no one person has ever controlled the Golia. They walk their own path," he said as he shook his head and examined the damage she had done through her link with Mikla, the large male wolf that was missing from the den and the temple.

"Yes, they do walk their own path. My grandson should take that to heart." She tried to sit up but couldn't. She took several deep breaths and then lay back down. "They also do not take deceit the same way as a human may. They cannot understand what a lie is. What cost comes with betrayal? These things they cannot comprehend unless they have the Jeddah spell cast upon them and then they see." She managed finally to raise her head enough to see Marko's eyes. "They see a great many things, even that which is hidden deep within your mind. They see, they understand, and they react like an animal would—to protect itself and those it loves. Not that much different from ourselves, wouldn't you say, grandson?"

"So you are helping sister find her way back home?" he said as he started wrapping the ankle.

"She will be here," the old woman said as she finally lay back down and closed her eyes. "There are a great many tasks for her to do."

Marko's eyes grew dark as he finished off the wrapping. He gently lay down his grandmother's ankle and then covered her with the blanket. He leaned over and kissed her forehead and then turned for the kitchen.

"I'll make you some bitterroot tea and then we shall await sister's arrival." He turned and looked at the woman lying in the bed in severe pain and then he tossed a match into the woodstove. "I even think Stanus and a few of the other Golia will be interested as well."

"And why is that, man-child?" she said as she started to drift off.

"Because Stanus just discovered you are responsible for Mikla being gone, and possibly even dead. You know Stanus may not like Mikla, but the animal is one of his Golia, and he takes their loss very personally."

As Marko delivered the threat, or warning, he turned to fill the teapot with water from the pump when he thought he heard his grandmother say one last thing. Then he shook his head knowing he must have heard wrong.

He gave the handle a few angry pumps and then stopped and looked back into the bedroom. He tried to think of what she had just said but knew he didn't hear it right.

"None of this will matter in two days?" he said to himself when he realized what the old woman had said in her sleep.

He turned back to the pump and filled the teapot with cold well water.

"What in the hell won't matter in two days?"

DANUBE RIVER DELTA, ONE HUNDRED MILES SOUTH OF PATINAS PASS, ROMANIA

The dark-haired woman lay with her head on Mikla's heaving chest. She heard the whining coming from deep inside the Golia's chest. For the first time in several hours the giant wolf lay still and was not attending to his broken hind ankle. The right rear paw and ankle was swollen to three times its normal size and walking on it the past night and day had only worsened a now critical condition.

Anya Korvesky used her Mossad field training to keep the injury as tight as possible and then releasing the pressure every ten minutes so the ankle could get its necessary blood flow. As it stood she was thinking that Mikla, a Golia she had known all her life, was critically injured and it was only the animal's raw strength that kept it going. If a Golia lost the use of one of its limbs it became a danger to all of its kind—for a Golia that could not climb the steep rocks of the Carpathian Mountains a broken ankle was like a blind man in a gun battle, all of the power was taken from it. The Golia had survived by not allowing humans to see it in its natural element. Discovery would be the death knell of a race of beings that had been living next to civilization since the small mammals known as men crawled from the rocks somewhere in Africa.

Anya eased the boy's head from her lap where he lay sleeping. They had traveled all night and were now just sixty miles from home.

During the daylight hours Anya was picking up vibes from Mikla. Random thoughts of the animal invaded her mind with a clouded picture of what was happening at Patinas Pass. She knew the animals were at once becoming divided, and then again together in a common goal, and Anya could not figure out the confusing picture she was getting. But the one thought she picked up from Mikla was the fact that Stanus, a beast Anya herself had never been close to, was the center of the troubles at home. Her brother, Marko, came and went in these thoughts, but she could not tell what his role was.

Mikla whined while deep in sleep and Anya placed her small hand on the animal and felt its intake of breath. She was tempted to slide her hand up and make the spell connection that came so easily to her kind. The one thing that linked the Jeddah with the Golia was the ability to become as one body and mind on a base level with one of God's greatest creations. Her hand hovered over the white-tipped ears of Mikla. She closed her hand into a fist as she decided that she couldn't afford to link wth the giant animal while it was hurt because it would incapacitate her to the same degree for as long as the link lasted. As she looked out from the stand of trees by the river she knew that losing control now could get her caught and the Golia killed, something she could never allow.

The hypnotic flow of the Danube seemed to calm the beast as it slept. This was the first time since the train that Mikla had rested without waking from the pain of its broken ankle. She decided it was time to wake and start the final run for home. She stood and looked down at the boy and the wolf. She nodded and then moved off to the river.

As she bent over to splash water in her face she thought about the general and the Mossad he ran. She couldn't help but have the feeling that it wasn't she who had betrayed the Israeli cause because she had been involved in something that was larger than the task and the road her grandmother had set her upon nine years earlier. She had not only lied to the Mossad, they had lied to her and knew far more than they should have about things involving the Golia and the cursed treasure wagons taken from the land of Egypt more than three thousand years before. She had many questions for her grandmother that would come after she warned her of Ben-Nevin—the colonel was closing in on her and she feared she was leading him right to the Patinas Pass.

She felt the presence behind her as her thoughts had betrayed her and allowed someone to come upon her without notice. She slowly turned and faced the intruder.

"Identification, please," said a man dressed in the gray and black uniform of the Poliţia, the local law enforcement. The policeman was accompanied by another who sat in the passenger seat of a small, white-painted patrol car parked by the river. Anya had walked right past them without realizing it. She tried to smile but she knew her appearance was a major concern to the policeman.

"I've lost all of my identification," she said trying to disarm the young man with her warm smile.

"Lost, huh?" The officer pulled out his notebook and rummaged through the pages as he searched for something. He stopped and read what it was he had written and then looked at the woman. He looked back to his notepad and then closed the book and fixed Anya with a stern look as his partner joined them at the river's edge. The sun slowly went below the horizon to the west. "You fit the discription of a woman who caused several thousand leus in damage to a train car."

Anya wanted to curse her luck.

"It happened on the Sarajevo limited from Bosnia. Have you recently been to Bosnia-Herzegovina, young lady?"

"No, I travel north. My home is there," she said hoping that their conversation didn't awaken Mikla and her nephew.

"And where is that?" The policeman continued the questioning as his partner moved to the side and then slowly started to get behind Anya.

She knew she was between the proverbial rock and hard place and also knew it would be far better, at least for these two innocent policemen, for her to be taken into custody. The alternative for the two law enforcement officials was not to be contemplated.

"We will have to take you in until we can be sure you are not the woman we seek." The first man held his ground while the second uniformed officer went behind her. Anya was going to allow them to cuff her and take her in because she was out to save the lives of these two innocents who didn't deserve to die for doing their jobs. She swallowed and waited.

Suddenly and without warning Mikla was there. The beast had jumped clear of the stand of trees they were hiding in and landed between Anya and the man in front of her. The action had been so fast and so unexpected that the second officer fell backward toward the flowing Danube. Mikla, his right rear foot and leg holding steady off the ground, bared its six-and-a-half-inch fangs at the men and then dipped its front half as it lowered its large frame closer to the ground. Anya knew Mikla was about to spring.

"No, Mikla!" she called out but it was too late as the beast jumped over the first policeman and then Anya herself and landed in front of the second stunned officer, who was still on his back trying to scramble away from the monstrous scene before him. As Mikla landed on the riverbank Anya heard the giant beast yelp as its injured leg came down hard after the leap. As she watched, Mikla quickly recovered and started limping toward the frightened man. The young policemen tried desperately as did the first to reach his holstered sidearm. Anya could only deal with one man at a time. Again she told Mikla to stop and then she spun and deftly removed the handgun that had just cleared the holster of the policeman that had questioned her. The man's eyes widened at the speed at which he had been disarmed. Anya then reached out and hit the policeman with the edge of her right hand, sending the young man to his knees grasping his throat. Fighting for a breath would incapacitate him for the time she needed to bring Mikla back under control.

She moved quickly as the great Golia forgot all about its own injury and started to slowly walk toward the man on his back. Anya saw the policeman finally clear his weapon from its flapped holster and bring it up.

"No!" she shouted and was raising the pistol before she realized she had been about to shoot an innocent over her stupidity at getting caught before she reached home.

Mikla reacted so fast that the man saw his empty hand before he realized the gun was being held by the animal's long and articulate fingers. The beast had narrowed its yellow eyes and was just holding the pistol in front of the man, who could not fathom what it was he was seeing—a giant wolf with the hands of a man? No, the policeman thought he may as well check out of this nightmare right now. He closed his eyes.

"Mikla, come now, we must leave," Anya called out.

The great Golia, its hind leg and paw still a foot off the ground, turned to face Anya. The yellow eyes narrowed at her. She could see Mikla was having none of it. The wolf again lowered its white-tipped ears and then tossed the weapon into the river. As the beast was preoccupied with trying to decide if it should obey the order it had been given by Anya, the second policeman gained his feet at the same moment the first recovered from the blow to his throat. Both men stumbled, fell, and stumbled again to get back to their small Audi police car. Mikla turned and growled. The Golia jumped once more toward the police car as the two men managed to scramble inside with shouts of fear, joy, and terror all mixed together.

"Let them go, Mikla!" Anya shouted but knew the beast had its hackles up and there would be no calming it. She knew how wonderfully wild the Golia were and how uncontrollable the entire family could be when confronted with danger. The two men would suffer for being at the wrong place at the wrong time.

Her nephew came out of the stand of trees with tears streaming down his face as the boy realized just what it was he was about to witness—the dismembering of two human beings. Anya tossed the pistol she had taken from the first officer toward the riverbank and watched as Mikla covered the thirty feet to the patrol car in one long leap. The animal landed on the hood of the small white Audi, crushing the metal into the engine compartment and sealing the two policemen's fate. As the front tires of the car exploded under the tremendous force of the animal's landing on the car, Anya could hear the terrified screams of the men inside.

"Mikla, leave them alone," she shouted, but the Golia was now frenzied through its pain and confusion at having awakened to find Anya gone and then finding out that two humans had successfully penetrated the animal's perimeter without it being aware of it. That told the Golia it was dying, something the Golia clan had learned as man had, that they, above all animals of the world, knew they would someday die.

Anya tried with all of her ability to link with Mikla but the distance was too great without the use of touch. It was enough to get the animal to spin on the hood of the crushed patrol car in confusion as its thoughts were invaded. It suddenly stopped and then faced Anya and growled knowing it was she that was intruding on its thoughts. Anya swallowed and tried her best to get the beast to respond.

Mikla stopped its agitation momentarily as Anya's thoughts entered its angered mind. The beast shook its head and then turned on Anya once more and this time the roar was something she had never heard in all her time with the Golia. Mikla was close to jumping from the car and killing her. He thought this was a betrayal. She made his mind see the men as they were. She forced the Golia to see that the men were not evil, but just men that meant them no real harm.

Mikla stopped moving in a circle and then jumped free of the hood as the men inside screamed again at the sudden departure of the wolflike creature. Mikla then used the crushed hood of the Audi and its humanlike hands to gain leverage and stood on both hind legs still favoring the broken ankle. Mikla towered over the crushed Audi.

"Mikla, let's go home," she said as calmly as she could and allowed her thoughts to change to the temple buried deep within the mountain. She projected thoughts of Patinas and the pass above it. Mikla seemed to calm with visions of home running through its thoughts.

When it looked as if Mikla had spent the anger and animal savagery it was feeling, the men inside the car made a horrible mistake. The first officer removed a shotgun from its bracket in the center console and when he charged a single round of double-ought buckshot into the chamber Mikla suddenly turned its attention back to the car. This time Anya couldn't control the Golia as it reached out with both hands and took hold of the Audi's bumper, lifting the front end of the car four feet off the ground and sending another wave of screams from the throats of the two policemen. Limping horribly on its broken ankle, Mikla roared again and this time used its massive weight advantage and spun the car up and over onto its top. The Golia roared as it limped back toward the upside-down Audi. Then with one last act of defiance the beast went to all fours and started ramming the smashed vehicle with the shocked and stunned policemen inside. The battering was horrendous as Mikla slammed into the patrol car again and again. Finally at the edge of the Danube the car slid into the river.

Anya saw the great Golia fall to the ground with an earth-moving crash and then lay still. Its energy was spent and it was in a total state of exhaustion. In the river the two policemen were still screaming as the white Audi started its run down the river.

Anya ran to Mikla and knelt beside the animal but before she could place a hand on its neck to soothe it, the right hand of the beast came up and took hold of her wrist, stopping her from making contact. The animal slowly let go and Anya withdrew her hand.

"Thank you. We cannot kill innocents; otherwise what good are we, Mikla? You're not Stanus, nor am I my brother. We are not like them."

"What is wrong with Mikla?" her nephew asked.

Anya stood up and watched as the sun vanished behind the mountains of Sarajevo to the west. She reached out and took her nephew and brought him to her and hugged the boy as she watched Mikla. Then she looked up and watched the police car vanish around the bend in the Danube with the shocked men still inside.

"He wants to go home," she said hugging the boy closer. "He just wants to go home and not die out here in the flatlands."

Mikla raised his head as Anya's thought struck its mind. It whimpered and then lay still for a moment and then just as suddenly it stood, still favoring its leg, which had swollen two times larger than it had been before the confrontation. The beast looked toward the distant mountains and then shook its massive head as it tried to clear it of the residue of thought emanating from Anya. The Golia eased into the Danube and started swimming across.

Anya and Mikla were only twelve hours away from seeing a home she had not laid eyes on in nine years.

EVENT GROUP 747-C 200, 650 MILES OVER THE ATLANTIC OCEAN

The 747-C conversion was broken into four distinct parts. The forward section housed communications, meeting rooms, and a research area. The center section was more of the same with small well-equipped laboratories complete with the latest carbon-dating equipment delivered special to the Group from the Sperry-Rand Corporation, and also a complete world library and hostile computer penetration expert thanks to the presence of Europa in the computer center at the top of the spiral staircase. The third area was for dining and the kitchen module. Complete showers and restrooms were next, followed by the sleeping area that could accommodate well over a hundred people in stacked and curtained private bunks. The bottom cargo area held everything from weapons hidden in the main and stern bulkheads and a complete document forgery section also run by the criminal mastermind Europa.

The soothing drone of the four General Electric engines had hypnotized most of the teams and they slept soundly in their bunks. The Air Force pilots attached to the Group had two full crews to man the giant jumbo jet on its long haul across the Atlantic and then over the boot of Italy to the eastern mountains called Carpathian.

Jack was sitting upstairs on the second deck reading a classified report that Niles had managed to get ahold of for him. They were national security briefing minutes from the White House. Collins sat and wondered as he read the report if the minutes to the national security meetings about the inclusion of Romania into NATO were offered voluntarily by the president or were they absconded by Niles, Pete, and Ma Barker—Europa? Jack was beginning to think the supercomputer was starting to like the criminal life, she was that good at it.

Jack heard someone coming up the spiral staircase to the second deck and he looked up from the small table that lined the communications center. It was Jack's watch in operations and he thought everyone with the exception of the Air Force flight crew was asleep. He lowered the report on the NATO concerns about the inclusion of Romania when he saw it was Alice slowly making her way to him.

"Well, company at last," Jack said as he tossed the highly classified report on the small desk in front of him. "Can't sleep?"

Alice looked around and decided to sit at the computer station. She turned the chair and then smiled at Jack. She said nothing as she studied him.

"You remind me so much of that old bastard, Garrison," she finally said as she looked away for the briefest of moments and then back at Collins. "You have the very same traits."

"Well, I think I'm quite a bit behind the senator in most departments," Jack said, embarrassed that she would compare him to Lee. "I think—"

"He was an ass at times also," Alice said with her smile still in place. "As a matter of fact, Jack, he was a real dick when he wanted to be." Alice batted her eyes at the colonel. "Just like you."

Collins was taken aback by the sweet and innocent Shirley Temple approach used by Alice to get his attention with false flattery. He smiled and wanted to laugh at the innocent way she looked at that very moment.

"Now wait, Alice, I have explained my reasoning to everyone concerned when it comes to my sister's murder. Everyone here knows what's going to happen and I will not drag them into it. I have an expendable asset and source that will be used to find her killer and that's it. None of my friends are going to get involved." He paused and then leaned forward in his chair to make sure Alice saw him and heard his words. "And that goes double for Carl. I have reasons beyond which you cannot imagine. No, I'll do it my way."

Alice reached over and patted Jack's knee and then leaned back in her chair with a sigh and closed her eyes.

"Jack, the one mistake Garrison Lee ever made was never explaining his feelings to anyone, including yours truly, almost until it was too late to do so." She opened her eyes and looked at the man sitting across from her. "It's not that you have not included your friends in your quest, Jack. It's that you haven't explained adequately enough on why." She smiled and held his blue eyes with her own. "You must allow Carl into your world because you made it his world when you arrived. You know after he lost Lisa in Arizona during the Matchstick Event, he would have resigned if you hadn't been in command at the time. You kept him going because no matter what, *you* kept going, even after all of the blood and heartache of your previous commands. The example was set and now you refuse to include the man who most admires you. That means that Lynn was his sister as much as yours. He admires you and looks to you as a big brother, and that, Jack, is all that man has."

Alice had hit him with her revelations about Carl and the blow landed somewhat below the belt. Jack never realized how badly hurt Everett had been at the loss of his fiancée, because even the stoic Jack Collins was engrossed in his sorrowful feelings for himself for being shunned by the Army after Afghanistan. Jack looked at Alice and then leaned over and kissed her on the forehead.

"How in the hell did the senator put up with you all those years?" he asked as he stayed close to her.

"Because he was always afraid I would murder him in his sleep." She batted her eyes once more and then stood up and patted Jack on the shoulder and turned to leave with a yawn. "And don't forget about Sarah, Jack—quit being an idiot about that goddamn Frenchman." She turned and faced Jack just before she arrived at the spiral staircase. "She could never feel the same about any man as she does you. Even if you do what you have to do, she deserves every minute you've got left." She turned away and started down the steps. "Or I just may have to give Lieutenant McIntire ideas about murdering some dumb bastard in his sleep—I mean it worked for me."

Collins watched Alice start slowly back down the staircase to her bunk. Jack smiled at the wit of the woman and how she could weave logic into any scenario.

Jack's thoughts turned inward as he examined the shaky-looking weather report coming from the Adriatic. It seemed the Carpathian region could be in for some serious rainfall. As he examined the swirl of black clouds closing on the resort and its mysterious inhabitants of Patinas, the 747 made a slow turn to the east as it started its run toward the Adriatic Sea and the night-shrouded mountains of Romania to the east.

PALMACHIM AIR FORCE BASE, TEL AVIV, ISRAEL

The air base sat on the coast just south of the capital and away from the prying eyes of the press and the public. The command center housed the Special Operations dispatch and security for the base and at the moment was the new home of Mossad Lieutenant General Addis Shamni. He had been at the base since early morning and now watched as the sun set on the day.

"No word yet, General?" a voice asked from behind the burly ex-army soldier.

"None." The general turned and faced the muscled man in the green T-shirt and desert camouflage pants. "There's been no communication from either agent. Colonel Ben-Nevin, well, he wouldn't contact us, would he? As for Major Sorotzkin." The general shook his head. "Well, she may be just as lost to us as that traitorous bastard Ben-Nevin."

The general paced to the coffee machine and poured another cup and then walked over to the window where he saw the Special Operations team rolling a giant Lockheed C-130 Hercules backward into a secure hangar area. Inside the darkened space waited the specialized equipment used by the strike team of twenty-three Sayeret commandos. The general knew for a fact that the men he was watching work silently inside the well-guarded hangar, ranked behind no organization in the world as far as skill in the art of death.

"I hope your men are patient, Captain." Shamni turned from the window. "It could be a while until we get the go order. Circumstances and timing will dictate when your team will go in."

"Yes, sir, we'll find things to occupy our time," the muscled captain said as he turned for the door. "We're used to waiting."

"The special explosives are secured?"

The bald-headed captain of the most elite fighting men in the world turned before opening the door. "Yes, it's under the watchful eyes of your Mossad agents."

"Do I detect some sort of disdain for my men and their capabilities, Captain?" the general asked with his coffee cup poised halfway to his mouth.

"Not at all, General Shamni, I mean it was your two people that have us sitting here at Palmachim awaiting the chance to invade a friendly country because they went bad on you. Disdain, General? Maybe that's not the proper word here," the captain said but left the rest of the sentence unvoiced as he left the office area.

"Yes, Captain, I can think of a few words myself that far exceed disdain."

The general's anger was directed at Ben-Nevin and not Major Sorotzkin. His thoughts about her were but flashes of worry in his mind. He could only hope the major made it home in one piece

Outside in the hangar a well-guarded fourteen-by-six-foot aluminum box was placed into the secured belly of the C-130 Hercules and lashed down tightly. That task completed, the men looked at the case with trepidation because for the first time since the Yom Kippur War of 1973, a nuclear weapon had been placed aboard an Israeli warplane and it and the Israeli elite commandos, the Sayeret, were ready for their flight to the great north where a legendary tribe of their own people vanished 3,500 years before and had never been seen again.

PATINAS,
CARPATHIAN MOUNTAINS, ROMANIA

Marko Korvesky sat in a large wooden chair near the dying fire as the embers burned down to near nothing. The woman next to him on the floor sat with her arm propped against his leg and watched the last of the flames they vanish. She wore nothing other than the gold earrings and necklace Marko had just given her this evening as a gift—which he was about to take back.

"The sun will be up in a few hours, you must not be seen leaving here." Marko leaned over and kissed the top of the girl's head and then smoothly removed the earrings and gold necklace with the unique inset that the young girl so loved. "And most assuredly not to be seen wearing these." He tossed the relics into the air and then closed his large fist around them. "Go now."

The girl whined and whimpered about having to leave her gifts here in Marko's house, but she did as she was told and slowly dressed as Marko stood and poked at the embers of the dying fire. She waited for the dark-haired Gypsy to say something as she stood by the door with her hands on her hips. Her red dress and blue blouse clashed with everything inside the cluttered house. When she saw Marko just continuing to poke at the fire she puffed out her ample chest in hurt anger and then left.

Marko put down the poker and then opened his left hand to look at the earrings and the necklace. The earrings were nothing unique, except for the fact that they were over three thousand years old. The necklace was a favorite of his and he thought the young girl would be impressed. The Eye of Ra was the same design as his grandmother's gold inlaid cane. The center pupil of the eye was a quarter-inch green stone that Marko had never seen before. But the artwork of the eye itself was something he couldn't get enough of viewing.

He held the Egyptian jewelry in the palm of his hand and then turned away from the fireplace. His eyes widened when he saw the Golia staring at him through his open shutters.

"God be with you my old friend, where have—"

Stanus vanished from the open window in a blur of black-on-black motion.

Marko lowered his head. Had the giant beast seen the artifacts he had removed from the temple? Had he known of the other thefts of the people's heritage? He shook his head but didn't open his hand again. He jammed the necklace and earrings into his red shirt. He looked toward the window once more but saw no sign of Stanus. If the Golia thought it had been lied to about the strange people far below Marko didn't know what Stanus would do. He thought he could eventually get the Golia to stay in the mountain and only come out when it was time to feed on their sheep and goats, but Marko also knew that he may have to do the unthinkable when it came to Stanus. The Golia was just too clever. And the same went for Mikla if the damn animal would ever show back up. Each of the two largest Golia disliked the other immensely. But the love they had for the rest of the beasts was unquestioned.

Stanus flew down the mountain at breakneck speed. The giant wolf was nothing but a black streak that could not be discerned as anything living as it made its way to the castle. If it had been seen as some of the Golia in the past had, the vision would have been spoken of as it were just another ghost that inhabited the Carpathians. Many rumors were started by the mere glimpse of a beast that was never really seen at all, and stories came and went of the unnatural things that roam the highlands of ancient and modern Walachia and Transylvania.

The Golia was on all fours as it neared the stone base of the castle. The back of the foundation was anchored to the rock wall of the mountain by three-foot-thick steel pylons. As Stanus came close to the edge of the castle where the side met the road which led to the villages below, the beast jumped and snagged one of the massive support braces that held the castle's foundation pinned to the mountain. It used its large hand to grasp the steel and allow its momentum to swing it to the next support beam, and then again to the next highest. Finally the giant reached the very highest parapet of the man-made copy of Dracula's Castle. Once braced it reached up and took hold of a facsimile of a steel weather vane that sat atop the parapet and watched the activity far below at the resort. The beast laid its ears back and growled low in its still heaving chest.

Suddenly the morning calm was broken by the thumping of a NATO Black Hawk helicopter as it flew low over the resort below.

Stanus watched the strange machine until it vanished beyond his sight to the right of the castle, which now blocked its view of the NATO encampment twenty miles away. The Golia shook its massive head in anger and then from side to side as the memory of the gold in Marko's hand came into its large brain.

For the second time in as many minutes the dark morning peace was shattered by a sound that woke many of the men and women as they slept far below. Workers who were now spending their last night at the resort heard the sound they had been hearing off and on for the better part of the three years it had taken to build the Edge of the World.

The ear-shattering howl Stanus unleashed from his lungs was a cry of anguish at the possible betrayal of its onetime friend—Marko Korvesky, the Gypsy crown prince and the inheritor of the tribal standard of the Jeddah.

Stanus became more confused, which allowed the beast to revert to an age when the Golia had no masters, a creature that had become a legend over the years that would not die in the Carpathian Mountains and in most of Eastern Europe— the mythical beast called the werewolf.

SARAJEVO, BOSNIA-HERZEGOVINA

As the 747-200 made a slow sweeping turn over the mountains of Bosnia the personnel on board were fully awake and doing their final prep work for the two Event teams. Niles and his people were poring over geological data supplied by Sarah McIntire, who explained to them just how amazing a geological mystery the Carpathians, and in particular the Patinas Pass, really was. There shouldn't be volcanic activity in the area and hadn't been in several thousand years, thus there was no real logical explanation for the hot springs and geysers that are known to exist there.

"Can this anomaly pose a danger to the people of the valleys above and below the pass?" Niles Compton asked, looking strange in his Group-issued khaki work clothes.

"If it poses a threat to them they are either oblivious to the danger or are not concerned. I suspect the latter because you cannot live near that pass or the village it's named for and not know that the mountain you are sitting on is like a bad molar in a mouth full of dead or dormant teeth. There is a connection with the hot springs and the mountain and it cannot be a good one."

"Thank you, Lieutenant. Has the Romanian government released any information about Patinas being seismically active?"

"With the land being privatized they now have a chance to get some geologists up there to see. They may not like what they find."

"Thank you, Lieutenant, you can join your team. If need be we will get you up to Patinas in the next day or so. You just may be the first geologist into the pass."

"Yes, sir," Sarah said, and then nodded at Alice, who sat beside Niles and Captain Everett. Will Mendenhall, fresh from the shower, stepped aside so Sarah could pass in the tight space.

"Lieutenant Mendenhall, you're late to my meeting. Are you pretty much up to speed on the people of the Patinas region and their customs?"

"All I know is that's where Dracula is from," Mendenhall said in all seriousness.

"Not exactly. You've been watching too many movies. Alice, explain to young Mr. Mendenhall the difference between legend and fact."

Mendenhall sat down and then waited as Alice pulled out her notes.

"Prince Vlad Dracul, or Vlad Tepes if you prefer, was born in the south of what used to be known as Walachia, or Transylvania, which encompassed the region from the east and surrounded what is now known as the Carpathian Mountains, the history of which is far more documented than one would believe. And nothing has ever dispelled the rumors that something was wrong in the high mountains of that warring state."

"For instance?" Will inquired, actually getting interested in what Alice was saying.

"For instance, in years 101 thru 102, and 105 to 106, Roman armies under the Emperor Trajan fought a series of military campaigns to subjugate the wealthy Dacian kingdom. By 106, under Trajan they succeeded in subduing the southern and central regions of Dacia but left one area of the very rich kingdom alone—Patinas. One of the most important passes in the entire country and the most experienced Roman commander under Trajan left it unguarded and undefended. No military commander would have left an avenue of attack that glaringly obvious to an enemy force without a garrison being stationed there."

"The Romans, Lieutenant, placed men in any area where they thought an attack could originate, and Patinas was one of those areas." Niles gestured for Alice to continue.

"After the Romans it was the Visigoths and Carpians, and after them Attila the Hun. But the one thing none of these invading and experienced war commanders ever occupied was the Patinas Pass. A Boy Scout could see the pass as an invasion route." Alice lifted her file and then rummaged through it until she found the report she had been looking for.

"What about Dracula?" Will asked with raised brows and a hint of a smile.

"In 1241 thru 1242 during the Mongol invasion of Europe, Transylvania was among the territories devastated by the Golden Horde. A large portion of the population perished, but one thing remained constant: Genghis Khan, the ablest general ever to invade Transylvania, never took the Patinas Pass and there was never anything written in history about the khan to explain why he didn't take and hold it. Something is not right on that mountain. It has remained inaccessible to invading armies since the dawn of written history. From Rome to the Habsburgs, the region was left alone for no apparent reason. Finally, after assisting Vlad the Impaler in his war with the Ottoman Empire and the invading Turkish armies, Prince Vlad," she looked directly at Mendenhall, "or Dracula if you insist, deeded the land as a protected area after the war was finally won. The mountain with no name officially began its protected status. An explanation was never given forth by the prince even until the day he was executed."

Will looked at the large satellite recon photo of the pass and saw that the winding road through the small village disappeared many times underneath massive ledges of rock and earth. He counted a hundred good ambush points for defending troops, and with the harsh terrain surrounding the Patinas Pass he could also see how rumors and legends of dark things roaming the Carpathians came about.

"As we deal with historical truth we must disallow any suggestion of the supernatural to enter the equation. Whatever is up there, and I believe my wolves are, they are not a legend or a myth, but something capable of scaring three of the most brutal men the world had ever seen, the Emperor Trajan, Genghis Khan, and finally, Vlad Dracul. I won't even mention the German army in 1943. All of these men feared something in those mountains. These facts are not in dispute, Will, nor is the fact that historically speaking we have ventured into a world we know nothing of, and there just may be monsters in the rocks. No, Will, no myths, no legends of vampires and werewolves, cold, hard, historical data tell no lies. And this is when we learn that superstition and science can be one and the same."

"I apologize for making light of it, I'm sorry," Mendenhall said when he saw that his banter had brought the academic wrath of Alice down around his ears and she responded as any good schoolteacher would: she backhanded him with fact.

Alice relaxed and then smiled at Will and stood and patted his chest as the meeting slowly came to a close. The 747 had started its descent into Bucharest.

The Event Group had arrived on station to confront the inhabitants of a mountain pass that has frightened the most prolific killers in European history, from Rome to the Waffen SS of the German war machine. As the 747 touched down all thoughts turned to an Event that was as unorthodox as any the department had ever been sent on.

Operation Grimm had officially been activated and the Event Group was now on the clock.

9

The sun had been up for two and a half hours but the resort looked as if it had several thousand guests in attendance as the workers who had toiled hard at their labors were now packed and headed for buses that would take them back to Bucharest, Prague, Ukraine, and other points of the redrawn Eastern European portion of the globe. They would return and struggle through their countries' worsening economies the best they could. Many of these men and women were more than happy to be leaving the wondrous resort they had built far behind them, never to be seen again.

Janos Vajic and general manager Gina Louvinski watched the line of chartered buses as they left the resort. Vajic glanced down at the woman, who had her clipboard clutched to her chest as she watched the last of the buses leave just as the first of the many hundreds of black stretch limousines started up the circular drive.

"This is like the return of Ceauşescu and his thugs," Janos said as he watched the first of the arriving guests. "Please inform our host that the first of the mob has started to arrive." Janos turned and allowed the sliding glass door to open automatically before he stopped and faced Gina with a wry smile on his clean-shaven face. "You can use a different descriptive for his friends if you like."

"I don't know, I think *mob* was a pretty apt description."

Janos pulled a cell phone from his suit pocket and opened it. The reception bars were at zero.

"When are the cell towers supposed to come online?" he asked as he angrily slammed his phone closed.

"Not until next week because of weather concerns."

"Damn, I don't like the idea that the only way we have of reaching for help is our antiquated phone system with weather moving in." Janos thought a moment and then turned to Gina. "Make sure our engineering staff is made aware that we need to keep the phone service up and running."

Janos looked outside and saw that there wasn't a cloud in the sky. He grimaced and had that horrible feeling in his gut that the gorgeous blue of the world would soon give way to darkness.

PATINAS PASS, ROMANIA

Several of the more burly men of her village managed to get the old woman out of bed and after the women had dressed her they had moved her while still ensconced in her large wooden chair out into the grassy square at the heart of Patinas. They propped her broken ankle onto a large cutting of firewood until she was comfortable. The breakfast fires had long been extinguished and the men for the most part had left for the high pastures. Madam Korvesky thanked the men and allowed them to depart for their chores. The women stayed long enough to exchange the morning's gossip about the doings far below, and then they too eventually drifted away in twos and threes and went about their task of making life livable in the pass.

The old Gypsy woman allowed the sun to caress her face as she stared upward into the crystal blue sky. To her the Carpathians were the most misunderstood mountains on the face of the earth, and she knew well that her people had worked hard to make them seem so. But in her opinion these mountains were God's last great masterpiece—beauty hidden amid the stone and steam of the pass.

She lowered her face as she heard the small bell around the neck of the goat at the gates leading to the road chime, and then she heard the goat bleat out a warning. Madam Korvesky turned and watched the goat for a brief moment until the animal went to its knees and continued to chew its cud, relaxing after an initial sound, or smell, had frightened it. She always ordered one of the young goats to be tied at the front and back gates of the village, just as a warning to the men, women, and children that there may be Golia about and to be aware of their thoughts.

"I see the pain medication and the antibiotics I got from that filthy Slav below at the resort have helped you. You survived the night."

She didn't turn to face her grandson but she did turn her face up to the sun once again.

"You sound almost disappointed, Marko."

"You know that isn't so. I want no harm to befall you. After all, you're all I have."

The old woman kept her eyes closed and her face turned to the warmth of the sun. She took a deep breath as the Percocet tablet she had taken earlier seemed to be helping not only herself, but she thought maybe it had also helped Mikla somewhere out on the flatlands.

"You also have your sister, don't forget," she said as Marko had already turned to leave.

"She isn't a part of my life any longer. She left the people to join a world we know nothing of and now she will never be a part of the people again."

"Unlike you, man-child, she did as she was told. She left her home because I said she had to." The queen finally lowered her face from the warming rays of the sun and fixed Marko with a harsh glare. "And she will always be a part of us, make no mistake, my prince," she said and then chuckled at the use of the title.

"If you say so, Grandmamma." He smiled. "Now you take care of that leg."

"You will not be tending your flock today?" she asked as he turned his back on her.

"No, I have other tribal business."

"And what is that?"

"Nothing you need to worry over."

"I believe your queen asked you a question, grandson," she added sternly.

Marko stopped and took a deep breath before he turned to face her with his smile still lining his features above the black beard.

"I and a few others will see for ourselves this new world that has arrived on our doorstep—after all, I am young and must keep up with my sister as far as knowledge of the outside world is concerned."

"I believe you have gained much of that knowledge the past few years, Marko. You have changed, and don't think that I don't know of your courting the evil that has arrived on our mountain."

Marko decided that he no longer needed to respond to her accusations. Soon the people would see that his way into the future was the right way. Not the old way, but the human way. He was their leader and there was no returning to the old ways. No longer would the Jeddah be subject to the laws of the ancients. They would now join the people of the world and they would no longer struggle in the mountains to live, they would reap their reward for three thousand years of exile and finally use that which they have guarded for so long. That was the real sticking point between him, his sister, and grandmother—they all knew the time had come to abandon the old ways, but it was only he who wanted the rewards they deserved.

The sound of the goat's bell sang out as the small animal stood and was looking nervously across the road and into a stand of barren trees and rock.

"The Golia seem to be agitated. They are out of the temple this fine day."

Marko ignored her comment and then turned for the front gate, sidestepping the agitated goat as he did. The small animal kept its sharp eyes on something hiding across the road.

The old woman watched for the longest time just as she knew she was being watched in return. She suspected Stanus was there and he was wary of something. She thought maybe it was worry, or even anger at Mikla for vanishing as he had on her orders. Either way, the giant wolf was acting strangely and that fact alone worried the queen of the Gypsies.

All around the village of Patinas the Golia watched every move made by man, woman, or child. They were starting to feel they had been betrayed by the men and women they had lived with since the time of Abraham and Joseph.

Things had changed in the pass and whatever it was had the Golia on edge like no other time since their arrival in the pass three thousand years before.

OTOPENI INTERNATIONAL AIRPORT,
BUCHAREST, ROMANIA

The Boeing 747-200 taxied into the secure area of the international airport that was home to the Romanian air force and its 90th Tactical Airlift Flotilla. The Americans were using their status as part of the current NATO alliance maneuvers around the eastern Danube. They were a part of that exercise and attached to the group mapping the Patinas Pass. The president had used the awesome weight of the Oval Office to get the clearances.

The white and red 747 was flagged into a large hangar by United States Air Force personnel stationed there to handle American airlift capabilities while the maneuvers were in progress. As the four massive General Electric engines spooled down from their long and arduous journey, the giant hangar door slowly started to slide closed. Outside the hangar the engine noise of the 747 was replaced by the high turbine whine of two U.S. Army Black Hawk helicopters and that noise was soon joined by the start-up sounds of a brand-new Sikorsky Executive S-76C^{++} helicopter borrowed from the State Department and the ambassador to Romania.

The procession down the rolling steps of the aircraft started with Niles Compton replete in khakis and baseball cap. He was followed by Mendenhall, Ryan, and then Alice, who was flanked by the much larger Captain Everett. Then the science teams led by Pete Golding and Charlie Ellenshaw came down the long set of stairs. Finally, Jack and Sarah dressed in casual attire followed. They carried clothing bags for the nights and days they would be at the Edge of the World. Pete Golding and Jason Ryan were also similarly equipped, with the exception of Collins's and Ryan's nine-millimeter sidearms hidden away in their suit carriers.

"Dr. Compton?" asked an Air Force loadmaster and his assistant.

"I'm Compton," Niles said as he reached the base of the stairs.

"Sir, your transportation is right outside for your flight to the Dacian Hot Springs bivouac area. We have a Sikorsky executive craft waiting as requested." This remark elicited a dirty look from Will Mendenhall that was directed at Jason Ryan over his chance inclusion as a passenger on the luxurious helicopter while he had to vibrate to pieces in the Black Hawk.

"Thank you. Is there any further communication from Colonel Guillen of the 82nd Airborne since last night?" Niles asked as he stepped by the two airmen.

"No sir, they are waiting on your team for the reconnoitering of the pass itself. We have a report that the storm we have been monitoring has caused a lot of flooding in low-lying areas along the Danube in the south and west. There's scuttlebutt that the maneuvers and the examination of the Patinas Pass may be canceled. The Romanian army could be called away for emergency relief. I'm afraid we have to rely on them to transport your equipment. They will follow as soon as we can get some of these people in line, just as soon as we can find someone that speaks English."

"Very good, the Air Force is as efficient as ever and my compliments to your team for the weather heads-up." Niles rubbed his chin as he saw their cargo being

removed from the lower compartments of the 747 and was sorry to hear that the
equipment would be out of U.S. hands.

As the Event Group personnel filed by the two watchful airmen, the American Air Force personnel saw the strange makeup of this NATO survey team. The
two men exchanged looks after a smiling Charlie Ellenshaw walked past and gave
the men a horrid open-handed salute and a broad smile until the crazy white-
haired professor was pushed forward by Pete Golding. The last was Jack Collins,
who looked the airmen over. They knew immediately that this man was an
officer—one that looked capable—very capable and that instinctual, self-survival
mechanisms that all private soldiers get when around a man they knew was a real
soldier.

"NATO assayers my ass," the smaller of the two airmen said as the door closed
behind Jack.

The sergeant looked up at the red-liveried 747-200 and shook his head.

"Just who in the hell are these people?"

THE EDGE OF THE WORLD HOTEL AND RESORT CASINO, DACIAN HOT SPRINGS, ROMANIA

At two that afternoon over a thousand of the specially chosen guests of Dmitri
Zallas were wandering through the hotel and the attached casino with mouths
agape. Never had they seen anything like the Edge of the World in all of Eastern
Europe. With the guests still flowing in for the first night of the three-day weekend they were matched by one attendant for every four guests—a major concern
of Janos Vajic. His bottom line was going to bottom out over the losses this party
would generate.

Vajic smiled as best he could as he stood inside the long covered walkway that
connected the hotel proper with the real moneymaker next door—the casino with
the name placed above the entrance in golden letters—the Dacian Room.

Janos stiffened when he saw Zallas approach with one of the five differing
women he had seen him with in just the past two hours.

"I must say your staff is exceedingly efficient. My guests thus far truly believe
they are in a Las Vegas–run facility. And I cannot wait for the grand opening of
the castle tomorrow night. I expect the staff will be as professional there as here."

Vajic nodded his head in acceptance of the compliment but deferred speaking
in front of the Romanian bimbo currently inhabiting the man's personal space.

"The interior minister has not arrived as of yet?" Zallas asked smiling as six
guests walked past dressed in their finery on their way into the casino.

"I have not been informed as such. I suppose he will wait until night has fallen
to make an appearance." Janos looked at Zallas. "That would camouflage his arrival to the press corps that is building up outside the gates. Another matter you
said not to worry about."

Zallas caught the slight toward his other partner in the tangled web of financing for the Edge of the World along with the sniping about the press near the front gate. He only laughed.

"Very good, Janos, very good." He stopped smiling as he leaned toward the Romanian. "Make sure your outstanding wit does not make an appearance in front of the minister. Am I understood? If not, that wit will bury you, quite literally."

Vajic watched the smile return to the bearded face of the Russian as he placed a protective arm around the girl and slowly walked into the casino without a look backward.

"God help me," he muttered.

Around him the excited guests of Dmitri Zallas knew they were in for the most interesting weekend in recent memory. And as fate would have it, they were indeed in for a most interesting and wild weekend.

EIGHTY MILES FROM PATINAS PASS

The man sat and waited for the fax that was incoming from his contact inside the governing body of the state of Israel. The person that was sending the information that he waited on was embedded in the Israeli Security Council and received every bit of sensitive military intelligence that the prime minister was briefed on every morning.

Ben-Nevin was close to the woman and her pet dog and he knew it. It was that very same unusual animal that had him concerned, as he had never seen anything like it in all his experience. The size alone was terrifying and even more worrisome was the way the beast was handled by the girl. Ben-Nevin could not believe the narrow escapes from death he had experienced in just the past two days. For a man who had never had to use a weapon in anger he had almost lost everything before he had a chance to complete his mission.

The small roadside gas station had an eating area where you could force down a cold drink and a sandwich from a machine. The colonel had forgone the plastic-wrapped sandwich stuffed with greasy-looking sausage and settled for a soft drink. He sat waiting for the only fax machine within twenty miles to beep behind the counter where the bored clerk leaned against the service counter looking at a filthy magazine. It had cost the colonel his inexpensive wristwatch and twenty euros for the use of the gas station fax machine, which the clerk was unsure how to use in the first place.

His men were waiting outside in the false light of the evening underneath blinking and burned-out fluorescent lighting. After the train incident his men were jumpy and every time the lights flickered they looked about nervously. Ben-Nevin was smirking at his men as he knew they would feel much more apprehensive if they knew what it was that was traveling with the major. An abomination from a horror movie was walking with the woman and if they had seen what he had on the train he likely would no longer have any men to command.

As soon as his information arrived confirming the woman's destination and the rest of the acquisition element being sent to him by friends of the organization, he would move.

As he sipped the Romanian version of cola through a straw he heard the phone behind the counter ring and then ring again in rapid succession. Ben-Nevin looked up and the burly man nodded his head. He disappeared toward the back of the small office adjacent the counter area.

Ben-Nevin used a napkin to dab at his thin mustache and then he pushed the can and napkin away and stood, careful using his wounded right hand with his missing fingers. By the time he reached the counter the clerk was back holding a sheet of fax paper. He held it out but just far enough out of the colonel's reach that the gesture was clear. The man thought he deserved more money for the fax. Ben-Nevin smiled and then moved his left hand and pulled back his sport coat only slightly, just enough to expose the handle of the Glock nine-millimeter he was carrying. The colonel shook his head.

The clerk froze for the briefest of moments and then he too smiled a toothless grin and handed over the fax. Ben-Nevin took the fax but held the man's eyes long enough that he soon lost the stupid smile and turned away.

The colonel quickly read the fax and smiled.

"I knew you were close, you little witch," he said as he folded the fax and placed it in his coat.

Just as he realized he was only miles away from probably the richest archaeological finds in the history of the world, several sets of headlights pulled into the gas station. The clerk's eyes widened when he saw how many men piled out of the seven cars. The new arrivals stretched and then shook hands with the men who had arrived earlier with the man with the mustache. The clerk turned and looked at the colonel, who was also looking at him. The heavyset attendant swallowed as the colonel raised his right hand. Then he smiled and raised his damaged and bandaged hand to his lips. "Shhh," he said as he turned and left the station.

He walked out and shook hands with the men who had arrived to assist him in recovering what was Israel's and although the men didn't know it, they were also going to help him kill the little witch and her abnormally large dog.

"Gentlemen, I assume our equipment is in the trunks, so let's move out. I want to make camp outside our target area and wait for our lady friend to arrive."

"And where is the target area?" asked one of the bearded men who had just arrived.

Ben-Nevin pointed at the dim outline of the Carpathians in the near distance.

"Up there is where our reward will be found, my friends."

"Does this place have a name?" the same man asked as he opened the rear door for the colonel.

"Yes, the Patinas Pass."

Fifteen miles from Dacian Hot Springs and the NATO encampment, the two Black Hawks flying in formation peeled off from the Sikorsky executive helicopter. Inside the large helicopter Jack Collins felt for the invitation Europa had forged from the sample that had been sent to Jack by Henri Farbeaux, who owed the Group more than he could ever repay for the way they assisted in the Frenchman's escape of American justice two months before. The invitation request was just the start of Jack's plans for Colonel Farbeaux.

Collins smiled as he watched Pete Golding fiddling with his suit. The green tailored garment came complete with a bright gold cravat, and it was this item that made Pete look like an out-of-place version of Hugh Hefner—minus the girls and add on the horn-rimmed glasses.

In the corner seat facing the front of the Sikorsky, Jason Ryan was dozing with his chin resting on his hand. He was dressed like a newly installed but well-to-do young criminal fresh off the boat from Spain. Why Ryan chose that nationality Collins couldn't fathom because as far as he knew Ryan had learned only one language in school and that was English, and at times even that talent was questionable.

Collins shook his head as he realized the newly promoted lieutenant commander could sleep through anything. It had to have been his naval aviation training that allowed the small man to tune out any noise after learning to ignore the jet engines of fighters. He smiled and then looked at Sarah, who was in turn looking at him. Her smile was magic to Jack as he took her in. She was dressed in an expensive Paris-made pantsuit that would be the envy of any woman at the Group if they had seen Sarah wearing it. It was white with a green blouse that just set off her eyes. Her hair, although short, was something Collins could never get enough of touching in more private moments, and it was now that he regretted any doubts that he may have had in regard to Sarah and the Frenchman. That smile she was currently hitting him with answered everything.

"Colonel?" The Air Force pilot's voice came over the speaker on the side of the bulkhead. "Get everyone awake, we're landing at the resort in two minutes."

Jack and Sarah looked out the window on her side and saw the lights of the massive resort complex. The colonel's eyes went past the hotel and up toward the mountaintop and remained there for a few seconds.

"Now that's something you don't see every day," Jason said as he yawned and nodded out the large window. "Halfway up the mountain," he said, pointing.

As they looked up toward the pass the purple and blue spotlights mixed with smaller white ones and enhanced by several blue and purple laser beams played a dance on the stone of Dracula's Castle. The massive structure sat high above the resort and was reached by the giant cable car line reaching upward toward the strangest site any of them have ever seen on the face of a mountain. The castle with its five large parapets and the actual working drawbridge was not the only star of the mountainside attraction; the cable cars that sat motionless were the largest anyone had seen. The whole scene looked as if it had sprung from the pages of an Alistair MacLean novel.

"Think old Vlad the Impaler envisioned this for his legacy?" Sarah asked no one in particular as their helicopter started to settle onto the landing pad where four valets awaited their arrival.

"You know, I'm really starting to think that the bad guys' side pays better," Ryan said as he noticed the richly appointed valets in their bright red jackets and black pants.

"But our side has a more reliable 401(k) and far better dental," Jack said as he unfastened his seat belt and then waited for the rear door to be opened.

"Well, here's your chance to see how those bad guys live, Jason. Who knows, I can see you getting used to this life," Sarah quipped as she released her belt.

Ryan shook his head as the other door opened. "As the colonel just said, we've seen a lot of these jerks retired early and permanently, so, no thanks, I'll take my Navy pay and call it a day."

As the four passengers stepped down from the Sikorsky, the valets emptied the baggage compartment and escorted the team into the hotel. They entered the main lobby and were stunned by the medieval artwork, weapons, and tapestries that lined the interior of the gorgeous property. Suits of armor of varying descriptions stood guard at every entrance and exit. Giant chains held a drawbridge in place that led into the breezeway connecting the hotel to the casino. Every detail was meticulously sculpted, carved, or molded.

"I think you were right the first time, Jason, I could get used to this," Sarah said as she stared in awe at the 180-foot atrium reaching up to the sky—the core of the immaculate design.

"You would think the hotel would be far more crowded," Ryan said as he followed their luggage.

"Yeah, but when you consider that this crowd here is only the friends and business acquaintances of Dmitri Zallas you have to admit it's a decent turnout." Collins also followed Ryan to the front desk with Sarah and an amazed Pete Golding in tow.

"I hope Mendenhall gets a cot next to Doc Ellenshaw, who'll talk his ear off all night and day. That would make this whole wonderful experience complete." He saw the colonel's stare. "For me at least," he added quickly.

After turning over their false passports and forged invitations to the front desk for laser scanning, the four Event Group personnel were escorted to their rooms, all on the sixteenth floor, the highest the hotel offered. Jack had requested the rooms for their excellent view of the castle and the mountain rising above. They all made plans to shower and then meet in an hour in the lobby for a tentative look-see at the property. Sarah wanted to get out to the spa area to take some readings on the hot springs and also take a sample of the mud that boiled up from somewhere beneath the hotel.

Jack opened his door and examined the room before stepping inside. He had warned his team to check their rooms very carefully, as he would not put it past the Russian mobster to bug his guests' rooms. Jack knew the criminal mind and eavesdropping was always a profitable move in most cases.

Collins skipped moving his luggage in until he looked at every wall socket, light socket, and even checked the headboard. On his way to check the window frame he caught sight of the castle above. The lights cast eerily moving shapes and shadows in tints of purple and blues on the giant stone blocks that made up the construction. As he looked on his eyes moved up the road toward the pass. Of course he couldn't see anything but he could imagine the hard life anyone who lived in the pass faced year in and year out. His eyes traveled back to the now empty Castle Dracula as it waited for its grand opening in just two nights.

There was a light knock upon his door. He went to the door and looked through the peephole and saw the top of Sarah's head. He opened the thick door and allowed her to quickly step inside.

Sarah had changed into an evening dress of blue with a low neckline. She smiled and entered his room holding her high heels. She faced Collins and then dropped her shoes onto the expensive carpet.

"Is it against Army regulations for a colonel to zip up a lieutenant's dress?" she asked as she turned around to expose her back and the open zipper.

Jack smiled and relaxed for the first time. He reached out and took Sarah by her shoulders.

"As a matter of fact it most assuredly is against Army regs, Lieutenant, but at the moment I'm a criminal on vacation and am also a sordid and salty character." He slipped his hands under the dress's two straps and pulled them free of her shoulders allowing the dress to slip from her body. He turned Sarah toward him and kissed her.

"Besides, for the next hour the U.S. Army can go—"

"At ease, Colonel," Sarah whispered as she pulled Jack's head down and kissed him—the maneuver successfully quieted her commanding officer and stilled his insults to the Army for at least the immediate future.

And for the next hour Castle Dracula—the nightclub, the Patinas Pass, and Alice Hamilton's Little Red Riding Hood tale along with her Lost Tribes of Israel theory—all were temporarily placed on hold as Jack concentrated solely on the woman he knew he loved in the most desperate of ways.

Marko stood at the front of the hotel and was watching the guests as they milled about laughing and pointing at every piece of exquisite artwork along the walls, on pedestals and easels, all placed around the immense lobby. Most were probably scheming how to steal some of the artwork from the man who had invited them there.

Marko's attire was all black. The shirt he wore was collarless and was buttoned to the top. The black satin vest and even blacker shirt gleamed in the false light of the front portico. The black head scarf was neatly tied in the back just over the foot-long ponytail. The goatee was freshly trimmed and his gold jewelry prominently displayed from his ears to his wrists. His larger Gypsy friends from the other villages were similarly dressed. The six men stood for a moment watching the guests wander the lobby through the twenty-foot-high plate glass windows. The Gypsy men brought many of the guests to a stop as they noticed the strangely dressed group in the exotic and a bit disturbing, peasant clothing.

Marko stepped across the threshold of the hotel he had financed though his theft of his tribe's heritage. It was now time to reap some of the benefits of that shameful act.

Gina Louvinski saw the six men as they entered the lobby. The dark-haired man with the intense look was familiar. She had seen him interact with Zallas from time to time and it seemed to her that this man was not frightened of the Russian one iota. She watched as one of the hotel's manager-on-duty staff approached the men as cautiously as he could and with a distasteful look on his face cleared his throat. Gina shook her head and then started forward to stop the trouble she was about to witness.

"May I help you gentlemen?" the shift manager asked Marko, who stood in front of his men.

The Gypsy looked at the manager irritably. "No, you may not."

"Gentlemen, do you have an invitation in your possession for this weekend's festivities?"

"No," Marko said as he faced the shift manager with a dead sort of smile that faded long before it hit the black-mascara-lined eyes.

"That is all right, these gentlemen don't need invitations—they are acquaintances of Mr. Zallas." Gina turned away from the manager on duty and faced the Gypsy, who only looked at her as if he found her distasteful. His companions though did little to hide their appreciation of the general manager of the Edge of the World Hotel and Resort Casino. "Will you gentlemen be requiring accommodations for your stay?" she asked, praying at the same time they would not be staying overnight, as they were still attracting the strangest and most insulting looks from the real guests of Dmitri Zallas.

"No. Where is the Russian?" Marko asked.

"Mr. Zallas is inside the casino I believe. Would you gentlemen like a draw of chips for play?" She saw the irritated look on the Gypsy's face. "On the house of course."

Marko turned and walked away without another word. His followers did the same, only they smiled at her as they passed and those smiles weren't that friendly. She was glad Zallas had to deal with them and not her.

Outside the moon started its slow climb into the sky, fighting its way above the rocky peaks of the Carpathians.

"Ah, Marko, and accompanied by our friends and neighbors as well! It was so kind of you to join us for our small celebration," Zallas said, breaking away from the roulette table before the band of Gypsies could join him and his guests. He smiled as he took Marko by the elbow and tried to steer him away from the gamblers, who were watching them with much interest, as most had never laid eyes on a Gypsy before this rather unusual intrusion.

Marko froze to one spot and made Zallas look the fool as he embarrassingly pulled on a stone wall that refused to give. The large-framed Gypsy didn't budge. The Russian smiled at the gawking guests and then leaned into Marko.

"What are you doing here?" he asked through clenched teeth and a false smile. "You said you weren't interested in the day-to-day operations of our investment."

"Remove your hand from me," Marko said while staring straight ahead. Zallas did as he was told and then looked around smiling and hoping the guests didn't see the hostility oozing from the dark man standing in the middle of his casino. "I am here to see the end result of that investment."

"Now that you have seen it you must not come here again, and most assuredly not with your friends. There would be too many questions asked inside capital meeting rooms and that would lead to people that have a high stake in the success of this operation. There will be government eyes here tonight that will report all they see here at the Edge of the World, I assure you."

Marko smiled for the first time as he turned and faced the Russian. "More eyes than you would ever dare to imagine, Slav. Sharp eyes that see much in the dark."

Zallas was pretty much fed up with the old Hollywood version of "I'm a scary Gypsy" act and so he stepped up to Marko angrily and began to remind him about the ethnic slur he kept slinging at him.

"I told you not to call me a Slav, I don't—"

"My friends and I shall tour the property and then I think we will eat. Make sure we are seated and well taken care of."

"I am not—"

"You are what I always thought you were, Zallas, and this is why I have come to see my operation." His smile grew as he took in the busy casino. "I mean the fruits of my investment, of course."

The Russian watched as the six men moved off to snickers and outright hostility from the guests. He saw that the Gypsy ignored the looks and whispered remarks, or just didn't hear them or heard them but couldn't understand them.

Five miles to the east of the Edge of the World was the NATO bivouac area. The Romanian army made up the largest contingent at 150 men, just a little over company strength. The U.S. contingent was the second largest with eighty-eight engineers of the elite 82nd Airborne Division. Several other neighboring nations had men attached but for the most part it was an intimate get-to-know-you task that NATO had always loved. The men thus far seemed to enjoy the air and the mountains and not one of them had any doubts as to the falsity of the myths and legends surrounding this absolutely beautiful area of the world. After the deserts of Afghanistan and Iraq, the Carpathians were like the Garden of Eden.

"What did you think of those strange ducks that came in on the Black Hawks?"

His partner laughed as he reached behind him and removed a sharp rock from beneath his butt. He tossed the stone into the darkness.

"Tell me, when doesn't a Black Hawk drop off some strange ducks, including us?"

"Yeah," the man watching said as he removed his Kevlar helmet and then hefted the small M-14 battle rifle and pulled out the magazine from the receiver and looked inside. "This is the one thing I can't get used to since we deployed back to the world," he said shaking his head.

"And what is that?" asked his hole mate as he rummaged to remove more painful rocks under his rear.

"Carrying around blanks instead of hot loads—there's something basically wrong with that."

"Well, we can't go around blasting away at out new allies, can we? Besides, those Romanians to our right over there aren't commies anymore, we served with them in Afghanistan—the boys are fighters."

"Yeah, well good for them, why don't you go ask them if they happen to have any real bullets, smart-ass."

Alice Hamilton pulled the collar of her green coat tightly around her neck as she looked past the soldiers and their equipment and brought the mountains into sharp focus. She couldn't believe she was actually here looking up at them. To her mind's eye the craggy scars of deep-cut rocks and small, time-worn grooves where water had saturated the stone through millions upon millions of years, all still looked beautiful. The scars in the rock reminded Alice of a perpetual covering of white snow and ice that remained year-round.

"Looking at them in the moonlight can almost allow your imagination to truly believe in the legends, can't they?"

Alice turned and saw Carl Everett standing behind her. He was dressed in a down vest and blue denim work shirt. His boots were a worn civilian brand and his pants Levi's.

"It didn't take this view to make a believer out of me, Carl. I've seen these mountains a thousand times in my thoughts while never really knowing it was the Carpathians I was looking at. I could never imagine a more beautiful range." She smiled as she turned back to face the imposing monoliths. "Especially when this old woman claims there be monsters up there," she said in a mockingly ominous tone.

"Ah, you're not old," Carl said hoping Alice took his small joke the right way. She did.

"No, not old, but very much a believer in fairy tales—is that what you're saying, Mr. Everett?" she asked, turning back and smiling at him.

"Yeah, something like that," he said as he stepped up behind Alice and placed his thick arm around her and looked with her at her mountains. She placed her hand onto his and they just stood in silence.

"Uh, excuse me, are you Captain Everett?"

Carl and Alice both turned to see a young staff sergeant standing next to them.

"That's me, Sergeant."

The camouflaged sergeant handed Everett a piece of paper. As Carl reached for it he saw a lot of activity near where the Romanian army had set up for their maneuvers. To his shock it looked like they were packing up.

"What are the Romanians up to?" Everett asked as he clicked on a small flashlight to read the message.

"They're leaving, sir. Because of the storm in the south there's been massive flooding along the Danube and since these boys are engineers they've been ordered out to assist in evacuations if it comes to that."

"What is it?" Alice asked as Carl lowered the note.

"He's right, the Romanians have been ordered to the south and the 82nd has been directed to return to the air base."

"That will leave us with no cover."

"We have to get word to Jack."

"Sir, we've been ordered to leave you with two Humvee transports and twenty men. The rest have to RTB."

"Damn," Everett cursed as his eyes roamed toward the top of the mountain. "With no cell connection we only have the Europa satellite link and even that is spotty because Europa will only be overhead twice a day. I'll get with Will and get a message off to the colonel, by foot if we have to."

Niles Compton walked up at that moment, hurriedly tucking in his shirt. Everett held the message up for him to see. Compton raised his hand.

"I've seen it—any suggestions?"

As they stood there watching, the cover and protection of the United States Army and the soldiers of their new Romanian ally continued to pack up their equipment. Soon several loud engine noises were heard as the large Black Hawks started to spool up. Everett nodded at Alice.

"Niles, we will have a short window in an hour to communicate with Europa, so I suggest we get Mendenhall and have him call Jack on the secure satellite cell and give them the heads-up that we just lost our cover. And be sure to remind everyone that with the weather moving in here this weekend we may even lose the satellite link with Europa."

"Where are you going?" Niles asked when he saw Everett reach for a small satchel and remove something. It was a handgun and he tucked it in his waistband.

"Charlie Ellenshaw and I are going to mosey over toward the resort and see what we can see. If the last of the 82nd is ordered out we won't have one bit of cover remaining. So I think we'll study the lay of the land and how difficult it would be to get past the locals and enter the pass on our own. After all, Alice didn't come all this way to not see her hard work pay off." He smiled and nodded at Niles, then turned and left the breaking camp of NATO soldiers.

As the helicopters continued to spool up their twin engines, Alice turned and watched the mountain high above her knowing her answers were there, in the darkness of Patinas.

THE EDGE OF THE WORLD HOTEL AND RESORT CASINO, DACIAN HOT SPRINGS, ROMANIA

Jack and Sarah walked the spaces between the three sprawling buildings. The hotel, the casino, and the Enviro Dome—which Jack thought was a bit of overkill—were all impressively designed. Sarah had been most interested in the mud baths and the bubbling waters of the open hot springs. She leaned closer to one of the pools of water and touched the surface with her fingers.

"Jack, if this spring is any indication of the size and flow of the natural aqueduct that allows the water to flow this far from its source and still maintain the temperature as it is now, this area may have a serious seismic problem. And I do mean a significant one."

"I'm not following," Jack said as he too touched the extremely hot spring water as it bubbled before him.

"The temperature should have cooled far more than this in its passage from under the ground, or possibly even from as far away as the mountains that look down on this monstrosity. If this water is any indication of the thermal variance in this region we could be looking at a significant seismological event in the very near future."

"In English, short stuff."

"Jack, the ground this resort sits on is seismically active. There is significant thermal power building up from somewhere, and I bet it's closer than these fools think. I suspect it's where Alice's pass is located. The direct line of flow is about right."

"You mean this could all just blow up?" he asked as he looked around at a few of the guests as they admired the plant life that had been collected for the dome. "Come on, really?"

Sarah looked around and saw the bubbling mud and a look came to her face that Jack didn't like.

"I mean, there would have to be some sort of warning, earthquakes and the like, right?"

Sarah looked at Collins with a raised left brow, a habit derived from Jack himself over the years and one that was becoming increasingly irritating.

"I know of a mountain that showed no significant activity for a 123-year sleep. There was almost no warning—no tremors or quakes, just a jump in mean temperature. Eleven days later the seismic activity started and on that day, May 18, 1980, the mountain exploded."

Jack nodded his head in understanding. "Mount St. Helens?"

"Yes, and that mountain also had no significant activity almost until the day it was shattered into a million pieces. We could have the same thing building up here."

"But in Romania? There are no volcanoes in this region."

Sarah smiled at Jack's naïveté. "My dear Colonel, there are over 692 dormant volcanoes in Eastern Europe alone. And remember, Italy, one of the most active regions in the world, is not that far away. Believe me, Jack, this place could blow and wipe this area clean of everything."

Collins looked around the giant and very much gaudy dome structure.

"That may not be so bad," he said as he took Sarah by the elbow and started walking toward the large escalator.

"What do you say we skip the escalator ride and get to bed and start fresh in the morning? You have to collate what you've seen here and I have to start running some names and faces through Europa. Maybe we can start marking some of the antiquities buyers anyway. We can start a file on every one we can get a real name for. It will solve a lot of problems in the future when it's time to bring some of these thieving bastards down or at least to justice."

"You mean we have to sleep in separate rooms tonight?" she asked with a false scowl.

"Knock it off, Lieutenant. You've had your fun for this trip." He smiled and then relaxed. "I'll tell you what, since you took advantage of your colonel earlier tonight, how about something to eat and then a nightcap?"

Sarah made a face at the trade of lovemaking for food and a drink, but she stopped and looked at Jack with her sad eyes.

"You know Alice is right."

"Yeah, short stuff, what's she right about?"

Sarah smiled up at Collins.

"You are a prick sometimes."

"Ouch!"

Jason Ryan had his short black hair combed straight back and was shiny with oil. He was resplendent in his navy blue sport coat with a gold shirt opened at the collar with as many gold chains as his neck could bear. The necklaces and other jewelry had been liberated from some of the finest collections at the Event Group complex. If Ryan underwent close scrutiny—which his training told him he had been receiving since he and Pete arrived inside the casino—his wares would hold up under close examination. The Eye of Ra pendant on his lapel should attract one of the bigger fishes swimming around the casino. As for Pete Golding, Ryan wished he would stop fiddling with his cravat.

"Why do I get the strange clothing?" the computer genius asked as he tugged on the irritating cravat.

Ryan paused by the row of blackjack tables that stretched far into the distance of the casino. He noticed that only a quarter of the tables were occupied with guests. The others had their dealers standing by with hands folded neatly in front awaiting the spoiled guests of Dmitri Zallas. Ryan decided that someone enjoyed throwing money away by overstaffing.

"Look, Pete, the suggested clothing for you came from your own computer system—are you going to stand there and tell me that Europa was wrong about matching your style to what she knows of gangster fashion?"

Pete stopped adjusting the cravat and looked at Ryan. "Europa is never wrong, Mr. Ryan," Pete said and then looked down at his green nylon knit suit with the yellow shirt and even yellower cravat. "But this time she's a little short on being right."

Ryan smiled at Pete's obvious consternation that his Marilyn Monroe–voiced computer had screwed him.

"Can I interest you gentleman in some champagne?" came a voice from behind the two.

When Ryan turned he saw the same woman he had seen when they checked into the hotel. She stood smiling with a clipboard pressed to her chest and a waitress standing to her left. The young Romanian girl held a tray of champagne glasses perfectly balanced with an equally charming smile etched on her face. Through Ryan's experience with almost every sort of woman in the world he could see that neither of the two could stand being in the casino with the current clientele. The taller woman was dressed in a black suit that showed off her long legs. Ryan could not help but stare at her.

With his current state of dress and attire, Ryan didn't realize that his normal charm had to be triple its normal strength to cover for the slicked-back hair and the well-trimmed three-day-old beard. When he saw a small hint of disgust on the dark-haired woman's face he almost went into panic mode and explained that this wasn't really him at all, that he dresses normal, then he realized he couldn't say anything because this woman was more than likely in on whatever deviltry was happening in the well-camouflaged den of thieves.

Pete Golding salvaged the situation by reaching over and removing two glasses from the tray with a smile and a nod of his head to the young waitress. He nudged Ryan until the commander reached for his glass without taking his eyes off the general manager, which her gold-plated tag on her breast pocket announced. The woman became uncomfortable when Ryan's gaze lingered on the nametag a moment longer than was necessary. She adjusted the clipboard to cover her chest area.

"Thank you very much," Pete said as he downed the champagne in one large swallow and then watched the tension develop between the woman and Ryan.

"Do you gentlemen require chips for the table games?" she asked just to see if the small man with the ridiculous gold chains and rings could speak or if his only

verbal skills were grunting and pounding his chest like most of the other Nean-
derthals at the resort.

"Uh, no thank you," Ryan finally managed to say as he handed over the un-
touched champagne to Pete, who switched hands with his empty glass and then
downed Ryan's offering. Jason leaned into Pete. "Why don't you go track that
waitress down and get another, Doc," he whispered conspiratorially to his Don
Knotts attired teammate.

Pete looked up and saw that the woman looked uncomfortable standing and
speaking with what looked like an evil little drug lord. Golding leaned back.

"Perhaps we should be moving along."

Ryan smiled and turned the computer whiz around and shoved him off in the
direction of the young waitress who was serving champagne to several hard-looking
men sitting at a blackjack table smoking large cigars. Ryan took an immediate dislike to the men but pushed them and Golding from his mind as he turned to face
the general manager once more.

"Now where were we?" he asked with his most charming "I'm only a little ole
naval aviator" look on his face. The sad puppy dog eyes were the kicker.

"You were about to go and join your friend—it seems he may have been a little
jealous of your attention toward me." She smiled and winked and then turned and
walked away.

Ryan took a moment to reflect on her comment and then it hit him right between the eyes. He realized as he turned and closely examined the way Doc Golding was standing with a glass of champagne halfway to his mouth and the way he
was crooking his arm as he did so. Ryan's eyes widened when he realized the
general manager of the resort, one of the best-looking women he had laid eyes on
in quite a while, thought he was gay and that he and Pete Golding were together
for the weekend. Ryan didn't know if he should run to his room at that moment
and kill himself or blow his cover immediately and confess his righteousness to
the woman and hope for the best. If it had been a man assuming he was gay, that
would have been fine with Ryan because he had nothing against that lifestyle except thinking that the lifestyle was flawed because it excluded the most important
assets in the known world—women.

"Hey, hey, whoa there," he said as he chased after Gina Louvinski to explain
how his being gay was a flat-out scientific impossibility. Ryan quickly caught up
with the general manager, who was busy perusing the casino floor.

"Hi again," he said when he caught her. Gina rolled her eyes but kept the smile
in place for as long as she could bear it. "I think you may have the wrong impression of me," he said as he stopped in front of her and stepped from one foot to the
other as he tried to keep her attention. She looked at his chains and his open collar
and nodded her head. "Uh, I'm not gay in any shape, form, or fashion," he said
with a smile that only elicited a raised brow from Gina. "Really. Not that there's
anything wrong with that."

"Mr.—?"

"Ryan, name's Ryan," he said like a schoolboy telling the hall monitor his name.

She made a show of looking on her extensive guest list and as she did Ryan realized he had really chased this woman down to explain to her, not that he wasn't gay, but that he wasn't like these other men. He would rather be gay than have her think he was one of the bad guys.

"Mr. Ryan, you don't seem to be on my guest list," she said as she ran her mani-cured nail down the list, checking once again. "You are American?" she asked when she looked up into Ryan's smiling face.

"Oh," Ryan said as he felt the color drain from his face. "Uh." He nodded his head toward Pete, who was speaking with the young waitress who looked to be explaining the game of blackjack to the computer expert. "My assistant is so used to me traveling using a false name that I forget sometimes not to use it."

"So, what is your real name?" she asked while out of the corner of her eye she saw trouble brewing. The young waitress this man's companion was speaking to was being touched and prodded by the men at the blackjack table. Pete Golding looked uncomfortable as he raised a finger and wagged it at the two Polish and two Romanian thugs as if he were a teacher admonishing a bad student. Ryan didn't catch the eye movement or realize the Doc was in over his head.

"Uh, Mendenhall," Ryan said as he forgot the cover name he had been issued as this woman's eyes erased all pertinent information from his frontal lobe.

Without looking for the name the woman allowed her full attention to travel to the table where Pete was standing and the young waitress was dodging the probing hands of two of the men.

"Thank you, Mr. Mendenhall . . . would you excuse me?" she said and then turned and left Jason standing and wondering how he had lost his magical charm with women on the flight over here. He shook his head as he watched the woman move with purpose toward the gaming tables.

"Gentlemen, our waitresses are quite busy and cannot linger with one table too long," Gina said to the thugs groping the young girl.

The man closest to the girl smiled and ran a hand up the girl's thigh, forcing her to balance her tray of glasses while trying to avoid the touch. Pete saw panic in her eyes. He stepped forward and slapped the man's hands away. That caught everyone's attention from several tables around. Across the aisle Jason rolled his eyes and knew there was trouble right here in River City.

"That's not acceptable, mister," Pete said as he straightened up and realized what he had just done as the large man in the black clothing stood up from his chair at the table. The burly brute stepped into the girl, brushing her aside and confronted Pete.

It seemed time was standing still for Golding as the bearded man took him by the cravat he hated. The resort's general manager braved getting between the two guests. When she did the other three men stood and started forward. The larger brute let go of Pete and then reached out and pulled the clipboard from Gina's hands and ostentatiously dropped it to the carpeted floor. His smile widened as he reached out and roughly handled her left breast just under the black suit jacket she wore.

Pete's eyes widened in shock at the way these men were acting. He had never been witness to anything so blatantly boorish. Pete slapped at the man's hand again, and in response the man took Golding by the throat and started pushing him backward.

Gina Louvinski panicked and wanted to call for her security but all she saw around the casino were Zallas's men, who not only weren't moving toward the ruckus but were watching with humorous curiosity. Knowing she was on her own, Gina reached out and took the man's large hand and tried to force it from Pete's throat. A second man came around and wrapped his thick arms around the general manager and lifted her away.

The next thing the woman knew was the sensation of falling, which came on her so fast that she thought she had blanked out momentarily. She hit the floor and then saw the second man's large frame, the thug who had wrapped his arms around her waist and lifted her off the floor, come crashing down beside her.

Ryan moved far faster than he had ever moved before. Seeing Doc being assaulted and the woman grabbed was far more than Ryan's mind could grasp at one time. The end result was that Jason Ryan reacted as he was taught by the colonel. The next move was to bring his hand up and into the thick wrist bone of the man holding Pete by the throat. The bent knuckles came up and smashed into the wrist of the mobster, separating the two halves of the bone. The man screamed in pain and shock and Golding slid to the floor gasping for air.

Gina tried to stand as she saw the two remaining men from the table charge toward the man she thought was called Mendenhall. She grimaced as she saw the small dark-haired man take a stance and as he did the brute whose wrist he had just shattered went to his knees holding his arm. Ryan kicked out with his new Gucci shoes and caught the mobster on the chin, sending him backward into one of the men coming to his rescue, knocking him over the blackjack table. Ryan readied himself for the fourth mobster to make his opening bid so Jason made ready to defend himself. His eyes widened though when the man pulled out a gun and brought it up toward the small naval aviator.

"Oh, shit," Ryan said. "There always has to be one pussy in the crowd that brings a gun." He waited for the bullet that would end his small adventure in the Carpathian Mountains.

Before the shot was fired, several men dressed in black suits swarmed the man with the gun and his three companions. One of the guards lifted the injured thug with the broken wrist to his feet and unceremoniously pushed him back.

"Gentlemen, gentlemen, this is only our first night together and we have this breaking out in the first few hours?" Dmitri Zallas said as he approached the gaming area with many of his security men in tow. Janos Vajic was with him and he hurriedly went to Gina and helped her to her feet. Zallas looked at Ryan for the longest time, even tilting his big head so he could get a better look at the man he didn't recognize. Then the Russian host looked over at the injured man, who was holding his shattered wrist and glaring at Ryan. "Leno Kurkovich, I should have known," Zallas said as he reached out and helped the man lean against the blackjack table. "This may be appropriate behavior in Krakow my friend, but we expect a little more restraint here at the Edge of the World." He leaned in close so the Polish mobster could see his face. "Misbehave again, my friend, and you and your companions will be living at this magnificent resort permanently—am I understood?"

The large Polish mobster only glared at the much smaller Ryan as the Navy man finally relaxed. Jason Ryan, USN, reverted to his aviator spirit and his natural way of looking at things—he winked at the killer, whose eyes suddenly widened. The man started forward but was stopped by Zallas.

"Enough!" Zallas said as he gestured for his security men to remove the four troublemakers. "See to it our friend here makes it to the infirmary." Zallas patted the injured man on the back. "We have an exceptional medical staff and we'll get you fixed up in time for the gala grand opening of Castle Dracula." His head tilted to the left and his men removed the four from the casino.

Ryan stooped down and helped a stunned Pete Golding to his feet while at the same time retrieving Gina's ever-present clipboard.

"Damn, Doc, you've been hanging out with crazy Charlie Ellenshaw too much for your own good—his and your confrontational attitudes are out of control." He slapped Pete on the back. "Just like your overwhelming sense of justice."

"Thanks, Mr. Ryan," Pete said as he pulled the wrinkled and damaged cravat from around his neck. "I thought that monster was going to rip my head from my shoulders."

"I think that was the object lesson he was trying to impart to you, Doc."

"Gentlemen, I don't know what to say," Gina said as she retrieved her clipboard from Ryan's hand. "But thank you."

"Yes, I must say I have never seen our friend Mr. Kurkovich subdued with such reckless abandon," Zallas said as he stepped up to Ryan and Golding. "And with such skill." The Russian looked from Ryan to the still shaken Golding. "Both of you, exceptional indeed."

Ryan didn't say anything as he turned to face the host of this freak show. Their eyes met and Ryan knew this man was used to getting what he wanted.

"If we had our own security teams in place—" Janos began.

"If we had your security in place our two heroes here would now be dead and bleeding all over my new carpet." He turned and faced Janos Vajic after cutting him off. "And we can't have that can we, Janos?"

Vajic gave Zallas a weary look and then placed his arm around the young waitress and his general manager and started to steer them toward the breezeway that led into the hotel. "No, we cannot."

Ryan watched the exchange and determined that the balding partner and his manager, Gina, were not too fond of the Russian.

The woman turned around as she was led away and caught the attention of Ryan, who was watching her leave. She mouthed the words *"Thank you."* Then Ryan mouthed the words, *"I'm not gay."*

Gina smiled as she was led away.

Zallas watched Ryan for the longest moment and then he too smiled: this small man wasn't an associate of his or anyone else's that was invited.

"Now, what can I do for two such exceptional gentlemen? I am deep in your debt. Especially since I don't know either of you, and since this is my party I feel slighted somehow."

Ryan looked over at Pete, who snagged another glass of champagne from a passing waitress to soothe his aching throat muscles, what was left of them anyway.

"Name is Jason Crubble." He winced as he said his cover name. "My friend is Pete Postlewaite, and we're here because we received an invitation." He made a show of reaching into his coat pocket for the gilded and very much Europa-forged invite, but Zallas stayed his hand.

"That is not necessary, Mr. Crubble, not at all. If you're here that means you were meant to share in this monumental achievement." Zallas smiled as two gorgeous women came up and placed their arms around his waist, one on each side, and then they both eyed Jason appreciatively. "I am deeply in your debt, sirs, if you need anything." He looked slightly to his left and then right at the two beautiful women at his side. "And I mean anything at all, you gentlemen have but to ask. I treat heroes with much respect." He smiled as his eyes took in Pete Golding as he finished off another glass of champagne. "And from what I have seen, no ordinary heroes."

As Zallas walked away he kept his eyes on the small Navy man and Jason knew they had blown their covers because of his stupidity and womanizing. Ryan saw one of the two women lag behind with a nodding glance from Dmitri Zallas as he did so. She stepped up to Ryan and took his arm and pursed her bright red lips. Ryan shook his head and removed her hand. He gestured toward Pete by tilting his head in the direction of the hotel, indicating it was time to leave. And then Ryan faced the woman Zallas had left for his enjoyment, but compared to the Romanian GM who had just been led away from the casino, this blonde would never be comparable to the dark-haired beauty.

"No thanks, beautiful, I'm gay."

Dmitri Zallas saw that the small man had spurned his chance for an easy partnership in his room with the young female offered to him. He watched the two Americans leave and then he gestured for one of his bodyguards to join him.

"Yes, Mr. Zallas?"

"I want the interior minister to check out these two Americans and any other Western men and women I don't recognize. I want complete workups on those two and any others I don't recall having met before."

"You suspect they are not here as your friends?" asked the big man.

Zallas laughed. "I have very few friends here." He gestured at the roaming guests of the casino. "These are all business opportunities. But these two Americans, no, not friends, I suspect they are something much more."

"Police?" the man asked. "Interpol?"

"Perhaps," Zallas said, watching the two American men vanish into the breeze-way. "Whoever they are, those two and anyone they converse with bear watching."

Anya couldn't move another step. She was carrying her nephew in both arms and had stumbled with the sleeping boy ten times in the past hour. She finally had to stop and rest.

It was a full five minutes later that Mikla came limping into their resting place. The giant wolf flopped to the ground, its massive chest heaving in and out in exhaustion. Anya reached out and felt the very tip of Mikla's nose. It was warm and dry and that worried her. The Golia was feverish and there was nothing she could do until they reached home. She leaned back and was startled when she heard noise coming from in front of her. She raised her head up and scanned the darkness. She saw blazing lights in the distance and wondered just how far off course she was. She knew of no lights that bright within 150 miles of Patinas. She shook her head angrily as she realized they must be lost.

She lay down and placed a hand on Mikla. The wolf must have been desperately ill to get so lost on his way home. That was something Mikla was good at, finding his way anywhere he was sent and returning without fail—with the exception of their predicament at the moment.

Anya was so exhausted she couldn't help it and closed her eyes thinking she would get just a couple of minutes of downtime. She went to sleep and for the next eight hours never realized that her home was only one mile distant and the lights she was seeing was the resort at the Edge of the World.

She had made it back home after nine long years, but for now she was too tired to care.

The six men sat at a large table in the very elegantly designed Roman Spring restaurant. The waitstaff was wondering just how many bottles of the $900 1995 Lafite Rothschild the strangely dressed men could drink. As it stood, the food and beverage manager had ordered a case out of San Francisco and another from a warehouse in France, so altogether the restaurant had eight bottles of the elite wine and six of them sat empty in front of the men. They had also dined on oysters, steaks, and a dozen other expensive entrées, most of which were picked up by the wait staff without so much as having been nibbled upon. They seemed to be content with Dmitri Zallas's expensive and personal Lafite Rothschild. The large man with the silver-embroidered head scarf raised a hand for the waitress and indicated that they wanted another bottle of the expensive wine.

Marko watched as the staff started buzzing around knowing that Zallas had to be informed of the wine usage of his personal stock. The dark-haired man smirked because he knew the wine was a favorite of the man he had set up in business.

The wine steward arrived and opened the wine for the men but one of them removed the bottle from the steward's hands after it was uncorked. Without waiting for it to breathe the large Gypsy started to sloppily pour the wine into their glasses.

Marko's eyes were drawn to a couple who was being seated in the nearly empty Roman Spring restaurant. The man looked to be a little over six feet in height, which made the beautiful woman in the blue evening dress stand out that much more because of her small stature. His dark eyes watched as the man held out a chair for his more petite companion. His eyes studied the couple as they accepted their menus and listened to what the restaurant had to offer.

One of Marko's companions held another glass of wine out for the prince of princes but immediately saw that Marko wasn't there, at least in the mental sense. The men around the table knew the look. He was probing someone close by. Each man in turn quieted and placed his glass on the table. Each turned and looked in the direction of the two who had just been seated.

"Are you feeling something?" one of the men asked as he looked at the small woman across the way and was impressed by what he saw.

After a minute Marko blinked and then tried to focus once more on the man and at that exact moment the object of his concentrated thoughts looked up and the two men's eyes met for the first time, and then the feeling slammed into the front of Marko's brain like a sledgehammer. His eyes widened as the man's secret opened up for Marko and for the first time in his life he was stunned at the feelings that came from someone he connected with. The man's penetrating blue eyes met Marko's brown ones and it was as if both men had an insight into the other. The stranger with the blue eyes raised a brow and then looked away. Marko did not, as his eyes were still wide. He was slowly feeling a knot grow in the pit of his stomach.

"Marko, you look as if you have seen Moses himself, what is it?" asked the man next to him, who removed the glass of wine from in front of Marko's shaking hands.

"Let us leave this place," was all Marko said as his eyes went from the man to the smiling woman. He watched her lightly touch the man's hand from across the table and then saw her pull her hand away after initial contact as if it were forbidden somehow for the two to come into physical contact. "Go and I will meet you outside." He looked at his men. "Go, brothers, I will join you soon."

The men did as they were told and stood to leave without looking back at the man and woman who had frightened Marko—a man they had never seen shy away from trouble of any kind, and since they were witnessing this behavior for the first time they were unnerved by it. They started to move off toward the exit much to the relief of the waitstaff and the wine stewards, who couldn't fathom how to begin explaining the missing wine to Zallas.

Marko sat alone at the table as his men filed out of the restaurant. The man and woman watched the Gypsy men exit.

As his men left as ordered, Marko continued to study the couple. The couple's eyes never left each other, but he knew they were aware of everything happening around them. These two were not the same kind of people he had felt around him for most of the evening. The man and woman weren't like Zallas and the other guests.

As Marko watched, his eyebrows rose as he caught a fleeting glimpse inside the man's head that never ceased its locomotion-like activity—he could tell the stranger was not used to any inactive periods in his life. He was a hard man used to action. Marko tilted his head and concentrated on his company. Once he fought his way through her feelings for the man in front of her, he began to get a clear picture of the beautiful woman in the blue dress. Marko smiled when he realized this young lady was nothing but a teacher or some similar profession. He kept getting the impression of stones, diamonds, gold, ordinary rocks—and natural hot springs. Marko's eyes widened again. This woman was here to study his lands—his mountain. Once that thought was clear he closed his eyes again and pushed his mind out toward the couple.

Marko again came awake and then stood and strode with confidence toward the man and woman. He stood next to the man and waited to be acknowledged. The dark-haired gentleman patted his mouth with a napkin and slowly sipped from his glass of water. He was intentionally waiting to look up at the man who had approached them.

"I was wondering if you were going to stare all night or come over and let us know what was on your mind," Jack Collins said as he finally fixed Marko with his eyes. Sarah took a drink of her wine and waited.

"You must excuse me for staring, I am a local of this area and I was just wondering why you are here," Marko asked with nothing more threatening than a dip of his head in acknowledgment to the woman, who nodded in a bored response.

"Well, we're here to enjoy this new resort and to celebrate that fact with our host," Jack offered, knowing that somehow this man knew he was lying. The smile remained above the well-trimmed goatee.

"American?" Marko asked as his eyes roamed over Sarah's low-cut dress.

"Yes, we're American," Jack said. "And you're Romanian, a Gypsy I would say."

"Yes, it's amazing how tourists to our lovely mountains expect the colors and the silk and the sitting around our campfires telling fortunes and stories of vampires, witches, and—"

"Werewolves?" Sarah asked. She saw the curious look on the Gypsy's face. "Can't forget the werewolves, I mean this is the Carpathian Mountains, right, vampires and werewolves and all that horror movie stuff?"

Marko's smile broadened as he looked down upon the American woman and then turned and looked at Jack. "Yes, we Gypsies are a rather quaint people. We mix well with the farmers and the sheep men that live here." He leaned over and looked from Jack to Sarah. "And we all like to keep the old folklore alive and well." The man smiled broadly and then spoke in a conspiratorial tone. "But I'll be honest with you, there really are no vampires around here. Vlad the Impaler came from the west of our mountains."

"That covers vampires, but what about . . . other legends?" Sarah persisted. She looked at Jack and he nodded his head only slightly.

"That's all they are, myths, legends, and people who have nothing better to do after the day's chores than sit around a fire and tell stories to frighten children and entertain the few tourists that actually make it up the mountain."

"I didn't mean to be insulting to your way of life. I find your heritage fascinating."

Marko looked at Sarah once more and then bowed. "Yes, Universal Studios and the rest of Hollywood has made quite a bit of money telling the world what they know of the Gypsy." He became serious at that moment and his gaze turned on Collins. "And I will say this: the world knows nothing of us." He switched his look toward Sarah and he placed both of his large hands on the table. "Nothing."

He straightened and then fixed the two Americans with his dazzling smile, which highlighted his whole amazing outfit of reds, blacks, silvers, and blues. The gold he was wearing was exquisite and did nothing to make Jack and Sarah any less confident that this was their man.

"I hope I see you again before the weekend is over. If you get out and travel the roads ask for me, and you will be allowed anywhere that the regular tourists are not. I will be happy to show you the true Gypsy life. Perhaps you can join us tomorrow inside the pass?"

"Thank you. But if I may ask, why would we be accorded such a privilege?" Jack asked with his own small smile. He slowly lifted his glass of water and drank.

"Because I know you are not here to visit Zallas or be with the fools he has invited. You are here for another purpose," he half bowed, "and that purpose shall remain yours and yours alone," he straightened, "but if you need help, please ask anyone on the mountain about me, they will get word to me that you want to . . . talk." Marko felt good letting them know that he was no fool. "Just ask for—"

"Marko Korvesky?" Jack said, throwing the Gypsy his own American-style curveball. He saw the smile falter a bit on the Gypsy's face. He recovered quickly and to his credit the large man held his questions for now.

"Yes, how intriguing that you already know of me and my family."

"Anyone who visits an area where they have never been would be wise to find out who is really in charge. And at the moment there are two powers in the area. Zallas, who controls everything from the castle to the resort, and the family Korvesky, the queen mother and her two grandchildren, Marko and Anya, who control the pass and everything related to the mountain."

"I am indeed impressed, Mr. . . ."

Jack was taking a risk showing his cards like this but they had been presented with an opportunity and he knew he had to chance it. The prince of the Gypsies seemed intrigued that they knew so much. Collins also knew that Korvesky would want to keep him and Sarah close until he knew what motivated the two Americans.

"That doesn't matter, just call me, Jack. This is Sarah."

Marko bowed and then looked at both. "I must learn how my family has become so popular outside Patinas. And for you to know of my sister, that is truly vexing. You must visit Patinas and allow my people to show you the hospitality of not only the Gypsy family Korvesky, but of our friends and neighbors as well. Tomorrow afternoon and into the evening we will be celebrating. I would be pleased to see you there." He leaned over and lightly touched Sarah on the arm. "I insist, as I wouldn't want to have to come looking for you."

"We would love to accept," Sarah said. "May I ask if we can bring some acquaintances?"

"Please, bring anyone you wish. It will be a real experience in the Carpathians." He gestured around him with distaste. "Not this."

"I think that would be a fine idea. We're here to map the pass for NATO. I'm sure you've seen the soldiers around?" Jack said.

"I do not understand the ways of the military world, Jack," saying the name as if he had just eaten a rotten piece of fruit. "But if it's information on the pass you seek, my grandmamma will be happy to answer any question you may have. She's what we would call a student of Patinas history."

"We look forward to it, tomorrow afternoon then?"

Marko bowed and left the table without another word. The waitstaff saw him coming and they parted like the Red Sea when they saw the look crossing his dark features. His eyes were aglow with what could only be described as pure fury.

"Well, I didn't expect that," Sarah said as she took a drink of wine.

Jack was watching the retreating form of Marko Korvesky. The man looked quite a bit more impressive than he did in his dossier photo.

"I'm sure he didn't either." He looked over at Sarah and tossed his napkin on the table and stood. He shoveled out a hundred-dollar bill for the waitstaff and then assisted Sarah to her feet.

"Okay, I know that look, Colonel, what are you thinking?"

"I'm thinking that when he was sitting at his table I was feeling like I was being spied on from inside my own head." He looked up as he waited for Sarah to step away from the table. "And don't ask because I don't know. I've never had that feeling before in my life." He took her by the arm and started to leave. "It's like he was draining information from me."

"Such as?"

"He now knows the faces of everyone on our team and suddenly he asks that we all come up to see the pass."

"Maybe I shouldn't have brought Niles and his team into the conversation."

As they walked he thought. He stopped and looked at Sarah as they waited for the elevator.

"He's dangerous, but in what way I just don't know yet."

"What do we do?"

"We have to allow Niles's team to do their jobs and we still have to accomplish what we set out to do. Our mission here is to track the artifacts and make a connection to the history Alice has put together." Jack pursed his lips in thought. "No, we stay and they go. We need to stick close to Zallas."

"Damn it!" Sarah said as the elevator doors slid open.

"What?" Jack asked.

"We get stuck here with gangsters and the lowlife scum of the earth, and Niles and his team get to spend time with a legendary people, and possibly even more legendary creatures."

"Yeah, they get all of the fun. Get in the elevator, shorty, before I do let you go dance with the wolves. And speaking of wolves I hope Ryan and Pete stayed out of trouble."

"It's Ryan, what could possibly go wrong?" Sarah said with a smirk.

Ryan was in his room and he had just stepped out of the shower after having been driven crazy by the oil in his hair and the scratchiness of his three-day-old trimmed beard.

As he toweled off, Ryan slid into one of the fanciest complimentary robes he had ever seen just as a knock sounded on his door. Ryan walked over and looked through the peephole and saw a nervous-looking Pete Golding trying to peer into Ryan's room through the same peephole. Jason let out a deep breath and then opened the door. The computer genius was still dressed in his green Don Knotts suit and looked distressed.

"Hey, Doc, what's up?" Ryan asked as he finished drying off his hair and then half turned and tossed the damp towel on a chair.

Golding danced from foot to foot and then looked up and down the hallway; Jason caught the meaning and then stepped aside for Golding to enter.

Golding stopped just inside the door and wrung his hands together. He turned to face Jason, who stood by the door with his eyebrows raised.

"Look, I know I'm not the physical man that you and the colonel, Will, and Carl are, I know that. And I just want to apologize for getting us into that trouble downstairs. I could have blown everything."

Ryan shook his head. "Look, Doc, you did what any one of us would have done. Treating someone who's just trying to do her job like she's a piece of furniture or someone's personal touch toy, well, I think you did what we in the Security Department would have done, only you did it without thinking. That's rare and it shows that you're starting to get field instincts." Ryan hoped the speech helped the doc, even though none of it was true. He took Pete by the arm and steered him back to the door. "Look, I know this is only your, what, third time in the field away from your mistress Europa? I think you're becoming a real asset, Doc, I really do."

"You really think so?" Pete asked, beaming.

"I never say things I don't mean."

Pete smiled and then stopped before the door, making Ryan run into him.

"Would you mention this to Professor Ellenshaw? He thinks he's the only one outside of the Security Department that's worthy of field operations."

Ryan laughed and looked at the professor and winked, leaning close as if to pass a secret. "Here's a little inside intel, Doc, for your ears alone. The colonel said that he would rather have you on loan from the computer center than ten Marines, because you think out of the box. And if he would rather have you than ten Marines, Doc, where does that leave crazy Charlie? Eatin' your dust, that's where."

"Ohhh," was all Pete could say.

Ryan patted him on the back to get him moving back toward the door.

"And Pete?"

"Yes, Commander?"

"Take that suit off and get back to your white shirt and black tie, it's more you."

"Oh, I see," Pete said as he started to unbutton his shirt.

"In your room, Doc." Jason managed to get the door open and then Pete started to step out rebuttoning his green shirt when he suddenly stopped. Ryan made a face and slowly glanced around Pete's shoulder and his heart sank into his lower abdomen.

Gina Louvinski stood at the door with her eyes neutral as she watched Pete suddenly lower his hands from his shirt buttons and then step back against the open door. As for Ryan he was frozen in what he thought was the most compromising position he had ever been nailed in, and that was including last month when he had been forced to dress as a candy striper to escape a Las Vegas hospital.

"Oh, excuse me, I . . . I . . . I just wanted to say," the dark-haired Romanian placed a hand over her mouth and averted her eyes, "I am so, so, sorry to have—"

"Doc, go to your room . . . now," Ryan said, recovering.

Pete squeezed past the stunned resort manager and went to his room.

"As I said, I am so sorry for disturbing your . . . your . . . I am just sorry. I wanted to thank you personally for what you did downstairs. I assure you if our own security were on the premises this kind of behavior would not be tolerated. You and your . . ." Gina looked lost for the right word and Ryan flinched when she finally found it, "Your friend."

Ryan pulled the woman into his room and closed the door, shocking her.

"Look, the doc is my friend, but it ends there," Ryan said.

The general manager of the Edge of the World looked Ryan over as he spoke. She noticed he was minus the oil in his hair, and the gold chains and jewelry were noticeably absent. And as she looked toward the dresser drawers she saw regular clothing neatly folded and not one was a garment of the garish variety. She looked at Ryan and suspected something was way wrong with her initial assumption about the small dark-haired man.

"Hell, I don't even know how to explain this."

The woman could tell he wanted to say something but then thought what was the use? She watched him take a deep breath and then a look of resignation came over his features.

"Oh, what the hell? Whatever you think I am, I probably am. Right now I'm too tired and my hand hurts too much to care." Ryan reached out and opened the door.

Gina reached out and closed the door and then looked Ryan over.

"Are all Americans as strange as you two?" she asked as she took in Jason's nice features without the cover-up of beard and oil and gold.

"Pretty much, yeah."

The general manager became serious and then took a step toward Jason.

"The men you dealt with tonight are the type that won't forget such a slight. The owner didn't have them removed, so please, watch yourself." She turned for the door but Ryan stopped her and turned her around and at the same moment kicked the door closed with his foot.

"I'm not afraid of those guys. After all, I'm loud, proud, gay, and I'm gonna stay." Ryan took her in his arms.

For the next four hours Lieutenant Commander Jason Ryan, USN, proved to one very perceptive general manager of the Edge of the World that, indeed, he wasn't gay, and also he was still Jason Ryan, naval aviator and king womanizer of the planet.

10

THE TEMPLE ARCH,
PATINAS PASS, ROMANIA

Marko stood silently at the camouflaged entrance to the temple. He felt the heat as it poured from the cracks in the scared strata of the mountain as he stepped into the entranceway. His eyes adjusted to the dim lighting of the oil lamps that stretched away into the infinite darkness of the immense staircase that wound down into the bowels of the mountain. He started down. Far below he saw the illumination of the temple lighting and he heard the flow of naturally boiled water as it bubbled up through the artesian pools far beneath the earth. The blast furnace of heat and steam made the walk down uncomfortable.

Marko was only halfway down the stairs when he heard a noise behind him. He stopped and peered into the flickering darkness cast by the oil lamps that lined the access to the temple. Seeing nothing, he was about to turn and start back down the staircase when he heard the low growl and this time he knew he had company. He reached out and removed the flaming bowl of oil that sat in a notch in the prehistorically carved tunnel. He held the bowl high in the air and that was when he saw the yellow eyes staring at him. They glowed angrily in the light cast by the oil lamp.

Stanus was standing on the steps twenty feet from Marko. His eyes were watching but the wolf wasn't moving. The growling low in Stanus's throat was unnerving.

"I've been searching for you, where have you been?" Marko asked as he gently placed the small bowl of flaming oil back into the notch.

Stanus growled once more and didn't move. Instead of asking anything more, Marko slowly lowered himself to the three-thousand-year-old hewed stone. He took a deep breath and then looked back at Stanus, who was still standing motionless on the steps high above Marko.

"I know you think I have betrayed you, the Golia, and our people." He held the wolf's yellow eyes with his own, darker ones. "That ridiculous castle is as far as the human encroachment is going to get." Marko made sure Stanus was looking at him. He was, intently. "But you will see that tomorrow soldiers will come. These are our soldiers, and a few Americans." Marko laughed and then shook his head as he smiled over and up at Stanus, who wasn't growling any longer, but had tilted its head as it tried to understand the words of the man without the spell being cast upon it. "You don't even know what an American is, do you?"

Stanus flicked his ears as if saying, "Does it matter?"

"They are mapping the pass, as your ancestors once did, as my ancestor Kale once did. They are mapping it for the defense of the north in case war comes to the people not of this mountain. Not us, but the lowlanders."

Stanus whined and then took three tentative steps down the staircase.

"The Golia must remain inside the temple for the next two days and then the men and soldiers will leave this place of the Golia and Jeddah. Do you understand me, Stanus?"

The wolf sat beside Marko and looked him in the eyes. The beast was a full four heads taller than Marko as he sat and looked down into the man's face. Marko slowly lifted his hand toward the left side of the massive head of the wolf but the great beast pulled back out of touch. It was as if Stanus would not allow the joining spell to be cast. That made Marko nervous, but not for the first time around the great alpha male.

"We have set in motion events that will secure the safety of our mountain, our people, and our babies. Babies you have in the temple. We will never have to worry about security again. We have discovered after all these years what it takes to make sure we survive—money." Marko held the gaze of the Golia and didn't flinch. "You don't know of money, do you? Think of gold, and gemstones—we have what the outside world craves. Like you crave the company of your Golia, they also must have things of material value."

The wolf, without Marko casting the joining spell, had to be made to understand.

"This is why we must make sure nothing happens to either the soldiers that will come to map our home, or those men and women down below. I promise you, my friend, there will be no men allowed beyond the castle, just the soldiers, and they cannot be harmed. I cannot say this enough, Stanus—leave them be. I and my men will handle anyone who strays from the path. Keep the Golia babies safe inside the temple."

Stanus didn't move. It was like he was looking for the lie hidden inside Marko's words.

"I know I told you that the newcomers would not breach the mountains and I swear to you it will not happen again. Grandmamma will have us destroy what is ours and abandon our home if threatened, but I say we can keep what is ours and remain where we have for the past three thousand years."

Stanus surprised Marko by leaning into him and then rubbing its muzzle on the side of Marko's face. Stanus was smelling him for any deceit, and luckily for Marko this time it was all the truth. He closed his eyes waiting for Stanus to disagree. It didn't. The great wolf huffed as if to say, "We'll see," and then with one leap hopped over Marko and disappeared into the cavern that housed the greatest temple complex ever built by man.

Marko sat for the longest time and prayed he hadn't made wrong choices in his partnership with the Russian. If he had, he knew he could end the entire dream that was their home and God's personal dream that is the Golia.

That things would calm after the resort below was up and running and his people had a steady flow of untraceable money and not the artifacts Marko had had to steal from the temple to bribe not only the Russian, but also the interior minister. Tomorrow was Friday and after that if he could survive one more day and night without the Golia showing their fierceness to anyone, they could slide into safety on their mountain again and live in the way they had been denied for three and a half thousand years.

Colonel Ben-Nevin had his men dispersed as he compared his map to the terrain in front of the new resort. He had stopped his small convoy three miles to the west of the hotel and well away from the crowd of reporters and TV crews camped outside the front gates. His secret conspirator inside the Knesset had sent him the coordinates of the area the Israeli army had been alerted to. This information had been taken directly from the mouth of General Shamni himself when he reported to the committee overseeing foreign intelligence. The information was helpful in the fact it gave him a new starting point. He knew if the major was heading for Patinas, this was the only way in.

"Sir," one of his men said as he approached the colonel.

"What is it?" Ben-Nevin asked as he looked up from the map.

"Our eastern team reports a NATO camp that is just breaking up on the far side of the resort. They say it looks like most of the contingent is leaving the area."

"Most?"

"There is a platoon-sized element still bivouacked."

"Our contact was right about NATO being interested in the pass, but I thought they would take a little more time in getting it done."

The messenger was about to turn away when Ben-Nevin called him over to the hood of the car where he had the map spread out. He hit the gas station–supplied map with a finger of his undamaged left hand.

"I want ten men right here." He jabbed at a spot he had been studying closely for the past two hours. "If she's near she will have to pass through right there. It's the only spot near enough to the foothills to even get close to the road leading to the pass. Yes, this is the spot. Tell the men I will join them soon."

The man nodded and turned away to gather the men when he heard the sound of an automatic weapon being charged behind him. It seemed the colonel was about to go hunting.

It had taken Charlie Ellenshaw over an hour and a half to fully awaken. He stumbled behind Everett as they slowly surveyed the area to the front of the resort. Carl stopped and studied the hotel and the security situation. Charlie knelt beside him.

"I hope Niles got through to Jack because I don't think we could get into that place. If that's their normal security force it rivals several small nations I've been to."

"Impossible to get in?" Charlie asked.

Everett smiled and looked at the professor of cryptozoology. "Impossible? Nah, just formidable, Doc, just formidable."

Everett stood and started walking once more to the west. The lights of the resort still lit the night around them and Carl felt exposed. Finally he spied the road that led up the steep mountain. He was surprised when he saw two men standing by the side of the trail leading to the road. They talked a moment and then a third man came up and said something to them and then the three left. Everett took a deep breath when he realized how close they had come to walking right into the two men. He shook his head and then waved Charlie forward, silently cursing his stupidity in worrying about the lights of the resort when he should have been concentrating.

"Why don't we just use the road?" Charlie asked when Everett continued to use the thin trees for cover.

"Well, Doc, if we—"

Before Carl could answer Ellenshaw, the noise of men shouting broke through the nighttime silence. They both heard men running. Everett reached up and pulled Ellenshaw down and they both waited.

"It seems awfully crowded out here in the woods for it being almost dawn."

Everett had to agree with Charlie on that point.

Suddenly there were two sets of boots standing just above the small ditch they had crawled into. Everett shook his head when Ellenshaw started to move. The men spoke in a foreign language and Everett knew that language was not Romanian. He had heard it just two days ago in Rome. The two men hurried away and Everett rolled over onto his back until his eyes could see the fading lights of the stars as it neared dawn.

"How in the hell did they know to come here?" Carl asked those disappearing stars.

Charlie was about to ask the captain to explain when they heard the yelp of a large dog. Then another pain-filled cry came bursting through the trees. They heard men shouting and then a woman screamed an obscenity.

Everett reached behind him and pulled out the nine-millimeter.

"Come on, Doc, this doesn't sound good."

"Hey, do you have a gun for me?" Charlie whispered as loud as he dared.

"Damn, I accidentally issued it to Pete Golding," Everett joked, knowing that would irk Charlie to no end. Then Carl slowly moved out of the small drainage ditch and into the trees. Ellenshaw looked lost for a moment and then frowned.

"Pete!" he cursed under his breath and then started after the captain.

It took several minutes for the woods along the road and adjoining trail to calm down from the excitement moments earlier, Carl and Charlie managing to keep out of sight.

Everett had a chance to see several of the men up close and he could see that they were not professional soldiers or even militarily trained. They acted like hired men from various professions and that made his job that much easier, as he could track the noisy men without being seen or heard.

After a long wait behind one of the larger pine trees, which were becoming far more sparse the nearer to the mountain they got, they watched eleven men as they started returning to the road in the same place they were before all the commotion began. *All but one man*, Carl corrected himself. This man silently stood his ground and listened to the early morning sounds.

In the weak light of dawn, Carl had a feeling of déjà vu as he watched the dark form standing just ahead of him and Charlie. The tall, thin man placed a hand on the tree and listened, and then suddenly vanished. Everett raised his head a little and tried to find out where the familiar form had disappeared to when he heard something. It was a small cry of pain as someone stumbled in the dim light of morning. Everett gestured for Charlie Ellenshaw to hold his ground and the professor nodded that he understood.

Carl moved slowly away from the last protected spot he had for a hundred yards. He kept close to the ground as he headed toward a large boulder that had tumbled from the mountain sometime in the past thousand years. Everett realized as he ran stooped over that he wasn't getting enough exercise as he struggled to keep bent at the waist. Finally he placed his hands on the giant stone and knelt to catch his breath. He had felt exposed in the dawn light and knew he had been foolish to try to get as close as he could to where he thought the noise had originated. He finally controlled his breathing enough that he could listen. He heard the birds singing their morning songs and several of them even sprang from the trees above them. But of the strange noise he had heard, there was nothing.

Carl was about to turn away when he heard another cry and then a curse as someone was pushed from the small thatch of trees fifty feet beyond where Everett had pulled up.

"Traveling with a child has never been Mossad policy, Major Sorotzkin, you should know that."

Carl saw the man and then the woman and boy. The child wasn't the same but the woman was Anya Korvesky—the Mossad agent from Rome. And the man who held the two at gunpoint was the very same colonel that had tried to kill him and Ryan in the small antique shop near Vatican City.

"Well, imagine meeting you two here," Carl muttered as he turned to make sure Charlie was still in his spot behind the large tree. His eyes widened when he saw that Ellenshaw wasn't there. He hissed at having lost the professor. He angrily turned back to the strange scene ahead of him in the growing light. He then turned and made sure that the men who had left the area earlier were not returning. He guessed the arrogant man holding the woman and child at gunpoint thought he could handle this alone—which was right in line with Carl's innovative plans.

"Did you not think we had the resources to trace your movements? All we had to do was watch General Shamni. Our people knew at the precise moment that the general discovered where you would be going. Did you know that he's assembled a strike team, which means I have very little time to expose the truth of this mountain to all of Israel, or the most important of those people anyway."

Everett watched the girl knowing she was fast and light on her feet. But as he did he knew she wouldn't do anything to risk the life of the boy who clung to her.

"That will be the day when scum like you thinks he has a real soldier like General Shamni figured out." The woman stopped walking but kept her hands where Colonel Ben-Nevin could see them. "I may not be his favorite right now, but he's a man who loves his country, and you couldn't think like him if your life depended on it."

Ben-Nevin ignored the slight. "Now, where is that magnificent animal that saved you on the train? I must see the beast and know that the old tales are true." He smiled knowing his captives couldn't see it. "Because if the animals are real that means that other, more viable legends are also true."

"Mikla died this afternoon in his sleep. He was too badly injured from a broken ankle that became infected."

"This is a shame. I was looking forward to dispatching the animal myself and then mounting its head on my office wall."

"You couldn't outthink or outfight Mikla with an army of mercenaries."

Ben-Nevin smirked, a gesture that Everett saw from his hiding place behind the large boulder. Then Carl winced angrily when the colonel shoved the woman in the back viciously with the barrel of his gun. She didn't let out a sound as she was pushed forward, dragging the young boy with her. They stumbled and fell to the ground and Ben-Nevin moved to kick at the two prone forms.

Everett was just standing with his weapon held with both hands as he took quick aim at the colonel before he could bring his foot down on the defenseless woman. Suddenly he felt the sharp jab of a weapon as it was poked painfully into his spine.

"Don't move," came a heavily accented voice in English.

The sudden noise didn't stop the kick that was delivered to Anya as she squeezed her eyes shut against the pain in her kidneys as the boot dug deeply into her. The boy, as brave as he could be, threw himself over Anya and waited for his turn. Ben-Nevin however had his attention drawn away by something beyond Anya's hearing. She managed to raise her head and see a man walking toward them and from her skewed viewpoint the man walking with his hands up looked familiar. She felt the air part as Colonel Ben-Nevin stepped over her and her nephew.

"This is fortuitous, I must say."

Everett was angry but he tried his best to hold it in check after being caught unawares by the two men who had managed to get behind him without him knowing it. He figured these two or more like them had also gotten poor Ellenshaw and that was why he wasn't by the tree. Carl felt as if he had let Charlie down by leaving him behind.

In the early morning light Everett saw Colonel Ben-Nevin turn from him to look at the woman he had just kicked. She was looking up at Carl and he could see her eyes shift as she recognized him from Vatican City.

"Is that the way you treat women where you come from, dickhead?" Everett said as the weapon at his spine was shoved a little harder at his insult. He half turned to the men behind him. "As for you, that damn thing has bullets; I suggest you use them instead of trying to skewer me with the barrel." That elicited another sharp jab.

"Are all you Americans so arrogant?" Ben-Nevin asked as he moved toward the three men. He gestured for the man with the AK-47 at Carl's back to back away, not out of any consideration for the captain but the fact that Ben-Nevin didn't want anyone too close to this man. He had seen him in action and had respect for anyone that can move as quickly as he had seen this man do. The two men took a step back and Everett was grateful for the relief and the maneuvering room in case an opportunity presented itself.

"Just the ones I know," Carl answered as he glanced behind to see how far away the two men were. They were better than he thought, standing out of arm's reach.

"Witty. Do you have a name, or just a number?" Ben-Nevin asked.

"I have a name, but only my mama's allowed to use it. You can just call me Popeye the Sailor."

Ben-Nevin raised his pistol but didn't aim it at Everett but just waved it slowly back and forth to make sure the large American saw the weapon.

"All right, Mr. Popeye, where is the funny-looking white-haired man you came into the hills with?"

"White-haired man? You guys must have seen a ghost because I—"

The AK-47 butt plate to the back of Carl's ribs ended his reply before it was finished as he went to his knees from the impact. He felt his breath leave his lungs and then he heard a woman's voice ask Ben-Nevin to stop. Everett shook his head and then managed with some difficulty to take in a breath of air. He slowly glanced back at the man who had delivered the blow. He was standing behind him with a look of satisfaction on his face. The man's accomplice reached down and pulled Everett to his feet where he did his best to steady himself as air slowly returned.

"You guys from the Middle East don't have a sense of humor do you?" Everett said as it felt as if his ribs shifted back to the right spot inside his body.

"I am not the kind that will stand here and bandy words with you, Mr. Popeye. I will ask once more who you are and who you report to. If you do not answer, as you draw your next painful breath the very next sound you hear will be that bullet you requested earlier as it enters the back of your head."

"My name is Popeye and I work for a man named Wimpy, and I hate him because he never pays me for my hamburgers."

"Shoot this man," Ben-Nevin said as he angrily turned away from the American to concentrate on the woman and the boy.

Everett knew he was had so he made ready to at least go down without the bullet-to-the-head thing. He would rather go out with his hands wrapped around the throat of the man who had hit him from behind.

Carl tensed as he started to spring, but before he could move he heard a loud whack and then an even louder grunt. Then another swish sounded in the morning air and after that a loud, painful yelp came as Everett rose and saw that Charlie Ellenshaw had came up from behind the two men and coldcocked them with a large tree branch. Now Ellenshaw stood there with the branch in his hands looking as if he had done something horribly wrong. It was as if he was sorrowful for hitting the men as hard as he had. Everett ignored him and reached for the fallen AK-47.

Ben-Nevin turned at the unusual sound and then his eyes widened when he saw the very man he had just asked the American about. He was standing with a large limb and the other American was reaching for one of the fallen weapons. The Mossad colonel quickly brought up his own weapon and just when he thought he had a shot at the American a sharp pain raced from his leg to his brain in record speed. When the shock settled he looked down and saw a small knife sticking from his left leg. As he brought the weapon over and around he saw that another small boy had once more saved the day for the man and the woman—at least momentarily. The gun went to the boy and that was when his legs were knocked out from under him by Anya, who had kicked out at the last moment before the weapon discharged in her nephew's face.

Ben-Nevin hit the ground and he immediately felt the gun fly from his hand. He rolled as fast as he could before the large American could aim the weapon he had recovered. He rolled until he felt his body hit an incline and then the speed of his roll increased. Ben-Nevin finally came to a stop and before anyone could take quick aim at him he stood and vanished into the trees.

Carl had tried to raise the automatic weapon and at least try a shot at the escaping colonel, but one of the men Charlie had laid waste to came to and grabbed Everett's ankle, stopping the aimed shot before he could pull the trigger. Carl hissed and then easily turned the AK-47 around and thumped the man on the head.

"That's for the hit in the ribs," he said as he started to turn away and then turned and hit the man again with the butt plate. "And that's for waking up at the wrong time." The man crumpled and stayed down.

Charlie Ellenshaw was wide-eyed as he watched an angry Captain Everett turn away and walk toward the fallen woman and boy. He gingerly stepped over the two men he had hit with the branch, which he still clutched. As he stepped over the men he tossed the branch away and his eyes widened when he saw the other AK-47 lying beside the man. He reached for the weapon just as Everett reached for it and removed it just as it touched Charlie's outstretched fingers.

"Sorry, Doc, this isn't an M-16, it's far more sensitive and one shock to my back is enough for one evening."

"Damn," Ellenshaw hissed as Carl turned away once more.

Everett saw the woman as she slowly rose to her feet. He turned and made sure no more surprises were imminent and then he removed the magazine from the weapon he held and looked at the loads. He reinserted the clip and then took in the woman.

"Looks like you had a rough trip?" he said. He didn't exactly aim the barrel of the AK-47 directly at Anya, but it wasn't pointed in the opposite direction either. Even the boy was scrutinized by Everett. It had been he who eventually saved Carl's life and that demanded respect.

The woman didn't say anything as she helped the boy to his feet. She looked around and then faced the captain.

"He will be back with more men, I must leave." She started to turn the boy away but Everett made sure she heard the safety being removed from the automatic weapon he now held on her. She turned angrily. "We must leave; he wants you as much as me. The colonel will be relentless, he has no choice now. He intends to kill you and anyone else in his way."

Everett raised the barrel of the weapon toward the sky away from Anya. She nodded her head in a quasi-thank-you motion and then pulled the boy further into the trees they had initially been hiding in when they had been discovered by Ben-Nevin.

Carl followed the woman, the boy, and Charlie about two hundred yards further into the hills. Finally he spied the road that led upward toward the strange-looking castle and the pass above it.

"Aren't we a little too close to the road?" Carl asked as Anya finally stopped and looked around her at the early morning landscape. "I would think that Ben-Nevin and his friends would use this to track you, I mean it's the most expedient route."

The woman looked at Carl. "The colonel would never be stupid enough to expose himself on the open road on this mountain. This is the one place on earth that is not controlled by men from the outside . . . no, we have to cross the road here and retrieve something I left behind."

"What in the hell is so important that you would risk—"

Everett became angry when Anya Korvesky sprinted across the road with the boy close behind. They soon vanished behind a small wall of stacked rocks.

"Damn it!" Everett said as he gestured for Ellenshaw to follow him across. The two men made it without anyone seeing them. Carl hopped deftly over the stone wall and was followed by Charlie, who hit the wall and flew over headfirst landing squarely on his chin.

"Jesus, Doc, can you make any more noise?" Carl said as he tried to see where Anya and the boy had disappeared to.

"Sorry, misjudged the height somewhat."

"Damn, if I lost that woman again . . ." Everett muttered and then left the sentence unfinished. "Doc, did you hear that colonel ask the woman about an animal?"

"I must have missed that," Charlie said as he looked for the girl along with the captain.

"Well, we can't find them by staying put, let's go this way," Everett said as he pulled Ellenshaw to his feet, but before they could take a step he saw the woman not ten feet from them just standing and looking at them.

"If we are not to be caught again you two will have to travel with a little more stealth than what you've shown you are capable of."

"Sorry, I'm afraid it's my fault, I'm not a real field—"

"That's enough, Doc. She has learned just about all that I care to give her for the moment. At least until she can explain why she was trying to out our agent in Vatican City."

"I wasn't outing him as you so quaintly put it. I was trying to discover what he had learned about the pass and my people. That is what I do."

"Yes, I believe you're part of a tribe called the Jeddah. Why you're part of Mossad is something we have yet to learn."

"And suddenly, you, whoever you are, know quite a bit about a subject that absolutely fewer than a hundred men and women outside this mountain have ever heard. Perhaps I was watching the wrong contact at the Vatican. Maybe I should have let the young priest be and waited to follow you, especially since you're quite the historian." The woman took two steps backward into the trees and vanished.

Everett didn't want to lose sight of her again, so he once more grabbed Charlie by his Windbreaker and pulled him into a large stand of trees where the woman vanished.

"Look, you're not losing us again, so why don't you—"

Charles Hindershot Ellenshaw III and Carl came to a sudden stop just as their hearts did. Both men felt their mouths go slack when they saw the girl, the young boy, and the largest animal outside zoo walls they had ever seen. The wolf was lying on its side and with its head off the ground and was staring right at the two intruders. The wolf tried to rise but Anya was holding its ears and talking softly to the beast.

"Oh, my God," Charlie said in a barely audible whisper.

The yellow eyes never left Carl or Ellenshaw as it continued to growl deep in its chest. Then it suddenly whimpered and curled into a ball and started licking one of its hind legs. Anya spoke to the beast once more and then she stood and faced the men.

"I have to get him home to my grandmother or we'll lose him. Right now the break isn't that bad but infection is soon to set in if my grandmother cannot get to him. Will you help me get my friend back to the pass?"

"Your friend?" Charlie asked as he took in the vision of the curled-up and very dangerous-looking wolf. "That animal has to weigh close to a thousand pounds!"

Ellenshaw said just as many of the old werewolf tales came flooding back. That was one legend that Charlie always took with more than a grain of salt because he knew the physical limitation of the human body and those of the standard wolf. Any change from wolf to human form had always been the most severe of impossibilities in his learned opinion.

Everett continued to eye the woman. Then his eyes went to the giant wolf lying at her feet. The boy continued to stroke the animal and talk to it.

"Answer me this first, and then we can talk."

"We have no time," she said pleadingly.

"You have time for this because it's very important to a person that's very dear to me."

Anya looked down at Mikla and then nodded her head at Everett.

"That is a Golia?"

"That is Mikla. The Golia know not the old name of their species. He cannot differentiate the difference by names, but by knowing."

Everett smiled as he thought of how Alice was going to react.

"If you're done with your questioning, can you help me get Mikla back to Patinas before Ben-Nevin returns?"

"I hope you don't want us to carry him, I don't think it would take kindly to the offer," Charlie said as he continued to stare at the giant Golia as it continued to whine and lick its wound.

"He will follow, I just need cover and you have to be it. It will take a while for Mikla to make the climb."

"Well," Everett said as he pulled his walkie-talkie out and tried to reach Niles once again but he received no signal. He knew he would regret not being able to inform Jack of his discovery. "Why not?" he said as he gestured for the woman to start leading the way.

As Carl and Charlie watched, the giant wolf slowly rose to its four paws and with the right rear one off the ground started to limp after Anya and the boy. Carl reached around and unslung the second AK-47 from his shoulder and then handed it to Ellenshaw.

"Don't shoot anything, just point it and if that doesn't work throw it and run for your life."

"Got it," Ellenshaw said as he hefted the heavy Russian-made weapon. "Eat your heart out, Pete."

Everett turned and watched as the woman, the boy, and the nightmare-sized wolf disappeared.

"Stay as close to them as you can. I'll be skirting the side to make sure we don't have any unwanted company closing in from the rear."

"Right," Ellenshaw answered as he smiled at Carl. "Alice was right, they do exist," he said and then left to follow the woman and her friends.

Right," Everett said as he watched Ellenshaw leave. "Now all we have to worry about is what else she was right about."

Everett shook his head and then vanished into the trees.

PATINAS PASS

The old woman used the door frame to steady herself as she gingerly eased her bad ankle out the door. She was careful not to slip on the morning dew that covered everything from the crags in the mountain to the high pastures to which all the men had left for two hours before sunrise.

The Gypsy queen had been dozing in her large chair with her feet propped on a small stool. She remembered hearing Marko snoring soundly on the small bed she had abandoned for the comfort of the chair. Her grandson had come in late and instead of going to sleep in his own house he chose to tend to his grandmother and rest there. He had been in a surly mood and she could tell he had been angered by something or someone. She had the distinct impression that he was troubled by something he hadn't expected. He had mentioned that they could have visitors tomorrow to at least the lower villages by a group of Americans. And it was this issue that was troubling the man-child and she had picked up the strong vibes and instead of saying anything she had lain awake most of the night in worry about what the boy had done.

She stood in the doorway and looked south down the mountain and the feelings she was receiving became stronger. She winced as she placed too much weight on her healing but still heavily wrapped ankle. Suddenly it hit her like a sledgehammer blow to her brain. It was Anya. Mikla was with her and so was the boy, Georgi, and someone, *no*, she thought, *two someones were with them*. She tilted her head as she tried desperately for more information. Madam Korvesky was still feeling Anya's fear of being caught but she also knew, or more to the point, felt, that the men following her were not the basis for her fear.

The old woman turned for the door and called out Marko's name twice, very loudly. After she heard her grandson stir inside she reached up and grabbed the thin rope that was attached to a bell she had Marko install years before in case she needed help. She needed help now. She started ringing the bell with purpose, which should bring several of the local villagers in from a few of the lower pastures. A moment later she saw a few of the men trotting briskly down from the meadows just below the pass. Then she stopped ringing the bell when she felt Marko step up beside her while still tucking his shirt in.

"What is it, a fire?" he asked, his head about to explode from last night's drinking.

"You smell of the grape, man-child," she said as she took a tentative step out of the doorway. Marko reached out and took her by the arm to steady her.

"Is that what you woke me and the entire valley up for?" he asked angrily.

"No," she said but waited till several of the men came bounding into her small fenced yard to explain further.

"What is it, a fire?" one of the men asked as he came sliding to a stop in front of Marko and his grandmother.

"Go quickly to your homes and retrieve your shotguns. Anya is here and she is in trouble. She's close by, down there," she said as she pointed down the mountain. "She is with Georgi and Mikla, they also have two men with them, they are not to be harmed. Bring them in. Kill anyone who is trying to harm them."

Marko allowed his eyes to roam to the men after his grandmother's rather brutal announcement.

"Kill them?" he asked.

"The evil men she is running from mean her harm. They mean us harm. Kill them all if they are near my granddaughter. Go now and bring her home."

The village men of Patinas didn't even look to Marko for guidance as they turned and ran for their own small and humble cottages to get their shotguns off mantels now cold from the morning cook fires. Marko was angry and disappointed that the men of the village still followed the old woman's orders blindly and without question. He wondered if he would ever get that kind of devotion and respect when she was gone.

"You could have awakened me before you sounded the alarm, Grandmamma. This could have been done quietly and without having to resort to murdering someone who is probably lost from the resort and not chasing dear sister at all." He turned to her in the doorway and escorted her to her chair. It irked him even more that she was smiling like a schoolgirl. "And why are you so happy? Is it the prospect of murder?"

"No, foolish man-child. I am happy because Anya has come home."

Marko frowned as he went to the mantel and grabbed his old double-barreled shotgun. He broke it open and saw that the ancient paper-encased shells were still in.

"Then when she arrives we will offer sacrifice as in the old ways," Marko said bitterly, "and feast as if it were harvest time, for this is the arrival of the prodigal daughter and the whole of the Jeddah should rejoice that she has come home to save us from the horrid and evil brother." He slammed the double-barreled shotgun closed as he turned and left the cottage.

"Marko, I didn't mean—"

Her words were cut off as the rickety old door slammed shut. She closed her eyes as she realized she had once again hurt Marko. She thought she could have handled the boy better after his parents died, but he had always been far too headstrong and jealous of the material things owned by those of the outside world.

Madam Korvesky knew in her heart that Marko, through trying to help his people, had allowed evil to enter their world and she no longer thought she could control the situation, and what was worse, control the Golia.

She was beginning to understand why Stanus was acting strange: the alpha male was feeling a change coming and he was preparing.

But what the giant Golia was preparing for exactly, she knew not.

Colonel Ben-Nevin kept his men well away from the main road heading to the pass. It was hard enough skirting the castle as early morning workers left behind continued to prepare for the next night's grand opening. The colonel shook his head in anger as he realized the girl could be anywhere by now. The two men that had failed him so miserably were now back at their small camp nursing a broken nose and three cracked ribs. Of course he could not be blamed for the loss, not as long as others were so conveniently close by to blame.

"Colonel?" one of his men called out. "Sir, this just came in from Jerusalem." He handed Ben-Nevin a fax from the machine at the local station.

"You can't tell me this isn't a government-run operation, we would be better off having Indians send up smoke signals." He took the message and read it. "Recall the men, we'll settle this problem from another direction," he said as he crumpled up the message from his contact inside the Knesset. He gestured for his second in command to join him. "Gather the men, it seems we may have a friend in the area we didn't know about." He smiled. "And frankly, neither does he."

The small man read the note after it was offered by the colonel.

"Who is Dmitri Zallas?" his man asked as he lowered the note.

"A man with as big an appetite as I when it comes to old things."

"And where is this savior to our cause?"

"Why, he's right down there," Ben-Nevin said as he pointed south.

The man looked down the road that led to the valley and what his eyes saw in the morning sun was the gleaming facade of the largest resort hotel and casino in the Eastern European portion of the globe—the Edge of the World.

"Smile, my friend, sometimes we cannot complain about who our bedfellows are as long as they can help us and our people," Ben-Nevin said as he gestured again, this time toward the north. "Besides, anyone with an imagination to build *that* will have an equally good time imagining what may lie in the mountains right above his head—after it's explained to him."

The man turned and looked to where Ben-Nevin had gestured above them in the mountains. "What in the hell is that?"

High above them stood the formidable presence of the new and improved Dracula's Castle.

Niles Compton paced in front of the idling Humvee. The twenty men of the 82nd sat around eating their MREs and waiting for word as to when they would move to map the pass. Niles looked at his watch once more and then turned and faced Alice Hamilton.

"If Mendenhall can't raise Jack or find out if they found our equipment with the satellite radios, this mission could fail before we even get a chance to see the pass."

Alice folded her arms across her light jacket and then smiled at Niles. "Will's all right, he has to be careful getting close to the resort and then he has to get Jack the message that Carl and Charlie are missing."

"Where in the hell are those two?"

Alice reached out and patted Niles on the shoulder. The director wasn't all that familiar with the vagaries of field operations. Oh, Niles knew the bottom line on what a mission costs and the organizational skills necessary to make a multi-billion-dollar operation run smoothly, but as far as his worry about field personnel was concerned he needed more practice—sometimes Alice wondered if Niles knew just how good every one of his people at Group was. She thought he just worried too much about his personnel.

Will Mendenhall approached Alice and Niles and he had Denise Gilliam along with him. She was eating from an MRE and frowning at the taste.

"Well?" Niles asked.

Mendenhall held up the small radio and tossed it to the director.

"Well, Sarah was right in her hunch, we are definitely having reception problems. I was able to contact the colonel and I managed after an hour to finally get the message understood. Colonel Collins suggested that we continue without the captain and Charlie. He said we should get Alice into the pass. If Everett turns up anywhere he said it would be there—the colonel said that is the one place where Mr. Everett knows we'll be. He suggested we get to the pass and wait."

"The colonel doesn't feel it necessary for his team to drop the surveillance of the resort and join us?"

Mendenhall saw that the director wasn't happy about Everett being missing or the fact that the colonel felt obligated to stay behind.

"He says that Sarah may have come across something that could be a danger to the entire region. Something about the venting of the hot springs, I couldn't get it all because of all the iron ore in these mountains."

Niles handed the small radio back to Will and then took a few steps away to think. He looked up as the twenty men left behind by the Airborne made ready for their foray into the pass. Niles shook his head and made his decision.

"As of right now we have little choice but to do as the colonel suggested."

Alice released the breath she had been holding because she had been afraid that the mission to the pass would be canceled.

Compton looked at his watch. "We have only today to look things over, Alice, because tomorrow I want all my people secure in one place with the storm heading this way. If we don't have radio reception now, just think how bad it will be tomorrow. No, we better get there and reconnoiter the pass."

Will nodded and he and Denise Gilliam left to load their equipment.

"What's wrong, Niles?" Alice asked.

Compton turned away from watching the two Army Humvees being loaded with surveying equipment.

"The radios, the satellite hookup with Europa, Captain Everett and Charlie coming up missing, Sarah sees something wrong geologically in this valley, and now we have one of the largest storms of the year heading our way." Compton looked up and into the crystal blue morning sky and shook his head. "First we lose our Romanian military escort, our Airborne element has been cut down to nothing, and the fact that they have no weapons whatsoever." He smiled at Alice. "I would say things could be going better."

Alice Hamilton returned the smile and patted Niles on the shoulder.

"Garrison told me once that sometimes after all the power, all the expensive equipment, and having the smartest people in the world working for you, sometimes all we have in the end is your brain and your . . ." Again she smiled and winked. "Balls." She turned away as Niles watched her. "In other words you can be the king of all you survey one moment and then you realize that the only real thing you have going for you is the fact that you are still sitting on nothing but your own ass in that exalted throne."

"Just what in the hell is that cryptic statement about?" he asked her.

Alice stopped and fixed Niles with her eyes.

"It means sometimes we just have to do this without all the fancy toys and do it in an environment that bodes ill for those who fail. Now you know what being the director of Department 5656 is all about. Making it work no matter what." She smiled and turned away to gather her notes and history of the pass. "And you just happen to be extremely fortunate, Niles my boy."

"And why is that, Mrs. Hamilton?" Compton called after her.

"Because you have the best people in the world working for you, and you know what? They always get it done. And you will, too. Now let's go see if this old woman's cheese has totally slid off her cracker, or see if there be werewolves in them thar mountains," she said in her best hillbilly accent.

Niles smiled as he watched the most brilliant woman he had ever known leave and get ready to fulfill her long dream of finding the Jeddah and then he turned and looked at the mountain high above.

"To tell you the truth, Alice old girl, that's exactly what I'm afraid of finding up there." He shook his head as the Humvees started their engines. "Damn it, Carl, where are you and Charlie?"

11

THE EDGE OF THE WORLD HOTEL AND
RESORT CASINO, PATINAS PASS, ROMANIA

The restaurant was somewhat crowded, mildly surprising Jack and Sarah. As they were led to a table Collins saw Jason and Pete as they entered from the far end. Their eyes met for the briefest moment and then Jack sat at the table and was handed a menu. As he sat he looked up and saw that the waitress was leading both Pete and Ryan right to their own table. Ryan had a troubled look on his face and Pete just looked lost.

"Excuse me, but I see plenty of empty tables," Ryan said as he ignored the menu offered by the waitress.

"Mr. Zallas left strict instructions to the restaurant staff that the four of you should be seated together."

Collins listened to the exchange and at that moment he knew their cover was truly blown, or at the very least Zallas suspected that something was afoot with the Americans.

"Is there any particular reason for that request?" Jack asked, looking at the young girl.

"We were only left the instructions, sir." She finally got Pete and Ryan to accept their menus as they acceded and sat at the table as the waitress poured coffee for the two newest guests while the hostess stood over them. The two waitstaff finally left.

"Well, this can't be good," Ryan said as he opened his menu.

"Very little is good at the moment," Collins said as he sipped his orange juice. "It seems Mr. Everett and our good buddy Charlie Ellenshaw came up missing last night."

"What in the hell—" Ryan started to say but Jack held up his hand to stay the question.

"We don't know. The radios are crapping out on us. We also have a major storm heading this way and the Romanian army pulled out late last night to handle flooding in the south. I won't even mention the fact we have missing trucks with our equipment inside of them, including our Sat system, so we don't even have the fallback of communicating with Nellis." He shook his head and then let out his breath in exasperation. "So that leaves us with twenty unarmed 82nd Airborne boys and two Humvees as backup if needed."

Sarah shook her head and then reached for her cup of coffee. As she did the deep, dark liquid in the cup shook and then settled, and then the cup vibrated once more and the brew moved again and then stopped. The geologist studied the tabletop and waited but the tremors didn't continue.

"If our cover here is blown I see no reason why we shouldn't leave and get out there and find the captain and Charlie. I mean we're back in the stone age here and believe me this Group isn't used to that. Our well-planned Event has suddenly turned into a royal cluster—"

Jack looked at Ryan, successfully cutting off the profanity-laced finish. But Collins knew the new naval lieutenant commander had a point. It was dangerous being in a place where the host suspects that you are not who you pretend to be. And now you have people missing in the field and no way to talk to anyone. *Yes, the stone age,* he thought. Jack took a sip of his coffee. He set the cup down and then he felt it. He placed his hands palm down upon the wood. He looked at Jason, Pete, and Sarah, each in turn.

"I think the mission parameters have changed in the last twenty-four hours, and priorities have—" Pete started to say as he dabbed his mouth with his napkin.

"Not now," Jack said. Collins threw his napkin on the table and started to stand.

"Where are you going?" Sarah asked.

"You and I are going to Patinas. The least we can do is make Zallas and his henchmen work that much harder to keep track of us. We're splitting up. You two stay and keep an eye out for Alice's artifacts. If Zallas starts to get cocky head north to the pass. I love Alice but getting people killed over this is a little much. And I'm afraid our Mr. Zallas may be a little more deadly than even the Interpol reports say he is."

"Why are we going to Patinas?" Sarah asked as her chair was pulled out by Ryan.

"Just as you did a few minutes ago, I felt the tremor."

Sarah was surprised that Jack had felt the earth move also before she had a chance to say anything.

"And besides, I have something else to show you, come on."

The others followed Jack out of the restaurant and as they moved they all saw the two men follow who had been sitting at a table away from the group of Americans. Collins allowed the others to catch up as he stepped toward the large escalator that moved people to the top of the atrium. Jack walked to the base of the 170,000-ton people mover. He acted like he was tying his shoe and knelt over.

"What do you make of this?" he asked Sarah.

Pete and Ryan crowded around so most of the patrons moving between the restaurant and the casino couldn't see what she was doing. Sarah knelt and examined the spot Jack was indicating.

"I saw that yesterday," Collins said as he finished with the act on his shoe. He stood and waited while Sarah examined the concrete that made up the base of the giant escalator.

"This concrete and the reinforcement steel are only a few months old." She ran her hand along the large crack in the concrete and then ran her small fingers deeper into the crevice and frowned. "Damn, this fault has to go all the way through to the rebar."

"As serious as I thought?" he asked.

"That is not normal expansion of drying concrete. That fault is not natural, you can see where the two halves don't line up and that means the entire escalator has shifted at its base and that indicates earth movement." She pulled Collins away from the spot and she waited for Ryan and Pete to join them. "Jack, this entire valley is shifting for some reason."

Collins watched Sarah walk over to the waterfall and the hot springs bath beneath it. Without hesitation McIntire knelt once again and tested the water with her fingers, frowning only momentarily before removing them.

"My best guess would be a five-degree rise since yesterday."

All four Event Group members knew time was running short.

PATINAS PASS

Everett waited for the large wolf to limp by him and Charlie. Anya was sure to walk between it and the two wide-eyed men. Mikla growled as it slowly slipped past. As it did, so, the two men had a chance to study the animal close up, something that would forever be etched in their memories.

Charlie nudged Carl and nodded toward the ground where the Golia laid its paws. For the first time they saw the one thing that made all of the legends, fairy tales, and myths come true for both of them—they could actually see the tightness of the fingers as they were folded into a paw form with the thumb tucked neatly inside. The pads were on the outside of the fingers and served as the contact point for the feet while on all fours.

Everett's eyes went from the strangely folded-in fingers to the right hind ankle of the muscled animal. He saw the swelling under the weed-, straw,- and cloth-wrapped leg. He could clearly see that the pain of walking was sapping the giant's strength.

The wolf moved through the underbrush and disappeared behind the boy and Anya. Carl tried his radio and for a moment thought he got the colonel. When he didn't raise him he reported their situation anyway in hopes Jack could hear.

Sarah, Ryan, and Pete stood in a half circle around Jack as he dipped his head trying to listen to his radio, which had suddenly come to life. Luckily he had the volume turned low so the passing crowd of mobsters, thieves, and killers couldn't hear. Collins was half in and half out of a small alcove that had a bust of Julius Caesar on a pedestal. Sarah heard Jack's frustrated voice as he tried to communicate with whoever was calling. Finally he hissed and stepped out from behind the group.

"Billions of dollars in budgeted money, the most brilliant men and women in the world, the best equipment money can buy, and now we have to search for a pay phone, of which there probably isn't one, all because we have these and no way to talk with any of our people."

"Who was it?" Sarah asked.

"It was Carl and from what I could make out he and Charlie are all right and heading for the small village below the pass, and before you ask that is all I got besides something very cryptic that I'm not sure I want to clarify at the moment. In any case, Jason and Pete, you're going hiking. Ascertain the situation with Mr. Everett and Ellenshaw if possible; if not, reconnoiter as far up as the castle. Report back the best way you can, if not, return."

"What was the message, Colonel?" Ryan asked as he and Pete leaned in closer to Jack and Sarah.

"The captain said to tell Alice that the three little pigs do have something to worry about on the mountain."

"What does—" Pete started to ask and then Ryan frowned and cut him off by holding up his hand.

"Who was the nemesis of the three little pigs, Pete?"

Light dawned in Golding's eyes.

"The Big Bad Wolf."

Everett stopped and listened when the birds stopped chirping and the insects went quiet. Charlie was starting to pick up on the vibes Carl was putting out that something wasn't right. It had been ten minutes since they were separated from the boy, Anya, and the Golia they called Mikla. Everett knew they couldn't have gone far, as he and Charlie were only separated from them for the few minutes they tried to reach Jack on the radio and satellite link.

"There are two scatterguns aimed at your backs and I would take it seriously when I tell you do not move."

Everett froze at the sound of the voice. Whoever it was that came upon them unnoticed was well practiced at doing so. He never heard as much as the laying down of a footstep. Carl slowly turned and he felt Charlie behind him do the same.

The eyes were the first things Everett saw when he turned to face the man, eyes that were as dark as the night. The man raised the ancient sawed-off shotgun a few inches to make sure Carl knew that one wrong move and he would find out just how serious this man was.

"Why are you here?" Marko Korvesky asked the two men.

Everett waited while three more men came into view and all were carrying the shotguns. Carl sensed even more men hidden in the trees.

"We're looking for someone we lost; a woman and a young boy."

The man in the brightly colored garb said nothing at the information provided. He tilted his head and looked from Carl to the crazy white-haired Charlie Ellenshaw, who, to Everett's immense pleasure had kept silent as he held his hands in the air.

"I too seek a young boy and a woman, they are from my village." The man continued to look at Everett but did not lower the lethal-looking shotgun.

"Hello, Marko," said a feminine voice from the direction of the tree line.

Carl saw the look come over the man's face as Anya spoke. He didn't know if the look was one of pleasure or one of stunned recognition. The man slowly turned and faced the woman who stepped into the small clearing. The captain relaxed when he saw the genuine smile of a man who was pleased, uncomfortable but pleased, to see the girl. The man lowered the shotgun and took a step toward her.

"Hello, baby sister. I would have expected you to come home with a bit more fanfare and not being chased through the woods by this rather large American."

Anya smiled. It was a tired expression on an even more tired body as she took the remaining steps to her brother and wrapped her arms around him.

"I didn't know how I would feel seeing you after so long. How I would feel about you being sent away and me having to stay." He smiled and hugged her again. "But I was wrong. It is good to see you again."

"Marko, what is happening here? There are more people who know about us now than there has been in the history of our people. What has happened?" she whispered as even more villagers came in. Carl counted seven men altogether and they were all armed.

"First, where is Mikla?" Marko asked as his demeanor changed faster than even Anya realized. "How badly is he injured?"

"How did you know he was hurt?" Anya asked as her eyes went to Everett as he watched the exchange while being guarded by the men from Patinas.

"Grandmamma broke her ankle—her right ankle."

"It was she?" she asked as she finally released Marko. "Damn it, why is she taking that chance, what if Mikla had been shot?"

Everett was having a hard time following the harshly whispered conversation.

"My concern exactly. I need to know where Mikla is, and I need to know why Grandmamma summoned you home."

"Mikla is—"

The bolt of an automatic weapon being thrown caught everyone's attention. Everett looked up and saw seven men all standing in a semicircle around the group. Marko's eyes narrowed when he saw the men all aiming weapons at them. He and his villagers had been taken unawares because of the happiness he had shown at seeing his sister.

"What is this?" Marko asked as he held his shotgun outward. He turned and gave Everett a menacing look. "I should have shot you immediately," he said as he dropped the shotgun on the ground. His men did the same, but the looks they gave the intruders were far more murderous than Marko's glare.

"They are not together," Anya said as she saw a few of the same men that had been part of Ben-Nevin's team of killers. "These men work for a ruthless bastard called Ben-Nevin, a colonel in the Israeli Mossad."

"The Mossad?" Marko asked, finally turning away to face his sister.

"Where is the wolf?" one of the men asked as he pushed by one of the villagers. Anya saw that is was a brutish-looking man who handed over his automatic weapon and then slowly pulled a knife from a sheath just under his shirt.

"You men need to leave this place," Marko said as he took a menacing step forward.

Anya saw the look in his eyes and feared for her brother. He took another step and that was when the man raised the knife and poked it into Marko's belly, but the small Gypsy continued with another step that actually sent the blade a quarter inch into his stomach. Marko just smiled as he leaned forward placing more pressure onto the blade. Everett grimaced as he realized this man was trying to goad the intruder into action.

"Oh, this is not going to be good," Charlie said as his eyes locked on something Everett couldn't see. He turned and looked at Anya, who shook her head and then she blinked her eyes toward the ground with a nodding motion. Charlie's eyes again widened when he realized what she was telling him.

At that exact moment Marko hit the ground. The move was so fast that the assassin's blade had no time to cut before the Gypsy was hugging dirt and grass. By the time the man realized what was happening the giant black wolf was on him. One minute he was standing with his knife poised to do its skillful work and the next the man was just gone. They heard a brief scream and then the men around them started shooting into the trees. Anya, Marko, the villagers, Charlie, and Carl were on the ground.

Everett managed to keep his head up and his eyes widened when he saw the Golia spring from the trees again. This time it took a man by the throat and tore it free before springing back into the thick line of trees. The other five men tried to aim and fire and that was why they failed to notice Marko and the others reach for their dropped weapons. Soon shotgun blasts tore at the forest around them. There was no screaming, no shouts, and no warnings. The villagers ruthlessly took every man left standing. As for the wolf, there was no trace.

The small clearing was silent and smoke filled from all of the shooting. Charlie was shaking badly, but it wasn't from the gunfire. He reached over and shook Carl's arm.

"Did . . . did you see the size of that wolf? That wasn't Mikla," Ellenshaw said as his words ended in a high-pitched squeak.

Everett saw Anya stand and run toward Marko and help him up and then he turned away and looked around him at the dead men as the villagers walked from corpse to corpse checking on the dead and dying.

"Well, we didn't need this," Marko said, shaking his head. His eyes soon went to Everett and Charlie. His blackened pupils narrowed as he locked eyes with the larger, blond-haired American.

"They saw Stanus," he said as he took a step toward them.

Anya saw the look in her brother's eyes.

"Yes, and they also saw Mikla. And they saved your sister's life just half an hour ago from these very same men."

Everett finally realized just who it was he was looking at. Marko Korvesky, the Gypsy heir apparent.

Ben-Nevin waited patiently for the rest of his men. They had not answered the radios even when the reception was good. The iron ore inside the mountains wreaked havoc on all communication outside of a landline. The colonel looked at his watch as he spied three of the men he had sent searching for the others come from out of the tree line. They shook their heads when they saw the colonel looking their way.

"Well?" he asked, tossing the useless radio to his second in command.

"We found what amounted to a sea of blood, and this." One of the men handed over an AK-47 assault rifle. The barrel was bent. Ben-Nevin examined the weapon and then handed it back with what amounted to distaste. "Our quarry has left the area and we haven't enough men left to search."

"How many men have we?" he asked.

"Counting us five, eighteen men remain."

Ben-Nevin once more shook his head. He reached into his coat pocket and brought out the message sent from Tel Aviv and held it in his damaged hand.

"This message was to convey to me that Tel Aviv has no more personnel to send us."

"So, what is your plan, Colonel?" the taller assistant asked as Ben-Nevin turned away and fixed his eyes on the resort sitting two miles distant.

"I plan on recovering the people's treasure, and the only way we can do that is to secure the ally recommended to us by our friends in Tel Aviv. Our contacts say he would be receptive to adding to his collection, and if not he dearly loves money. In either case we have no choice, it's the Russian or we go it alone."

"What if this . . . this . . . casino owner already knows where the temple is, wouldn't we be exposing ourselves if we brief him on what we are really after?"

Ben-Nevin had a smile on his face when he turned back to face his two men.

"What is life without a little danger and intrigue?"

"Colonel?" his man asked, confused.

Ben-Nevin wiped his face on a handkerchief and then removed his coat and brushed at the dust and pine needles that had become attached to the material.

"When you have nothing left to lose, danger becomes a moot point." Ben-Nevin placed his coat back on and then turned and looked at the Edge of the World resort once more.

"I don't follow, Colonel."

"Tel Aviv is betting, and I concur with their assessment, that that stupid Russian has no idea the greatest treasure in the history of the world is but a few miles away sitting inside a mountain he only thinks is a nice place for gangsters and thieves to rest and relax."

"Do you think he will assist?" the man persisted.

"Oh, yes, and he may also become a convenient scapegoat if things fall apart." Ben-Nevin turned and opened the car's front door and then they were on their way to meet a possible partner in the assault on the mountain and he knew that he had very little time before General Shamni in Tel Aviv decided to act.

Operation Ramesses would be launched and the mountain and the temple would be destroyed—not by God's fire, but flames with the power of the sun.

Niles wanted the Group represented in the lead Humvee as they set out past the main road that led to the resort. Will Mendenhall was riding with the lead element of 82nd Airborne engineers as the two vehicles started out. They left five men at camp to hopefully wait for the soon to arrive Romanian army trucks with their Event Group equipment. As far as they knew, the trucks and their rather expensive satellite equipment and weapons were still on their way to the Danube.

Niles always heard about government-run operations outside of his Group as being sloppy at times, but this was the first time he had seen it happen in his department and it frustrated him no end. The perfectionist inside him made him realize just how hard his field teams had it at times and how fast they had to think on the fly.

Compton reached into his pocket and pulled out a weather sitrep supplied by the 82nd as they accidentally scanned a Romanian army alert that the storm had stalled in the south and that the weather system might miss them completely. And even the parts of the massive front that hit the Danube region had not been as severe as they first predicted. Compton reached over and handed the message to Alice, who was squeezed in between Denise Gilliam and a rather hefty engineer in desert camouflage. Alice read the note. She smiled and shook her head as she handed the message back to Compton.

"So our equipment is down south assisting a region where the massive storm never materialized, and the entire cover story and Romanian army fronting us hightailed it to that same region. Do you think that anyone will have enough common sense to send at least our equipment back? Or maybe even a few troops?"

Niles laughed, a short burst brimming with sarcasm.

"Yes I do, just as soon as we won't need them anymore."

"See," Alice said smiling back at the director, "Jack's field humor is starting to rub off on you."

He looked at his old friend. "Honestly, I don't know how that man and his field teams survive sometimes with the dumb, bad luck those boys run into on a daily basis."

"Amen," Alice said as the Airborne Humvees turned onto the road that paralleled the resort and led the way to Dracula's Castle and then the pass beyond.

As they passed the main gates of the resort they saw the reporters and protesters standing by as the festivities at the exclusive resort continued into the second day of the private grand opening.

"I hope Jack and Sarah watch themselves in there."

Niles didn't comment on Alice's worry; he was looking at the giant steel towers that were the first of many that supported the gilded cable car system. The skyway was operating at only half capacity bringing men and women to the top where they could tour the outside of Dracula's Castle. After they toured they came down, as they were not being allowed to take a sneak peek inside the gaudy nightclub. The large cars moved simultaneously up and down the giant eight-line cable support.

"Now that is something you might see in Bavaria or someplace like that. Very impressive," Denise Gilliam said as they watched the sixty-two-foot cars glide easily along their stretched cables.

"Yes, and we now know how at least part of that was financed," Niles said as his eyes moved over to Alice. "Let's not lose sight of that in the midst of werewolves and Lost Tribes of Israel, shall we. And I hope Jack watches his back inside that den of thieves."

Alice knew Niles was right. Discoveries or not, there were still dangers to the game they were playing, the Russian mobster not being the least of them. As they made the turn onto the large and winding road, the Humvees suddenly came to a stop due to oncoming traffic. The column of cars, trucks, motorcycles, and broken and battered travel homes cut the corner sharply and headed in the direction they were currently going. The lead car was a battered and very old Citroën sedan. As Niles watched the cars stream past he saw that each vehicle was filled with women, children, and men. They were all dressed brightly and every dented and rusted-out car or truck had loud music blaring from open windows. Niles even saw a rather large pig riding shotgun inside an old Mercedes truck.

"What in the world?" Dr. Gilliam asked as they watched the Gypsy caravan move off ahead of them. They too were heading for the Patinas Pass.

"It seems the Gypsies are gathering," Alice said as she leaned forward to examine the caravan more clearly. "I cannot believe we are seeing this."

"What's so special about a caravan of locals?" Denise asked.

"I could be wrong, and this is a rather large guess," Alice said as her smile grew with every passing car or battered camper, "but I think Mr. Everett's young and very former Mossad agent from Rome has arrived."

"You mean they know about her and are coming back to greet her?" Denise asked, finally removing her eyes from the road where the last of the twenty-two vehicles slowly passed by.

"I believe so." She looked at Denise and then slapped Niles on the knee as the Humvees fell into the back of the caravan's long line of color and sound.

"What?" he asked.

"The Gathering?"

"What's that?" Niles asked as the Humvee started up the long road toward the Pass.

"Gypsies hardly ever gather in one large group. These travelers are not just your typical Gypsy band. What we have here is the extended royal family if you will. They travel as a small family or as a caravan as they move safely together from one place to another. But they ordinarily never congregate at any location where they are exposed as a whole. The special ones—the Gypsies that are royalty, for the most part they never left Europe. They stayed and they separated and never do they come together as a people. Now here they are and there can only be one explanation for it," she said as she reached for a small journal she kept in her jacket pocket. She thumbed through it until she found the entry she was searching for. "The family of man is getting ready to have a change of power. Someone is stepping down as the king, or the queen." She smiled broadly. "I suspect that's why they are gathering."

As Alice began to believe in her dreams coming true, the two U.S. Army Humvees followed the motley group of Gypsy revelers as they climbed past Dracula's Castle and the high mountain beyond.

12

After Collins had sent Ryan and Pete out to see if they could get a hint of where Captain Everett and Charlie Ellenshaw had disappeared to, he decided he and Sarah needed to start getting close to some of the seedier characters in the resort. Perhaps that way they could get a line on the antiquities that seemed to have flooded the world from this not so very sophisticated criminal, Dmitri Zallas.

He and Sarah had been studying the man's dossier for the past two hours try-ing to find a common thread with any of the names of Jack's security watch list for antiquities theft. Thus far they had discovered several very familiar faces in the milling crowds of gamblers and revelers. As the couple roamed the grounds freely they did spy several of Dmitri's henchmen keeping a close eye on them.

As they strolled along the mud baths and steam rooms of the atrium they saw men and women used to the decadent way of life soaking in the hot mud and natural steam baths of the mountain. Zallas was placing no mind to the cost of this expen-sive weekend as every guest seemed to be attended by one or more of the hotel staff. They were approached no fewer than three times and offered drinks, towels, robes, and any other accouterment that comes along with the filthy rich and pampered in the short time they walked through the beautiful spa area.

"Do you think we could talk Niles into building one of these for the com-plex?" Sarah jokingly asked as she dipped her head at a rather large and bulbous-looking man with a beard as he slowly sank into the mud with an appreciative glance toward Sarah. Then as she watched the man's face became a scowl as he quickly rose from the mud complaining about the excessive heat.

"You bet. I'm sure he can scrape together the extra $45 million in the budget somewhere."

Sarah smiled and then just as quickly lost it when she saw Zallas with his ever-present group of men and women around him approach with a wide smile. Jack's worst fears about a blown cover came readily to her mind.

"Tell me my friends, are you enjoying your stay at the Edge of the World?" he said with a smile that said he just ate the cat that ate the canary and there wasn't anything anyone could do about it.

Jack and Sarah both knew the sole purpose of this little run-in was for Zallas to gauge who he was dealing with when it came to Americans. The colonel knew Zallas suspected, but for right now that was just about all. He would play his little hand to the end.

"One of the more hospitable resorts I have ever been to," Jack said, even though he had never been to a resort in his life. "And also one of the more gra-cious hosts I have ever encountered."

Zallas tilted his head and laughed as he held out his hand to Jack.

"I don't believe I have had the pleasure, Mr.—?"

Collins, as did Sarah, studied the man's demeanor and they both knew at that exact moment that their fears were not unfounded. Zallas, while he may not know just who they were, suspected they could be some sort of law enforcement, and he was gauging the two to see what steps he would need to take to make sure his in-terest was protected.

"Collins, Jack Collins, Colonel, United States Army, and this is Lieutenant Sarah McIntire of the same organization."

Zallas had a hard time not showing his surprise as he quickly and deftly by-passed Jack's offered hand and instead took Sarah's and harshly kissed it, making Sarah wince at the wetness of the action. Between Zallas kissing her hand and the utter shock she was feeling after Jack had suddenly blurted out exactly who they were, Sarah was flustered enough that she froze after Zallas kissed her hand and then finally reached for Jack's.

"Now this *is* surprising. How does a soldier, and one so beautiful," he said, shaking the colonel's hand and then quickly looking at Sarah in her expensive pantsuit that no longer fit the cover they had blown, "find their way to my resort?"

"That's easy enough, uh, Mr. Zallas is it?" Jack asked.

The Russian stepped back and smiled. He nodded his head and then fixed Collins with a look that bordered on distaste.

"Yes, Dmitri Zallas, I am the owner of the Edge of the World."

"As I said, Mr. Zallas, there is a simple enough explanation. We were assigned to the NATO forces and had some time off. By a fluke we decided, what the hell, let's see if we can get a reservation, and here we are. I admit to using absconded invitations but they can only kick us out, right?"

"Yes, but kick out is harsh term. I'm sure we could come up with something better than that." Jack heard the veiled threat buried in the comment. "Strange though that our reservations center isn't in operation yet and all of my guests and business acquaintances were all informed of the pre–grand opening by courier."

"If that's the strangest thing you run into all weekend, I'd call that pretty good," Jack said as he returned the stare of Zallas.

The Russian raised a hand and gestured toward someone Jack couldn't see. Soon enough Gina Louvinski strode up to the group.

"Yes, Mr. Zallas," she said, nodding her head at Jack and Sarah, wishing they would have stayed clear of the mobster.

"This is our resort's general manager, Ms. Louvinski," Zallas said.

Jack and Sarah knew that the Russian had obviously been informed that they had exchanged words early this morning with Ryan and Pete in attendance.

"Yes, we met Ms. Louvinski this morning before breakfast."

"Ms. Louvinski will make sure your time at my resort is an enjoyable one. Gina, please make sure the colonel and the lieutenant have passes for the show tomorrow night at Dracula's Castle. Make sure their table is close to mine," he said smiling as his eyes went to Collins. "Shall we also make arrangement for your two companions to join the fun?" he asked in almost passable English.

"The more the merrier," Sarah said as Collins and Zallas continued to face off. Both men were smiling but neither was showing any mirth in their eyes. Finally Jack held out his hand to the Russian.

"My thoughts exactly," Zallas said as he quickly brushed Jack's hand with his own and then nodded his good-bye as he took Gina by the arm and he and his entourage moved away. Gina nodded her head at Jack and Sarah as she was pulled out.

Collins and McIntire watched the group leave. Zallas looked as if he wanted to kill the general manager right there in the spa. She was shaking her head and Jack knew the woman might pay for their subterfuge. Maybe he shouldn't have told Zallas exactly who they were, that could only mean trouble for the Romanian woman.

"Jack, if I may ask, have you gone totally insane?" Sarah lost all pretense of being his subordinate and turned on him. "'I'm Colonel Jack Collins and this is Lieutenant So-and-So of the United States Army.' I ask again, have you lost your mind?"

"Look, he knows we are not his friends, and he knows we don't do business with him, so it would have been foolish to keep up the facade. That man knows bad people and he would have seen us coming from five miles away. He knows for a fact that Ryan and Pete are with us, so why lie? If he was that worried about us he would do something about it. Since he didn't we have bought some time while he tries to figure out what to do about us. Just maybe being that he's Russian he would be hesitant about killing any NATO representatives."

Sarah rolled her eyes at the colonel, letting him know in no uncertain terms what she thought of his exercise.

"Have you considered that maybe that man is just a nutcase and would order us killed anyway, just because he didn't like or trust us? What makes you think he had the sophistication to think beyond the fact that some people tried to penetrate his security and did? And do you think he's smart enough to order us buried someplace up there?" She gestured toward the mountain.

"That's what I'm banking on."

"He's not Henri Farbeaux, Jack, this man has not one ounce of honor, he reacts, he doesn't think."

"Well, I hope you're wrong."

Zallas stopped admonishing Gina about the reservations deceit Collins had just told him about and then pushed her away to see to the guests.

"Those two, and their two companions?"

"Yes, Mr. Zallas?" the largest of the five bodyguards asked.

"They are never to leave this valley. U.S. Army my ass. If they're not Interpol or American CIA, or FBI I will give Janos Vajic the deed to this resort."

"Sir?"

"I want all four of their heads, hands, and teeth removed, and then buried amongst the rocks where the crows can't even find them."

Pete Golding and Jason Ryan were just two of the twenty guests of the resort who stood looking up at the majestic sight. The cable car wasn't even a quarter full and that left plenty of viewing space for the men and women as they gasped at the setting high above them at Dracula's Castle. While Pete marveled at the modern architectural materials used to create the illusion of age and strength and noting that the castle was something to behold, Jason was trying to figure out just how many of the men and women inside the car were actually there to view the castle, or who was there to keep their eyes on him and Pete. Thus far he had counted at least two of them as Zallas's people. They just weren't quick enough to look away when Jason turned toward them several times.

"Do you think the captain and Charlie came up here?" Pete asked.

"It's a place to start."

As the cable car rose to its optimal height on its way up the mountain, a hidden speaker system kept the guests informed as they studied the design of the castle. It was a recording by a very familiar Hollywood actor who seemed to narrate anything that came down the pike these days and it surprised Pete and Jason very much to hear his voice explaining the Vlad Tepes legend and the cross-reference to the Dracula tale, and all of this was done in English, Romanian, and French. As the castle grew larger the words of the narrator was starting to have its effect. As the voice explained why Vlad was deemed insane Jason and Pete felt the history of this mountain come alive.

The car climbed and Jason jabbed Pete on the side as he gestured out the window and down. Far below on the wide road parallel to the castle and winding upward to the pass high above, they saw a long line of over a hundred vehicles of every make and description. Jason nodded his head and suggested Pete look in the center of the long column. Pete nodded when he recognized the two Humvees that stood out like new cars at a wrecking yard.

"Well, at least someone is sticking to some form of the plan we had going in."

Pete looked at Jason and nodded just as the car approached the large platform where the passengers would be discharged. There was a mild bump as the car gained the platform, which was built to look like large embedded stones and thick, fire-hardened wood. There were wrought iron torches lining the wall, and while they were gas fed and burned brightly, it was still an adequate effect. Pete was impressed. Jason was not as he saw the two men who had been eyeing them step off the car with the rest.

Ryan and Golding stepped from the car and watched as the two men hesitated and then when they knew they couldn't stay behind the crowd without being noticed, moved off with the oohing and awing men and women as they examined the lobby of the giant nightclub.

The interior was done like a Hollywood movie set and even Ryan had to gasp at the decor. It was something right out of a Bram Stoker novel. The expense shown in decoration alone proved to Pete and Ryan once and for all that this place required inordinate amounts of cash.

The stage was enormous and rivaled anything seen in Las Vegas. A trapdoor system built along the lines of a Broadway stage for raising and lowering musical sets was in operation as they watched the final touches being put in place for the big grand opening tomorrow night.

"You would think this would be the place you would want to see in operation until you realize the possibility that stolen antiquities may have been the financing plan behind it."

Ryan had to agree with Pete. This was a wad of money and to come up with that inside a country that was still trying to see if it was viable after the collapse of communism was nearly impossible. Not many banks are willing to loan money when their people are in danger of having no heating oil for the hard winters here. No, bad money was here and on display.

"Wow, I saw his show in Las Vegas!" Pete said as he walked up to the large cardboard cutout of Drake Andrews as he stood clad in a garish purple tuxedo and was crooning to an audience that rarely came to see his shows in the desert any longer.

Pete gave the cardboard cutout one last hug across the shoulders just as if he were a tourist getting his photo snapped with the legendary entertainer. He smiled at Ryan, who only stared at Golding.

"Sorry, it's just that I'm like an oldies nut."

"Believe me, between you, Doc Ellenshaw, and the colonel I can never take music seriously again."

Pete shrugged his shoulders. "Where to now? I don't see either the captain or Charlie."

Ryan took a breath and looked around the large nightclub. He shook his head. "Yeah, this was a waste of time," he looked back at Pete, "but at least we found out Drake Andrews will be here. Come on, we may have better luck outside," Ryan said, making fun of Pete's man-crush on the entertainer.

"Well, he used to be big."

As Pete and Ryan turned to find an exit that led out onto the mountain, the two Zallas men followed them, brushing by the life-sized cardboard cutout of Drake Andrews, spinning it, and then knocking it to the floor where several men and women inadvertently stepped on it.

OTOPENI INTERNATIONAL AIRPORT, BUCHAREST, ROMANIA

The Russian-made Mi-26 Halo is a twin-turbine heavy-lift helicopter. It is the world's largest production helicopter and was a source of worry for NATO planners for years before the ancient helicopters fell into old age and disrepair and were shipped off to Russia's satellite nations just before the collapse of the Soviet Union. The amount of equipment and personnel it could transport is still a source of pride among its builders and designers. As it sat on the tarmac waiting for the last of the equipment and passengers to be loaded, the heavy engines vibrated and shook the old airframe as if it were in a blender.

As he sat in his seat toward the rear of the old aircraft, American singer Drake Andrews glanced over to his agent, who sat staring straight ahead, afraid to move as the ancient Russian helicopter shook, rattled, and rolled as it idled.

"Remind me to kill you when we get back to Vegas in fourteen months," Andrews said as one of the turbine engines actually backfired, making both men in their expensive clothes jump and yelp.

"I'm not the one that got busted for tax evasion. It was either this or lose that menagerie you call a house in Vegas."

"Yeah, well that two million bucks ain't going to do diddly for me if we crash and burn in something the Wright Brothers wouldn't have climbed into."

"You should have finished school and not been a child star, Drake. The Wright Brothers built airplanes, this is a helicopter," his agent said like he was explaining things to a child.

Edwards looked over at his agent and raised a brow. "Are you getting smart with me after dragging me to Romania of all places? That's ballsy, I'll tell ya."

"Paternity suits, taxes, bar brawls, all because you're mad at the world because it passed you and your show by. Let's just collect your performance fee and get back to Vegas, okay, then you can fire me. Until then just shut up."

"How many acts before me, and will they be in line with my program?" he asked as he closed his eyes.

"You have five acts before yours and they will be doing medley comps to set your show up. They'll do songs from your era, and—"

Drake looked over sharply. "They won't being covering any of my hits, will they?"

"No, Drake, they won't, just hits from the sixties, seventies, and eighties, nothing newer than that and certainly not as old as your stuff," the agent said with a satisfactory smile etched on his face as he too lay back. "As a matter of fact, here are your cover bands now," he continued with an even larger smile.

As Drake looked up he saw the motliest group of men and women he had ever seen marching into the interior of the old helicopter. They had long hair and looked as if they fell right out of a Volkswagen microbus in 1967. There were sixteen of them and some were women who looked as if they took their clothing, hair, and nail advice from Alice Cooper. Suddenly one of the men broke free from the boisterous group and made his way to Drake Andrews with a killer grin on his face. The clothes the man wore were certifiably different from the $2,000 suit that Drake had on. The long-haired man started jabbering in what Drake could only assume to be Romanian or Russian, he wasn't sure.

"Whoa, there, slow down, chief," Drake said as he harshly nudged his agent.

"Drake Andrews, hey everyone, here is Drake!" the man screamed at the top of his lungs to be heard over the increasing engine noise of the vibrating helicopter. "Oh, we look forward to making everyone ready for the big Mr. Drake Andrews, you see, we make men and women hungry to hear you." The man smiled and slapped Drake on the shoulder sending him into his agent next to him. The American watched the enthusiastic young man move forward toward his seat.

Andrews stared at the large group of men and women who were doing everything from wrestling in the aisles to pounding on the window glass to see if it would hold. His eyes widened when one of the Russian band members was escorted to his seat after offering the pilots a bottle of vodka.

"My God, I've died and this is hell. I just didn't realize that hell would be 1967 Haight-Ashbury on an old and broken-down Russian helicopter." He turned and looked at his smiling agent. "The guys warming up for my act are the Manson Family!"

His agent couldn't help, after all the years of hell Drake Andrews had put him through he was finally getting some payback.

"Remind me when we get home to fire you, and then I'm going to kill you!"

PART THREE
THE GOLIA

Even a man who is pure in heart and says his prayers by night may become a wolf when the wolfbane blooms and the autumn moon is bright.

—Curt Siodmak,
The Wolf Man (1941)

13

PATINAS PASS, ROMANIA

The old and battered panel van traveled slowly up the road. Anya wanted them to stop at the small village before reaching Patinas so Mikla could be taken care of. Marko however wanted to get Mikla back to the pass as soon as possible. Not only to get him help, but to also keep Stanus at bay. The giant Golia had only been seen once since the encounter in the woods and that was but a brief moment when Marko observed the wolf watching them from a large crevasse in the mountain while blending in almost perfectly with the dark geologic makeup of the area.

With Mikla taking up most of the floor space in the van the crowding was nerve-wracking to say the least. Anytime someone would move inside the cargo compartment Mikla would raise its large head and growl with his eyes narrowing and his ears laid back. The sight was enough to make even Anya nervous at being closed in with the wounded Golia.

"Are you going to tell me about your American friends?" Marko asked as he rewrapped the bandage around Mikla's ankle. His eyes never rose to meet his sister's.

"This man saved my life in Rome." Anya looked at Everett and then just as quickly her eyes moved away.

"So you bring him home like a stray cat?" Marko said as he tore the very end of the cloth wrapping and then tied it lightly around the wolf's ankle. Mikla for his part only winced. "As you can see, little sister, we have more than enough stray animals running around." He patted Mikla on the head as lightly as he could. "As for you, Mikla, I would advise you to stay clear of Stanus for a while." Marko eased back when Mikla raised its brows and growled very deep in his chest.

Anya looked quickly at Carl and Charlie and wondered if she should broach family business in front of the two men. She then looked at Marko.

"Why did Grandmamma bring me home?" she asked as her eyes drilled into Marko's.

"I can no longer answer for the reasons why our grandmother does anything. It may have something to do with my investments for our people."

As her brother answered, a look of stunned surprise crossed Anya's features. The emotion wasn't lost on Carl.

"Investments?" Her eyes shot toward Everett, who sat and watched the exchange as the van hit a bump in the old dirt road that shook Mikla and made him whine. "Marko, the people need only themselves and the Golia. We lack for nothing."

"We lack for nothing because we have never had anything. This will change. Grandmother's ways are the old ways. And I will not discuss this in front of uninvited guests." He looked at Everett alone and his brown eyes held no compassion for the American even though he had saved his sister's life.

"Tell me, what has changed in three thousand years that would make your people start selling off a heritage you have been guarding since the time of Joshua?" Carl ventured just to see the look on Marko's face.

Next to Everett, Charlie winced as he knew that information shouldn't have been readily available for any American to just read in a history book. Either the captain knew what he was doing or Ellenshaw feared they may have invited this rather unpleasant man with the strange eyes to slide a knife across their throats—something he looked quite capable of doing.

Marko patted Mikla one last time and then straightened and sat leaning against the sidewall of the van. He took a deep breath and looked from Everett to his sister.

"And suddenly this man you just met knows all there is to know about the . . ." He smiled. "Our people."

Anya didn't hear what Marko said, her double-colored eyes of green and brown were on Carl and they didn't move.

"Yes, suddenly he seems very informed." Her left brow rose as she took in the large American. The silence was palpable.

"We try not to go into anything without first knowing the basics." Everett said, allowing his own sight to adjust to Marko. The two men sized each other up and they both found they could not read the other's ability.

The Gypsy raised his left brow and then he reached up and toyed with the hoop earring as he thought.

"We?" Marko asked as a smile seemed to break slowly across his lips. "By 'we' I take your meaning to encompass your four friends staying at the resort? Friends that have already stood out like coal on a snowy landscape, so much so that whoever you and your people are have brought the unwanted attention of a very unsavory man who just happens to own the resort."

"And suddenly you know an awful lot about us, or at least enough to know what that unsavory character is doing. Or should I say, Dmitri Zallas—your business partner?"

Marko swallowed and then looked from the American to Anya. The sad look in her eyes told him that she saw what he was doing. Marko always dreamed of his people being normal. That they could also be human, live side by side with the rest of the world, and he always told his dreams to his baby sister, who used to be sympathetic to those dreams. But as he looked at her now he knew Anya was now just as his grandmother *was*—dedicated to keeping the old ways intact.

"Marko, what have you done?" Anya lowered her head, no longer able to look her brother in the eyes.

"I did what many leaders before me should have done. Why would these so-called leaders of a nation keep us in abject poverty while the rest of the world thrives? Our lives have never changed. We are still subservient."

"And the Golia?" Anya asked.

Marko smiled for the first time and he placed a gentle hand on the back of the resting Mikla.

"They are strong once more. They do not need us to live. They are home, and they will remain. Now we shall join the world as a people and live the way we should have for these many years. We owe others nothing."

"Let me tell you, my friend, as a man that has been in that real world you're talking about, I'll tell you this, it's bleak at times and everyone, and I do mean everyone, fights for survival out there." Everett pointed toward the wall of the step-van. "And from what I can see out there this is a real home—the only kind of home that ever made sense. Don't just toss that away for a few of the finer things, because, buddy, the finer things are right in front of you."

Ellenshaw was stunned to silence and looked away. Anya on the other hand was looking at Carl as if a light had been shone on his features for the first time. She tilted her head to the left and studied him until he looked her way and then she closed her eyes and took a deep breath.

Marko glanced at his sister and didn't care for the way she watched the American when the van came to a stop.

Anya looked up and knew she had finally returned home to Patinas. And as the doors of the van were thrown open the mountain came alive with the sound of the Golia as their howls rent the daytime skies of the Carpathians.

THE EDGE OF THE WORLD HOTEL AND RESORT CASINO, PATINAS, ROMANIA

Jack watched Sarah on the grounds of the hotel just inside the sprawling pool area. The geologist had made sure she wasn't being spied on by the one sunbather, obviously a woman not interested in the goings-on with the underworld inside the casino. Sarah bent at the waste and stuck a small thermometer attached to the thinnest of wires into the chlorinated water. She looked at the readout on her small watch. The expensive equipment was some of the only tools Jack and Sarah had left to them after their trucks had been diverted to the south.

"Well?" Jack asked.

"A one-degree rise since eight this morning."

"Short stuff, they obviously had to have known this was a seismic area, or why in the hell would they build it here?"

Sarah slowly and expertly replaced the small probe and the wire spooled neatly into the watch base.

"The simplest and best explanation could be they just didn't check. Remember, this area was under government control for close to two thousand years. I don't imagine many seismologists or geophysicists have been nosing around this region."

"You mean they just skipped over the land's geologic appraisal?"

"Jack?"

"Yeah," he said as he looked to the distant front gates at the milling news reporters and protesters who still remained despite the slowly moving black clouds coming their way.

"What do you think the cost of this resort is?" she asked as she looked around the vast property.

"Niles placed the estimate at somewhere in the two-and-a-half-billion-dollar range for the resort, the castle, and the property. Plus no telling how much was spent on bribes to get the land." He turned away from his view of the far-off front gates and then faced Sarah. "Why do you ask?"

"Why would he built it here, it's that simple, he had to have known this area was seismically active, he had to."

"What in the hell are you getting at?" Jack finally asked.

"He could have bought property anywhere in Romania, and better, more access to the resort, why build in the middle of nowhere?"

"Because you said it yourself, the land was cheap."

"No, Jack, the land wasn't cheap. It's all in the reports. Possible bribes to the interior minister, negotiating with the locals for use of the roads. No, Jack, he could have gotten by with half of his money spent. No, he bought here for a specific reason."

Jack turned away and examined the men and women walking through the resort on the far side of the glass. His gaze wandered from the casino to the restaurant and then to the giant atrium.

"Do you think he knows about the Jeddah? Maybe not Alice's wolves, but the Jeddah themselves?"

"Why would he care?" she asked.

"Remember what the reports said about the ancient tales of the Lost Tribes? The disgraced professor in Los Angeles said that one of these tribes was rumored to be carrying the vast treasures of countless campaigns from the Exodus. The biggest rumor was the one about the great temple being erected in a far-off place that housed the greatest treasures of not only Egypt, but of the ancient Hebrew people."

"Jack, that's stretching it somewhat, isn't it?" Sarah said as she realized that not even she could fathom someone risking that much money over a rumor.

"What would the antiquities alone be worth?" he asked instead of answering her.

"Priceless. You couldn't place a worth on something like that. The cultural and historical aspects alone are worth . . . worth . . ."

"Far more than two and a half billion dollars I would say."

"Still too thin, Jack, so thin I could see through it. I mean two and a half billion dollars in the hand is worth far more than speculation of trillions in the bush."

Jack looked down at Sarah and smiled as he shook his head. "Nice turn of phrase, short stuff."

"I have my moments."

"Still, things just don't add up. This place will make money, there's no doubt of that. But I just don't see our Russian friend as a real hotel entrepreneur, do you?"

"No, Conrad Hilton he isn't."

"Then let's hope Alice and Niles come up with more information when they hit the pass." Jack shook his head and then walked away a few paces as the sun broke through a few of the clouds.

"What is it?" she asked.

"I was just wondering how far Zallas would go to see if the rumors of the treasure of the Lost Tribe are true. I mean we know he was being fed antiquities from someone, more than likely a Jeddah. Marko—maybe, maybe not. But the *one* thing we do know is that he has to believe that his supplier has access to a cache of treasure. Maybe it wasn't in his original plan, but things may have changed. We know from the dates of the building permits that Dracula's Castle was a last-minute expense. That could have been built far lower on the mountain for far less money."

"Hey, it's me; tell me what you're thinking."

"Just four or five trinkets from the Exodus may have earned this man close to a billion dollars, just think what avarice-filled dreams he has running through his head. Again I ask—how far would he go to get his hands on the treasure if he suspected it was real?"

"With his history, I shudder to speculate."

"Well, let's just hope he can never confirm where those antiquities are coming from."

Dmitri Zallas was eating his lunch. His constant womanly companionship was missing as he always preferred to eat alone. That was the only time he had to think and he didn't need inane conversation.

Zallas was small for a Russian mobster. Most men in his line of work got things done through sheer brute intimidation and usually they got this way because they were bigger and stronger than most. But Zallas had to do things differently. Because he was so short and stocky he had to think his way out of trouble. He had to plan accordingly and he gambled the same way. This was why he was in the Patinas region of Romania—speculation. Oh, the resort was a fantastic investment and he would make billions on it. That wasn't what Dmitri really cared for, he wanted the risk—the problem solving that comes with the search. He knew his affliction wasn't greed, it was power. Those antiquities gave him power; the power of knowledge.

He looked up and saw Gina Louvinski standing at the entrance to the restaurant watching him. He tilted his head and the general manager held up something and pointed at his table. Her clipboard was still pressed against her chest. Dmitri took a sip of coffee and then gestured for Gina to join him. He looked at his two bodyguards and they allowed the tall woman to pass. Zallas took his napkin and wiped his mouth and then tossed it on his still full plate.

"And what can I help you with, Ms. Louvinski?" he asked in a bored sort of way.

Gina held out a small card. Zallas looked at it and raised his brows. He didn't reach for it.

"A rather dirty and unkempt man at the front gate gave your security detail this."

Zallas looked at the business card but still didn't reach for it.

The card didn't waver as it was held firm in front of Zallas.

Zallas sipped more coffee and then placed the cup down and snatched the card from her grasp. When he looked it over he saw that it was plain white with no bordering or fancy lettering—white with black print.

"Avi Ben-Nevin," he said as he read the card. He held it up and then looked at Gina with his brows raised once more—he was running short of patience.

"Read the back," she said and then turned and left the restaurant.

The Russian watched her leave and then deftly flipped the card over.

"Colonel, Israeli Mossad." The hastily scrawled note below it was written in Cyrillic—the Russian alphabet: "The Treasure of the Exodus—I know the location."

For the first time that weekend, Dmitri Zallas and his smile were genuine.

"Yes," he said to himself. "Real estate speculation could be very rewarding."

The bright red Toyota Land Cruiser with the Edge of the World logo on both front doors pulled up to the hotel's main entrance. Colonel Ben-Nevin wondered if the advice he had received from Tel Aviv was sending him to disaster instead of a possible ally.

Zallas was standing by the large one-hundred-foot glass window that looked out onto the pool area. He was speaking with one of his men and didn't turn to see Ben-Nevin as he waited to be noticed. The Russian said something to the man and the bodyguard nodded and then walked away. With one last look at the couple standing by the swimming pool Zallas turned and faced the colonel. He wasn't smiling but he was holding the business card. Zallas held the card in front of him and then snapped it twice with his fingers creating a popping sound. The Russian took a few steps toward the man in the dirty suit.

"I would usually tell a guest dressed such as you that we adhere to a strict dress code in certain areas of the resort." Zallas looked around him at the guests passing through the front lobby. "And this is one of those areas."

"Apologies," Ben-Nevin said as he examined the bearded man in the white suit and red tie. The colonel knew the type of man this was before he even opened his mouth. As a Russian the colonel knew the man wasn't fond of his ethnic background. The man's dark little eyes washed over the Israeli with a look of distaste.

"You have an interesting way of introducing yourself, Colonel. One that would sway me to believe that you had this card printed—a lie perhaps," he smiled for the first time, "to go with the meaningless phrase you have scrawled on the back." Zallas popped the business card again.

Ben-Nevin felt the eyes of his bodyguards on him but he took another step forward, closing the space between him and the Russian. His smile matched his hosts.

"If I had the audacity to lie to a man with your reputation and resources on your property with no backup, I think I would listen to this audacious gentleman until you could decide for yourself if he *is* a liar."

Zallas finally placed the card in his silk jacket pocket and then gestured for the colonel to join him at the window.

"All right, Colonel, let's say you are this man and have earned this title for this particular organization, what can I do for you except to explain I am not a big follower of the Exodus. My knowledge is limited to that old American film I am afraid."

Ben-Nevin could see immediately that the man was an expert liar. He could see the mind working inside his thick skull on how to get the information from him without giving away anything in return. The man was a moron who was as see-through as the glass they were looking out of.

"If I were a man in an intelligence position, I would undoubtedly have information on antiquities smuggling and the sale of same." Ben-Nevin continued to look out of the window at the couple standing by the pool. They seemed engrossed in deep conversation, and for some reason they looked out of place to the trained eye of the colonel. He watched the couple as he spoke. "I know you have come in contact with certain items that I and many people are interested in. We are willing to offer compensation to the individual who assists my organization in this quest."

"Treasure hunting in Romania?" Zallas turned and looked at Ben-Nevin, his eyes roaming over his dirty clothing. "I'm waiting with great expectation, Colonel."

"You have never heard of the spoils of Egypt taken by the Hebrews during the Exodus? Vast amounts of gold, jewelry, and other finery—the spoils of countless battles and wars. A treasure so vast that no one can begin to speculate its true worth. And that is but the tip of the iceberg." The colonel was speaking in passionate Russian. "The antiquities you have auctioned off to finance this . . . this . . . playground," Ben-Nevin gestured around him, "were but a minuscule portion of what awaits inside the great temple of the Jeddah."

Zallas turned fully on to face the Israeli. "Great temple?" he asked, not knowing Ben-Nevin had expertly drawn the shallow gangster out of his lie about not knowing anything.

"One so large it had to be hidden inside a mountain."

"A mountain," Zallas repeated as if he were almost dozing.

"A temple built by the great artisans of the Hebrew nation, and the engineers that once designed the great halls of Ramesses II."

Zallas remained silent as he looked into the eyes of the colonel. Ben-Nevin saw a small twitch at the corner of his mouth and knew that at least he had the idiot's attention. Finally he saw the small man smile and then shake his head.

"A nice fairy tale indeed, we have many like them stemming from the czars of lost treasures hidden by the despots of old." He laughed. "I must ask where you came across such a story, and finally, how you may prove it really exists."

This time Ben-Nevin was the one to smile as he finally removed his eyes from the couple by the pool.

"The proof you're looking for is with the man you have relied on in the past to invest in your joint venture here."

Zallas outright laughed. "My partner, you mean Mr. Vajic? I'm afraid you have failed to convince me, Colonel."

"That is not the man I speak of. Your not so silent partner is in the capital and should arrive sometime tonight. Your *real* silent partner and the man that made all of this possible for you, lives up there." Ben-Nevin turned and pointed north toward the pass. "His name is Marko Korvesky. You know this name, yes?" The smile remained on the colonel's face. He knew his connections inside the Knesset had come through, as the Russian's artificial-light-induced tan drained from his face and the smile vanished.

"And suddenly you know much about my business affairs, Jew."

"Ah, that hurt." Ben-Nevin also lost his smile. "But very much off the point, Mr. Zallas. The real edge of this sword is that your man Marko knows where the temple is. He was supplying you with antiquities that could not have come from anyplace else but the temple I have just described. And now I will let you in on a little bit of intelligence that may help you decide in a timely manner if you should assist me and my associates in this endeavor—or if you will bury me in those lonely mountains someplace and throw away a chance at immortality."

"I'm listening," the Russian said menacingly.

"Good, now that's productive, Mr. Zallas."

"You are beginning to irritate me, Jew Colonel."

"Yes, I can see that. The temple has stood for three thousand years." Ben-Nevin leaned in closer to Zallas. "And I can guarantee you that elements outside my control will be coming for what they consider their property in less than forty-eight hours."

"And just who are these elements?"

"Members of my government you wouldn't want visiting your resort, I assure you."

The Russian turned and watched the two people by the pool walk away toward the entrance to the hotel. His eyes watched them with intent.

"Do you know this man and woman?" he asked, nodding toward the man and woman and also taking Ben-Nevin off guard with the sudden change of subject.

"No." He hadn't let on that he also thought the two by the pool looked out of place.

"They are American." He turned and faced the Israeli. "I suspect law enforcement of some kind. American FBI, CIA, or perhaps Interpol."

"That man is no policeman," Ben-Nevin said as he watched the way the dark-haired visitor carried himself. "That gentleman is military."

"Yes, that's just what the American said. I don't believe him."

"Then by all means you must watch him." Ben-Nevin finally turned away as the man and woman walked in through the entrance. "My tale, Mr. Zallas, does the recovery of the subject matter interest you?"

Dmitri Zallas turned and then gestured toward one of his men. The guard left the area and was back very quickly with Gina Louvinski in tow. She stepped up to Zallas and the man with the filthy suit.

"Yes, Mr. Zallas," she said, trying to mask her irritation at having to jump every time the Russian commanded.

"Have our friend here see our medical staff for that hand and see to it that he has credit at our clothing shop and set aside a suite of rooms for him and his men on a vacant floor as I'm sure they also could use some cleaning up. I wish them to be kept away from my other guests, is that clear?"

"Yes, Mr. Zallas," she answered blandly as she turned away toward the front desk.

"A wise decision," the colonel said as he watched the American man and woman disappear into the hotel, "and one that should profit you to no end."

"I always profit. I have a way of securing my investments."

Ben-Nevin turned on Zallas and became deadly serious. "But I must warn you that we may be up against a considerable force of will when it comes to this Gypsy and his people. I hope you have sufficient numbers to take what it is we came for." Ben-Nevin wasn't even considering the human element in the equation, but he surely wasn't about to mention the extremely large wolf that seemed to be protecting the Jeddah.

"Colonel, when you are at the front desk, ask to see the guest list, tell Ms. Louvinski you have my permission."

"And why should I do that?"

"That, Colonel Jew, is my army." He turned away and started for the casino. "That and a hundred armed men who will die on my command."

Ben-Nevin watched the Russian walk away as if he were a god amongst mere mortals.

The colonel turned and walked into the hotel lobby. He immediately saw the same man and woman from outside as they strolled toward him and the elevators beyond. The dark-haired American never made eye contact with him although they came within a foot of touching.

Jack lowered his eyes as he placed an arm around Sarah and pulled her close as they walked.

"Oh, shit," Collins hissed as they walked past the front desk.

"What?" Sarah said, avoiding the temptation to turn and look at what Jack had just spied.

"The hotel is filling up with the saltiest-looking people."

"You mean the man in the dirty suit?" she said low enough that only Jack could hear.

"Yeah, that man just happens to be Colonel Avi Ben-Nevin, Israeli Mossad, the man that tried his best to kill Carl, Ryan, and our man at the Vatican. And a man I can only assume is on the run."

"And now he's here."

"It just may turn out to be an explosive weekend."

"What are we going to do?" she asked.

"We do our job and hope that Ryan and Pete find Everett." Collins stopped and waited for the elevator but turned and faced Sarah.

"That may be hard to do with you telling Zallas who we are. But you're right," she said, easing her look toward the filthy man at the front desk and then just as quickly looking back at Jack. "This is trouble."

Jack frowned as the elevator doors opened.

"That is an alliance we didn't see coming."

"Well, we're not fortune-tellers and we're sure as hell not Europa," he said with a smile as they stepped into the elevator.

"Or Gypsies."

VILLAGE OF PATINAS

Carl and Charlie had been unceremoniously pushed into what amounted to a small barn. The place smelled like goats or sheep, Everett couldn't decide which, or if it even mattered. Anya, Marko, and quite a few of the men who had captured them had eased Mikla onto a makeshift stretcher made from the front door of a nearby house. The door was far too small to accommodate the size of the animal but the men managed to get him out of the stuffy van.

The strange thing was that when Mikla was exposed to the outside for the first time after being moved into the open air, the mountain around them came alive with noise and Everett and Charlie could swear they heard howling. Carl hoped it was his imagination because the sounds had to have been made by, many hundreds of wolves.

The captain watched the small house in the center of the town through a break in the wooden slats that made up the facade of the barn. Everett knew he could punch out one of the slats with ease, but he had decided to play this out and hope that the woman made someone listen to reason. He watched as even more of the villagers made their way to the house where Marko and Anya had vanished.

Ellenshaw tapped Carl on the shoulder.

"Look at this," he said pointing out a small window on the south side of the barn.

The captain stepped to the small window and saw a hundred people on the road leading to Patinas. They were men, women, children and they had goats, a cow, a wagon with several pigs inside, and they were all smiling and looked as if they were on their way to a large picnic or small fair. The music they played as they walked along the road was festive and was made up of tambourines, violins, flutes, and horns. The music grew louder as they came upon the village.

"They must be from the nearby towns," Everett said as he watched the progression of brightly dressed Gypsies.

"What are they here for?" Charlie asked as he strained to see over Carl's shoulder.

"I don't know, but I'm sure we'll find out soon enough."

Madam Korvesky held her granddaughter to her chest and cried. Marko, feeling uncomfortable at first, softened as he watched both women, his only true blood in the world sob over the years that had been lost.

Marko turned away and ran his hand through the thick black fur of Mikla. The wolf lay still and allowed Marko to stroke him. The beast closed its yellow glowing eyes and that was when he placed his hand on Mikla's head and pressed ever so slightly as the animal dosed. Marko tilted his head as his hand moved by small increments around the beast's skull. Mikla winced once in his sleep and then settled.

A fleeting vision of Anya came to his mind and then the face of a man he didn't recognize. The tan face and thin build, the pencil-thin mustache, nothing was recognizable. Of course he knew he was seeing this vision through the muted gray-green spectrum of vision that the Golia used, but the vision was clear in Marko's eyes. Mikla saw this man as a threat, one that meant harm to Anya, whom Mikla had been sent to protect. Words intruded into Marko's thoughts and the spell was broken. He felt the small headache but it wasn't as severe as the spell he would have normally used with Stanus, which would have drained his mind of all activity for hours. He felt a sharp but momentary pain in his right ankle and then he turned to face his grandmother.

"Marko, are you listening to me?"

He blinked and then smiled. "Yes," he said simply and as matter-of-factly as he could after seeing the man that was trying to kill his sister far more distinctly than her mere description of him.

"Well, are you going to tell them that now is not the right time for song and dance? There will be ample time for them to celebrate after I have seen to Mikla."

Finally Marko heard the cacophony coming from outside the village. The locals were starting to gather, something he had been fearful of ever since his grandmother had mentioned Anya was returning home. The music was loud and the people boisterous, which caused Marko a pang of jealousy and also of worry that there were now too many Jeddah eyes around Patinas for what was happening far below at the resort. The gathering was not wanted or needed at this time.

"I will see to it," he said as he turned and patted Mikla one last time on the cheek. The wolf whined deep in its throat and then stilled again. Marko left without looking at either woman.

"Your brother has brought great trouble upon us I fear," Madam Korvesky said as she watched her grandson leave. "He has done this for a cause that he sees as just, but I fear will bring the world down upon us."

Anya wiped tears from her eyes as she stood and faced her grandmother.

"This is why I am to stay?"

Madam Korvesky smiled and then looked her grown granddaughter over as she held out a hand for assistance to stand from her large chair.

"No, your mission for the Jeddah is at an end. We have no more reason for eyes on the world, and especially eyes placed in Israel."

"I do not understand," Anya said as she helped her grandmother over to the door that had been placed between two large sawhorses from the barn. She watched as the old woman placed a weathered hand on Mikla's shoulder, being sure to stay away from the animal's head. She wanted him sleeping for what she had to do. She patted him easily and the wolf huffed and then went still.

"We are at a crossroads, my child. The world has started to gather more knowledge than we can suppress." She turned and faced Anya with a sad look. "And I'm afraid your brother is the cause. He was blinded and now he is beginning to gather his wits about him and truly see that which he has set in motion." Madam Korvesky looked down at Mikla and stroked his thick fur as he slept. She ran her hand easily down the full length of the beast, limping as she moved.

Anya stepped over to assist but the old woman shook her head as her hand came in contact with the break in the right hind ankle.

"He did this thinking he would make life easier for the Jeddah. And now the world has learned many things, and this knowledge cannot leave here."

"Fool," Anya said as she shook her head at the naïveté of her older brother. "What are we facing?" she asked, now afraid of the answer.

The old Gypsy queen stopped as she felt the small break in the bone. She tilted her head and closed her eyes. She was feeling her own touch in her swollen ankle and she knew it was comforting not only to herself but also to Mikla. She nodded her head and then took a deep breath.

"It's not as bad as I thought," she said as she smiled and then rubbed the muscled leg of the Golia. "We'll have you fixed up in no time, you clumsy wolf," she said laughing at her own words.

"Grandmother, what are we facing?" Anya insisted.

"Nothing but the total end of our way of life." The old woman said it far too easily for Anya to be sure she heard the statement correctly.

"Surely things are not that—"

"And I'm not sure if that is a bad thing."

Now Anya was totally stunned. She grasped the old wooden door to stabilize her wobbly legs as she felt her heart break at the thought of losing the mountain and what they have protected for thirty-five hundred years.

Before Anya could say anything the old woman held her hand up to still the questions she knew was coming.

"We can discuss this after we take care of Mikla. We must hurry him to the temple as soon as he is able. The other Golia may relax when he returns unharmed."

Anya watched as her grandmother prepared for the healing spells that would not only make the pain easier to bear for Mikla but also herself. She stepped up and took hold of her by her elbows and helped her walk to her kitchen that was only a few paces away.

"And then we can discuss this rather large American stray you brought home."

"He saved my—"

Again the smile and the hand stopped Anya from speaking.

"And you know how I feel about strays. You were always bringing home some animal for healing or for loving." She turned with her smile still in place. "But I feel this particular stray means something a little more to my granddaughter."

The hand again stopped Anya from speaking and she became frustrated as her grandmother started rummaging through her boxes and cabinets for the items needed for the healing spell.

"I'm a Gypsy, my dear, and some of the stories about us are true. I know you've been absent for a long while, so I'll let you have your doubts. But I can feel this man has caught your heart." She stopped rummaging and turned to face the young woman who looked just like her when she was at the same age. "Hear me, girl," she said, losing the smile and becoming deadly serious. "Things are going to change, and now may not be the best time for such things as your American stray to be near the Jeddah."

Anya didn't want to go into any form of denial with her grandmother. She was old and she wasn't reading things like she used to. But the news about her brother was now starting to weigh heavily on her. She smiled and then kissed her grandmother on the cheek.

"Your visionary aptitude has gone astray, Grandmamma, the American has no interest in a Gypsy from the mountains."

The old woman chuckled.

"You have been gone far too long. I have missed your smile so much. And I won't even say what a horrible liar you are."

Her grandmother took Anya in her arms and hugged her as if for the last time.

From what Niles could tell, the five men in the Army Humvee liked being in the procession of cars, vans, and other old and rusted vehicles. They nodded and pointed at vehicles they recognized from bygone days. Everything from rusted-out Chevys to French-made Citroëns.

"This is amazing," Alice said from the backseat of the hard-riding Humvee.

"That's one word for it. I thought most of these cars and trucks would have been scrap sometime after the Kennedy assassination. What do you think is happening to draw so many Gypsies to the pass?"

"I've always heard about it, but no one I have ever spoken to has ever seen a Gathering."

"It's a gathering all right," Niles said as he watched an old and battered Toyota pickup slide by them with ten children and several more adults in the back. They were jabbering away and laughing. Niles shook his head. "A gathering of what I don't know. Look at their clothes, the styles they're wearing, it's like I'm looking back in time at several different ages. The sixties mostly, but maybe even as far back as the eighteen nineties. It's amazing."

"Gypsies," Alice said beneath her breath.

"What was that?" Niles asked leaning closer to her.

"These are what the real Gypsies are like, Niles. This isn't Hollywood or what others perceive them to be, these are the real thing." She looked at Compton and smiled and he saw that she was loving every minute of what was happening. Alice was finally in her element. "These aren't the Gypsies you find in Paris, London, or New York. No, these are the ones that stayed close to the mountains."

Niles watched the motley group of Gypsies inside a truck as it went past.

"Are you saying that these people are—?"

"The Jeddah."

Compton was about to respond when the driver of the Humvee gestured forward.

"We have a village here and it doesn't look like the others below, this one seems a little crowded."

As Niles and Alice strained to look out of the front windscreen, the multitude of men, women, and children could be seen crowding around the small village of Patinas. Many were lined in the roadway and many more in the trees surrounding the town. Many were playing and laughing as they waited, while others sat around and smoked pipes and cigars and discussed the year's shearing and butchering that would be handled come fall. The women were gossiping about this and that and the children were watching the many entertainers winding their way through the crowd.

"I think this is about as far as we're going to go, sir."

Niles reached up and patted the driver on the back. "Okay, let's go see what's going on and ask if we can visit the higher reaches of the pass."

As Alice stepped out of the vehicle she was amazed to see the friendly smiles and faces that greeted them. This was not at all like the closed society of Gypsy bands that roamed the Western world—these people were open and very much unsuspicious of others.

The men of the 82nd, along with Niles, Alice, Will Mendenhall, and Denise Gilliam, all watched jugglers and vendors, and then their eyes widened when a small brown bear with a collar around his neck and being led by a small Gypsy child with a gold shirt and black vest walked upright to many laughs from the children.

Denise had to smile when Mendenhall's mouth came slightly agape at the sight. Even the engineers from the 82nd looked as if they were kids seeing a circus for the first time. One staff sergeant pulled on the sleeve of another and pointed to the two teenage girls dancing and swirling to the sound of a horn as they beat tambourines. The men were awestruck and Alice could do nothing but clap her hands together and smile. All the while Niles watched. It felt good to the director of Department 5656 to see her smile again. It had been a long haul since the senator's death and she deserved this last Event call.

"What do you think, Alice?" Niles asked as he turned away and studied the milling crowd of happy Gypsies that must have traveled from every village and town from the Czech Republic and the Russian steppes to get here. As Alice said, these people were the real thing.

Alice smiled and looked around her and then up at the mountain peak. She was trying to envision the interior and spy the true and hidden secret of the Jeddah.

"This is a Gathering to announce something. Or maybe to welcome someone home," she said looking over at Compton with a wink.

"You mean this could be for our missing Mossad agent?"

"Yes, that's exactly what I mean, and if I were to think clearly on this with her here and Captain Everett missing . . . well, there could be a connection."

Niles got a worried look on his face as he glanced at the empty web belts of the 82nd Airborne engineers. It was what wasn't on those belts that concerned him: They had no weapons of any kind.

"Well, shall we pay our respects?" he said instead of voicing any concerns about their vulnerability. He would allow Alice to ride the wave a little while longer.

"By all means, let's."

Alice and her Event Group walked three thousand years into history.

The sun was slowly sliding behind the mountains to the west bringing on a false evening that cooled the milling crowd of Gypsies outside the gate of the small house. Charlie Ellenshaw was studying the activity through the slats in the rickety old barn. He blinked when he thought he saw a familiar face in the crowd standing a head taller than the rest. Charlie removed his wire-rimmed glasses and rubbed his eyes and then replaced them and looked again. A smile slowly crossed his lips.

Everett was examining the barn for weaknesses in case he decided not to play gentle captive any longer. Thus far he figured he could be out in about as long a time as it took to raise a boot and kick out one of the ancient slats that had seen far better days. They were open on three sides of the barn. The fourth and back side was butted right up against the mountain which served as its rear wall and which must have played hell during the rainy season. Carl looked up and saw that the hay loft reached all the way to the broken roof where he spied the craggy rocks as they climbed high above the barn.

"I'll be damned, they made it to the village," Ellenshaw said as he turned and got Everett's attention.

"The director?" Carl asked as he stepped down from a small shattered corral gate. "Well, Will is out there anyway, and a couple of the Army guys."

Everett walked to the wall while brushing remnants of hay and Lord knew what else from his blue denim shirt. He went to the widest crack and looked out. He saw Will standing among the large crowd of Gypsies. He smiled when he saw Alice and Niles wedged between the engineers of the 82nd.

"Come on, we'll go out the south side, there are fewer people over there and the wall seems ready to fall down anyway."

Everett turned to face the cracked and broken wall and started to raise his right leg and boot. That was when he froze. He slowly lowered the foot and his hands which had been spread for balance during his kick. The yellow eyes staring back at him made the blood freeze in his veins. Ellenshaw slowly turned to Carl with a smile after viewing their friends.

"I can't wait to report what we've seen to Alice, she's going to . . . oh, shit," Charlie said when he saw what had frozen Everett in mid-kick. The wolf was actually standing on the far side of the wall and was looking in at them. To Charlie the operative word was *standing*.

"Don't move, Doc," Carl said as he never allowed his eyes to look away from the beast that was staring in with those menacing yellow eyes. Its ears were up and the size of the animal as it stood on two legs made the captain feel as if he were but a small child facing a Great Dane.

Before Carl could blink an eye the animal leapt up and away out of their view. Everett took a quick step back as he heard the wolf on the top of the barn. Dirt, leaves, pine needles, and other debris collected over time fell on them from the massive weight being applied to the old wood above them. Their eyes watched the giant animal move across the roof, each beam of wood shaking and then bending under the wolf's massive weight.

"That's the big one, isn't it?" Charlie asked as he leaned further back against the wall he had just been looking through. "The one Marko and Anya called Stanus . . . I don't think he's very friendly."

Carl didn't voice it, but he had to agree with Ellenshaw. The animal that had come to their rescue earlier seemed to him to be the surly type. And it hadn't been too pleased to see him and Charlie with Anya and Mikla. And now here it was paying the prisoners a visit. Carl winced as he heard nails being wrenched free from where they had been secured for a century or more. Then before either could move a muscle the beast jumped into the barn and landed in the shadows and light beams coming in from the outside. The black giant came to its full height after absorbing the impact of its landing from thirty-five feet up. They both heard the deep growl coming from the wolf's throat. Everett allowed his eyes to cover the distance from the angry countenance of the beast to the long and very articulate fingers as they curled and uncurled at Stanus's sides as the animal moved its weight from one foot to the other keeping a balance that had been practiced since birth.

"This is the most amazing thing I've—"

"Doc, now is not the time for a Carl Sagan narrative."

Stanus stepped forward into a large sunbeam that was slowly starting to dim as the sun moved further behind the western mountains. The ears were up but the growling was intensifying. The large head swung from the more formidable Everett to that of Ellenshaw, who managed to hold his ground even though he was facing a thing he said could never exist.

Before Everett could react, the beast moved with lightning speed and took the captain by the neck and then raised the 235-pound man clear of the dirt floor. Carl took hold of the thick muscled arm to alleviate the stress on his neck as Charlie made a move to assist. Stanus simply leaned forward and growled, this time his long black ears laid flat against his skull, giving every indication that it was no longer tolerant of the men that didn't belong. Stanus brought its ears up as Charlie took a step back against the far wall. The giant wolf that couldn't possibly exist just two days ago finally brought its full attention back to Everett.

"Uh, can we talk about this?" Everett managed to squeeze the words out against the growing tightness constricting his breathing.

Stanus growled and then relaxed its hold on Everett's throat as it leaned in and smelled the captain from the top of his blond hair to his neck. The intake of air was deep and slow as the Golia seemed to be deciding something as it breathed deeply. The mouth slowly opened and came forward. Everett was looking at the largest set of teeth he had ever seen. But yet the captain realized that the animal wasn't threatening him, he was testing him to see if he would panic—at least he was hoping that was what the beast was doing. Everett opened his eyes and steeled himself to make the beast blink first. He was so intent on doing this that neither he nor Charlie heard the sound of the barn door being opened. Only Stanus allowed its eyes to flick in that direction as its large and sharply pointed brow rose as Carl seemed to have passed some sort of ritualistic test.

"Put the American down, Stanus."

Everett, though he couldn't breathe, recognized the voice that came from behind him.

Stanus turned its head to face the man Everett couldn't see. The growl was deep and this time very menacing. The ears lay down once more and then Stanus unceremoniously allowed Carl to slide through its fingers until he landed on the dirt floor where the captain took a grateful breath as he leaned over massaging his neck.

"The mountain, Stanus, go home, you shouldn't be down here, there are far too many who don't know the Golia are here. Even amongst our own people there are eyes we would rather not behold the miracle. Go home, Stanus."

Carl watched as Marko held his ground as Stanus took a menacing step toward the Gypsy. The arms were outstretched and the long claws were working to get at something. Everett could see Marko's dark eyes looking at the moving claws. Then the confrontation seemed to end as Stanus stood straight and then the long, powerful arms relaxed as it took two tentative steps back into the shadows of the barn. It took two more. The yellow eyes going from Marko to Everett and then back again until the only thing they could discern in the darkness of the barn were the yellow eyes and then in a flash of black-on-black movement, Stanus vanished up and into the rafters and then they heard the weight of the beast as it crunched onto the wood of the old roof as it scrambled onto the mountain to vanish.

"Maybe a leash law would help," Carl joked as he slowly picked himself up off the ground. He rubbed his neck and throat trying to ease the pain of having his larynx crushed.

Marko looked from Everett to a very scared Charlie, who moved quickly to assist the captain. The dark eyes roamed over both men.

"A leash, that's very humorous. I think I would like to be the one to watch as you put that leash on Stanus, or any Golia you come across." Marko turned and gestured for the front door.

"My sister insists that you be allowed to join your friends who have arrived from down below." He turned and looked at Everett. "The man and woman I invited are not among them. I suspect your dark-haired friend scares the Russian at the resort."

"And you know this because . . . ?" Carl said as he went to a pail of water and splashed some of the stagnant liquid on his face.

"Because I am a Gypsy, and I know your friends mean Dmitri Zallas harm. For right now I cannot allow that. In later months, yes, maybe you can take him, but for now he is needed. So after tonight, collect your friends and leave this mountain. You do not belong here."

"You're not a very friendly fella, are you?" Carl said as he stepped up closer to the much smaller Gypsy. He swiped at the water still on his face.

"After tonight my word will be law. My plans for the betterment of my people will begin as soon as the power is mine to direct our new course."

"And your sister, just what is her opinion on this new course for the Jeddah?"

Carl could see that knowing the information on the Jeddah was a little unnerving to the Gypsy prince. He could tell that he wasn't used to an outsider that had so much accurate information on a legend that had been hidden successfully for thirty-five hundred years.

Marko made a face and smiled as if the question had been asked by a small child.

"My sister, what does that have to with my plans? She is an outsider now, maybe not trusted by her own people any longer. She is the younger and could never be crowned queen as long as I am alive."

"Then all of these people are here to see you get your deserved reward?" Everett persisted as he noticed that Marko was losing a little of his cool demeanor when the subject of his sister came up.

"You may join your friends, but make no move to go into the pass. I think we can drop that ridiculous pretense." Marko looked into the taller captain's eyes. "NATO, it never ceased to amaze me how easily the Russian sold the Romanian government a bill of goods by getting NATO to cooperate in getting the land grant settled. And you're supposed to be the light of the shining world? I think I would rather do business with the Slav." Marko turned and left and they noticed the barn door was open.

"What a great guy," Charlie said and then looked at the spot from where Stanus had vanished. Dirt was still falling from the damaged areas of the roof where the beast had walked. "It's like that wolf and that young man have the same temper problem."

"Yeah, well, here's one for the books Doc," Everett said as he finally faced Ellenshaw. "When that wolf had me by the short and curlies I had the distinct impression it was trying to see if I was a part of something it didn't like very well, and as these thoughts struck I kept picturing the man who just left here."

"So what are you saying?" Charlie asked as they started walking toward the barn door.

"What I'm saying, Doc, is that I don't know if Stanus is very trusting of his friend Marko. It was smelling me and trying to decide which side of the line I would fall on." He smiled and laughed. "Hell, I don't know, but that wolf and Marko are connected somehow and it's not in a very friendly way. Marko has lost something with that animal and Stanus feels lost. That's what I felt, Doc, now call me crazy."

"How can I do that, the name's already been taken."

Both Carl and crazy Charlie Ellenshaw laughed and made their way out of the barn and into one of the largest celebrations in Jeddah history.

PALMACHIM AIR FORCE BASE, TEL AVIV, ISRAEL

The three Mercedes cars sped onto the old tarmac and vanished beyond the old hangar. Moments later the side doors opened and several black-clad security personnel entered the darkened structure. They saw the gray and white camouflaged men of the commando unit and studied each before they stepped aside. All eyes watched as the prime minister stepped over the threshold of the sliding door. He had his hands behind his back and his head was lowered in thought, just as every picture of the man ever taken seemed to show. He was dressed in a simple blue sweater that covered a white shirt. He had no tie and his gray hair was not covered in his customary black hat. The prime minister finally looked up from his thoughts. The eyes were sympathetic to the man as each soldier knew what a daunting task it had become to be the leader of a nation that had enemies on all sides. The commandos knew and respected the man even though he seemed to be far left of the political center—something the military of Israel had started to embrace.

The prime minister of the state of Israel moved silently toward the communications area of the hangar as each commando watched him. He looked up and nodded his head as the door was opened for him.

General Shamni moved in his sleep and then he opened his eyes when he felt the presence in the room. He looked over from the cot he was sleeping on and saw that the prime minister was sitting in a chair not three feet away. His glasses were perched on his forehead and he was leaning forward and smiling.

"May I ask what is so humorous?" the general asked as he slowly placed his feet on the floor and sat up. He rubbed his burning eyes and then tried his best to focus on his old friend.

"You sleep like a big child, do you know that?"

"Anyone below the age of eighty is a child to you," Shamni said as he tried again to focus. "Why are you here?"

"I wanted to tell you myself."

"Oh, this is going to be good. If something were bad enough to take you away from your books to come all the way down here we must be at war or damn near it."

The PM reached out and slapped the general on his knee. "It is good to see you can still be funny." He lost his own smile. "Not war, but trouble is brewing in Romania."

"You mean more trouble, don't you?"

"Yes, more trouble. Our radical friends in the Knesset have been in contact with your Colonel Ben-Nevin. As far as your people know and mine, the bastard separatists have directed Ben-Nevin to make inroads to the owner of that cursed resort. This is a development that needs to be attended to."

The general rubbed his hand over his face and then stood and walked over to the coffeepot. He slapped the radio operator on the shoulder and told him to excuse the PM and himself. The old man watched the commando leave and then watched as the general leaned over and turned up the volume on the long-range radio set that was being monitored.

"Going deaf, I'm afraid," Shamni said as he smiled in embarrassment and then went and poured himself a cup of cold coffee.

"No word at all," the PM asked as he turned in his chair to face Shamni.

"No, but that is expected. We won't be contacted until the very end, when need outweighs common sense."

"I am detecting quite a bit of animosity coming from you, old friend."

"This should have been taken care of long before you and I took the seats we currently hold." The general looked down at the cold coffee and made a face and then placed the cup on the desk he was sitting on. He looked at the silent radio and shook his head. He stood and walked to the window that looked into the hangar and the clean-looking lines of the Hercules C-130 as it sat waiting in alert status. "I don't think the lives of one of those boys out there are worth one thing buried inside that damn mountain."

"I agree, old friend, but send them into harm's way is just what we will do. We cannot allow this discovery to give our radical friends the ammunition for separation from our neighbors, this has to end. If they get ahold of what's there we will be fighting for a thousand more years, or until someone delivers a little atomic package on our doorstep."

The general saw the worry in his friend's face. The problems of the old world intruded on what they were trying to achieve in the region and they couldn't have that. The beliefs of the tribes had mellowed over the years and now the extremists wanted the world to think that, indeed, they were the true chosen people. The PM and the general both knew that the old prejudices would begin anew if that mountain spilled out its secrets.

"If we don't receive word by midnight tomorrow, we move with or without a signal from Patinas."

The general nodded his head. "Will this never end?"

14

THE EDGE OF THE WORLD HOTEL
AND RESORT CASINO

Sarah watched as the huge helicopter that had seen far better days as it touched down roughly on the lawn outside of the large pool area. Her eyes lingered a moment by the window and then she smiled as she recognized the brash—and broke—Las Vegas entertainer Drake Andrews as he stepped off the helicopter. It looked as if he were very irritated at everyone around him. She shook her head and then turned away from the window.

Sarah walked to the room's dressing table and studied the experiment she had running. The tall glass of water sat motionless. Floating in the center of the glass was a golden aluminum candy wrapper shaped like a small cup. Attached to the floating foil was a small wire that Sarah had connected to her cell phone, which was open and broken into three distinct pieces on the table next to the glass. Next to the phone was what remained of the thermostat that controlled the temperature inside their room. The small vial of mercury sat in the bubble of the floating foil where Sarah had attached the leads from the cell phone. She concentrated on the digital readout on the screen. The application was for a musical tone graph used in many areas of downloading music for variance control and noise level.

"Well, Mr. Wizard?" Jack asked as he stepped out of the bathroom drying his hands on a towel.

Sarah held up her hand as she studied the makeshift seismograph she had constructed in place of her more expensive equipment accidentally absconded by the Romanian army. She shook her head as the numbers slowed down from their previous high.

"The movement has increased by point one since four o'clock."

"I take it that's bad?" he said as he tossed the towel onto a chair in the far corner. Jack then started putting on a button-down shirt as he stepped up to Sarah and watched her write down her current set of numbers.

"No, bad is the fact that I just saw Drake Edwards arrive and that means he's the entertainment tomorrow night." She looked up and smiled—Jack didn't. "Okay, the readings are bad, but with no previous record to compare it to I have no way of knowing just how bad. But we have earth movement here and it's due to the natural hot springs. We may not have a severe volcanic situation happening here but we do have a pressure buildup of some kind. I just wish I had the seismic history of the pass before I make any conclusions. I need Europa."

"Well, you don't have Europa or any more history than you already have, so I need a best guess from our resident geologist and I need it now. We have people up on that mountain and very little time to warn them if you think there's trouble up there."

Sarah bit her lower lip and turned her back on Jack. He shook his head and then reached out and zipped up the back of Sarah's evening dress. They had received an invitation for dinner from the general manager as a thank-you for Ryan and Pete's assistance the night before. They were to be joined by Dmitri Zallas's partner, Janos Vajic. Jack figured they could try and get as much information as he could before he declared Zallas too hostile for him and Sarah to remain at the resort. Once her dress was zipped she turned and wrote down her final set of numbers.

"I just don't know where this is headed, Jack. It could be just tremors we're facing or it could be a disaster the size of Mount St. Helens. I really need to get into the Romanian Interior Ministry."

"Believe me, we would like to get inside and find out how much cooperation Zallas really received from their interior minister. We give it tonight and then I figure it's time we left the resort and find our people. I don't think Zallas would try anything out in the open even with such a seedy guest list. But that doesn't mean he won't either. More than likely he would wait until after his nightclub opening tomorrow night, so if you don't mind, short stuff, I would prefer not to be here for those festivities."

Sarah slipped into a light satin shawl and then looked up at Jack, who was just sliding into a casual navy blue sport coat. His eyes found Sarah and he had to smile as he took her in. If this mission had taught Collins one thing it was the immutable fact that he loved the small woman standing in front of him like he had never loved anything in his life.

"Well, rock hound, would you like to go and show ourselves to the seedier side of the underworld and try to blend in? Let's do what we came to do to and see if we can make a provenance claim on any antiquities there may be on the property. That would make our job of proving theft a lot simpler when we give the proof to Interpol. We may as well act like crooks after dinner and break into the big man's office."

Sarah laughed as she placed her arm around Collins.

"The strange thing is you seem to slide right into the category of crook rather seamlessly."

"Yeah, I'm a regular Scarface."

"More than you think, Colonel Darling."

They were about to step out the door when Sarah froze and then her head perked up as she suddenly turned and ran for her notes on the table by the window. In her haste she bumped it and spilled the water that was still attached to her useless cell phone.

"Hey, what's wrong?" Jack asked as he took a quick look into the hallway and then eased the door closed.

"Jack, I've been looking at this thing from the wrong angle. The figure I'm seeing on earth movement is a constant and that is an impossibility. The power of an eruption or any sort of seismic event has to build up over a period of time. That's why we get tremors and then suddenly the big one. But this, Jack," she said as she reached for her notes and started jotting down a new formula, "this is too damn steady. It's more like I'm calculating for a mud slide or something similar. It's earth movement all right, but on a smaller scale. This is too localized, if it wasn't close by we would have picked up on it all over the world from monitoring stations."

"You have totally lost me."

"Jack, this is like it's man-made. It's a constant and there are no constants in seismology." Sarah ripped her notes free of the pad and then scanned them. "You're right, Jack, we have to get into the office of Dmitri Zallas and while you look for your artifact thief I've got to get into the geology report on this resort." Sarah stepped to the window and pulled back the multicolored drapes and looked up at the swirling blue and purple colors of Castle Dracula. "If the foundation of this building is shaking like this I need to know what's happening up there. How in the hell was that thing built? Look, Jack, it clings to the side of the mountain like it's glued on. I need to know how they set their anchor studs."

"What are you saying? That the instability we're feeling could be brought on by a shoddy geology workup?"

"The movement is less the further south we go on the property. It only stands to reason that the problem is north of our current location, and the only thing that has changed on this mountain in a few thousand years is—"

"The castle."

"Right. We need to know if the construction up there has caused any environmental damage to the mountain it's anchored to."

"Sometimes you professors scare me. All you needed was a broken cell phone, a glass of water, and a few sheets of paper and you come up with this?" Jack said as he turned for the door.

"Yeah, now all I have to do is calculate how we find Carl and Charlie and warn everyone else about not to climb the mountain because it just may come tumbling down."

Collins was silent as they stepped out into the hallway.

"What are you thinking?" Sarah asked as she linked her arm through Jack's.

"I'm thinking we may have to get out of here in one hell of a hurry if this thing goes south on us. And that will entail finding Captain Everett, Alice, Niles, and the others, and we need Pete and Ryan for that."

"Yeah, and just where in the hell are they?" Sarah asked as she nodded at a portly gentleman with a nineteen-year-old on his arm.

"Knowing Ryan's work habits he's probably lying by the pool."

THE EDGE OF THE WORLD HOTEL AND RESORT CASINO, PATINAS, ROMANIA

It seemed to Pete Golding that he had picked up every species of burr and sticker known to nature in the Romanian region. By the time they were allowed through the very much heightened security by having their IDs checked against their reservation and their invitations, Pete was about to die for a bottle of calamine lotion.

As they walked up the long circular drive they were both grateful the sun had slipped beneath the mountains and their fruitless day of searching the lower elevations for Captain Everett and Charlie Ellenshaw had come to an end. The only thing they may have possibly confirmed was that they were more than likely up in Patinas where the colonel had suspected they would be.

"I am tired and worn out and I think I have a burr in my sock about the size of a baseball bat." Pete limped along as the hotel grew closer.

"All I want is a beer and cheeseburger, and then nothing more than sleep," Ryan countered.

As they approached the hotel's entrance they spied the troublemakers from the night before, only this time they had grown in number. Ryan nudged Pete to the left and headed for the pool entrance around the side of the hotel. As they made the turn Jason pulled up and placed his back against the building and made Pete do the same.

"This isn't doing anything to relieve my legs of these naturally formed torture devices I have embedded in my socks. I thought—"

"Doc, be quiet and listen," Ryan hissed as he took a fast peek around the corner of the building. He counted eight men and as he did a ninth walked up with his two bodyguards. Dmitri Zallas stood speaking in hushed tones with the brutes from the casino. As Ryan strained to hear, his eyes widened when another man approached the group. He was smoking one of the Russian's larger-than-life cigars and he seemed very interested in the conversation between the gathered men.

"Regardless, we will manage to get him here. We will seal off the basement and work from there."

"If this man is taken so easily, why don't you have your men do it?" one of the large Romanian men asked Zallas. It was the same brute that had been molesting the waitress that had started all of the trouble the previous night.

"The man will be hesitant and extremely untrusting around me and my people. He will not see you or your men coming. Just get him here and my people will handle it from there. I want this business finished before the grand opening of the castle tomorrow night." Zallas reached into his coat pocket and brought out a thick envelope. "Here is your advance payment and ten thousand dollars' worth of gaming chips. Make sure when he arrives tomorrow that it's done quietly. I don't need this man's people learning what happened to him."

The Romanian criminal placed the envelope in his coat pocket and then the brutes left. Ryan watched the group of eight miscreants walk away, leaving only Zallas and his guest, whom Ryan recognized immediately.

"You must remember this must be done with the utmost secrecy and stealth. If Tel Aviv gets intelligence that we're moving on the temple, they—"

"They will what? Drop in commandos from a stormy night sky into some of the most rugged terrain in all of Europe in pitch blackness? This is not 1976 Uganda, Colonel Jew, this is the twenty-first century and we have ways of dealing with arrogance brought on by military success." Zallas turned and faced Ben-Nevin. "I and my men will have every ruble of treasure out of there and have the temple stripped long before your magical commandos hit the earth."

"You seem to take the threat of military intervention lightly, Mr. Zallas," Ben-Nevin said as he puffed on the horrible cigar, and with distaste forming on his features he tossed the offensive smoke into the grass. "If I were you I would not wait until tomorrow night. I would take this Gypsy this very evening and make him disclose the location of the temple. Move tonight, take everything before Tel Aviv has time to react." He faced Zallas with a smile etching his mustache into a mocking thing that made the Russian want to backhand the intelligence officer. "Because, make no doubt, they *will* react, and react with swift—and deadly—force."

Zallas smiled and looked the tall man over and then turned and faced the large Olympic-sized pool, which now sat empty with the arrival of night.

"The man will be busy tonight and hard to draw away from his village. To-morrow is the only time we can act without alerting every Gypsy inside the valley as to our plan. If you wish you can gather your men and make the attempt your-self, this very night if you wish."

Ben-Nevin held the Russian's arrogant glare but at the same time realized there would be no way he would ever venture up that mountain in the dark, or even the daylight hours with those wolves up there. He thought about mentioning the animals to Zallas but had decided earlier why complicate the moron's thinking process.

"Very well, I hope you have enough men because these Gypsies—"

"—Cannot stand up against my men. And I have more than two hundred men available to me." He smiled and then started to walk past Ben-Nevin. "And they will die on my command, as I suspect many of them will." He kept walking. "Shall we get a drink, Colonel?"

Colonel Avi Ben-Nevin had decided just two minutes after meeting the Russian mobster that he would not leave Patinas Pass without placing a bullet into the anti-Semitic head of the Russian mobster. The colonel smiled from his inner thoughts. *Maybe two in the kneecaps before the bullet to the head.*

The two men vanished around the corner and Ryan turned back to think about what he had just heard.

"Wow," Pete said as he and Ryan finally stepped away from their hiding place. "Were they talking about us, the colonel, Alice, and them, or were they speaking about one of the Gypsies?" Pete asked.

"Well, our team's not sure where any temple is, so we have to assume he was speaking about one of the locals, maybe this Marko guy the colonel briefed us on."

"What do we do?" Pete asked as he turned and tried to catch up with Jason.

"We're going to report to Colonel Collins and then we're going to get that cheeseburger."

"Maybe we can get the cheeseburger and calamine lotion first? I mean that damn temple has been here for over three thousand years."

VILLAGE OF PATINAS

Carl and Charlie eased their way through the crowd as they followed Marko away from the barn. Everett would reach up to his neck every few minutes and rub the area that Stanus had assaulted. His throat was throbbing as he remembered the unnatural strength of the animal and that it had every opportunity to kill him if it had really wanted to.

Niles and Alice were watching the house just as were the thousand men, women, and children with them as they waited in anticipation for something Niles couldn't wait to see. Alice tapped her toes nervously as they waited as Niles turned to see a smallish man in a black vest, bright red shirt, and black head scarf standing before them. He was flanked by two much larger Gypsies that had a menacing look about them.

"You are the Americans that have a man and woman staying at the resort, a Colonel Collins?" Marko asked with his dark eyes boring into Compton's, who stood stunned that this man knew Jack's real identity. "And you are Alice Hamilton? The colonel asked my permission last evening for you to join us here in the pass, and as a courtesy to our newest NATO ally, of which my people care very little for, I grudgingly gave permission for you to bear witness to my home of Patinas."

"Thank you, we are grate—" Alice started to say but was cut short.

"I must insist however that you remain in the village and keep your other charges under control. And keep these two men away from my family," Marko said as he stepped aside and allowed Carl and Charlie to squeeze through the crowd of humanity.

"Carl! Charlie!" Alice said as she placed her arms around Everett and then patted Charlie Ellenshaw on the chest. "We were so worried." Alice let Everett go and then turned to face Marko but he and his two men had already left.

"That guy's a piece of work," Everett said as he smiled down at Alice and Niles. Charlie was gesturing wildly as he tried to explain all they had seen since they had been separated. His arms were going high into the air and then would form into the shape of claws as Will's eyes grew larger as he listened to the professor's latest exploits in the field.

Carl took Alice by the arms and looked her in the eyes as men and women bumped past them to get closer to the house they had surrounded. The music was almost deafening.

"We saw them, Alice," he said as easily as he could. It was hard keeping the smile off of his face.

"Them?" Niles asked for her when she didn't respond.

"The Golia, we've seen two of them, and one viewing was rather close and personal," Carl said as he gingerly touched his reddened and extremely sore neck muscles.

Alice felt her legs go weaker as she reached out and took Everett's arm. The question was in her eyes but the words could not be formed.

"Yes, everything you thought about them is true. The hands, the thumbs, the upright walking, the climbing, but most importantly, Alice, they're smart. One saved our asses not long ago. But I can tell you this also, they are dangerous. I think it could have killed all of us and not really have given a damn one way or the other."

"Oh, my," was all she could say.

Carl was about to go on when the men and women around them started cheering for something they couldn't see far ahead of them.

Then they saw Marko and his men standing close to the old front door of the cottage everyone was watching. He was looking at the gathered villages of the Patinas region. Niles watched as fathers placed children on their shoulders so their young could get a good look at the happenings. Suddenly the door opened up and two large men wearing head scarfs and large boots stepped out carrying a large chair between them. In that chair was an old woman. Her head scarf was a soft blue and her smile glowed as she was carried from the house. She waved and raised an old cane up in the air as the admiring crowd erupted at seeing Madam Korvesky.

Compton and Everett, along with Will and Charlie looked over at Alice Hamilton as the Gypsy queen was brought out to greet her people. They could see the smile that stretched from ear to ear. Alice was in what she considered heaven. All the years of research, of disappointment, all washed away in these final few moments of discovery.

The two men set the chair down on the small cobblestone walkway that led to the small house. Marko stepped up to the chair and then knelt before it. The old woman smiled and raised her hand into the air and then brought it down on Marko's covered head. He dipped his head lower and then stood as the crowd erupted again. Marko looked taken aback as he momentarily thought the sudden crowd noise was for him. Then he slowly stood and saw why the people were cheering. His sister was standing inside the doorway and then the closest men and women saw her and started cheering.

The noise grew like a wave as Anya stood rooted in the doorway. Her grandmother gestured for her to come out into the open and she slowly and hesitantly responded. Finally Anya, cleaned and refreshed, walked out onto the walkway and then smiled at the people. The small village erupted in rapt admiration for the little sister that had been gone from home for so long. Anya turned her head away feeling embarrassed for doing nothing more than coming home.

Her eyes searched the crowd until they fell on the man she was looking for. Carl Everett stood far back and away from the small house but she could see his eyes boring into her own. She halfheartedly raised a hand into the air but before she could wave at Everett several of the larger men took Anya up and into their arms and held her high as the Jeddah people launched into a euphoric dance and applause as their Gypsy princess was finally home.

Everett watched Anya as she was paraded through the milling and cheering mass of modern-day Jeddah. He fought to keep his eyes on the beautiful woman, who was fighting to do the same. As Anya was twirled from strong hand to strong hand she fought to lay her eyes on the only man she had taken notice of in the past nine years. She finally spied Everett as he tentatively raised his hand as she was lifted high into the air by several of the farmers and sheep men.

Alice nudged Niles's arm and nodded at Everett as he watched the girl being celebrated. Niles had never seen the captain this way. He was actually straining to see. As they watched a smile slowly crawled across Everett's face as he finally locked eyes with Anya. This time he did raise his thick arm into the air as she was twirled and tossed by the people. Her smile grew as they looked at each other in the dying light of day.

Many hundreds of torches were soon lit and the food from many hearths started to be set upon long tables of wood. People broke off into smaller groups, mostly according to village. As preparations were made the Event Group personnel watched the old woman carried back inside and Anya was soon to follow after having to pull herself away from the adoring people.

Carl felt his heart hitch as his eyes watched the closed door to the small house whose windows were now glowing with the soft glow of electric light. He finally turned and looked at Alice and the others who were all looking at him. All he could do was mouth the word: *What?*

All around the Event Group, Patinas came alive with the smell of food and the sound of music and celebration, even as far below at the resort the extinction of the Jeddah had already been planned.

The old woman was placed on the floor by the table where Mikla was still resting. She placed a hand on the beast as the men left the room and Anya stepped inside. She watched her grandmother run her hand up and down Mikla's large frame and then she turned and faced her granddaughter.

"Do you see the adoration of your people?" she said as she reached out and took Anya's soft young hand into her own aged and aching ones.

"I was ordered home, Grandmamma, by you. It wasn't my choice to rejoin the people. I believe I was being far more helpful in the position I was in than being here where we constantly play the king and queen game for a people that place far too much emphasis on that particular position."

"You have learned the gift of talking without saying anything, child." Her grandmother allowed Anya's hand to fall free as she looked into her eyes. "Is my status but an empty position, young one?" The smile was still in place and that made Anya feel bad for the way she had just trivialized her grandmother's entire life.

"You know I didn't mean anything by that. I'm just tired and worried about Mikla. And Stanus, I have never seen him like this. He scares me and he's never done that to me before. Even as a child Stanus could play rough but he could always be trusted not to be Golia when he was with us. Now he seems lost as to what's happening around him."

"When I was in the temple, every one of the adult male and female Golia were missing. I have never known them to leave their young completely alone before. Where they are I do not know. They vanish for hours at a time and Stanus is leading them. When they return from the caves and springs they are covered in mud and wet from their exertions."

"If they are leaving the young undefended this means trouble, Grandmamma. What are they doing? Have you ever known them to be so secretive before?"

"No." The old woman closed her eyes in thought as she tried to remember the Golia ever having behaved in such a manner. "Marko has done something to make them distrustful of us. I was only able to link with Mikla because of his closeness to you." She looked at a far younger version of herself many years before. "Otherwise, Marko is the only Jeddah that has been able to cast the spell with them. And now I even suspect Marko has lost their trust. The Golia will not allow us to see what they are doing, and this is not natural to them. If we have lost the trust of the Golia, we are truly lost."

"And this is why my cover in Rome was no longer viable." She said it as a statement and not a question. "Why forewarn of trouble for our people if there is nothing to come home to? Is treasure being sold off as the Americans have said?"

The old woman took her granddaughter by the arm and squeezed. "Now is the time for us to move on. I need you here."

"What is happening?" she persisted.

The old woman took a deep breath as she watched Mikla breathe.

"Why I brought you home is not really at the forefront of your thoughts, girl-child." She again reached out and took her hand and this time she squeezed. Madam Korvesky tilted her head and then faced Anya and for the briefest of moments she felt her granddaughter. "Your thoughts are on the American."

Anya pulled her hand free of the older woman's grasp. "Don't do that to me, you always promised you wouldn't try to read me, ever. Now tell me what is wrong here." Anya knew her grandmother was dodging the question, at least for the time being.

"Calm down, girl-child, I want to meet this man—this man from the sea."

"What man, I don't—"

"Oh, he's right outside and his thoughts are near to battering down my already aged door." She stopped talking and a funny look came over her features. It was if Anya was seeing her grandmother leaving her body for the briefest of moments. "Keeper of Secrets," she said as her eyes opened and she smiled. She looked up at Anya with a curious arch to her brows. "Your man has come from America accompanied by the Keeper of Secrets."

"What are you talking about?" Anya asked, worried that her grandmother had not only lost the ability to see into her mind accurately, but that maybe she was starting to lose it mentally as well.

"Bring them in, Anya. Marko, are you out there?" she called out, knowing he had been standing in the shadows listening to their conversation.

"Yes, you know I am," he said as he stepped past his sister with a look that wasn't pleasant.

"Get a large quilt from my room, no, make it two. Take one from the bed if you have to. Cover Mikla as best you can." She smiled and gestured for Marko to hurry.

"Anya, I asked you to bring your man and his friends inside. Marko, when you are done make the soldiers that have accompanied Anya's companions comfortable. Feed them and make sure they are watched. And it makes me wonder, Marko, why none of the adult Golia have ventured down to the house to see Mikla, this is most strange. Perhaps they are not inside the temple just as they have not been the past few months."

Marko removed a quilt from the bed and stood before Madam Korvesky not answering her query. Then he tilted his head and leaned over and kissed his grandmother.

"The Golia have been vanishing for close to a year now," Marko replied. "I have asked Stanus about it but he has become overly distrustful since the con-

struction began at the castle. He has thus far kept his promise to me and not mo-
lested any more of the Romanian workers on their night crews. Stanus will have
to change with the times just as we will. He must learn how to protect the Golia
and still live among mankind. This is something he must do or the wolf-kind will
perish."

"I will not allow that to happen. You know this. We will speak with Stanus
tonight and decide how best to proceed. Now, girl-child, bring me the visitors to
Patinas. I will now speak with them and the Keeper of Secrets."

Anya looked from her grandmother to Marko, who only shrugged his shoulders in just as much consternation as his sister as to their grandmother's intent.

Marko spread the blankets over Mikla and then brother and sister left for
their tasks.

As for Madam Korvesky, she sat in her chair and smiled at the memory of a
long-ago night in Hong Kong harbor and the young American woman and the
handsome one-eyed scoundrel she had met that seemingly ancient evening.

"Welcome to Patinas at long last, Keeper of Secrets."

Stanus sat high on a ridge with his massive head on his front paws as his eyes
scanned the scene below. The wolf had just recently settled on the ridge after in-
vestigating the two men held in the barn. From the scent of the two humans
Stanus knew them not to be a part of the defilement of his valley. Still, his instincts told him the outsiders needed to be watched closely.

As Stanus studied the revelers below, another Golia, this one female and the
mate of Stanus, lay down beside the giant alpha male. Stanus leaned over and
sniffed her muzzle. The familiar smell was there and it was pleasing to Stanus.
The beast allowed his eyes to roam to the small house where he knew Mikla lay in
pain. The huge yellow eyes blinked twice and then the large male nuzzled up to
his mate. He licked at her filthy paws as she lay against his thick, muscled body.
The claws were ripped and torn and the pads were bloodied in a few places. Stanus
licked the wounds and the female allowed him.

The adult Golia had been working at a task Stanus had set them to not long
after he had figured out that Marko had lied to him. While connected mentally he
had told Stanus that the construction was a benefit for the Golia and the Jeddah
together. Against its instincts Stanus had allowed Marko to have his way and the
resort had started going up. Stanus allowed this without fighting back. And then
Stanus had realized that he had been deceived by Marko. The castle started going
up and Stanus went on the attack. It wasn't until Marko had convinced Stanus
that would be the very last encroachment to the pass. The castle was the last insult they would have to endure and then their lives could settle back down to
normal. Marko had assured Stanus mentally of this.

The one thing that Marko never figured on was the Stanus's intellect. The
Jeddah had always known the Golia to be the smartest animals ever created, but
the one thing he didn't know was that you could deceive a Golia, especially one

such as Stanus, just once. After that he would never trust you again. Stanus had made a decision that went far beyond that of joint protection between the Golia and the Jeddah, because when it came down to it, Stanus would protect that which is most important to him—the Golia, nothing else in the world mattered, and that was what the alpha male's role was. Not the protection of the Jeddah, but the right for the Golia to live on in this world of men.

Stanus was finished cleaning his mate's paws when he held out his own outstretched fingers to allow the female to wrap her smaller, more feminine fingers over and around his. The two Golia sat like that for an hour watching the village below and the activity of the Jeddah as they celebrated the return of their princess. The female laid her head against the thick chest of Stanus. She breathed deeply as her mate watched the activity far below.

Alice, Niles, Charlie, Denise, Will Mendenhall, and Carl all stood watching the men and women around them they went into action. In a practiced act of precision the Jeddah had turned the small village of Patinas into any small county fair found anywhere in the world. Hundreds of torches lined the streets and the music was everywhere as people danced, ate, and talked about the return of the young princess to the mountain. It was as if everyone in Patinas knew that night that they would be safe for the next generation because now brother and sister were united as one and they would lead the Jeddah into their future. Charlie Ellenshaw jumped as a firecracker went off and several small boys went running by laughing as they were chased by an irate mother with a broom.

The door opened and Marko stepped out and was joined by his two companions and they quickly left. Anya then came out of the house and looked around and spied Niles and the others and then started walking toward them. She had to almost push her way through the adoring Jeddah to reach the Americans.

Marko watched the way the men and women of the Jeddah reached out to touch Anya. His eyes took in the fact that the people had missed her far more than he had ever realized. He never took into account the effect her return would have in vitalizing the way the people felt about their heritage and how much they would like to maintain that, even above Marko's own grandiose plans for the tribe. He knew the people craved news of the outside and of Israel. But soon Marko had realized the people would be satisfied with a brief description of the outside world's happenings and then they would return to their everyday routine and well-ordered lives.

As he watched the faces of the people as Anya passed by, the way their eyes followed her every movement, was a dagger into the heart of her older brother. He felt the gains he had made in supplying his people with the basic gifts of modern appliances and electronic devices that amazed the children were now lost among the euphoria of having their princess back among them.

Marko allowed his eyes to move to the tall blond American. He saw the way the man with the sharp blue eyes watched his sister. Could this be a way in which Marko solidified his power? He wondered as he watched the crowd part as Anya guided the Americans to their grandmother.

"She is far more popular among the people than we believed she would be," the large man to Marko's right commented as he too watched the adoring Jeddah fete Anya with praise and welcoming smiles and touches.

"Soon it will not matter. Anya is far too late to stop the Jeddah from moving out of the stone age. Even if my grandmother went mad and tried to name Anya queen over the leadership of the true heir, it is too late. Soon there won't be a treasure to guard and thus no need of tribal leadership in that regard. The true leadership of the Jeddah will be established by the man that guides the Jeddah into the future to take our place among the people of the world. No more being the guardians of a culture that has long past slipped into history. No, she will not matter. The people will eventually see I mean to gain status for them after all of these years of servitude."

"Are you capable of doing what needs to be done, Marko, if and when the need arises?" the man asked, watching the Gypsy prince closely for any deceit that may spring from his mouth.

"My sister will never be harmed. I don't need to do that. I can see," as his eyes continued to follow Anya as she squeezed past the crowd of adoring men and women, "that Anya has little interest in continuing with this ancient farce." He turned and looked at all three of his companions as they stood near the gate. "Leadership will fall into my lap and then we can start using the proceeds from our tribal investment and move into a far brighter future than we have ever known on this mountain. The old days are done."

The men watched as Marko looked back one last time at his sister and then turned and left, walking toward the temple entrance.

Anya finally made it to the front door. Niles leaned aside as one old woman reached out and touched Anya's hair. The girl dipped her head and smiled but Niles could see that this situation of people admiring her didn't make the young woman comfortable. She tried to smile and nod but the old woman continued to hold Anya's long black hair in her hand. Finally it was Everett who stepped up and gently removed the woman's hand and smiled down at her. Anya felt bad but she reached for the door latch and stepped inside. The others followed. Everett waited until everyone was in the house and then he let the woman's hand slip free. For her part the old Jeddah grandmother was still watching the door with adoring eyes for Anya. Carl was amazed at what he was witnessing.

As Everett stepped into the semidark house he closed the door. Denise Gilliam, Charlie Ellenshaw, Niles, and Alice were standing just inside as they watched Anya as she leaned over and was hugging someone they couldn't see. Anya finally stepped away and that was when they saw Madam Korvesky for the first time close up. The woman Alice was looking at was the same young girl she had met many years before in Hong Kong harbor aboard the yacht *Golden Child*. The woman had aged far more than Alice had. The years of worry and of protecting her people were etched in every deep-cut line and wrinkle in the woman's face.

Madam Korvesky tilted her head as her eyes locked on Alice Hamilton. The two women were meeting across a vast crevasse of time and the reunion was one that made them both realize that time had not stood still for either of them.

"It has been many years, Mrs. Hamilton."

Anya was the first person to register her surprise that her grandmother knew this American lady. She looked from face to face and was shocked that none of them was registering the same surprised expression that she was.

"Indeed, we were never really introduced before our evening was cut short . . . when you blew up the *Golden Child* right under our feet."

Niles Compton allowed Alice to play this out her way. She was the closest to the investigation and knew what had to be said where this woman was concerned. He was still apprehensive because he didn't know how the intrusion of his team would sit with the queen of all Gypsies.

"Actually, Mrs. Hamilton, I used far less explosive power than my great-grandmother wanted to use that night in Hong Kong. She had ordered no survivors." The eyes were locked on to Alice's own and they didn't flinch.

"Well, if it's any consolation my date that night took good advantage of your light batch of explosives and managed to get us out, as you well know."

"Ah," the old woman said as she used her cane to stand, shrugging off the helping hands of Anya. Alice looked down and saw the Eye of Ra emblazoned in gold on the handle. The same cane her great-grandmother had used that night on the *Golden Child*. "The Keeper of Secrets," Madam Korvesky said as she reached out and took Alice by the hand.

"Yes, that's what you called him that night: the Keeper of Secrets. But he wasn't the only keeper of secrets aboard that yacht that night, was he, madam? I believe you tend toward keeping things rather tight to the vest yourself, correct?"

The old woman smiled and then looked over at Niles, ignoring the statement Alice had just made. Madam Korvesky released Alice and then reached for the hand of Niles Compton. Niles felt uncomfortable and he stepped from one boot to the other. Charlie Ellenshaw stood next to the director and was smiling from ear to ear as the old woman closed her eyes.

"The watcher. So much weariness, so much concern for those . . . for those . . ." She smiled and then opened her eyes. "No, you gather, guard . . . you are also a Keeper of Secrets." She looked away at nothing and then back at Niles. "To have so much knowledge is not a comfort to you most times, is it?" she asked as Niles felt as if she not only read him perfectly, she felt the drag his position had on his thoughts, his personality, and the ever-present feeling of being overwhelmed by the massive responsibilities he carried with him on a daily basis. She patted his hand and then released it. "One comforting thought for you, Keeper, the job doesn't get any easier and one day you will realize that it's not the task, but the people who do the task that is what's important. I learned that a very long time ago." She patted Niles on the chest and then moved over to Denise Gilliam.

Denise for her part was not a big believer in any form of clairvoyance or prophecy. She was an old-school MD that knew what she could feel or see was the real version of life, not mysticism in any form.

"Ah, a healer . . ." Madam Korvesky smiled and then looked into the young doctor's eyes. "But you're here to watch . . . watch this one," she said as she turned to face Alice with a smile. Alice looked at Niles and gave him a dirty look as she realized that Denise was babysitting her and it angered her to no end. "But I may have something you may very well be interested in, healer, something that will amaze and maybe even frighten you."

"Does it matter that I'm already frightened to beat all hell," Denise said as Madam Korvesky let her hand slip out of her own.

The old woman moved on to Charlie Ellenshaw. As she did, Anya took a quick look over toward Everett. Carl saw her and they looked at each other for the longest moment. Anya swallowed at the exact same moment as Everett did and then they both realized they were staring at one another and looked away.

"My gracious, funny-haired man, your head inside is a mess."

Charlie looked confused at first and then glanced at Niles, who only shrugged his shoulders as if saying, *I told you.*

"Oh, here it is . . ." she said as she moved her hand to the front of Charlie's head, just under a swatch of unruly white hair. "You are a man who is a believer in myth and legend." She tilted her head and closed her eyes. "You believe when all others don't see. You try to bring to light the unbelievable. Yes, a true mess inside there," she said as she lowered a tired hand and touched Charlie's smooth jawline. "But that's the way you like it, isn't that right?" She didn't wait for Charlie's embarrassed nodding of his head. She moved down the line until she finally stopped at Carl. The small woman looked up into Everett's eyes and Madam Korvesky froze as she took him in.

Anya felt uncomfortable. It was if she were terrified of what Everett would reveal. Did the large American hate her for what happened in Rome? What were these men and women here to do? She moved from foot to foot as her grandmother confronted the American.

"The Man from the Sea," she said as she again closed her eyes, only this time she took both of Carl's hands into her own. The cane was held between both sets of hands and Everett could swear he felt the age of the wood thorough his skin. "Troubled. You are troubled by a friend, the loss of . . . of . . . confidence toward that friend . . . Jack. Yes, you are troubled by a friend named Jack who will not allow you inside . . ." Again she tilted her head. "He will not allow you to be too close for there is danger."

Carl raised his brows as he watched the old woman standing before him. She opened her eyes and patted Carl on the chest as she had the others.

"How is that for Gypsy mysticism?" she asked smiling.

"Truly insightful," Everett said as he looked over at Anya.

"Is that right, Man from the Sea? Well here is something that will really make your lantern burn brighter." She once more looked up at Carl and then over at Anya. "You have to stay away from my granddaughter, Man from the Sea. There is nothing there for you."

Anya was stunned. She allowed her jaw to drop as she took an involuntary step forward to try and silence her grandmother.

"She has many tasks to perform and she cannot be sidetracked. The time is not right for Anya." She watched Carl for a reaction.

For Carl's part he could see that the old woman didn't like what she was saying as Madam Korvesky turned and faced Anya. "I'm sorry, girl-child, but things have changed and as you know a queen cannot take an outsider as a husband, or even as a mate."

Anya was frozen to the spot where she stood. The words that had just been spoken aloud by her grandmother had made her heart stop.

"Have you gone crazy, Grandmother?" she said as she finally broke the spell she was under. She stepped up to Everett. "I am sorry, Captain I don't know where this is coming from." She turned and faced the old woman, who stood by motionless as she leaned on her cane. "And what do you mean, queen? There is no way I would ever do that. Marko is destined to lead our people and you know that. He's my brother and I will not go against him."

"You will do as your queen decides, young one, now lower your voice before—"

They all heard the breathing behind them. None of the Event Group personnel had ventured a look into the small room to their right as they had entered the cottage. Standing in the small doorway and leaning over so it could view the interior of the kitchen, Mikla stood with his arms outstretched and bracing himself against the pain in its ankle. It was on two legs with the right foot barely touching the floor. The beast was breathing in and out as it eyed the visitors.

"Oh," was all Niles could get out of his mouth. Denise almost went to one knee as her legs could no longer support herself. Alice Hamilton smiled and looked from the impressive Mikla to Madam Korvesky. The old woman was not surprised that not one ounce of shock registered on Alice's face. It was if she had expected to see Mikla at any moment.

"Golia," Alice said beneath her breath.

"You seem to know much about us, Mrs. Hamilton. That is good, now I don't have to explain why my orders must be obeyed as far as my granddaughter is concerned."

The room was quiet as they all watched Mikla breathe in and out as it scanned the faces before it. The beast was weak and they could see its struggle to remain standing in the doorway.

"Alice, this is Mikla," Carl said as he eased himself toward the giant Golia. The animal growled as Everett moved. The captain stopped and waited for Anya. He knew the beast was about to collapse.

"This was what I wanted you to see, healer," the old woman said as she looked at Denise Gilliam. The Gypsy woman stepped forward and placed her small hand on Mikla as the beast wavered and almost fell. "Not all healing is done through potions and medicine. Sometimes a little something more is called for."

"What is wrong with it?" Alice asked as she also took a tentative step forward to see the Golia better.

"If we don't get his broken ankle set and spelled before too long Mikla will die," Anya said as she stepped forward. Her eyes momentarily locked with Carl's as if in apology for her grandmother's words a moment before. She finally reached Mikla and the beast lowered its head in pain and frustration as it allowed Anya to take it back to the bedroom.

"We must get Mikla into the temple, the spell will have to be cast soon," Madam Korvesky said. "Anya, we will discuss my words to your friend later," she looked at Everett, "when we are alone. For right now I will take Mikla into the temple. You are to stay with the people and show yourself to them. They will be needed when the time comes to face your brother about my decisions."

"This cannot be your decision, Grandmother. This is my life and I have done everything for the Jeddah that you have required and enough is enough. Marko is king and will lead the Jeddah forward. His offense cannot be as grievous a crime as you claim."

"You will do as I say, Anya. This is why you have been brought home. Marko has the Golia so confused and angry that Stanus and the others cannot be trusted any longer to do right by the Jeddah. He has lied to them and they will not forgive. You are the only person that will correct the wrong that has been done to them by Marko." She held up a hand when Anya stopped with Mikla hanging on to her to prevent the disagreement from becoming a full-blown argument between granddaughter and queen. "If our burden inside the mountain has come to light we will have to act, and Marko cannot be trusted to do this. His position with the Jeddah and their safety has been compromised."

The door opened and several of the village men stepped in. Mikla growled as the men reached for him and the beast actually took a weakened swipe at the lead man, who easily dodged the long sharp claws. They were all lucky that Mikla was worn out and too drained of energy to defend itself. The Gypsy men took Mikla and placed him on the door that had been utilized as a bed and lifted the Golia for the trip into the temple where he would either be healed and live, or suffer a bad spell casting and die horribly. Mikla sensed this and was troubled.

"You will all come with me, Mrs. Hamilton; I will show you and your friends where real secrets are kept."

"The temple of gold and Egyptian finery," Alice said, repeating the legend of the Lost Tribe and its temple of riches.

The old woman smiled and then laughed aloud.

"Yes, exactly, Mrs. Hamilton, the treasure of the Exodus and the palace built to keep it safe, all wrapped up inside our most magic of mountains."

Everett looked at Anya and found she could not look up and face him.

"Man from the Sea, stay and watch over my granddaughter. If you truly feel about her the way I know that you do you will make sure she is undeterred from what has to be done for her people." She took a painful step in his direction by using the cane to lean on. "I assume you have the dignity to allow over three thousand years of history to play itself out without interference?"

"Madam Korvesky, I assure you—" Niles began to speak for Everett but she didn't allow him to.

"The West has done quite enough interfering by allowing your NATO hooligans to sell my land to an outsider, a Russian outsider at that. No, you and your people have harmed mine enough, Man from the Sea. Amend some wrongs and keep Anya safe until I return. Now, go inside Anya's marriage chest there," she smiled when her granddaughter blushed, "and hand me a quilt, young man."

Carl swallowed and then with a last look at Anya nodded his head as if he were afraid his voice would fail him at this most inopportune time. He walked a few steps toward the foot of the small bed and saw the large trunklike box. He did as he was asked and pulled an old comforter from the five-foot-by-four-foot-square box that had seen far better days.

As Carl lifted the blanket he saw something square wrapped in another old, moth-eaten quilt. He saw part of what looked like a headstone and before he closed the lid he looked at Anya and wondered just what kind of woman would keep a chunk of stone in her hope chest. Everett closed the top of the box and then attempted to slide the chest back against the bed. Whatever was inside wrapped in the old quilts was as heavy as a dozen gold bars. Carl again pushed it against the bed and this time the chest moved. He straightened with a curious look on his face and then placed the blanket in the old woman's hands.

"Mrs. Hamilton, if you and the others will come with me I will take you to the place you came to see and the very special life that protects the heritage of the Jeddah."

15

THE EDGE OF THE WORLD HOTEL AND RESORT CASINO

As Pete and Ryan walked through the connecting hallway leading to the hotel's lobby, Jason spied Collins and McIntire as they stepped off the elevator. With a look at the way he was dressed and with mud covering half of his pants, Ryan decided that the information he had to pass to the colonel was far more important than his desire to impress.

"Come on, Pete, there's the colonel and Sarah," he said as he tugged on the computer genius's elbow.

Pete lowered his glasses from where they had been perched on his forehead and squinted toward the elevator area. Pete shook his head.

"No way. I have to get to that restroom, Commander, or my legs will itch right off my body."

Jason glanced down at Golding's burr-encrusted pants and shook his head.

"Okay, Doc, you stay right in there and don't go to the room until I'm finished telling the colonel why everyone is out to get rid of us."

"Right," Pete said in haste and then turned and practically ran toward the men's restroom.

Ryan again shook his head in wonder at how uncomfortable these academic types became at the least little bit of irritation to their physical being.

He turned and made his way toward the restaurant.

Pete pushed the restroom door open and stepped inside not noticing or caring if anyone was present as he was in such a hurry to get into a stall. He immediately closed the door and sat upon the toilet and started removing his shoes and socks. As he pulled he felt the tearing of his skin as the burrs and foxtails slowly relinquished their hold on him. As the socks finally peeled away, relief flooded his system. He stood and raised the toilet seat and tossed the socks inside and then flushed. As he closed his eyes relishing the pain-free feeling, he became aware that something wasn't right. He felt water rushing at his feet.

"Oh, crap," he said when he saw that his socks had clogged the toilet and water was flooding from the top and splashing at his feet. "Damn!" Pete said as he reached inside with a grimace and fished around until he pulled first one and then finally the other sock from the clogged toilet. Pete felt the cold water still flowing around his feet as the bowl started to empty, but still he closed the lid and then hopped on the stool to get out of the rush of freezing water.

Pete cursed his luck as he watched the water finally stop flowing onto the tiled floor. He sat and felt like an idiot instead of a graduate from MIT and Stanford. He heard the bathroom door open and at least two men step into the restroom. He was about to call out a flood warning to the unsuspecting restroom users when a voice spoke up that he recognized immediately. It was the man from the night before and the same roguish gentleman that had received orders to keep him and Ryan under wraps not a half hour before. Pete froze when the men headed his way and stopped before the sinks on the opposite wall.

The men were speaking in Romanian and Pete was lost as to what it was they were talking about. He thought he was safe when the two men had finished washing their hands and sounded as if they were moving off when one of the men stopped talking. Pete heard some splashing and then silence filled the restroom. Golding squatted on the toilet lid as silently as he could. He felt his chest start to burn as he held his breath. He heard footsteps and his heart froze as he looked up and saw that he had not locked the stall door. As he reached for the slide lock, the door suddenly opened and the man he had confronted in the restaurant the night before was standing in front of him. A smile slowly creased the man's bearded face.

"Ah, a little shithouse rat. Are we trying to hide among the overflowing toilets?"

Pete slowly lowered his legs and placed his feet in the cold water that was slow to drain from the floor. The large Romanian thug stepped back and held the stall door open.

"Running into you was fortunate—we don't have to scour the hotel looking for you. Now we will find your little smart-ass friend, who I want to speak to very badly." The man gestured for Pete to step out of the stall. "Come, I have instructions to take you to a place where you can do no more damage to Mr. Zallas's hotel. Please come with us."

"Pete didn't know how the rest of the field teams did this without getting into as much trouble as he and Charlie Ellenshaw did the few times they had been allowed out of the complex. Now here he was being taken away by two very large Romanian men that looked as if they ate Ph.D.'s for breakfast, and on top of that he was now barefooted.

He knew Charlie would never let him live this down.

Jack and Sarah had just turned the corner of the lobby when they saw the person they needed desperately to speak to. She was the one employee who looked as if she wasn't happy about Zallas and the way he ran things. As they didn't know how close her operations partner, Janos Vajic, was with Zallas, they could only hope that the general manager of the resort, Gina Louvinski, would be approachable with their rather bizarre request.

Jack took Sarah by the arm and moved toward Gina, who was instructing one of her staff on something. She looked up and saw them approaching and hurried the employee off. The general manager looked around nervously for a moment and then smiled as Jack stepped up to her.

"Colonel, I would have thought that you and Miss McIntire would have found a safer holiday weekend somewhere else." She looked around with the false smile still on her face. "I mean with the trouble from Mr. Ryan and all, I thought staying someplace else may have been preferable to . . . certain things."

"You're blathering, Ms. Louvinski. What made you think we would be leaving? Because of a small altercation? No, we have business here and we think you're the only one that can help us."

Gina looked around nervously. She nodded her head at Janos as he walked past on the far side of the hotel. He moved on without a second's thought to the two people she was speaking to.

"Help you do what?" she asked without really moving her lips or breaking her fabricated smile.

"My friend here thinks your resort is going to blow up or something and she would like to look at your original geology reports on this land the resort sits on."

Gina was shocked Jack had said all of that in one breath.

"I guess that took you a little off guard," Jack said with a little smile. "But I had to get your attention. Ms. McIntire here needs to see the original geologist's report on the valley."

"Ms. Louvinski, the entire Patinas area is getting severe and continuous movement in an area not known for seismic activity," Sarah said, cutting in. She quickly explained the situation.

The general manager was speechless. She looked from Sarah to Jack and that look was a lost one.

"Uh, uh, those plans and reports would be in Mr. Zallas's engineering office adjacent to his own. He would never allow an outsider." She thought for a second. "Not even me, anywhere near there."

Jack smiled, taking Gina by the arm, and then he and Sarah walked her clear of a few of the guests as they made their way to the restaurant.

"Look, we can do this now and maybe stop something terrible from happening, or we can wait until we can contact NATO command in Germany and have this whole area sealed off, but that would take time, Ms. Louvinski, time we don't have." Jack looked around with the smile still on his face and then he looked back down at the general manager. "We have a selfish reason for asking this. We have friends lost on that mountain somewhere and we don't know where they are or if they need help. We can't look for them or help them with this seismic event hanging over our heads."

Gina swallowed and looked around. The surroundings seemed unfamiliar as her heart raced. She knew these people were serious but she also knew that Zallas would kill her if she allowed them access to his office.

"I'm sure if you explain to Mr. Zallas your suspicions he would—"

"Your boss is a criminal and our original intent was to prove he is an antiquities thief and to discover where these artifacts were coming from. Now that has to take a backseat to what my geologist friend here has discovered."

"You are police?" Gina said as she involuntarily took a step away from the two Americans.

"No, not exactly," Sarah said as she closed the distance between herself and Gina. "My friend is telling the truth. We need to see the geology report and we need to see it soon. Mr. Zallas would not allow that, so you have to, or you will be just as responsible as your employer if what I'm sure is happening, happens."

Sarah's words hit home but Gina was still frozen because of her fear of Zallas. Without a word Gina turned and pushed her way past Jack and then brushed by an approaching Ryan without taking notice to him.

"Well, that didn't go at all well," Jack said.

"What did you expect," Sarah said, "with that bare-my-soul tactic of yours? You could have been just a bit more subtle, GI Joe."

"Well, we don't have a lot of time here, we have to—"

"Boy, do I look and smell that bad, or did someone tell her I was a cad of the first order?" Ryan said as he glanced back at a very frightened Gina as she walked away.

"No, I'm the one that scared her off. We may have a bigger problem than antiquities theft on our hands here, Mr. Ryan."

"Yeah, I think we may. I think the owner of this place wants us out of the way."

"Any more good news?" Sarah asked Ryan as she angrily stepped between the two men.

"Well, until a second ago, no, but as of this very second, yes," Ryan said as he pointed to his right in the direction he had come.

As they watched, Pete Golding was led out of the men's restroom and herded toward the elevators. Jack lowered his eyes when he realized who was escorting the good doctor away. He could see the large Romanian smiling as they waited for the elevator and poor Pete Golding looked horrid with no shoes and filthy clothing.

Sarah looked at Jack and he shook his head in disgust at allowing the doc to be taken right under their noses.

"Commander, we have to get into the engineering area of Zallas's office. Sarah thinks there's a significant problem with the geologic makeup of the ground here."

"Well, from what we overheard outside that may be hard to research if we're dead and buried someplace. I don't think our host is all too thrilled with us being around, it's like he knows we're not invited guests."

"Boy, I wonder where he got that notion," Sarah said, looking at Jack with a raised brow.

"This is certainly turning into a banner day," Jack said as he started to move forward toward a shaken-looking Pete Golding but was stopped by an outstretched arm. Ryan shook his head at Collins.

"You and Sarah do what you have to do, Pete's my responsibility. I'll get him out of whatever trouble he's in and meet you back at the rooms later."

"And how do you plan on doing this, Mr. Ryan?"

Jason took a deep breath and then smiled. He then aimed himself at the bank of elevators.

"Like you, Colonel, I'm making this up as I go."

As Jack's eyes followed, Ryan made a beeline for the men waiting for the elevator to arrive. Collins shook his head and then took Sarah by the arm and they made their way to the main lobby.

"Well, I think now would be about the best time to head to the office area before we go into the restaurant." Jack looked around and then nodded toward the front desk where a lone employee stood at a computer terminal. "I guess we can assume the managerial areas are back there."

"What do we do, just stroll up to the front desk and ask for the key to Dmitri Zallas's offices?"

"That wouldn't be the best course of action in this case."

Jack and Sarah turned and saw the resort's general manager as she returned. Gina slowly removed her glasses and they could both see she was frightened by what she had been asked to do. Sarah saw the hand holding the glasses shaking almost uncontrollably.

"Mr. Zallas is out on the grounds and his goons are with him, with the exception of those two men there." She nodded behind them. "I don't know where Zallas is exactly and since he has scheduled dinner with you, you will only have a few minutes inside the offices. I suggest one of you do your artifacts search and the other take the engineering office for the geological report. If we are caught we can expect . . . well . . . I have heard stories about Zallas and his business practices."

Jack looked at Gina and reached out, and with his own hand stilled her shaking one. "He's the kind of man that promotes his own legend, it's business, it's meant to frighten. The man is a fool, but these sorts of men we have discovered are the most dangerous and unpredictable. He thinks we're a part of NATO and that will make him a little less likely to off us while we're here. You let us in and then disappear, go eat dinner, and we'll be out before you know it."

Without another word Gina gestured by nodding her head and then she walked toward the far end of the front desk and was through before Collins and McIntire could move. Gina turned and smiled in their direction and held her hand out toward the rear of the front desk area, as she attempted to act normal for the desk clerk's benefit.

"Right this way and we'll get you started looking at our honeymoon packages," she said with her large and very false smile in place. Her eyes moved to the front desk clerk and she winked at the young man, who returned her smile and then turned back to his work.

"Don't get your hopes up, Jack," Sarah said as she haughtily walked past him to a waiting Gina Louvinski.

Jack's eyes followed Sarah and he shook his head.

"Newlyweds," he muttered as he followed the two women into the back offices where their burglary would commence against one of the more ruthless individuals in the world.

VILLAGE OF PATINAS

Anya was not happy about having to stay in the village and watch out for Marko. Her grandmother wanted him kept an eye on and she was it. As Madam Korvesky prepared to leave for the temple, she gathered the things she would need for the healing of Mikla, who had already been removed by several of the trusted Patinas men and taken to the temple. The Gypsy queen was using her cane more heavily than before. Dr. Gilliam had offered Madam Korvesky pain medication but it had been explained to the MD that any introduction of a toxicant or opiate right now would interfere with the spell casting to be done.

"Mr. Everett," Niles said, "Charlie and Denise are insisting they join us inside this temple of Alice's. I think it best you and Lieutenant Mendenhall stay here and see what you can find out about this Marko and what his plans truly are. If you're thinking like me, his sister can tell us a lot about the power play going here."

Everett nodded as Anya vanished into her grandmother's room to dress and clean up.

Niles watched as Madam Korvesky was finally eased into a large chair and then four men raised it from the floor of the cottage. She smiled down at Alice, Denise, Charlie Ellenshaw, and Niles, and then gestured for the men to take her out.

Everett saw the bright red satin, lace-lined head scarf that was placed on the woman's head. The garment was simple yet elegant. Its color matched that of her red dress and for the first time he could see the young Anya in the old face that looked down upon her people as she was carried from the house. The music became louder and the cheering of her people reverberated throughout the small house. Carl stepped to the doorway and saw the people reaching for Madam Korvesky as if she were Jesus entering Jerusalem. The men carrying her beamed at the honor of carrying the queen to the temple.

"We tend to overdo things here," said a voice from behind him.

Everett turned and his eyes widened. Anya was dressed in a bright sky blue dress that went down to her mid-calf. It was made with a light weave of soft cotton. The blouse she wore was equally blue in color with red piping along the sleeves and a very low-cut collar. Anya had her jet black hair straight and brushed to a high sheen. The bright blue head scarf was covering just enough of her hair for Carl to feel disappointment. She wore rings he hadn't seen before and her bracelets were many and bright on both arms and wrists. Her boots were the old-fashioned button-up kind with the spiked heel that was popular in the eighteen hundreds. The top of the boot was white and the bottom black.

"Well, does this meet with your expectations as to what a Gypsy girl looks like?" she asked with sarcasm lacing her voice.

Everett couldn't help it and he smiled.

"Yes, it does," he said as he kept his eyes on her dual-colored ones. "Only the Gypsy girls I've seen never looked like this."

Anya looked taken off guard by Everett's compliment. She was momentarily flustered and then shook her head negatively.

"Well, unfortunately, this is the way we dress, and don't be a smart-ass about it, Captain." She stepped around his large frame with a huff.

"Never," he said as he turned to follow Anya from the house.

As several of the mothers and aunts and other admirers crowded around Anya, Carl finally spied Will Mendenhall and waved him over. As he waited he noticed that the 82nd men were being well treated by their hosts as they ate to their heart's content. Will came near to saluting as he stepped up to the crowds and squeezed past them until he was next to the captain.

"Will, watch your fellow Army boys and make sure they don't cause an international incident with the Jeddah," Everett said as he saw Anya finally break free of the women and start away from the house.

"Yes, sir, do you want—" Will started to ask but Everett walked away as if he had been sleepwalking. "I guess not," Mendenhall finished.

He found Anya as she was standing and watching the mountain above them. Several men and women walked past but left her alone as they knew she was getting reacquainted with her home. Carl stepped up to her and he also looked up.

"You know I was hoping for a little bit more of an explanation about just who in the hell you really are. I mean are you . . ." Carl looked around to make sure no one was listening in to his conversation—they weren't. "Are you Jeddah or are you Jewish? I mean Mossad, that's a strange place for a country girl like you to end up."

Anya didn't exactly face him nor did she look away either.

"I am not Jewish, well, not in the sense that you mean anyway," she said as she nodded at several well-wishers and admirers as they streamed past and the large blond-haired American. "Captain, we really can't even claim to be Jeddah any longer." She finally looked fully at Carl as the large bonfire in the center of town reflected off his tanned skin. Men and women were dancing and playing music and the laughter of everyone put Everett ay ease more than anything had in years.

"I'm not following you," Carl said as he saw the way the firelight played off her black hair.

"I am not as angry at my brother as my grandmother is. I see what Marko is doing and I want him to succeed, but not the way he has planned by bringing outsiders into it. The selling off of . . . certain things cannot be allowed to happen." She gestured around her at the men and women as they danced around the fire pit. "We are not like we were once upon a time. Marko is right, these people deserve to serve themselves, not some ancient promise made to a people that has forgotten them as surely as if we never existed. Marko should have done it another way. Now all of this may vanish, my grandmother will see to that."

Carl stepped closer to Anya as he realized she was telling him all as if she had to release the pent-up emotions of her past.

"I have been gone for so long I have become cynical of my own kind. And there is another problem. I haven't told my grandmother yet that I believe certain people in Mossad, besides Colonel Ben-Nevin, have much more knowledge of the Jeddah and our mountain than we initially thought. Why the knee-jerk reaction to a simple report about an American spy inside the Vatican archives? Someone panicked when they saw what was sent in that message."

"The wolf's skull?" Carl asked.

"As you said, back in Rome, Captain, I'm not a big believer in coincidence in this business. And now I have all this information and something else is happening that has me so angry that I want to spit." She accepted an offer of a large wax-lined sheepskin bag. She squeezed something red-colored into her mouth and then slammed the bag into Everett's chest. Everett drank.

"You will have to spit if you keep drinking this stuff," Carl said as he held the bag out and looked it over.

Anya turned on Everett as if he were the cause of all her pain.

"I cannot be queen. I am not in the direct line of succession after her and never have been. My grandmother will be breaking the law by appointing me heir to her throne."

"Maybe you can do some good, where your grandmother thinks Marko can't."

"My brother is not as stupid as most would like to make out. He can lead the people into a new future and my grandmother has to realize this."

"What's your solution?"

Anya bit her lower lip. "I would ask Marko to cut ties with this resort and its ownership. Then we can move into that future with a clear conscience. The selling off of the assets in the mountain will only bring discovery of the Golia down on our heads. I hope to say these things to my brother."

"Well, why don't we go find him and ask him, it can't hurt, can it?"

"Believe me, Captain, with Marko it can hurt when you least expect it." Anya took Carl by the hand, which surprised him. He stepped close to her as she studied him. "I am more worried about the Golia.'

"I know what you mean, they worry me also."

She smiled for the first time and that made Everett feel a hundred percent better. For some unknown reason he felt he needed to make her smile and laugh, as if she had been missing that small joy for some time.

"I guess an outsider would see them that way," Anya said as her smile grew with the warm feeling of the wine in her belly. "All the Golia ever wanted was to just live, Captain, that's all. They hunt what we supply them so they never have to leave their sanctuary. They have their families to care for and they felt safe here. But now Marko's plan has Stanus and the others acting like I have never seen them before. Stanus read something in Marko when he cast the joining spell and the Golia took something away from that coupling and has resented Marko ever since."

"First I think you better explain just what in the hell a joining is."

Again Anya turned her head and nodded. "I keep forgetting you know absolutely nothing about us."

At that moment a small man with a barrel chest and impressive handlebar mustache danced his way toward Anya. He was sliding a bow across a small violin and smiling to beat the band. He stopped playing long enough to take Anya by the arm and spin her toward the large fire pit, and the gathered revelers erupted with adulation that their long-lost daughter had joined them.

Carl watched Anya as she stopped and then slowly started to dance around the fire pit. Everett stepped lightly between two older men who stared and clapped with the others as Anya moved around the fire. Someone tossed her a tambourine and she started hitting it in accordance with an old-world-sounding European tune. Violins and flutes played as she danced and spun and banged on the tambourine in time as she twirled, sending her bright blue dress flaring wide as a flower would opening up to the morning sun. Many more men, women, and children were starting to drift over from other areas of the village as they all wanted to witness the return of the first daughter of Patinas.

Will Mendenhall and several of the engineers from the 82nd stepped up to Everett as he continued to be mesmerized by Anya and the seductive way she could move.

"Wow," was all the young lieutenant could say, his mouth agape.

As Anya spun around the fire pit she came close to Everett on a turn and their eyes locked. She was sweating and her black hair was laid flat on her forehead as she came to a sudden stop as the music slowed. She continued to look at Carl as her chest heaved with the effort to catch her breath. Everett had never witnessed such an innocent dance become so incredibly erotic. It seemed they faced each other over the two feet that separated them for an hour as everything inside Patinas slowed to a crawl and time stood still. Carl could barely hear the cheers of the men and women around them. He didn't even flinch when Anya was finally picked up and carried away by her many admirers.

"Now that was something I assumed only happened in the movies," Mendenhall said as the engineers moved off back to the long tables brimming with food. Will smiled and then looked over at the captain. Carl just stood watching Anya.

Mendenhall shook his head as he realized that Carl had not heard one word he had said. His blue eyes reflected the firelight as they followed the throng of people around the fire. *He was someplace other than here*, Mendenhall thought.

As Everett watched, Anya was finally placed on the ground and she spied Carl looking at her. As she breathed in and out still exhausted from her dance, she realized that her grandmother had been hinting in the right direction. There was something about this American agent that stilled her heart every time she looked at him. It had been that way since the first moment she had laid eyes on the large Navy man.

Anya finally broke away from the crowd and walked over to Everett, who just stood watching her. Mendenhall, never one to be slow on the uptake since his time hanging out with Ryan on his runs into Las Vegas, knew when to exit stage left.

"I'll be over here with the vampires and werewolves eating supper." With one last look at Everett, Mendenhall put his hands in his pockets and strolled away.

"Vampires and werewolves, right," Everett said, not even realizing what it was he had repeated.

The former Mossad agent stepped up to Carl and brushed some wet hair off her forehead and then reached out and took Everett by the hand. Shocking him, she then started running through the crowd as if she were starting to feel strangled in the midst of the adulation by the Jeddah.

She and Everett ran until they were through the front gate of Patinas.

Alice, Niles, Charlie, and Denise Gilliam were in a straight line as they followed the two Gypsy men as they carried Madam Korvesky up the small sheep trail that wound away from Patinas and into the pass. The trail looked old and the dirt they walked upon had been worn to the bare rock of the mountain. As they neared a large granite-faced rock they started to see small symbols etched into the stone. Niles looked at Alice questioningly as he held a small gas lantern close to one of the symbols.

"Hieroglyphs of some kind," she said as she too was intrigued.

"That is the language of the Jeddah," Madam Korvesky said as the men carried her in her chair up the steep incline.

"Why in hieroglyphs? Didn't the Jeddah speak ancient Hebrew?" Alice asked as she realized for the first time that the real schooling about the Jeddah and the Golia was about to begin.

"The Jeddah, the warrior clan of the tribes of Israel, did not speak the language of Abraham, Joseph, Moses, and Joshua. We had our own tongue," she said as she was moved past stone and bush on their way seemingly to nowhere. "We were always separated from the rest of the tribes by the elders. We were feared for no other reason than we were warriors not only for Israel, but for Ramesses II and his fathers before him, and many other fathers before that."

"So you developed your own language?" Alice asked.

They heard Madam Korvesky laugh. "Well, we have to assume that. It has been a while and quite a few of the old tales have vanished from Jeddah memory."

Alice was about to ask further questions on the origins of this language but was stopped when she looked up and saw that Madam Korvesky and the men carrying her had disappeared from the trail.

"Just walk up to the large boulder and step inside," came the old woman's voice seemingly from nowhere.

Niles held Alice back as he and Charlie Ellenshaw stepped past the two women and up to a large boulder that seemed to block the path. Then their eyes widened when they realized that the giant boulder was nothing more than a gate into the mountain. From the angle of the trail it looked as if the house-sized boulder was intact, but upon closer inspection they saw the archway that had been carved in the stone many thousands of years before they had arrived in Patinas.

"Now this is camouflage, Jack would love to see this," Niles said as he ran his hand along the boulder as they passed through. "You could walk right up on it and not know it was there," Niles said but realized that Charlie wasn't beside him, nor were Alice and Denise. As Compton looked back he saw that all three had stopped and were staring at something beyond. As he turned and looked, Alice slowly raised a finger and pointed with her eyes wide. Charlie had a smile on his face as if he had just caught Santa Claus pilfering cookies and milk. The director froze as he saw a giant Golia standing in the archway, blocking his entrance. The beast was breathing hard and its fingers gripped either side of the entrance as its bright, nighttime glowing yellow eyes watched Niles. The dark silhouette was enough to make Compton freeze.

"I think we have run into one of the temple guards," Charlie said as he went to one knee to get a better angle.

"Nadia, leave them be, they are friends!" the voice of Madam Korvesky was heard saying loudly from the far side of the entrance.

"Nadia?" Denise asked in a whisper. "That six-and-a-half-foot animal is a female?"

The eyes of the Golia narrowed and then its ears came up in a more relaxed posture. The beast awkwardly moved aside but did not leave as the others slowly squeezed past.

Alice swallowed as she came nearest to the Golia. She could feel the heat of the beast's breath and the feel of its fiery eyes as she moved along the stone entranceway.

"Easy, Nadia is in heat and that is why she has been left at the temple. Nadia, go to the babies now."

The beast leaned over and with one hand outstretched and long fingers splayed, it touched Charlie's wire-rimmed glasses, once, twice, three times, until they fell from his face. The Golia's eyes went so wide at the shock of seeing Ellenshaw lose his eyes that the giant bounded away and then using the strength of legs and arms scaled the rock walls and vanished.

"Left behind? What do you mean?" Alice asked as they entered what looked to be a huge gallery of open stone carved ages before. It was the size of a theater lobby and was lined with old wooden torches that burned brightly as they illuminated the hieroglyphs on the walls. They were Egyptian in context and construction and without closer inspection neither Niles nor Alice could decipher what they spelled out

"That seems to be the mystery of the day," Madam Korvesky said as she sat and waited for the newcomers to join her. The two men waited patiently beside the chair. They watched the Americans as they examined every area of the gallery. "It seems all of our adult Golia have been vanishing at night and we don't why or where. It has something to do with Marko, but for the life of me I don't know where the wolves are going at night. Nadia because of her condition was tasked to watch the baby Golia."

"I must admit I'm somewhat disappointed in the temple structure," Ellenshaw commented. "I thought after so many thousands of years that it would have been larger, maybe with more than just this one room."

Madam Korvesky laughed and shook her head at Charlie Ellenshaw's naïveté.

"The temple, no," she said, trying to still her laughing at the poor American scientist. "This is not the temple. The temple is hundreds of feet inside the mountain. This is just the gallery, of which we could fit over a million of these in the cave system we utilized to build the temple."

The two men didn't wait for orders, they took the large arms of her chair and once more lifted up the old woman and then started down the massive staircase that had been hidden behind the giant Golia. They were silent as they continued down. The heat was tremendous the deeper along the staircase they went.

The two men finally stopped at the edge of a great cliff and waited. The visiting Americans stepped up and then looked down into the most amazing sight any of them had ever seen. Stretching out before them was an entire city. Egyptian spires and columns. Smaller gods of the ancients were depicted in the most massive relief drawings they had ever seen. The human and animal hieroglyphs were at minimum a thousand feet in height and fifty in width. The pictographs ringed the giant city that was laid out before them like the city of Los Angeles. Buildings, many never before occupied, sat empty and dark. Small temples to God had been erected. Massive grain bins sat like beehives on the outskirts of the city. The dominant feature was the large pyramid at the center. The entire scene was illuminated by large fire pots on standards throughout the well-designed temple.

"My God," Alice said as she stood on the edge of the six-hundred-foot cliff looking into the past of a people long thought to have vanished from the face of the earth.

The most amazing thing about the Egyptian-inspired architecture was that most of the city was built from the stone of the immense cave system. Pillars were hewn from solid rock with only their fronts exposed to the stone carver's tool. The four small pyramids ringing the larger one were solidly built and stood against the far wall of the temple. There were giant stone statues of deities or ancient Hebrew tribesmen that Alice, Niles, Denise, or Charlie had not seen before. The giant statuary was arranged around the great gallery of the temple and all stared down at a central location in the center of the small stone city. The altar stone was mounted by four sets of stone steps and had been carved from an outcropping of lava that had sprung from the cave's floor in the ancient past. Just behind the altar was the largest of the pyramids.

As the Americans gained the ground floor of the six-thousand-foot-deep excavation of a natural cave system, they examined the very special place of the Jeddah. But it was crazy Charlie Ellenshaw that noticed that something wasn't quite right about the temple. As he examined the stone statues closer in the flickering light of a thousand torches he saw that the coloring used to paint the images was old, chipped, fading away to nothing. Most looked no better maintained than the current ruins at Luxor. Many of the statues were missing large and small pieces. Some of the temple housing had collapsed in on itself and the stalactites had oozed their way down onto the largest pyramid almost to the point of covering it whole. The great Eye of Ra that was etched into the flooring was covered in fecal matter that he imagined was deposited there by the Golia. Finally Charlie looked at Niles and Alice, who were conferring with Denise about something. Charlie tapped on Niles's shoulder and pointed to the pyramid and the enormous stalactite that covered it. Niles nodded.

"We were just discussing that very thing. It seems the Jeddah have been negligent in the upkeep."

"The Jeddah don't come here often, do you?" Alice asked the old woman, who was looking up.

"No, this is the city of the Golia. This is their home."

As the four Americans turned and looked high into the cave system they saw hundreds of Golia pups and innumerable little glowing dots of yellow that were the eyes of the young as they watched the intruders far below their perch. For the first time Alice realized that the Golia were alive and living well in the mountains of Romania.

Charlie looked up at the glowing dots of light looking at them from above. It seemed the young of the Golia had been taught that silence was to their benefit.

They didn't move, they just sat and watched. He was amazed when he saw from the great distance one of the small pups stand on its two hind legs and wobble a few steps before collapsing. Ellenshaw realized that he was looking at the ancestor of the very myth he as a cryptozoologist said could not possibly exist—he was watching what amounted to a baby werewolf taking its first steps.

"I present to you the city of Oraşul lui Moise."

The Event Group looked down upon the City of Moses.

THE EDGE OF THE WORLD HOTEL AND RESORT CASINO, PATINAS, ROMANIA

Jack waited just outside the office as Gina and Sarah made it look like they were just having small talk while Gina unlocked the outer door to the private suite of offices which were set well away from the regular offices of hotel management.

Gina turned the key and as it clicked it made her wince as if the entire resort could hear it. She gestured for the two to go in. She stood at the door.

"The office Zallas uses is right there, the one with the double doors," she pointed with her manicured nail. "The engineer's office is over there, both are unlocked."

Collins nodded.

"I'll be right out here keeping an eye on the desk."

Again Jack and Sarah nodded that they understood. Gina eased the door closed and left.

"Okay, I'll take El Creepo's office and you take the engineer's."

Sarah moved off as she was in a hurry to see the geology report. Jack watched her leave and then turned for the large double doors that led into the office of Dmitri Zallas.

As Collins eased the door open he peered inside at the blackness. The only light came from a softly illuminated globe in the corner. Jack stepped in and closed the door. He reached in his pocket and pulled out a small penlight. He clicked it on with one hand held over the top allowing just enough light to filter through his fingers to see. He smiled. Only Zallas could be this arrogant. Around the office on his desk, credenza, and other glass shelving specially built for them sat hundreds of little artifacts that could only have come from the heritage of the Jeddah.

Collins wanted to laugh at how easy proving provenance for theft was, it was as if Zallas dared the world to come and get him. Jack was used to dealing with antiquity thieves like the slickly professional Henri Farbeaux. Henri would never have anything that could connect him with theft inside his home or office.

As he moved over to a brightly polished credenza, Jack opened the topmost door and saw the most advanced shortwave radio system he had seen outside military circles. This setup had everything from radio to satellite transmission capabilities.

Well, at least the idiot set up for emergencies, this may come in handy, he thought as he checked to see if the equipment was operational.

As he closed the door to the credenza he heard the office door swing open and Jack turned and his world in that moment spun out of control.

Sarah was having a hard time in the architect's drawers looking for the correct plans for the resort's foundations. She had found the geology report almost immediately and also saw that the interior minister had signed off on the report. She raised her brow at discovering that it wasn't a geological engineer that had signed off on the report, but the interior minister, that's one powerful signature. And that signature had stated rather mundanely in geologist speak that the ground, the mountain, and the flatlands the resort was to be built upon were safe.

Sarah closed the drawer in frustration, and as she looked over the hotel's foundation plan she saw that it was built at least fifty miles from the nearest abnormality in the strata. She picked up the thick file with the geology specs inside and then turned and looked at the architectural drawers again. Did she miss something? She again returned to the drawer and pulled it open. She rummaged through what seemed thousands of drawings and then she stopped as one heading caught her attention. Castle Dracula was one of the last sets of drawings as they were placed in the drawers. Sarah pulled the plans from the drawer and spread them out on the floor. She was looking at an amazing drawing of the castle. Every intricate detail of its construction was laid out before her. She shook her head at the cost of the structure.

It was on the third page of the bedsheet-sized drawings that Sarah raised her eyebrows. She ran her penlight up and down the engineer's grandiose plans for the unique way the castle was to be built directly into the side the mountain. Sarah had been impressed earlier when she had examined the castle from their room. The way the structure was molded into the craggy sides of the mountain made it look as if it had been built directly from the stone. Now by studying the plans she knew how it had been achieved.

She turned the page and ran her hand along the inked representation of the sixteen giant, eight-foot-in-diameter, three-hundred-foot-long solid steel anchor pins that ran from the castle's foundation, linking the structure with the mountain as the anchor pins had been sunk three hundred feet into the side of the Jeddah home. The anchor pins were what held the heavy castle in place, securing it to the mountainside.

"Amazing engineering," she muttered as she noticed the small note paper-clipped to the top of the plans. As she pulled it free and opened it she saw that it was a drawing from the original engineering firm located in Moscow. She read the note and her eyes widened. She started racing through the plans until she found the one she wanted. Then she opened the geologist's file and pulled a report that normally would have been mundane on its surface. She read the report and then looked at the placement of the anchor pins once more. Sarah grimaced and then turned the thick file folder over and spilled its contents on the carpeted floor. She rummaged through the papers until she found the one she had spied earlier that she hadn't paid attention to. It was a report and drawing about a large fault found in the strata of the rock facing the mountain was built into. The crack, as it were, was stretched across the entire width of the facing. It ran two hundred feet into the mountain—and the anchor pins ran right through the fault. The pins were in essence holding the two halves of the mountain together, and one half included the castle that was built upon it.

"Son of a bitch," she said as she found the original geology report and the engineer's follow-up. Sarah slowly lowered her hands to her lap as she sat on her knees inside the Russian's office.

The report had been doctored to show that the fault that sat behind the rear wall of the castle, and in basic engineering parlance, held it in place by the giant anchor pins, was not there. She looked at the engineering schematic once again and saw that the anchor pins did run right through the crack in the mountain. Zallas was sitting on a disaster waiting to happen. Sarah shook her head and started gathering her data. No matter what was to happen to their investigation, this report had to be brought to the attention of people that could shut that castle down before thousands of people were killed.

Sarah heard the door to the engineer's office open. She excitedly stood with the castle's drawings and the geology report.

"Jack, this place is in big trouble, they have—"

The words froze in her mouth as she saw Zallas standing in the office. He had two men beside him and Jack was behind them with three others. Gina was standing beside him and Sarah could see that she was scared witless. Sarah looked at the Russian, who in turn looked around and saw the engineering schematics spread on the floor.

"This place, as you put it, Ms. McIntire, is not the only thing in serious trouble."

Sarah let the plans slip through her fingers as she felt her heart trying to keep the blood pumping through her system.

Zallas nodded for Sarah to join them in the common area of the office space.

"Yes, we seem to have quite a bit of trouble here tonight," Zallas said as the door opened from the outer office. "And as you can see, more has just arrived."

Standing in the doorway was the tall man Jack had recognized earlier. The newcomer smirked. It was Jack who said his name before Sarah.

"Colonel Ali Ben-Nevin." Jack returned the arrogant smirk and then looked at Zallas as the men guarding him tensed with their guns pointed at his sides and chest as the man before them half bowed.

"I don't know you," Ben-Nevin finally said.

"No, but I know a man that has met you and would like to do so again."

"Believe me, that is in the plan, my friend."

Jack didn't like the way Ben-Nevin smiled at all as he was unceremoniously pushed toward the rear entrance of the office area.

"There is good news, we have decided to upgrade your accommodations somewhat," Zallas said. "You'll be staying in the yet to be christened Vlad the Impaler Suite. I think you'll enjoy it."

THE CITY OF MOSES,
PATINAS PASS

As Niles, Alice, Denise, and Charlie were led down a carved stone ramp to the bottom of the temple, the heat had increased by at least fifty degrees, making it somewhere around 110 as near as Niles could estimate. As the men placed Madam Korvesky before the altar the Americans got a better look at the architecture of the city. Madam Korvesky raised her head, weary from the unsteady gait of the two men in their descent into the temple, and saw her guests' confusion.

"The men who designed this place wanted the temple to last a thousand years. Well, it has lasted three and a half." The old Gypsy looked around her at the decay of the temple. "We have been weary of the task for many generations. Losing life in its protection and in the pursuit of cover-up has gone on for too long, my grandson is correct in that."

"I'm not following," Alice said as she saw the old woman was on the brink of announcing something.

"Our tribe has spread like butter on far too much toast. We are speckled throughout the globe. We have become bastardized with the modern world. A sad thing but one that was inevitable, as you Americans can attest, like the destruction of your Indian tribes, it doesn't really matter how and why, it just happened. For us our loss of faith was inevitable as our desire to eventually be free of ancient things. Like your American Indian we are fading from history, but unlike those noble people, we want that to happen. Maybe not this soon, but we do want it eventually. And now with my grandson's arrogant actions it is coming to pass."

"I don't understand," Alice said as she saw the tiredness of the woman before her, so very different from the vibrant hellcat that once upon a time blew up a very expensive yacht in Hong Kong harbor.

"I'm afraid Marko may have dealt with the devil and we are about to pay for that sin. I'm afraid he has allowed outsiders to learn of the temple, and that cannot stand."

"The Russian?" Niles asked getting his hackles up.

"Yes," the old woman said.

Alice could only nod her head.

Niles nudged Alice and turned as the two men, accompanied by six others, carried the old and cracked door inside the temple. On it was Mikla covered by the quilt. They placed the beast on the stone altar and then nodded and bowed toward the queen and moved away into the darkness of the city.

Mikla was breathing deeply. They all saw the quilt rise and fall. Each breath seemed a labor for the great animal.

"We have to act now and cast the spell before Mikla's injury becomes gangrenous," said Madam Korvesky.

Charlie elbowed Denise as he gestured with a nod of his head toward the high gallery of stone and a strange fluorescing mineral embedded in the rock. Denise could not help but gasp.

High above them the Golia young had started to howl. It was a pathetic attempt as far as the power of their parent's call went, but they were trying nonetheless. Each pup was attempting to stand. Each fell in turn, and the ones that could stand pawed at the air as they sensed the sleeping Mikla far beneath them.

Madam Korvesky looked up and then closed her eyes.

"The power of the Golia will help us with Mikla. They feel his pain and will quiet and settle to assist me in what needs doing. We will become one and we will set right what has been done to Mikla."

As they watched, the giant wolf clenched its muscles in a spasm of pain. The quilt slowly slid off the beast and they saw that the black fur was matted and crusted with sweat and dirt from its passage to Patinas.

Suddenly the gallery high above erupted with more howling from the pups and other young. This time they all managed to attain their mature voices and it sounded unlike anything the Americans from the Event Group had ever heard before. It sounded as if hundreds of children started crying and screaming at once.

"My God," Denise Gilliam said as she thrust her hands over her ears as the cacophony assaulted them.

"They are receiving signals that Mikla is in serious trouble," Madam Korvesky said as she slowly stroked the black fur of the injured wolf.

"Signals?" Niles asked as he grimaced at the wailing and mewling coming from the Golia young.

"They are all connected. Some can pick up emotions from other Golia as much as several hundred miles away." She smiled and looked up, her small hand slowly wrapping into the black fur of the beast. "And soon you will see a far more substantial connection the Golia possess." She looked away and gestured for the one remaining villager. She nodded that he could do as previously instructed. "Your Man from the Sea, your . . . I believe you call him Mr. Everett?"

"Carl?" Alice said, wondering where the old Gypsy was going with this.

"Yes. My granddaughter seems quite taken with him, and just two days ago they were in Rome with thoughts of killing each other. Life is strange, is it not, Keeper of Secrets?"

Alice looked from Niles to the hundreds of milling Golia offspring restlessly scurrying around above them and then he looked at the old woman.

"Your plan for Mr. Everett?" Niles asked.

"He is a very healthy man, he reminds me of your tall man in China," she said, looking over at Alice. "The first Keeper of Secrets."

"You'll find that both men have a lot of the same qualities," Alice said and then a knowing look came to her face as she looked at the Gypsy queen. "And a lot of the same flaws I'm afraid."

"That is what makes them who they are, does it not, Mrs. Hamilton?"

Alice did not reply.

"In answer to your question, Mr. Compton, your friend is needed. Needed by your companions down at that stone monstrosity they call a resort."

"What's wrong with our companions?" Niles asked.

"It seems they have encountered the men that my grandson has been doing business with and I am sensing that they need assistance. I need your Mr. Everett to find out for me," again the crooked smile, "and then you will see the very special power of the Golia, and why God placed them here. The one true link."

"I don't understand what you're saying—one true link?" Alice said.

"The true link Mr. Everett will have with him," Madam Korvesky said as she glanced up into the high stone gallery that sat just beneath one of the three stone pyramids.

As they turned and looked up they saw the beast. It stood at least eight and a half feet tall. Its left arm was outstretched as the animal was leaning on a stone outcropping. The Golia stood on its two hind legs and the yellow eyes stood out in the darkness as the giant wolf stared down upon them.

"Oh," was all Alice could say.

"Wow," Charlie Ellenshaw said as he stepped forward to see the sight that stood high above them. Denise for her part decided that she was close enough and took three tentative steps back. Niles held his ground but like Charlie, Alice took steps to get closer to the far wall so they could look up at the legendary alpha male of the Golia.

Before anyone could move, Stanus leaped from his high perch and flew through the air until its large feet struck the stone flooring of the temple. Stanus went down to its knees, as the leap from the gallery was at least a hundred feet. The beast slowly started to straighten and as it did the massively long claws came free of the hands and the Americans could see that Stanus was anything but happy about them being inside the temple.

The four Americans stepped back as Stanus took first one, and then another step toward the dais and the spot where Mikla was lying. The eyes never left the Americans. Madam Korvesky was impressed because most would have seen Stanus and run just as their ancestors had done at the awesome sight.

Suddenly the Golia growled deep in its throat as it approached the old woman and Mikla. The beast looked from Niles, Alice, Charlie, and Denise as it raised its right hand and with outstretched fingers placed its claws into the fur at Mikla's neck. Stanus's ears slowly came up and they could hear the whining of the giant as its claws ran through Mikla's dirty, wet fur.

Alice saw the humanity in the Golia's touch. The eyes, made to cast fear into any beast that saw them, were slowly moving over Mikla as Stanus examined it. Finally the large hand made it down to the broken right ankle of Mikla. The ears lay down and then they heard the deep castings of the wolf's growl. It was as if Stanus could sense, or even smell the infection that was starting to grow from Mikla's injury. Madam Korvesky slowly and gently reached out and placed her much smaller hand on that of Stanus. She closed her eyes and the wolf quieted and became still. The yellow eyes seemed to roll up into the Golia's head and the ears came up like a set of antennae. Then the eyes opened and with one last look at Mikla and then over at the visiting Americans, the alpha male turned, ran, and scrambled up the rocks to the gallery and then vanished.

"That was amazing," Alice said as she stepped closer to the dais and then with a questioning look in her eyes at Madam Korvesky, silent permission was given and then she too laid her hand on Mikla's heaving chest. She felt the heat of the animal and the infection was starting to smell bad.

"Can you do anything for him?" Niles asked as his mind shifted from the trouble that Jack and then others were facing and the immediate problem before them—the wounded Golia.

"Yes, we may very well have Mikla up and running by tomorrow. If not and he dies we may have a serious problem on our hands as Stanus would not take the death of his only remaining brother very well at all. The people that did this would never make it home. So I need your Mr. Everett. I need Stanus, his strength, his power, and his cunning. I need your friend because he can evaluate the situation where Stanus cannot."

"I am not following you at all. I need to make sure my people are safe." Niles looked at Alice. "We have to leave, we can't take a chance that Jack and the others aren't in some kind of trouble."

"You will stay, Stanus will go and your Mr. Everett will go."

"I will not place the captain close to that animal, that doesn't seem like a smart thing to do," Niles said, finally getting a little put off by the mysticism talk and the unscientific way this was unfolding.

"What are you planning?" Alice asked as Mikla whined in its sleep.

"While we help Mikla, your friend and Stanus will perform the miracle and discover what is really happening with your friends and our common enemy."

Charlie Ellenshaw felt the flutter of his stomach as he realized what it was that Madam Korvesky was getting at.

"The miracle? The miracle is—"

"Tonight you will learn that there truly are monsters in the world of men."

"Riddles are a hard way to discover the truth, madam," Niles said as his anger was turning inward to the old Event Group failing—curiosity.

She smiled and then cocked her head as the offspring of the Golia started howling again in their small, screechy voices.

"Tonight you will see the transformation."

"Transformation?" Denise asked, not liking the sound of that at all, especially being an MD.

"Yes, my dear, there is only one thing that can tell us what we want to know and has the stealth to get that information."

"And that is?" Niles asked, almost afraid to hear the answer.

"The werewolf." The smile was large as she took in the astonished faces around her.

"A were—"

"Yes, a lycanthrope," she answered, cutting off Niles and his astonished reply, "and tonight the beast will run, and your Mr. Everett will run with it."

"You don't mean—?" Charlie started to ask, amazement lacing his words.

"The change will come upon your Man from the Sea and he will run with Stanus, becoming one with the beast, and the magic of the Golia will be shared."

"You can't mean that he will—" Alice said but stopped when the old woman laughed.

"Tonight, the most ancient of beings comes alive and the werewolf will walk the mountain once again."

THE EDGE OF THE WORLD HOTEL AND RESORT CASINO, PATINAS, ROMANIA

As they were escorted down the hallway Jack saw that the men watching them had no weapon of any kind, at least none that he could discern. With one man on the outside of Sarah, another on his left, and one behind and the follow-up element of Zallas and his new friend Ben-Nevin, he knew he could take the two men next to him and Sarah, but Ben-Nevin was no fool, he would have ample time to draw a weapon.

As they were led down the sixth-floor hallway, Sarah was relieved to see Pete Golding and Jason Ryan coming around the corner from the opposite direction. Sarah held up a hand to warn them that they weren't alone when she saw the four men behind them. They were in as much trouble as themselves and they were being led to the same suite of rooms.

"Good job, Ryan, I see you got Pete out of trouble," Jack said as they were made to stop before two double doors with the number 66-6.

"Yeah, these four armed men with very ugly automatic weapons dissuaded me from any inappropriate reactions where the rescue of the doc was concerned." With that one of the small Uzis appeared and jabbed Ryan in the back.

"I see your point," Jack said as Ryan was pushed forward.

"Jab me with that thing again and what I gave you last night inside the casino will seem like a kiss, dickhead," Ryan hissed at the thug from the night before. The man smiled and was about to raise the small Uzi and pop Ryan again.

"Stop that," Zallas said from behind them as he produced a keycard and then swiped it in the lock. Then as a second security procedure he entered a code on a keypad. "This is my private suite of rooms." He smiled as he threw the door open. "I think you will be most comfortable here until the Romanian authorities arrive to take you into custody."

"Into custody, you have got to be—"

Collins held out a hand and that stopped Sarah's outrage.

"Yes, what did you think, I'd be foolish enough to kill three American soldiers and one," he looked at Pete Golding, "whatever this is? Maybe you are with the NATO contingent, maybe you are not, but if you were it would be very stupid of me to kill four representatives of the organization that made the construction of all this possible. No, I don't pick fights with NATO. You'll be arrested for breaking and entering and then expelled from Romania. That may or may not sit well with your employers, whoever they are, but it should be enough to keep you quite busy explaining yourselves."

A knock sounded as Jack stared at Zallas. He knew that the man, while brutish and a gangster, was smart enough to realize his limitations as far as attracting attention to himself. For a man that dodged the old KGB and the newer version of that organization, the NKVD, to escape Russia and then organize here, well, he knew Zallas was a man that wasn't as dumb as many would believe.

One of the Romanian thugs opened the door and allowed the hotel's other owner into the suite.

"What is this?" Janos Vajic asked as he saw the Americans in the center of the suite.

"These people have been caught breaking and entering into my and the engineer's office. They will be arrested and then expelled from Romania after the weekend's festivities are complete."

"These guests do not seem the burglar type," Janos said as he worried that Zallas was going too far.

"Mr. Janos," Sarah said, "your partner has placed a death sentence on this resort. The whole thing can come crashing down at any time thanks to his bribery and faulty engineering."

Janos looked from Sarah to Zallas, who was shaking his head.

"What is she talking about?" he asked.

"What I'm talking about is the fact that the castle up there is secured to the mountain facing by giant anchor bolts that pass right through a major fault that was uncovered and is in the original geology report from your Ministry of the Interior."

"And that means?" Janos asked as his eyes stayed on Zallas.

"The construction of the castle has caused irreparable damage to the rock that makes up the face of the mountain. The face your new castle is anchored to."

"I'm not following," Vajic said as he finally looked away from Zallas.

"It means the situation is fast deteriorating and that castle could come tumbling down the mountain like Humpty Dumpty."

Janos turned and looked Zallas. A light came on behind his eyes and he felt as if his blood had frozen in his veins.

"The Interior Ministry? Our partner, Kenly Václav, that is why you brought him in on the deal because you had to bribe him to keep the geology report away from the state," he said as everything dawned brightly as if the sun sprang from the dark clouds. "Otherwise the deal with NATO never would have been approved and the valley never would have been opened up for lease."

Zallas smiled and then looked over at their newest partner, Ben-Nevin, who was watching the turmoil with mild interest.

"Jesus, it took you long enough to grasp the reality of your partnerships, Janos."

"Then it's true?"

"The original report was, yes, but the updated report from a better engineering firm covered that which we needed covered." Zallas took a few steps forward and then touched Sarah on the cheek, which brought Jack to full attention. "No, the castle will not fall. Even our engineers acknowledged that the pilings were driven through a fault, but they say the fault is strong and the anchors will secure the two halves and thus make the castle's foundations as safe as if they had been grown into the mountain."

"You idiot, that is what I'm saying, there is another element at work here, whether it's a natural degradation of the anchor steel inside the mountain or the rock around the pins are loosening.—whatever the reason the entire facing of that mountain is loosening."

"That is quite enough. The castle is on far safer earth than the ground down here. I have been assured of that," Zallas said as he placed his arm around Janos and walked him to the door. "Now, I will worry about the mountain and the castle, and you worry about the resort."

"Gina is missing and I don't know where she is," Janos blurted.

Zallas stopped as he opened the door. He placed his small girlish hand on Janos and then smiled.

"I am sure she is out and about, you'll no doubt find her soon."

With a worried look at the Americans, Janos Vajic left the suite. Zallas closed the door and then faced Jack, but it was Ryan who took a menacing step toward the Russian.

"If you hurt that girl, I'll—"

One of his Romanian brutes cuffed Ryan in the back of the neck and the naval aviator went down to his knees. Jack swung out and caught the man's hand in midair before he could bring down the weapon a second time onto Ryan's head. Collins twisted the small Uzi from the thug's hand and expertly ejected the ammunition clip, and then with one hand ejected the round that had been chambered and then tossed the weapon to Dmitri Zallas, who caught it with his eyes wide.

"Don't ever touch one of my people again," Jack said, not looking at the offender but instead straight at Zallas, who shook his head when the disarmed man turned to face Collins. The man backed away and then caught the Uzi as Zallas tossed it back to him.

"Next time, the colonel here has permission to rip out your throat." Zallas took a menacing step toward the five Romanians. "Without any recriminations from me."

"What did you do with Gina?" Ryan asked as he was helped to his feet by

Jack and Pete and was vigorously rubbing his neck where the Uzi had connected solidly.

"Her employment was terminated." Zallas smiled as he took in Collins. "After all, she is not NATO and will not be missed."

"If you hurt her, I'll—"

Zallas had already turned for the door as he waved his men out.

"Hurt? My young friend, she is very much dead. My mercy and understanding of the world clearly has its limits." He turned and looked at Colonel Ben-Nevin.

Ben-Nevin caught the drift of the threat and knew when the time came Dmitri Zallas would have to be dealt with. But until that time he had to satisfy the Russian.

"I need to know what information these Americans have on the temple complex," Zallas said. "If they know where it is, taking this Marko Korvesky would be a moot point, we wouldn't need him to learn the location of the temple." Zallas again looked at Ben-Nevin and shook his head.

"The people that live on that mountain are far more adaptive than you could know," Ben-Nevin said. "I imagine since they have been defending this mountain for three thousand years they can do it rather efficiently if the need arose. Are you following?"

"They are nothing but peasants."

"Yes, but then again it was nothing but peasants that fought off everyone from the Hittites, Visigoths, the Romans, and then finally Vlad the Impaler, not counting the entire Ottoman Empire, but yes, they are nothing but peasants," Jack said, trying his best to irritate the two men.

Zallas and Ben-Nevin turned and looked at a smiling Collins.

"As a matter of fact, I would think it would be wise to stock up on silver bullets if you're going up there." His smile grew as he studied the two.

"What in the hell are you talking about?" Zallas asked as he was confused by what Collins just said. He was hoping it wasn't a reference to the nonexistent wolves of the mountain again.

"Mr. Zallas said we will have enough men and firepower to get anything off that mountain if we so choose. I don't think old legends will frighten this man," Ben-Nevin said with hope.

Zallas looked from Ben-Nevin to Collins and then shook his head.

"I will take your suggestion and think about it," Zallas said, smiling wide at what he thought was an attempt by the American to get him to second-guess his action against the villagers. He opened the door to the suite.

"Wait!"

Zallas and his men, along with Ben-Nevin, turned and looked at Ryan, who was still in the process of rubbing the pain from where he had been struck on the neck.

"Out of professional courtesy, and for later reference, just who was it who killed Ms. Louvinski?" Ryan asked as he moved closer to the men and Jack allowed

Jason to play out whatever he had in mind. He normally wouldn't but he could see that the reported death of Gina Louvinski had affected the Navy man. And Zallas's business associate was also stricken by the news.

"If you must know, little man, it was me," said the big Romanian from the night before, the one who had manhandled Pete and the waitress. He stepped forward with a broad smile on his bearded face. Ryan allowed his eyes to flick toward Collins and he didn't read any dissent there.

"Good, I thought it would have been you," Ryan said as he moved so fast no one could stop him. The right hand went from the back of his neck and out to cross the bridge of the Romanian mobster's nose. The hit was so hard that the man froze in place and his features went slack almost immediately. The palm of Ryan's hand had hit the nose so hard that an explosive combination of bone and gristle was sent directly into the man's brain pan. The mobster's face turned white and then went slack. He went to both knees and then slowly fell forward onto his face—dead. Ryan rubbed his hand and waited for the bullet that would kill him. One of the Romanians saw his friend and raised an Uzi up but Zallas stayed the move.

Zallas looked down at his dead guest and again shook his head as he nodded to the gunman to collect his fallen leader.

"Now that was impressive," he said and looked back at Ryan. "I will allow you that one." He grinned. "But just that one." He turned and left after demonstrating how cheaply he valued human life.

Ben-Nevin also shook his head as he stepped over the dead body as his friends were trying to lift him. The door closed and then Ryan turned to face Jack. He was still rubbing his hand from the trick of death that Jack had taught him more than five years before.

"I never killed a man like that," Ryan said as his eyes never left the closed door.

"You don't get used to it," Jack said as he assisted Ryan over to the center of the large suite. "But if anyone here needed killing, it was him."

"She didn't deserve to be murdered," Jason said as he finally sat down at the large table as Collins went back to the door and tried the lock. It wouldn't move. Sarah for her part walked over and placed a hand on Jason's shoulder.

"Calm down, Mr. Ryan," Jack said. "It was me who got Ms. Louvinski in trouble, not you." He turned and faced Jason. "I think we may want to find a way out of here. Zallas said he won't kill us, he's lying. We're a backup plan if the questioning of Marko Korvesky doesn't go as planned."

"Plan for what?" Pete asked.

"I have a sneaking suspicion that they're going to try to take the temple built inside the mountain."

As Sarah turned and looked out the large plate glass window she saw the swirling colors of blue and purple as they played off the stone of Dracula's Castle.

"Alice's little adventure has suddenly taken a turn for the surreal," Sarah said as she watched the swirling spotlights that illuminated the castle.

They all heard Ryan chuckle. It was almost a sad sound, especially coming from a man who never had a bad word to say about anyone.

"When has one of our missions not turned out to be surreal?"

Jack chuckled as well, a sound that made them all nervous.

"But then again, that's what we do, people. Now let's start thinking about how to get the hell out of here and up to that mountain."

16

PATINAS

Carl sat with Will Mendenhall and Anya inside the relative calm of her grandmother's front yard. The small picket fence wasn't much of a defense against the onslaught of well-wishers and anyone else who just wanted to smile at Anya and say hello, but the villagers seemed to be respecting the separation of the small wooden pickets.

As the hour grew late the men and women of Patinas and the other six villages of the mountain started gathering their sleeping children, who were long since worn down from the excitement that so seldom came to Patinas. The children had gone to sleep knowing that things would be better now that brother and sister were together again.

Anya waved good night to several of the families and then smiled at Carl, who sat on the small one-step stoop of the cottage. A fire slowly burned behind them in the fireplace and warmed their backs. Mendenhall slowly stood and stretched and then nodded his head at Everett and then Anya.

"Well, we better get the shelter up or we'll be swimming in dew by morning. I guess we'll see if these Airborne boys know how to set up a camp."

"I'll be along as soon as the director and the others return," Carl said as he stood.

"If you place your camp closest to the barn you will find that the morning sun will wake you." Anya looked from Mendenhall to Everett and smiled. "One of the more pleasant experiences about living in Patinas."

"Will do, ma'am, and good night, Captain." Mendenhall gave Carl a two-fingered salute and slowly moved off while refusing more food from one of the older women who waited just outside the gate.

"You and he are close?" Anya asked as Carl watched Mendenhall smile, nod, and refuse yet more food from yet more women.

"Yes, the lieutenant and I are very close. That kid has worked his way out of some tough times to make something out of himself," Everett said as he slowly sat back down on the small stoop next to Anya. Carl stretched his legs and then looked up at the stars that seemed far closer than he had ever seen them. "Talk about a place getting a bum rap from Hollywood, this is it. I've never seen such a beautiful spot." He looked over at Anya, who watched Carl as he spoke.

"You are troubled about me," Anya said, looking away as Everett turned again to face her as he realized it was a statement and not a question.

"From Patinas to the Mossad, that's quite a stretch. And also quite industrious on your part, to spy on an organization that prides itself on never having an agent penetrate their organization."

Anya shook her head. "My grandmother set me on my odyssey. She has not, and never will, tell me everything. I made connections inside the Mossad that I should not have been able to make. I was noticed in training by all the right people, chosen for just the right assignments to move up in rank. No, very little about my Mossad history was brought on by me. My grandmother needs to tell me the truth of what she is doing."

"I don't mind saying you have totally lost me," Everett said, shaking his head and looking away.

Anya reached out and placed a hand on his shoulder and closed her eyes. Everett felt her touch and for the first time in a while felt as if a flock of birds was let loose inside his stomach.

"May I see your hand?"

"Are you going to tell my fortune?" he asked and then immediately regretted it.

"That is not a politically correct thing to say." She cocked her head to the right. "I believe you are laughing at us Gypsies, Captain," she said as she pulled her hand away from Everett's in a mockingly insulted way.

The blond American kept his hand in place. Anya again took his and turned the palm up.

"Besides, I don't tell fortunes, Mr. Everett, that's my grandmother." She smiled and then closed Carl's hand and wrapped her small fingers around his. "I will look into your past."

"My past?" Everett said as he was tempted to pull his hand away.

"Yes, all of us Gypsies are strange like that."

"You mean all you Jeddah?" Carl asked, watching her closely.

Instead of answering Anya closed her hand more tightly around Everett's. "I don't actually tell you anything about the past, you tell me and I don't hear, I see. The mind is powerful as I am sure you have learned in your many travels. But two minds linked is something that is powerful beyond description."

"I'm not a big believer in prophecy or the foretelling of bad things."

"You Americans are always so narcissistic. You only believe in yourselves and in nothing else. The world has many things to offer, and the ancient world has *even* more than the heavens could ever supply in words and stories. I want to show you what the world, my world can offer you."

Carl felt the heat of her touch and he closed his eyes as he kept her face etched in his mind. He felt Anya raise his closed fist to her lips and then he felt the warmth of her soft breath as she blew on his hand. He felt as if water was oozing though his clenched fingers and the sensation made him chill with excitement. He felt himself floating for a moment.

"Open your hand," Anya said as she released him.

Everett opened his eyes and looked at the raven-haired beauty as she smiled at him. She was backlit by the fire and Carl could swear she was aglow with a heat that only he could feel. He lowered his eyes and then slowly opened his fist. He felt his mouth open as he gazed upon the image that seemed to be written in bloodred ink. It was an exact likeness of the woman he had been secretly engaged to seven years before. He had lost her in a desert mission that seemed long ago, but the memory of her death was as if it occurred only weeks before. The smiling face of Lisa Willing stared back at him from his own palm. Everett raised his other hand and rubbed at the image.

"Minuscule blood vessels have burst just under the epidural layer. The blood vessels were guided by your own brain power and memory. As I said, there are powers that the world has never understood."

Again Everett rubbed at the image as if he could erase it.

Anya reached out and placed a hand on Everett's cheek and he looked at her and she saw the pain at his loss from so long ago. She smiled softly and then pulled his hand to her mouth and once more enclosed Carl's large hand and then kissed it. She shut her eyes and as she did Carl felt his heart flutter. He also shut his eyes as he felt his heart come into his throat. He felt Anya lower his hand and remove her own from his. He slowly opened his eyes and the image of Lisa was gone. The pain he had always felt and the sense of loss he had every day seemed to vanish from his mind and heart. He slowly stood from the stoop and walked into the small yard. He felt Anya watching him and so he turned to face her. She sat on the stoop and then raised her hands to her mouth as she seemed to come to a realization. She stood and waited.

Captain Carl Everett saw Anya Korvesky and nothing else.

Later that morning Carl stood with Anya just outside the gate to Patinas. He glanced up at the darkened mountain as he placed his arm around the woman he had been doing battle with not two days before in Rome. Everett didn't try to analyze what it was he was feeling so he just attempted to let his mind and his heart wander free of his common sense. He turned and looked at her and was about to speak when she held a hand up and cocked her head.

"Someone is out there," she said as she slid from Carl's arm and looked into the woods and then up the side of the craggy mountain. They heard the snap of a twig and they both turned to see one of the village elders that had accompanied Madam Korvesky and the others into the temple. He stepped up to Carl and Anya, looking from the woman to the large American.

"Your grandmother wishes to see you inside the temple. You are to bring this man with you," he said and then dipped his head and doffed the small black hat he wore and then moved off toward his home.

Anya watched him leave and then took Carl's hand. She smiled up at him and that look told Everett all he needed to know about how she felt. It was the same gut-wrenching feeling he was having.

As she pulled Everett toward the trail and the temple higher up, she turned and looked into the woods knowing that the person that had been watching them was still there. She turned away and held Carl's hand that much tighter.

Marko stepped out of the tree line and onto the trail as Anya vanished with the American naval officer around the bend in the trail. His eyes narrowed at the memory of his sister coming from his grandmother's home with this man close beside her. He didn't need his vivid imagination to know that his sister had been compromised by this man. Where that would lead him he knew not. But one thing he did know, he could never allow his little sister to control his people, which would only lead to more of the same for them.

For over three thousand years they had done the bidding of tribes they no longer knew nor loved. The days of slavery and bondage to Pharaoh had never really ended for the Jeddah; it had just changed from one cruel and uncaring hand to the next. The time for the Jeddah to break away clean had come and they would all reap the reward of thousands of years of bondage that was once called freedom, and what Marko and most Jeddah called the biggest lie. The treasure was there for them to use and the Jeddah would start to flood the world with their artifacts.

Carl could not believe what he was seeing as they descended the long and wide staircase that had been carved from solid rock 3,500 years before Everett was born. As he looked down he could see the worn areas that told a tale of millions of pairs of feet over the ages treading this way. As they entered the temple's main gallery, Everett had to stop and take in the carved magnificence of the Temple of Moses.

"I don't believe it, it's actually here," Carl said under his breath.

"Yes it is, but before you get to impressed just remember it took the Jeddah two thousand years to get this temple built, and all at, or just below your minimum wage," she teased as she stepped past Carl and into the temple.

"I take it you're not as impressed with your Jeddah's achievements as outsiders are," he said as he caught up with Anya. His eyes roamed to the three pyramids that made up the backdrop of the temple. The columns and the obelisks lined every nook and cranny of the magnificent structure.

"My people have been a slave to this menagerie for far too long, my brother is right about that. A palace built to honor the Exodus from Pharaoh, it is nothing but trouble and should have been buried long ago." She looked around at the illuminated temple and sighed. "I'm as tired as the people are of maintaining this museum of our history and I just can't do this anymore." She looked at Carl. "I'm with Marko on that one point."

"Why don't you come over here and explain to me what you can and cannot do, granddaughter."

Anya turned and saw her grandmother as she sat next to the dais where Mikla was still lying and breathing hard.

"I was explaining how a backward people need to embrace those that they fear the most."

"As we are the backward people you speak of, the people we fear must mean the rest of the world, is that what I understand, girl-child?"

Carl saw the uncomfortable way that Anya shifted from foot to foot as she faced the queen of the Gypsies. He looked over at Niles and Alice, who were watching the small power play without comment. Charlie and Denise were there also but they had their attention on something behind Carl and Anya.

"I didn't mean—"

"Yes, child, you did mean. Marko has done a horrible thing and now it must be corrected, so I guess you will get your wish sooner rather than later. This life we have on the mountain is coming to an end. Just what that particular end will be for our people remains to be seen." Madam Korvesky then nodded to a place behind the newly arrived pair.

Everett and Anya slowly turned. Sitting on his haunches and up about six wide steps from the temple floor was Stanus. The beast was growling and staring at Everett. The yellow eyes were intent and the captain could see the giant wolf curl a black lip over gleaming white teeth. Anya took Everett's arm and then took a step in front of him.

"Grandmamma, why is Stanus here?" she said as she placed her back against Carl's front and watched the dangerous beast before them.

"He awaits you and your Man from the Sea. I have a task for both."

Carl managed to turn his eyes away from the giant sitting menacingly before them. He then noticed Niles standing not far away with the others. He only shrugged, indicating he had no idea what the old woman had planned.

"They have work to do just as you and I have with Mikla this night. We must work soon as the sun is only three hours distant."

Anya swallowed and saw that Stanus was listening to every word that Madam Korvesky was saying. Its eyes would flick from the two in front of him to her grandmother, all the while the low growl emanating from his throat.

"The work with Mikla must be completed before the first birdsong of the new morning, or he will not survive." Madam Korvesky laughed and patted Mikla's sleeping form. "By the bones of Joseph, I may not survive it." She waved Carl over to her side. Stanus continued to stare from his sitting position on the staircase, its glowing eyes following Everett's every move. "Stanus isn't going to care for this all that much," she said as she took Everett's large hand into her own.

"Grandmother, what are planning?" Anya asked, worried.

"Your Man from the Sea will walk with the werewolf tonight, and now you must prepare him for the journey."

"You can't, Stanus would kill him." Anya turned and faced Carl. "He could never control him, the beast will out. You remember that saying, Grandmamma? The beast will out. The captain cannot control him."

"He needs not control, just influence. I need to know the disposition of this man's friends."

The old woman smiled and then squeezed Carl's hand tighter as she looked up and into his eyes.

"Move and prepare your Mr. Captain for his walk. Then we will send him and Stanus on their way and we can get down to the business of spelling Mikla."

Anya Korvesky closed her eyes and then blindly held out a hand toward Carl, who broke his hold with Madam Korvesky and went to her. She linked her fingers through his.

"I am sorry, I didn't mean for this to happen to you."

"If it's to help my friends down below at the resort, I don't have a choice but to listen to your grandmother. Whatever it is she wants me to."

"Didn't you hear a word she said, you are to walk with Stanus tonight."

Everett looked over at the spot where Stanus was sitting. The giant wolf never allowed its eyes to leave the form of the big American. It just sat and stared.

"Well, if I'm walking him, I hope you have one hell of a big damn leash."

"She means something else, Carl," Alice said as she pushed Charlie Ellenshaw toward the couple in order for him to assist Anya and Everett. Carl looked from Alice to Anya, who looked away and then pulled him toward a small stone enclosure that had no windows or openings save one. Charlie, with an uneasy yet excited look back at Niles, soon joined them.

As for Niles Compton, he and Alice turned away and watched as Madam Korvesky became still and silent. He watched her hand run through Mikla's fur and the giant wolf whined in its uncomfortable sleep. Alice nudged Niles in the side and they both saw the Gypsy's eyes rolling underneath the lids.

"It's as if she's in a deep sleep and rapid eye movement has started."

"Look," Niles said, pointing to Mikla. The wolf was still asleep, but its eyes were working rapidly underneath the lids. Mikla was also starting to dream.

Across the way Carl allowed Anya to pull him inside the small rock-hewn house.

"What does that mean?" Everett asked as Charlie Ellenshaw winced at the answer he knew was coming.

"She means you are to become one with Stanus. My grandmother obviously has a concern for your friends down below. I believe she thinks if anything happens to them even more attention will be cast toward the Jeddah. She can be very selfish."

"And to become one with Stanus means?"

"Tonight you are going to learn what it's like to be in an old horror movie."

"And just what in the hell does that mean?" Everett asked as she took his hand and pulled him inside the torch lit room.

"Tonight you will become a werewolf."

Inside the small stone-carved room Ellenshaw watched as Carl lay down upon an old Russian-made army cot. Charlie's eyes roamed the room and that was when he saw the deeply gouged claw marks that were sunk deep into the stone walls. Large swipes had been battered through pure stone from something that looked as if it hadn't liked being in here.

Carl lay staring up at the ceiling as the five torches inside the enclosed structure issued forth a smoky, dark visual of what Anya was doing. She stood next to a small table and was in the process of mixing a few herbs into a small clay bowl. She used a stone that was worn over the years until it fit perfectly into her small hand, or the hand of the necromancer, whoever was using it at the time. Anya was silent as she mixed her strange concoction.

"The spell will cause small stomach cramps at first and then they will settle as the poison is introduced to your system."

"Poison?" Charlie asked.

"Yes, there is a small amount of mandrake and nightshade in the mix," Anya said as she placed the bowl down and looked at nothing, keeping her back toward Carl and Charlie. "I would like to say that the experience is without pain, but that would be a lie. The first five minutes are excruciating as the minds join. Stanus will not like you in his head and you will most definitely not like Stanus in yours."

"Sounds like some of the drugs working their way through Berkeley in 1969," Charlie said, "and a lot of those people never came back." They all looked at Ellenshaw and wondered if he had been one of those that were lost in 1969. "How does the joining, or this spell, work?" Charlie asked, as he knew Carl was thinking about the pain.

"The mixture," she said as she turned with the small clay bowl placed firmly into her hands, "will open the captain's mind. Free it if you will. He will feel like he has taken a mild hallucinogen at first, then he will sleep."

"But how do the minds connect?" Charlie asked, ever the curious scientist. As for Everett he wasn't sure he wanted to learn that little bit of information.

Anya gave Charlie a sad, knowing smile. "It's in the hands of the Golia—quite literally. Stanus will join with the captain through touch, the special gift of the werewolf—the joining of two minds that are connected through a million years of evolutionary survival together. The symbiosis allows Carl to hitchhike on the mind of Stanus. He will feel the power of the wolf and also see what it sees. He will be the wolf and know the power of what it is to be feared."

Anya placed her hands behind Carl's head and raised it. She placed the small earthen bowl to his lips and tilted it until the dark, viscous liquid flowed into Everett's mouth making him gag. He coughed and tried to swallow the horrible mixture. Finally he got it down and then he placed his head back on the old, rickety cot.

"Stanus will become Carl's eyes and ears as he remains here with us. The captain will be able to assert some direction to Stanus, but never, ever depend on his following your every request. And he will not follow orders. As you can see by my grandmother's ankle there are inherent dangers to the spell. You will receive the same wounds, the same pleasures, and the same pain the Golia will feel. And I must warn you, Carl, you will find the mind of the Golia vast and disturbing. The species has been mistreated since the dawn of time. Men have hunted them, driven them from the beautiful parts of the world until they have been pushed to the very edge of the map by mankind."

Suddenly the doorway was filled. The light from the outside torches had been blocked off. Charlie and Carl turned their heads to see Stanus standing in the small doorway. It was so tall that it had to lean forward to see into the room. The beast growled and that sent cold chills down Charlie Ellenshaw's back and arms. He took an involuntary step back.

"Don't move, Professor, please," Anya said as she placed the empty mixing bowl on the small wooden table. She turned and faced Stanus, who was breathing hard and looking at Everett.

"Do the Golia like being joined with men?" Charlie asked.

"They love it. Well . . . sometimes they love it, sometimes not." Anya finally approached Stanus and then slowly raised a hand to its massively large head and rubbed. The beast leaned closer so Anya could scratch deeper. Then the wolf slowly slid down onto all fours as it entered the room, forcing Anya to step inside. "Stanus is allowing this only because he is curious about not only the captain and his intentions toward me and Grandmamma, but because it wants to know if you are here for the purposes of deceit. That would not be good. Your mind has to be open, Carl. Do not try to hide anything. Stanus will tear down any barrier you have to get at the information he wants. That was where I believe Marko made his mistake in his attempted fooling of Stanus and his lies about the encroachment of the Russian investor; the wolf knew it was being lied to."

Charlie squeezed up against the rough wall as Stanus went to all four legs and then came into the room and filled it with its bulk. While on all fours it was still face-to-face with Ellenshaw as the beast sniffed and then huffed. Then Stanus moved on to Anya and sat before her. Anya without any extra movement placed the remaining potion from the bowl in front of the wolf. The beast lapped up the foul-tasting liquid.

Anya was breathing hard and wondering how Stanus would accept the stranger into its mind. The beast walked around the table on four legs as it continued to examine Carl. For Everett's part he lay as still as he could as the fuzzy effects of the homemade hallucinogen took hold of his mind as the wolf stopped and then licked the remainder of the liquid from its muzzle using its wide tongue. Suddenly Stanus raised a right paw to the cot and used its anchored weight to lift itself from the floor until it was standing on two powerful legs as it looked down upon Carl. The ears lay down and then sprang back up as the beast was starting to get glimpses of the man's mind.

Anya motioned for Charlie Ellenshaw to slowly back away from the scene played out before them. As he watched and slid down the wall at the same moment, Charlie saw the large hand with extended, claw-tipped fingers as it settled onto the head of the large Navy SEAL. The beast closed its eyes as he felt the pulse of Carl's beating heart for the first time. Its breathing became steady and the grip on the captain's head intensified, eliciting a small gasp from Everett, who now looked to be in a deep dream state.

Everett felt the beast inside him. He felt himself inside the beast. Carl was confused as he felt his eyes roam over his own prone body. He could actually feel the touch of his two-day-old beard as the hand of Stanus felt the minute pores and flaws of Carl's skin. On several instances the hand would pause over a few of the deeper scars from his time as a SEAL. The beast would whine as the fingers felt the pain from Carl's past. Then Stanus hit upon Everett's sadness in regard to the loss of Lisa Willing, then the beast moved past that and into Carl's present. It was if the animal were getting a feel for who and what Everett was. The hand would settle on a new spot on Carl's skull, linger for a moment, and then move off to another spot. Finally the beast opened its eyes and then without warning it leaped over the cot and stood before Ellenshaw. Charlie felt his bladder partially let go. After all of the amazing things he had seen in his many years as a cryptozoologist he had never beheld a more frightening, purely beautiful sight as he was witnessing at that moment. The beast sniffed.

"Don't be frightened," Anya said. "I think that is the captain. Stanus is there but he is allowing Carl to take over for the moment. I think he wants you to know that he's all right and inside Stanus."

"You have got to be kidding me," Charlie said as he half turned away from Stanus as the muzzle of the animal came within inches of Ellenshaw's face. The hot breath of the beast was washing over him as a waterfall would.

"Chaaaaarlllllieeeee," the sound came out more as a jumbled cacophony of baritone mumbling, but the name was clearly understood.

"Now that is something, never has a Golia spoken before with a man they didn't know. Stanus must feel comfortable with your Mr. Everett," Anya said as she slowly and cautiously approached Stanus from behind. "Carl is exhibiting amazing strength in controlling him."

Charlie's eyes widened as the beast raised a large hand and with just the long claws turned Ellenshaw's head toward its yellow eyes. Then the beast took Charlie by the collar and lifted him off the stone floor. Ellenshaw felt his feet dangling as the animal secured its viselike grip on Charlie's throat.

"Oh, oh, that's not the captain." Anya moved quickly and placed both hands on the back of the giant wolf. She could feel the muscles underneath the black fur working as the beast was slowly getting its blood up. "Captain, if you can hear me reassert your influence and tell Stanus that Professor Ellenshaw is a friend, it hasn't connected that part of your memory yet. He wrested control away from you when his part of the mind didn't recognize your friend. Introduce them to each other."

Suddenly the beast relaxed its grip, but the hand was still there around Charlie's throat. The strange thing was Charlie wasn't trying to breathe at all. Stanus sniffed Charlie once more. Then an amazing thing happened and Ellenshaw was lowered to the ground as Stanus lowered its large frame so it could look into Charlie's eyes and then without warning he went to all fours and sprang not through the open doorway, but through one of the larger window openings and was gone. Charlie heard Dr. Denise Gilliam scream as Stanus leaped from the window.

Carl found out that he was just a passenger on the ride of his life. He could actually feel the earth beneath his paws as he ran. Stanus he found out had a favorite pastime and that was running. The Golia felt free when its legs were stretched to their limit. Stanus, Carl knew, hated the life he led with having to stay on the mountain and never venturing forth. But Everett also felt that the beast was content as long as its clan was safe. That was the foremost vibe Carl was picking up from Stanus.

Everett felt the beast stop and then rise to his hind legs as it gripped a large pine tree and examined the world around it. Carl could actually smell the odors of the woods and mountain. He could smell birds high up in their nesting places. He could see better in the dark than he could ever see in the daylight with his own eyes. Everything stood out in grays and green contrast and he could see anything that moved or broke its cover. And it seemed every animal that was lying in its burrow or nest knew that the werewolf was roaming the mountain this night. Everett had never felt the power he was feeling at that moment. And the amazing thing he felt was the fact that he knew Stanus was enjoying showing off.

Carl felt the attention of Stanus drawn to something below. As Everett focused his mind along with the mind of the wolf, he could see the swirling purples and blues of Castle Dracula.

Carl felt free and for the first time he felt Stanus grip the tree he was leaning against for support and then the howl let loose and it actually exhilarated Everett. It was like he was proclaiming to the world that something special was coming their way—one of God's greatest creations was on the move.

Stanus lowered himself to all fours and with his fingers curled inward made his hands into the running pads of the animal. Stanus shot off down the mountain at a full run at breakneck speed. Carl felt as though Stanus was about to make an example of just how powerful the werewolf really was.

Its direction—Castle Dracula.

Will Mendenhall woke and was very confused regarding where he was. He had been far more exhausted than he had realized and went right to sleep after he had laid his head on the air mattress and sleeping bag supplied by the Airborne boys. He had been told they would only run a 10 percent watch of their small three-tent camp.

As he struggled in his sleep his eyes came wide and he realized finally where he was at and what had awakened him. It was no animal noise or strange bumps in the night for Mendenhall, it was his bladder. If he didn't get up at that exact moment there would be incident he would never live down—especially from Ryan.

Will thanked the heavens he had been too tired to even unlace his boots before he had zonked out. He stood and bounced off the air mattress and crawled and ran quickly through the tent flap barely missing the two men who were just changing watch.

"Hey, Lieutenant, it looks like the party settled down about an hour ago and we were—"

Will ran right past the two men, who watched him vanish into the small stand of trees beside the old barn and just below the craggy face of the mountain.

"Can't talk now, emergency," he said as he sped past.

Mendenhall finally made it into the trees and had his jeans already unzipped. He started to relieve himself against the lower, very rough face of the mountain. He closed his eyes and whistled.

"Lord Almighty!" he hissed, "that was close to—"

Will froze when he looked up after the initial relief of making it to the trees and saw the two yellow almond-shaped eyes as they gazed down at him. The beast was upside down and because of the darkness of the morning hours Will could not see anything else because of the black fur. He was looking at a perfectly camouflaged Golia. And he realized as his relief dried up on him that it was Stanus who had all four sets of claws buried into the rough rock wall of the mountain. Will realized he was seeing what the beast did best of all—it was a climber just as Alice had said these animals had developed into. Stanus was hanging upside down and Will saw the Golia slowly open its mouth and start to lean forward while the teeth grew ever closer.

Will thought he could at least swallow when the first attempt at screaming went afoul, but he couldn't muster enough saliva for that. He felt the dryness of his throat as the beast was now only inches from Will's upturned face. Suddenly Stanus released the hand closest to Will's head and then the giant wolf slapped him playfully against the right side of his head, knocking him to the ground. When Mendenhall rolled over he saw that Stanus was gone. Will just lay there staring up at the now empty facing of the mountain as a breeze sprang up and moved the trees.

Inside the temple in a room that sat only twenty-five feet from the greatest rumored treasure in biblical history, Captain Carl Everett stunned Anya and Charlie by snickering in his sleep at something that happened with Stanus. His eyes were moving rapidly and they knew Carl had just enjoyed something in his very unusual ride.

CASTLE DRACULA

Drake Andrews stood on the front section of the enormous stage and winced at the loudness of the sound system. He glanced at his agent and gave him a dirty look. The Russian musical troupe had all lined the front and back part of the stage just to witness Drake sing a few bars from an old standard of his for a sound check. Even with the deep booming sound system an engineer had managed a bad connection someplace and a piercing screech sounded through the nearly empty nightclub. Drake placed two hands to his ears and the Russians did the complete opposite, they actually clapped and cheered at just the opening refrain of a hit he had back in 1967.

Right at that moment several of the Dracula props they had arranged mechanically around the gothic-laced dressing of the stage popped free of their ancient-looking coffins and one even fell all the way forward and crashed into the front row of the arranged tables. The mechanical dummy hit the table, rolled off, and then something inside fizzled and smoke rose into the air. Again Drake looked at his agent and without a word, and as the Russian musicians were still applauding at three-thirty in the morning, Drake Andrews stormed off the stage and headed for the large stone balcony that looked up and onto the mountain. His agent followed as one more mechanical Dracula dummy half opened its casket door and an arm broke off and fell free much to the delight of the long-haired Russians.

The American entertainer looked out across the expansive outdoor patio and knew that this gig would be a disaster and once word of this got out he would be lucky to get Knott's Berry Farm.

His eyes roamed to the mountain rising above the club. *Well, at least if he was going out he would go out in relative obscurity*, he thought. His anger spent at the screwups, he turned and bumped his face directly into a wall that hadn't been there just a second before when he walked out onto the patio.

"What the—" His voice caught in his throat as he saw nothing but pure black, and his nose, although pressed against something warm, could smell a heavy animalistic musk. His eyes traveled upward and then widened as they saw the yellow glowing orbs with the ring of black around the pupils. Drake took a step back and his eyes grew even wider.

Stanus stood before the failed crooner and watched as if he was nothing more than a mild curiosity. The large head tilted first right, and then left as its ears stayed upright and long. The wolf stood over six and half feet and Drake had to strain his neck to get in the full extent of the creature before him.

"Whoa, now that's better!" Drake exclaimed as he reached out and touched the thick black fur of Stanus, who took a precautionary step backward. "You really need to be in there instead of those mechanical monstrosities they have malfunctioning everywhere. This is impressive."

Slowly the long silver-tipped ears of Stanus lowered until they were aligned with its skull and its muscles started to bunch up underneath the thick fur and skin. Then the beast just as quickly closed its eyes and the ears came back up. It was as if the animal were in conflict whether this man was a threat or a joke.

"Well, maybe a little tightening up of the suit here," Andrews said as he pulled out an inch of skin and fur from the giant animal only a foot away. Stanus growled. "Yeah, other than that, the only thing I can see is to maybe tone down the headlights some." Drake Andrews patted Stanus on the belly and then stepped around the agitated beast and yelled into the club, "Now this is a prop, and you guys have him stuck out here to scare the tourists, he should be in there!" He smiled as he turned back to his visitor. "Yeah, a little work and you can become pretty convincing . . ." The last words trailed off as Andrews realized that the actor in the smelly werewolf suit was gone.

The Las Vegas veteran ran to the parapet that surrounded the patio and looked out over the steep crevasse that the castle was built over—nothing. The man had just vanished.

"Figures, one class prop in this whole menagerie and he quits—just great."

Stanus sprinted downhill after the brief confrontation with the human at the castle. The wolf had the initial impulse to do what it had done on his previous visits to Dracula's Castle, and that was to rip the man's throat free of his neck. It was the presence of the traveler that had stopped him from his bloody impulse. The large American inside its head, while it could not stop Stanus from doing what he wanted, could influence and sway him down another path. The Golia had always accepted the spell and the traveler that came with it because the beast had always yearned for more information from the Jeddah.

It had been Carl to ease the animalistic instincts of Stanus when the human had grabbed its fur, which did not hurt him in the least, it was the fact that the beast hated being touched by anything outside the Golia clan. Everett was reading this. In his sleep he felt the path that wound beneath his feet. He had felt the smoothness of the stone patio and even had the sensation of smell. There was one thing though, and Carl knew it could be a serious problem. He was feeling everything, even down to the smashing of pinecones underneath the Golia's paws as it ran. The sharp pain Stanus didn't seem to notice, but Carl did. To him that meant if he could feel the smallest thing, he could also feel when the animal was truly hurt or injured. He now knew why Madam Korvesky had a bruised and swollen ankle. It was broken when she had traveled with Mikla. He realized then that this little excursion to the resort could get a little dicey and he surely hoped he could control Stanus enough to avoid getting shot.

Everett had been amazed at how agile and precise Stanus was when he traveled. The beast was as expert at climbing as any ape species. The animal was blindingly fast and had such an efficiency of movement that his gait was like riding in a car with great suspension. The appeal to do this on a regular basis was at the forefront of the captain's mind.

As Stanus bounded onto a tree the beast stopped and rested as it took in the large and imposing shape of the giant L-shaped hotel and casino. The beast sniffed and Carl then felt the strangest sensation. It was like the animal was reaching into his memories of something and then sniffing for those memories. The Golia grabbed the large tree and the claws went deeply into the wood producing a dark musky odor of pine sap. The deep breaths Stanus was taking brought in so much air that Carl thought the giant wolf would burst, and then when he thought it would, Stanus slowly allowed the air to escape its lungs. Everett was shocked when the eyes shot to the highest section of the hotel and the Golia didn't move as its glare examined each and every window of the sixth floor.

Before Carl could even realize what was happening, Stanus broke from the tree line and made straight for the resort and the enemies of the Golia.

PATINAS

Madam Korvesky watched Alice for the longest time and she realized the concern the American woman had for the man that was traveling with Stanus. Soon her eyes moved over to Denise, Charlie, and Niles as they were busy examining one of the small pyramids that had been carved out of the stone. The temple had been everything Alice had ever dreamed it would be.

"This was not the time for you to come here, as bad things are about to happen, to this mountain, and possibly to my people."

"What has changed for the Jeddah after all of these thousands of years, the encroaching world?"

Madam Korvesky laughed and squeezed her hands. "Not the world, it's never been about the world, nor has it been about the treasure of the Exodus. Not about faith, not about God, not about Israel. No," she looked up at the gallery high above them and the offspring as they played and fought amongst themselves, "it's been about them. The protection of the Golia is our only concern, and I have used many despicable tricks in my time to do just that. We have great respect for what the Golia protects make no mistake about that, Mrs. Hamilton. But we will not sacrifice the Golia over what we have kept secret here—never."

Alice felt the power and conviction of the old woman's words and realized that indeed the Jeddah had come to a crossroads thanks to Marko drawing attention to the pass and what lies beneath.

"You expected temples of gold and columns made of granite and a gold treasure more vast than a thousand King Tut tombs, am I correct?"

"I rarely thought about the great treasure of the Exodus. And the only time I ever thought about that was when in search of you and them." She indicated the gallery.

Madam Korvesky nodded her head and then released Alice's hand. "The mountain belongs to the Golia now and I must see to it they are never, ever disturbed."

"How do you plan to do that? Do you realize the political forces arrayed against the Jeddah and Golia? Do you know the power used to bring that resort into being? You are not used to modern politics. You now have NATO concerned about the pass. The Golia will have to find a new home eventually."

A serious and deadly look came over the old woman's features. "Not if the pass is no longer there to have to defend."

Alice was about to ask for a clarification when Niles Compton and Denise Gilliam approached. Niles had worry written on his face as he pursed his lips.

"Dr. Gilliam is concerned about the symbiosis that Captain Everett is going through," he said as he knelt down and examined Madam Korvesky's ankle. He shook his head and made room for Denise to take a look. Niles stood and faced the Gypsy queen. "The exact same location and injury our very impressive friend Mikla has. You and he were injured in the same incident, weren't you?" Niles asked as he kept his eyes on the Gypsy.

"Well, I don't know how you're coping with it," Denise said, "but that ankle is broken in not just one, but three different places. How you can withstand the pain you must be experiencing is beyond me." The doctor waited but there was no explanation forthcoming.

Alice Hamilton knew the answer but waited for Madam Korvesky to answer Dr. Gilliam's inquiry.

"I put up with it because if I didn't the infection inside Mikla's ankle would have taken him to the precipice; I am currently taking the brunt of the infection into myself."

Denise Gilliam shook her head and crossed her arms over her chest and paced a few steps away, not accepting such magic.

"We will discuss this at another time. Right now we have to see if we can save Mikla. Dr. Gilliam, will you assist me?" Madam Korvesky waited while the color slowly drained from Denise's face. "The three of you also," she said looking from Alice to Niles and Charlie Ellenshaw.

"All of us?" Alice asked, excitement lacing her words.

"Mikla is quite ill and will die within the hour if we don't get in there and fix things." She reached out and took Denise by the hand and pulled her closer to the dais. "This will be harder on you than anyone. Well," she said with a sad shake of her head, "almost anybody. To be honest," she said as she allowed the doctor's hand to slide through her own, "I am very happy an American doctor is among us. Sometimes I think those old ladies in the village don't care for me all that much, and I would rather have a steady hand helping me do what it is I have to do."

Niles and Alice exchanged looks of discomfort and Denise Gilliam was flat-out white-faced as she realized what the plan was.

"And what is it you have to do to make Mikla better?" Alice asked.

Madam Korvesky gave Alice a sad smile in return and then stroked the black fur of the giant Golia once more.

"We will have to remove the offending break from Mikla's leg. Dr. Gilliam will have to amputate."

All eyes went to the wolf lying on the dais. Mikla was breathing harshly and his tongue was lying outside his mouth.

"Will he survive the procedure?" Charlie asked, genuinely concerned for Mikla.

"Mikla will survive," she said as she looked down upon Mikla with tears in her old eyes. "But without a hind foot his life will be far shorter than the rest of the Golia. He will not be shunned by the other Golia, but Mikla would eventually wander away from the temple and die among the mountain. A Golia cannot survive without the ability to climb and run."

Every face was saddened.

"Now I must prepare the spell and the potion, we have little time."

"I had better get Mikla's ankle cleaned up as much as possible so I can at least see what I'm doing," Denise said as she nervously wrung her hands while looking at the great wolf before her.

"Mikla is fine, leave him be," Madam Korvesky said as she started to stand with the aid of the cane. Niles and Charlie ran to her side and assisted her to her one good leg. She smiled and nodded her thanks at the two men. "It's me you have to prepare for."

"I don't understand," Denise said.

Niles and Alice figured it out first.

"Mikla would never be able to survive the surgery," Madam Korvesky said as he looked at Denise. "There is too much damage and we were a little late getting to him. My injury is purely, although realistically, in my mind. I have no *real* physical damage to my ankle. Oh, it looks that way but my mind only made it seem so."

"Don't be ridiculous. I felt the breaks in that leg."

Madam Korvesky only smiled.

"Denise, she is saying that her wound is not actually infected and the break is only an illusion—a powerful one, but one that the brain can produce all on its own. Since Mikla's damage is severe she is saying we will bypass repairing the damage done to Mikla and go to the safer route—thus maintaining the life expectancy of the wolf."

"You have totally lost me," Denise said. Even though she knew what Niles was talking about she wanted someone to come out and say it directly.

"Mikla's is not the foot and ankle you're amputating, Doctor," Alice said as she took Madam Korvesky's hand and along with Niles and Charlie moved off to the small hut where Carl was sleeping and being watched by Anya.

"It is mine you're cutting off, Dr. Gilliam, not Mikla's."

THE EDGE OF THE WORLD HOTEL AND RESORT CASINO, PATINAS, ROMANIA

Ryan ran his eyes over the double-paned glass and shook his head. He turned and faced Collins and Pete. Sarah was busy running her experiments on one of the expansive suite tables. Thus far they had only been checked on four times in the past three hours by Zallas and his men. Ryan walked up to Jack.

"Sealed. Hell, we would make so much noise they'd think the second invasion of Normandy was taking place in here if we tried to break through it."

"The sun is starting to come up, maybe we should wait and try to find an opportunity when they feed us," Sarah said as she jotted down some notes on the hotel's stationery concerning the strange and growing vibrations coming from the ground and the mountain beyond. She shook her head and bit on her lower lip.

"Well, what good news have you got to share with us?" Jack asked as he finally turned away from trying to find some way out of the massive, well-appointed presidential suite where they were being held prisoner.

"We have an increase in vibratory influences raising at increments that leave little doubt that the earth movement is not only continuing but increasing." She once more bit on her lower lip, a habit that Jack usually loved because it meant Sarah was in deep concentration and once that happened it was hard to get her to answer questions.

"And that means?" Collins asked, leaning over until his face was in line with her vision.

"Jack, all I can say is that something bad is going to happen. I suspect its origins are up there," she pointed out of the giant ten-foot plate glass window that looked out onto the castle and the mountain high above the hotel, "or right here under our feet."

"How long?" Pete asked, wishing he had access to Europa. She would make the guesstimates they were producing at the moment irrelevant and would provide the exact time and place of any seismic event. But Sarah knew her business and if she said there was going to be a problem, Pete believed there was going to be a problem.

"Who knows, I don't know what the parameters here are without an extensive look at that geological report and the hydro-strata findings." She looked at the others in the room one face at a time. "Look, guys, this place could fall into the bowels of the earth at any time. I mean anytime."

"Jesus, suddenly this fun little excursion into Romania looking for fairy tales and antiquities thieves has become a little more serious than we realized." Jack turned and looked out at the darkness of the predawn and shook his head. He and Ryan could just open the door to the suite and eliminate anyone who was in the hallway, but what good would that do? They had to wait and allow Alice and Niles to get what they needed at the mountain and then return and get them out of here, because right now they had absolutely zero options. Jack turned and looked at the others. "Recommendations?"

"We don't have a choice but to allow Zallas to make the next move," Ryan volunteered. "He and that asshole Colonel Ben-Nevin will eventually make a play for the temple, that much we know. But when will they make the attempt and then how do we warn the people up in the pass so they can defend against them?"

Jack knew Ryan voiced correctly the two serious questions facing them. He turned and paced away toward the large living room of the suite and then sat on the edge of the sofa and lowered his head in thought.

"Colonel?" came the voice of Pete Golding.

Jack didn't respond at first. He kept his head lowered and was thinking of the most surefire way to get Niles and Alice, or at the very least Mr. Everett, word that the village and the pass at Patinas would be under serious threat in the next twenty-four hours.

"Colonel Collins?"

"Oh, shit!" came the startled voice of Ryan.

"Jack, I think the fairy-tale aspect of the mission you just mentioned just reared its ugly head," Sarah said as the room became deathly still and quiet.

Colonel Jack Collins, United States Army and Congressional Medal of Honor recipient, slowly stood, turned, and faced in the direction of Sarah, Pete, and Ryan as they stared at the large plate glass window. Suddenly all of the old wives' tales and stories invented to scare the little children of the world was at the window and looking at them. For the first time in the storied career of Jack Collins he allowed his mouth to go slack and he felt his stomach do a back flip as his eyes met those of a true and very much real Golia.

"My God," Sarah said as she wanted to move but felt her feet glued to the floor. It was if the giant beast was holding them in place with just a look.

The wolf was looking in through the left side of the large window and that told Jack and Ryan that the beast was hanging off the stone wall of the hotel with no handgrips other than the claws on its hands and feet. *True mountain climbers*, he thought. The animal watched them with its yellow, piercing eyes. The ears flicked once, twice, three times as it looked from face to face. The mouth came partially open and that was when Pete, who was standing closest to the window, saw the gleaming white teeth and impressive strength of the Golia's jaw. He took an involuntary step away from the glass.

The beast growled and the four heard the deep and booming baritone as the glass shook. The animal looked again from face to face and then finally settled on Jack, who, unlike Pete, took a few tentative steps toward the window. This made the beast react even more as it released one of its handholds and then held the open palm toward the glass.

"I may be crazy, but I don't think it wants you to get any closer," Sarah said as she went back a full step.

Collins couldn't help but smile as he examined the large digits of the animal. The claws were as long and as strong as any natural defense he had seen in nature. The fingers and thumb were articulate, and the hand, although humanlike, still held the wolf quality that had been shown in movies for more than a half century. He smiled even wider as he realized that everything that Alice had said about this beast was true. It was spectacular.

As they watched, Stanus reached out and placed his hand on the cold glass. With the double panes they saw the outer one bend in and at that time, and they would all report it later, the animal seemed to smile. The hand came away and then they all were shocked beyond words when the Golia, with the use of only one securing hand, swung away from the hotel and dangled in front of the large window. Jack and Ryan saw the bunched muscles and knew without further examination that this animal had to be one of the strongest land creatures in the world. Collins estimated the Golia to be no less than eight hundred pounds.

Suddenly the Golia spread the fingers of its right hand wide and held it to the glass and then that strange turn-up at the corners of the wolf's mouth occurred again just as if the joke was on the people standing stunned inside the hotel suite. As they watched in shock the animal raised its hand and brought it up to its thick, curled brow and then the hand went up, paused as if it were shading its eyes, and then smiled even wider making Jack freeze. Then they all witnessed as the yellow glowing eyes dimmed for the briefest of moments, so minuscule was the change that they would all wonder later if it had happened at all. The yellow actually changed to blue, and then almost as quickly back to the yellow color of the blazing sun. The hand came to the window one last time and then one claw appeared and was placed against the outer pane of the weatherproof glass. The single claw and its sharpened tip scratched the window and before their astonished faces the number 6 appeared. Then the beast fell away.

The room was absolutely still and silent. Every face was turned to the window and the number 6 that had been scratched there. The personnel of the most secretive agency in the American government and members of teams that had countless excursions into the world's most bizarre situations and members of a Group that found amazing elements about the real world and people that were hard to scare, continued to stand in shock. Pete leaned against the wall and then allowed his knees to buckle as he slid down into a sitting position.

"As much as I love Alice Hamilton, and as brilliant as I know she is, I really thought she was nuts on this one," Pete said as his eyes went back to the now empty space at the window. "But that, boys and girls, was no wolf species that was ever found in the fossil record."

"Why should it be," Sarah said as she finally forced herself to turn away from the window. "It's a Golia, just as Alice has said all along."

Ryan slowly turned and was about to say something and then stopped. He instead went over to the large bar and poured himself a small shot of whiskey and then downed it. He was used to all sorts of danger, as most ex-fighter jocks were. But to face something like that with only a few millimeters of glass between you and a myth that could not possibly exist really placed a crimp in Ryan's self-image of being unafraid of most things.

"What is it, Mr. Ryan?" Jack asked, knowing exactly what the naval aviator had seen. He had seen the same thing and was wondering if he was slowly losing his ability to interpret what he was seeing correctly.

Ryan slid the small shot glass so hard down the bar that it hit a bottle and nearly shattered it, bouncing off the bottle and onto the floor.

"You'll think I'm nuts," he said as he tried his best to avoid the eyes of Sarah and Jack. Pete was still ensconced in staring at the large window.

"Well, then we're all heading for the insane asylum because I think I saw what you did," Sarah said. "Jack?"

Collins smiled and then joined Ryan at the bar and figured he could allow himself one on-duty drink—after all, how many times do you actually see a werewolf at your window and know for a fact that it was real? He poured himself a shot and then quickly drank it. He set the glass down and smiled.

"You mean when the Big Bad Wolf changed its eye color to one that matched Captain Everett's perfectly, or was it the fact that the damn thing saluted me?"

Pete Golding looked over at Jack, who poured himself a second shot and sipped at first, and then finished the whiskey.

"You mean the captain is—"

"Yes, I think that was Carl and he's . . ." Collins laughed and then poured a third shot, thought a moment and then pushed it away shaking his head in wonder. Pete lowered his head and said the words that Collins couldn't.

"He's a werewolf?"

"Oh, man, this is way too much, way too fast. You mean this thing Alice has been talking about is actually real. I mean, a Lost Tribe of Israel, all right, yeah, sure, I can buy that, after everything we've seen the past few years, no problem. But the captain a werewolf? Okay, I have to really consider quitting this job."

The mission was taking a turn they never really believed could happen.

"Well, it proves one thing," Sarah said as she walked over and picked up the shot glass that Jack had sent flying off the bar and then placed it back near the colonel and placed a hand over the lip.

"And what's that?" Jack asked eyeing the glass and the hand over it.

"Operation Grimm," she said and then finally smirked and looked at Ryan, Pete, and then back at Collins. "Alice was damn near perfect in naming her Event, wasn't she?"

The question went unanswered as the morning broke on the day of the grand opening of Dracula's Castle, and the last night of the Jeddah.

17

PATINAS

Carl had felt the beast stiffen and fight against his suggestion of contact with Jack and the others. Everett had not known if the Golia would allow him to manipulate his body control long enough to give Collins the heads-up. He did manage to see the astonished faces of his friends through the double-paned window and knew that either they saw the signs he had given them or they had just been too shocked to see an actual Golia that they hadn't registered anything from Stanus other than the enormous teeth and muscled body. But Carl knew the whole experience had been worth it when, for the first time in the many years he had known

Colonel Jack Collins he saw the man actually take a step back from a situation and his eyes widening. It would make for great conversation in the complex mess hall.

Stanus was running at full speed up the side of the mountain, as if the large brain of the animal knew something was happening up at the pass and the Golia needed to be there. Carl was trying to see what the Golia was seeing but only succeeded in bringing the animal to a complete stop a mile past the castle. The sun was up and the morning rays were being diffused by the large storm slowly coming up from the south. Stanus shook his head while staying on all fours. Everett felt the animal start to fight him. The beast continued to shake its massive head hard enough that saliva was starting to fly from the growling mouth. Suddenly in his sleep state Carl felt his stomach heave, once, twice, and then a third time.

Stanus struggled to get to his hind legs, and using one of the large pine trees for support raised its muzzle to the morning sky and let loose a howl that frightened the man inside the head of the giant wolf. The large, thick, purple-colored claws dug into the bark and tore loose a four-foot section of the tree as Stanus struggled to get Everett out of its head. The beast hit the ground and rolled. The activity was forcing Carl to place every ounce of his sleeping mind into calming Stanus. Anya had said that a Golia can only be hitchhiked on for sometimes as little as five minutes before it will start to become uncooperative about hosting the traveler.

Carl felt the sensation of the animal's being start to fade from his vision as Stanus not only hit the ground hard and rolled, but the animal was actually shaking its head as if that alone could shake loose the stranger that was inside it. Suddenly Everett felt the power of the Golia ebb into nothingness as his strength left his body. He no longer could feel Stanus around him. He could no longer feel the raw emotion of the animal and knew that the spell was done. His mind seemed to tumble as the power of the wolf left and did not return. His body was deflated, his mind now putting out useless information of confusing thoughts and animalistic rage.

Captain Carl Everett's time as a werewolf was over.

PATINAS PASS,
THE TEMPLE OF MOSES

Carl thrashed and rolled half on and half off the old Army cot. His arm flew off and hit the stone floor. Madam Korvesky had just been brought in and laid upon a hardwood bed that was higher than the cot Everett was on. The old woman reached out and took Anya by the hand and stilled her from going to Everett.

"No, girl-child, let him come to the surface on his own, do not interfere, you know better than that."

"But Stanus has dislodged him completely; he's never done that before."

The old woman smiled and then lay back on the wooden table just as Niles and Charlie Ellenshaw walked inside. Niles held up the large black bag and showed it to a very nervous and angry Denise Gilliam. She nodded her head and then gestured for Niles and Charlie to enter.

"Stay close, I'm going to need you two."

Ellenshaw exchanged an uneasy look with Niles Compton, who knew what the doctor was going to ask.

On the cot Everett finally vomited onto the floor of the small stone enclosure. The red substance spewed onto the stone blocks and then when he thought he had most of the souring potion out of his stomach it heaved once more and then the last of the poisonous fluid finally convulsed from his stomach. Anya wrested her hand from her grandmother's and hurried to Carl's side and with the aid of Niles and Charlie lifted Everett back to the cot.

"That is worse than waking up the morning after a Shanghai drinking binge," Carl said as he squeezed his eyes closed against the flare of the several torches that lined the walls. He blinked and saw that an electric light had been strung into the small hut and was focused on the table next to his bed. Anya held Carl's hand for the longest time as his mind attempted to come back fully into his head.

"Stanus has shown you the ability of the wolf, and now you will pay for that," Anya said and placed a hand on his forehead and then wiped off the gleaming beads of sweat.

"Captain, did you find out the disposition of your people at the resort?" Madam Korvesky asked.

"I . . . think I did . . . hell, now I'm not too sure."

Anya smiled as she looked down at him and then worried over his lack of color. The spell had taken far more out of Carl than she realized it would. She now knew that the strength Everett was using to hold the mental link with Stanus had proven far too much for the large American. He was now exhausted and there wasn't anything he could do now but rest.

"What is happening here?"

They all turned to see Marko Korvesky standing in the doorway. Two large Gypsy men were on either side of the smaller Marko and all looked angry.

"Grandmother, you know bringing them in here is strictly forbidden by Jeddah law."

The small laugh from the old woman made Marko cringe as he took in the face of his sister as she stood over the American.

"And it looks as if this man has been traveling." He looked down at his grandmother with an angry expression. "Did you order this?"

"Yes, and now I have orders for you, man-child," she said as Denise started prepping her swollen ankle and leg for the impromptu surgery. "A storm is coming," she said, finally looking at Marko. "Tonight you will see your fondest wish fulfilled, my grandson: you will prove your worth and become king of the Gypsies, and join the long line of Jeddah going all the way back to Kale Al-Saul."

Marko and Anya were both shocked at the statement.

"The future of our people and of the Golia will be in your hands, Marko, in the next few hours. Many Golia and Jeddah will not be seeing the dawn after this coming night."

Marko looked back at Anya, who was watching the exchange while holding the American's hand. It looked as if she were struggling with his grandmother's decision.

"Do you plan on cutting off my grandmother's ankle or Mikla's?" he asked the doctor as she brushed past him with a pan of water that Ellenshaw had retrieved from the mineral hot springs that spewed forth the steamy liquid from deep beneath the mountain. She stopped and stared angrily at the arrogant man.

"Your grandmother needs to be in a hospital," Denise said as she handed Niles Compton the bowl of water. "I don't have the right equipment and the sanitary conditions are off the scale in here. I've got dust and dirt falling from a three-thousand-year-old ceiling and I'm performing major surgery on a woman in her eighties when her grandson could place her in one of those broken-down pieces of crap you people drive and get her to a real facility where they can treat her!"

Niles saw that Denise was close to losing it. He was asking too much of a medical doctor to suspend her belief long enough and actually cut off the old woman's lower leg to save another that a scalpel would never touch. He stepped up to her and gestured outward by holding the pan of water. Denise nodded and understood that she had just lost it. She gestured for the director to place the water at the head of the table. Denise reached into her bag and brought out a small bottle of morphine and then looked at Madam Korvesky. Denise halfheartedly smiled, shook her head, and then started arranging her instruments.

"Do you think my grandmother would listen to me?" Marko asked. He sniffed and huffed. "If she is choosing Mikla over herself so be it. She hurt herself by being secretive about her plans when all of this could have been avoided by naming me the heir many years ago." He stepped closer to the table and looked down upon the old woman. "Now we will do things my way," he said and then shocked everyone by leaning over and kissing her on the forehead.

"You are not king yet, man-child, I have one last task for you."

Denise slowly pushed a syringe into the small brown bottle and then looked at Niles and shook her head in anger. She knew the old woman could not survive the amputation, she was just too old and the infection had spread too far. Her fate would be the same as Mikla's, only Mikla would die before the surgery was completed. Denise eased the needle into the old woman's arm and then she locked eyes with Marko.

"Say your good-byes, because your grandmother has chosen suicide over common sense." Denise angrily threw the needle against the far wall of the room. Charlie Ellenshaw eased over to the young doctor and placed his arm around her.

Marko ignored the indignant American doctor and returned his attention to Madam Korvesky as her eyes started to settle into a far more relaxed state.

"Go to your new friends at the resort and have them release the Americans." The Gypsy queen ordered her grandson as she allowed her eyes to flutter shut as the morphine was starting to take effect. "Explain to your partner that if this is done, he will be rewarded in the ways of avarice. The trinkets you have delivered to him are nothing compared to what the Gypsy queen is prepared to give him for the favor of releasing the Americans."

"I do not have to ask, I will order their release." Marko once more leaned over and spoke directly into his grandmother's ear. "After that, the Jeddah will begin a new life, one we deserve. Do you understand me, Grandmamma?"

She lightly patted his hand as she started to slide into unconsciousness. "You will be king so you will be able to do anything you want. Now go and free the Americans, they will not want to be at the resort after the day ends tomorrow night."

The last words were nearly unintelligible as Marko allowed her to sleep. He closed his eyes and said a small prayer for the woman that raised him, one that he respected and loved like no other, but also one that he had always feared as being the one who would always make the hard choices and decisions. That was something Marko himself hoped he had inside of him.

Suddenly Marko's demeanor changed completely. He turned to Anya and then looked down at the American.

"These people must be gone from Patinas tomorrow." He looked from Niles to the faces of the others. He stopped at Denise and then said, "Please help my grandmother, I would not want to see her go out this way."

"Listen to me, you little backwoods jerk, I'll do what it is I—"

"Doctor!" Niles said louder than he had intended.

Denise cut off her angry reply and then just shook her head.

"I will gather my men and we will pay our partner a visit, have lunch, and wish him well on his grand opening of his ridiculous castle. Then I will order your friends released. Then you will leave Romania and never return. This mountain is not yours."

They all watched Marko leave the room, quickly followed by the two large men, who hesitantly patted their friend on the back at his new honor.

"Well, we have little time, her fever is up to a hundred and five degrees. We have to remove that leg now."

As Marko climbed the large staircase he stopped and looked back down to the four village women who stood silently around Mikla in the center of the temple. His eyes traveled up to the gallery high above and saw that every single one of the Golia young were lined up and watching Mikla. Marko then turned with a smile and started outside.

As one, the Golia started howling as Mikla yelped and started growling as the amputation had started.

With the pain-filled howl of the sleeping Golia echoing inside the lost Temple of Moses, the last twenty-four hours of the ancient tribe of Jeddah were about to begin.

Denise Gilliam fought for one solid hour to remove the shattered lower right leg of Madam Korvesky. The blood loss had been tremendous. Dr. Gilliam was amazed at how the old woman seemed to control not only the pain, but also the flow of her own blood. At first Denise was willing to chalk the strange ability up to a fluke, but she was now convinced that Madam Korvesky actually managed to control the speed at which her heart was operating. That told Denise that the Jeddah had more than just unusual control of their minds, but of their bodies as well. It would be later that Denise, Alice, Charlie, and Niles would conclude that the Jeddah had the ability to not only control the Golia to a point, but also the physical and metaphysical world around them. They thus came to the conclusion that the rumors of vampires, werewolves, and other strange in the Carpathians were the kind of stuff that made legend seem like fact.

As the surgery was taking place, Niles and Charlie Ellenshaw stayed as close to Mikla as they dared. Several of the village's biggest men-folk had managed to slip restraining ropes around Mikla to hold him to the stone dais. The ropes had been passed around the eight-hundred-pound beast several times because the men of Patinas knew what it would take to restrain one of nature's most tenacious killers.

Mikla had calmed down when Madam Korvesky was given the morphine injection by Dr. Gilliam. One minute Mikla was snapping and snarling at the men around it and the next the bright yellow eyes became dull and the great Golia listless. The men still kept their distance. It was crazy Charlie and later he would admit to being pressured by the bravery of Ellenshaw that pushed him to follow the nutty cryptozoologist toward the now still yet perceptive animal. Charlie's eyes were fixed firmly on the dais and the ankle of the Golia. Compton wrung his hands together as he too watched the wolf for the reaction that they knew was coming.

"I've always heard of remote healing, Niles, but never remote healing with a pinch hitter before. I mean to take the leg of someone who wasn't actually injured, only psychosomatically, and that removal of the offending limb is supposed to heal the actual injury that occurred to another entity—amazing."

Niles looked at Ellenshaw, who was excited at what was happening since they entered the temple. Compton, as was his habit, always watched and then calculated his opinions. And thus far the director of Department 5656 wasn't completely satisfied that Madam Korvesky could be trusted. Her sudden turnaround on the appointment of her grandson, Marko, spoke of a plan that Niles had yet to figure out. It was like the old woman had become tired of the struggle and surrendered the leadership of the tribe of Jeddah to Marko and not the better-equipped Anya.

Charlie looked from Mikla to Niles and then at the four men standing around but still far away from Mikla. Charlie gulped and then placed a hand near the break in the beast's right lower leg. The wound was swollen and Ellenshaw could clearly see the break in the bone. One bend was larger than the others but he still counted three separate breaks. He shook his head as the odor hit him. He turned back to Compton with a sad shake to the head.

"Gangrene has set in; Mikla's whole leg has gone bad." Charlie removed his glasses and closed his eyes. "There is no way this wolf can survive. Even I cannot believe in this . . . this—"

"Magic?" Niles said, cutting off Ellenshaw's logical conclusion.

"Okay, I'm glad you said and I didn't. I would have—"

That was as far as Ellenshaw got in his explanation when Mikla suddenly strained at the offending restraining ropes. The beast thrashed and twisted, threatening to rip the thick ropes holding it down. The mouth opened and spittle flew and then the loudest howl any human had ever heard shattered the interior of the temple.

Compton and the men from Patinas saw them first. The adult Golia were everywhere. Whatever strange mission the adults had been on was clearly not a priority for them today as they were all streaming down the steep walls of the temple, coming from someplace only the Golia knew. They came down headfirst, sideways, and backward, each holding on to the rough-hewn walls of the temple. They were all coming to Mikla's aid. The four men of Patinas knew it was time to leave. They sprinted from the center of the temple, leaving a startled Charlie and Niles to watch their retreating forms. Compton looked from the running men to the flailing body of Mikla thrashing on the stone table.

"I think we better follow suit and get the hell out of here," Niles said as he grabbed Ellenshaw by the arm and started pulling him away from the injured wolf. Just as Charlie nodded that he thought Niles's assessment of the situation was spot-on, they both turned and saw Stanus standing at the bottom of the stone steps leading to the outside. The Golia was standing with one arm raised and holding the wall for support. The claws had actually dug into the stone. The animal was breathing hard and staring at the two Americans.

"You know what, Mr. Director? I don't think he looks all that happy and I suspect that the captain is no longer a passenger aboard that particular thrill ride."

Niles couldn't answer as he felt the other adult Golia start to settle onto the floor of the expansive temple complex. There were at least a thousand of the amazing wolves. The males ranged in weight from a few hundred pounds to close to a thousand as they walked on all fours toward the dais where Mikla was thrashing horribly. One by one the Golia took up station in a circle around the injured Mikla. For the moment Niles and Charlie were ignored, but Compton figured that would last only as long as Stanus allowed it to. Still, the alpha male watched. Its breathing was calming somewhat but the animal was still clearly angry at having been host to a stranger.

Suddenly Stanus strode with a purpose toward Niles and Ellenshaw. The beast came close to a large stone block and angrily swiped at the ten-by-ten slab. As they watched in amazement only feet from their own deaths, Compton and Ellenshaw saw a large chunk of the stone fly off and strike the wall. With a single blow the angry leader of the wolf pack had shattered solid stone. Compton was near to closing his eyes when Mikla let out a howl that sent shivers down the director's spine. It even made him forget the immediate threat of Stanus and turn to look at Mikla. At the same moment Stanus stopped and stared as the other adult Golia, covered in mud and filth, started to repeat Mikla's painful howl.

As they watched, the ankle of the great wolf popped and straightened. Mikla screamed in absolute pain. The center rope restraining him snapped with an audible twang as the two halves separated. The Golia thrashed and growled. Stanus raised his muzzle to the ceiling and let loose a blood-curdling howl that made Charlie cover his ears. At the same moment the other adult Golia and then the offspring high above started howling. The noise was deafening as the healing of Mikla continued. Compton could only wonder at what the old woman was enduring for the sake of the animal she had sent to protect Anya.

Before anything could be figured out by the two men from the Event Group, Mikla screamed in utter pain. The body stiffened and the animal rolled onto its back and the legs went straight into the air. The large mouth opened and they saw the amazing whiteness of the teeth as a howl of pain came through with not a sound. Then Mikla's body went limp. Charlie winced as he realized the pain of the spell of healing had been just too much for Mikla, and Ellenshaw was starting to suspect that things didn't go well inside for Madam Korvesky.

Stanus stood before the two men with its yellow eyes bearing down upon them.

With Niles and Charlie watching in stunned and terrified silence, Mikla suddenly tore free of the remaining ropes that held him down. He slashed with his claws and with his teeth until the ropes were in tatters around the dais. The giant wolf sprang from the table and landed on all fours. The rear right ankle looked as if it had never been injured. Charlie felt his will to advance science was at stake as he took a tentative step toward Mikla as it stood watching the men and shaking its head to clear it of the painkillers that had been given it by Dr. Gilliam. In response to Ellenshaw's bravery, Mikla roared in anger and then stood on two legs. The right hand bunched into a fist and then it came down on the stone dais. The enormous block of stone cracked but stayed intact.

Stanus moved before either man could realize what was happening. The giant beast jumped over Niles and Charlie and stood between them and the newly revived Mikla. Then without another sound all the other Golia vanished up the walls. Mikla stayed behind as did Stanus. Then even Mikla, with a last look at the stone hut where the surgery was taking place, sprang away into the flickering light of the torches. Stanus stayed.

"Uh oh," Ellenshaw said as Stanus looked directly at them. The claws of both hands were clicking together at the animal's sides as it took a malice-filled step toward the two men.

"Stanus, that's enough!"

The voice of Anya coming from behind froze the beast as it slowly turned its head to the woman who stopped its actions. Niles and Charlie could clearly see that Stanus was growing very tired of listening to orders. As the two men looked out the corners of their eyes they saw Anya standing in the doorway with Carl Everett beside her. He had an arm around the Gypsy princess and looked weaker than anyone could ever recall seeing him. He was haggard but his eyes still held the deep blue and they could see that he had survived the spell.

"Go with the babies, Stanus. Go!" Anya shouted angrily. The night and morning were taking a toll on her.

Stanus turned and walked with purpose toward Anya and Everett. Charlie took a step forward but Niles held him back. Whatever was going to happen to Anya and Carl there wasn't anything either Niles or Ellenshaw could do about it. The beast tossed Anya aside and then snatched Everett off the floor until the large Navy man's feet were dangling three feet off the stone.

"Stanus, no!" Anya shouted and as she did the ears of the beast lay down as it started to raise its right hand into the air for a decisive swipe into Everett's tired and haggard face. Anya tried to seize the right leg of Stanus to get its attention away from Carl, but the beast ignored her.

"Stanus, come," came a weak voice from the room. "Stanus, come to me."

The Golia froze. The hand was still in the air and the sharpened claws were only a foot away from ending the captain's life when the ears came up.

Niles felt he understood what was happening. The animal had been afraid that Madam Korvesky had died and that was why it was in a killing mood. That coupled with the betrayal felt by Stanus by Carl's traveling with it, had made the animal barely controllable.

Stanus let Everett slide through its fingers as it turned and ran into the hut. Moments later the Golia stepped from the enclosure where Madam Korvesky was lying in a drug-induced weariness and looked at the two men and Anya. Everett was still on the ground looking up at the wolf he had been running within only recently. The beast suddenly reached down and snatched Everett off the floor and then brought him to its face. The beast sniffed, once, twice, and then a third time. It allowed Carl to slide through its fingers and then the Golia vanished just as the others had done. The temple was now as silent as a tomb.

Niles and Charlie ran to Carl and Anya and they assisted them to their feet. Carl was shaken and Anya was mad.

"The Golia are getting too hard to control. I've never seen Stanus and the others acting like this. Where are the adults disappearing to and why in the hell are they so filthy?" she asked herself out loud as she walked over and picked up one of the torn ropes and looked it over.

"How is your grandmother?" Niles asked as he finally got his shaking under control.

Anya looked at Compton and then tossed the frayed rope away as she helped Carl over to the dais where he leaned heavily against the stone.

"She will be dead by midnight. She gave her life for Mikla."

Denise Gilliam walked out of the room and threw herself onto the stone floor and swiped at the sweat on her face and forehead. She was shaking her head. She looked up at Anya.

"She wouldn't be so weak if we had gotten her to a hospital. Hell, we can still save her if we move now," she said, pleading with Anya.

"My grandmother has made her choice. She will live until this is settled, and then she will go the way of Kale, of Joshua, and of Moses."

"I cannot believe you, you are an educated woman. We can save her."

"No, Doctor, we cannot. This night has been foretold since Joshua. It has been foretold since the time of the Exodus. We either live after tonight, or we go the way the Golia were always meant to go, to extinction. My grandmother's life will ensure their survival."

"You are all insane," Denise said, standing and turning to check on her dying patient. "And you, Director Compton, are guilty of backward thinking just as much as the Jeddah."

"We don't have a right to interfere," Niles started to explain but stopped. He lowered his head. "Tonight the Jeddah pass into history."

Stanus allowed its anger to be placated by his claws sinking deeply into the stone wall of the temple as it leaped from the ground to the twenty-foot mark of the wall. It hesitated as its claws sought purchase in the porous rock. Small jets of steam escaped the stone where the deep, purple-hued daggers sank deeply. Stanus thrust forward with its hind legs, clearing the stone by inches as it leaped another thirty feet, and then the long, strong fingers and toes found purchase once again. Then it repeated the climbing maneuver until it sprang onto the gallery shelf where the young Golia crowded around the alpha male, who snapped, slapped, and pushed the smaller wolves away as it went to all fours after landing.

Stanus shook its head as its eyes looked around at the young. Their parents had vanished once more after their initial curiosity over the fate of Mikla had been satisfied. Stanus turned and looked down into the temple and saw the man being helped to the dais by Anya. The wolf was feeling more confused than ever at the appearance of the strangers. For a reason the beast could not fathom the Jeddah queen had taken them in and by the way her thoughts met his told it that she trusted these humans where the Golia feared them. Stanus had been confused by the man that had traveled with it. At first the Golia hated the intrusion of a mind it did not know. Nor could it ever fully understand the dimensions and deepness of the man that had been inside its head. The human was like Stanus himself and that was odd for an outsider. However, he had the feeling that the man and his companions were here to determine the fate of the Golia—and that was not understood. The difference between the spell making with Marko was the fact that although Stanus knew Marko, he never fully trusted the man prince. On a more unstable note to the Golia was the fact that the human tonight eased Stanus to the point where it allowed the traveler to see and feel it. This man was trusted among his own, and the difference between him and Marko was what was confusing Stanus.

The alpha male stood and slowly rose to both feet and then sniffed the air. It stopped and ran until it cleared the young and then went to all fours as it started to run even faster for the very highest point of the temple structure. The many holes that had been dug in the past year were evident throughout the upper reaches. Hundreds of holes the size of small doorways dotted the walls. The darkness in this area was as if bright daylight in the night vision of the Golia. Stanus pushed through one of these and ran down the length of a Golia-dug tunnel.

Stanus traveled the excavation for two miles until it reached a chamber where it opened wide enough for a thousand of the Golia. Stanus broke into the open and ran for a strange-looking object that ran the entire length of the chamber. Several more of the long, rounded objects protruded from the stone. The chamber was five hundred feet high and as many long. It had taken the wolves nearly a full year to reach the spot that Madam Korvesky had put into their minds almost eighteen months before.

Stanus was joined by Mikla. The once injured wolf sniffed Stanus up the length of his brother's body. Stanus allowed this. Mikla was not much smaller than Stanus but the alpha weighed almost a quarter more than its little sibling. Once the greeting was done, Stanus and Mikla rose to their hind legs and then resumed their digging just as the other Golia adults were doing. Every once in a while growling was heard as the wolves struggled with the pile-driven steel.

The steel-reinforced anchor pins of Dracula's Castle were now fully exposed and the anchors' foundations was crumbling far faster than in previous days and months. The strange vibration Sarah was trying desperately to get a handle on was increasing as the enormous anchor pins started to give way.

Castle Dracula was being undermined from the mountain itself by the deteriorating hold that the anchor pins had on the cracked and worn rock it was attached to.

A thousand animals began to dig out from around the massive steel pins in their continued undermining of the engineered foundation.

The new and very much improved Castle Dracula was doomed long before the first guests hit the dance floor.

Madam Korvesky was lying on the cot after Denise had finished with the procedure. The morphine drip she managed to handle with her minimal equipment made Niles proud of the young MD as she went about the field amputation on the eighty-eight-year-old woman.

"Young miss, I would like to thank you for giving me the extra time I needed."

Denise Gilliam threw down a bloodstained towel and then braced herself against the old and worn table her instruments had been placed on. She pushed the offending stainless steel utensils off the table where they crashed to the floor and then lowered her head as she cried. Without saying anything the very tired and angry doctor turned and left the enclosure.

Alice, who was sitting next to Madam Korvesky on a small stool, knew they had asked Denise to do too much. Doctors become angry when patients think they know more than they do. And Dr. Gilliam was angry knowing she had just killed an old woman for no other apparent reason than the belief she would save the injured wolf, even after Niles had explained that the strange trade-off had worked as Mikla had bounded away after being on death's door.

"I must speak with you," Madam Korvesky said as she raised her head off the makeshift pillow made up of two worn blankets, "and you, Keeper of Secrets," she said first to Alice and then Niles, who walked over to the small cot.

"I do not expect you to understand the ways of the Jeddah and the Golia. To tell you the truth we have not understood ourselves for so long that we have become lost. Today you will learn the secret of the Jeddah tribe and why we settled here in these mountains and why our mission here thirty-five hundred years ago was one of survival. You will learn of the secret, but you will never leave here with it. It all ends here, tonight. If what I believe is going to happen, indeed comes to pass, this will all be gone by sunup tomorrow. You will take the truth to your place of secrets and there you will have the knowledge that we choose no longer to have."

"We do not understand," Alice said as she held the woman's hand.

Madam Korvesky tried her best to laugh but the constant throb of her missing right foot and ankle kept her from it.

"The treasure of the Exodus will be the reason the Temple of Moses will fall by the hand of the unbeliever."

"If we can get down to the resort we can get the authorities here," Niles started to say.

Madam Korvesky held a hand up. "Bring in the Man from the Sea," she asked Niles, who went to the door and vanished momentarily.

Two minutes later a weary Carl Everett stepped into the enclosure where he had been just five hours before. Alice smiled up at the captain and he nodded. Anya stepped in behind him and placed an arm around his waist and helped guide him into the room.

"Who can understand the ways of the ancient world better than the traveler who has experienced it?"

Carl was confused as he looked from the dying woman to her granddaughter.

"You have seen your companions?" she asked in an increasingly weary voice.

"Yes, I think they are being held against their will. I'm sure about that but . . . but . . ."

"What is it?" Alice asked when Everett became confused.

"It wasn't I who sensed that Jack and the others were being held against their will, it was the wolf, Stanus, who knew for a fact they didn't want to be in that room. He sensed it." Carl shook his head as he never would be able to figure out the metaphysical properties of just what it was that happened to him that night.

The old Gypsy closed her eyes and everyone thought she had drifted off from the heavy influence of the drugs. Alice was getting ready to tell Anya to run and get Denise when the old woman looked up into the face of Alice Hamilton.

"You miss him?" she asked with a tired voice.

Without even thinking about it Alice knew exactly whom Madam Korvesky was talking about.

"I miss Garrison every minute of every day," she said as she wiped away a small tear.

"Yes, I know you do. He was a good man. I knew it back in Hong Kong and I know it now. This, and only this, is why you are allowed to know about us, because soon we will not exist as a people any longer. The Jeddah will finally venture forth from this valley and experience the world for the first time."

"I don't under—"

Alice was stopped. "The young ones have never understood the stories of the old days—the old religions and even older leaders that fated them to a backward existence for three thousand years. Oh, the old will stay and struggle to exist and live among the Golia because that is all that they know to do. But the young," she smiled and looked at her granddaughter and the man she was holding on to, "they have earned the right to join the human race. That is what I have always wanted since I was a girl, not running around the world trying to keep secret a lie that was perpetrated many thousands of years ago. No, they need to love, and live." She squeezed Alice's hand tighter.

"Tell me what your plan is," Niles Compton said.

"They will be coming."

"Who will be coming? I think I can pretty much guarantee that NATO will reevaluate their strategic plan for this valley and the pass. I do have a connection in government circles," Niles said as even Carl had to shake his head at the way Compton alluded to the fact that he was best friends with the most powerful man in the world—the president of the United States.

"No, not soldiers—the Russian criminal below has learned our secret and will be coming with my granddaughter's Hebrew Judas."

"Ben-Nevin has allied himself with Dmitri Zallas?" Niles Compton asked.

"The colonel works for some very ruthless Jewish hard-liners that have infiltrated the Knesset. They are powerful and in their pursuit to prove that the Hebrew nation was the chosen people they are willing to sacrifice everything Israel has fought for nearly the past seventy years. They will once more alienate the Israeli nation over ancient history that never made any sense to begin with. This is not what Moses and Joshua had intended. Israel must be friends with their neighbors or the Exodus will never end. My ancestor the great Kale knew this thousands of years ago. Joshua eventually learned the truth and this is why the Jeddah were damned. Why a magnificent species of animal like the Golia has been relegated to securing the truth of a people long espoused to be the chosen. To hide from mankind and do the bidding of men that haven't walked the earth for an age."

Before Anya could finish her explanation there was a loud explosion of barking and growling coming from the interior of the temple. They heard Charlie outside yelling at someone, then Will Mendenhall's scared voice coming from some distance away.

"Nice doggy," came the frightened greeting.

"Miss Korvesky, uh, my friend needs a little help," Charlie yelled as Anya and a very tired and bone-weary Everett went to see what was happening.

"Oh, God," Anya said as she saw what Everett saw and they both tried to get close to the downed Will Mendenhall, who had at least six or seven young Golia the size of year-old German shepherds bouncing around him and licking him, one even pulling his boot free and running off with it.

"Help, I'm being mugged here," Will called out as he rolled onto his belly to keep the cold tongues off his face

Anya placed her two small fingers in her mouth and then produced a loud whistle. The Golia pups stopped roughhousing with Mendenhall and their ears perked up. As a group the black-furred babies scrambled up the wall next to the staircase. Will rolled over onto his back and closed his eyes as he tried to get his racing heart under control. Charlie ran to the lieutenant and helped him to his one-booted foot.

"Well, at least they weren't the size of the dog I saw earlier," Will said as he brushed at his dusty clothes.

"Uh, those weren't dogs, Will."

Mendenhall stopped slapping at his clothes and then looked at Ellenshaw. "I'm not following, they were right there, you saw them, all the big dogs."

"Not dogs, werewolves."

Mendenhall smiled and then patted Charlie on the back. "I suppose they were Golia?"

Charlie waited until Will stopped chuckling and then tapped him on the back and pointed upward. Will's eyes went where Ellenshaw was indicating and his mouth fell open. Mikla had returned and was standing at the top of the gallery and was looking down. It was on two legs and the arms were stretched out at its side as it watched the activity below in the temple. Mendenhall turned and faced Ellenshaw and a look came over his features as he realized he had not been playing with dogs, but baby werewolves. He closed his eyes and swallowed.

Suddenly a boot struck the stone flooring of the temple. Will looked up at Mikla.

"I guess he remembered you from yesterday and wanted to return your shoe," Charlie said as he laughed and then walked away.

"Great!" Will said as he retrieved his boot and with one last look up at Mikla, who growled and then bounced away again, limped to the enclosure where Anya, Niles, and Carl waited.

"Why are you here, Lieutenant?" Everett asked as he placed his arm around Anya one more time.

"It took me over three hours to find the entrance here. The guys who designed that camouflaged doorway are better than anyone we have."

"So what made you brave the pass?" Carl insisted.

"We got part of a radio message from the NATO force assisting in the flooding down south."

Niles and Everett became instantly concerned.

"The storm has turned and is heading north. The local radio station is warning everyone that this has the potential to produce flash flooding all over the southern and central Carpathians."

Everett voiced what everyone other than Anya was thinking.

"We have to get to Jack and get everyone the hell out of here."

Before anyone could move several large pieces of stone fell from the ceiling of the immense cavern and smashed to the floor. Dust and dirt settled from high above after what seemed like a solid fifteen seconds of shaking.

"Tell me you get tremors from time to time?" Carl asked Anya as he examined the gallery where all of the Golia young had vanished.

"No, never. This region, outside of the thermal hot springs produced by a vent of very deep origins, has no seismic activity at all."

Everett looked from Will Mendenhall to Niles Compton.

"I swear we must be bad luck, because every time we show up, a mission parameter or something else that has stood for thousands of years, is suddenly going to come down around our ears," Mendenhall said in frustration.

"Well, this is what we do at the Group, young lieutenant," Niles said as he turned and went back into the small enclosure.

"Next thing they'll tell us we have to disarm a weapon of some kind," Will said as he wandered away and then sat hard to replace his boot.

Charlie Ellenshaw knew what Will was thinking.

"I know exactly how these things turn out," he finally finished.

18

THE EDGE OF THE WORLD HOTEL AND RESORT CASINO, PATINAS, ROMANIA

It was past four in the afternoon and not one of the staff employees had seen Gina Louvinski since late the night before. Janos Vajic steeled himself for the worst as he went searching the hotel and casino grounds. He had heard a rumor that she vanished at the same time the Americans had but thus far he had been unable to find out any information and the hotel's smooth functioning was starting to wane without her.

He spied Dmitri Zallas in the mud springs and spa area. He was wearing a white terry cloth robe and smoking a cigar as one of the spa employees massaged his small feet. Colonel Ben-Nevin was close by looking irritated as he waited for Zallas to finish his afternoon spa session. His bodyguard as always was nearby and tried to step in between Janos and his partner. The balding Vajic felt the heat of the spa start to penetrate his blue suit as he was escorted to where Zallas sat with mud rubbed on his face and wearing a set of dark sunning glasses. Ben-Nevin looked him over and then just as quickly dismissed the man as no threat to either himself or the Russian, whom he needed for the next twelve hours. After that he didn't care what happened to the Slavic gangster.

"Janos, why are you not preparing for the festivities at the castle?" Zallas asked, not really caring about his answer.

"Gina is missing. Since last night I have been unable to locate her. The four Americans have also vanished."

"Perhaps the Americans checked out, and Ms. Louvinski went with them. My men tell me she was rather intimate with that small and very arrogant American with the black hair."

"Gina would never leave the resort, not with the grand opening tonight. I would think you would be a little bit more concerned since we desperately need her if tonight is to go off with minimal setbacks."

Zallas finally lowered his cigar and then removed the dark glasses. His eyes went from Janos Vajic to the Israeli and then he smiled as his attention once again focused on his partner.

"Oh, I plan no setbacks for tonight. I expect everything to go off without a hitch as the Americans are fond of saying."

"And the fifty new men who arrived by car this morning?"

"Nothing gets past you, Janos. Yes, this is why I expect little or no trouble to-night, as I have brought in extra security."

"You mean more than the hundred men you already had here?"

"Yes, tonight is very important to me . . ." He looked back at Ben-Nevin, who remained unmoving and unsmiling. Zallas's eyes never left Janos Vajic. "And many, many other new friends."

Vajic knew Zallas was up to something and that something was what had changed the demeanor of the Russian in the past twenty-four hours, and the reason for that was the tall skinny man staring at him.

"And the television is saying that the storm that has devastated the south has taken a turn to the north and is coming straight for us. This does not bode well for your grand opening."

"My guests are not afraid of a little weather, Janos. Now quit being a bitching little Romanian and get things ready."

"No matter what, I *will* find Gina," he said as he started to turn away.

"Janos?"

He stopped and without turning fully, waited. Ben-Nevin stepped up to Vajic and placed his hands on the smaller man's shoulders and turned him to face Dmitri Zallas.

"Our friend would like your full attention," he said and then stepped back as Janos stared at the man and his audacity.

"Look for the woman, but not to the detriment of my grand opening. You will have to be present around midnight as I have other business to attend to." The look in the Russian's eyes was frightening. "Do I make myself clear, Brother Janos?"

"Very," he said and then with a last look at the Israeli left the spa to the smiles of the two men watching after him.

"It is too dangerous to keep him alive after tonight," the Israeli said. "He has seen me and we don't need outside influences muddying up the water."

"Janos came to me after his investment group heard we were forming this limited partnership, he can be trusted. Anyway, as you can see, the man is terrified of me."

Ben-Nevin watched the retreating back of the man he thought was familiar to him but he didn't think the Romanian was not someone he had met before. Still, the man had something in his brown eyes that Ben-Nevin didn't like at all. It was a look of silent confidence.

"Terrified is a word that I have not come across much in my business, and that man is hiding something."

Janos Vajic knew it was time. The extra men Zallas had sent for coupled with the fact that the man who was now spending an inordinate amount of time with him was none other than Colonel Avi Ben-Nevin, a man he recognized after some raking of his memory. He had thought for a moment that Ben-Nevin had also recognized him, but he had relaxed when the suspicion in the Israeli's eyes vanished. Now Vajic had no choice. Gina was gone and it was time for him to slip away as well. With a last look into the hotel lobby he stepped into the reception area in the back and made for Zallas's office.

Janos glanced through the small partition and saw the two desk clerks looking bored as most of the guests were either getting an early dinner or playing craps before the time was right to get into the cable cars and make their way to Zallas's precious grand opening. Once he saw their attention was elsewhere he used his special key that Zallas did not know he had and opened the door to the office. He froze in horror when he saw what was waiting.

"Gina!" he said, knowing he had spoken too loud.

Gina Louvinski was sitting in a chair. Her head was slumped forward on her chest and there was blood pooling around her feet. Janos swallowed when he saw that her wrists were cut. He closed his eyes as he slowly stepped into the office and then closed the door behind him. He lowered his head and then went to his partner. He gently lifted a wrist and checked the woman's pulse. There was none. He saw that most of her fingers and expertly manicured nails had been broken. She had been held down as someone sliced her wrists.

Vajic slowly lowered her arm to the armrest and then he closed his eyes and said a silent prayer for his partner of the past five years. He was about to turn away when he heard a key sliding into the lock. He turned and silently and deftly stepped to the wall and waited.

One of Dmitri's larger bodyguards opened the door and stuck his head inside. That was when Janos Vajic moved. He used both hands and took the man by the head and pulled him inside the office until his foot caught on a Persian rug and the man went sprawling only inches from the seated body of Gina Louvinski. Vajic very slowly closed the door and then threw the locking mechanism. He unbuttoned his suit jacket and pulled the garment from his body. He placed it on Zallas's desk and then before the man on the floor could recover he kicked out viciously and caught the man in his stomach, which doubled him over into a tight fetal position. Vajic reached down and pulled the man's weapon from his now exposed shoulder holster. He made sure the weapon was charged and then shoved the gun into his pants as he kicked out at the man once more.

"That's to get your attention," Janos said as he knelt beside the man, who was struggling to get air into his body. "You had a hand in this, yes?"

The bodyguard moaned and continued to roll back and forth in pain. The man could not believe the small Romanian nerd had crippled him like that.

Janos took a deep breath and then reached out and took the man's right thumb and quickly snapped it in two. "Again, you had a hand in this woman's death, yes?"

"No . . . I mean . . . we were following orders!" the man cried out in hopes that would be enough for the man kneeling over him.

"Ah, following orders," Janos said with a sad smile. "Haven't we all heard that one before?" He looked back down at the man and made a quick decision. "We no longer tolerate men and women who do things blindly and who just follow orders. This is no longer tolerable." Janos reached out and took the man's jaw and turned his head until could see into his brown eyes. "The men who arrived today, what does Zallas have planned for them? They are not added security. These men are too heavily armed."

"I . . . don't know . . . it has something to do with the mountain pass, that's all I know. The regular bodyguards weren't in on the meeting. I do know . . . it's supposed to happen at midnight."

"I want you to know that you have murdered the kindest and most professional agent I have ever had the honor to work with, and for her to die like this— for this nonsense? Well, I am a thousand miles from home and no one is here to give me a countermanding order, so . . ." Janos reached out and took the moaning bodyguard's head and snapped his neck. He stood and with one last look at Gina went to the office of the Russian mobster.

It was time for Janos Vajic to end his partnership with Dmitri Zallas.

PALMACHIM AIR FORCE BASE, TEL AVIV, ISRAEL

Mossad General Shamni was dozing on the cot as the radio operator placed his right headphone into his ear and pressed hard as the words he struggled to hear barely made sense.

"General, I have Demetrius; he's coming through but very weakly. The storm is starting to play hell with the atmospherics in the Carpathians."

The general shot to his feet and ran to the radio. He pulled hard on the operator's headphone line until it popped free and then suddenly the far-off voice became clear as it wound its way through the speakers. The door opened and Major Donny Mendohlson popped his head in. The noise was loud and hard to understand.

"Demetrius, this is Duke, do you copy, over?"

There was an immense amount of static and the operator played with several knobs a moment and then they heard the voice of the Mossad agent eighteen hundred miles to the north.

"Duke . . . Demetrius . . . Forestall is dead, it looks . . . Czar is moving on the city, over."

General Shamni lowered his head and then took out his cell phone at the mention of Dmitri Zallas and his code name, Czar. The number he punched in was as secure as a phone call could ever be in the Middle East.

"Hold on, Demetrius," said the radio operator.

"Mr. Prime Minister, the Russian is moving on the City of Moses just as we suspected he might. Suggest we go to phase two immediately."

General Shamni became silent as he listened to his old friend on the far end of his secure cell phone.

"Thank you, my friend, the best of luck to all of us." The general shut the phone and then took up the microphone for the radio. Before he keyed the mic he looked at the Israeli commando, who was waiting expectantly. "You're a go for immediate departure and insertion. Major, remember you're a relief flight for the flooding, NATO-approved. Good luck, my boy."

"Thank you, General."

The major left the office and the general heard the hangar come to life as the turbine whine of the C-130 started to sound in the cavernous space. He shook his head as once more he was sending Israeli boys into harm's way.

"Demetrius, this is Duke, over."

"Duke, barely . . . hear you . . . atmospherics are getting—"

"Demetrius, Operation Ramesses is a go. I repeat, Operation Ramesses is a go. The strike initiates at 0215, HALO drop into the village below Patinas. Be there for extraction, at the conclusion of Ramesses, Duke out."

The static-filled response came through the air and Shamni gave the mic back to the operator without caring what was said in response to the historic strike order.

He stepped to the window that looked into the hangar as the ear-piercing scream of the four Pratt & Whitney turbofans of the giant Hercules started spinning up to idling power as the C-130 started to raise its rear loading ramp. Major Donny Mendohlson bounded up the personnel ramp to the pilot's door just aft of the cockpit. He turned and faced the general and then gave him a quick salute and a smile. He turned and entered the Hercules just as the giant hangar door started to rise.

General Shamni turned away as the Hercules started its roll out of the hangar for Israel's part in the flood relief for southern Romania.

Mossad had long anticipated the building of the resort when Marko started selling off antiquities from the Exodus through the Russian's contacts. Shamni knew the destruction of the temple was now of the utmost importance to the state of Israel.

Tonight the past would get buried forever and the one weapon that Will Mendenhall feared the most was now on its way to a country once called Transylvania.

General Shamni took one last look at the secure storage area that would pop open automatically at certain coordinates over Romania and then it would be jettisoned over Patinas where the device would be recovered by the Operation Ramesses forces and then placed into the Lost City of Moses.

That device was nuclear in nature.

PATINAS PASS

The first of the rain started at sundown and the dark clouds bled the sun away early as the storm that initially had been forecast to miss the pass came directly toward it. The village of Patinas was unusually quiet as most of the farm-folk were settling down to a cold dinner. The apprehension felt by everyone in the small village was palpable as Niles Compton toured the single street that ran down the center of what would have been called a Romanian thoroughfare. Three of the 82nd Airborne combat engineers followed close behind. Niles removed his glasses and looked up at the black sky that was now hidden behind a roiling storm front. He refused one of the waterproof ponchos offered by the staff sergeant. Niles replaced his glasses and then looked at Will.

"You three, gather the rest of the men, we'll stay here tonight, it may be a little drier than those tents," Niles said, looking at the engineers. "Besides, I want us all in one place. Charlie will join us later. Alice and Denise insist on staying with Madam Korvesky."

The three Airborne troops started to salute and then thought better of it and left the cottage as Will Mendenhall found the single light in the house and pushed hard on the old push-button switch. Nothing happened. He tried again and still nothing.

"Power's out," he said but then he saw the glow of Castle Dracula two miles down the mountainside through the opened window. "Huh, the castle looks like a Hollywood premiere is going on," he said as he turned and looked at Niles, who was busy drying his glasses.

"Did you see the single phased power line running up the mountain? Well, you can bet your commission that it only runs here. The hotel and casino complex received all of the new stuff."

Will understood now. "It must be nice being friends and limited partners with the interior minister."

Niles nodded his head. "Something I plan to have changed as soon as I can get some reports filed. NATO and the president won't be too happy to realize they became silent partners in an international land grab sponsored by antiquities thieves and mobsters. I think the new president of Romania may wish to speak to her interior minister."

Mendenhall went to the open window and pulled closed the old wooden shutters and then slid down the even older lead glass four-paned window. He turned and looked at the director and hoped he was thinking the same as himself.

"What are we going to do about getting the colonel out of that resort?"

Niles put his glasses on and then walked over to the dead fireplace and started placing pieces of wood inside. He stopped and his shoulders slumped.

"It looks like for now we have to depend on that Marko character to help Jack, Sarah, Pete, and Mr. Ryan." He shook his head and then angrily tossed the last piece of firewood into the dark hole.

"Yes, sir, but which side is he on exactly?" Mendenhall said as he only voiced the same doubt that Niles was thinking.

The lives of their friends depended on a band of Gypsies that should have died off over thirty-five hundred years before.

THE EDGE OF THE WORLD HOTEL AND RESORT CASINO, PATINAS, ROMANIA

Dmitri Zallas stood on the sixth-floor expanse of the loading platform with his arm around a dark-haired woman who obediently nodded a greeting to every lowlife that came to ride the cable car to the castle. Zallas was dressed to the nines in a black tuxedo and was dazzling with a bright red scarf wrapped around his thick neck. His cigar was smoking and he was beaming. The man next to him was not however. Colonel Avi Ben-Nevin stood silently in the new suit that had been purchased, after he had signed for it of course, and waited for the last of the guests to leave the casino. The last sixteen laughing and now ready to party guests stepped onto the ornate car where drinks were already being mixed by the car's bartenders. A man approached and looked around as the car was preparing to leave.

"He has arrived, Mr. Zallas," the man said and then gestured out the large geodesic dome that housed the atrium and the cable car barn.

Zallas smiled when he saw the approach of the old cars from the north. They made their way through the falling rain with little trouble. The Russian then removed the cigar from his mouth and smiled at the dark-haired woman next to him.

"My dear, I will join you at the castle shortly, I have immediate business to attend to."

The woman made a fake pouting face and then smiled and hopped onto the cable car, smashing the illusion that the girl had any class at all. Ben-Nevin shook his head as he waited. The doors slid closed and the car with its anticipatory guests started the long climb toward Dracula's Castle.

"Come, let's meet our royal highness," Zallas said as he himself almost bounded down the escalator to the spa and garden area where they would confront Marko Korvesky.

The eyes watched from a hidden corner of the darkened casino. The man had just returned from making his covert radio call to Tel Aviv. He saw the cars approaching the resort and knew it was the Gypsy, Marko. The man had also seen the armed men just outside the patio area earlier loading automatic weapons. He had counted over 135 hardened mercenaries.

Mossad agent Janos Vajic was now officially running out of time.

Ryan stood at the door and listened. He half turned and held up his hand and then just as quickly lowered it. He shook his head.

"It's no one. I thought I heard the keycard for a second."

"Give up, we were hoping they would bring us food and then we found the fully stocked refrigerator so there went that plan. They don't even need to check on us."

Ryan straightened from the door and looked at Pete Golding, who withered from his glare.

"Doc, they know we're something other than NATO inspectors, so they will be in to check on us just like the colonel said they would. Just be patient."

Golding flinched and then nodded that he understood. He turned and looked at Jack and Sarah, who sat silently at the small table and waited.

As they watched the lights flickered once more. It was the same flicker they had been noticing for the past three hours. They had finally learned it was the giant cable cars stopping and starting from their large barn. Jack took the fork and made another mark on the cloth napkin. Thus far he had made over twenty-one hash marks.

"Well, it's only a guess but the hotel should be near empty by now."

Ryan looked at Collins and then walked to the large window, which still sported the wolf-etched number 6. The cable car was now visible as it cleared the sixth-floor barn. He could see the ornate lighting inside illuminating the party-goers as they anticipated a great night at the grand opening of Dracula's Castle. Jason allowed his eyes to go to the swirling lights that came through clearly even on this stormy night. He turned and then walked back to the door.

"You think they've waited to do something about us until the hotel was empty of guests?" Sarah asked as she reached over and removed the fork Jack had been using to mark the number of times the northern-traveling cable car left the barn. She laid the fork down and took his hand.

"If not, this time will give us our best chance of busting out of this joint," Jack said with a wink.

Pete nodded his head feeling better every time the colonel explained things. It was between those moments that doubts started to creep in.

Once more Jason held up his hand and the room went silent. This time Jack stood from the table as he had heard the same thing Ryan had. There had been a definite thump coming from the hallway. Collins reached over and took the small kitchen knife he had lifted from the fancy kitchenette. He walked to the door and waited with Ryan. Pete just stood rooted to the center of the room. Another bump sounded and then the door cracked open an inch. Jason prepared himself.

The door swung open and a man fell backward through the opening. Then another limp body was thrown in the room on top of the first. Ryan stood ready but then relaxed when he saw Janos Vajic step into the room and then close the door. He kicked at the legs of the last man he had thrown inside and then looked at the astonished faces around him.

"Colonel Collins, may I suggest you and your people leave this place immediately," Vajic said as he quickly stepped to the double-paned window and looked out. He angrily shook his head as he looked around the suite.

"Mr. Vajic, do you mind telling us what is happening?" Sarah asked while Collins and Ryan looked out into the hallway before closing the door and facing the man that was not just a mere hotel owner.

The man they thought was Romanian walked over and took one of the suite's Queen Anne chairs and walked back to the window. He took a deep breath and then looked at the two men who had inched closer to him as he was walking to the window. He finally smiled.

"Colonel Collins, suffice it to say that we in the Mossad are not fools. Just because we cannot find out your current assignment or duty station, do not think for a moment we believe you would be relegated to a NATO fact-finding mission. Not with your reputation and record of military service. We would have found you out even if you hadn't told us your real name."

"Mossad? Is everyone we meet here in Mossad?" Ryan asked, now not trusting the man at all, especially after the way he and Mr. Everett had been treated in Rome by that particular organization.

"How about it, Mr. Vajic?" Jack asked, keeping the small knife handy in his right hand, which was not lost on Janos Vajic.

"The name is Janos Schumann, Captain, Mossad," he said as he kept his gaze on Jack's right hand as he half bowed in military courtesy. "Colonel, you must leave this place, we would hate to have an American Medal of Honor recipient killed when we take down this mountain. That wouldn't read too good in the newspapers."

Before Jack could respond to the cryptic threat delivered by the Mossad deep cover agent, the Israeli raised the chair and smashed through the first pane of glass. The two Americans jumped back as he raised the chair again and brought it into the second, much thicker glass, smashing through it until the chair went flying. The Israeli captain then bent at the waist to catch his breath as rain and wind started pouring in through the smashed window.

"Take the small ledge to the cable car barn. It's on the same floor. Then climb down and get out of here."

"We can't. We have people in the pass and we won't leave without getting them out."

"But you have to—"

"Save it, Captain, you heard what the colonel said, we're not leaving without our people," Ryan stated flatly as he confronted the Mossad agent.

Janos Schumann shook his head angrily and then wiped rainwater from his face. He came to a quick decision.

"You still have to go out this way, you have no choice," he said as he relented and faced Collins. "The only way to get to the pass is on the cable cars. The weather is turning bad and walking or driving without knowing the road is too dangerous."

"I would rather take my chances on the road," Ryan said, looking from Janos to Collins.

"That won't work. Zallas and Colonel Ben-Nevin have an army out there and throughout the hotel. They'll catch you and that would be that. I don't think they'll leave anyone behind to tell the tale after they find out what they have sitting right under their feet."

"You mean the treasure of the Exodus that sits inside the City of Moses?" Jack said before Janos could.

"Okay, Colonel, you seem to know a little more about my business than you should," Janos said menacingly.

"Touché, Captain. Now what is Zallas planning and what is his manpower disposition?" Jack asked as he tried to ease the tension in the room.

"He has well over a hundred armed men."

"Do you have a plan for that?"

"We have a strike team currently en route to Romania."

"The Sayeret will be here in a matter of hours, won't they?" Jack said as he remembered the alert Europa reported the Israeli army was under.

"Yes, they will bring down the temple and there will be nothing to stop them. They know they are expendable in pursuit of that goal."

"They're going to HALO jump through this storm?" Jack took another menacing step toward the man. He knew that if the Sayeret commandos were going to use a high altitude, low opening, or HALO, parachute jump, they meant some serious business. And Collins knew that business included his friends in the pass.

"Okay, we'll go out the window. But make no mistake, Captain Schumann, we are going to get our people out of that pass, and if I have to go through you and the best fighting soldiers in the world to do it, I will."

"And he can," an angry Ryan said, stepping close to the Israeli.

Janos looked at the two Americans and knew immediately that if something happened to the people in the pass because of something his men did he would surely see the sharp end of a long knife as Collins would keep his promise. Yes, Janos had indeed heard of the reputation of U.S. Army Colonel Jack Collins.

"And you allowed Zallas to murder Ms. Louvinski so you could keep your cover?" Sarah ventured.

"Gina was not only my friend, she was my partner on this mission for the past five years. I would easily have given my life for hers."

Ryan shook his head in wonder at the world he lived in. He now knew that no one was who they seemed.

"She was a good agent and I know she had wished to help you and your team, whoever you are. So, please, go get them out as we are fast running out of time."

With that Jack turned to Sarah and held out his hand and then looked at a soaking wet Pete Golding.

"Come on, Doc, let's go find out if Charlie is having as hard a time as we are with this crap," Collins said as he slapped Ryan on the back and pushed him toward the window and the brightly illuminated castle far beyond.

The grand opening of Dracula's Castle had started and Jack and the others wanted to be there.

Marko stood before Dmitri Zallas with his twelve burly men standing menacingly beside him. The Gypsies were dressed as they have been for the past two hundred years while living in the pass. The brightly colored clothes stood out starkly against the Russian's black tie and tux.

"I have been expecting you since this morning, Marko, what took you so long?"

"I am not here to play games with you, Slav."

At the word "Slav" Dmitri flinched but the smile remained. Ben-Nevin for his part smirked at the racial epithet thrown at the arrogant Russian by the Gypsy. The man at least had balls.

"I want the four Americans to be brought to me, my grandmother wishes for them to be her guests at the pass."

Zallas smiled wider and then looked at Ben-Nevin. The Russian then turned back to face Marko.

"Of course, anything for your grandmother, you know that. I will release them as long as I have assurances the Americans will not be allowed back onto resort property. Fair?"

"I'm not here to discuss what is fair, Zallas, I am giving you an order," Marko said and for emphasis his twelve men spread out just a little further while staring down Zallas and his men.

"An order promptly obeyed, old friend, I assure you," Zallas answered as his smile continued to irk Marko no end. But one thing was for sure, the smile never reached the Russian's eyes.

The appearance of twenty heavily armed men and then the loud report of a discharged weapon made Marko flinch. As he looked around one of his men was lying facedown in the mud pit where bathers had frolicked not three hours before. The man slowly sank into the hot surface and then vanished. Marko saw that he and his men were surrounded as he slowly turned back to face Zallas. The man was still smiling as Colonel Ben-Nevin had produced an old Colt .45 automatic. The gun was pointed at Marko's belly.

"I'll be the one giving the orders today," Zallas said as his men came forward and started disarming Marko's men of their small caliber guns and the obligatory arsenal of knives and other stabbing instruments Gypsies were fond of hiding on their person. One man struggled to get a man's hand off him and Zallas nodded and that man was executed with a large caliber bullet to the back of the head. Marko didn't turn to witness the murder as he was focused totally on Dmitri Zallas and Ben-Nevin. The dead man that had been used as an example was pushed off into the mud.

"Now what did you do that for?" Zallas said as he reached over and used a towel to wipe some imagined dirt from his hands. "You'll just have to dig him out of the mud later, think gentlemen, think." Zallas tossed the towel away, relit his cigar, and then looked at Marko Korvesky. "Now, as partners we must have a talk, Marko. It seems you have not been exactly forthcoming with me concerning the acquisition of the antiquities you have been delivering."

Marko refused to believe he had been fooled by this man, this idiot gangster. His grandmother had been right. He had brought this evil to the pass by selling their heritage. He wanted to be sick as he heard his men being pushed and shoved and slapped toward the hotel area. The desk clerks saw what was happening and ducked out of sight.

Dmitri watched Marko and knew the man would never reveal the location of the hidden temple, but Zallas had ways around that. He started to place a hand on the shoulder of the Gypsy but when he saw the black eyes look up at him he thought better of it and lowered his manicured hand and instead gestured toward the hotel.

"Come, Marko, this shouldn't take long. We just need to ask a few questions about the location of the treasure of the Exodus."

Marko managed to move his eyes to the one who had obviously fed the Russian the temple information—the tall man with the pencil-thin mustache was the obvious choice, as he was smirking at Marko and still pointing the gun at him. Marko then looked back at Zallas.

"I will kill every one of you for this," he said as he was pushed in the back toward the lobby.

"Yes, yes, I'm sure you will, but you have some talking to do first." This time Zallas did brave touching Marko on the shoulder as he was escorted out of the garden-spa area. "When I was a boy, it was explained to me by some very determined men of the Moscow police force the disadvantages of being a criminal in a closed society. I am a student of the techniques used back in the day and believe me, my friend, you and your men will end up telling us everything we want to know." Zallas slapped Marko on the back and stopped and watched as the Gypsy leader was led through the lobby to the elevator that would take him and his men down into the cavernous basement of the hotel where the screaming of Marko and his men would be lost in the immense spaces below.

"I do not want the Gypsy hurt or killed at this time, we may have need of him after all of this is over," he said without turning to face Ben-Nevin. "Are you sure you can break him your way?"

Zallas heard the chuckle of the Mossad agent but still didn't turn to face him.

"I will be at the castle," Zallas said as he adjusted the bright red silk scarf. "Assemble the men at midnight and we will then pay a visit to the pass."

"Do you not think this is a priority over your Castle Dracula's grand opening?" Ben-Nevin asked as Zallas moved off toward the escalator.

This time Zallas did stop and finally turn to face the Israeli.

"I have spent over $5 million on tonight just in entertainment and special effects for that club and I plan on bringing it in with what the Americans call a bang."

As Zallas smiled and walked away, Ben-Nevin was thinking the same thing. He had yet to inform Zallas just who it was that would be coming after them. If the Russian knew that he wouldn't be so cavalier about what was about to happen up in the pass. Ben-Nevin had no illusions that if somehow word got back to General Shamni that he was here, the Sayeret would explain it to Zallas and his men in no uncertain terms.

Ben-Nevin knew that Satan was in the air somewhere above the black storm clouds and he was coming their way.

Ryan was about to be the first to step out into the storm but Jack pulled on his arm until Jason was forced to hop from the sill of the large broken window.

"At ease, Mr. Ryan, I'll be going out first. If I happen to fall take the interior route and get Sarah and the doc out as best you can."

"I don't mind saying, Colonel, that maybe Captain Everett has a point."

"And what would that be, ol' wise one?" Collins asked, knowing he was about to be slammed for privilege of command authority. He wasn't disappointed.

"That maybe you should let us start sharing in these harebrained chances you seem to take." Ryan looked at Collins and the normal, joking smile was absent this time. "With all due respect, of course."

"Of course," Collins confirmed. "Still, I'll take this one. You go the way of our new Israeli Mossad agent friend and get these two the hell out of here. If not, join me on that three-inch ledge outside in a few minutes." Collins raised his brows until Ryan couldn't hold the colonel's gaze any longer. He nodded that he understood. Jack slapped Ryan on the shoulder. "Please don't be in a hurry to get killed, Mr. Ryan, there will be plenty of time for that in the near future, believe me." Jack hopped up on the sill and then looked back at Sarah. "You be careful, short stuff, this wind will blow you right to Oz."

"One fairy-tale land at a time, thank you," Sarah said but Jack had already stepped out onto the ledge and into the driving rainstorm. "Ass, Colonel." Sarah looked at Pete and stared him down until the computer expert looked away. Then she gestured to the doctor that perhaps he had better step out there and follow Jack.

Ryan watched as Jack stepped free of the room and started inching his way toward the distant cable car barn that looked like a domed stadium far ahead. He assisted Pete onto the slippery ledge and as Golding fought for a handhold against the falsity of the gray stone blocks, Ryan deftly reached out and slipped off Pete's horn-rimmed glasses and then placed them in his shirt pocket.

"What you can't see can't hurt ya, Doc."

Pete squeezed his eyes shut and then started inching his way along the three-inch ledge.

"After you, my dear," Jason said, bowing at Sarah.

Just before Sarah stepped onto the sill she looked at Ryan, who wasn't that much bigger than the diminutive lieutenant.

"You know, smart guy, since you're trying your best to scare the doc, you know how far it is to the ground, and I believe some hotshot jet ace doesn't have a parachute, does he?" she mocked and then deftly hopped onto the sill and started to walk along the ledge as she quickly caught up with a struggling Pete Golding.

Ryan had to smile at Sarah's quick-wittedness. He stepped up to the sill and then took a cursory glance down to the now rain-washed grounds of the resort. He shook his head two times quickly as he realized McIntire was right—it was a long way down.

The jail break was on.

When Ryan finally made it to the corner of the hotel he saw Collins squatting just over one of the large square windows that made up the partial geodesic dome of the cable car barn. Sarah was sitting on the roof talking softly to Golding, who was still embarrassed at having slowed them down so much. Ryan bypassed the two and advanced to Jack's location where he knelt beside the colonel.

"What have we got?" Ryan asked as he tried his best to turn his head away from the driving rain, which had threatened on more than one occasion to throw one of the four from the ledge on their trek across the sixth-floor ledge.

"We have one hell of a dandy-looking Russian getting ready to wow the world of entertainment."

"What?"

Jack turned and faced Ryan. "The Russian is getting ready to join his guests up in the castle."

"That means we have to wait until the castle car comes back?"

"We don't have that luxury," Jack said as he quickly came to a decision. "Well, we're all wet anyway, a little more water won't matter. Get the others and come on."

Ryan gestured for Sarah and Pete to follow, but by the time he looked back Collins had already threaded his way through the mass of piping and other hazards as he made for the top of the cable car. He waited as the other three caught up.

"Jack, I think you've lost your mind," Sarah said as she tried to catch her breath. Collins had to smile at the drowned rat look she was now sporting in her fancy dress. He shook his head at his private joke at McIntire's expense. "We can't ride the same car as Zallas!" she whispered with authority.

"I'm open to suggestions, people."

Pete managed to rise up enough to see over Ryan and the cable car beyond.

"Excuse me, Colonel, but how do we get inside without that Russian guy seeing us?"

"Come on, Doc," Ryan admonished just as Jack took off for the now moving car as it started its run for the castle. It had just cleared the interior area when Collins easily stepped onto the top. He turned and assisted Sarah on board and then at Ryan's urging, Pete. Jason was the last one on.

"Boy, and I thought we would have it easier than Mendenhall down here at the resort. I was sorely mistaken."

With Zallas below in warmth and comfort sipping champagne, the Event Group hitchhiked on top of the cable car with the lightning flashing around them.

Up ahead they saw the swirling spotlights that cast the castle in blue and purple through the driving rain.

They all realized at once the surreal situation they now found themselves in. Sarah smiled and looked at Jack, who was holding on to the cable pulley system that stood as high as a man. The wind picked up as the large car broke free of its enclosure and the four started getting pummeled by the storm.

"Are you thinking what I'm thinking, Colonel?" Sarah said as she tried to shield her face from the raindrops.

"I think I do. Here we are riding a cable car toward Dracula's Castle on a dark and stormy night in an attempt to save one of the Lost Tribes of Israel and a subspecies of wolf that had been mistaken for werewolves for three thousand years and then we have to pull our friends off a mountain that may or may not blow up in the next six hours. Did I leave anything out?" He grinned as the rain started becoming serious as they all hung on as the car swayed a bit.

"Yeah, you did leave something out," Sarah corrected.

"What's that?"

"That our duty, as the Event Group charter points out, is to discover just what in the hell is so important to the Jeddah and the Hebrews that they had to bury it two thousand miles away from their homeland, and whatever that is why are they are willing to destroy it so readily."

Jack smiled and then leaned closer to Sarah.

"I didn't want to use that many words."

Sarah just stared at Jack as the cable car carrying Dmitri Zallas made its way to the nightmare scene far above as Castle Dracula waited.

CASTLE DRACULA

The guests were seated for the most part as the wait staff filled glasses of complimentary champagne to the elite crowd of thieves and bankers, in this case the same profession. The waterfall curtain was a particular favorite as the crowd oohed and awed over the multicolored display of falling water drops that changed hue every few seconds to the sound of recorded rock music. It was now ten o'clock.

Backstage Drake Andrews sat in a chair as his manager went over his play list. His part of the show was still two hours off and Drake had sworn he wouldn't step foot out on the stage until the last minute. He had never felt as humiliated as he did on this rainy night in Romania. He heard loud laughter and he stepped to the curtain and looked.

"They actually have a white man dressed as Stevie Wonder? Oh, God, I'm going to be ruined."

As they watched the Russian group take their places, Drake felt a slight tremor under his fingers as he held on to the door jamb. He rolled his eyes at his warm-up band. The vibration started and then stopped. He looked at his hands and cursed his luck once more.

"The music hasn't even started yet and we're already getting the shakes out of this place."

PATINAS PASS

Niles had returned to the temple to retrieve Charlie Ellenshaw as he was sure the professor's questions were driving Anya insane.

As he made his way down the torch-lit steps Niles thought he heard something behind him. He stopped and listened but nothing moved. He only heard the sizzle of the oil-encrusted torches. He turned away and started back down the steps but stopped once more as he realized this time he was not alone. As he slowly looked up the reason why he hadn't seen anything behind him was due to the fact that the wolf was hanging upside down with its claws firmly dug into the rock stairwell. Mikla didn't move as its nose twitched, smelling Niles.

Compton couldn't help but moan under his breath. The Golia up close were the most frightening, most amazing creatures Compton had ever seen. If there was one thing that must come out of this unscathed it had to be these animals. In his opinion the Golia were the priority and once out of here he would try to make sure they always had a protected home—if he survived this current encounter that is.

Mikla whined deep in its throat and then released its right hand and brought it down to Niles's head. The long, articulate singers and claws wrapped around his skull like a normal-sized man would hold an apple. The beast seemed amazed that Niles had no hair on the top of his head. The animal then clicked a claw up against his glasses, producing a clack. Then it hit the glasses again until they went askew on Compton's face.

"Mikla, stop that! I swear your curiosity will get the best of you someday."

Niles knew it was Anya but he refused to turn that way as Mikla quickly withdrew his hand. The Golia barked once, twice, and then hopped free of the wall and then Niles heard the popping hip joints and the way the Golia arranged its skeletal frame to accommodate its amazing ability to walk upright. The Golia stood before Niles and cocked its head. The beast sniffed at Compton one last time and then reached out and with one, long, sharpened claw clicked his glasses one last time until they were sitting straight on the director's face and then the beast leaped to the wall and with the grace of a wall fly crawled up and into the darkness of the high reaches of the City of Moses.

"Thank you," Niles said as he wiped the cold sweat from his brow.

"Mikla never means any harm. Unlike Stanus, Mikla has the ability to see things differently. He's far more curious about humankind than is good for him. He has been the only Golia I have ever known to actually seek out a traveler." Anya stepped into the torch light. Charlie Ellenshaw was with her and they both looked up and into the darkened upper reaches but Mikla was gone. "My grandmother wishes for you to join her. She says we have little time to explain our history so that the Keeper of Secrets can place it into proper historical perspective."

"And just what does that mean?" Niles asked, looking up into the smiling face of Anya.

"She wants you to know why this place was selected by God for the Golia to live, and why this is the hiding place of the greatest discovery in the ancient world, and one that will vanish in just a few hours."

Niles straightened and then fixed the young woman with a look that said he still didn't fully understand.

"You will now see what it is you came here to see, Dr. Compton, and what it is that my grandmother and every ancestor of ours since the great Exodus has kept safe for over thirty-five hundred years here in these once forsaken mountains."

"And that is?" Niles persisted.

"Have you not wondered why this temple is named the way it is named, doctor?"

"The City of Moses?"

"Exactly," she said and then turned and went down into the bowels of the temple complex.

Niles looked at Charlie and then they both turned and followed in far more of a hurry than they intended.

The City of Moses was about to give up its ancient and devastating secret that some men in the world deemed important enough to kill an entire tribe over, and other men that were willing to destroy an entire historical heritage of that people for the mere threat of having their secret exposed to the world.

The Great Exodus was finally coming to a conclusion almost four thousand years after the fact.

FLIGHT 262, HEAVY COMMERCIAL AIRCRAFT, SQUAWKING FRIENDLY OVER ROMANIAN AIRSPACE

The Hercules C-130 bumped and ground its way through roiling clouds that sparked brightly with electric streaks of lightning that came close to striking the airframe of the American-built heavy transport. The plane bounced and tossed the men around inside the cavernous belly of the aircraft, which elicited a loud yahoo from the commandos as they tried to shake off the nerves of the impending HALO jump from the ramp of the Hercules.

Major Donny Mendohlson sat at the small navigator's table going over their flight path with the air force specialist. They had come to the conclusion that they couldn't make the jump as high as they initially wanted because of the high altitude of the storm—they would land at least two miles downwind if they jumped at 32,000 feet. They would have to chance it at half that.

"Any contact from Demetrius?" Mendohlson asked as he placed his map into a plastic-lined cover and then put it in his jacket pocket. He and his men were dressed in black Nomex and were self-equipped to handle most anything thrown at them—if they all made it down through this backbreaking storm. It would be a first for all of them.

"There has been nothing coming from either the south or the north of Romania since the storm hit. The authorities are reporting that they are having a hard time evacuating the populace from the low-lying areas of the Danube."

Major Mendohlson nodded his head as he zipped up his black body armor.

"Well, I guess they'll be far too busy to be concerned about one small relief flight straying off course a little, especially in the storm of the century."

"Get a flash priority one message off to Tel Aviv. Tell General Shamni that Operation Ramesses is a go." The major looked at his black-painted watch and pushed the small timer. "We HALO in five to eight minutes."

The call went out to Tel Aviv explaining that the world's fiercest killers were about to jump headfirst into the cauldron of swirling blackness and exploding electrical strikes to finally end centuries of cover-up.

The black-painted C-130 made a final turn and headed for the far peaks of the Carpathians.

A futuristic form of Pharaoh's once fierce and unbeatable chariots was heading the way of the Jeddah with the same intent as the once historical goal of the Egyptians—to make it all go away.

PATINAS PASS

Everett slowly sat up in bed and watched as Madam Korvesky was given a large injection of painkiller from a protesting Denise Gilliam. Carl just sat and listened as just moments before the Gypsy queen had been dreaming and shouting about the Golia. It was unclear what she had been trying to say when her eyes had sprung open and she sat straight up on the rickety cot. She awoke as she slowly blinked her eyes wide. She looked at Denise and that had been when the argument had started about the amount of morphine Denise thought appropriate.

Now Everett waited and watched as the old woman seemed to be in a deep trance of some kind. His eyes went to the doorway when Anya, Niles, and Charlie stepped in.

"She's been this way for the past five minutes," Everett said as he tossed the old Army blanket aside and then placed his feet on the floor and then started pulling on his boots. He was feeling much better after the energy-sapping ride with Stanus eight hours before.

Anya stepped to her grandmother and looked at Alice, who was still holding the woman's hand. Alice shook her head indicating that she didn't know what was happening. Anya whispered her grandmother's name and then ran a hand over her open eyes. They stayed staring straight ahead and never flinched.

"She's somewhere other than here," she said as she turned and watched Carl get dressed. "Are you rested enough to be getting up?"

"With the crap that's getting ready to come down I think Doc Ellenshaw may need some help, what do you think?" he asked as he was quickly becoming agitated with everyone's concern over his little trip with Stanus.

"I think so, yeah," Charlie said as he looked from Carl to the director.

Madam Korvesky blinked and then turned her head and looked at Alice. "They are coming for the treasure. They are coming now. They have Marko, but Marko is brave and strong. He will resist, but the men he thought were as strong as he will betray him, and then the Russian and the Israeli will come."

"They are coming to the City of Moses?" Anya asked as she tried to get her grandmother to lie back down but she resisted her efforts.

"We must gather the menfolk and hide the women and children, Pharaoh is upon us."

"Now is not the time to prove you're a mysterious Gypsy woman, Grand-mother, tell us what's happening," Anya said as Everett had to smile at her modern way of getting to the point. The old woman blinked again and looked at the much younger twin of herself sixty-five years before.

"Marko's men will break under the torture of an Israeli traitor."

"That damn Ben-Nevin," Anya hissed.

"Yes, that's the name I get, Ben-Nevin, a weak sort of name if you ask me. I believe he is the son of a man I once knew many years ago." The old woman tried to move her legs in order to stand up but Alice and Anya were much too fast and strong for her. They held her in place.

"Send the Keeper of Secrets to Patinas to rouse the men by ringing the village bell. Arm them, as we must hold the temple until help arrives."

"What are you talking about? What help?" Anya asked as she held her grand-mother at arm's length and looked at her.

"A very old and dear friend is coming." She finally looked at Anya and her smile grew and her features cleared up as if the drugs and the effects of her amputation had vanished. "You know deep down inside of whom I speak, don't you, girl-child?" Madam Korvesky turned her smile on Alice. "And so do you, do you not, Keeper of Secrets?"

Alice looked up at Niles and was worried that the old Gypsy queen had finally lost it.

"Come now, or should I ask Dr. Compton to explain it to you? I think he understands the situation."

All eyes turned to Niles, who had turned away and paced back to the doorway deep in thought.

"Mr. Director, you have something to say?" Everett asked as he struggled shakily to his feet tucking in his denim shirt.

"Yes, Alice should know whom she is referring to, as we have dealt with the man many times over the years; he just didn't know who we were." Niles turned and looked at the expectant eyes. "His name is General Addis Shamni, if I'm not mistaken."

The old woman cackled a funny-sounding laugh and then lay back down. "Yes," she said, "the Keeper of Secrets knows all."

Niles Compton ignored the statement and then walked back into the stone-walled room.

"No, not all, but I'm beginning to understand. General Shamni is head of the Israeli Mossad." He looked at Anya for confirmation, but her silence was enough for Compton. "He is responsible for young Anya here being husbanded through the system of Israeli intelligence until she was ready to assist in covering up all there was to know about the Jeddah. She was one of many such plants around the globe, I would suspect."

"I'm not following," Charlie said as he looked at the smiling old lady as she listened to Compton.

Niles fit one of the final pieces into place.

"What is the general to you?" he asked Madam Korvesky as Anya felt her heart go still at learning that her grandmother knew the general.

"He is my baby brother by twenty years," she said as she placed a weary arm over her eyes as she silently sobbed. "I have not seen Addie since 1947."

"Yes, that makes sense," Niles said, looking over at Anya. "You were working for your great-uncle the entire time you were in the Mossad." He turned back and looked at Madam Korvesky. "How long has the Israeli leadership known about the City of Moses and how long has a pact been in place to destroy what is here if discovered?"

Anya was so shaken that she stumbled and Carl reached out to steady her. She shook her head as she looked up into his face as if she was as lost as a small child.

"The home tribes have always known about the temple. Have since the time of Joshua. It was Joshua himself who sent us into the wilderness to hide what the world could never find. Men have searched and failed, sometimes they even made it to the mountain only to find the Golia there to greet them."

"Marcus Paleternus Tapio," Alice said as she looked over at Niles Compton as the old woman just confirmed that her research was spot-on.

"Yes, Mrs. Hamilton," Madam Korvesky said as she went to a place in her mind none of the others could see. She slowly blinked and then she once more looked at Alice and squeezed her hand. "Not only Rome, dear Mrs. Hamilton, but Troy, the armies of Alexander, the brutes of Genghis Khan, even that little thug Hitler was trying to kill us all for the secret of the temple, but not knowing like the others that the secret lay with only a few of the true Jeddah, not our kind that broke from the tribe hundreds of years ago. No, many have searched and some have found, but none ever lived to tell the tale, as they say." The smile was creepy to Charlie but he kept his mouth closed. The woman was enjoying laying her soul open for all to see.

"What are you protecting here?" Niles asked.

The old woman slowly sat up with the help of Denise and Alice.

"Girl-child, take them to the temple," Madam Korvesky said as she reached up to her neck and then pulled sharply on something and then held it out to Anya. It was a small but thick five-starred medallion. She blindly reached down and felt for her came. Denise saw what she was reaching for and picked up and handed it to her. The old woman held both items out to Anya. "Take them so they shall know the truth."

All four Americans exchanged apprehensive looks.

"Go, the truth awaits and shall explain all."

THE EDGE OF THE WORLD HOTEL AND RESORT CASINO, PATINAS, ROMANIA

The engineering section of the basement was large and very nearly empty as most of the supplies that maintenance would be using had yet to be delivered. The group of men stood in a circle around the central figure in the center of the room. The man was held up by a car winch and cable. His wrists were nearly severed due to the weight being placed upon the bone and sinew. Marko Korvesky was near death.

Colonel Ally Ben-Nevin used a small bottle of spring water and poured it into one hand and then tossed the empty plastic to one of Zallas's men. The colonel began to rub his hands together, washing free the blood. He accepted an embroidered Edge of the World towel and dried his hands. He then walked up to a shirtless Marko and placed the towel around his neck and then held on to its ends as he spoke. The man's long black hair was free and soaked through with perspiration. Nearly all of the Gypsy's teeth had been knocked out.

"Now you see what unpleasantness could have been avoided if you had only listened to reason?" he asked as he leaned in close to the broken man while pulling on the towel. "The location of the temple had already been disclosed by one of your men more than an hour ago. But still you would not speak to me. Now look at you."

Marko attempted to raise his head but his swollen eyes didn't know exactly where the Israeli was. The last vision he had was of his men being piled into the far corner of the engineering spaces after being executed one by one until the last man, a farmer not from Patinas, broke and told the torturers exactly where to find the hidden entrance to the temple and the City of Moses that sat beyond.

"Ah, you wish to say something to me now?" Ben-Nevin asked.

Marko attempted a smile, showing his broken teeth as he did so. Blood poured from the broken lips and gums. With a mighty effort the new king of the Gypsies spit in the Mossad agent's face. Ben-Nevin quickly stepped back and just as one of the Russian's men raised his weapon to dispatch Marko, the colonel stayed the barrel of the gun and shook his head as he swiped at the towel around the Gypsy's neck and wiped his face.

"Leave him to bleed out," he said with a calmness that made the Russian thugs respect the man from Tel Aviv far more than they had. They watched as Ben-Nevin grabbed the Gypsy's black hair and pulled him forward making the chains securing his wrists dig in that much deeper. "Be sure you hear this before you die, Gypsy—know that I will kill your entire family not because you insulted me, but because I was going to kill them and any Jeddah that get in my way anyway." With a harsh shake of the dying man's hair, Ben-Nevin turned and left the basement followed by all but one man.

Marko felt his head start to swim and the sounds he was hearing seemed distant and far off and that was when his addled brain realized that he was dying and this was what it felt like to do so. The scenario was not an unpleasant one for Marko because he had failed his people so miserably in trying to make their lives better than they had ever known. But now he knew he had been mistaken. The transformation should have been done over a period of years, not months. He knew he would never be able to tell his grandmother how wrong he had been.

The single thug left behind was whistling and for the oddest reason the whistling infuriated Marko. He tried to raise his head to see the man that was whistling and walking toward him but his swollen eyes refused to focus. Suddenly a loud bang sounded at the loading dock door. The sliding aluminum panel that made up the delivery entrance for engineering was fronted by a drive that actually sank into the ground whose road led to the loading dock that was hidden from view. It was this door that shook in its frame. The man, who was whistling and screwing a silencer onto a thirty-five-millimeter Glock pistol, stopped and looked at the still shaking door.

Marko Korvesky smiled a toothless grin as his head perked up at the sudden stillness of the man that had been left behind to ensure his last breaths were taken before dawn. The door was slammed again and a large dent appeared. Then again, and again. The man with the pistol stepped back and brought up the gun and aimed at the door. The sliding aluminum panel door didn't move.

Marko managed a laugh through his pain that froze the large Romanian thug's blood.

"The Big Bad Wolf is at the door, little piggy, oh, what to do?" He laughed again, this time louder as the man's eyes grew wider as a large hand slipped under the door and he saw the very long, very sharp claws thrash at empty space for a moment and then the fingers wrapped around the rubber weather stripping of the bottom edge and started to pull up. The door was locked in place at both ends so the force being exerted brought the center of the door up like a window blind being raised but with the shearing and grinding of aluminum against the steel door frame. The eyes of the man widened further when he saw what was standing on the other side of that door.

Marko was laughing hysterically and coughing up blood at the same time.

Stanus stood breathing hard and staring with its yellow glowing eyes at the man standing before it. The wolf's left arm was still holding the shattered door as it examined the men inside. The eyes moved from the frightened criminal to the chained and bleeding figure of Marko. The beast's eyes narrowed as it took in the bloodied condition of the king of the Jeddah. The muzzle opened wide and all thought about holding the door up left the animal as it roared and came forward toward the man, its long fingers curling in and out of fists. Its gait was two-legged and long. The beast roared a second time as it closed the gap. The arms swung back and forth as it came on.

The man attempted to raise the gun and just managed to do so as he fired prematurely. The bullet pinged off the concrete floor just as Stanus reached the man. The Golia rose to its full height and then reached out with its right hand and grabbed the man by the throat and raised him off the floor. He was taken by surprise so badly that all thought of the weapon left his mind and hand as the Romanian tore at the claws and strong fingers now suffocating the life from him. Stanus shook the man once until he heard the snap of the neck. The alpha male brought the mercenary close to its large snout and the beast leaned over and sniffed. Satisfied the man was dead, the Golia threw him against the far wall as it reached for Marko. The man cried out in pain as Stanus tried to free him. The wolf stepped back and whined as it bent at the waist and came to eye level with the Gypsy. The wolf sniffed once more and then growled in anger as it knew, unlike any animal ever created in the natural world, that the man was doomed. Stanus shook its massive head and roared as it raised its muzzle to the rafters of the basement. The roar was so long that it eventually turned into a sorrowful howl. The animal finally stopped and then the distinctive pops were heard as the beast dislocated its hips and then brought the bones free of the frontal socket, and then snapped into place on the back ones. The beast then curled the articulated fingers under and they formed a paw as it went to all four legs. The animal silently curled up in front of the dying Gypsy.

Marko didn't know how long he was out. When he opened his eyes he saw Stanus lying at his dangling feet, curled up and whining. It was the saddest sound Marko had ever heard and for the first time in his life he truly listened to the Golia. He realized then how much the two species—Jeddah and beast—meant to one another.

"No time for sadness, old friend," Marko struggled to say through his broken mouth. "I have one more thing for you to do," he said as blood continued to pour from his mouth. He knew his lungs were filling with blood ever as he spoke. "You must leave me now, brother," Marko said as his head dipped even lower as his strength ebbed.

Stanus whined and started walking in a circle and the cries were emphatic as the wolf knew that it would never see Marko again. Even with the distrust the wolf had of the Gypsy, the man was still loved by all Golia.

"Stand up, brother wolf. Stand up and take me into you for the last time. No potion, no magic to be said. Take me fully and allow me to make right that which I have broken."

The words trailed off as Stanus roared and shook his large head in anger. Then the beast hitched up and then stood in one smooth, very fast, and fluent motion. The alpha male was now face-to-face with Marko.

"One . . . last . . . time . . . old . . . friend . . . allow me . . . to run with . . . you." The words were so weak that Stanus leaned in and its ears perked up. Then the beast slowly brought its right hand up and placed the long fingers over Marko's head and the Golia pressed the claws into the thin skin. The pain was light and the connection was made for the last time, and for the only time in recent memory a Jeddah had chosen to die within the mind of a Golia.

Stanus soon released Marko and the beast staggered to the far wall as Marko's head hung down to his chest. The heart had nearly stilled the moment Stanus had made the connection. Marko was gone and only his broken body remained.

Stanus became still as its eyes once more narrowed to bright yellow slits. The Golia suddenly turned toward the door and its roar shook the building as Marko made Stanus aware of all that was happening.

Stanus took three large strides back to the damaged door and then started smashing the aluminum in with both of it balled-up fists as it worked the anger from its system. The door was battered to pieces in his frenzy and anger. Finally Stanus stood in the open doorway.

The howl was heard as far away as the pass. Will Mendenhall and the rest of the Airborne engineers stood in the driving rain and looked to the south.

At the same moment Marko's mind died inside of his battered and broken body, Madam Korvesky choked back a sob. It was a thick feeling around her heart and she couldn't help but think about Marko as a small child. The way he used to play with the Golia pups, Stanus and Mikla among them. Now he was leaving them and she knew they would never see the man-child alive again. As hard as the old woman tried to keep her emotions in check her heart was breaking for the boy who only wanted a better life for his backward people.

CASTLE DRACULA

Jason Ryan flinched and grit his teeth as the cable car rocked back and forth on the massive cables that hung four abreast over the heavy transport. The lightning was starting to make strikes along the ridge of mountaintop and every time one struck the earth Jason was amazed to see the night illuminated like day. The car slowly moved into the protection of the car barn that led to the old-fashioned-looking wooden dock. The car slowly pulled in and that was when they could all hear the thump of music coming from the club. The brightness of the heavy fluorescent lighting made Jack squint as he motioned for the others to follow him along the top of the car.

Collins soon spied the maintenance ladder and started to climb. The others quickly followed and not a moment too soon as the automatic doors on the cable car closed and then the car started moving backward to return to the hotel just as its twin started the opposite run to the castle. Pete came close to falling because of the heavy vibration of the pulley equipment and the electric motors driving the $27 million system. Pete steadied himself with a reassuring hand from Ryan, who was beneath him on the ladder and securing him with his strong right hand to Pete's ass.

Jack finally made it to a small platform that led to a catwalk which looked as if it led inside the castle. Jack looked at Sarah and her soaking-wet clothes and at Ryan and Pete, who looked even worse. Outside the storm started in earnest.

"It looks like the only way off the upper floors is through that door and we don't exactly know where that door leads or what's behind it."

"The way things are going and based on what sort of animals live around here, I'm betting that it's nothing good," Ryan said as he looked around to make sure they weren't being observed, as it would be a little hard to explain why four people are hanging out where only bats fear to tread.

Jack ran his fingers through his hair to straighten it a little.

"Oh yeah, that's much better, Jack," Sarah said with her eyebrows raised.

"Yeah, well you're no runway model at the moment either, missy," he said as he squeezed past her and made his way down the high catwalk to the wide door.

Jack closed his eyes as he pressed his ear to the door and listened. He heard the loud music but that was all. With a shake of his head he tried the steel door's knob. He was afraid it wasn't turning but realized that his hands were wet so he gripped harder and the knob turned and cracked open and Collins and the others stepped through.

As the door hissed closed on its hydraulic spring, a large hand shot out and caught the heavy gauge steel door before it closed. The black wolf wedged its fingers in the frame and kept the door from closing as it hopped down from the upper reaches of the catwalk cage. It had ripped a man-sized hole in the steel mesh screen and waited for Jack and the others to pass by. They were the same humans Stanus had seen earlier at the resort. The beast was curious as it took station in front of the door while standing on its hind legs.

Stanus flicked its large ears when the music assaulted him. The beast slowly opened the door and stepped through into Dracula's Castle, right behind an unsuspecting Jack, Sarah, Pete, and Ryan just as the large audience broke out in applause deep inside the nightclub.

Dmitri Zallas had arrived and Castle Dracula was truly getting ready to rock 'n' roll.

PATINAS PASS

Niles had called in Will Mendenhall and equipped him with the only weapon they had available and that was one of the small Uzis that had been taken from one of Anya's assailants. The other two were useless, as the only rounds they had left in their clip Everett had ordered placed into one weapon. The storm was getting worse by the minute and Will had reported that the villagers were starting to gather at the large abandoned barn that sat in the lee of the mountain for the small protection it afforded from the driving rain and smashing thunder.

As the group followed Anya away from the center of the stone temple, Niles saw that Carl was slowly regaining the strength he had lost during his spell with Stanus. He was now walking without the aid of Anya, who walked beside him anyway. Director Niles Compton had never seen the captain so comfortable around any woman other than the friends he worked with. He knew it had been a bad stretch for Carl over the past seven years since the loss of his fiancée, Lisa, and he knew Mr. Everett deserved to enjoy the friendship of a woman once more.

Niles waited for Charlie Ellenshaw, who was looking around like a schoolboy inside a circus tent. He marveled at the designs carved into the solid rock of the mountain. Beside Charlie was Alice, who had her arm through the crook of Ellenshaw's and they looked as if they were just a couple on a stroll through the most amazing park in the world. Niles saw the justification on Alice's face and he was happy for her. This one last chance to prove a theory had been a godsend and he was happy to have had Jack talk him into the Event—*If they made it out of there*, he thought. Denise Gilliam was in the stone enclosure looking after a weakening Madam Korvesky, who had seemed to wither away faster than before right in front of their eyes after crying for no reason that Anya or the others could see.

Anya walked past the twenty-five-foot-high double wooden doors that were set deep into the stone wall of the largest chamber. Niles had thought that was the area she had been taking them to but saw now that their destination was far beyond what was visible inside the temple. He watched as Anya walked up to a seemingly impenetrable stone wall. She reached over and dislodged a torch that had seen better days. She held the weak flame to the wall to allow her visitors to see the design that had been carved by one of the master stonecutters of the ancient world. It was a beveled, deep-cut image of the Eye of Ra. Anya lowered the torch and raised the five-pointed star that was still attached to her grandmother's chain and then placed it against the image of the most famous eye in the history of deities. The bronze five-pointed star was pressed into its twin facsimile in the stone. A depression formed and then Anya turned the star until there was an audible click that echoed in the small enclosed area of the temple.

"A key," Will Mendenhall said when he turned to see what the Gypsy woman was doing. He had been watching the area above them where he kept hearing the rustling of something running around.

"Yes, part of one anyway," Anya said as she raised her grandmother's cane and then deftly snapped the handle free of the old wood. "Sorry, Grandmamma, I don't have the time to be gentle," she said as she placed the handle with the image of the eye molded in its center against the stone and again pressed until the handle turned and sank into the stone. Anya turned the handle with her hand to the right and then released it and stepped back. "Watch out, this may not have been opened in a while and I don't know how much thermal pressure has built up."

Before Niles and Charlie had a chance to ask, a wide seam opened up in the stone as a false facing of solid rock separated from the wall. The square was about twenty feet by twenty feet and now stood separate from the wall by five inches. Steam escaped from the precise cut of the hidden doorway. The hissing continued and steadily grew louder until the Americans had to cover their ears from the piercing noise. A loud crack sounded and steam blasted from the cuts in the stone and then du amazing thing happened: the wall rolled forward and then swung open with a blast of vented steam. Beyond the darkened doorway it was dark and hot.

"That is the most amazing piece of engineering I have ever seen in my life," Niles said as he examined the technology necessary to get such a precise cut in the stone so as to seal it against pressurized steam. He shook his head in wonder.

"Yes, the Jeddah had the best master builders Ramesses could supply. One of the spoils of Egypt so many have talked about," Anya said as she took the torch and with her arm through Mr. Everett's she stepped through the doorway and into the darkness beyond. "Please come through but be careful not to step any further than the torch light can reach."

Niles and the others stepped through the barrier of heat and rising steam. The temperature had to be hovering above 120 degrees. When Anya could see everyone in the weak light of the torch she lay the burning wood against a wall trough filled with kerosene. The flame caught and traveled the two square miles of hidden points where a large flame caught and illuminated the interior. As the view below them came into stark reality, Anya tossed the dying torch away and stepped to the ledge. She smiled and gestured for them to see what it was they came to Romania to see.

As they stepped cautiously to the ledge, Alice took in a sharp intake of air as the view came into focus. Stretched out before them was a city the likes of which no one had seen since the time of the Pharaohs. These were not carved replicas like the ones inside the temple, the buildings were stone blocks and the statues real. The colors caught them off guard. The monuments were painted in bright whites and stark reds and blues. The reptiles that stretched above and wrapped around the city must have taken a hundred years to carve. The pyramids were not like the small ones in the temple. The three stone structures were three hundred feet high and looked out of the small city like sentinels watching their young.

"My God," Niles said as Carl Everett whistled.

The city was an exact replica in every detail of an Egyptian city. The buildings were not the same in number as a larger population would have, but they were exact and they had been built by the very same hands that had constructed the ancient Egyptian cities of Thebes, Memphis, Ra-Ramesses, and Luxor.

There were six giant stone lions with the heads of bearded men that guarded the largest structure other than the three pyramids. The depictions were a cross between an Egyptian sphinx and a Hebrew with a long and curling beard.

The columned building was built into the far end of the mountain and had fifteen large stone steps leading through the hundred columns. The giant statue of Anubis stood guard in front of the lions, only this time the Event Group had no illusions as to what the giant black statue represented—the Golia. The wolf head topped a headdress of red and blue and green and other colors that were so bright as to be celebratory. The gasps that came from the astonished Americans were just as Anya expected.

"Welcome to the real City of Moses, the Law Giver."

CASTLE DRACULA

Jack Collins was stumped as how to get to the lower levels of the castle without being observed. They had to find a back way out to get to the road that traveled along the mountain. They needed to get to Patinas and get Niles and their people the hell out of there. He knew he was pressing and not thinking clearly in his anxiety to get out. They were on a main catwalk that supported the lighting system for the club. Sarah, Pete, and Ryan were staying as low as they could, expecting a lighting technician to come upon them at any moment. Pete was listening to the music below and nodding his head.

"These guys aren't that bad," Pete said as he heard the refrains of "Mustang Sally" coming from the stage.

"I hate to agree with the doc, but he's right, they are good," Ryan said, looking at Sarah, who was shaking her head.

"If you two fans of the truly weird are done, I think this is the way out."

Ryan frowned as he hadn't realized Collins could hear his opinion.

As they moved they were amazed at the decor even in the uppermost sections of the castle. There was everything from shields of old to long wooden banquet tables filled with exotic food lined the club. The expense of building and outfitting the castle had to have been tremendous.

Jack saw what he had spied a moment ago. It was a small vent exposed to the fresh air outside. Jack saw that the fan that would be placed over the vent for exhaust purposes had yet to be installed and that would be their exit point. As he moved he saw that the catwalk ended and the top floor opened up into a medieval balcony. Collins hadn't seen the gap earlier. He shook his head as he saw no one near so he stepped off the catwalk and onto the rug that ran the length of the balcony. The others eased themselves down and followed Collins to the vent. Jack immediately went to prying it open. He finally managed to free it from its frame and they were all immediately hit by rain as it pummeled them through the opening. Jack nodded his head.

"Well, we were soaked anyway, let's go."

As they stepped free of the castle they realized they were on the north wall and it was only a short step down onto the rocks that led to the trail below.

"That was just a little too easy," Ryan said.

"Look," Pete said as he was pointing down onto the road they were soon to be upon.

As they looked a line of vehicles wound its way past the castle and then continued toward the north. The drivers didn't seem to fear the massive streams of water that was now washing out the very edges of the dirt road. The sixteen four-wheel-drive vehicles moved steadily toward the pass.

"Damn it, they're not wasting any time. That's Colonel Ben-Nevin and his assault force," Jack said as he wiped at the rain running down his face. Lightning rent the night sky and Sarah saw the look of near defeat in Jack's eyes. It only became worse from there.

"Move and that will be the last thing you ever do," came the heavily accented English voice. The sound was emanating from the mouth of one of Dmitri Zallas's personal bodyguards.

Jack turned and saw that they were surrounded by ten men in heavy weather gear.

"Mr. Zallas expected you would be along sometime tonight. Only he expected you to make a little better time." The men laughed as they kept their weapons pointed.

"Yeah, well, you try riding on top of that cable car and see how fleet of foot you are after braving that storm, asshole," Ryan said as he recognized that one of the men was the very same thug he and Pete had the run-in with.

"Yes, I'm sure it is a thrilling ride. Unfortunately the situation here in Patinas has changed and Mr. Zallas can no longer guarantee your safety because of the severity of the storm," the man said as he smiled and gestured with the gun for them to move back into the castle. "We cannot have NATO representatives sliding off one of our more rugged roads and dying in a most horrible accident."

"Yeah, that would be a tragedy especially with our bodies riddled with bullets," Jack said just as he realized they could not be taken back inside. He was going to have to do something stupid so the others could have a chance.

Jack turned around just before he came to the steel door and that was when he saw the wolf jump from the top of one of the castle's parapets. The leap was a good thirty feet and the beast landed with a heavy thud, which got the attention of their captors; only it was far too late for them to react as Stanus waded into the men tearing and slashing at skin and bone. It was like the beast was possessed as it killed every man that stood on the castle wall. The Golia roared in triumph as the last man fell to the stone floor as rain washed the blood and gore quickly away. Stanus looked from the slaughtered men strewn about like so much roadkill and then focused its attention on Jack and the others, who stood frozen in shock at the sudden turn of events.

"Oh, shit, that thing does not look happy," Jason said as he took a step back from the heavily breathing animal. His eyes traveled to the curved claws that moved as the animal clicked them together. None of them could look away from the blood as it slowly dripped from the purplish-looking eight-inch claws.

Jack eased toward the far wall and the trail just below it but Stanus growled and stepped forward to block his move. Ryan tried the same maneuver but the beast growled again and then moved to block him.

"I don't think it wants us going that way," Sarah said as she watched Stanus narrow its yellow glowing eyes.

Finally Stanus growled loud and jumped to the opposite wall and then, with one last look back at Collins, leaped over the stone parapet. Jack and the others ran to the wall and saw that there was another smaller trail on that side and it led to the mountain and then vanished into nothing.

"Look!" Pete said pointing through the rain.

As everyone turned their eyes toward where Pete was pointing, a large bolt of lightning streaked across the blackened sky. As the ground illuminated into a bizarre landscape of shadows and things that were blacker than evil itself, they saw Stanus vanish into a large fissure in the side of the mountain. They watched and waited but the wolf never returned.

"Well, I guess we'll go with the Golia's plan," Jack said as he eased himself over the wall and then started to follow Stanus into the heart of the mountain.

"I never thought I would be taking orders from a large dog," Ryan said as he leaped to the top of the wall and looked down and then smiled and looked at Sarah McIntire. "But I've woken up with a few," he laughed and then disappeared over the side.

FLIGHT 262, HEAVY COMMERCIAL AIRCRAFT, SQUAWKING FRIENDLY OVER ROMANIAN AIRSPACE

The C-130 Hercules transport circled on station alternately climbing to 28,000 feet to raise and lower the aircraft over the roughest of the storm front. Thus far they had done everything but declare an emergency in order to be able to hold station as close to the HALO point as possible.

"Otopeni Tower, this is Israeli Civilian Heavy 262, our inertial navigation system is still a little screwy, we'll need another few minutes to get it straightened out before we turn for the south, over."

Israeli Army Major Donny Mendohlson stood between the pilot's and copilot's seats and listened. He adjusted the headphones so he could hear the irritated response of the Romanian air traffic controller from Bucharest.

"Israeli 262 Heavy, continue orbiting at current altitude and speed, report any change in situation, and remain off the air until a disposition of your emergency can be determined. Over."

"Thank you, Otopeni Tower, this is Israeli 262 Heavy, out." The air force pilot half turned and looked at the major. "They don't seem too happy, but we should have a few extra minutes, as they're in no hurry to deal with us. At the moment they have over two hundred commercial flights and then the extra flights added on for the flood relief effort. But soon enough someone's going to get suspicious in Bucharest and then we may get a close-up of those brand-new F-16 Falcons the Romanians just bought from the Yanks."

"What do you figure?" Mendohlson asked.

"Maybe thirty minutes before we have those all-weather fighters on our asses, no more. After that we have to head south or risk a Sidewinder up our tail ramp."

The major patted the pilot on the shoulder. "That will have to do. We go in no more than thirty."

As the major made his way below he saw his sixty-two men of the elite force. They were busy checking the three-minute oxygen supply it would take for the jump. Two of those minutes were added for security reasons, but the air should be sufficient to get them to the ground, in what kind of shape after a HALO jump in what amounted to hurricane force winds no one could say. He knew this jump would kill some of his men and he knew that was what was expected of them.

In less than thirty minutes the far-off land of Transylvania was about to be invaded by the new and vastly improved Hebrew army.

PATINAS

The expanse of the City of Moses was the most impressive sight any of them had ever laid eyes on. As they examined the city they saw the young Golia playing in the massive temple structure that was the actual vault of secrets for the Hebrew tribe. Golia were everywhere and they cared not one ounce that the City of Moses had come alive with light and the strange voices of men.

Anya took Carl's hand and started down the steep ramp that led into the city. Everywhere they looked steam vents of massive proportions were spread throughout the buildings. Everett squeezed Anya's hand as they neared the bottom of the ramp and for the first time the Americans stepped out and back into history. The city could have been a miniature version of Luxor. The lions with the heads of long-lost bearded men and the statues of Anubis that they now knew had nothing at all to do with the furry little creatures thought to have been Jackals—they now knew they were the Golia. And everywhere there were the Golia pups. Everett lost track at trying to count them.

As they approached the many columned temple Alice realized that the first temple was nothing more than a ruse to keep trespassers at bay just in case someone found their way in. Security for the complex was as straightforward as a sword point. They knew who kept watch on this place and they were running and playing around them right at that moment. Anya started to climb the stone steps.

Niles walked next to Alice, who was in between him and Charlie. Will Mendenhall brought up the back and kept his eyes on the ramp behind them. Will was starting to feel that something wasn't right.

"Wait, stop!" Mendenhall said as he raised a hand and then looked around him. "Do you feel that?" he asked as his hand and arm slowly lowered.

They all did. As they walked the steps leading to the temple the entire city wavered and shook. The sensation of movement ceased but it worried them nonetheless.

"I have never felt that before," Anya said as she squeezed Everett's hand tighter. She shook her head and then smiled at Carl, who could not take his eyes off the woman with the raven hair and the blue head scarf. She finally turned and walked to the giant bronze doors and stood waiting.

Alice was in her element. After all the years of waiting, searching, and arguing with Garrison Lee over the temple and the very tribe's existence was almost too much for her. She was nearly stomping her feet in her effort to see the actual treasure of the Exodus spread out before her eyes.

"King Tut ain't got nothin' on this," Charlie said as the double bronze doors were opened wide.

"The true treasure of the Exodus," Anya said as she stepped aside and allowed the Americans to pass into history.

The sight that met them was one they would never forget.

The fissure in the mountain wall behind Dracula's Castle was a tight fit, but Jack thought if the wolf could make it through they could too. A mile in he thought he had figured wrong.

"Jack, this crack in the world is a little too straight to be a natural phenomenon. It's tight, but look at its lines. This fissure was excavated."

The fit was so tight Collins couldn't turn his body to respond.

"Your point, Lieutenant?" he asked in frustration.

Before he could get an answer in the darkness around them he felt the grip as it wrapped around his throat and he was pulled forward and thrown into open space.

"Colonel?" he heard Ryan say as if from a great distance.

Collins shook his head as something heavy landed next to him. He felt around and then discovered someone had thrown an unlit torch onto the floor. He heard the others as they squeezed through the last large crack and into the open space. A hard breeze took Sarah's hair and pulled it back toward the tunnel.

"There's quite a draft in here," she said as she placed her arms out in front of her to keep from bashing into a wall.

"No one move—not one inch," they heard Collins say as a brilliant flash of light illuminated the small cave they were in. The torch caught and then Jack fanned out the entire book of matches he had used to start the flame burning. As he brought the torch around it almost came into contact with a solid object that stood directly in front of him.

"Oh, crap, he's big," Ryan said in amazement.

Stanus stood in front of Jack and the giant Golia was sniffing at him as if the smell of Jack was a reminder to the beast that the man he had traveling with him earlier was close to this human. It sniffed the air and Stanus knew this to be true about all four of the humans inside the cavern. The animal went to all fours with an audible adjustment to its skeletal frame and confidently strolled over to Ellenshaw, Sarah, and Ryan. The beast was eye-level with the Navy man and taller than Sarah. Charlie was the only one tall enough to see over the wolf's shoulders. Sarah slowly brought her hand up so Stanus could sniff her. Jack froze, wondering if she had lost her mind.

Instead of sniffing at Sarah's hand, Stanus sat hard on his haunches and then brought his right front paw up and then the fingers unfolded before her eyes. The fingers reached out and the large humanlike hand stroked Sarah's face as gently as any lover could have. Then the Golia blinked and walked to something the torchlight had failed to show them a moment before. Stanus jumped eight feet from his sitting position and landed on something round and black. Jack's eyes widened as he stepped forward with the torch flickering and sputtering.

"Oh, my God," Sarah said as she recognized what it was that Stanus was pacing alongside of as the Golia watched the four humans below. The earth had been taken from around the structure leaving it totally exposed to the air. The giant steel anchor pin was one of sixteen that secured the foundation of the castle to the rock strata of the mountain. The giant anchor pin ended with a drill bit that had dug its way into the almost solid stone of the pass. Steam vents had weakened the area around the pin and it had been easy to dig out the rest.

"What is it?" Pete asked as he placed his hand on the cold steel.

"It's one of the sixteen anchor pins used to secure the castle to the mountain. If the other fifteen are like this we have just discovered where that strange vibration was coming from. It's not the steam or the natural hot springs bringing this seismic activity, it's them," she said as she pointed upward in the darkness.

Above them and joining Stanus on the top of the steel anchor pin was the remainder of the Golia adults. Even Mikla was there sitting on his haunches looking at the visitors.

"I think this big guy is trying to tell us something," Jack said as he placed the torch next to the area of the cave where the pin had penetrated. "Look at this, short stuff; it's just like you described when you saw the engineering specs and the geology report."

Sarah placed a hand on the pin and felt it not only moving up and down but it actually felt as if the steel was attempting to back out of the hole that it had forced open in the mountain like a knife wound.

"These thermal vents have weakened the strata of the mountain, making it almost porous. Thus it's very weak and any geologist worth his salt would have seen that on his initial survey."

"Unless that geologist had access to Zallas and his millions."

Sarah had to admit that Jack was right. Through bribery this mad Russian had doomed at least part of the mountain, namely the pass at Patinas.

"I'm not following," Pete said as he too saw the giant cracks in the rock as the pin passed through.

"Look, Pete," Sarah started to explain as she removed the torch from Jack's hand and then placed it by the pin and lowered it to the bottom where fresh dirt had been piled along the fissures floor. "The pin has nothing to bind itself to. It's like shoving a sharpened knife through a cracker, no matter how sharp that knife is it will eventually compromise that cracker and it will break. The same thing here," she said as she ran the torch along the lines of the pin. "The constant pressure of the castle being secured by these pins to the facing of the mountain wall is bringing too much pressure to bear on the sixteen anchor pins holding the building in place. And now our little amazing animals here have been undermining the locations where the pins were most secure."

"What are you saying?" Pete asked as his mind started to grasp what the Golia's plan was.

"They're bringing Dracula's Castle down, and possibly the entire resort below it."

"No animal could possibly figure out the displacement dynamics involved," Pete said, envious of the computing power that the brain that thought that scenario up had inside. He shook his head in wonder.

"Maybe for the Golia alone, but I suspect that the first strike of the wolves against their intruders to the mountain was thought up by something other than a smart wolf."

"Madam Korvesky?" Sarah asked.

"That would be my guess, as I don't think that Marko character had it in him to think this up."

"On the other hand, I never thought it took too much explanation for the reasons why a dog digs," Ryan said as the simple truth of the matter always hit him in the most easily describable ways. "Maybe the Golia just didn't like these ugly steel pins in their mountain and they are trying to dig them out. I would rather believe that than think that a rather large timber wolf could outthink me on a battlefield."

Jack smiled and looked at the young Navy man. "From what I've heard from Alice, these damn wolves seemed to have amassed a reputation for being just that, great warriors and tacticians. I'm leaning toward collaboration between the Jeddah and the Golia to stop this encroachment by destroying the only thing they can."

"But an engineering failure on that scale would bring far too much attention to this area of the world for the Jeddah to cover up," Sarah reminded Jack.

"Not if their plan was to destroy the entire pass," Jack said as he realized the Jeddah and the Golia may be giving up their home of over thirty-five hundred years. The end for both may be near.

Above them they heard the Golia move off with the clicking of their claws on the steel pin. Jack took the torch from Sarah and then pointed it down the long anchor pin and saw that the dirt and rocks had been moved away from the steel by at least five feet in all directions. The anchor pin was basically suspended in mid-air with no support. And as they watched, the massive steel pin moved up and then down a good five feet. The movement of the pin was getting worse and to

Jack's horror he saw that the pin had backed out of the mountain by at least three inches since they had been standing there.

"Let's get to Patinas and get everyone the hell off this mountain."

They all followed Jack as he squeezed past the opening between the exposed anchor pin and the side of the mountain. Now it was a long clear run to the pass.

As they ran the mountain shook beneath them as the anchor pin in another area slid further away from its support. The mountain was now dying from a knife wound through its heart.

PATINAS PASS

Sergeant Jimmy Forester watched the line of vehicles approaching and was wondering what fools would brave that horrible dirt track at night and in the middle of the storm of the century. He leaned forward and pushed open the wooden shutters of Madam Korvesky's house. As he watched the line of cars approach the village he was wondering where the Army officer was. For whatever reason the engineer felt better when the officer was giving orders. And that was hard to admit for an Airborne soldier such as himself. But still, this mountain was not conducive to positive thinking.

Suddenly bells were heard clanging from every corner of Patinas. Lights were coming on in every home as doors flew open and men, women, and children started streaming forth in various stages of undress. Men were carrying shotguns and the women their children. They were running toward the gate and the mountain beyond. The sergeant ran to the door and opened it just as one of the Patinas village elders stepped onto the small porch.

"We must go to the temple, immediately, bring what weapons you have and that shotgun over the mantel. I believe the queen has shells in her kitchen," the white-bearded man said as he pulled on the camouflage jacket of the American. "Bring your people, now!" the man said in very bad English as he turned and ran.

"Jeez, I don't know about you, Sarge, but when the local populace starts heading for the hills and until we know who these assholes are it might be wise to do the same. From the frightened looks on the faces of those men and women I would bet they're not very welcome here, whoever they are."

The sergeant knew his man was right. He looked down at the two nearly empty Uzis and knew they had not much firepower to make a stand there.

"Right, let's boogie," the sergeant said as the sixteen men of the 82nd gathered up their equipment. The lone shotgun and its shells was packed and even a large meat cleaver and butcher knife from the old Gypsy's kitchen. The men retreated from the shelter of the small cottage and joined the exodus out of Patinas just as the first cars made the village.

Colonel Ally Ben-Nevin stepped from the large Toyota four-by-four and examined the small village of Patinas. He watched as his men fanned out around the town. The men were each heavily armed with a brand-new AK-47 supplied by Zallas and his people in Bucharest where the men were hired.

"Check every house. Bring along whoever you find. They may make our task easier if we have them."

He looked up at the swirling night sky and the almost constant streaks of lightning that crisscrossed the heavens. He was feeling better than he had at any time in the past few years. The storm was so bad not even the great General Shamni could get a relief force in here. He knew he would have the run of the mountain for the next few critical hours until he gathered the proof his superiors needed for their fundamentalist movement. No, there would be no cavalry riding over the hill to save the day. Not this time.

FLIGHT 262, HEAVY COMMERCIAL AIRCRAFT, SQUAWKING FRIENDLY OVER ROMANIAN AIRSPACE

"That's it, Major, we've been made," the pilot said as he struggled with the yoke as the Hercules jumped a hundred feet into the roiling storm.

"What's up?" Major Donny Mendohlson asked as he came forward.

"We have two F-16s out of the Ploesti region and they are heading right for us. They're not buying the navigation screwup any longer. We have to exit out of Romanian airspace ASAP before they get a visual on us. They won't take too kindly at seeing an Israeli air force Hercules instead of the Airbus they were expecting."

"Yeah, I can see where that would be kind of bad."

The major turned and went to the communication shack just aft of the cockpit. He nodded at the operator as he gestured down to his men by waving his right hand in a circular motion. The silent team of professionals went about finalizing their jump preparations. The radio operator, who also served as their jump master, handed Mendohlson a pair of earphones.

"The signal is secure through our satellite," the operator said as the major nodded.

"Seti, this is Broadsword, do you read? Over."

"Broadsword, this is Seti the Great, read you five by five," came the clear and encrypted voice of General Shamni.

"Seti, it is time to play or get out of the park, some rather nasty-looking local bullies have arrived by air," the major said as he told Shamni that the Romanian air force had decided to pay them a visit. He spoke cryptically out of habit and he knew the general would do the same. Nothing is ever secure enough for the elite forces of the state.

The general knew that no matter what occurred down in Patinas he had to have eyes on the ground and a decision had to be made whether to jump. To him that was the simplest thing in the world and an order he wanted to give since learning about this nightmare as a child.

"Understood, Broadsword, you are clear to commence Operation Ramesses, I repeat, you are clear to launch operation Ramesses. Over."

Mendohlson swallowed and then without turning from the radio raised his right arm into the air and his thumb went high. The men below moved like lightning as the go order was now official.

"Roger, Seti the Great, Broadsword confirms, Operation Ramesses is a go."

"Good luck, Broadsword, end this thing," came the weary voice of General Shamni.

Sounding through the cavernous aircraft was a loud warning bell and the lights inside switched to dull red in preparation of the ramp being opened to the harsh elements outside. Each man had a full face mask and supply of oxygen. Each was also equipped with 190 pounds of extra gear, but mostly killing tools of the trade. They never jumped into a situation they felt they had no hope of escaping, it may be delusional but psychologically it was helpful.

In exactly two minutes the sovereign state of Romania, America's newest NATO partner, was about to be invaded by a friendly nation and they were coming to kill a legend.

The ancient City of Moses had an hour to live.

PATINAS PASS

The giant room that was illuminated with a thousand oil lamps was brightly inlaid with gold leaf on the walls instead of the normal paint used on most of the statuary. The ancient story the hieroglyphs told was related in stark gold relief and the highlights trimmed in emeralds, rubies, and diamonds. The depictions of the Exodus were there.

The treasure room was just that. It was what Alice Hamilton always envisioned. With one altering factor—there was no treasure. The room was completely empty with the only exception being three wooden boxes the size of coffins that sat on carved stone pedestals.

Niles looked at Alice, who had a look of confusion on her face. She looked at Anya, who was whispering something to Carl Everett.

"Anya said she is ashamed and embarrassed. She knew you would be disappointed," Carl said for the woman who had wandered away and sat next to the center stone. She took a deep breath and waited for the laughter at what a foolish people she lived among.

"Disappointed?" Alice asked. She separated herself from Niles and walked up to Anya and stood before her. "My dear, what in the world do you think we came to see? We're here because of the mystery of your people and a story that must be documented, but written so the truth of your kind can be placed beside those of the rest of civilization. Not for any treasure."

"I don't mean to be the material one here, but just out of curiosity, there is gold and jewels all over this chamber, so where is the rest of it?" Will Mendenhall asked as his fingers slid lightly over a diamond the size of a dove's egg that had been expertly embedded into the wall.

Anya finally laughed out loud and only Carl smiled with her.

"This *is* the treasure of the Exodus, Lieutenant. All the spoils of Egypt."

Carl laughed as did Niles and Alice. Charlie looked from face to face and joined in the laughter simply because he was amused to see them all actually lose it. Only Mendenhall looked distressed.

"The real spoils of war were farming tools, animals; mundane things that we think were everyday items but that they thought of as riches. Grain, water, food—all of the things of normal life were the real spoils—the reward for hundreds of years of near servitude. These small things were all that there was of any avarice from the two lands of Upper and Lower Egypt."

"I suspect the real treasure and the need for secrecy is right there, isn't it?" Alice said as she placed a hand on the first ancient wooden box and ran her fingers along its worn top.

"My grandmother told me the story of your meeting, Mrs. Hamilton; she said she believed you to be the rare woman to understand what the Jeddah were about, and all from that one brief meeting in Hong Kong."

"Your grandmother wasn't only beautiful, but perceptive, young lady," Alice said in appreciation.

Anya smiled in return and then allowed Everett to assist her to her feet. She locked eyes with Alice and then hugged her. "Now you will know why the world and especially our own people in Israel can never know about this place," she whispered into Alice's ear.

Mendenhall, Charlie, Niles, and even Everett jumped when Anya suddenly and unexpectedly slid the top of the box off until it crashed to the floor. Without looking inside Anya walked away into the shadows cast by the flickering torches.

Alice watched the young woman leave and then her eyes went to the contents of the box and then she gasped. She had expected to see something of immense religious value, perhaps even the lost Ark of the Covenant, but what she saw amazed and frightened her. It was a mummified corpse. The wrappings were rotted and most had peeled away thousands of years before, exposing leathery remains that had petrified due to the conditions inside the buried temple.

As the others stepped up to view the mummy inside, Anya turned suddenly and walked to the left-side box and pushed that cover away until it hit the stone flooring. Then she repeated it with the third box and then, looking tired, Anya went toward the far wall and waited for the questions that would follow.

Alice looked toward the high ceiling of ornate wood and stone and went deep into thought.

"What is it, Alice?" Niles asked but it was Charlie who smiled and knew what she was going to say.

"Moses climbed Mount Nebo from the plains of Moab to the top of Pisgah, across from Jericho. There God showed him the whole land and said unto Moses, 'This is the land I promised on oath to Abraham, Isaac, and Jacob when I said, "I will give it to your descendants. I have let you see it with your eyes, Moses, but you will not cross over into it." And Moses the servant of the LORD died there in Moab.'"

"The Book of Moses?" Niles asked, lacking a little in his Bible studies of late.

"Deuteronomy," Alice said as she stared into the center-most wooden box. "It also says in the Bible that Moses was buried by the Lord and the place of his burial was kept secret from all men. After the death of Moses, his body became the focus of a battle between Michael the Archangel and the devil but that's all mired in controversy, isn't it, Anya?"

"Yes, the legend states that at some point Moses was resurrected by the Lord of Hosts and brought to heaven. That was what all of Israel was told by Joshua. His divinity was intact even after death. It was the first of many—"

"Cover-ups," Alice finished for her.

"I understand you Americans are uncommonly attached to that word, but maybe fudging the truth is a better phrase."

"Wait, I'm not getting this. If there's no treasure, why build all of this?" Will Mendenhall asked.

"To house the body of the greatest Hebrew of all time, and also a man that served the court of Ramesses II," Alice said as her eyes went to the center-most mummy with the simple cloth blanket of reds and blacks lying across the bulk of it. "Anya, he's your direct ancestor, would you explain to Lieutenant Mendenhall who this is?"

Anya walked up to Will and then smiled at his naïveté.

"The Egyptian name of this man was Munius, which the Torah translates into Hebrew as Moshe. But he was also known by no fewer than ten other names in his time of power, both Egyptian might and Hebrew might. He could be called Yered, Avigdor, Chever, and seven other names that are as equally unpronounceable."

Alice smiled and then put an arm around Mendenhall.

"Hard to take it all in isn't it, Will?" she asked.

"You mean to say that this is—"

Anya cut him off by standing and talking as she stood by the second wooden box.

"And this is the body of Joseph, the man responsible for Israel's bondage into Egypt." She walked past the second box to the third. "This is Joshua, whose body my ancestor Kale stole from the people not long after his death to be hidden with his brother and mentor."

Will Mendenhall just realized what it was they were saying to him as he looked back into the box with the small five-foot mummy lying inside. Alice chuckled and looked at the stunned lieutenant.

"Say hello to the Prophet Moses, Will."

Crazy Charlie Ellenshaw placed the U.C. Berkeley 1969 stamp of approval on the discovery.

"Now *that* is far out!"

Colonel Ben-Nevin watched as the men completed the sweep of the village and he saw that not one of the locals had been found. This was a little unnerving as he would have thought to catch them unawares at this time of night. He gestured angrily for the men to move toward the gate and the mountain that sat waiting for them to rape it. He was about to move when a pair of headlights crossed the path of his men. He squinted into the bright lights made far eerier because of the sideways rain that pelted them. He cursed when he saw it was a black Mercedes SUV and then the man that was being assisted out of the backseat became recognizable. The man was wearing a full-length wool overcoat and was dressed in a black tuxedo. The cigar was blazing as Zallas stepped into the raging storm. Ben-Nevin angrily approached.

"I thought we had agreed to allow me to recover the treasure. You were not to be here."

Zallas removed the cigar from his mouth and saw that the rain had killed it cold and then angrily tossed it into the flowing water that was quickly becoming a lake.

"Yes, plans change. I was content to sit it out and wait for my reward, but that luxury changed when ten of my men were slaughtered down at the castle while trying to detain the not so innocent Americans. It was a god-awful mess and an insult to me personally and I'm here to see that the people responsible for it pay dearly, NATO be damned." Zallas flinched and ducked when a close strike of lightning sent a small tingle of electricity through their shoes.

Ben-Nevin saw that it would be no use in arguing with the idiot so instead he turned and made for the hidden passage to the City of Moses and its treasure rooms.

19

PATINAS PASS

The first gunshots echoed off the stone walls of the large staircase. The first few rounds were fired blindly at the fleeing villagers as they scrambled down the stairs in a mad flight to escape the unknown attackers. Two of the 82nd Airborne sergeants and three of the locals took up station at the first large bend in the staircase.

The two Uzis in the hands of the engineers would be useless in just twelve shots apiece. Besides, combat engineers were excellent shots with a regular M-16 or 14, but an Uzi? They fully expected to be wiped out in a matter of seconds. The sergeants both looked at the ancient long doubled-barreled nine-gauge shotguns held by the three bearded Gypsy farmers and then they looked away, not very confident of their rearguard action to protect the villagers. The Americans figured since they didn't know who was who in this case they would stick with the families that had fed and sheltered them. Besides they actually liked the Gypsy clan for no other reason than they treated them as family. Yes, when in doubt just be a good guy.

The first man to breach the wide corner was startled to see the bearded men along with two uniformed men waiting for them. His eyes widened in startled wakefulness as the first Gypsy standing over one over the sergeants fired not just one, but both barrels into the man's chest sending him flying backward into the stone wall where blood and gore splattered in a wide arch.

The Gypsy cackled as he broke the nine-gauge open and tossed the still smoking shells onto the floor and then easily pushed in two more.

"I think you enjoyed that too much, cowboy," the sergeant said as another blast of the shotgun silenced him.

One more man went down as the second Gypsy in line had opened up on the intruders.

The second sergeant fired the Uzi and bullets sprayed everywhere but where he had aimed.

"Damn it!" the man shouted at his poor accuracy.

The third Gypsy farmer said something loudly as he stepped around the sergeant, obviously cursing his poor aim, and fired his shotgun. The pellets struck another of Ben-Nevin's men, spinning him backward. Then the old man suddenly grabbed his face and went down. The bullet hole was clean and precisely in the center of his head.

The first sheep man checked his friend and then angrily stood and discharged both barrels into the stairwell. Then he yelled something Romanian and turned to the Americans.

"We run now," he said and then took off. The Americans exchanged startled looks and then followed suit, running as fast as their feet could carry them down the long flight of stairs.

Jack heard the gunfire coming from somewhere ahead. In the darkness of the trench that had been dug by the Golia he could barely discern the walls much less the end of the excavation. The walls had closed in so tight he had been forced to extinguish the torch, as it was in danger of choking them all to death.

"Uh, oh, it sounds like someone may have company," Ryan said from his position at the rear of the line.

"Damn it, Jack, Alice and Niles are in there!" Sarah said as she inadvertently tried to push Jack faster than was able to go.

"Hey, hey, if you push any more we're going to get ourselves wedged in here," Collins said as he tried to move faster

Suddenly he broke into an open space and he saw a light in the distance. As he stepped forward in the darkness he just hoped he wasn't heading for a precipice he couldn't see.

"Colonel, I don't think we're alone in here," said Pete Golding as he too stepped into the open space.

"Yeah, well let's not wait around until we get surprised by something else that comes straight from a nightmare," Jack said as he grabbed Sarah's hand and moved down the passage toward the light.

As Jack neared the light he saw that it was just a round hole and it looked recently dug. He smelled the ripe richness of the dirt and knew that the Golia had been hard at work in the temple. Collins eased his head out and saw that he was in a large room with three boxes and golden depictions of Egyptian or some other deities in relief on the walls. Jack eased out of the hole and then helped Sarah. Outside the enclosure the gunfire continued, sporadically at first and then a thunderous exchange. Collins released Sarah's hand and then pulled the stolen nine-millimeter from his wet and muddy pants. He waited for Ryan and Pete to do the same.

"You have the extra weapons we took off those wonderful people?" he asked as he handed one of the Glocks to Sarah, who charged the weapon and then looked at the colonel.

Ryan took the lead as was fast becoming his custom under Jack's training. The gunfire started again and then the sound of men shouting in Romanian and then in another unknown language. Ryan peeked out of the column doorway just as several women and children broke from a large empty stairwell toward a city the likes of which Ryan had never imagined was possible to build. As they all watched the small group was covered from a location they couldn't see from their vantage point. The group of villagers made it to cover as one last running circle of men broke from the high stairwell and headed down a ramp toward the strange city below. Ryan and Jack saw three other men break into the open and they were firing down at the running men before them.

Jack looked to the right at whoever had been covering the women and children, but whoever that was was not covering this group. Perhaps they were out of ammunition.

"Cover fire, Mr. Ryan," he said calmly as he trained the front sight of his nine-millimeter on the second group and fired. Ryan opened up at the same time. Bullets struck the three men almost simultaneously and they went down, one even sliding on the ramp so far that he went right off the edge two hundred feet down to the stone floor. The first three men made it to the bottom of the ramp and then broke through the opening and into the city, running for the far cover where the others had vanished.

"Let's go," Jack said as he headed to the right taking cover as far as he could along the columned temple. He made it to the end and then saw the huddled masses of the villagers and then he saw Niles, Mendenhall, Everett, and Charlie Ellenshaw as they hunkered low along the trim lines of the smallest of the three pyramids. It looked as though they had empty weapons lying beside them and were now holding the most ancient shotguns he had ever seen. He shook his head and broke cover.

Collins didn't make it three steps with the others close behind when the entire upper gallery above them came alive with gunfire. Bullets struck every inch of the city as close to 120 automatic weapons opened up at once. Jack waited and then pushed the others ahead of them until they had cover behind the first pyramid.

"That was close," Jason said as he ejected the clip of his Glock and made sure there were still rounds inside before slipping it back in. "But I have to admit to not minding shooting those bastards for what they did to Gina."

"Yeah, I reckon they have some killing coming their way for that," Jack said as he straightened and looked around as the gunfire eased off to nothing. He then sprinted to the next pyramid and then finally to the third where he slid in next to Captain Everett. Ryan and Pete hurried and took up position next to Will and Charlie Ellenshaw.

"Have a good time at the resort?" Carl asked Jack as he broke open an ancient-looking cardboard box of shotgun shells and spread them on the ground for easy access.

Collins shook his head. "You bet, we were just in the mud spa as you can see," Jack said as he tossed Everett one of the extra Glocks.

"Liar, I know for a fact that you were locked up inside a rather nice hotel room with hot food and a wet bar. What was that room, the Dr. Frankenstein Suite?"

"I think you're going have to explain to me how you pulled that one off, Captain," Jack said as the truth of what they saw at the hotel was just confirmed by Everett himself.

"Nah, it's a SEAL thing, Jack," Carl said and then raised the Glock to take aim at the men who were again starting to filter out onto the gallery ledge.

Charlie Ellenshaw was sitting and making sure the assailants weren't getting ready to charge the city when he turned away from his view of the gallery long enough to look at Pete Golding.

"So you're all done partying at the resort and thought you would finally go to work?" he asked in a nonjoking manner.

"If you knew what we have been through, Charles, you would not be looking so smug. Do you know there are werewolves out there?"

"Really, just wait until you see what's in here, I fairly think that you will shit yourself, Dr. Golding."

Stanus was the last of the Golia to leave the temple. The young were all safe and secure five miles from the pass and well out of harm's way. Stanus had even snarled and bit until every adult was safe and well away from the temple on this night of nights. The long-laid plans of the Jeddah and Golia were now coming to fruition and although the great animal could not connect the intricacies of the scheme, it knew that Madam Korvesky's plan was the only hope for the wolf-kind. Now remained only Mikla, the younger sibling of Stanus, who was the last to enter the cave system that the Golia had discovered many centuries before and kept the location secret even from the Gypsy queen.

Mikla was on all fours as it would have been considered a challenge if Mikla confronted Stanus on two legs. Mikla was paying his brother the respect due, but he was refusing to join the other Golia in hiding inside the caves. Mikla whined and then took a tentative step toward Stanus, who held his ground but made no aggressive move to stop the now fully healed and rested Mikla. Soon the two giant wolves were nose-to-nose and it was Stanus who moved his yellow eyes to his brother and then for the first time in both the Golia's long lives they connected as leaders of the pack. Stanus was letting Mikla know that he respected the way Mikla had traveled with the old one, and for saving the life of the young princess. Stanus snorted and then dipped his head and playfully slapped its near twin along the jawline. Mikla jumped up and then brought both paws down onto the back of Stanus and then the two wolves rolled on the floor as other Golia watched the strange exhibition between the brothers from the safety of the cave.

Stanus stopped playing in the mud and rain and then the large alpha slowly untwined himself from his younger brother. With one last look back at the caves where the clan of Golia was now hidden, Stanus and Mikla broke away at full speed toward the temple shaking the ground as their eight-hundred-pound bodies came into contact with the earth.

The hour of the werewolf was close at hand.

Outside on the main road a lone figure stepped into the falling rain and ventured a look up into the swirling storm. Janos Vajic was dressed in black Nomex and carried a submachine gun strapped across his back. He saw that no one was near the village of Patinas and just hoped the wind and the rain allowed the drop to happen without getting anyone killed. He quickly set up the tripod that had been strapped to his back and then placed a small black box in a slot at the top. He raised a small compartment lid and dialed in a series of coordinates. Soon a bright green laser light shot straight into the sky and then the beam adjusted itself as it vanished into the clouds. As he watched, the laser beam started to move back and forth at ever increasing speed. It formed a fanlike illusion as it vanished into the storm. The laser was creating a cone for the HALO jumpers to follow if and when the beam broke free of the swirling mass of clouds.

The laser system was only the backup for their GPS system each man carried on his arm as he flew at breakneck speed through the air toward the ground at over four hundred miles per hour.

As Janos watched he heard a pop that sounded loud even over the crash of thunder. Then he saw the first chute as it broke clear of the clouds only two hundred feet above his head. The man braced himself and then slammed into the road and then rolled as he tried to break his momentum. Then he slipped and fell face-first into the mud.

"That was bloody graceful," cursed the first man down as Janos ran to assist him with his chute and harness. As he did the now familiar loud pops of deploying canopies sounded overhead as the rest of the Ramesses strike team made it through the storm.

Major Donny Mendohlson shrugged out of the heavy gear and then tossed his oxygen system on the discarded equipment.

"Sergeant Major, gather the gear and destroy it, please," he said as he made sure his weapon was ready to fire. He looked up when Janos Vajic stepped up to him and nodded.

"I take it you're Demetrius?" the major asked as he waved his men into position making sure that light discipline was maintained.

"Actually I'm Captain—"

"Please, let's keep this on a first-name basis, my first name is 'don't ask.' That way," he looked over at Janos and smiled widely, "we can remain friends."

"Did you bring *everything*?" Janos asked.

The young major quickly looked at his watch and then replaced his gloves.

"If the air force is worth a damn at navigation we should be getting a letter from home right about now," he said as he pointed toward the sky.

Janos looked from the raging storm to the young commando. Then he heard the last loud pop of the night and saw the small bright red parachute as it broke cloud cover and landed squarely in the center of town where it was quickly wrestled into submission before the storm could snatch the parachute away. Lord only knew what route it took to get here from the C-130 and then because of all of the GPS math involved in figuring air currents and wind shear he was amazed the package had arrived at all.

The major shrugged his shoulders.

"Air force navigation is great, their timing is for shit," he quipped, embarrassed.

Vajic watched as the commando moved quickly to get his men into the temple complex.

Operation Ramesses was on the ground and hell itself had landed just a few seconds after.

Jack knew it was going to end fast. He was down to four rounds and they had managed to knock off less than 10 percent of the attacking force. The men Zallas had may have been thugs and brutes but either they were some of the bravest men he had ever seen or it was due to the fact that they were all terrified of facing Zallas.

"We just may be in some serious trouble here, Jack," Everett said as he ejected his last full clip.

"You are the master of understatement, Captain. And why do you keep looking back at that girl, you and she have another gunfight or something?" Jack asked as he took aim and fired. He nodded his head, satisfied when he heard one of the thugs yelp and then fall.

"Or something," Carl said with a smile that Jack didn't miss. He tilted his head and then returned to his work.

Madam Korvesky was feeling no pain as Denise had loaded her up on morphine when the men from the village had broken in and taken her, table and all, away into the City of Moses.

Alice Hamilton was still at her side as the firefight raged around them. Bullets pinged and ricocheted off the stone monuments and the noise made the children scream as they huddled around their mothers as their fathers and older brothers and sisters battled the men from the world. The men were fighting with everything they had. The women fought also with shotguns and slingshots and not a few thrown rocks from the teenage Gypsy clan of Jeddah. Alice watched as the history of these people unfolded before her. Like the American Indian of the past they were now fighting for existence. She was actually proud as they came together as one and fought. She knew that Madam Korvesky had ordered Stanus not to take part. That he should lead his clan to his safe place and not return to the valley—ever.

"It looks like the men are running out of ammunition," Alice said and then was shocked when she saw a smiling Madam Korvesky holding a good-sized meat cleaver in her right hand that she had hidden under the blanket she was covered in.

"I'll hold them off until help arrives, as the old films say." She laughed and then looked at Alice and her eyes were so dilated that Alice was worried Denise had been so angry at the amputation that she intentionally overdosed the ornery and very perceptive Gypsy queen. Alice reached out and lowered the cleaver but didn't try to take it from her. After all, she may need it. "I'm glad you chose to join us here on our little mountain, Mrs. Hamilton." Madam Korvesky slowly deflated. "You did see the magnificence of the Golia, didn't you, Mrs. Hamilton?" she asked as her eyes seemed to plead with Alice to understand the thing she had done by sending the Golia away from here forever.

"They, like the Jeddah, will always live, I swear to you that I'll use all of my considerable influence to see that this comes to pass as a gift from me to you, just a thank-you for protecting such a species and guiding them through history until they could live amongst themselves and be free of all men. No, old friend, it was time to call it a day."

"Yes, we will call it a day." Madam Korvesky closed her eyes and as she went under knew that at least one person understood what it was she had done.

A shot hit one of the lower blocks that made up the smaller left pyramid and then slammed into the left dress shoe of Jason Ryan. The bullet had hit so close that it tore the rubber heel from the low-cut designer shoe.

"Damn it, I signed for these shoes!" Ryan said and then fired two quick shots in the direction of his shoe assassin.

Mendenhall rolled over and lay in the prone position next to Jason and then fired two rounds of his own into the upper entrance to the city, once more knocking not just one but two of the attackers down onto the ramp.

"Kind of like ducks in a shooting gallery, huh?" Will quipped just as five large-caliber rounds struck the large blocks of stone, forcing Mendenhall to curl up into a fetal position.

"Yeah, only these ducks shoot back in case you haven't noticed," Ryan answered, loving the fact that their attackers' timing could not have been better to silence the cocky Mendenhall.

"Yeah, well, that pair of shoes you have to pay for serves you right for getting the cushy job at the resort while we're roughing it out here in the damn wilderness being attacked and chased by everything from wolves to Hansel and Gretel."

"I hate to break this up, but how many rounds do you girls have left?" Jack asked as he flung away the last empty clip. Will reached into his pocket and tossed Collins his last clip of ammunition. "Now if you ladies care to stop your bickering for a few minutes I have an idea. By the way, did you see that ass Ben-Nevin after the fighting started?"

Both Ryan and Mendenhall shook their heads as Jack slid by the two and made his way toward the back of the city wall that encompassed the entire area. As he passed, Will gave Ryan a dirty look and then both men followed the colonel.

As the Sayeret paused just outside the area the map told the major the entrance would be, he still placed his men until the entrance could be confirmed. The emptiness of Patinas had foretold danger ahead. Major Mendohlson pulled the waterproof card from his pocket and then a compass. The tritium-faced dial told him he was right in front of the giant rock screen that camouflaged the entrance.

"Okay, from here on out your fire is free, let's move, gentlemen, and—"

That was as far as the major got in ordering his advance into the temple. It seemed the entire facing of the mountain erupted in fire as the ambush was set loose upon them. Major Mendohlson could not believe he had walked blindly into an unknown force and been caught off guard. His arrogance had proved disastrous.

His men took cover and started to return fire. From here on out his men would need no direction from the major or even their team leaders as each man knew his job and each also knew what was expected of him.

Major Mendohlson lowered himself to the muddy road and then crawled to a ditch that lined it. He tried to raise his head to see through his night-vision goggles what they were facing but a streak of lightning hit close by and forced the commando to jerk the night-vision glass from his head.

"Damn," he hissed and then brought his scoped M-14 carbine up to his eye and quickly scanned the area before him hoping to see what they were up against in the muzzle flares of the weapons arrayed against his team. Lightning helped at the last second and the view made Mendohlson roll onto his back and curse. He had counted at least fifty or sixty weapons up ahead at the entrance to the temple. He closed his eyes and let the rain wash over his face as he desperately tried to think.

Before he could throw his arm over his eyes a bright flash of an aerial flare burst overhead and Mendohlson again rolled over onto his stomach to take advantage of the illumination. The light cast shadows that moved everything in front of them as if all bushes and trees were attacking enemy.

"Cease fire . . . cease fire!" came a voice through a bullhorn.

Major Mendohlson scanned the area but saw no one. He waited.

"I am now speaking with the leader of the Sayeret strike team currently breaking Israeli law by attacking a foreign nation," the voice said in English, so only the major could understand the lie.

"Oh, man, that's good," the major said as he waited.

"I am now speaking on behalf of the Israeli Knesset; you have been ordered here illegally and must cease this unlawful incursion. Lay down your arms and the Romanian authorities will take you and your men into custody for return to Israel. You will not be harmed."

The unit's sergeant major slid to a stop beside Donny Mendohlson.

"Whoever that is up there has the gift of bullshit," he said as he waited for his commander to say something.

"I think I know who's delivering that bullshit," the major said as he leaned forward and then eased his head up hoping the rain kept him hidden well enough from the inevitable snipers he knew to be out there. "We came for the grand opening of the resort."

"I know you are Sayeret. I've seen your alert orders. This operation is illegal and will bring the most dire of—"

Mendohlson opened up on full automatic, sending twenty rounds of heavy-caliber slugs into the facing of the giant rock screen. He looked over at his sergeant and then smiled.

"That is one irritating voice," he said and then rose up again and fired until he was empty. His men took the cue and a raucous fire erupted that slammed the mountain and created bright flashes as bullets bounced from stone and tree.

Jack stopped his trek long enough to explain to Everett and Anya what he was thinking. Anya thought he was on to something. Then something caught everyone's attention. There was additional gunfire coming from outside the city. The firefight was distant and only a military-trained ear could discern the gunfire through the thunder that shook the entire mountain.

"I think the bad guys have company," Jack said as his eyes locked with Anya's. Carl looked at her also with a raised brow.

"Something you might want to share?" he asked, knowing the look she was wearing was one that said indeed she knew something.

"I think my grandmother and my former employer may have some hard explaining to do," she said as she raised her head to see what was happening but the ramp leading to the outer temple was too far away and the entrance even further.

"Try again, Ms. Korvesky," Jack insisted. "We're all ears."

"I think the Mossad has sent us help, well, maybe help, or maybe someone else who will try to destroy the temple complex, and maybe kill us also. With General Shamni and his friend the prime minister you never know. Those men may be the Sayeret."

"That's what I thought," Collins said as he lowered his silhouette and then thought. "We had a report from the CIA that the Sayeret had been placed on alert, now I guess we know why."

"They're not here to rescue anyone, are they?" Everett asked, hoping Anya would tell them the truth.

"No, they are here to destroy the mine. But I didn't know for sure until tonight. It was my grandmother and General Shamni, my boss in Mossad. The time has come that Israel will no longer tolerate those bodies being there. They must vanish forever."

"But why?" Carl asked, not understanding her at all.

"Because the fundamentalist movement taking root inside Israel could possibly upset the peace process that is now gaining momentum, isn't that right, Anya?" Alice Hamilton put in as she and Niles lowered themselves next to the three. The gunfire was starting to pick up once more.

"Explain," Jack asked Alice as she smiled at Anya, indicating that what was happening was understood, at least by Alice and Niles Compton.

"The prime minister," Alice explained, "does not need a civil war over whose religion is the right one. Those bodies, if proven to be who the Jeddah say they are, would ignite a fundamentalist war against the men and women who want this hostility stopped, not reignited over ancient history. All because Moses was nothing but a man and that makes the cover-up of three and a half thousand years ago a major problem for religion in general when all anyone has to see is the fact that no matter how you look at Moses he had divine help. The Golia? Indeed. God— well, who created the Golia but nature and that has always been God. But that explanation is never simple enough. Moses was a man who spoke with God and now a man that became a myth that we have to hide simply because people cannot grasp the simple fact that the story of the Exodus while true has many more complicated facets than meets the eye, or even the biblical text."

"Yes," Anya said as he smiled and nodded at Alice. "Mrs. Hamilton is exactly right."

"Surprise, surprise," Charlie Ellenshaw said.

"The temple and the City of Moses will cease to exist after tonight."

Jack shook his head. "Not if what we're hearing outside is that relief force you're talking about, because it sounds like they ran into an ambush," Collins said as he saw more and more men easing themselves down the ramp and the villagers and Americans had little or no ammunition left. "There has to be another way out of here," Jack said as he looked around him at the frightened faces of the women and children as their menfolk started filtering back after their meager defense had failed. The men tried to comfort the children as best they could. Collins could see that most of the men had abandoned their empty shotguns for large knives and pitchforks. Collins shook his head, knowing what he was seeing was insane. He couldn't allow these people to be hurt because someone thought there was a vast treasure inside.

"Hey, remember this afternoon, Captain?" Ellenshaw said as he took Carl by the arm. "The barn, Stanus?"

"How do the Golia get into the village—is there an unseen entrance to the temple above the barn?" Everett asked Anya.

"I don't know. Was Stanus above the barn?"

"He could have only have come from the mountain, the village was so full of revelers trying to see you that a wolf that size could come close to the barn only one way."

"From the mountain," Anya confirmed.

"We have to find that exit, it's going to be the only way out of here." Jack turned and suggested heading south behind the giant stone lions with the heads of bearded men. "That's the only way it could be," Collins said as he waited for confirmation that his guess was best.

"I have never seen the Golia back there."

"From what I understand the Golia have been doing a lot of things lately the Jeddah know nothing of." Sarah reminded everyone of the anchor pins they had been undermining for the past year.

"Okay, gather the families and keep them tight. Get some men and get Madam Korvesky moving. We go until the temple won't let us travel anymore." Jack looked at Will and Jason. Before he could say anything Charlie and Pete stepped up and squatted next to Ryan and Mendenhall as if to tell Jack that their orders were their own. Ryan was proud of the two super-nerds but this was no place for the two professors.

"You two give us as long as you can. Then get the hell out, don't be heroes and die here," Jack said as he looked at Ellenshaw and Golding. "They only have two weapons with ammunition, so get moving and help with those kids and older people."

"But, Colonel, we can—" Pete started to say.

"Did you men hear the colonel?" Everett nearly shouted to scare them into listening. "Obey orders and get these people out of here."

"Yes, sir," both men said and then hurried in a crouch to assist the women and children as the entire village of Patinas started to move away into the darkness.

"Good luck, you two," Jack said as he moved off. Everett nodded his head at Ryan and Mendenhall and Anya smiled. Alice Hamilton hurriedly kissed both men on the cheek and then Niles Compton tilted his head and shook it as if to say he'd skip the kiss on the cheek. Instead he nodded and then left. He knew his people realized he cared for each and every man and woman inside his complex—but kissing them good-bye was a line drawn in the sand.

The newest exodus of the Lost Tribe of Israel known as the Jeddah was off in search of a safe haven once more.

Major Donny Mendohlson knew he would have to take a chance as he saw several of the ambushers move away from the camouflaged opening to the temple and disappear to their rear somewhere.

"Do you see what I see?" the sergeant major asked as he squinted through his scope.

"Yes, they've been moving off in twos and threes for the past five minutes. They're weakening their core defense by trying to flank us. That has to be a Mossad agent leading these idiots."

The sergeant major laughed at the running joke that the Sayeret had with their intelligence service, just as American soldiers usually had very little good to say about the CIA.

"Okay, you and I are it. We have to get into that temple and place this bad boy," he said as his gloved hand tapped the aluminum case that housed a small piece of the sun. The rain was still coming down in torrents as the major signaled for the remainder of his men to give them covering fire to the left of the entrance as they would try and flank the right and enter the temple complex on their own.

"And what do we do after we get inside and find out we're outnumbered a hundred to one?" the sergeant major asked.

"Well, with our bodies riddled with foreign bullets we will do our duty and kill them all, or blow up the temple around us and them."

"Sounds like a plan to me," said the old veteran of almost every conflict Israel had been involved in the past ten years, "except for the part where we die."

"Goes with the territory, Sergeant Major, it goes with the territory."

The hand signal was given and every weapon they had opened up on full automatic.

The final assault on the City of Moses had started.

Colonel Ben-Nevin ducked just as the fusillade of bullets struck the outcroppings of rock near him. He tried to rise to see what was happening but the incoming fire was so intense that he couldn't move. He looked to his left and saw that most of the Russian's men had started to try to flank the men to their front. Ben-Nevin knew the tactic was foolhardy and told the men so, but being like Zallas himself they ignored the warning and moved off in force. Now the colonel found he was in command of only twenty of the original seventy-five he was using for the ambush.

The colonel needed to move the remainder of his men to the entrance to ensure no one got by them. Ben-Nevin's only salvation was to get into the temple and recover at least part of the lie Israel was covering up. That alone would satisfy his superiors and get him that nice retirement villa along with a hefty piece of the spoils. He started to shout his new orders over the force of the driving rain and wind when something bounced off the stone screen that guarded the entrance to the temple. Ben-Nevin wondered if the Sayeret had been reduced to throwing rocks when he saw what had been tossed it his way. A grenade came to rest only three feet from him. The colonel didn't hesitate as he threw himself behind the stone screen just as the grenade went off. The explosion rocked Ben-Nevin. He shook his head just as another grenade sailed over the berm and then clanked off the stone screen. This time the colonel turned and ran for the temple entrance as he realized he didn't have enough men to cover the assault that was about to happen.

The intense burst of fire that slammed any defender brave enough to pop their heads up had succeeded in opening up the front door long enough for the two men to stealthily run into the temple. Together they carried the one weapon that rivaled the power of God himself.

Major Donny Mendohlson was the very first Israeli soldier to carry a weapon that Israel has always insisted they didn't have in their arsenal—a 1.2 kiloton tactical nuclear weapon.

Jack took point and Sarah was right behind him. The rest of the village was spread out for close to half a mile as the refugees from Patinas made their way along the ancient excavation that had long been forgotten by the Jeddah. Only the Golia knew the temple complex better than any living thing on earth. Jack could see the weariness of the villagers as fathers who were not used to anything more exciting in Patinas than that year's wool harvest or the number of calves a certain herd had produced over the winter tried to keep their children calm as the explosions and bullets ripped the air around them. As they moved along the back wall of the City of Moses Collins felt the heat from the natural steam vents getting hotter.

Sarah tugged on Jack's sleeve and with her eyes indicated that he should look up. He did and that was when he saw Stanus and Mikla. The two brother wolves as giant as they were had been nimble enough to maneuver the large frames into the tight spaces on boulders and outcroppings above their heads. Soon they were joined by Anya and Carl. Everett seemed to be animated about something. Collins stopped and waited as Anya and Everett made their way through the mass of scared children and frightened women and farmers and sheep men who didn't understand why the outside world was trying to destroy their way of life. Carl winced as he heard the rearguard action formed by Jason Ryan and Will Mendenhall start in earnest. They were out of time. Ryan and Mendenhall, great shots though they were, would still be out of ammunition and still have over a hundred criminals to deal with.

"Colonel, the captain is saying he's picking up Stanus's thoughts . . . and also that of my brother," Anya said, not understanding the dual aspect to what Carl's mind was receiving stemming from Stanus as the beast watched the progress of the village as they moved out of the City of Moses.

"Now you've really lost me," Jack said as he turned his head and scanned the rocks above him looking for any opening that could lead to the outside.

"The captain wants to ask Stanus for help, but every time he attempts a connection Marko is there in the Golia's mind, it's as if—"

"Your brother is dead, Anya."

As they all turned and looked they saw three men from Patinas, one holding a sputtering torch and the other two had Madam Korvesky in a chair and they were carrying her. Alice saw this and became furious at the men.

"Put her down before you drop her," Alice said as she moved past Niles.

"I am not leaving the temple. I will remain." She looked at her stunned grand-daughter. "Marko was killed earlier tonight by his new friends."

Carl watched as the true feelings Anya had about her brother came through. She was in shock and angry that this was happening. She shook her head and placed it against Everett's chest and then took a deep breath. She looked up at Carl and then made a decision.

"What is left of my grandson now inhabits Stanus," Madam Korevsky said. "Soon the alpha will shrug off the memories of Marko and the man-child will be absorbed completely by the wolf, and this is how the Golia maintains its intelligence."

Everett looked at Anya and she nodded her head and explained, "Each of us will bond with a Golia upon the arrival of death. Our bodies will become part of nature and join the earth, but our soul, our memories, and our love of the wolf and of the people will be taken into the memories of the Golia, thus we live on in a far simpler form, one that does not have the travails of man to contend with—the Golia are us and we are them."

"Now, Captain, would you ask my grandson if he would help your colonel in leading my people from this mountain, for tonight God ends all here in this place," Madam Korvesky said as her pulse was being taken by Denise Gilliam, who ordered the men to put her on the ground and place the torch closer so she could see. Niles Compton watched and knew for all intents and purposes that the old woman was already dead and it was just her tenacity that was keeping her motor functions operating.

Jack and Sarah looked at Everett, who shrugged his shoulders that he didn't understand, but he would try. Anya took his elbow and stopped him.

"Carl, if Marko's mind is traveling with Stanus I don't know how my brother will react to you. Stanus will accept you into his head, but Marko may create a conflict. I don't know if he suspected anything about . . . well, about my having any feelings for you, but you have to be careful. Stanus could rip you apart and not understand why he's tearing your arms off, not knowing Marko has a great deal of influence on his thought process. If my brother hated you because of me he could kill you."

Jack, Sarah, Niles, and Alice saw the small smirk on Everett's face.

"What would Marko have suspected about us?" Carl asked, not caring who was watching or listening as Carl slipped off his long-sleeve shirt in his preparation to climb the sheer walls and speak with Stanus and then possibly be killed by a mind hiding inside the wolf, all pretty straightforward stuff to the captain's way of thinking. Meantime the gunfire from the city was starting to grow heavier; Jason and Will were now in serious trouble.

Anya looked embarrassed at the question. She looked from the stark blue eyes of the American and then found she couldn't hold them. In that instant Carl realized that this woman had never even considered falling for a man. Everett smiled and then with a look at his friends who were watching with interest, Carl leaned down and kissed Anya firmly and deeply. He pulled back and the woman still had her eyes closed. Everett felt other eyes on him and he half turned and saw that Madam Korvesky was watching the two and the look on her face was not a pleasant one.

"Well then, maybe I better have a sit-down with brother Marko and straighten this out and explain that I plan on making an honest woman out of the Gypsy princess?"

Anya opened her eyes and then the smile she gave Everett made Sarah want to tear up as she took Jack's arm.

"Until then, if I'm not back in twenty minutes," he looked at Jack, "call the president," he joked but before he could take his first handhold on the rough rock that led upward, Collins stopped him.

"Not this time, Jack." Everett slapped Collins's strong hand away and started climbing. "This one is mine, I have more at stake here," he said and vanished into the darkness of the cave system. The colonel looked over at Anya and saw that her eyes were still locked on a form of a man that was no longer there. Anya slowly walked over to her grandmother and as the men placed her on the stone floor Anya sat beside her and then placed her head against the weak shoulder of the old woman. Madam Korvesky gently placed her arm around the girl-child and spoke with her softly about Marko.

The gunfire coming from the city a half mile distant slowly started to ease and Jack knew that Ryan and Mendenhall were now on the move trying to make for a harder target. Jack knew that the two professionals would hold them for as long as possible, they were that good at what they did. No, the two men would never give up to a bunch of gangsters.

"Think we should give up?" Will asked Ryan as he tossed the empty Glock away and then faced his friend.

"Nah, let's hang out a little more," Jason said as he squirreled his head around the corner of the foot of Anubis, or as they knew now, the statue of the Golia, and fired his last four shots and was rewarded with the cry and yelp of another criminal biting the dust. He looked at Mendenhall and raised his brows twice in appreciation of his own shooting prowess. Then the smile left when he noticed the Glock was frozen in the empty position. He frowned and tossed the gun away.

"Good, I just wanted to make sure the Navy wasn't bailing out here,"

Mendenhall said as he ventured a look over at the men streaming down the foot ramp from the outer temple. "One thing's for sure, it's getting a little crowded in here. May I suggest we take up station with Moses and Joshua, those doors seem a little more stronger than these toes of Anubis," Will said as he burst from the hiding spot and ran for the columned temple of Moses.

Ryan watched his best friend run past him and then he sighed in relief when he saw that Will made it through the thick doors of the temple.

"You're right about one thing, buddy, the Navy is going to bail out of this jerkwater place," Ryan said and then with a burst of speed ran across the last hundred feet and then into the temple.

As Ryan and Mendenhall started bracing for the assault they knew would come quickly, the ground beneath their feet shook and then stilled. They exchanged looks and knew their situation was about to go from bad to worse.

The anchor pins holding Dracula's Castle to the side of the mountain slipped three feet to the south.

The expansive engineered castle leaned forward far enough that drinks on tables shook, settled, and then if one looked and was paying attention, anyone could see the un-level surface of those drinks. The castle was now leaning forward by eighteen inches from where the building had started out earlier that evening.

The mountain was beginning to shed the shame of Dracula's Castle as the American entertainer Drake Andrews took the stage. His opening set was so loud that the vibrations were sent through the foundation to the compromised anchor pins buried inside the mountain. The decibel level blaring from Castle Dracula started to eat away at the remaining earth securing the pins to the mountain.

The castle was close to rocking and rolling itself down the mountainside.

Carl Everett paused on the way up the sheer wall and swiped the sweat from his brow. The temperature had risen by at least thirty degrees since he had started climbing. The captain was about to place his hand in a better and more secure location when his left hand slipped free of the rock securing him and that was when he knew he was going to fall a great distance and that would be that. Suddenly he was in midair as he fell backward. Just as his hand slipped from the rock he was grabbed hard enough that his wrist almost broke. He was yanked upward like he was nothing more than a child and then before he realized it he was dangling over the ledge with Stanus holding him and staring right into his face. The wolf seemed to be smiling as the corners of the mouth turned upward.

"Oh, hi," Carl said, as it the only thing that came into his head.

Stanus lost the good-natured look on its fur-covered face and then pulled Everett up so hard that he felt his shoulder almost pop from its socket. He was unceremoniously tossed to the floor. The area was so black that the only thing the captain could make out clearly were the yellow glowing eyes of the Golia. Carl backpedaled a few feet until he bumped into something. He stopped and then leaned his head back and looked up. In the upside view of the dark world around him he saw another set of glowing eyes looking down at him.

"Mikla," Carl said nervously, "I'm glad to see—" Mikla cut him off by reaching down and pulling the large American to his feet. Everett brushed himself off and then wiped sweat from his face. Carl chanced looking away from Mikla and then turned and looked at the larger Stanus as the beast stood on both hind legs and was placing weight from one large clawed foot to the other. The breathing was deep and steady and their ears, much to Everett's comfort level, were straight up and not lying along the side of the skull in an aggressive stance. No, if Marko was in there someplace he wasn't inclined to kill him right off the bat. He glanced back at Mikla, who went to all fours with the loud popping sound of the skeletal frame adjusting. "Uh, Anya says hello," was all Carl could think to say.

Stanus didn't move. The animal just stood and swayed as if it were listening to a tune only the Golia could hear.

"Look, bad men are here to destroy the Jeddah and take their heritage from them. They must be stopped."

Stanus growled, as did Mikla behind him, which made Carl close his eyes in hopes he wasn't about to be raked by Mikla's claws straight down his back until his spinal cord was exposed. Still he tried again.

"We have to get the Jeddah to safety. We have to leave here, now," Everett said as Stanus suddenly went to all four legs.

The great Golia slowly closed the distance between man and animal. The eyes remained locked on Carl as it approached. Stanus was as close to Carl as Anya had been only minutes before, only the captain did not feel the same emotions coming from the Golia leader as much as he had from Marko's little sister. Stanus, although Everett knew it was really the curiosity of the traveler inside, Marko, sniffed the man up and down and then the yellow eyes settled on Mikla. There seemed to be a symbiosis of silent commands and then Mikla sprang from the ledge and vanished in the direction of the temple.

"No!" Everett shouted. "That's the wrong way, the bad men are that way, we have to go to the barn, Stanus, the barn!"

The Golia tilted its head as it tried to understand. Then the wolf nudged Carl and then nudged him again, almost knocking him into the wall. Suddenly Carl knew this wasn't about an escape route to Stanus, but of a more personal nature to the man inside, Marko Korvesky. The Golia reached out and took Everett by the neck and then squeezed. The whole time the animal remained on three legs and the reach was simple to accomplish, especially since the captain submitted to Marko.

"Go ahead, that won't change a thing about my intentions, fella, my mind was made up the minute I met your sister in Rome," he said, as the grip of Stanus, or as Carl knew it to really be, Marko, increased until the air was cut off from Everett's lungs. Carl became angry and held his breath as the beast slowly applied pressure to the human. The captain saw his vision start to narrow and knew before too much longer he would be hanging like a damp washrag in Stanus's grip.

The whine was loud enough that Carl's eyes flew open as Stanus released him and allowed the large American to slide to the stone floor. In the dark Everett could see the golden glowing eyes blink in confusion as Stanus whined again and then turned and looked around as if he were lost.

"You want what's best for your people? This all has to end tonight or the world will descend on the Golia and the Jeddah and the people of the world will not understand. Believe me, we all know how the mob reacts to things that scare them. That's what we do, my friends and I, we protect the world from our own fear of the unknown. Let me help Marko save his people, Stanus. Let me inside, we have to find a way out of the temple and get the Jeddah to safety."

Stanus growled deep inside and Carl thought he had pushed the wrong button. The Golia looked at Everett and then reached outward, but instead of Stanus grabbing Carl and finishing what it had started, the beast grabbed the rock wall and leveraged itself to a standing position. As Carl sat in wonder, the beast raised its muzzle to the ceiling and in the darkness at the edge of the City of Moses, Stanus roared until rocks fell from the ceiling.

From the City of Moses to the entrance to the first temple, the roar brought every man, woman, and child to stillness. Zallas, who was nearing the columned temple complex, stopped and looked at the men around him. The roar of the animal bounced from wall to monument, from pyramid to obelisk, until it finally faded to nothingness.

Major Donny Mendohlson and the sergeant major stopped their travel down the long staircase to the temple when the roar froze their blood.

"Do you think command authority forgot to mention something about this mission?" the sergeant major asked as they continued their flight into the first outer temple.

As for Carl, he watched as Stanus reached down and took him by the neck once more and instead of pinching his head off like a tick, Stanus threw Everett onto its back and started to climb.

This is what the Golia did, and did very well.

Zallas was standing behind one of the smaller statues of the Egyptian god of the underworld. Anubis posed in an imposing posture wielding an Egyptian battleax and was standing legs apart and ready for battle. As Zallas looked at the statue he ran his hand along the gold leaf that had been pounded into the stone over three thousand years before. He smiled as he realized if the ancients had placed this much gold on mere statue finery, what lay in wait in the temple. He motioned for his men to redouble their efforts at getting inside. The return fire has ceased more than two minutes before. Zallas saw Colonel Ben-Nevin running down the ramp from the upper temple. It looked as if the devil himself were chasing him.

The Russian was perplexed as he leaned out and watched the Israeli gather four men at the bottom of the ramp and placed them facing the top. He gestured wildly and then his eyes looked the Russian's way. The colonel ran to Dmitri's position.

"Your fool men need to learn how to follow orders. We had the Israeli assault element pinned down and then your idiotic men decided to take matters into their own hands and now we have commandos inside the temple," Ben-Nevin said angrily into the face of Zallas, who looked at him with a blank expression. "They are here to blow it up, you idiot. You must get more men up here and take that unit out!"

"Israeli commandos?" Zallas asked with an astonished look on his face. "What in the hell have you done to me? First I am eliminating members of NATO and now I'm up against the Israelis?"

"You knew what was at stake, did you think the men and women that have secured this place for almost four thousand years were going to allow you, a moron, to just waltz in here and upset an apple cart that is teetering on the brink anyway? Get men up here or we will have nothing." Ben-Nevin braved reaching out, and taking the Russian by his tuxedo collar said, "You will have nothing, not even your little casino, it will all be gone. You have killed NATO members, you idiot." Ben-Nevin smirked. "Do you think that any legalities will be observed when some black operations type smashes through your bedroom door in the middle of the night and places an ice pick in your brainstem? You have no choice now but to see this thing through and gather as much treasure as you can."

"What is your game?"

"All I need is the proof of what's inside this mountain; I couldn't care less in whose possession it's in. My mission is to prove the existence of the City of Moses, that's all. Men in power only seek the current government's downfall before they give back everything Israel has earned through blood and death."

"You are insane, and the men you work for are maniacs," Zallas said, regretting ever having listened to the spy, a man that was more highly trained at deceit and maneuver even far better than he could ever have been. "But as you say, I may as well get something out of this."

"Sensible. Our only break is the fact that the Sayeret were caught off guard and most of them will not make it out of the ambush. Unfortunately we cannot get them all, they are too good. So may I suggest we either kill the commandos inside the temple, or we get what we can and escape to the resort, the one place our highly secretive Sayeret cannot go."

Zallas knew he had totally misjudged his opportunity with this man. But he also knew he had come too far to let the chance slip of recovering some of the antiquities the Gypsy was selling off. Even if the temple collapsed he would still own the lease on the land and he would recover anything the Israelis buried.

"Look, the men they left behind, they must be out of ammunition, tell your men to advance into the temple."

The mobster braved a look and saw that it had only been two men defending the front of the temple and now they had abandoned the defense and were running it through the large doors. He shook his head in anger as he realized one of the men was the American from the resort. His suspicions on the NATO aspect of the Americans' story were now confirmed. He stood up in anger once he realized his six-plus men had been pinned down by only two defenders and he gestured wildly for his men to advance into the temple. Zallas was tired of this and needed to be at the castle not here in the middle of a storm deep inside a mountain in a temple he hadn't known existed twenty-four hours before.

"Kill those men, now!" he ordered. Zallas then looked over at Ben-Nevin and then used his eyes to signal one of his bodyguards. The man turned his AK-47 assault rifle on the Israeli. "Shall we see what the temple holds, Colonel?"

Ben-Nevin looked from the barrel of the weapon and then over to the Russian, who was busy brushing some dust off his expensive coat. He decided that just the antiquities in the hands of the Russian would be enough for him to complete his mission, as the proof that the treasure of the Exodus existed would be enough for the old legends to be proven as real, upsetting the lies of the left-wing government. Now he knew it wouldn't matter if the Russian was dead when the authorities uncovered the antiquities. No, he thought, it wouldn't matter at all.

"Yes, let us see what the Jeddah have hidden away for us."

Jack called a halt as the air was becoming far too hot for the band of escaping Gypsies to breathe adequately to maintain the fast pace. Collins placed a small girl on the nearest outcropping and then raised the torch high and looked along the wall that was no longer hewn from the mountain, but this was virgin stone. They had left the temple complex and were now deep in the mountain inside a natural cave system. As he moved the torch around Jack could see the many thousands of footprints in the fine dirt of the worn train. He then understood that the path they were following was worn that way because this was the train of the Golia and how they traversed the mountain without being seen by the human inhabitants on and below the peaks.

"How are we doing, Colonel?"

Jack turned and saw Niles Compton with Sarah in tow. The lieutenant was carrying the twin girl of the child Collins had been carrying. She placed the girl down next to her sister and the two Gypsy children held each other as the American strangers discussed their options.

"If we don't get these people out of here soon we're going to have a mess on our hands as far as heat exhaustion is concerned."

"We can't go back and we can't keep moving deeper into the mountain. Bullets or steam vents, not much of a choice," Niles said as he cleaned his glasses the steam kept fogging.

"Jack, the shooting back in the temple has stopped," Sarah said as she realized what that meant. Jason and Will were either dead or captured.

"I know," Jack said worriedly. "Those two are on their own." He looked at the worried faces of Sarah and Niles. "Don't worry, they know the better part of valor when it's called for. They'll be all right," Jack lied as best as he could for his benefit as much as for the others. It was Niles who voiced the far more immediate concern.

"Where is Mr. Everett?"

Alice watched the old woman sleep as she lightly dabbed at the sweat coming from Madam Korvesky's brow. Anya held the old woman's hand on the other side of the makeshift cot. Four of the village men were carrying a scythe, a long butcher knife, a large club, and of all things a wrist rocket slingshot. Alice could see that all were tiring. She was about to remove her hand when Madam Korvesky took hold of it and then turned her head to face Alice. Then she weakly turned and looked at Anya.

"Your hope chest," she said in a barely audible whisper.

"What, Grandmamma?" Anya asked.

Before Madam Korvesky answered her granddaughter she turned and looked at Alice. "The chest in my home, it is Anya's hope chest, it must be saved."

"Grandmother, I don't think we'll be going back for my hope chest."

Alice Hamilton listened to the exchange and remembered the heavy chest that Carl Everett had retrieved Madam Korvesky's blanket from and how hard a time Carl had moving it.

"You must, and Mrs. Hamilton, the chest is yours, Keeper of Secrets," she said as her voice was growing weaker by the minute.

"Grandmother, we cannot return to Patinas, it's far too dangerous, Colonel Ben-Nevin and that Russian gangster have the town and the temple."

"Mrs. Hamilton, promise me you will return to my home and take this gift I give you. Take it to your desert temple and place it among your greatest secrets. Hide well what it is you find."

Alice looked from the closed eyes of Madam Korvesky to Anya, who looked as confused as herself.

"Promise me this, Mrs. Hamilton."

"I promise," Alice said knowing that Anya was right, there was no going back to Patinas. That way was forever blocked to the retreating Gypsies now. The only way was down the mountain, either through it or under it.

Alice looked down and Madam Korvesky had fallen asleep again. She watched as Denise Gilliam came over and checked her pulse and then felt the old woman's forehead. She shook her head and then went to several old women who were holding children on their laps. She gave the adults salt pills for the heat and she handed out what little water they had to the smaller children. The long line of Patinas refugees stretched out for almost half a mile and only the flickering of a few torches announced they were hiding in the dark at all. The heat was growing the deeper they went.

———

Will tried to close the large double doors to the temple but they were too heavy and had not been closed in the past century. They creaked and groaned and then Ryan helped by throwing his weight against them. They finally managed to get them closed just as several large-caliber rounds struck the ancient wood.

"Jesus, I think we're trapped," Mendenhall said as he turned and faced the interior of the tomb. The three makeshift sarcophagi stood sentinel in the center of the large temple but other than that the room was bare of anything to fight with.

"Then may I ask why you led us in here?" Ryan asked as he ran to the far wall and started looking for an escape route.

"It was the only place I was familiar with."

As they ran around looking for something to fight with, the double doors bent inward as the men outside started to force them open.

"Oops. I think they figured out we're not shooting back anymore," Ryan said as they both stopped and watched the doors slowly open.

"Gentlemen, you can still survive this night, we have no wish to kill Americans, so stand still with your hands where they can be observed, and we can end this."

"Can I assume I am speaking with that traitorous little bastard, Colonel Ben-Nevin?" Will asked tauntingly as Ryan made the "what in the hell are you doing" face.

"You may assume. Now I am out of patience. We can just as easily bury your bodies up here among the rocks and the sheep, and believe me, my friends, no one will ever find you. You'll be just another mysterious disappearance in the dark and dangerous Carpathian Mountains."

Ryan looked at Will and shrugged his shoulders.

"Crap," Mendenhall said as he realized the jig was up for him and his friend. "You know, this is your fault, I mean you could have come to the rescue with just a little more firepower," Mendenhall said as he turned toward the double doors as they opened all the way and Colonel Ben-Nevin and sixty Romanian and Russian criminals rushed into the oldest vault in the history of the world.

"What we brought would have been enough if you ever learned to shoot straight, popping off rounds like we had a million of 'em," Ryan shot back as he raised his hands into the air.

"Well at least I can say I didn't spend my time getting mud baths while the rest of us—"

"Hands up," one of the thugs said as he roughly shoved Will and turned him around.

Both Will and Jason looked at each other and each was far more worried about his friend than himself.

"This really sucks," Jason said, resigned to the fact that he and Will were now out of the game.

As the men filled the room, Avi Ben-Nevin came through the door and Dmitri Zallas was close behind. The Russian stood in the doorway and lit a cigar and then looked at the two Americans. He shook his head and gestured to the Israeli to speak.

"Thank you, gentlemen, now we can conclude this business and be on our way," Ben-Nevin said as the ground shook around them and dust filtered down from the stone cut ceiling. "Because one way or another, for some reason or other, I don't think this mountain is entirely stable."

Will and Jason looked around and then exchanged uneasy looks as the tremor was far longer than the last.

The colonel was right, the mountain was feeling its oats.

Jack knew he had to get the people up and moving. If Sarah was right he knew they were fast running out of time. If any kind of detonation in that temple were set off it would likely trigger a massive shift in the strata and that would result in the anchor pins holding the castle's foundation to the mountain snapping off or pulling free of the mountain.

Sarah and Niles stood when they saw that Jack was about to order everyone forward once more. Sarah knew upon looking at the people they would never make it through the heat of the natural steam vents dotting the mountain.

"I know what you're thinking, but we haven't a choice, we have to keep moving and assume Mr. Everett has—"

The wall next to Jack and behind Niles Compton started to crumble as something was battering the stone and earth. The entire stone wall caved in and what was standing there froze everyone in place. Stanus roared and then stepped away from the hole it had made. The giant wolf vanished and then Carl Everett stepped through.

"This way to ladies' linens, housewares, and ancient Egyptian passageways," he said.

The line of displaced Gypsies erupted in cheering and crying as the cool air of the outside world started to flow into the mountain and cooled their heat-induced fear.

The second Exodus of the Jeddah had found a new route to salvation.

Major Donny Mendohlson could tell by the lessening volume of fire coming through the noise of the storm that his men were seizing control of the rabble that had held them at bay for far too long. He was angry that the intelligence on the part of the mission planners had failed to foresee an armed force of defenders. He was far angrier at himself for considering the HALO jump the most dangerous aspect of Operation Ramesses and not the actual demolition of the site.

"As far as I can tell we were singularly lucky these weren't trained soldiers," the sergeant major said as he aimed his weapon toward the entrance of the temple they had just entered.

Major Mendohlson heard the noise and then aimed his own weapon at the entrance where a bright flash of lightning illuminated the opening just as a man ran through. They were getting ready to shred the intruder to pieces when the major held up his right hand.

It was Janos Vajic. He was soaked and mud-covered and realized that he had about been shot to death. He shook his head.

"We have about fifty percent casualties. We are setting up a dry place for the wounded and your medic is working on them."

The major held the Mossad agent's gaze waiting for the other shoe to fall.

"Eleven of your men are dead, Major."

Mendohlson had just been handed an indication of what the butcher's bill would be for this little foray to destroy something that couldn't even be explained to him and his men. And now he had the dead to prove just how messed up the world had become. He turned on Vajic.

"Who in the hell are we fighting and just who is leading the defense inside that mountain?" Mendohlson asked.

For the first time Janos Vajic heard the firefight going on far beneath them in the temple. He couldn't imagine it was the villagers of Patinas putting up such a spirited fight.

"You're up against a ruthless bastard who is one of the richest mobsters in Eastern Europe. The man will stop at nothing to get anything he already does not own."

"And this man has sided with this Russian?" the major asked, waiting for the Mossad agent to tell him that they were facing not only the mobster but a well-trained agent as well. Now he understood why the ambush had been so complete, the son of bitch knew his team was coming. He wanted to backhand the agent in front of him for not seeing this coming. His men were always at the mercy of pencil-pusher agents in the field that didn't know their ass from a hole in the ground. His complaint was the same as that of any black operations soldier in the world.

"Colonel Ben-Nevin is not to leave this place alive."

"That I can pretty much guarantee, spook," the major replied. "Now who is fighting him, it can't be the locals, not shooting like that."

"It must be the Americans. I saw their vehicles near the village. I helped them escape earlier and I knew they would come here to get their people. My partner died to assist them, so don't give me that look, I'm going in with you."

"What in the hell are the Americans doing here? Do they have to complicate everything in the world?"

"I thought they were the NATO contingent mapping the pass, but they're far more than that."

"Obviously, those aren't engineers and surveyors in there."

"Gentlemen, we're about to have company," the sergeant major said as he again raised his weapon and made ready to cover the opening. "May I suggest we make our delivery and get the hell out of here before the Chinese show up—I mean everyone else is here."

"I hear that, let's go. We place the weapon as deep into the temple system as we can get without getting our asses shot off."

"And then?" Vajic asked as he chambered a round into his handgun.

"Then we get the hell back to the village and hope General Shamni can get us out of this Romanian nightmare."

As the three men moved deeper into the upper staircase leading to the first temple, the mountain started to shake in earnest.

Pete was one of the last to step up to the hole and peer inside. He turned and faced the captain, who handed him a small boy, wide-eyed and frightened at the prospect of going into the darkened hole. And Pete sympathized with the child, as he was terrified himself. The long line was now being led by the engineers from the 82nd, their uniforms making the farmers, herdsmen, and womenfolk of Patinas feel safer. But Pete was feeling none of this at the moment.

"That wolf isn't in there any longer, is he?"

"We don't have a hell of a lot of time here, Doc," Everett said as Charlie Ellenshaw finally stepped up and then looked at Pete.

"It's okay, Pete, I'll be right there with you."

"Carl and Jack exchanged looks as they realized that Pete was actually fearful of the closed-in space far more than the wolves running around. They let Charlie handle the computer man. Soon the three eased off with Charlie speaking to Pete about all the magnificent discoveries they made.

Finally the four burly men of Patinas came up with Madam Korvesky on the makeshift cot. Alice was with her and then Anya was the last in the long line of refugees. Denise Gilliam walked with her low and Jack knew the old woman must have been on her last legs.

As Collins watched them ease the old Gypsy through the large hole he turned to Niles, Everett, and Anya. He nodded at Sarah for her to explain what was running through both their minds.

"I understand the dynamics of what's happening here. The anchor pins will not hold. I suspected the vibration was getting worse and now I think I know why. The wolves are not digging any longer. Anya, you said the Golia have been hidden by Stanus and Mikla?"

"Yes, that is right. Stanus knows the mountain is unstable because that was what he and my grandmother had planned all along."

"If they've stopped undermining the foundations of the castle why are the vibrations and the tremors getting worse?" Niles asked, hoping there would be some good news somewhere.

"The castle's grand opening. They are playing live music in there and that cannot be helping the foundations. By the frequency of the tremors the face of that mountain is getting ready to let go."

"What are you saying, Jack?" Carl asked as he wiped sweat from his brow.

Collins turned and faced Anya.

"Look, I don't know how the Mossad plays it, but my people and I try not to kill innocents, and that even means people that thrive just below the what is the legal line."

Anya suspected at what the American colonel was playing at but said nothing as long as Jack's intense green eyes bore into her own. Carl watched the exchange with growing concern as he saw Jack's demeanor change once the villagers were out.

"I'm saying those commandos are here to destroy the temple, but how are they going to do it?"

Anya looked uncomfortable because she knew the destruction of the City of Moses by the commandos was the only fallback position they had of assuring the destruction of their home in case the wolves failed at sabotaging the foundations of the castle.

"There are over four hundred people at the castle, Major. Now I don't mean to be unsympathetic to your plight but your concern about the world knowing your secrets has to have boundaries. Now, what weapon is being used by your people?"

Anya looked from Collins and then found Carl. She wanted him to tell her, order her to disobey not only Mossad's orders, but worse, her grandmother's wishes. She swallowed and knew they were short of time as the mountain trembled again, this time it lasted ten seconds longer than any other shake to that point.

"A Forger," she said ashamedly.

Jack closed his eyes and Everett shook his head. He reached out and placed a hand on Anya's shoulder and squeezed. She felt deflated that their secret was out to the Americans.

"Get them out, Captain," Jack said as he looked at Niles. "I'm going back to get those boys out of there and try and get some sense talked into anyone who will listen."

"What is a Forger?" Niles asked, as he was unfamiliar with the term.

"It's a weapon that's going to turn the interior of the temple into a ten-thousand-degree inferno in just about a millisecond," Sarah explained. "It's also enough firepower to shear the entire facing of the mountain off from the major fissure point just a quarter mile from the castle. That means the castle with all of those men and women inside is going to tumble like a house of cards if we don't stop her people from setting that thing off. If not, the vibrations will do it anyway, just a little slower."

"And we need that extra time to get those guests out of there," Jack concluded.

Carl stepped forward with the torch and was about to protest but then he saw Anya and knew he wanted her out of there. He nodded once at Collins and then held the torch toward the open maw of the black hole and Niles bobbed his head and entered and then Sarah placed a hand on Collins's arm and smiled.

"Don't be a dick and leave me outside all alone, you hear me?"

Jack winked and then pushed Sarah through the hole. He looked at Everett and Anya.

"Good luck, Jack, see you on the outside," he said as he gestured into the hole with the torch for her to go. Anya looked at Jack and nodded.

"Cancellation code Matilda, 112, you have that? That will get the commander of the Sayeret to cancel Operation Ramesses, but once the sequence is initiated on the Forger apparatus there is no stopping it."

"Someday I'm going to find the guy that designed those damn things and their safety systems and break both of his arms," Jack said as he thanked her and then left the way the long line of refugees had just fled.

"I hope the commander of that unit listens to him, the Sayeret tend to make up their own rules."

"Well, your man is about to meet the guy that doesn't follow rules at all."

Everett nodded for Anya to go and then he went after her.

Mikla was waiting for his brother, Stanus, just above the temple. Mikla had been getting visions that were coming from the sleeping mind of Madam Korvesky and he was feeling confused as Stanus ran up to him. Stanus suddenly started feeling the push also from the old Gypsy and Stanus himself started rolling on the hard rock floor of the Golia path just above the City of Moses. The last vestiges of Marko Korvesky tried in vain to sort out the confusing messages being sent by the Gypsy. There were flashes of many humans running, screaming, and dying under the stormy night sky. The wolves rolled on the ground as the horrible visions penetrated both of the Golia's minds. They were being asked to sacrifice one last time for the Jeddah. Stanus was refusing, Mikla was not. The wolves wrestled and growled. They snipped at each other and then they both became still as the vision was completed. They saw the mountain come down around them and their young.

Three miles away three adult male Golia poked their snouts out of the cave system in which Stanus had placed the clan. They had picked up on the troubled mind of Madam Korvesky also. The babies inside the cave system started howling and crying and the females lent their voices to that of the young. Suddenly twenty of the largest males sprung from the cave and ran headlong into the raging storm. A flash of lightning gave a strobe effect the side of the mountain, which for the first time in centuries saw the Golia moving out in force.

If there had been witnesses they would have seen the wolves heading south, toward Dracula's Castle and the unsuspecting revelers that would never realize that myth and legend were coming to visit.

The Temple of Moses was fronted by two great gates with two charioteers facing one another done in various paints that had faded over the centuries with age and dust. The giant wooden doors were seventy feet high and almost four feet thick. As Ryan and Mendenhall watched, Zallas and his men streamed through the opening. The bright handheld floodlights they used illuminated objects missed in the torchlight.

They watched as the Russian's men fanned out inside and were eyeing the Americans, really not knowing what to do with them. Zallas made things a bit clearer.

"You and your people have cost me considerable time and trouble. I am afraid I was a bit too hospitable to you before. Now I'm afraid, what do you Americans say? Oh yes, you have truly worn out your welcome," Zallas said, as if he were proud of his Americanism.

"Well, excuse us all to hell," Ryan said, making Mendenhall wince and take a deep breath.

Colonel Ben-Nevin walked up to Ryan and backhanded him. Ryan spit out blood and then faced the colonel.

"Captain Everett said you hit like a pussy, now I see that he wasn't lying."

Ben-Nevin brought his hand down again but this time Dmitri Zallas caught it in midair.

"We do not have the time for your dramatics, Colonel; let's get what we came for."

Ben-Nevin gave Ryan a dirty look and Jason blew him a kiss. Then he and Zallas walked over to the far left of the three large containers. Zallas had to suppress a smile as he closed his eyes and envisioned the treasure to behold. He opened them and the smile quickly left his face. Ben-Nevin got a confused look as he took in the mummified remains in the hand-hewn box. Both men turned to the center box and studied the remains inside.

"What is this?" Zallas asked as his eyes never left the wrapped and disintegrating corpse of Moses the Law Giver.

"This isn't right—where are the antiquities, the gold, this isn't what's supposed to be here?" Ben-Nevin went to the third box and then turned away, his face white with shock. He looked around at the men staring back at him. Then he ran to the far wall and started feeling around. "There have to be hidden storage areas."

"Looks like the Jeddah spent a lot of money over the centuries, huh?" Ryan quipped, making Mendenhall flinch once more. He sensed Ryan was really trying to get them shot faster than would be normal.

Ben-Nevin stopped searching and then took five quick steps toward Ryan and then pulled his Walther automatic and placed it against Jason's forehead and pulled back the hammer.

"Where is the treasure of the Exodus?" he asked as Ryan smiled.

"Right here in my left front pocket, dickhead," he said just as the barrel of the gun whacked him on the side of the head. Will started forward but one of Zallas's men pointed an AK-47 at him and stopped Will from helping his friend.

"Ow," Ryan said as his knees buckled. "That hurt."

"Where is it?" Ben-Nevin insisted.

"You are wasting your time, spymaster," Zallas said. "The villagers of Patinas have obviously emptied the temple of anything valuable and left us nothing but these rotten corpses," he said as he kicked out with his black Armani shoe and knocked the box containing the body of Joshua onto the floor. The mummy rolled out and then came to a rest. Ryan looked at the mummy and then slowly stood up and faced Ben-Nevin. Will had his brows raised as Zallas looked from each man.

"That probably wasn't the best thing to do, my friend," Ryan said. "That was a very important man to a few people a while back."

"A stinking corpse," was all Zallas said.

"Look, I'm not a big believer in biblical teachings, but one thing I've learned is that everything has a basis in fact, and that little fact you just kicked over scares the hell out of me. If I were you I would quit while I was ahead. Nothing good ever comes from desecrating something that can bite you in the ass."

"You bore me with your old wives' tales," Zallas said. He turned to Ben-Nevin. "Finish your business here and let us see what the backward Gypsies took out of here. Come, they only have one direction to go, and we shall meet them there."

Ben-Nevin smiled and then as Zallas and his men started to file out of the temple and head for the ramp, he stepped up to Ryan.

Mendenhall didn't think the Israeli colonel was the type to get long-winded and tell Ryan how bad his killing was going to be and thus affording Will a chance to help Ryan out of that killing. No, Ben-Nevin raised the barrel of the gun and his smile widened and that was when the bullet hit.

Will was shocked when he saw the weapon fly from Ben-Nevin's hand. The colonel turned and looked but saw no one. He started to run just as another round pinged off the stone flooring. This time the colonel sprinted for the door holding his injured right shoulder.

"Damn it. Clear?"

"Clear!"

"Clear!"

Mendenhall heard the all clear calls coming from to the left of the doorway. That meant while Zallas and his men's attention was on Ryan getting questioned by the colonel, someone had entered the temple unseen and taken up station behind Zallas and his people and then lay in silence until the men had left and had only exposed themselves when they had a chance.

Will went to Jason and helped him up.

"You can get him talking by doing something other than insulting him, you know," Will said to a bleeding Ryan.

"Yeah, but pissing him off was more fun," he said as he staggered and then caught himself. They looked up when three men came down from the high wall just to the left of the large door frame.

"Sorry, sweat rolled into my eyes at the last second, and then I missed him again. I must be getting old."

Will and Jason looked the three men over and then Ryan's eyes widened when he saw that one of the men in the black Nomex was none other than Janos Vajic.

"The hotel owner?" Jason asked.

"What?" Will said.

"Sorry, as I said, just dumb luck I missed. I guess you were right, Sergeant Major, I should have let you take the shot, but I wanted that bastard."

"Next time I shoot," said the burly man as he slammed another magazine into Vajic's appropriated AK-47 and then handed it back to him.

"Uh, who in the hell are you guys?" Mendenhall finally asked.

The small man in the front reached over to his left shoulder and then pulled up a Velcro patch. Underneath was a black and gray version of the Israeli six-pointed star and that was enough not said for the two Americans.

"They are Sayeret, Lieutenant, and they are not very friendly."

All eyes turned to see Jack Collins hop down from the back wall of the temple where the villagers had vanished over an hour before. Jack walked up to Jason and lifted his chin.

"You okay, Commander?"

"Yeah, I'll be better when we get after that asshole colonel."

Collins patted Jason on the back and then turned to face the three men and one in particular.

"Who's in command?" Jack asked as his eyes searched all three. The three remained quiet as the small standoff went on.

"Colonel . . . Collins, is it?" Janos Vajic said as he stepped between the American and the Israeli major. Jack said nothing, as he had fixed the smaller man holding his glare as the commander of the Sayeret strike team. He ignored Janos.

"My compliments on what had to be one scary HALO through that storm." Jack tilted his head and studied the man a moment and then finished, "Is it major or captain?"

The smaller man held eye contact. "Major, and you'll forgive me if I leave it at that."

"Yes, I understand the game, Major, and how it's played. And you, sir, are not playing the way you're supposed to."

Jason and Will saw the sergeant major tense and raise his weapon just an inch or two as he watched the colonel talk.

The smaller man looked at his watch and then looked at his sergeant major and the man lowered his weapon.

"I am here to do a job, Colonel. If you are who I think you are you can understand that."

"In order to follow your orders, Major, you will have to kill over three hundred innocent people. If you blow that weapon this entire mountain comes down on that resort."

"I am assured that the destructive power is only sufficient enough to bring the temple down and to incinerate everything inside."

Jack could have leaned over and kissed the mountain at that precise moment as the entire temple shook harder than anytime previous.

"There have been elements at work here that have guaranteed the destruction of not only the Temple and City of Moses, but the entire resort down below in the valley."

"Elements?" the young major asked.

"Yeah, elements the likes you would never believe," Ryan said for the colonel.

"I have my orders, Colonel, please, you and your men must vacate the temple."

"Yes, I understand what a stickler for following orders General Shamni can be."

All three Israelis froze at the name.

"Yes, I know the general very well. We taught commando tactics together at Sandhurst in England for a semester. Now, cancellation code Matilda, 112. Abort Operation Ramesses, Major."

The three men again exchanged looks of distrust. Never would they have given this man any credence until Shamni's name was mentioned. Only the prime minister knew the name of the man that headed the top secret Mossad.

"I'm sorry, Colonel, no dice. You know I cannot accept anything from you. I would like to trust you but this mission must succeed."

"Listen, your mission is guaranteed to succeed, you don't need that damn weapon, now stand down, Major!" Jack said taking a menacing step toward the Israeli.

The Uzi came up and Jack stopped but didn't flinch.

"As I said, Colonel, we must—"

Before the major could finish a roar filled the inside of the temple and reverberated off the stone walls. The three men flinched as something jumped down into their midst and grabbed the small aluminum box. Before a shot could be fired, Stanus had taken the small device and hopped to the wall holding the case by the strap. The beast roared as it stopped and looked down. The major quickly raised his weapon after his initial shock at seeing the animal and fired. The bullet hit Stanus in the lower back and Jack heard the giant wolf yelp in pain as it leapt clear of the wall and disappeared high above. Jack lowered his head and then shook it.

"Damn fool."

"Just what in the hell was that?" the sergeant major asked.

"That was one of the elements that are going to bring the castle down and you idiots just shot him," Mendenhall said as he realized he was now concerned for the injured Golia.

Jack wanted to take the young officer and shake him until he understood that every mission is never dependent on just one's orders. You must evaluate as you go to make the right choice. Collins had done that a number of times and paid for it in the end, but it was better using common sense than being a nonthinking automaton.

The mountain shook as the echoes of Stanus's pain-riddled yelp slowly echoed to nothing. The ground shook and this time the left-side wooden door broke free from its bronze hinges and then dangled a moment before it fell to the ground.

"What in God's name was that?" Major Mendohlson asked wide-eyed.

"That's a long story that your friend Mr. Vajic can answer at a later time."

"Colonel, I don't want to be considered the cowardly one here, but I would rather not wear this mountain as a hat," Ryan said as he and Will were ready to go.

"Major, you and your team can stay and convince the wolf to give you back your weapon, or you can run like hell and help us save these people down at the castle."

Ryan and Mendenhall started for the double doors.

"Hey, what castle?" Major Mendohlson called out as Jack turned and started after his two men.

"Dracula's Castle," Janos Vajic answered as he too turned and followed the Americans.

The major and sergeant major looked at each other and it was the older man that finally said it as he turned and started after the others.

"This I have got to see," the sergeant major said excitedly after seeing the largest land animal he had ever laid eyes on.

Mendohlson watched the enthusiastic sergeant start following the Americans and Vajic.

"I think I've seen quite enough already."

20

PATINAS PASS

It had taken over an hour to get the villagers to safety through the animal paths inside the mountain. Stanus had made sure Everett knew the way back before the large wolf had vanished. The last of the women and children had been handed out through one of the ancient steam vents that dotted the mountainside by the menfolk of the village. Niles had been impressed by the movement of the entire village as not one child made a cry or complaint. The men had been silent also as they moved their families without complaint. These were hardy people that needed little help from Niles or his people. These men and women had courage in abundance. They and the Golia were the ultimate survivors.

One of the last to be moved from the inside of the mountain was Madam Korvesky, who had to leave the makeshift cot inside as it wouldn't fit through the vent. Alice, Denise, and Sarah held a blanket up over the vent hole to protect the old woman from the slashing rain. Once the men were out Carl took notice on where they had come out. Niles called his team over to the side.

"Where are we?" he asked. "Best guess."

"I would say we're only a mile from the castle and a mile south of Patinas, and we better get moving before Zallas and his people return."

Niles nodded as he turned to look for Alice. She was gone along with Sarah and Anya. He spun in a circle as he realized every one of the Gypsy villagers had vanished into the storm.

"Where did they go?" Pete asked as he and Charlie ran across the road to see if they had gone that way.

"They know this mountain better than anyone. I think they know where to go to be safe," Everett said as his thoughts turned to Anya, Sarah, and Alice.

"But they'll kill Madam Korvesky even faster, we must find them," Denise said.

"For right now we have to get some help. Charlie, you and Pete get to the castle and do what you can to warn everyone. Smash dishes or faces, I don't care, get them out. Captain, get back to Patinas, I don't know why but I think that's where they went. Madam Korvesky has something to do with it, I know it. Dr. Gilliam, you'll come with me and set up a triage station at the resort in case we don't get those people out in time. We'll need a lot of medical help if the worst happens."

"You?" Carl asked as he flinched when a flash of lightning streaked overhead.

"Jack says there's a shortwave radio inside Zallas's office. I think it's time we call a friend for some help."

As everyone broke up and went their different ways into the storm, Everett wondered just who in the hell can come and help them at a time like this.

But Niles Compton knew just whom to call.

Alice was barely able to climb the road back to Patinas. Her legs had given out three times and Sarah had to assist her back to her feet. Anya helped by taking Alice's other arm and together they battled the raging wind and rain and barreled headfirst through the storm to Patinas. Finally the village came into view and Anya asked the obvious, as Alice had refused to tell them why she had to return to Patinas with the mountain getting ready to fall down around them.

"Why are you doing this? My grandmother was delirious, we cannot go back there, Zallas and his people are still there."

Alice continued to struggle against the wind and then when she stopped it caught Sarah and Anya off guard—standing before them were twenty armed men in black clothing.

Anya feared this almost as much as running into the Russian and his men. They had run straight into the waiting arms of the killer elite of Israel.

"I am Major Mica Sorotzkin, you men are ordered to stand down."

The men just looked on and said nothing. Anya could see that most of them were bloodied. The leader of the remaining commandos was about to step up and address the major but instead he ducked as automatic fire opened up behind them. Bullets hit everywhere as Alice, Sarah, and Anya dove into the rushing water and mud for cover. Sarah chanced a look up and above the village saw streaming out of the temple the Russian's men making a mad rush for their waiting vehicles. The Israelis turned, hit the mud, and started to return fire, but not before three more of them had been hit. Bullets struck to the left and to the right as Alice suddenly stood up and started running. Sarah screamed for her to stop but she kept running through the blaze of gunfire. Sarah had no choice but to go after her and that spurred Anya into action to follow.

The first SUV tore out of the village and that was followed by others as the volume of fire became less and less and more of the men from the temple made it to their vehicles.

The man left in charge of the outside assault element was mentally kicking himself for not disabling the vehicles.

Alice tripped, stumbled, and then fell into the rushing water as she reached the front gate to the village. A large black SUV nearly missed her as she dove through the front gate of Patinas. Sarah was soon there as the last of the black SUVs tore down the mountain.

"Are you insane?" Sarah yelled as she helped Alice to her feet.

"Please, we have to get to Madam Korvesky's cottage, now," Alice said as Anya reached down and helped them both. In the falling rain she faced Alice and then shook her.

"My grandmother is wrong, what you're going after isn't worth it, believe me. It's something she won't share even with me," she yelled as rain poured from her face and hair.

"She says it's important," Alice said as she struggled to get away from the hands holding her.

"Nothing here is that important, you saw what it was the Jeddah were protecting all these years, it's nothing to die for. That is why we were going to destroy it. Please, let it go, Mrs. Hamilton."

Alice twisted away and then ran for the cottage. Anya screamed in anger and then she and Sarah followed.

The front door was open and several men raised weapons and aimed them at Alice as she stumbled through the doorway. The men were all injured by either bullets or from the HALO jump.

"No!" Anya shouted at the men in English so they would understand without really thinking.

Alice ran past the men with Sarah's help and stumbled into the bedroom and then practically fell onto the old hope chest. Anya came in after them with an oil lamp and waited for Alice to catch her breath. The ground was now in constant motion this high up.

"There is nothing in there but a bunch of shattered dreams my grandmother had for me at one time. There is nothing in there of value, Mrs. Hamilton, please, let us get these injured men off the mountain now."

Alice threw open the top of the chest and then started tossing blankets, sheets, and other items that Anya once thought were important. Then Alice hit upon something metal and hard. She took a moment and studied what she had discovered. Anya got a strange look on her face, as she hadn't known there was anything in the bottom of the chest. She held the lamp closer as Alice reached in and opened the steel box. Inside was an old burlap bag that was tied at one end with a length of rope. She slowly reached in and brought out the bag. It was heavy and felt as if it held nothing but rocks. Alice lifted it free of the chest and was about to open the rope end when several men came into the house. As Sarah looked up she was relieved to see Jack, Jason, and Will. They were soaked and Ryan was bleeding. Will looked scared half to death.

"Ladies, I believe I told you to get the hell off this mountain, what are you doing here," Jack asked angrily.

"Collecting something Madam Korvesky wanted us to have. Now may I suggest we do as Jack here says, I think the mountain is falling down."

With that they were all amazed when Alice bolted from the room and out the front door.

"I'll tell you something, she cannot come on field operations anymore!"

As Pete and Doc Ellenshaw climbed the stairs to the cable car platform they turned left into the lobby area of the castle and Niles and Denise boarded the southbound car just as the doors started to slide closed. Compton looked at his watch and worried it had taken them too long to reach the castle.

Pete and Charlie heard and felt the music long before they breached the club. Drake Andrews could be heard belting out his most famous cover song, Creedence Clearwater Revival's "Green River." The crowd was raucous and the backup band blazing. Pete opened the door to step in and a rather large and brutish man placed a bear-sized palm on his chest and then gave the filthy computer genius a dirty look. He just shook his head when he saw the condition of his clothes and his person.

"Listen, you have to get all of these people out of here!" Pete said, trying to push past the doorman. The man wouldn't budge.

As the music played even louder, Charlie looked over and saw the raging storm outside as the cables for the massive cars were swinging back and forth. He then felt the thick stone blocks beneath his feet shift. His eyes widened and then he started running and pushed past the large man at the door, knocking him and Pete to the floor.

"Everyone get out, get out now!" the crazy white-haired Charlie Ellenshaw screamed at the top of his lungs, but it was to no avail, as everyone was locked in on the famous American crooner gyrating on the stage. The backup band was having the experience of their lives playing with the once top star. "Stop, stop playing and get out of here," but it was like Charlie was speaking into a vacuum.

The doorman was finally on his feet and had Charlie by the back of his filthy shirt and was in the process of pulling him back toward the cable car platform when he backed into something unmoving. The man turned and raised a hand to hit the other filthy man when his eyes looked straight into nothing but black hair. He saw the chest rise and fall and he heard the heavy breathing. His eyes slowly moved upward as his grip on Ellenshaw loosened and Charlie fell to the floor.

Mikla was standing on the platform and was looking down on the large doorman. The man was frozen in fear as the freshly healed Mikla leaned down and looked the man directly in the eyes and then the mouth opened to show the man the business end of Mikla's touch.

The man felt his knees buckle as Mikla roared. The ears lay back and the hand came up but the doorman had already fallen to the floor.

"Good, Mikla, good!" Charlie said, not knowing how or why the Golia had saved them but wasn't about to thumb his nose at the chance to get the people out as the castle really started to move under their feet.

The Golia seemed like it was a beast on a mission as it shook its massive head and with ears laid to the sides of that head started walking through the open doorway to Castle Dracula's.

Drake Andrews was having the time of his professional life as he felt the subtle nuances of an audience that was lost in his music. He hadn't felt the power of his music for almost a quarter of a century. It had become stale and predictable, even to the point where the MGM Grand and then the Mirage in that order canceled his upcoming gigs.

He was just finishing up when he heard a commotion in the upper reaches of the club. He glanced up at the balcony and heard several shouts, but the American figured they were just yelping for more. He turned to the band and said something and then the strains of the old rock 'n' roll standard by Tommy James and the Shondells, "Mony, Mony," began. As the heavy music started its heavy beat they heard another scream and then another and Drake smiled as he knew the song was getting their attention.

Andrews stepped up to the microphone and was just starting to open his mouth when he saw one of the club's guests get onto the railing that ringed the upper balcony where the rich would sit and listen, drink, and do the kind of things you can't do on the main floor. Drake saw the man and wondered just what he was up to when he suddenly jumped over the railing and fell the eighty feet to the tables below where he hit hard and then rolled to the floor amid screams of terror. Drake Andrews looked up still stunned when he saw the wolf from the night before jump up and then roar out over the crowd. Drake, instead of singing the first few refrains from "Mony, Mony," watched as the crowd started cheering at what they thought was part of the show. Drake knew that if it was part of the club's show that something pretty bad had just gone wrong.

The beast roared again as two more people jumped. The Golia roared for a third time until the band stopped playing and just stared up at the surreal scene above their heads. A man with crazy white hair stepped up next to the black, upright wolf that had everyone in the house amazed.

"In case you hadn't noticed, this very big wolf wants all of you OUT OF HERE!" Charlie shouted at the top of his lungs just as Mikla roared and then jumped clear of the railing and onto a table, crushing it. The men and women sitting there just stared up at the amazing creature standing on the remains of the table and looking around curiously at the startled men and women. Mikla reached out and slapped at a frightened man in a tux, making sure his claws were retracted far enough that he didn't decapitate him.

Some of the patrons of the grand opening became aware that this was not part of the show or a prank: there was a wolf standing in the middle of the club—and the wolf standing before them was as real as it gets. They panicked and started running in all directions screaming and yelling as Mikla added his voice to the confusion and started swiping at the passing stampede of humanity.

Charlie Ellenshaw looked down from the balcony as Pete joined him. They saw men and women running everywhere. They saw Drake Andrews try to help a lady who was attempting to get on the stage to escape the monster wolf that had just crushed her table, but her hand slipped out of Drake's and she fell back into the maddened crowd. Andrews turned and started pushing the young Russian kids off the stage. As Charlie and Pete watched from above they exchanged looks and Charlie made a face. The panicked people below saw the first filtering of dust from the ceiling as it came down but no one inside Castle Dracula could care at the moment. Still the panicked guests streamed toward the stairs and the cable car platform seeking any way out of what had quickly become a nightmare.

"Wow, maybe you could have handled that just a little bit differently, Professor."

The SUVs blasted down the slick, wet road as fast as they dared. Several of the all-terrain vehicles went flying off into the storm-driven night when they failed to take a corner at a reasonable speed, but each car was afraid of being the last to get to the castle. Dmitri Zallas was not feeling at festive as he had earlier that evening. In the first car was Zallas and Colonel Ben-Nevin, who was still holding his damaged shoulder from his near miss at the hands of the Israelis. The colonel sat in the backseat scowling, believing that no matter what happened from this point on his mission was a failure and now it wasn't just his career that was over, but also his life, as the proof saying the City of Moses really existed had never been there in the first place. The legend was a lie, a falsity that held many of his people chained to the past, and one that he had come to despise above all else in Israel.

The black SUV swerved in the road as they came around the last bend. Zallas's eyes widened when he saw the men and women running into the night. They were streaming down the staircases on the outside while many others were pushing and shoving to get inside one of the cable cars that had just arrived. He saw the heavily overloaded car sag on the large, thick, four-cable lines. He screamed in anger as the automatic doors on the car slid closed, surely injuring several of his guests. He watched all of this from far below as his four-wheel-drive pulled up to the first cable tower as the car high above them broke free from the car barn.

Zallas saw people streaming on and off the two small elevators and he decided to bypass them and run for the stairs. Rain made the going slippery as even more of his men pulled up and joined him in their run up to the club and possibly the escaping villagers of Patinas. Ben-Nevin joined him in the enclosed stairs thankful for being out of the storm with his arm throbbing because of the bullet having ripped into him from his own people . . . *Well, what used to be his own people*, he corrected himself. The Mossad colonel knew what they were doing now was a

waste of time. It was just the Russian not wanting to be made a fool of. There were
far worse things in the world than that, and a hanging rope for traitors was one of
them.

The Russian stopped when they reached the top as his guests were screaming
and yelling trying to get down the same stairwell. Zallas started angrily pushing
them out of his way and as he crashed through the top floor door he even heard
one of his men shoot someone below. Dmitri Zallas was now beyond caring about
his guests. He wanted what was his and he wanted his resort protected, and right
now neither was happening. He walked quickly to the entrance, pushing a dark-
haired woman out of his way and then kicking at her angrily, and when her escort
tried to stop Zallas, he pulled a handgun from his large coat and shot the man
without a second thought. Several more shots were heard behind him when his
men saw the example being set by their employer. With the rumors of a vast treasure lost, the men had become murderous.

Pete turned and saw Zallas just in time as the men walked into the club and
onto the balcony section. Golding, with no warning at all, pushed Charlie over
the railing and then he jumped after him. Ellenshaw struck the floor and felt his
ankle bend in a manner that wasn't conducive to walking upright. He rolled and
yelled while grabbing for his injured leg.

Mikla was near the stage roaring angrily at the frightened people as they ran
one way and then saw Mikla and then turned screaming running in the opposite
direction. Drake Andrews and the terrified Russian band had abandoned everything and were battling to get through the wings just offstage, but every time
they thought they found an exit they were stopped by the humanity trying to flee
the now shaking castle. The American singer heard the roar of the animal and that
turned into a long howl. He screamed for no other reason than he wanted to, as he
and the others battled for their lives to get out. One second there was nothing but
shouting and panic, and the next everyone went silent as they swore they could
hear gunfire—quite a bit of it.

The only operational vehicles they could find were two very old cars used by the
Gypsies to travel the lower valleys. One was a thirty-five-year-old Citroën and
the other a beat-up, faded red 1962 Chevy Impala that came to Romania in God
knows what manner or circumstance. Jack, Sarah, Anya, and Major Mendohlson
were in the Chevy's front seat with Mendenhall, Alice, her potato sack with her
rocks, and sitting beside her was Ryan. Jack was cursing the slipping clutch as he
downshifted the old standard transmission. Anya screamed next to him as someone ran into the road waving his arms.

"It's Carl!" Anya shouted, happy to see him as he skidded to a stop beside the
sliding Chevy. Major Mendohlson hoped the Citroën behind them didn't slide
into them as they waited for the American to get out of the storm. Carl quickly
squeezed into the back by almost crushing the Israeli commando when he pushed
the front seat up.

"Nice car, Jack," Everett said as he pushed Mendenhall over.

"Yeah, I'm afraid shit red was all they had," he said as he put the car back into gear and peeled out in the mud and running water.

Carl saw Anya turn her head and look at him, happy he was still alive and ashamed she had left with Alice and not said anything to him. He shook his head and then winked. She turned back with a smile on her muddy face. Only Jack noticed the look as he tried to keep the old Chevy on the road.

He couldn't prove it, but Collins could swear the road was starting to move under the worn tires of the Chevy.

Two miles deep into the mountain the music of Drake Andrews and his new Russian backup band had finished the sabotage the Golia had started. The vibrations caused by the amazing sound system installed at Castle Dracula had started to shake away the last restraints holding the anchor pins in place. The six-foot-thick steel pins started to rotate as they lost their hold on the earth. As they turned, the heavy gauge steel snapped at several points along the two-mile anchorage. The next thing to tear loose was the foundation settings that connected the anchor pins to the castle's main foundation. The castle slipped a foot away from the facing and tilted toward the resort far below, making the highest parapet shake and actually break into three separate sections that barely hung on.

The furthest, deepest anchor pin gave way with a totality that would have been heard in Bucharest if it hadn't been buried deep in the mountain. After the steel broke in two, the whiplash fractured the remaining strata that kept the thermal vents intact. The underground geyser erupted into the cracks of the mountain where it built up enough pressure that the resulting explosion blew out the strong but now loose anchorage of the sixteen foundation pins. The force of the collapse pulled the top of the mountain toward the south, creating an avalanche of massive proportions. The rock fall started and continued rolling as it picked up speed and debris. The top of Patinas Pass turned to a viscous substance that resembled a wave as it collapsed, sending the pass into Patinas, burying the small village for all time.

The resulting release of energy had only one place to go, and that was through the area of least resistance and that meant through the thirty-five-hundred-year-old City of Moses. The explosion rocked the city, knocking over the wonderful obelisks and columns. The giant walled gate with the proud depictions of the Jeddah in their heyday of service to Pharaoh collapsed and then the stone carved ceiling came down upon three of the most famous men in the history of the world and crushed their remains to dust and buried them forever.

In just seconds the work of two thousand Jeddah and numerous engineers of Ramesses II came down, never again to see the light of day.

Pete Golding struggled to get Charlie Ellenshaw up and running when several people ran past with three of them stopping to help them up. Drake Andrews didn't wait for a thank-you as he and the other Russian musicians fled as Mikla roared again right next to them. They hadn't seen the wolf when they had stopped and didn't look back now. Ellenshaw watched the panicked people for a moment and then shouted to Pete.

"I think that's about enough, maybe we should split now, want do you think?"

Golding nodded that yes, he did think that was quite enough.

"Mikla, go!" Charlie shouted. "Run!"

The wolf suddenly went to all fours and looked around him as if he were confused. The Golia howled and then ran for the front with people screaming and jumping from the path of the giant.

Charlie saw Mikla jump onto the high stage and threaten several of the guests as they tried desperately to get away from what they thought was a Castle Dracula special effect gone awry. Ellenshaw saw two couples in the far darkened corner of the club still sitting, talking and drinking among the chaos. Ellenshaw hurriedly ran to their table tripping over several men as they tried to push themselves as far away from Mikla as they could get. The beast was standing upright, roaring and swiping at people as they ran by. Charlie was worried that instead of leaving, the giant Golia was starting to get its blood up and was becoming so excited that the claws would start slicing people in two soon if he and Pete didn't get out of there.

The two men and two women finally looked up as they saw Ellenshaw with Pete close behind running and stumbling toward them. One man stood from the table and as he did three bullets stitched a line across his white tuxedo jacket sending the man slamming against the wall, spraying blood on his companions as he did. The women screamed and then two more rounds hit the tabletop shattering glasses and sending the remains of their cocktails flying. Charlie fell facefirst and then covered his head. Pete looked up and saw Zallas and his men standing at the railing of the balcony firing down. The bullets hitting the floor and walls around them were aimed at him and Charlie. Pete reached out and pulled Ellenshaw as close to the wall as he could for protection.

Mikla roared again as Drake Andrews with several of the young Russian musicians in tow had somehow not found their way out to the cable car platform where men and women were pushing and shoving to either get to the front of the line or they were slapping and shoving each other on the twin stairwells that wound down to the ground from the platform. Even these were causing more casualties among the guests than Mikla ever could as they were tumbling down the steel steps as if they were doing it intentionally, and it was one of these men that Jack nearly struck with the front bumper of the old Chevy as they skidded to a halt.

Even above the din of screaming guests and running feet, Jack could hear the sound of gunfire over the tremendous pounding of the door. Then they all heard the roar of a Golia and every man and woman inside the Chevy thought the worst—that one of the wolves was loose inside the club and was now in the process of killing everyone and that would not do for the secrecy needed for the species. Collins was thrown an Uzi without the silencer attachment as he, Carl,

Mendohlson, Mendenhall, and Ryan all scrambled out of the car and into sheer madness as men and women in their finery splashed, screamed, fell, and rolled in the flooding mud caused by the raging storm.

As Collins hit the first step in the long stairwell to the top of the platform, the next cable car pulled in and Jack could hear the screaming, the jostling, and the cursing as men and women fought to be the first inside and away from the terrible things happening inside the club. As he hit the second platform of stairs on the way to the top with the others beating the steel stairs behind him, Jack flinched as first the body of a woman in an evening dress struck the side of the stairwell and spun off into the storm to strike the ground far below, then the body of a flailing man flew past striking the handrail on his way down.

As Sarah and Anya left Alice in the car with the smelly burlap bag, McIntire ran to the woman who fell to the ground. She checked for a pulse and in a flash of lightning Anya saw Sarah shake her head. Then she quickly checked the body that had landed only inches from his date. He too was broken and very much dead. Sarah knew if they didn't get Zallas and his people under control soon they would have a disaster on their hands that would be capable of shining too much light on the Event Group. They had to save as many people as they possibly could and then get out of there without the Romanian authorities asking too many questions about the strange group of men and women that had attached itself to the NATO survey.

Another roar of the Golia sent Anya flying up the stairs as she realized one of the precious and irreplaceable beasts was actually inside the club and they were hearing a lot of gunfire.

Zallas stood next to the balcony railing and surveyed the disaster that his precious Castle Dracula had become. The Russian was so angry he failed to feel the massive stone blocks beneath his feet shift, and again most did not see that the liquid in the half-filled glasses was beginning to lean to the south with a prominent tilt.

Zallas turned and took the wounded Ben-Nevin by the coat collar to pull him to the railing and then shake him as he gestured at the catastrophe below.

"What have you done to my club?" he yelled as spittle flew from his mouth and into the Mossad agent's face. "All of this and nothing from you!"

Ben-Nevin watched as the women and men continued to try to get out of the giant nightclub, most fearing the animal as it ran from spot to spot in a frenzy of excitement. His eyes widened at the familiar sight of Mikla, the beast that had rescued Anya on board the train just two nights before. Ben-Nevin slapped Zallas's hand away from his coat collar and then pulled a nine-millimeter from his waistband. He took quick aim and fired into the crowd in an attempt to hit the wolf. Mikla went to all fours and practically flew up the wall and into a dark vestibule and vanished. Ben-Nevin then sighted a new target. The white-haired man and the strange fellow from the hotel were huddling in a far corner by the stage.

It looked as if they were waiting to make a break for the rear door and the cable cars outside. Ben-Nevin took aim at the crazy-haired man.

Charlie Ellenshaw and Pete Golding had finally given up trying to separate the guests from the armed men that were in the mood to kill everyone in the confusion caused by Mikla. Charlie pulled Pete down closer to the floor when Ellenshaw had spotted the thirty or so men streaming into the club. They were Zallas's as the automatic weapons attested. Charlie was getting ready to pull Pete to his feet when he was knocked down just as three bullets punctured the stone wall next to his head.

"Wow, man, I think that cat was trying to kill you!" Drake Andrews said as he rolled off of Ellenshaw. Charlie managed to look up and see the harried and now very much crumpled American entertainer. His black show jacket was covered in blood and the young people behind him didn't look any better.

"Thanks," was all Ellenshaw could say as more bullets struck the tables and the walls behind the group of frightened entertainers.

"Are you an American?" Andrews asked.

"Yeah, we're Americans, but if we don't get out of here we'll never see the golden shores again," Pete interjected.

A bullet pinged off the black wall behind them and one of the young Russian singers screamed in pain as she grabbed her arm. Drake pulled her closer to him and then covered her.

"We have to get these kids out of here," Andrews said.

"Yeah, any suggestions?" Charlie asked. "If I'm not mistaken there seems to be a pretty angry Russian up there!"

Ben-Nevin had the white-haired man in his sights again and this time that American singer wouldn't help him. Suddenly several angry hornets crossed in front of his face. He turned and looked and saw several men and to his surprise running along with them was Anya Korvesky, or as the colonel knew her, Major Mica Sorotzkin. She took cover quickly behind a large pedestal with a suit of armor on it. Zallas pushed Ben-Nevin away and then his men returned some of the fire directed at them by the Americans.

Zallas gestured for his remaining men to advance on the Americans and he didn't care how many men he lost taking them out.

"Kill them all," he screamed as he looked around at the shambles of his castle. He could not believe he had been talked into this by that Israeli traitor. He knew he always had to go for the brass ring even though he had enough money already to buy the factory that made the brass rings. He always had to have what others had, and now here he was. The castle was going to be a complete loss and now he had to make sure this disaster didn't touch the much more valuable property below—the Edge of the World. That had to be saved after this fiasco. He looked at the cowardly Ben-Nevin and knew this man would die slowly in his hotel's basement just as Marko Korvesky had earlier in the evening.

Jack chanced a look down over the railing and saw that the only guests left in the club were Charlie, Pete, and a group of terrified-looking young people huddling together by the stage. There was no way with the minimal firepower at hand they could extricate Ellenshaw and Golding.

"Jack!" Sarah shouted as she held the handgun out and pointed to the far wall closest to the cable car platform.

Collins looked to where Sarah was pointing and then he jabbed Mendohlson and then yelled for Carl. He pointed to the same spot as McIntire. Their eyes widened. As they watched, the rip in the stone blocks where they had been cemented together was separated by a good eight inches and the gap was widening. Sarah knew the castle was starting to separate from the mountain. The tremor hit and that made all the gunfire magically cease for the briefest of moments as everyone realized at the same moment that something was starting to go terribly wrong with Dracula's Castle. Even Zallas remembered Sarah's dire warnings about a catastrophe in the making. Now the Russian was starting to see—and feel—her point. He was thinking maybe it was time to leave and sort this out in a better location, like his offices.

"The doc is pinned down by the stage, it looks like they may be the last ones to get out, he and Pete are with a bunch of kids."

"Kids? Here?" Carl said as he accepted another nine-millimeter clip from one of the Israeli commandos. Everett popped up and downed one of the mobster's hired killers, who grabbed his face and then fell over the balcony and then his body smashed into a table in the center of the room. "If we have to do this one at a time we may be here when this damn castle falls down," Everett finished and then fired one more round at the mass of killers fronting them.

"If you don't mind me asking you gentlemen, just who in the hell are you?" Mendohlson asked.

"He's Navy, I'm Army, and that really doesn't matter at the moment, Major," Jack said as he looked at the man. "What does matter is that I have two men down there protecting a bunch of kids. I have to get them out."

"Well, we're down to fifteen men. The rest are wounded or assisting the evacuation. We're it."

Jack grimaced.

"Here they come, Jack!" Everett said as he fired blindly into the men who were trying to make it to the cable car platform. "Damn!"

Bullets started slamming into the floor and the walls around them. The suit armor finally toppled over, narrowly missing a rolling Anya as it crashed to the floor. Collins saw that the Russian was done, he wanted out but they were in his way. Collins wasn't about to raise his hands and give Zallas free passage to the cable car that was just pulling in. As Jack tried to get Ellenshaw's attention below a bullet hit the colonel in the left shoulder and he felt the sting. Sarah saw him go down and there was nothing she could do about it.

Jack and his rescue team were about to be overrun.

Zallas knew he would make it with the human shield in front of him. He turned and grabbed Ben-Nevin once more and pulled him close.

"You will stay with me, my friend, until I have in my hands what I was promised. I want those men and I want what those Gypsies took from the temple!"

One of Zallas's men fired a long burst from his AK-47 and the mobster looked up in time to see the dark-haired American go down. To the Russian that was a start. He had bad vibes ever since meeting the American with the intense green eyes. He smiled again as he shook Ben-Nevin and pointed. "Now you'll see how we conduct business in Russia!" he said smiling maniacally.

Mikla was standing on the highest parapet on the east side of the castle. The giant Golia reached up and took hold of the ornate weather vane for balance and let loose a howl that was heard even over the building storm. Mikla was calling for help.

The mountain above the castle suddenly came alive with a black-on-black movement that looked as if ants were heading down the side of the mountain. The Golia had arrived to battle one last time against the forces of Pharaoh.

"That's it, I'm out!" Sarah said as she looked around hoping that Mendohlson and his men had something extra to give. They did not. Their volume of fire diminished. They were done for.

Zallas was seen pulling the Israeli colonel around by the collar as his men kept up the withering fire as they worked their way to the platform. The cable car was there looking none too good after the wild ride down with screaming guests that had been terrified by what they still thought was a special effects show gone awry.

"You better pray that old Gypsy and her backward people are down below or you will never leave here, Jew Colonel," Zallas said as his anti-Semitism came flowing from his mouth like corruption from a wound. "They better have what you have promised me." He shook the colonel once more as he walked behind his curtain of men, dodging from fake castle appointment to potted plant. "Look at this, you are responsible for this!"

As Zallas looked around, his club was a shambles and as it stood he knew he would at least lose millions in a delayed opening. Dmitri Zallas was the type of man who never looked at the legal ramifications of anything he came across, he always had the fix in, just as he did at the moment with the interior minister. The damage could be controlled but that didn't mean that the Jew had made a deal and he was going to stick to it if Zallas had to kill every last Gypsy inside Romania. And then he would start in the neighboring countries—nobody lied to Dmitri Zallas or ripped him off.

"Doc!"

Professor Ellenshaw heard the shout coming from behind. The din of battle from up top was starting to slacken as their rescuers ran low on ammunition. Charlie eased his head around the woman he was protecting with his body. He saw Jason Ryan and Will Mendenhall lying on the cold stone floor looking at them from a small cubbyhole at the end of the stage. It had taken them ten minutes to work their way outside and then to one of the ornate leaded glass windows where it took another three minutes to break through the lead that held most of the stained glass in place.

"Come on, Doc, we gotta split, man," Ryan said, frantically waving Ellenshaw and his charges away from the main floor.

Ellenshaw started with the girl beneath him. It was the young woman dressed as Janis Joplin, and that made crazy Charlie give her a double take.

"Must have been one hell of a show," he said as he pushed the young girl, who was still wearing her sunglasses, toward Ryan, who also gave Janis a second look.

Next Pete was pushing Jim Morrison, and holding on to his long fringe-lined vest were the three Supremes screaming as bullets stitched the thick brick walls. Each of the Russian performers, all dressed as past greats for Drake Andrews's performance, was sent through the small opening to the rear of the stage and the false front of the castle beyond. Ryan and Will exchanged astonished looks as the evening just became far stranger.

"Okay, come on, Johnny, move it!" Ryan yelled out as the second to last performer, a kid dressed all in black like Johnny Cash, almost got stuck in the small opening.

"Wow!" Mendenhall said as the last man through was none other than Drake Andrews.

"Hey, dude, thanks a lot," he said as he started crawling through the hole and into the small passageway.

"Come on, Doc!" Ryan said as he finally assisted Ellenshaw and Pete through the opening. "Good job getting those kids out of there," Jason said to Ellenshaw and Pete as bullets slammed into the hole from upstairs.

"Where to now?" Pete asked as he waited for the others.

"The drawbridge in the front, it's the only way out to get to the platform, we can't take a chance getting to the stairs from the main room," Mendenhall answered as he pushed Pete forward through the tunnel beside the stage.

"The drawbridge?"

Jack, Carl, Mendohlson, Sarah, Anya, Everett, and three of the Israeli commandos were forced to break off and make a run for the far corner away from the platform, as they could no longer stand and fight.

Before Jack realized what was happening he was taken off guard by the brass of the Russian, as he not only directed men to the cable car to hold it, he was actually sending twenty men after his small retreating unit. As he watched the men turn down the balcony hallway the castle gave a giant lurch as the concrete sealant around the foundation and stone block walls finally gave up its hold on the mountain. The castle slipped forward on its foundation by one and a half feet. This time the undermined anchor bolts twisted free of the earth until there was no longer anything holding the castle tight to the mountain. It was starting to come down and Jack knew it.

"To the roof, we'll catch the cable car from there and hope Mr. Ryan finds a way up, let's move, people," he said as Major Mendohlson took the lead and rushed for the stairwell at the end of the hall and just hoped it went up at least one more floor to the castle's promenade at the top.

Zallas and his men immediately realized the Americans had broken completely off. They made a mad dash for the giant cable car that had docked just moments before. It was still partially in motion as it swung into the loading area. Three of the Russian's men ran to the ornate wooden door but the automatic system had failed and the double doors remained closed. The men batted on the clouded window but the doors remained closed. The first man tried to look inside and found the view obscured. He stepped back and that was when he noticed that every specially etched glass window was covered in a thin film of red. The man's eyes widened when the doors suddenly hissed open and before he could stop the first two men they ran inside.

The Russian heard the screaming men just as they broke into the promenade for the cars. The men inside were screaming and the large, heavy car was rocking on its cables. As the remaining men stopped short of the car, Stanus broke free of the doors and stood silhouetted in the ornate lighting from the interior. The beast was in the standing position. Its black muzzle shining with the fresh blood of the two men that were now scattered all over the Queen Anne decor. Stanus was breathing heavy as it took in the startled men standing before it. The yellow eyes were now dulled by pain and its two bullet wounds were bleeding heavily, one from its upper right back and one in the back of the neck. Stanus shook its massive head back and forth sending saliva and blood flying in all directions and then it gathered its strength and raised its muzzle high and roared. The sound shook the platform and had the toughest men in Eastern Europe reversing as quickly as they could.

Ben-Nevin was the only one to react since he had become used to seeing these creatures. He allowed Zallas to step behind as he removed his nine-millimeter. Stanus lowered his head and fixed the colonel with his eyes as if daring the man to shoot.

Four more men turned and decided they would rather face this strange giant dog than face Zallas. They slowly brought up their AK-47s and took aim.

At that precise moment all the hell stored up in the history of the dark Carpathian Mountains broke free. The Golia struck the castle in force. Mikla was the first to jump from the top of the cable car where it had hidden amid the pulleys and platform cables and leaped onto the roof and then to the floor, crashing through the thin aluminum manufactured to resemble thick wooden beams. It was on all fours and was taking up station in front of his older brother, Stanus, growling and making the men hesitate just long enough for the rest of the male Golia to strike from the open sides of the promenade. They hit with such force that the men had no time to react. While backing away, Ben-Nevin fired blindly, missing Mikla by inches as the Golia moved and struck, barely missing the colonel as he turned and ran with Zallas and the last fifteen men.

The rest of his assassins were facing the wrath of the Golia and started losing very quickly as one man would go down and three of the giant wolves would strike as a team and the man was soon rendered in pieces. The frightening screams of the men covered up the sound and masked the movement of the castle as it broke completely free of the mountain, tearing the electrical conduits that snaked through the cement foundation, making the lights flicker and then go out completely.

In the sheer blackness in the few seconds it took for the emergency lighting to come on, Zallas heard his men being torn to pieces by something out of a nightmare. Suddenly Marko and his Gypsy band didn't seem so foolish. Water mains ripped from the mountain added to the flood of rain from the pass above. The final collapse of the City of Moses shook the mountain one last time as if God were saying an end had come to all.

Zallas and his force of personal bodyguards knew they had only one way out of the frightening scene now visible in the weak emergency lighting. They had to get to the top of the castle and then work their way down and hope the Americans had decided to take another route. They ran for the stairwell that was well camouflaged as a thick wooden castle door. Ben-Nevin thought it best to stay with the only firepower left on the mountain and followed as the wolves of God finished off the evil that had invaded their lands.

Stanus collapsed inside the car and didn't move. The push it had received from Madam Korvesky, who had vanished with the other Gypsies, had brought him to the cable car tower and that was where he climbed to the top and waited for the return car to the castle. The other Golia had met Mikla and joined him on the roof of the castle and had waited patiently to spring their trap, which they pulled off to perfection, just as it always had. Now Stanus was nearing the end as his blood flow was starting to ease for lack of pressure. On the roof Anya stopped and felt the sudden loss as Stanus started breathing heavy and as Mikla stood over his brother whining as it sniffed the giant Golia. Stanus raised his head, smelled Mikla, and then lay back. Mikla looked at the remaining male Golia and then it stepped from the car as the doors slid closed behind. The Golia used its special eyesight and saw the imprint the retreating men had left on the cobbled

stone flooring. The prints stood out as a shade of gray brighter than their surroundings.

Mikla growled and then anger over the wounds to Stanus overcame the calmer
of the two brothers and forced the shape shifting to begin. Mikla roared as it tried
to stand and failed. Then it roared again as its hips finally popped free and the
thigh bones fell free of their sockets, and Mikla, roaring in pain, finally gained his
hind feet and then looked and lowered his large ears and howled. The other Golia
stopped and then as one they tore through the cable car promenade heading for
the stairwell door.

Jack was balanced on the outside wall on a small ledge that wrapped around the
back. The cable car promenade was a hundred feet below and the only way they
could reach the cars was to jump from the castle wall just below one of the massive parapets to the cable car roof and then down into the car. Jack wished they
had the time to just run away on foot but knew that the flooding on the road pre-
vented any foot traffic to the resort. They were now forced to brave the cable car.
Sarah was behind him as she saw him stop and listen. The screams coming from
inside the castle had startled even Collins. The Golia were inside and he didn't
know if once their blood was up they would differentiate good guy from bad.
Luckily Anya was in front of Everett straddling the six-inch ledge.

"Anya, what is it?" Carl asked when he felt the woman hitch up and then almost fall from the wall. Everett quickly reached out and took her and held her.
Mendohlson saw Everett's struggle and assisted in holding the woman. She finally
opened her eyes and then fixed them on Everett.

"Stanus is dying."

Everett didn't know what to say. He helped her straighten as Jack started moving again.

Collins was nearing the parapet rising high above them when the first shots
struck the wall next to him, sending stone chips into his face.

"Damn!" he said as he almost lost his grip on the ledge. Sarah winced as she
braved removing one hand from the mortar gaps and taking Jack by his belt.
She closed her eyes not knowing for the briefest of moments if they both were
going over into the chasm between the road and the castle. Jack finally caught
his balance as more shots pinged off the stone facing around them. "Thanks,
short stuff," he said as he completed the ledge walk and made it to the open
window of the parapet. He assisted Sarah inside and then the others. He chanced
a look outside and saw Zallas and his men starting to step out onto the large
ledge.

As they moved through the darkness they all lost their footing as they searched
for a way out to the opposite ledge and then the short jump to the promenade roof
as the castle broke into two distinct halves. The top half broke free from the foundation and came sliding five feet over the club below. It stopped just as the mountain quit convulsing. Jack got to his feet and felt the tilt of the castle. The movement

was now constant as mortar and stone started splitting apart in unseen places, evidenced by the constant scraping they were now hearing.

"I do believe we are out of time, Jack!" Carl said as he finally sped to the door in the darkness.

Everett threw the door open and Mendohlson stepped through and vanished. Collins's heart froze as he reached out and was barely able to take the Israeli commando's sleeve preventing him from falling the four hundred feet to his death. Carl and Anya with Sarah holding Jack's belt again pulled the major.

The entire wall of the west side tower was gone, leaving a gap of twenty feet to the promenade roof. Jack and the others finally managed to get the major back through the open doorway.

"Whoa, many thanks," Mendohlson said as he tried to get his heart going again. One HALO jump in a year was enough, much less doing one without a chute.

"I think we have to find another way, the jump is too far," Collins said as Everett looked out the doorway and confirmed what the colonel was saying.

"Where is Stanus when you need him," Carl said as he put his head back in. "Jack, you know when those assholes get here they are going to place so many bullets into this room it'll be like a shooting gallery with these stone walls. We have to go up even higher and try another way. We won't have time to scale down from here."

"You lead the way this time, swabby; I think I've lost my mountain goat skills."

Carl nodded, took Anya's hand, and then looked out the open doorway once more. He saw a small ladder just outside the door, what was left of one leading to one of the skylights now lying four hundred feet below in the gully. Everett leaned over and kissed Anya on the cheek and then reached out and took hold of the ladder that would lead them to the highest portion of Castle Dracula.

They were unaware that it was the portion now dangling over the remains of the club and teetering over the abyss.

Charlie, Ryan, Mendenhall, Pete, Drake Andrews, and the sixteen Russian musicians and performers had found getting to the promenade platform would be impossible so they took the only route available. The many stairwells leading to the base of the cable car tower had taken almost ten minutes to travel as they slipped and fell on the wet steel as the storm continued around the steel towers. Ryan could feel the short jolts of electricity flow through the handrails as lightning struck close by on several occasions. Finally they spied the bottom.

Pete was the first one to step out of the stairwell and into the inky blackness. He vanished as the water took him. The rainwater was now turning the roadway into a debris-swollen river. The collapse of the temple complex had opened up the pass sending a wave of mud cascading down the mountain. Now the raging river had Pete. Charlie had to be pulled back as he tried to leap into the water to save his friend.

"No, Doc!" Ryan shouted into the fierce mouth of the raging storm. "You've done enough, it's my turn," Jason said as he turned to Mendenhall. "Get them down the best you can, Will," he said and then saluted him with a smile and without another word dove into the swirling water and was swept away.

Mendenhall and Ryan knew when playtime and the joking ceased and when it was time for the junior officer to take orders from a superior and this was one of those times as much as Will hated to admit it. He shook with anger that Ryan had gone without hesitation. He knew he had to move as the tower they had just climbed down was swaying the whole time they traversed the stairs.

Mendenhall moved his charges out of the tower to ease along the rim of the road, which was now only inches above the water. The first girl, the one dressed as Janis Joplin, slipped and nearly went in. Mendenhall and Ellenshaw caught her and pulled her back. The girl was shaking so badly Will knew he would never get her to attempt it again.

"Damn, Doc, we need a cab in the worst way!"

At that precise moment the dull red 1962 Chevy Impala bumped against the cable tower and careened into the stairwell doorway narrowly missing Mendenhall and Charlie. Will acted quickly, as he never looked a gift horse, or in this case, a gift boat, in the mouth. He reached out and used the door frame as leverage and jumped onto the hood of the car and then scrambled up the windshield and through the open window. Luckily the old and battered Chevy lodged momentarily against the cable tower, the bumper digging into the doorway. Mendenhall waved at Charlie, gesturing wildly for him to get all sixteen people into the car. It was going to be a tight squeeze but knew it was any boat in a storm. The Russians started jumping onto the car's hood and top. The trunk sank in the water as even more jumped onto the car. Charlie was the last one on and got stuck on the top as he kicked out several times with the help of Drake Andrews until the Chevy dislodged from the tower.

Soon the Impala was moving rapidly down the most recent rapids to come into existence in the Eastern world—Dracula's Wild Ride, Will would call it later when telling the tale.

The men and women of the Russian musical troupe, with Drake Andrews and Charlie Ellenshaw adding their weight, screamed as the car started twisting in the rapidly moving floodwaters as it rushed for a collision date with a doomed resort.

Zallas finally made it through the open window and it was another ten minutes of nearly falling ten times until they finally made it to the now silent promenade deck. Zallas took a head count and found he had only ten men left. He had lost another three in the harrowing climb down to the car. He gestured for his men to advance and make sure all of those insane dogs were gone.

As they approached the door it slid open automatically and then men jumped back with a start when they saw the prone body of Stanus. The giant wolf wasn't moving as it lay on the Persian carpet of the car's interior. Ben-Nevin, angry at seeing one of the animals that could no longer take his head off at the shoulders, stepped up and placed two bullets into the still animal's back. The Golia didn't move. Ben-Nevin gestured for them to get inside the car but had to brace himself as the castle shifted once more. It stilled but they all knew it wouldn't stay that way as they all saw the very long, very deep crack in the cobbled flooring of the promenade.

"Come, you fools, get aboard, this castle is no longer destined to stay attached to this mountain." He looked at Zallas as he stepped past the Israeli. "I guess the little American woman was right, you should have paid for a good engineer instead of the one you paid off."

Zallas gave the colonel a filthy look as he stepped over the bleeding Golia. He should have noticed the large hitch in the beast's chest as the automatic doors slid closed and the car started its slow push out from the covered promenade.

As the car below started to leave the barn, Jack knew they weren't going to make it. It was too far down. They could possibly get Anya and Sarah and maybe the major on board the roof but that would be it. It was Anya and Mikla who settled it.

"You three go, Mikla will carry me, now move!" she shouted just as Mikla jumped onto the roof of the promenade. With another leap he easily managed to jump to the large window overlooking the moving car below. Without hesitation Mikla took a struggling Anya by the arm and tossed her roughly onto his back and then the Golia jumped free of the window and vanished.

"I guess he has his priorities," Sarah said as she leaned out the large window and saw the Golia deposit an angry Anya on the cable car's roof and then he started to climb again away from the frantically waving Gypsy and frustrated woman.

"I think maybe the wolf is coming back to—"

Sarah was unceremoniously yanked from the room by Mikla, who repeated the process until Sarah was standing next to Anya as they both looked up at the three men.

As they watched the wolf start its amazing climb once more, the floor cracked straight down the middle and this time the top half of the castle tilted to the far front and Jack felt it slipping free of the lower half.

"That's it, out the window now!" he screamed as the tower started to crumble under their feet.

The three men scrambled out into the open storm as fast as they could but even as they gained purchase on the sloping wall they turned and saw the east parapet tilt. In the storm and lightning it was upright one moment and then during the next flash the tower was falling right past the man hanging on to the wall and just hoping the falling tower missed not only them but the entire cable car platform. It did as it went whooshing by them, splitting the rain and wind and creating its own storm as the large building blocks slammed into the club below.

That force of impact finally sheared the foundation away from the mountain and the club went next, sliding and tumbling down the mountain heading straight for the resort far below.

Collins, Everett, and Mendohlson felt the wall they were holding on to ripple and start to give way.

"Well, it's been one hell of a night, gentlemen, but it's time to see if we can fly," Mendohlson said as he leaped to the car now free of the barn and snagged a large cable. He was hanging on for dear life and then Jack and Carl breathed a sigh of relief as Mendohlson slowly made his way to the roof. Without comment, Jack, and then Everett, both let go of the wall as the same moment and snagged the same cable and went hand overhand to the car's roof. Just as their feet touched down several bullets came smashing through the roof forcing the new passengers toward the centerline where the cables attached to the car and the huge pulley system. Jack looked down as the car went out over the abyss and their descent into the valley began.

Sarah and Anya were trying to see in the darkness just when the remains of the upper half of Dracula's Castle would fall and crush them all to death when they saw in a flash of lightning the south parapet lean forward and then fall. It was like something out of a Hollywood movie about the wrath of God bringing down a stone monstrosity that dared rise against his mountain and his animals. The tower flew past the moving car and smashed into the main tower, shaking the cable and thus the car. It rocked back and forth with the force of the collision almost sending Jack and the others slinging off into the storm to their deaths. More bullets flew through the ornate wood ceiling as Zallas and his men continued to take potshots at them.

Suddenly in a bright flash the power lines exploded as part of the east parapet struck the second tower just as the cable car passed it, knocking free the power lines and shaking the car and the men inside enough that the intruders on the roof became a moot point as they all realized that the world was going to come crashing down upon them any second.

Finally the mountain gave one last tremendous shake and the remains of the castle, club and all, broke away, sending engineered stone blocks the size of houses and made in Hungary careening down the mountainside. The first twenty-two-ton block hit the first cable tower knocking it free of its cement base. The cables that ran through the pulley system on the tower unraveled sending the car plummeting to the road now three hundred feet down. Jack and the others barely held on to the heavy pulley block on the top of the car as they fell through the air. They waited for the crushing impact as they hit the bottom. They felt the tremendous jerk and then they all fell hard into the steel. The last cable had hung up on the next tower and the cable continued to play out. They were moving but no longer falling, but being lowered like a slow elevator as the cable hung on tight to the second tower. They were now only a hundred feet off the rushing waters below.

Finally it was the 800,000-ton foundation that came next. The anchor pins the Golia had painstakingly undermined for months came free of their pilot holes and the entire structure, foundation, and sixteen hundred-ton steel pins came free with it. Together they came down the side of the mountain like a runaway block of stone connected by giant lawnmower blades. Both slammed into the second tower hitting it with so much force that it not only knocked it from its base but bent it double. The next tower was even easier, as the agglomeration of Dracula's Castle's remains sent the cable car the last hundred feet into the swirling waters of the flood.

As Jack, Sarah, Anya, Mendohlson, and Everett hung on for dear life, the car turned in a large circle and sped down the ravine toward the hotel. They all wanted to scream when Mikla jumped onto the top of the car. Anya reached out and grabbed the wolf by the ears and pulled it closer to her. She thought they had lost Mikla when the castle came down, but he must have jumped from damaged area to damaged area until he had reached the third tower.

Together with the Russian and his men below in the darkened car and screaming like schoolgirls on an amusement park ride, the Event Group, Anya, and the Israeli commando held on tightly as the cable car shot down the growing rapids, careening from bank to bank as they rushed toward the Edge of the World—literally.

Will couldn't believe he was actually trying to steer the car in the rising water as the Chevy flew down the flooded road. The car smashed into the right berm, and then spun in a circle and then struck the left side. The Chevy was dangerously close to being sunk by the mass of humanity inside and on top of the car. Drake Andrews saw disaster coming their way first and started pounding on the roof as if Mendenhall could actually do something about what he was panicking over.

"Whoa, whoa, look out!" Andrews yelled and then watched as several hundred-ton blocks of stone bounced past them on their way to crash into the hotel. Then Drake and Charlie both started pounding the car's roof when they saw the next little fright headed their way.

"Will!" Charlie screamed from the roof, not knowing that Mendenhall was busy turning the wheel of a car that was now floating faster than it ever drove.

Mendenhall looked in the rearview mirror past all of the wet heads inside the car and took in a sight that froze his blood. The cable car was right behind them and was coming on fast. He could see people inside and outside on the top. He braced for the impact and it soon came.

The cable car smashed into the Chevy sending Ellenshaw, Andrews, and the girl dressed as Janis Joplin free of the car and into the water. The cable car's rear end flew up and that was when Major Mendohlson lost his fight with centrifugal force and followed them into the rapids.

Jack and Sarah tried to hold on to Everett and Anya but they too went over the side and into the water and they were quickly followed by Mikla, who went after the Jeddah princess. Jack cursed and then held on to Sarah as the car went straight for the geodesic dome of the large spa and nature center.

Niles Compton and Alice Hamilton had finally made it to the hotel to warn everyone of the disaster but all they saw of the remnants of the grand opening at the castle was the screaming, bloody, terrified guests from Castle Dracula running through the hotel. The staff had evacuated with them. Everyone was gathering at the front gate and trying desperately to get as far away from the Edge of the World as they could.

Niles pulled on Alice's hand knowing the older woman was near to collapse, but still she clung to the burlap sack containing whatever it was she had removed from Madam Korvesky's home. It had taken Niles another five minutes to find the radio in the office of Dmitri Zallas.

"Yes, Virginia, I'm sure," Niles radioed Virginia Pollack at the Event complex in Nevada, "if we do not get the emergency evac in the next hour we'll have an international mess on our hands that won't end. We have the proof of theft and we have evidence that supports the Event call. Yes, immediately, we have to—"

Niles felt the rumble just in time as Alice dropped the sack she was carrying and then pushed Compton out of the way as the first stone block from the falling parapet struck the hotel and veered into the casino, smashing through to the far side where it landed in the Olympic-sized swimming pool.

Niles looked up as he felt the rain on his face and the howling wind coming from the space where the outer wall used to be. He was still holding the microphone from the radio in his hand. The cord had been sheared off as the block not only took half the office away, but the radio also.

Alice quickly retrieved the bag and then helped Niles to his feet.

"I think we did what Jack wanted, maybe it's time to beat that hasty retreat they always talk about," Alice said as she gingerly eased herself over the remains of the office.

Alice and Niles Compton had made it clear of the hotel when the remains of the castle's foundation smashed into the hotel. The top floor collapsed into the fifth until the combined weight of both floors created the pancaking effect seen in building collapses. The hotel came down and pulled the casino into the water with it.

The Edge of the World had slipped completely off the grid.

The Chevy, the cable car, and those who had managed to hang on during their harrowing ride down the mountain slid into the cornerstone of what was left of the casino. The men and women inside and outside the Chevy jumped free but quickly went for cover as gunfire erupted from inside the cable car. The bullets smashed windows as the doors opened and several men jumped out into the water wanting to make it to the remains of the casino. Then several more men jumped free. Mendenhall watched as Jack Collins and Sarah McIntire jumped into the water from the top of the car. He opened his door and then allowed himself to taken by rushing water. The Russian musicians soon joined Will in the water as the last of Zallas's men made a break for safety.

Dmitri Zallas was fuming. Not only had he been as frightened as a child and demonstrated so on the way down the mountain, but his most trusted men deserted him. Only Colonel Ben-Nevin remained. He gestured for Ben-Nevin to give him his gun. The colonel only smiled and rubbed the wound on his shoulder. He raised the pistol and pushed the barrel against Zallas's ample chest until the scowling Russian stepped aside. Ben-Nevin shook his head as he passed the stunned gangster.

"I'm afraid our deal is off," he said as the gun never wavered from the Russian's chest.

"You have failed at your mission, your future will be as bleak as my own," Zallas hissed.

"Possibly, but I believe that we may have caused enough of a mess for the world to notice that the current Israeli soft-liners have sent an illegal force of Israeli soldiers into a friendly nation and killed Romanian nationals, so in the end my benefactors will come to power anyway, so at least I have a fighting chance. And you? I'm afraid you have nothing. Now, excuse me as I find a ride out of here."

Zallas watched Ben-Nevin as he stepped off into the rushing water and was gone as the car started to fill with muddy, dank water.

"I will kill you!" Zallas screamed as he made for the door in the darkness.

As he readied to jump into the rushing torrent, his shoulder was grabbed from behind. The claws dug deeply into the Russian's shoulder, sending the nails so deep that they struck the man's collarbone. He screamed in pain as he was suddenly jerked around. Standing there bleeding and wet was Stanus. The beast was still alive and well enough to stand upright in the rising water of the flood. The Golia was breathing heavily, trying to force life-giving air into its collapsing lungs. The animal had actually lain there and accepted the two bullets from Ben-Nevin's gun and not moved an inch. Zallas realized that this was no ordinary dog—it was not only the largest wolf he had ever seen in his life, but it was also the smartest creature he had even known, including most of his business associates. Then he looked into the yellow eyes.

Stanus leaned in so close to the Russian that its breath fouled the man's breathing. Stanus was near death, he could see that, but he also knew the beast was staying alive long enough to corner him before he could escape. Then he saw it. The eyes first flashed to brown and then back to the glowing yellow. Then he saw Marko in the reflection cast upon him. The Gypsy was there, inside the wolf, and the Russian knew this as a fact just as surely as he knew this nightmare from his childhood was going to kill him. Zallas shook his head just as the beast slowly opened its mouth and bit.

The screaming stopped almost as soon as it started as the cable car broke free of the remnants of the hotel and then circled once near the pool and then slowly went under the water.

Stanus, the alpha male of the Golia, was gone.

Jack saw Ben-Nevin leave the car and had jumped into the water to follow. Of all the people in this nightmare he knew that this man was at the root of what happened here tonight. He had tried to kill his people and Jack would never let that go. Sarah yelled after him and then carefully jumped into the swirling mass and followed him and Ben-Nevin into what was left of the casino.

"Hold it!" Jack yelled as his feet hit dry carpeting for the first time in what seemed hours. Ben-Nevin turned and without aiming fired three times, taking Collins by surprise. Jack's reactions were barely fast enough to move out of the way. Luckily the casino was dark with only a few of the emergency lamps still operational. "Missed, Colonel, typical spook shooting, not very good. I see the Mossad doesn't train their agents any better than the CIA," Jack yelled as he tried to get the desired effect. He did.

Ben-Nevin angrily fired off three more shots and then Collins heard a curse as the firing pin on the colonel's handgun came down upon nothing. Jack stood from his cover and saw Ben-Nevin standing there. He was looking past Jack and at something over his shoulder. Collins slowly turned and saw Carl standing there with Anya. They were battered and bruised and covered in mud but very much alive. Then Jack's eyes traveled to where Anya stood and saw in the weak battery-driven lights that Mikla was standing next to her. The wolf was only looking in one direction—straight at Ben-Nevin, the man Mikla had saved Anya from on the train, and the Golia had a very long memory.

"While taking our swim in the new river outside," Jack said, "we came across Pete Golding and Ryan trying to break a swim record for speed. They're outside with the remnants of a very strange group of funny-dressed Russians and Drake Andrews."

Jack looked from Mikla to Carl and then back at Ben-Nevin.

"You have a lot to answer for, Colonel. I should probably let Ms. Korvesky return you to Israel, but that may cause some embarrassment for a few people, so it looks like things will be settled a little more quietly," he said as he took a step forward.

"You may think you have stopped our faction for now, Major, but you have not. The truth of this place will come out. There is no stopping that now and then we will have the full power to bring the left-wing government down and replace it with those who know and understand the power of the past, and remember that we are God's chosen ones."

"I think you will find that scenario flawed somewhat," Anya said. "And the name is Korvesky, and I am the queen of the Jeddah."

Collins started forward but Carl reached out and took Collins's shoulder and stilled him.

"Not this time, Jack. I insist on the honors, well, my friend here does at any rate."

Ben-Nevin's eyes went wide as Carl turned away with Jack and along with Anya left him alone with Mikla. The wolf didn't move or make a sound. The beast suddenly stood on its hind feet and advanced in four long strides until its face was inches from Ben-Nevin. Mikla soon explained the real facts of life to the traitorous Ben-Nevin.

As Carl assisted Anya over the ruined casino wall he waited for Jack as the roar of Mikla was heard over the wind and thunder of the storm. Colonel Ben-Nevin had just learned the real magic of the Jeddah and why they had never been found—the Golia had always been there to protect them, just as Mikla was doing at that moment.

As Jack looked around him he saw what remained of his team and the night's entertainment. They all turned when they heard someone splashing up behind them. Major Mendohlson was standing there as wet as everyone else and he wasn't alone. The remnants of his team of fifty-six men were with him and Jack only counted thirty-two. Most were injured but at least they were alive. Collins nodded to his colleague and then watched as the Israeli approached. Anya and Carl joined them as the storm for the first time that night started to taper.

"Gentlemen, Major Korvesky," Mendelsohn said, "as we have no way to get a dust-off from the area, I am placing me and my men into NATO protective custody until such time as we can be sent back to our country to face charges."

Collins and Everett knew how the game was played. The Israeli government would never admit to authorizing the mission to destroy the City of Moses so they would have no choice but to hang the major and his team out to dry and call the action unauthorized.

Jack shook his head in understanding. "Major, we all may be headed for a Romanian jail, so why don't we hang out a while and see what happens."

"Yes, but if I may," the major said and turned to face Sarah McIntire. "I overheard you earlier explaining the dynamics of the temple and the mountains and the castle's engineering flaws. Can you assure me that whatever was buried inside that mountain is buried forever?"

Jack knew immediately what the major was referring to and decided to help Sarah.

"The last we saw, Stanus had the weapon, Major, what he did with it will be a mystery that went to the grave with him."

"You mean that wolf?"

"Yeah, that guy," Jack answered.

Carl took Anya by the hand and walked her a few steps away until they were well out from the rest of the survivors. They were now standing in the rain. Everett leaned over and kissed the new Gypsy queen and then just held her. As he did the thumping sound started from the sky and overrode the distant thunder. Carl looked up at the noise.

"What in the hell is that?" Mendenhall asked as he stopped applying the bandage to Ryan's head.

"That's the result of my phone call home. I see Virginia got through to the president, who in turn got the NATO commander in Cologne, Germany, to get us some transport in here. After all, we had a little problem with flooding ourselves."

All eyes turned to a filthy Niles Compton and Alice Hamilton. They looked as if they had been through a blender. They heard the six Black Hawk helicopters of the 82nd Airborne Division as they made their way through the diminishing storm to what remained of the most expensive hotel and casino Eastern Europe had ever seen.

"And Mrs. Hamilton, I think I'll sit out your next little foray into the world, this is rough," Niles said as he sat hard on an overturned craps table and waited for the American Army to rescue them from what used to be known to the world as Transylvania. A place the Event Group would not soon forget.

The sun struggled to break through the early morning clouds as the first of the five Black Hawks lifted off carrying the more severely injured of the small group left near the hotel. With Dmitri Zallas missing the security element had deserted the property.

Jack was getting ready to send Mendohlson and his remaining Sayeret team to the next Black Hawk when they were approached by several men in the blue and black uniforms of the Romanian National Police. Collins exchanged looks with Everett when they saw that the police had come in force and most were already standing by two trucks that had been brought in to remove the major.

"I am Captain Ceustantz of the National Police, Major Mendohlson. I have been ordered to take you and your team into protective custody pending a hearing for illegally entering Romania to cause anarchy upon our citizens."

Anya started to step forward to protest but Everett held her back with a shake of his head. It was no use getting herself arrested.

Mendohlson half bowed in compliance, letting the officer know that he would have no trouble with him or his men. He turned to face Anya and Everett and smiled.

"Major Korvesky, the best of luck to you in your new life. Captain," Mendohlson held out his hand and Everett shook it. The major then turned to Jack and offered his hand. "Colonel, I recognized your name as soon as I heard it. I would someday like to see you in action against something other than creatures from a fairy tale and mobsters that fell out of a bad movie."

"Someday soon, Major," Jack said, taking the man's hand and then shaking it. Collins watched the major leave and he was smiling as he wiped more mud from his face.

"What's so funny, Colonel?" Mendenhall asked when he saw his boss looking at the two trucks and the policemen who assisted the major's wounded and worn team into the back. The major turned and looked at Jack just as a large man with a barrel chest and police uniform stepped up to the major. They both were looking at the group of motley Americans. The big man smiled and waved as he helped the major into the back of the truck.

"I think we just saw Ms. Korvesky's former boss," Jack said as Anya stepped forward to view the scene better. Her mouth fell open as she was witnessing the impossible.

The second invasion of Romania was on as General Addy Shamni smiled and gave Anya a half salute. She saw a worn and weary Janos Vajic standing next to the general. And then to her shock she saw her grandmother's body as it was loaded onto the truck. General Shamni walked toward the stunned group of Americans and up to Anya. He eyed Everett and gave him an appreciative nod of his head. The general then faced his former charge.

"Major, I am going home now and taking my sister with me. She can no longer remain here. She will be enshrined with every king and queen the Jeddah have ever known in Jerusalem with the rest of her kind. She will lie next to Kale, the Great One. She's going home to a place denied to your tribe thirty-five hundred years ago. She's coming home with me." He leaned over and kissed Anya on the forehead. "Good-bye, niece." General Shamni turned and walked out of the life of Anya Korvesky.

"I never knew before tonight," she said as she watched the trucks with the counterfeit Romanian police drive away after rescuing their assault teams before the real police arrived.

"Well, it's all over now," Carl said as he knew his life was also never going to be the same after tonight.

Two hours later everyone was accounted for, including Denise Gilliam, who had ended up with the Israeli rescue force after Madam Korvesky died. She recounted how the old woman knew for a fact that her grandson was still inside Stanus. She then added what little she could to sustain the wolf's life while he lay in wait inside the cable car. She was there just long enough for Marko, herself, and Stanus to send Dmitri Zallas off to the afterlife with an attitude adjustment.

The last of the Black Hawks started spooling up their twin turbo-driven engines. As the four-bladed rotors started to turn the Event Group loaded up.

Collins watched Charlie and Pete board after making sure Drake Andrews and his new band had made it safely aboard another Romanian helicopter. Jack then walked to the last Black Hawk where Sarah, Mendenhall, Niles, Alice, and Ryan were waiting with Denise Gilliam. Collins stepped aboard and then turned and waited for Carl. He was holding Anya and saying something to her, and then with a final kiss they parted. She never turned away from Everett's back as he moved to join his friends. He made it to the doorway as the sharp whine of the

Black Hawk's twin engines started turning over. Carl stepped up to the doorway and looked at each face inside the chopper before his eyes settled on Jack and Sarah. He hesitated and then looked as if he wanted to say something.

"What are you doing, Captain?" Jack asked loudly as the engine noise built up to a deafening roar. Carl looked over at the colonel and they locked eyes. "Get the hell out of here."

Everett looked from Jack to Niles, who nodded his head in understanding. Then he looked at a shocked Will Mendenhall and an even more stunned Jason Ryan. He smiled and then saluted his friends. He then saw Sarah, who was already tearing up and getting angry for doing so. He gave her a look that told her "thank you for everything." All her hard work to get Carl back to living a real life again after the death of Lisa, his fiancée, had not been wasted. He kissed her. Then he leaned over and kissed Alice Hamilton on the cheek. He patted the burlap bag on the seat next to her and then winked. She smiled with tears in her eyes and found she couldn't speak. Everett straightened and then held out his hand to Collins.

"Thanks, Jack, you'll get my paperwork started, right?"

Jack Collins nodded that yes, he would get his retirement papers in order. He shook hands with his friend of eight years for the last time.

"Good luck, swabby, and take care of that girl. I understand she has some pretty rough in-laws that may not take to you." He smiled and Everett followed suit. Their hands parted as the Black Hawk spun up in power and the wheels lifted free of the earth.

They all watched as Everett walked back and placed his arm around Anya as his friends flew away to the south over the remains of the Edge of the World.

Captain Carl Everett watched the U.S. Army Black Hawk until he couldn't see it any longer. He then turned to Anya and together they walked away into their future.

EPILOGUE

PARTING

Hark, now hear the sailors cry
Smell the sea and feel the sky
Let your soul and spirit fly into the mystic

**—Van Morrison,
"Into the Mystic"**

EVENT GROUP COMPLEX,
NELLIS AIR FORCE BASE, NEVADA

The group that sat around the conference table was pretty much silent as the individual departments had been excused after their daily morning meeting, with the exception of Jack, Sarah, Will Mendenhall, Pete, and Charlie, Alice Hamilton, and Virginia Pollock. It had been two weeks since their return from Romania. Mendenhall, Sarah, and Ryan were still bandaged up in several places, but other than that the Event Group had come through the ordeal with minimum pain outside of Carl's departure. They all sat around the conference table as Niles Compton stepped back to the table from his desk. He punched a button and the small screen next to his seat slid up from the table. Very soon after that the picture of their commander in chief appeared. The president nodded a greeting to all in the room.

"I believe you're ready, Director Compton?" the president said into the screen. "Make it quick, I've got a meeting with the Israeli prime minister in ten minutes."

"First off, I wanted only essential personnel to hear the forensic analysis of Alice's find inside Madam Korvesky's house. Alice, if you would."

Alice, resplendent in a new knee-length blue dress and looking like her old self, stepped up to the large screen in the center of the room. She looked embarrassed.

"Europa, please present Slide 445789, Operation Grimm, on the screen, please."

"Yes, Mrs. Hamilton."

On the monitor what looked like six large chunks of stone of varying sizes were displayed on a stainless steel table. Alice allowed everyone to look them over.

"The stones were analyzed by our Nuclear Sciences Department and Virginia can validate all her findings. And they are extraordinary, I assure you. First, these were found stored inside an old chest that I am sure you are aware of. These were the only items prized by the Jeddah, and Madam Korvesky knew, or should I say sensed, that we would know what to do with them. These stone fragments were more valuable to them than the bodies of Moses and the other great Hebrew leaders, and far more than any of the spoils they collected during their Exodus from Egypt."

"First of all, just what are they?" the president asked.

"Sarah, your report on the material, please," Alice asked.

Sarah stood at her chair, noticing how silent Jack had been this morning and for the past for the past few days.

"The material was easy—granite, solid granite from the Arabian Peninsula. The manufacture concerning its attributes cannot however be verified."

"What attributes?" Mendenhall asked and then quieted quickly when he forgot the president was listening in and he knew that the commander in chief liked asking the questions. But this time it looked like the president was uncomfortable in doing so.

"The lettering inscribed in the granite," Virginia answered for both Alice and Sarah. McIntire nodded and then sat, brushing Jack's hand lightly with her own to get some sort of reaction out of him. He didn't respond but stared straight down at the table.

"Lettering?" This time the president did ask the question. "What sort of lettering and why is this important to the Jeddah?"

"The lettering is in ancient Hebrew," Alice said as she turned as another shot of the pieces of granite came on the screen. This showed the lettering up close on a section of stone that was somewhat curved in its carving. "As you can see, there is quite a bit of the text on this first line on the largest section of broken stone. We can actually read what it says." Alice waited for all eyes to focus on the screen as she wanted the impact of what she was about to say to hit home and hit hard. She waited until a close-up of the lettering appeared on the giant screen.

יִנְפָּל סִיהוּלָא יל וְיָא סִירְדָּא דְל־הֹיהִי

"It has been translated and verified by our Ancient Languages Department and Religious Studies confirmed it also. It is in ancient Hebrew and is clearly understood. It says '*Thou shalt not have no other gods before me.*'"

The room became still as Alice allowed her discovery to finally sink in.

"It is what we know as the First Commandment as given to Moses by God."

"Are you saying . . . what *are* you saying?" the president asked in confusion.

"That we are in possession of what remains of the original Ten Commandments as first given to Moses by the Lord of Hosts, and that legend said was destroyed on the slopes of Mount Sinai, of which the real mountain is in a secured location inside the borders of Saudi Arabia and not the Sinai Peninsula as history always said. There were not one, but two mountains of God. This has been a bone of contention with biblical scholars for almost a century, but the tale has been confirmed by our newest member of the Event Group, Professor Avi Feuerstein of Los Angeles. The Jeddah must have come into possession of the shards after their destruction and kept them. This is what they considered the real treasure of the Exodus, not dead men or riches, but the law of man as given to him by God."

The room was silent as most became uncomfortable with the news. Even after all the Event Group had learned over many years, they were still a little shocked at the report.

"One last thing before the shards go back to the lab and Virginia's team. The report from the Geology Department places the carving of the outer edges of the granite at four thousand years plus or minus five centuries, and that places these shards clearly in the time frame we were looking at—right at the time of the Great Exodus."

"And the writing?" Virginia prompted.

"The lettering was placed there by a heat source that could not have originated almost four thousand years ago. The edges of the stones were carved as we indicated, but that's where the ordinary become the extraordinary. The lettering was burned into the stone by something that would have to bring to bear the power of one of our modern argon laser systems, Virginia and her team can verify that."

"So you're saying—" the president began.

"That this lettering wasn't made by any known form of cutting used at that time in the ancient world. It was literally burned into solid granite, and unless Moses had an inside source at Raytheon Corporation, he didn't carve this."

"If that's what the lettering is." The president said what everyone else was thinking. "I mean, this is all pretty much speculative as far as the provenance of the shards is concerned. I mean, all you have is the word of an old Gypsy woman."

The room was again silent as Alice gathered up her paperwork and then sat.

"Alice will have the complete report on the Jeddah soon" Niles said. "Right now we do know that the interior minister of Romania has been charged in connection with his cooperation with the Edge of the World Hotel and Resort Casino. The land has been reverted back to the hands of the Romanian government for leasing to the original inhabitants of the pass—the Jeddah. Since the collapse of the pass itself and the temple under it, NATO soon discovered that the pass was no longer a weak point on the Romanian frontier and thus the plans for its defense were scrapped and a new threatening area was soon located for NATO to concern itself with."

"What of the species of wolf that you have verified as actually existing?" the president asked.

"The official Department 5656 report on Operation Grimm," Alice explained, "states that the quest to find a supposed new species of *Canis lupus* was unfruitful and the plans for any more incursions to search for this species have been shelved. The offshoot of wolf known to legend as the Golia do not exist, nor have they ever existed in the fossil record of any country." Alice cleared her throat as the cover-up for the benefit of the new alpha male, Mikla—so he could keep his clan of amazing creatures hidden from the rest of the modern world—became apparent. "As for the Jeddah, well, as Anya said, they are no longer that, but ordinary citizens of the world. The power of the link between species will continue to be studied by our Neurology Department and the potion sample returned is under strict quarantine on Level 72."

"We haven't learned enough to keep these highly volatile compounds out of this facility?" Sarah asked in reference to the disaster of eight weeks earlier in the Event Group complex during the Lawrence Ambrose investigation when a chemical compound was accidentally released into the complex bringing on death and damage.

"Director Compton authorized it," Alice said, "in order to keep this compound as secret as we can without the Centers for Disease Control knowing we have it. The properties of these ordinary plants work in combination with the human mind's natural endorphins and the end result once the two differing species have committed to the spell is a chemical balance that allows one mind to electrically attach itself to the other, in more than just the mechanical sense. As we saw with Madam Korvesky and Mikla, the mental link was so strong that when Mikla broke his ankle, Madam Korvesky's ankle snapped through the sheer power of her own mind and through the distress that the Golia felt at the time of his injury. In essence Madam Korvesky saved Mikla by accepting a large portion of his injury and thus dooming herself. As I said, we have years upon years of research as this can be a beneficial approach to advancing noninvasive surgery and for certain mental disorders."

When Alice was finished with her report she relaxed for the first time in weeks since the push to get this Event up and running. This was the last mission she would personally be a part of and wanted to end with what she considered one of the top Events in the department's history. She had proven not only the existence of one of the Lost Tribes of Israel, but also that of the most wonderful species of animals the world has ever seen. She thought of Garrison Lee and also of Madam Korvesky and the night they all had shared together in Hong Kong—the night that started it all for Alice Hamilton. She shook her head, silently saying *We did it* to Garrison Lee.

Two minutes later after the president had signed off with a "well-done," Jack, Sarah, and the others sat around the conference table not saying anything as Niles knew Collins was about to say what he had to say to the group. He cleared his throat and stood.

"Two questions are swirling through your minds about our last Event call. Why I let Mr. Everett go and why I allowed him to stay with Anya for as long as he possibly could. Niles agreed that it was for the best."

"I don't understand how losing the best man in this command is for the best," Ryan said, still angry and hurt over the captain's recent departure.

"Believe me, Mr. Ryan, that was the last thing I, Niles, Garrison Lee, or the president of the United States wanted. Captain Everett is integral to the plans of this nation in the next two years' planning for future Events. He had been picked by Garrison Lee and Dr. Compton last year for a mission that could help us in the near future, a mission being put together by the U.S. Navy, one that has serious ramifications for the defense of this planet in regards to the Event in the desert over seven years ago. However, last month things changed rather dramatically."

"What are you saying?" Sarah asked, as Virginia Pollock, who knew what Jack was about to say, reached out and patted Sarah's hand as the small geologist was starting to be frightened at the tense way Collins was delivering this news.

Colonel Jack Collins looked over and sadly nodded toward Niles Compton, who returned to his desk and removed a small metal box that was fingerprint-coded for security.

As Niles returned to the conference table with the small aluminum and steel box that was only a foot long and half that deep, Collins continued with his eyes averted and not reaching out to anyone. Now they would learn why the colonel had been so silent about Captain Everett since their return from Romania.

"You have all wondered why I excluded everyone in this room from assisting me in the search for my sister's killer, especially Mr. Everett. He was hurt that I would not include my best friend."

All in the room saw Jack's hesitation as he stated for the first time that his best friend in the world outside of Sarah McIntire was Captain Carl Everett. "There is a reason for this. Carl and I have to be separate for the foreseeable future." He finally looked up and saw the confusion on their faces. Will Mendenhall and Jason Ryan were the first to see the distress written on their colonel's face. A nervous Pete Golding and Charlie Ellenshaw exchanged looks but waited for Jack to continue.

Niles Compton now placed the small box on the tabletop and then used his right thumb for security verification as the pad read his thumbprint and the locking mechanism snapped and the lid opened with an audible hiss of air from the hermetically sealed box. A fine mist of frozen air exited the container as Niles sat hard into his chair, not wanting to see the contents. He pursed his lips and nodded at Jack after wiping his hands on his black pants.

"Last month in a dig in Antarctica, the United States Geological Survey team stationed 622 miles from McMurdo Station found this item just under one thousand feet of solid ice that the geologists say froze solid over three hundred thousand years before, covering a prehistoric rain forest. They excavated the site by creating large tunnels that were carved into the continent and the team brought up extinct plant life from Antarctica and this was enough to cause a stir at McMurdo Station to say the least. A bore hole was sunk next to the original site after magnetometers picked up on metal buried in the ice. Once down in the borehole the engineers discovered wreckage of what can only be described as a ship of some kind. Not only metal but they also started bringing out larger and larger specimens. They even unearthed a sabertooth cat—well, portions of one anyway." Jack fell silent and then closed his eyes as he pulled the box over to him and then with a look of distaste he removed the item. "Before the president of the United States put a clamp on the findings and sealed the area off with United Sates Marines, this was brought up." He handed the item over to Sarah, who placed it front of her as everyone who knew Captain Everett recognized what they were looking at.

"Oh, my God," Sarah said as she eased back down into her chair as she no longer trusted her legs. Charlie and Pete exchanged that look of utter impossibility once more and Ryan and Mendenhall just sat in silence.

On the table before them were the remains of a wristwatch. The band was missing with the exception of several broken, golden, links. On the back side of the stainless steel and gold watch was the inscription they all knew by heart since most in this very same room helped compose it for the gift watch not long after the Event in Brazil.

To Captain Carl C. Everett—next stop
Flag Territory—your family at 5656.

Each person in the room had seen the watch the day they had surprised Carl with it after his promotion to captain. It was well-wishes toward his next rank adjustment to admiral. Everett had beamed at the gift and thanked everyone as he slid the watch over his large wrist.

"What is the meaning of this, what does this artifact mean?" Charlie Ellenshaw asked.

"This watch stopped working when the man wearing it was killed, or died, or dropped it." Niles looked up into the astonished faces of his friends and now his most confused staff. "The watch stopped functioning over three hundred thousand years ago."

The silence in the room said it all. Now they understood why Carl couldn't be there. Jack was protecting him by keeping the captain tucked away in Romania with the illusion of happiness until this thing could be studied further.

"But why keep you and the captain separated?" Pete asked, fearing the worst, as was expected at the Event Group at all times and this he suspected was no exception to that rule.

As everyone read the words they all knew so well, Niles opened a second lid on the box and then acting as though he were afraid to touch it slid the box over to Collins. Collins took a handkerchief from his pocket and removed several gold links that at one time made up the wristband for the expensive watch. He held them and looked the links over and a sad smile crossed his lips as he set the items down.

"What is it?" Ryan asked, standing to get a better look at it.

"That, Mr. Ryan, is the reason Captain Everett and I have to stay separated until we reach some conclusions here at Group. I have been suspended from duty by Dr. Compton and restricted to base for the foreseeable future. Commander Ryan will take over my duties."

The room erupted as all questions were directed at Niles Compton, who sat next to Alice not looking at anyone.

"Again, what are those?" Ryan asked, becoming scared because for the first time he was seeing extreme unease in the face of Colonel Jack Collins.

"Those, Mr. Ryan, are the remaining links to the wristband of that watch. And as you can see they are covered in a brownish stain that we analyzed. Virginia, would you explain your findings on what kind of stain that is on the links?"

Virginia cleared her throat, as she hated discussing this with anyone, much less the friends inside of this room.

"The stain consists of O negative blood. The bloodstain was preserved by being frozen for such a long period of time."

"Captain Everett's blood?" Jason asked.

"No. The DNA profile was matched to a person here at Group, but not the captain."

"Who?" Sarah asked, knowing she wasn't going to care for Virginia's answer.

"Mine," Jack said as he finally sat in his chair.

The shocked faces around the room made Collins feel terrible as he knew he had just turned the worlds of everyone in the conference room upside down.

"At some point approximately three hundred thousand years ago, Captain Everett and possibly myself may have been killed in the prehistoric past."

Sarah felt as if her blood had stopped coursing through her veins as she looked at Collins in stunned silence.

Director Niles Compton rapped his knuckles on the conference room table to get their attention.

"Ladies and gentlemen, the president has authorized an immediate Event alert for this department—the location to begin the investigation is Antarctica. Pete, your departmental team will lead the investigation. Virginia, we have to have all theories no matter how ridiculous or mundane on the science of time travel and I need you to figure out with the rest of the engineers just what in the hell that ship is under the ice and where it came from. The president has authorized any expenditure in this endeavor. Until then as the colonel said, he has been relieved of command and is under house arrest. We cannot take any chances having him out in the world. As for the captain, we think he's pretty safe for the time being inside Romania."

The room was silent.

"We all know about the theories of time travel and their obvious flaws. However, if Albert Einstein said it was theoretically possible to travel backward in time, then we can assume that somehow our friends ended up in the past, especially after this discovery in Antarctica."

Sarah took Jack's hand and didn't particularly care about military protocol or who was watching.

The friends and colleagues of Colonel Jack Collins and Captain Carl Everett had a new mission—find out how both of their friends ended up buried under a mile of solid ice that hadn't seen the sun in three hundred thousand years.

The Event Group was now on a war footing.